Raves for *Regenesis*:

"The long-awaited, intricate sequel to Cherryh's Hugo-winning *Cyteen* brings events full circle. Complex and rich, with beautifully rounded characters, this novel can stand alone, but will delight fans of *Cyteen* with extra layers of meaning that resonate between old and new."
—*Publishers Weekly* (Starred Review)

"In the vast Alliance-Union universe, Ariane Emory, protagonist of *Cyteen*, seeks the murderer of the scientist of whom she is a clone, and anything less like the usual quest tale is hard to imagine, despite high rates of suspense and conflict between good, evil, and everything that lies between them. In Alliance-Union, there is lots of room between moral absolutes, and in this big book, lots of space for absorbing characters; for adventure, intrigue, and violence; and for plausible extrapolations of current technologies and institutions."
—*Booklist*

"Set against the richly developed future involving political, social, and sometimes military battles between the Union and Alliance interstellar organizations, this latest novel by the author of the Alliance-Union Universe novels serves as a sequel to both *Cyteen* and *Downbelow Station*. Cherryh's storytelling talent remains unmatched for its clearness of execution and its exceptional readability. Highly recommended."
—*Library Journal*

"Long-delayed sequels can often run aground because the author has forgotten important details or has changed so much that she's a different person form the one who crafted the original. This is not the case here. Cherryh's latest remains true to her original dystopian vision."
—*Romantic Times*

"It has been twenty long years since *Cyteen* was first released and happily, the continuation *Regenesis* was worth the wait. A fine piece of work that displays Cherryh's mastery of the storyteller's art."
—*Monsters & Critics*

C. J. CHERRYH

REGENESIS

DAW BOOKS, INC.
DONALD A. WOLLHEIM, FOUNDER
375 Hudson Street, New York, NY 10014

ELIZABETH R. WOLLHEIM
SHEILA E. GILBERT
PUBLISHERS
http://www.dawbooks.com

First Printing, January 2009.
1 2 3 4 5 6 7 8 9 10

DAW TRADEMARK REGISTERED
U.S. PAT. AND TM. OFF. AND FOREIGN COUNTRIES
—MARCA REGISTRADA
HECHO EN U.S.A.

PRINTED IN THE U.S.A.

To Betsy's determination

HISTORY OF UNION: The Post-War Period
Novgorod Publications

2424

Union came out of the Company Wars with both territory and political integrity, not beholden to Earth or Alliance for either. The Treaty of Pell, which ended active hostilities between Union and Alliance, left Earth independent, though militarily reliant on Pell's Star. The Company Fleet had defied Earth's authority, rejected the Treaty of Pell, and continued acts of piracy, as apt to prey on Earth's ships as on Union's, and now lacking a safe port.

The Treaty incidentally left the merchanter Council of Captains with more power than Pell's Star Station held in the affairs of the Alliance.

And the same Treaty ceded the greater expanse of human-explored space to the authority of Union . . . but placed merchant trade exclusively in the hands of the Alliance Council of Captains.

It was an agreement equally unpopular on all sides— which spoke a great deal to its fairness—and it was immediately followed by a period in which all former combatants maneuvered for advantage, everyone dreading a resumption of hostilities, but most convinced that war would break out again, probably within a lifetime.

The Hinder Stars, that bridge of closely lying, generally barren stars between Earth and Pell, became a zone of renewed interest for the Alliance, which governed that region. The Council of Captains, whose livelihood was their ships and their trade, looked to revitalize the mothballed stations on that route—stations that had collapsed economically with the advent of faster-than-light engines. Alliance thus moved to set itself as middleman between Earth and Union, and to profit from that trade . . .

if it could re-establish viable populations to consume the goods it wanted to trade along the way.

Union enjoyed the manufacture, mining, and prosperity of its own widely scattered stations, from Mariner and Viking to outlying Fargone, and it had the colonized world of Cyteen, with its major exports: the rejuv drug, embryos, genetically enhanced biologicals, azi workers, and concentrated foodstuffs.

In the viewpoint of the merchanter captains of the Alliance, that was a somewhat reasonable model for what the Alliance could create around Pell's World—Downbelow— by repopulating the abandoned starstations of the Hinder Stars, and revivifying trade with, not one, but two *living worlds within their reach—Downbelow and Earth itself.*

It was a reasonable model in all save one respect: the Alliance plan for the Hinder Stars relied on recruitment of station citizens and the natural human birth rate to provide population. This meant luring the poorer of the residents of Pell and Earth to live in frontier conditions at outmoded, pre-FTL stations.

The natural human birth rate is slow: that was one flaw in the plan; and, the second, the poorer residents of Pell Station, who had suffered most in the war years, were not generally optimists about government promises. Spacers would never give up their ships and family connections to settle permanently on stations. Earth residents were barred by laws restricting emigration of its educated and essential. So a consumer population, particularly of educated and prosperous classes, was very hard to obtain in the Hinder Stars. Subsidies began to drain Pell's economy and raise taxes on Pell Station itself, a source of great discontent.

There was also a basic conflict between station interests and spacer interests: stationers were not anxious to see their power further diminished by spacer exploitation of the planet beneath their feet. On the one hand there was no great enthusiasm among stationers to visit their sole Earthlike planet—it had its hazards, and *intelligent inhabitants. And secondly, there had begun to be a strong green party. That party, combined with those stationers fearing the Council of Captains would dominate the station itself, passed legislation making Pell's World a protectorate un-*

available for colonization. That cut one leg from under the merchanter captains' plan.

Contrast this situation with Union, which exited the Company Wars with an abundance of thriving stations, two stations at Cyteen's own home star, besides Mariner and Viking, which posed a convenient bridge to the Alliance trade. The terms of the Treaty of Pell demanded Alliance merchanters serve those routes, as a condition of Union not building merchanters of their own. And this, of course, provided sorely needed markets for Alliance, but not as profitable markets, counting Union tariffs, as they would be if Alliance owned the cargos and the stations.

And, while Alliance merchanter ships plied Union space, serving chains of Union starstations down various strands of stars, it was universally Union industry which benefitted from the transport. From Pan-Paris, on one route, to Fargone, on the other, with Cyteen itself at the center, Union had come out of the Company Wars with the kind of trade network and consumer base that the Alliance only dreamed of building.

Union stations numbered populations in the multiple hundreds of thousands, though Union was far younger than Pell. Cyteen itself, which did allow humans onworld, counted population in the millions... but the largest population center in Alliance space numbered, officially, counting both the remote and the near station at Pell, around half a million. Counting the merchanters on ships and miners at various outposts, the whole population of the Alliance numbered probably a quarter of a million more. So the bulk of human population in the universe might still be still centered at Sol, with its billions, but the population of Union now had to be counted as a major alternate center. The exponential increase challenged the economic power that Alliance had once considered unassailable: If that rate of growth continued, one day there would be more humans in Union than presently lived on Earth itself.

Union did not rely on natural human birth rate, or on emigration. Union used birthlabs. Union could create a station and, within twenty years, raise up thousands of highly motivated, trained inhabitants—inhabitants ready to meet the difficulties of station-building, perfectly content with barracks conditions at the outset, and ready to teach their naturally born children their values of hard work, adequate leisure, participation in the group, and, in due proportion, independent analytical thinking.

More, Union had rejuv, a product of Cyteen's biology, which doubled and tripled the productive years of its workers and thinkers. Natural reproduction might stop at forty, when a person went on rejuv, but work and economic production went on . . . and the birthlabs could enable individuals to reproduce into their next century.

Alliance efforts to revive the Hinder Stars, even starting with prebuilt residencies and mothballed businesses, were slow and subject to supply and personnel shortages. They failed to meet immigrant expectations of quick riches and reasonable living conditions. Only the smallest, marginal traders were willing to ply those routes, while the richer Alliance ships engaged in the far more lucrative trade within Union space. Factor in the occasional appearance of Mazianni pirates—former Earth Company Fleet—at these lonely, largely undefended stations of the Hinder Stars, and the reluctance of Alliance stationers to undertake the risk of living there was understandable.

Union, seeing that the Mazianni were deriving supply and new personnel from those stations, offered to assist the Alliance in patrols there, but old suspicions died hard. Alliance rebuffed Union offers, convinced that Union was seeking to control all these stations, which represented their route to Earth.

Besides, the Alliance was engaged in another, secret project: it had long known of an Earth-class world within its grasp, and it mounted an expedition which the Alliance captains saw as finally giving the Alliance the exploitable world they so greatly wanted.

The expedition arrived at that planet, and found it already occupied by a human colony . . . a Union colony.

The timing of the revelation could not have been worse for Alliance-Union relations. During the negotiations for the Treaty, Pell had strongly insisted on acquiring adjacent territory . . . knowing that world was there.

But a secret Union operation at the close of the War had

landed not a military occupation, but a colony. The CIT supervisors of the colony, largely military, had perished early. The azi workers, however, had survived, multiplied, and scattered into the outback, incidentally commingling Terran-origin biologicals and highly engineered microbes with the native fauna . . . and ultimately making accommodation with the native life.

The revelation of the Union colony on that world—which came to be known as Gehenna—came close to shipwrecking the Treaty of Pell. Alliance held that the Union signers of the Treaty had kept Gehenna a secret, and that the Treaty had thus not been negotiated in good faith. Union responded that its negotiators had not known about the colony, and that, within the framework of Union government, all knowledge of the settlement had been sequestered within two of the branches of government, Science and Defense. Thus the Bureau of State, which had negotiated and maintained the Treaty, had had absolutely no knowledge there was a problem.

Further, Union argued, the administrations of Science and Defense, under Emory of Science and Adm. Azov of Defense, had profoundly changed personnel since the War, and with the present Council of Nine pressing strongly for peace, it made no sense even to the most hawkish of the Alliance political parties to lead humanity back to a state of war. Union formally apologized for the situation and offered amends. The situation was so volatile that Union accepted the Treaty of Gehenna, presented by Pell, virtually without amendment—to wit, that there would be no future manned landing on a biologically complex world except by joint participation of Alliance and Union on the mission, and there would be no landing on a world with a native intelligence until that intelligence could meet humans in space and speak for itself.

By the same treaty, Union offered access to certain restricted technology in a joint Alliance-Union mission to be settled in orbit about Gehenna . . . a watchdog mission designed to preclude any biohazard getting off the planet. Regulations for any persons in contact with Gehenna became the standard for any future exploratory missions.

Though the Treaty of Gehenna was accepted by both

sides, the matter of Union assistance at the Hinder Stars was quietly tabled "pending future study," and, as the third component of the treaty, certain trade concessions and tariff reductions were given to the Alliance Council of Captains, as a confidence-building measure.

Scholars tend to mark the Treaty of Pell as the beginning of the post-war cooling-off period, and the Treaty of Gehenna as its close, as if the era could be summed up within those parentheses. But between those two events, the death of a single human woman, Ariane Emory, and her rebirth in a Parental Replicate, could ultimately prove of greater import in human history. As the rumor reached Pell and Earth that the Architect of Union—and of Gehenna—had died, there had been reaction clear to the ends of human space.

The war years, in which stations and whole planets had become logical targets, had threatened the existence of humankind, from the motherworld to the most remote colony of Union space. That state of affairs had remained true for much of the first Ariane Emory's tenure in various offices. She had been a genius in genetics and psychology, served as Director of Reseune for a number of years, was the principle theorist behind Union's strong population push during the War . . . and she had served as Councillor of Science during a critical period of the post-War era, including the Gehenna operation. Her political views were pro-Expansionist. She had been instrumental in the push of human population and commerce to the farthest reaches of explored space. She had founded the genetic Arks, in which genetic records of every available Earth species were preserved. She had steered the development of the planet of Cyteen from a largely vacant wilderness to a continent-spanning network of towns and research centers, and the establishment of ecological studies on the second continent. She had begun her career in full accord with Union's early intentions to terraform the world of Cyteen into a new Earth, but her opinion had evolved over time into a determination to preserve its native fauna.

The Centrist party of her day, which had crystallized around Emory's change of opinion about terraforming, continued to press for terraforming Cyteen and basing

Union around a strong central authority. Emory and the Expansionists contrarily argued against further alterations to Cyteen, and in favor of further colonization, with a strong emphasis on local autonomy of governments thus formed, a de facto decentralization of power.

And Emory prevailed.

Then, as a war-weary universe foresaw Emory's life winding down to a natural close, and as powers jockeyed to position themselves for a quieter post-Emory era of consolidation, Emory advanced a process called psychogenesis, the cloning of a psychologically and intellectually identical offspring. It was a procedure that had conspicuously failed before.

When Emory was assassinated, many in Alliance and even in Union assumed that her final project had been aborted, incomplete, or that if ever attempted, it would fail—that, in effect, it had been the last, forlorn hope of a dying woman.

Within two years, a child named Ariane Emory was born at Cyteen.

BOOK

ONE

MARCH 27, 2424
1328H

Hundreds of babies floated in their vats, in various stages, in Reseune's largest birthlab—azi babies, CIT babies, much the same. Azi were in one section. CIT babies—for Citizen mothers who for physical reasons, job reasons, or personal preference, didn't want to handle pregnancy the old-fashioned way—occupied another section of the same lab. The only difference between the two groups at this stage was a doorway, and whether a number or a CIT name tagged the vat. The data of real pregnancies bathed all the fetuses in a perpetual sea of appropriate chemistry and sound. The machinery of artificial wombs rocked them, moved them, kept them close and safe and warm.

There was, on one side of that doorway, Abban AB-688, an azi. It would take a close look to see him floating in his tank. At six weeks, Abban AB was about pea-sized, though growing fast. He'd be tall, someday. He'd be dark-haired, and very, very clever, and cold as ice.

In the tank beside him was Seely AS-9, who had been conceived in the same hour. He would be of a slighter build, pale blond, eyes fair blue, and, like Abban, he would be an alpha, and very, very smart. The 9 should have meant he was the ninth of his exact geneset and psychset combination: in fact he was the tenth.

The ordinary naming conventions did fall by the wayside at times, especially among highly socialized alphas, whose Supervisors named them whatever they liked, or among very old, foundational sets, whose numbers and alphabetics didn't always conform to modern usage. Abban, for instance: his personal alphabetic was B. But he had been given a name starting with both his letters— someone's whimsy, perhaps.

That was the first thing that was odd about Abban AB. Another was that, just like Seely AS, this Abban reused a sequence number: 688.

And that, all other conventions aside, should never happen.

On the other side of that doorway, Giraud Nye, conceived within minutes of the others, would be born a CIT, Citizen class, for no other reason than that he had a CIT number and came with no manual, no set course to take him through his first years. He would learn in chaos, being a born-man; and after he reached adulthood he would become responsible for himself. In his sixth week, just like Abban AB and Seely AS, he had just the start of a bloodstream. Last week he'd been nothing but a tube, the beginnings of a backbone and a spinal cord. This week he had a tail, had spots for eyes, had the beginnings of a heart, and the faintest discernable buds for arms and legs. He didn't have a brain yet. He didn't have eyelids because he didn't really have eyes. Any of the three of them could have been almost any mammal: Giraud could have been a piglet, as easily, or a horse. He could have been Abban or Seely. He could just as well have been a little girl, for that matter. But the DNA in his cells and the tag on his vat both said he was Giraud Nye, a CIT, and he'd be a square-built man with sandy hair, large bones, and cold blue eyes. Going on rejuv at age forty or so, give or take how well he took care of himself, he'd live to be around a hundred and thirty-three Earth Standard years before the drug played out on him, and then he'd probably die of a heart attack.

That was the blueprint of the last Giraud Nye, and this one was destined for the old Giraud Nye's power, someday, unless someone threw the switch and stopped him.

Ari Emory visited him today, out of curiosity, and with mixed emotions. She came with her two bodyguards, Florian and Catlin, and she created a stir in the labs. Even at eighteen, she had power, and she could throw that switch.

She could also create Giraud's brother Denys, completing the set, on any given day. She still had seven years' leeway in which to do that, that span of time having been the gap between the brothers. In her own untested opinion, any day would do. But doing it at all was, personally, a very hard decision.

For one thing, psychogenesis wasn't going to be a sure thing in the Nyes' case. ReseuneLabs didn't have the data on the Nyes that they'd had on her, whose predecessor's every living day had been documented down to the hormones, the chemistry, the actions and the reactions, for at least her formative years. The first Ariane Emory had been her own mother Olga Emory's living lab, and all her predecessor's data was out there in a vault under a grassy hill, just beyond the sprawling city-sized complex that was Reseune, with ReseuneLabs and its adjacent town.

This Ariane Emory was the second of her own geneset. And all her data was being saved under another such hill, so she was already pretty sure there'd someday be a third of her set. Like an azi, she supposed she could view continuance of her geneset as a vote of confidence by those who made such decisions. But whether they'd clone the original, or her, well—that was still to determine, wasn't it?

Successful cloning was a given for ReseuneLabs, an easy job. Cloning human beings or rare animals, with gene-manipulation tossed in for variety, or, more to the point, for good health—that was what Reseune and other labs did every day of the month, for the whole star-spanning state that was Union.

You wanted a child of your own genotype, or just a roll of the dice, the old-fashioned way? If you passed the psych exams, male or female, you could have a child, two children, as many as you liked—or as many as your local law allowed. You wanted a genetic problem fixed? Reseune could do that. Embryos shipped constantly, shuttled up to station, dispersed as far as Union reached . . . even, though rarely, to Earth. It was a huge industry. Reseune had the largest of the CIT birthlabs . . . but it had competition.

Psychogenesis, however, replicating a mind—that was a whole new twist on an old process . . . and only Reseune had done that.

It was the year 2424, and this Ariane Emory was the first success of *that* kind.

She could create Denys, if she wanted to.

She'd killed Denys—at least her bodyguard had.

Giraud and Denys had created her, right after they had, perhaps, killed the first Ari Emory.

Turn about, fair play.

BOOK ONE   Section 1   Chapter ii

APRIL 21, 2424
1509h

"If you do exist, third Ariane, and if you're hearing my record, with or without the first Ariane's, be warned that I intend to shape the world that you will inhabit, but be warned too—I can never utterly guarantee the outcome of what I do, or the outcome of what I am. Fixing anything that's wrong will be your job, the same way the first Ari created me to fix her mistakes.

"So I give you this advice: you have my geneset, and you may be shaped by many of my experiences, as I was shaped by the first Ariane's. But remember you're no more me than I am you. You're no more me, than you—or I—can ever be the first Ariane Emory, no matter how carefully they pattern us. Why? Because we don't live in her time. We can't live her life exactly as she lived it, and we shouldn't try, because then we wouldn't fit into the world we live in. You don't live in my time, and should never try to.

"This I do have in common with her: mine is not a peaceful time. Not all the decisions she made were the best ones, and she knew that long before she died. In many cases we both did as we could, too late for good sense.

"But I am certainly more the first Ariane than you can be, since the times in which I exist are directly linked to her time. The times I'll shape, with whatever power I can get into my hands, will link me to your time. I don't know how I'll feel decades from now, but it's my opinion that you'll ultimately need to hear from both of us—because the first Ari invented herself, and I'm the bridge between.

"Do the math. The first Ari died twenty years ago. I'm eighteen. I've been living on my own since I was twelve, because they preferred me to any other alternatives they had, most of which were bad. And, never mind that your records may insist I was fourteen when I set out on my own, I was twelve. The program just wasn't ready for me, so it said I was fourteen and I had to scramble to catch up.

"I owe my current situation to Dr. Yanni Schwartz, who saw Reseune through difficult years—and who followed the program laid out in the first Ari's systems. If you know the records, the first Ariane came to adult rights early. So did I. Both events were driven by legislators who feared their alternatives far more than they feared a child . . . or her overseers.

"Mine is still not an unlimited power, in my eighteenth year. I wasn't born with a Parental Replicate's rights. I didn't even have my CIT number. I had to prove genetic identity before I got possession of Ari's old CIT number and became the owner of everything attached to it—everything the first Ari owned. And I got it primarily because Reseune wanted those rights to stay in Reseune. So Reseune backed my claims.

"But it didn't prove in all senses that I was Ariane Emory. I'm still doing that, and people still question. Yanni Schwartz is Director of Reseune as well as Proxy Councillor of Science for Union, a situation which won't last forever—possibly not much beyond two years, or maybe longer. You'll know by your own lifetime how that transition of power played out—what I had to do, what I chose to do, and whether it was the best thing to have done. I'm pretty sure you'll get the CIT number attached before you're born: I'll try to see to that, since I fought that battle and there's no longer an issue. But no matter how much I can smooth the way for you, you'll likely face your own crisis of maturity, because money and power in the hands of a child make for powerful politics. Just say that right now my uncles are both dead and I'm alive.

"This, too, you should know. The Council of Nine always preferred me over the alternatives—one of which was for the Council to actually make a decision and plot a course away from the world that the first Ariane created.

They didn't do that. Possibly that lack of initiative was planned into them: you know that Reseune had a hand in Novgorod's population. I've not gotten anything from my predecessor that gives me a specific clue about that theory . . . but then I don't have access to all of the records that exist, even if I'm told I have it. One can't prove a negative, and if I haven't got it, it's hard to know if it exists—but I'm still searching. My best theory says the Council might have hated the first Ariane, but they were scared of life without her. And getting her back, in me—that felt much safer for them. At least the court voted to give me my identity, even if they couldn't give me control of Reseune: Denys was responsible for pushing that; nobody knew it then, since Giraud was the face they saw, but don't believe the histories: it was a combination of Giraud and Denys who really ran things, and Denys was brighter, but he was, let me say, a little odd.

"When Uncle Denys died, I overcame his Base in the house systems. I'd already opened up all of Base One—Ari's computer system—and gotten it to give me its records. I investigated all sorts of things that Denys had put under seal.

"Denys wasn't the one who'd walled me off from knowing things. Base One had done that. But when it was time, Base One was really his downfall. He couldn't seal the things the first Ariane had done, when Base One was ready to tell me: the little surprises in the computer system, the sudden appearance of which to this hour I can't predict, just happen, and they began happening years before Denys died. That's how she got past Denys, posthumously, by installing the program that taught me step by step what she wanted me to know. She created areas of the house system no one knew existed, and she did it so that, after she was dead, Base One would wait, intact, never letting Base Two rename itself. Then when I reached the right age and the right circumstances, Base One assembled itself. In my case, I suspect the trigger was not my birthday, as I used to believe, but a combination of moves by my caretaker.

"I'm pretty sure Denys thought he could turn me into a useful but much safer version of my predecessor. But that didn't happen. Understand: Base One isn't a com-

puter. It's always a moving target within the software of the main house system—and there's no knowing what it will be by the time you inherit it. Denys' experts couldn't find its parts, they couldn't shut it down without consequences, and it self-heals and adapts. So far as I know, it will still go on triggering things in your time—and I don't think that Uncle Denys' experts could do anything on their own that ever matched it, but I'm never sure—so I am careful, and so must you be. Never take Base One entirely for granted. You have to ask it very good questions to get its best and truest answers. And never assume the other Bases won't maneuver to get past it.

"*Evidently Base One has opened some of my files to you, so I assume you have reached a birthday or a crisis of some kind, and that your own accession to power is very near. Are you, in fact, eighteen as you read this? I have no way to know. At this stage I can't govern the age at which you get this, because I can't create the complexity of program that the first Ari wrote into Base One. I'll learn. For now, I just make the records.*

"*So maybe you're twelve. Maybe you're out on your own. Maybe not. I do assume that I'm dead by this time in your life, and that I have been since before your life began—by a few days, or maybe by some few months. It may have been my murder that brought about your birth. I shouldn't actually be surprised at that. And if that is what did happen to me, consider your own safety. They may have decided to create you—thinking they can control you, and Reseune's money—and when they find out to the contrary, they'll change their minds fast. Uncle Denys certainly did.*

"*Look around you. Ask who profited by my death, whether or not it was natural causes. I'm still asking that question about Ari One. Someone killed her. Someone ordered the termination of the first Florian and the first Catlin, too, and curiously that makes me madder than someone killing my predecessor. If you don't feel much the same on that matter, we're different, and you should think really carefully about that. You have the intelligence to see why it should be dangerous, or we are very, very different indeed, and something critical to our nature has failed.*

"Whoever killed Ari One, the plan to create me was already far advanced when she died, and my life went forward, in one sense, with the push of a button. You may know a lot about that by now, and likely you'll hear more about me as the years pass. You may know how I grew up, and you may know how I reacted to what they did. I learned to play their games. I was cute at the right moments—Uncle Denys saw through that, because cuteness was completely wasted on him. He was a very inward person pretending to be a good, sweet uncle. He relied on me for his power, because he couldn't hold it without someone to do the public things, and for a long time that was Giraud and at the last it was me. He didn't know how to be nice, just how to act nice, and people believed he cared, but he didn't. When I figured that out, things changed.

"When Uncle Giraud died, I think that was when Denys really began to be scared, because Giraud had always been his protection and his public face. I'm sure Denys was more and more afraid of me as I grew. He was so afraid of me—and, I think, of Yanni—that he never found a way to kill me in time . . . and I think that was his game. I think he wanted to have me get the first Ari's CIT number; I think he wanted me to get everything I could, and convince everybody I was real, which put a lot of money and power into his hands. When I nearly broke my neck, he was really, really upset. But he always planned I'd die before I got smarter than he was. He never knew when the right moment was, because he could judge how to make people trust him, but he couldn't do that so well once they got older and began to pretend to trust him. That was a very, very great weakness. And if the Denys I create grows up to be Denys the way he was, he might or might not be better at his games. So be careful.

"I do have ultimately to make a decision about Uncle Denys. Brilliant as he was in his field, he's not essential to the universe. But I'm nearly certain Uncle Giraud may need him, once he's born. Giraud is important to us, and it might be important that my Giraud have a brother he can take care of, speak for, and protect obsessively. Not to have Uncle Denys born might change Giraud, maybe not for the better . . . though I have as long as seven years before I *make the ultimate decision on that. I won't prejudice your thinking about Giraud, supposing my version of him is in your life—or maybe a third is, who knows? He could outlive me, and you might well have to deal with the Giraud I created. How I create him and whether I ultimately create Denys for him to focus on has bearing on what kind of Giraud you'll have. So pay close attention to what I say on that subject. If you're not in power yet, you need to start taking measures to protect yourself and stay alive. Giraud can be pleasant, but he's capable of killing you.*

"So I am leaning toward yes on the matter of Denys. Ultimately, I liked Giraud. I didn't like him most of the time he was alive, really, not as much as I like him in retrospect. One thing I know: I have to keep myself somewhat distant from the Giraud yet to be born, and not let my feelings for the old one enter into his upbringing. He has to oppose me: that's what his use is.

"The first Giraud always wanted to belong to something. Or he wanted something to belong to him. He had to serve something. He wasn't inclined, like me, like you, like the first Ari, to covet a solitary eminence. He had an azi's need to serve, in a certain sense—in his case, he served Denys—and I find that need fascinating . . . proving, I suppose, that one of the most universal and limiting traits we instill into the azi we create is actually a profoundly human one.

"Giraud served his brother long before I existed. And after Giraud died, Denys was, I think, a sad and very unbalanced man. Denys began to take actions, being afraid of me, and not having Giraud any longer to keep the world away from him. That was what Denys most feared, you should know. Not me. Not even dying. Denys was afraid of the world outside his world. And when Giraud died, Denys started having to do things for himself. He had very good azi: Abban, of course, who had belonged to Giraud first, and he had Seely, but they weren't Giraud. Worse, Denys didn't ever respect azi, not even alpha azi, and that lack of respect colored everything he ever did with them. They were loyal to him; they wanted to serve him; they did everything for him; but Denys couldn't respect anybody but Giraud. Born-men, CITs: they were even more of a *cipher to him, and he knew it. He had the program manuals for Abban and Seely; he could read them very well, so he knew them as well as he knew any azi, and I'm sure he thought he understood them, the way he thought he understood me.*

"But to really understand either born-men or azi, or me, you have to understand feelings, and Uncle Denys was all turned inward. He understood what he wanted. He could predict what Uncle Giraud was going to do most of the time. He actually trusted Giraud, and after Uncle Giraud died, Denys didn't trust anybody. He probably had confidence that Abban and Seely would do what their manuals said they had to do, but here's the salient part: he didn't, I think, have the least idea why they would do it. He was so far from being able to deal with azi on an individual level, it's a wonder he got a non-provisional Supervisor's certificate; I'm sure he finagled it, or Giraud got it for him. But don't ever think he didn't know azi, in the macro sense. He really did. His writings are brilliant, on economics stemming from azi populations turned CIT, macrosets in the largest sense, and profound integrations. I very, very much respect that work and I'm still reading it.

"And personally, one on one, he could smile and be sweet. He did favors for people, and he could tell in talking to them just what they wanted to hear—oh, he'd give them just exactly what would make them relax and believe him, and he could read that the way you'd read a book. But all that understanding of what people wanted to hear never got inside him, where he really lived. Inside he was all numbers, just numbers, and all the macroview, nothing micro at all. Much as I loathed Abban and Seely, I know he mishandled them terribly, and that may be their destiny again, because they'll be his when he needs them.

"Maybe you see the situation clearer than I do, because emotions both make things clearer and obscure the truth. You can understand and manipulate people without experiencing empathy—sociopaths do that really well; but if you don't know very clearly what your own objective is in the transaction, you can't really understand what your own emotions are doing to you, and it's easy to get confused. You can think you're being really smart, when

you're really just getting by. I think that was Denys' central trouble: he had a lot of the traits of a sociopath—totally self-interested, no empathy even for Giraud. . . . And it's not a flaw in him I feel safe correcting yet, or we could lose everything he was, intellectually.

"I'm just beginning work on my section of the tape you'll get. And maybe I won't tell you everything I could say right now, because you have to figure certain things out for yourself.

"My current decision is to let Ari One talk to you first, with the very same tape she gave to me, starting with your first log-on to Base One—for one thing, because it exists, and I can't predict how long I'll live. If things turn out the way I plan, you'll have heard her voice for years before you hear mine.

"So you'll come to know me, starting with this tape, if I haven't created any others to precede it.

"One thing is relatively sure: that you won't remember me. But you may know Justin, and Grant, and Yanni, and maybe you'll deal with my Amy and Sam and Maddy. And maybe even my Florian and my Catlin, whom I love above all the world, though I may have to order them to die. They're too powerful, and I honestly don't know what they'd do without me, or if they could love an Ari who isn't theirs. Most of all, they couldn't be children with you. But I don't want to think about that. Of all the things I suspect Ari One did, that's the one I can't stand. And yet it may have been absolutely necessary. It may have been the hardest and the kindest thing she ever did. I can't think what would have happened if I hadn't had my Florian and my Catlin when I was growing up. It would have changed everything.

"You see why, with all the questions I haven't answered for myself, I may let Ari Senior talk to you first. She never grew too old for questions. But she could give you answers from a much longer view. That isn't my perspective yet.

"I hope I have her years, to gain that sense. I hope I leave things in better order for you than she did for me. But I can't promise it.

"So hello, Ariane, in case we've never met before. I can't call myself your mother, because we're probably both eigh-

*teen, and maybe when I'm old I'll make early tapes for you,
the way Ari Senior did for me, and you can decide what to
do and which to give your own successor, or whether your
successor should exist at all. The world shouldn't just repeat itself. The advice the first Ari gave me may not apply
to the world forever.*

*"Most of all I'm sorry for all you've been through.
I understand. Of all people who've ever existed, I know
what you've been through to get here. Hello, from a sister.
Maybe that's the way to think of me. Hello, and don't trust
anybody but your Florian and your Catlin.*

*"If you don't have them, then someone has betrayed
you."*

BOOK ONE   Section I   Chapter iii

APRIL 21, 2424
1448H

Ari flicked the camera off. Session ended.

How would she look to future eyes? Like mirror into
mirror, for a girl who wasn't born yet? Someone in an odd,
outmoded style of dress telling another eighteen-year-old
things she didn't want to believe were true?

She couldn't help the outmoded part. Her successor
would see that tape at least on reaching her majority. That
was the current plan—granted she, or someone, authorized her successor to exist. She would be the one to lay
down the protocols under which her successor would get
full access to that tape or any tape. She would decree the
time at which the data and operational system that was
Base One would open up to her successor.

On some future day of upheaval, or simply on an otherwise significant birthday, her successor would log on to her
computer for the day, and Base One would start to tell her
things that would shake her world.

Her own wakeup had come early. The program Ari Se-

nior had written had made decisions and advanced the date
of her majority *and* her assumption of power—catching
Denys totally off guard. Was it wise of Ari to have done
that?

Yes. She was alive. And Denys wasn't. She hadn't exactly killed Denys. But her defenses were indisputably
lethal.

Fingers flew on the keys now that she hit the programming part, which she liked far better than talking into the
camera. She'd keyboarded and coded since she could remember and did this part without thinking too much about
the process, at least in replicating routines she'd lifted
from the files that had taught her. The hands flew very fast
as she linked modules, which was like taking chunks of
thinking, like building blocks, and dragging them all together into a coherent program. Her moves dictated what
would flow from that first session, and moved the defcons
Ari Senior had created for her own tapes into position to
protect and assess and seal that session from anyone's future deletion—even her own later second thoughts. That
was the way it worked—at least on the level she worked at,
inside Base One. She needed to be better than she was, but
she was good enough for this. She wouldn't be able to get
in and tamper, no matter if she had better thoughts later. If
she interfered with what she was now, she couldn't get her
successor to be who she would be. . . .

How was that for klein-bottle thinking?

BOOK ONE   Section I   Chapter iv

APRIL 22, 2424
1121H

Pre-lunch meeting, in a small conference room, not on the
agenda: Dr. Sandur Patil, Yanni Schwartz was notified,
had entered the Bureau of Science, was downstairs at the
moment, and on her way up.

It wasn't an extraordinary event: a professor registered in Science entered the offices of that bureau in Novgorod. But it was uncommon that such a visit would reach the attention of the Proxy Councillor for Science, and more unusual still that it would bring said Councillor to put on his coat and head down the hall to the back entry to an anonymous conference room.

In the capital, in an environment rife with media ferrets and political gossips, Yanni Schwartz found time, personally, to meet with Patil by a circuitous route. Technically she was one of his constituents, since Dr. Sandi Patil was a scientist, still registered to vote in Science, and he was Proxy Councillor of that Bureau . . . de facto Councillor. Lynch, erstwhile Secretary of Science, had been Proxy Councillor when Giraud died; Lynch had become Councillor for Science by succession, with the right to appoint a new Proxy Councillor: Yanni. So Yanni sat and voted in sessions, even though Lynch was in the city: it was a valid vote unless Lynch should rise up and repudiate it, which Lynch wasn't going to do, being a timid sort; and the office stayed, de facto, in Reseune, where it had always been.

And being Director of Reseune as well as Proxy Councillor—Yanni wielded a certain power as head of the Expansionist Party, which meant what he did politically was usually policy-setting in that party.

That was why, if any of the reporters outside the building had seen him meeting with Sandi Patil, it would have drawn notice—Dr. Patil being a particular darling of the Centrist cause, adored by the radical fringe of that group, though the majority of those registered in Science were Expansionist. She had voted against Giraud Nye, that was a near certainty. Now she arrived and proceeded as if she had business somewhere in the mundane administrative offices downstairs, some matter of records or certifications . . . then took the lift straight up to the administrative third floor, where a good Centrist was decidedly in foreign territory.

Yanni entered the conference room: his azi companion, Frank, was with him, but Frank went on through to the foyer. He had no other security present, unusual, in itself, for a Director of Reseune. His visitor, upward bound, didn't have a wire or a bug: the moment she walked into the lift, Frank had made sure she was clean. She likely would expect someone like Frank to sit in on the meeting, but she had seemed skittish of this dealing, Yanni was forewarned of that, so he stationed Frank in the anteroom and settled alone at the head of the conference table, waiting—about, he trusted, to find out what Patil thought of the offer she'd gotten three months ago.

I need time to think, she'd told the Reseune aides who'd initially contacted her. They'd warned her that any indiscretion would cancel the offer. And for three months she hadn't talked to anyone—not that they'd been able to track. That was encouraging.

Are the papers I have still valid? she'd asked, via the same contacts, after Denys Nye's assassination.

Yes, she'd been told. She'd asked for a meeting with other aides last week—which was too much potential for noise: Yanni had insisted she meet with him this week, face to face. The Council of Nine was in session. The vote on a critical bill was at hand. So she came to the Science offices, and hadn't talked to any reporters.

That cooperation didn't surprise him. Patil had lived very quietly, avoided the news so far as she could, had gone silent when controversy had tried to attach to her name—and she'd been one around whom political storms could very easily have formed. She had common sense. She was an expert in her field. Centrists backed her. He had everything arranged to make it a bipartisan deal, if the interview went well. It was just the reporters and the public they didn't want informed.

The woman who entered the conference room—Frank showed her in and left again—was fortyish in appearance, but the record said she was past a century: on rejuv, clearly. She was blonde, wore a chignon of braids—which might be her own—with a stylish brown tweed suit and high black heels. Fashion plate. Compulsive in that regard. He'd heard that about her.

"Dr. Patil," Yanni said pleasantly, rising to offer his hand. "Have a seat. Coffee?" Staff had provided a carafe, with two cups. Yanni poured one, for an opener.

"Thank you," Patil said, and he poured another for himself.

"Quarterly break for you, isn't it?"

"Yes," Patil said in a flat tone, and took the coffee he handed her.

Straight to business, then, with the warmth of a desert night. Yanni had a fortifying sip of his cup and sat down.

"I know you've read the offer," Yanni said.

"I've read it," Patil said. The beginning didn't augur well. He had his own notorious temper, he knew Patil's reputation as a bitch, and he wasn't going to react. They were safe here, however, from the media *and* less stable elements of the population, and his contacts had indicated the woman was leaning toward acceptance. Discreet, difficult to read: and that was a plus, in terms of the offer they'd made her.

"And?" he said.

"Not going to change your mind on *this* project?" she asked.

Sore spot.

"I assure you. Giraud Nye set this one in motion. It still moves."

"The position would be Wing Director in Reseune, at Fargone."

"Yes."

"Inside ReseuneSpace."

"Yes."

"Under an azi director."

Well, there was a nasty little tone. Prejudice on that score occasionally did come from stationers, which she had been. It even occasionally turned up in the halls of Reseune, in certain places. It grated on him, in a major way. "Oliver Strassen is a CIT now, Dr. Patil. He's been a CIT for some time. Social as they come and I'm sure you'll enjoy his company."

"Supposing I take this post, I'm to have this signal honor."

He was, for one heartbeat, not sure they wanted her anywhere near azi, let alone in charge of a program where there would be thousands. She was the best at what she did: that was one reason they'd approached her, that, along with her Centrist connections.

But she wouldn't be dealing with that aspect of the program. She'd be presiding over a station research installation, for cover, and she'd be well-insulated. "The deal has sat on the table for three months, Dr. Patil. We've answered all your questions, I trust. You've been free to consult certain advisors. We appreciate your discretion. Now do you have an answer for us?"

"Your influence, ser, got me hauled down onto this planet two and a half decades ago, cancelled a guaranteed program, shoved me into a teaching position, which is another honor I'd rather not have had. So now you want me to set up a lab, and I suppose you expect I should gratefully vote for you, if you stand in the next elections."

Oh, she was absolutely everything his aides had said. Brilliant, a Special, a mind ranked as a national treasure. Specials weren't necessarily nice people—a lot of them were downright eetee. The woman's students either worshiped or hated her—according to their skills and personal tolerances. But they still enrolled. Nobody cared about a Special's manners, where it came to her work.

"We haven't said a thing about your voting your conscience, which I trust, being an ethical woman, you will do wherever you're based. Hell, stand for Science yourself. You always could have done that."

"Correction. *Not* easy in a military bubble, where politics has kept me for decades. Equally inconvenient to do that from a Reseune Security bubble at the end of space, where you want to send me. I detest the military. I detest Reseune. And you want me to work under a local Reseune director who's absolutely guaranteed to be a by-the-book rule-follower."

Ah. *That* was the concept. Maybe not an entirely irrational prejudice.

"If you knew Ollie Strassen you wouldn't hold that opinion. And I'd have thought you'd gotten tired of graduate theses. You got caught in a situation, let me remind you, I didn't personally choose. I still support the decision, for the record, but this post I'm offering you is vastly different; and it may, I hope, make some amends for your time in purgatory. Fargone is a very comfortable place."

"And I'd be under stringent security."

"You were under that security at Beta, which has far fewer amenities than Fargone."

"And how long would I be there? Eventually I foresee a hardscrabble station orbiting a snowball."

"A living laboratory. Your laboratory, should you ever choose to view that world in person. But I think the proposal makes it clear—you'll never be required to leave Fargone Station. You'll work in a civilized, state of the art laboratory, handling everything from there ... a three-month lag in information, necessarily, six on a query *to* the object of your operations and back again, but you'll be in civilized surroundings, under perfectly innocuous cover, so long as you yourself choose to be." Give it a few years, and he'd bet that Eversnow would draw her out to the site. Hands-on work, a whole world for a lab, would draw Sandi Patil like an addiction: he knew her history. She'd eventually get exasperated with the six-month timelag on her results and go to Eversnow herself ... if she'd take the post in the first place. And nothing he had thus far heard from her discouraged him from enlisting her. "Let me be perfectly open with you," he said quietly. "Yes, you got an infamously bad deal during the War—"

"I got an infamously bad deal, damned right. Yanked out of my own research. Lured onto this dustball for a huge program I worked on for fifteen years—that got canceled six weeks before it implemented, largely thanks to Reseune. Pardon me if I have just a little apprehension about agreeing to another Reseune operation."

"There'll be no going back on this."

Patil stared at him, dark eyes in a pale face surrounded by pale hair, and right now there was no beauty, nothing but harsh, hard assessment. "And how long will you stay in office, Proxy Councillor? And how long until this kid comes along and cancels everything I'm working on, just the way her predecessor did?"

Blunt question.

"We advance it now," he said carefully. "We get the project implemented. That way there'll be no profit in *not* going ahead, and there'll be, let me remind you, nothing like the die-off zones, nothing like woolwood. Or platytheres."

"It's a damn snowball!"

"It's a Cyteen-class planet in a million-year deepfreeze. Remember you'll sit at Fargone, safe and warm and in all the comforts. You can socialize with Reseune staff—or not—at your pleasure, so long as you maintain cover. And you'll have a planet to work with, a thirty-billion-cred budget, for the next several years, and the warming—let me breach a little security here—is advanced beyond our first projections. We're going to jumpstart it with a few limited impacts this year, followed up by five more solar satellites as well as the research station. How fast *can* you push it, if we gave you a wide-open budget? And, once it's that far advanced, how soon until you no longer *have* to maintain cover?"

Lips went thin. But the eyes held thought. A lot of it. Fast. "Still a lot of practical unknowns with the snowball. Deep ocean. How much life is in the sea floor? How complex? You've got samples. The military is dialing up the heat with not a notion in hell what they're doing, beyond polluting it with the Earth biome and making themselves a nice little salt puddle. Brilliant. Is Eversnow life going to fight back, and how hard? And what kind of a mess do we have if you change your mind on *this* one midway?"

"This will be a centuries-long program . . . with a massive budget, on a bipartisan agreement. It incidentally gets you out from under Defense, back into Science, and gives you absolute authority about what drops onto that world— which may be some little incentive."

Guarded look, after a furtive spark. He had her. "Maybe."

"So do you want your name on it? Yes or no? It's yours, if you want it."

"No communications restrictions. Free access to Fargone, free access to Cyteen Beta by shipmail, no damn censoring of my articles for publication, once the lid comes off. And a two thousand-standard-kilo personal-goods allowance."

That mass was a heart-stopper, if it had been just any

traveler. The usual was forty standard kilos. No censorship on publication or scientific cross-communication, even with Earth and Alliance: that was worrisome—but it was no longer wartime and the lid was off. They just weren't used to it.

And the ridiculous personal-goods travel allowance was minuscule, compared to the equipment they'd be moving out there—a whole lab, containerized, to the farthest station down that strand of stars. "No communications restrictions," he agreed, "no publication restrictions—once the cover goes off, not from Reseune admin, not from the legislature. For what we intend to have known publicly, for the short term cover story, you'll run a new Reseune-Space lab division at Fargone, having to do with medical nanistics, in a very secure facility. Reseune itself will pay transport out. And it will pay transport back, if you decide at any point that you want to resign the post. Your two thousand kilo freight allowance, all right, granted. I'll throw in a resettling bonus, apartment paid, station share paid—unless you go out to Eversnow, and then you'll have to take that station as it is. But you'll be in on a founder's station share, on what's slated to be a major waystation down that strand of stars—tell me where you can get *that* nowadays. You'll have 10k a month, with equal pension when you retire. That's the same as any Wing Director in Reseune. Out there, in Fargone's economy, that 10k *and* apartment and station share is pretty damn extravagant."

"Money's not the issue. Freedom is. I'm spied on. Followed. For twenty-five damned years I'm hounded by Cyteen police, Reseune Security, Defense MPs . . ."

"I'm aware of that. And you know why."

"I don't control what shows up at the public library!"

"What shows up at your lectures is a problem you didn't choose and don't cultivate. We know that. Here, you're a magnet for people with agendas. You won't have that problem at Fargone—for one thing, you won't have to give any public lectures. I don't, frankly, encourage any publicity, for the initial period without cover, when, shall we say, political interest in your project is likely to be intense—even on Fargone. But there's no Paxer problem on Fargone, no Abolitionists to speak of; or if there are, they're the polite sort who simply write condemnatory letters to the station bulletin board, nothing violent. We appreciate that you've been discreet throughout your career. We have no doubts of your character, your credentials—" Give or take a certain bias toward voting the opposition in Science. "We certainly have no doubts of your administrative abilities in a lab operation, and none about your scientific expertise. You'll be able to pick your staff from Beta: you have absolute authority there. But I do need an answer, or I need to start looking out at Beta very quickly, because we are going to a vote tomorrow and I'm going to have to have some idea who we can put in. The bill will pass. I can present it for a vote with your name attached by cloakroom rumor, or not. We have a few Reseune personnel we could send out there, with less need of security, but you're our first choice, one both sides of the aisle can agree on. And this is your one chance to ride it all the way from tomorrow's vote to fund a 'medical nanistics lab'—the project you're signing onto."

"What time frame for my going out there?"

"Your departure within three months."

"I'm not sure I can make that deadline. I have a residence. I have classes . . . I have to pack."

"You'll receive considerations. If you can't sell the residence in the time provided, someone will buy it. That's no problem. Set aside what you want to take. If you're close, but a little over, between you and me, we can forgive a few kilos. Someone will have to take your classes."

A shift of position in the chair, a deep breath. "Tell me. Does the Emory girl have any idea what you're doing?"

Lie? He shrugged. "While I'm Director of Reseune, I *am* Director of Reseune. We have an understanding."

A line deepened between her brows. "You mean I'll be racing the next administration of Reseune. I do appreciate the honesty. It's been rare, from your district."

"I think the level of support you'll have from her lies partly in your hands. Did I mention to you that Oliver AO Strassen is a person she regards as a father—and his word carries an enormous weight with her?"

God, he loved delivering that small punch. It got a blink of those dark eyes, a sudden reassessment of biases, realities, and the worth of Oliver Strassen. It drew her deeper and deeper into visualizing herself integrating into the society she'd live in—first step in a good sales job.

"If your operation is running well," he continued, "well documented, all the earmarks of the project it ought to be—I'm sure Ollie Strassen's word will carry an enormous weight with her. It's a big boost for Fargone's economy— that's a great plus. I think when sera Emory assesses what *is* out there now, and what you'll have done by then, she'll agree. This is your project, on a platter. All the work you did back at the turn of the century can go into practical application. That is, if you want the job."

"A snowball. A damn snowball."

"A snowball third from its sun, with liquid water, an Earth genome puddle, and warming fast. And I assure you Fargone Station is absolutely the equivalent of Cyteen Station, all the amenities, an active social scene, every luxury you could ask. You'll be well able to afford it. You know how a Wing Director can live."

She drew a deep breath. "Have you got the paperwork?"

"I have it," Yanni said, and quietly opened the folder on the table.

The next meeting of the day was not on Science turf. It was over across the ring of Bureau towers, under a hazy seaside sky, in the Defense Tower, and Yanni went there with his full entourage, pursued by an unruly handful of reporters who'd followed him over from Science—into a reception made doubly noisy by reporters hanging about the portico of Defense.

The news services sensibly hoped an unannounced visit from the Proxy Councillor of Science to the Defense Tower might have some meat to it, with the Council of the Nine in session and now in a one-day recess for reading and consultation. It was a particularly good story, since elections were in progress in Defense, and Khalid, who had had a notably bad relationship with young Emory, was running against Spurlin, who was only slightly friendlier to Reseune. Current Councillor for Defense, Jacques, who'd been chair-warming for the old warhorse, Gorodin, who had just died in the post of Proxy Councillor—it was all very tangled—had not opted to defend his seat, but he had appointed Spurlin to be Proxy Councillor in the interim, so it was a wide-open and nasty contest. There had been talk Jacques might even resign and let Spurlin run as an incumbent. But it hadn't happened.

"Are you pressuring Jacques to resign?" a reporter shouted at him. And another: "Do you have any comment, Proxy Councillor?"

He wasn't throwing morsels of business to the media. Not on this. Not before the public deal was done. But he stopped, faced cameras, smiled in the sunny way he'd learned to put on when he was wearing his legislative persona. "There are a few items on the agenda that make sense to discuss with the outgoing councillor."

"This is an unscheduled meeting, right?"

". . . wide-ranging discussion on a number of issues where we can reach consensus, a few on budgetary matters." If there was anything to make a reporter's eyes glaze over, budget was it. Budget could lead to absolutely unmarketable footage, unless corruption was in it. And it wasn't. Actually, and for once, corruption wasn't the issue, and Jacques himself was never news.

Frank and black-uniformed ReseuneSec had meanwhile opened an avenue for him toward the door and during that second of glaze-over, he took it, while building security held the doors: press was allowed to besiege the outdoor carport. They couldn't, however, block the lobby.

Upstairs via the lobby lift, in relative calm, up to the fourteenth floor. As Proxy Councillor for Defense, Spurlin had an office there. Khalid's was somewhat higher up—clear up on Cyteen Station, as happened—and that was about as close as Yanni hoped to see him.

It wasn't a loving relationship, even so, his personal acquaintance with Spurlin. His own predecessor, Giraud Nye, had had a relatively cozy relationship with Defense, when Gorodin was in office, much less so with Khalid— the first Ari had had at least a reasonably good one with Azov, and then Gorodin, during the war years when Defense had had to rely heavily on Reseune. But young Ari had started a war with Defense and ruffled some egos mightily—especially Khalid's. Spurlin remained a bit of a cipher . . . but he was far more acceptable to Reseune.

Votes were coming in electronically, ship-mailed from time-lagged stations, to be opened simultaneously on Cyteen Station as polls closed on Cyteen itself. That would happen in July, given the longest round trip of messages, which was Fargone. But he owned one advantage in going into a negotiation with Defense, whoever ended up at the helm: Defense could look forward to a few years of fairly reasonable, low-key Yanni Schwartz before they had to deal with a sharp witted and adult Ari Two, whose agendas were as yet unknown—and the military didn't like unknowns. It preferred the devil they knew. Khalid, if he won, certainly had rather deal with him; and Spurlin certainly didn't want him making any cozy deals with Khalid. Jacques—nobody cared, nowadays, what Jacques thought.

He took Frank in with him on this one, Frank carrying a briefcase that never strayed far from his side. Communications, that was. Defense knew it, probably had a truther aimed at the room, would run electronic surveillance to see if any signal went out from that briefcase, and God knew what other probes it brought to bear, trying to penetrate the secrets in it.

Yanni didn't sit down. Since there was no Spurlin as yet, he made himself at home. He drew Frank a cup of coffee, indicated a chair to the side, where Frank ensconced himself—they'd been together lifelong, he and Frank, close as brothers. He wasn't comfortable outside Reseune when circumstances excluded Frank, was much more at ease in a room where Frank was, and he took himself and a second cup of coffee to a seat at the oversized conference table.

Spurlin came in, a walking stormfront of a man, with uniformed aides, who dispensed papers, water, glasses, and old-fashioned pens and notepads, God knew what they were supposed to do with those.

The aides settled primly around the edges. An ache hit the roots of Yanni's teeth as Spurlin lowered his wide-shouldered, uniformed and be-medaled bulk into the head chair. A silencer had started running, to prevent any eavesdropping.

"Admiral," Yanni said with a dip of his head.

"Ser," Spurlin answered. It had a note of question.

"Patil just agreed to terms," Yanni said plainly. "No alterations worth mentioning, except a two thousand-kilo mass limit and freedom to publish after the cover's lifted." He eased back in his chair, a little less ramrod straight. "Well. So we're all go."

"We're go."

"We'll handle communication with our own people at Fargone. There's a freighter going out on the twenty-fourth."

"Skip the freighter. No Alliance transport." Freighters were that, Alliance merchanters, plying the routes between Union stations. "We have a courier. It can leave after the vote tomorrow."

Low mass, big engines, faster by a classified number of days—especially if the courier was ready to launch. And no Alliance snoopery, though if they black-boxed it, there was no likelihood Alliance would snoop at all. Yanni nodded. "If speed is an issue. We have the appropriate orders ready. We can make your schedule."

"You were that convinced she'd do it," Spurlin said.

"I thought she would, yes," Yanni said. "A research scientist, with a life's-work project backed up on hold for decades? I was very sure she'd do it."

"Her Paxer constituency really isn't going to like her taking a Reseune post. Domestic security had better take hold and look sharp when that news breaks."

The Paxers, the peace party, had fallen on hard times after the War. They weren't the threat they had been. They'd had a spate of bombings. A certain number of their intellectuals showed up at Patil's public lectures. So, shadier and more violent, did a few of the Rocher Party, the Abolitionists. But it was a public forum, the Franklin Lecture Series, sponsored by a Centrist-leaning agricultural processing consortium, and as much as Patil's speeches usually generated web chatter, *she* didn't participate in the fringe-element chat. She more or less politely dealt with everyone who actually showed up; but she had a sharp manner when asked a stupid question, and only the intellectuals tended to ask her questions, *not* the subway-bombing lunatic fringe—they probably lived in terror of her. So did the tea-sipping social set who'd attend any function on the library circuit.

"ReseuneSec is going on alert when Patil's acceptance of a post goes public," Yanni said.

"My office will be on it," Spurlin said. Spurlin's specific office was system defense. He was a post-war admiral, never in combat. Khalid had that advantage, that he had fought against the Mazianni, the former Earth Company Fleet. "But this is supposing it goes through. Corain's not entirely a surety yet. It could all fall apart."

"I'm pretty confident he'll go with us on this," Yanni said. "Lao's with us." That was no news. Lao of Information was battling rejuv failure herself, another election they were going to suffer, but she was at the session, holding out on painkillers, Reseune's old friend. "I'm scheduled to talk with Corain this evening. But don't give any interviews until after the vote. It'll look bad."

Spurlin had no sense of humor. At all. "Your man at Fargone. The azi . . ."

"CIT," Yanni corrected him.

"Ex-azi. Emory's man. Is he up to handling the security aspects of this? And what will he be telling the girl?"

"I have less doubt of Ollie Strassen than I do of anyone else involved in this undertaking, ser. And he doesn't communicate with young Emory, never has. We have very efficient management out there. Check your records."

"So now you have a program."

"We will have a program." Yanni gave a small shrug. He wasn't really comfortable with Spurlin. The privacy screen made his sinuses ache. And he was anxious to have the meeting done, in token of which he drank half the very expensive cup of coffee at one go. "Patil will be drawing her own complement from Beta Station, perfectly current with the research. So you'll have plenty of sources who'll talk to you very nicely, I'm sure."

A brow lifted. Spurlin looked marginally happier with that thought: the military fairly well ran Beta, and that was insystem, definitely familiar territory, familiar channels. "So you get your new lab."

"And you get a planet," Yanni said wryly.

"Humanity gets a planet," Spurlin said. That was the theory. Humanity couldn't live on Pell without supplementals, and the fungi were lethal over time. Humanity couldn't actually live on Cyteen—if the weathermakers and the precip towers ever failed, they were all dead in a day. Humanity did *too* damned well at surviving on Gehenna, and if all of them could turn up dead in a day, it would make everybody sleep easier at night. They hoped eventually to do better at Eversnow—a viable planet, one they could entirely terraform and render completely habitable, right down to the oxygen balance—*and* where people could come and go without turning themselves into such deeply acculturated specialists they couldn't integrate with spacefaring society.

And not the only such planet, hereafter: once they'd proven the case and established the precedent for terraforming a marginal world, once they'd gotten past the emotional nonsense that bacteria counted as life on a world, young Emory *would* see the benefit.

That meant activation of the Arks, a use for the stored genetics. A new Eden.

A reserve Earth, in case the unthinkable ever happened.

"I have Patil's name on the contract," Yanni said. "But first out there and setting up at Fargone Station . . . will be ReseuneSec."

That didn't make Spurlin happy, but Yanni said it anyway: "ReseuneSec, for a Reseune installation. We'll establish connections, set up the labs. Our setup won't bother your military 'hospital' there in the least. But where it regards our tech and birthlabs, we don't admit anybody but Reseune personnel. That never changes."

"I wouldn't expect it to," Spurlin said, and, as if the admission were physically painful, added: "Good. We're happy. We can back this."

If we're elected, was the unspoken context. And Science was backing him as far as it dared. "Thank you, ser," Yanni said.

"I take it you're going to call on Jacques, upstairs. Give him my regards. And Khalid."

There it was. The direct challenge.

"I'll of course send the proposal up to station," Yanni said. "And of course present it to Councillor Jacques. But I'm very glad to have this particular discussion face to face."

Meaning Jacques was all but an afterthought, and the face to face he'd chosen had been with Spurlin, not Khalid. That had to please Spurlin.

"Good luck in the vote," Yanni said. He didn't mention the name Emory. "Will of the people. Civilized understandings. We'll hope to keep in touch, however things turn out."

There was a little flicker from Spurlin's eyes, a little consideration of that point, in the long-term realities of Union politics, that Councillors could be challenged every two years, and narrowly rejected candidates often came back repeatedly—if not this time, then next. Yanni's bet, personally, was on Spurlin—who, whatever his lack of combat experience, was the better politician. And the polls were running that way.

"Pleasure," Spurlin said.

"Mutual," Yanni said, and rose and shook hands.

No trail of documents—no outside witnesses. There would be a vid record, to be sure—Defense was rife with bugs—but he now had to go upstairs and explain to Jacques, who would actually cast the vote, that there was an understanding, and thank you so much for your help getting this far. Jacques' permanent retirement was a few months away, resignation from the military—given a sinecure of a corporate position. That had taken a little maneuvering, but Khalid would have beaten Jacques hands down, and no few people had moved to see Jacques step down fast and first, to make Spurlin look as attractive as possible.

Subordinates would work out the details from this point on, and settle such things as a launch time for the military courier, bearing orders for Ollie Strassen, but not, of course, anticipating the formal vote in Council.

Those orders, on a datastrip, he did leave with Spurlin, in a sealed envelope. The envelope, that old-fashioned precaution, wouldn't in the least stop Spurlin's people from getting into it, but it would occasion them just a lit-

tle hesitation—a point of satisfaction, just to tweak their
sensibilities—and they wouldn't learn a damned thing
once they did. What he'd told Ollie Strassen in that message, he'd told Ollie in plain words, because Ollie had his
training, had gone CIT, and, canny old Reseune hand that
Ollie was, from the inmost circles, he knew exactly what to
make of the message:

*You're getting a new wing and a director who'll be under
you. Keep it that way: she'll have notions of her own, but
you're in charge. She'll have a hell of a budget: a detached
module, cleanroom and security lock, all on Reseune's
ticket, all strictest security. We're reviving the Eversnow
project, total security: she'll run it. She's all yours.*

He had his little pro forma meeting with Jacques, who
was looking tired and overwhelmed these days, talking
about his impending retirement and an apartment on
Swigert Bay, and then Yanni ran the media gauntlet to the
car, which delivered him and Frank back to the hotel in
ample time for a little relaxation, a drink at the bar.

And that lull offered a little opportunity for a side ex-
cursion. The hotel had a shop and the shop window, on his
way to the tower lift, had a certain trinket he wanted. He
sent one of his staffers back down to buy it, gift-wrapped,
and meanwhile Frank ordered supper catered to his
suite . . . supper for two, with a choice of entrees, with a
later supper for himself: this was pure business. Critical
business.

He had time for a shower, a change of clothes, nothing too informal, however. He was combing his hair—no
haircut really improved it—when hotel personnel arrived,
dogged by ReseuneSec, who'd have superintended the
meal from the start, and Frank let them in.

They wheeled a cart in, set up the small table with a
politely low arrangement of flowers, and set a pair of wine
bottles onto cooling cradles, with two more in reserve . . .
not that they might crack a second one, but it was available, a choice of dry or not; and by the time they'd finished, Frank would deserve at least one survivor.

Mikhail Corain of Citizens arrived on time at his door,
with no aides, no entourage, and, hopefully, no reporters in train, unless someone had followed him up to the

twentieth floor. It was a meeting that would have drawn attention—if reporters had been able to get past VIP security, or accurately figure which of fourteen high-profile guests Corain might be visiting. Corain was, besides Councillor for Citizens, the head of the Centrist Party, and he'd been in career-long opposition to Reseune. Certainly if he could have consigned the first Emory to hell, Mikhail Corain would have been happy to see her off. Relations with Giraud Nye had been better, but they hadn't been warm. Relations with the second Emory? Guarded. Very guarded. It wasn't good politics to attack a kid.

Corain didn't look at all comfortable in coming here. But Yanni put on his own best manners, pleasantly offered his hand, offered Corain a seat at the small dining table, while Frank politely and firmly stationed ReseuneSec personnel outside the door, not inside.

Salad was local; the pork loin and the chicken were both Reseune's, and the wines were from Pell. The after-dinner coffee would be an Earth import. The meal encompassed a significant half of human space.

"So glad you were willing to come," Yanni said. "Pell Sauvignon? Or Riesling?"

"The Sauvignon," Corain said, and Frank quietly prepared that bottle. "Frank," Corain said, by way of greeting, and question. "Good evening, Frank."

"Good evening, ser." Frank smiled at him, perfectly at ease in his unaccustomed role. "I'm doing the honors this evening. My discretion is impeccable. My service may not be, but I hope you'll forgive my slips."

Corain nodded. Given his constituency, which compassed some of the Abolitionist types, he might be uneasy about the unegalitarian situation that surrounded the dinner, but thoughts passed through his eyes, one of which was surely that he'd rather Frank do what he was doing, and *not* have a leak of what they said here.

Yanni reckoned so, at least, and lifted his glass. "Who'd have thought we'd sit at one well-stocked table? Here's to . . . what shall we call it, ser?"

"Common sense," Corain shot back, quick on his mental feet, and glasses touched. They drank. "Did Patil agree?"

"Agreed and signed this afternoon," Yanni said, while

Frank served the salad. "She's on board. I've sent a message to Ollie Strassen, at Fargone; I just finished a meeting with Spurlin, and he's on board."

"Busy day you've had, ser."

"Very."

"So," Corain said. "How is Reseune faring these days, without the Nyes? A lot more decision-making on your desk? Or do we perhaps represent someone else? I haven't had that ever made clear, and I'd like to have, before the vote tomorrow."

Not a stupid man, Corain: sensing, correctly, that his own position, though he'd been in on the planning—not something Defense knew—now came down to the one vote that could and would stop the Eversnow project. His having the critical vote held advantages very much worth exploiting . . . judiciously, getting full value for the transaction.

What Corain surmised was unfortunately quite true: Reseune under the Nyes, while powerful, hadn't wielded the power it had under the first Ari; Reseune after the Nyes was perceived as yet another degree weakened. People believed, to a certain extent correctly, that the Schwartz administration was even more of a caretaker administration, but certain people saw that he was not averse to putting his own agenda forward, and hoped that it might represent a third force inside Reseune. It was a period in which concessions might be gotten, in which Reseune's power might be trimmed a bit, in which difficult agreements might be forced—conditions the first Ari, or the Nyes, would never have agreed to, and Yanni Schwartz might, to get what he wanted. That was the notion Corain seemed to have about him.

But he had held these sessions with Patil, Spurlin, and now Corain, in a chosen order and for a very good reason. He was a psychmaster, as the popular term was, out of Reseune, and sensible people in Corain's position, whatever their personal feelings, were open to a presentation of simple, career-affecting facts. He'd laid the foundation for this move. He'd gotten Corain interested before he went to Patil, he'd gotten Defense aboard, which Corain couldn't do—and flatly told Jacques to resign and throw his support to Spurlin or see consequences to his reputation and his retirement income. Science was a key player, and Yanni played this one for all he was worth.

"This is your chance," Yanni said pleasantly, "to get something. By the time my successor gets hold of the project, which will be some few years yet, things will be underway, *you'll* see the terraforming underway, and there'll be nothing much worth remediating at Eversnow. We've extracted microbes from the deep probes—not highly varied, at four widely separated sites. That's the total local life. We have the samples. So it's my estimation that young Emory won't try. She'll go with what's easiest, and she won't do a thing to stop it."

"Seems she already does things. Huge expenditures. New building at Reseune. The new labs upriver. My informants say they're both her projects."

"Keeps her busy," Yanni said.

"Pricey toys, ser."

"Useful in the long run. Reseune had a proven security problem. It won't, hereafter."

"Security problem." The breath of a laugh. Then total sobriety. "So you've just brought the first Ariane's murderer back to Reseune. That just baffles hell out of me."

Oh, the man wanted to know about that.

"Shouldn't baffle you at all," Yanni said. "He wasn't guilty."

"You admit it?"

"Jordan didn't like Ari. But he wasn't guilty of murder."

There was a small pause in Corain's demolition of the salad. The fork went down.

"And he agreed to detention," Yanni said. "In his best interest."

"And you admit that," Corain said. Frank took the nearly empty salad plate. And Yanni's. Corain never looked down. Just sat, with a troubled look on his face. "Why did he agree?" Corain asked finally.

"He had no choice. It was an assignment. For us? Expediency. The need to get Reseune going again. It was paralyzed. The Nyes were trying to get contracts honored, agreements handled . . . He'd broken no laws. But he'd violated Reseune policy."

"Do you know who did kill Emory?"

"No," Yanni said. "It's not actually important, in modern context."

"Context! I don't see it as a question of context. Maybe somebody should bring it up before the Judiciary and ask about your *context,* ser!"

"Well, you and I can certainly do that, and settle a question of history, or we can proceed on a cooperative project that can benefit all of us."

"I still find it troubling."

"So far as I can do justice in the case, I've done it. Jordie Warrick is back at Reseune. Not my doing, since we're being quite forthright here. Young Emory did it. The possible perpetrators are dead and out of reach, so, outside of correcting history, there's no point."

"Correcting history has some value."

"Actually, I agree. More than that, Jordan's a friend of mine and I personally assure you we'll be engaged in that, once we've gathered some records that someone attempted to bury. I simply signal you that there's more to the story and I don't want to surprise you with any sudden revelations."

"*That* would be a welcome change."

"Among other things that may improve our working relationship—I want something to write down as an accomplishment for my own tenure, and righting that old wrong is one thing I intend to do. Improving relations with Citizens is another. Part of that is carrying out this Eversnow business. It was one of Ari's last projects—and one she was willing to cede to terraforming. I agree with her, and I think you do, though I don't think you'll be making it a major point for your constituency's consumption—we can't make Cyteen a laboratory. That's just out of the question, nowadays: too many complications, including the major city out that window—"

Night had brought up the lights of Novgorod, other towers above the hard-roofed arcology that was the subway, the undergrounds, the deep digs, coffer-dammed against Swigert Bay and safe as a pioneering city could be in an atmosphere that could kill you, if you got much above the twentieth floor, outside the bubble. The handful of skyscrapers *were* precip stations, pillars of the sky, guardians of human survival.

Corain's look was involuntary, and snapped back with a deep frown. "We won't ever settle that argument, I'm afraid."

"We may not. Say what you like for your voters. We're here, however, to talk about a safe laboratory that we can both agree on. Eversnow can prove whether or not terra-forming can ever be done anywhere, and produce an ecology we can live in. And it will prove in the affirmative, I'm firmly convinced. I think there is a place for that science. The effort will teach us things, for the benefit of my constituents. For yours, Eversnow will *be* that new Earth everybody dreams of."

"Off in the far dark," Corain said. "At the end of the universe."

"For now. You know the charts."

"Expensive, godawful expensive, at a time when your successor is busy spending your budget in advance. This is going to cost tax dollars. The whole remediation budget. How is my constituency going to benefit in the near term? I really want to hear it in words."

"Immediate jobs, at Fargone, where the big construction will start."

"No azi there. None of this moving in your own personnel and calling it proprietary."

"No azi in construction except inside the labs: building of the module, all open to bids. Then there'll be station construction at Eversnow, give or take a decade. More jobs, right down to the first off-hours snack bar, shopkeeper and supplier that pioneers it out there. Then more and more of them. Ultimately a new trade route for Fargone. A military base outflanking any possible Alliance expansion. Spurlin is aboard. Science is; you are; Information is; Trade will be. There are no losers in this project. Not even the local microbes, who are going to get an infusion of heat, light, and a chance to grow and adapt right along with our imports. We're not going to wipe them out. We're going to use them, bootstrapping our way up. But that gets into technicalities."

"Huh." A grunt. The atmosphere had slowly eased.

After a brief hiatus in the dinner, in which Frank hadn't moved, Frank deftly offered the choice of main course, pouring more wine.

"So," Corain said, and ate a few bites of chicken. "This is good."

"Reseune farms," Yanni said.

"No political objections," Corain said, and the mood lightened considerably.

Until, over coffee, Corain said: "Patil's in vogue with the Paxers—that's going to create a stir when she takes a Reseune post." Paxers wasn't a word the head of the Centrist party liked to use in public. But Corain used it here. And then he added: "They're already fairly stirred up, not knowing what to think of you in charge of Reseune. They were caught off-guard by Reseune's recall of Jordan Warrick—they'd been for that. They'll like the terraforming notion. They'll see certain of your recent actions as unraveling the Nye era. But certain of the leaders are going to be sitting up at night wondering what you're actually up to, and wondering what they ought to be up to, quite frankly. *Are* you unraveling the Nye era?"

"Yes," Yanni said. "In some ways, I am."

"Then why can't you admit, publicly, that Warrick wasn't guilty?"

"I don't *think* he was. I think I've got a timeline that proves it. We're digging. But as I said, everyone who could have done it is dead, now, simple process of years."

"Process of the girl's security, you mean."

"Nobody came to Denys Nye's defense," Yanni said. "ReseuneSec didn't, more to the point."

"Meaning you didn't stop her."

"Denys Nye's best effort couldn't stop her." He really didn't want to discuss his thought process during those hours. And he charitably didn't mention that he damned well knew Corain had been getting Jordan's version of affairs straight from Jordan Warrick, via a Planys tech with unspoken Centrist affiliations. That wasn't the only leak at Planys. Defense had its own network. But he didn't bring that up.

"And you're his friend?" Corain asked. "Don't you want to see him exonerated?"

Jordan had opposed the first Ari, opposed her philosophically—bitterly—and politically. Jordan wasn't happy with the second one.

"I don't think," Yanni said considerately, "that raising that question at this precise moment, with Eversnow at issue, can in any way benefit him or us. All it will do is stir up the Paxers at a time when we'd rather not have them stirred up—or gaining membership. Not to mention Rocher and the Abolitionists. Let me be completely honest with you: one strong theory I'm pursuing is that it was a directed killing by an azi. And that an azi can suddenly kill, in civilian circumstances, is not something we want bruited about. Nor, I hope, do you, ser. You know, on an intellectual level, that it is possible. Of course it's possible. Frank, you'd kill to protect me, wouldn't you?"

"Absolutely," Frank said pleasantly.

Corain looked unsettled.

"Downriver," Corain said, "we tend to rely on civil institutions to protect us."

"Upriver," Yanni said, "we occasionally find our isolation leaves us without other recourse. Not often. And Frank is a bodyguard. He doesn't advertise the fact, but he is. The point is, it's not going to happen without an expert intervention and some CIT's involvement."

"Whose?" Corain asked. "That's the question. If an azi did it, who directed it?"

Yanni hesitated over the answer. Then said: "Jordan is certainly one who could have done it. That's why it's not so simple to say he's guilty or innocent. Denys Nye could have done it. Possibly Giraud Nye. Or Ari herself."

Corain's brows lifted. "A variation on the suicide theory?"

"She had cancer, ser. Nothing serious, except her rejuv was going. Probably the cancer was a symptom—it might have eventually caused her death, but that wasn't a sure thing. I'll tell you something about the first Ari, which I think you know very well: she liked to control the timing of events. And her death was a major, major event—for which it turned out she had amply prepared."

"So that's why you say the perpetrator is likely beyond justice."

"It's one theory."

"But why in all reason did Jordan Warrick agree to take the hit? Yes, it was a transfer—but he could have appealed."

Oh, that was disingenuous. Mikhail Corain hadn't spoken up for Jordan, back then, hadn't spoken up loudly at all, and had politically hoped for Jordan's silence, since the immediate precursor to Ari's death had been Jordan's meeting with Corain and with Defense. Jordan had been cutting a deal to trade Reseune secrets and go public with charges—if Jordan could get himself and his son out of Reseune and under Defense Bureau and Citizens Bureau protection.

"Who knows?" Yanni said, equally disingenuous.

"So is his return a controversial matter in Reseune?"

Interesting question. Clever way of putting it.

"Not very. He's settling in; he doesn't yet have a practice. His son, you may know, runs an important office in Reseune. Young Emory's studying, mostly, not directly concerned with external affairs. You could say I want to deliver her a more peaceful universe. I want a universe in which she doesn't have to start out opposing you . . . a cooperative universe, with less and less motive to destabilize what works—you know, that antiquated notion of progress by compromise? I think we've had enough of fringe groups and extremists. I know you don't like them any better than I do. I've tried to initiate compromise in my tenure. Personal legacy, ser. Personal legacy. That's my ambition."

Corain nodded quietly over his coffee.

Whether Corain bought it all was a good question. Nobody trusted a psychmaster. Urban legend invented the word, and amplified it into crazy notions of mind control and telepathy, all sorts of nonsense. The answer was, like most things, complicated. Yanni's reasons were complicated, and the manipulations were complicated: a little truth, aptly distributed, with very few outright lies.

Divert and divide. Redirect the perception of profit involved. Create a little wedge, Defense interests and Citizen interests—those were easy to split. Defense was naturally Expansionist. Citizens was naturally Centrist. The Paxers' interests, however, weren't remotely divisible down that great divide of War years politics. Their name meant peace—but their war being over, nowadays they just wanted the power a large movement offered. Paxer rhetoric and Paxer violence could influence events. Violent acts could recruit the young and disaffected, while the old, canny, and astute Paxer leadership, some of whom were openly interviewed on the news these days, drew satisfaction from the fear that surrounded them.

A clever old warhorse like Corain, head both of the Centrist party, and of the Citizens Bureau—the very constituency that happened to contain most of the Paxer movement—did know what grief his party would come to if the Paxers ever got their wish. This might be the time, Corain might well be persuaded, to move the Centrists closer and closer to the same interests as the Expansionists—at least for this generation. Together, Defense, Information, Science, and Trade, the Expansionists had a strong bloc in the Council of Nine: add Citizens to that, and they had an unbreakable majority—on issues that Citizens could remotely favor.

And when the Nine swung that definitive a weight, the Council of Worlds historically fell into line.

That wrapped it up neatly enough. Yanni sipped his coffee, reminisced a little with the first Ari's old adversary, and listened as much as he spoke.

They didn't get into the second bottle of the Sauvignon.

They weren't *that* friendly.

BOOK ONE   Section I   Chapter v

APRIL 22, 2424
1545H

Ari *wasn't* in a good mood. The smile was bright enough, a broad grin, a second or two in duration, and then it was gone. She went over paper printout with a forced concentration that just wasn't up to its usual enthusiasm.

Justin Warrick didn't ask why. It wasn't profitable to ask, but her mood was bothersome. Ari wasn't sulking, nothing to do with him, he sensed. She was just trying hard not to be elsewhere this afternoon, and didn't volunteer the information that anything was wrong, but there was, somewhere in her universe.

Which, if it wasn't his doing, he had to take as not his business. Her universe in one sense had widened when Denys had died; in another, in the weeks after, it had gotten a lot more focused, more down to the task at hand, and he was fairly sure she was dropping weight. He saw it in the hand that gripped the stylus, in the angle of the back—backbones showed under the silk jersey. She had a few people on her domestic staff, people who were supposed to be seeing to her welfare and making sure she got meals. She certainly had Florian and Catlin to look out for her and serve as confidants. But something wasn't right, and he'd begun to suspect it was a troublingly unusual complaint in an eighteen-year-old genius-level CIT: far too *much* study, obsessive study. Too little real sleep. Taking the cataphoric drug too often, trying to let deepstudy hours sub for sleep, and giving herself no time for dreamfunction. That could lead to some real eetee behavior. Ari didn't say so, but the signs of that were increasingly there, in the weight loss, the slight rawness of nerves.

"I don't see it," she said, after scanning page after page. "Justin, I don't see it."

"Maybe a little sleep would be a good thing."

"I sleep just fine."

"Sure you do," he said. "Ari, do me a personal favor. Have a little more of it."

Now he got the frown, full-force and directed at him. "There's nothing *wrong* with my sleep pattern. I'm just not seeing this problem, is all."

"Well, possibly I'm wrong." Not likely. He knew the psychset represented in that printout very well, and he knew the particular case in question, and the right answer was obvious to a much lesser operator. On the other hand, he was dealing with a mind that was capable of taking a new approach to a classic problem, and capable of not pinning the solution where every other operator thought it was. It was an interesting point, whether the obviousness of the answer would make her miss the question ... or whether she had rejected the classic answer and was after something else which no other examiner had ever caught.

They weren't going to find it out in five minutes.

"I want you to take this home," he said. It was near the end of their regular session. "Don't look at it again until tomorrow morning. And, young sera—"

"Don't call me that!"

"Ari. Get some sleep. No study tonight. *That's* your assignment."

A quick flash of dark, sullen eyes. "I'm fine."

"Sure you are. Take the evening off. Take the night off. Think about it."

"Too damned much thinking," she said. "I can *get* this, dammit."

She had a real bent for macrosets, the big picture, a very, very rare skill; he was an expert at microsets, and he taught her what he knew. It was what he did, these days, regular one-on-one sessions, five days a week. He gave her cases, she figured them, they discussed the answers and sometimes argued them. They were working on actual integration work, putting psychsets together in a community, letting them run in the original generation and two or three more, and seeing how the interface worked.

But the one he'd given her, and also slipped into the latest mix, was an azi named Young AY-4, who wasn't theoretical. AY-4 had blown up and attacked his teammates ... lethally ... during the War. Justin hadn't told her that. He just pointed out something had gone wrong in the integration, and she'd correctly picked up on AY-4 as the problem. The real-life AY-4 had gotten the self-defense part down, all right, but it had gone bad, véry bad, and he had taken himself out along with his teammates, for reasons still debated. The Defense Bureau had trained their own so-called Supervisors for a certain period during the War, over Reseune's protests. They'd messed with azi psychsets, thinking they'd turn out a better, more obedient soldier, who could work with *any* officer, not just a Reseune-trained Supervisor. *That* hadn't worked outstandingly well—witness the AY-4 case. It was a famous case in his generation—an azi designation most anyone of his age would recognize.

One thing was certain: Ari hadn't cheated and looked the case up in Library. She'd rather be stumped. She'd rather do it herself. That certainly had echoes of her predecessor. So did the temper. But do-it-herself was characteristic of young Ari, too: passion for knowledge was one of her better attributes, so long as she wasn't sleep-deprived.

"I know you can get it," he said. Then he added, because she looked so tired: "Do you want a hint?"

"No," she snapped back, and then the frown mitigated into a worried expression. "I'm sorry, Justin."

"Sleep's good," he chided her. "Try it. You'll like it."

The worried look stayed. "It's not study, it's Yanni."

Yanni Schwartz. *That* shed a different light on her week-long mood. "Oh, well, a lot of people have said that."

"Sometimes I just want to break his neck." She gathered up her papers, shoved them into the folder she was taking upstairs and got up slowly. "And you're not supposed to hear me say things like that, so I didn't, but it's so, anyway. Damn him!"

Yanni was off doing legislative business in Novgorod. And Justin didn't want to ask what had happened. He just folded up his briefcase and wished he had a quick fix for what bothered his sole student. By what she said, it wasn't kid business, though her reaction wasn't helped by lack of sleep.

"You just take care of yourself. Don't take any kat tonight. Relax."

"I'm trying," she said, and sighed and gave him a pat on the arm as if *he* were the child, at thirty-odd to her eighteen. "You're right. I know you are. Probably the answer's obvious as hell and I'm being terribly thickheaded. *Is* it a trick question?"

"I'm somewhat interested to see what you'll come up with. I don't want to spoil it."

"You think I'm a fool."

He laughed; that proposition was so unlikely. But it was the perpetual self-doubt of a young genius mind that never found peers to compare to. "You're my science project. I'm determined to see the outcome. Keep going on it."

A very heavy sigh. She took up her briefcase and hit the door button. Florian and Catlin were waiting for her, dark and light, doubtless having tracked the whole four-hour session with the endless patience of their profession. Grant was on his feet, too, across the hall, not in possession of the coms Florian and Catlin used, but taking his cue from them. Grant was supposed to have been busy in the Education Wing office, but he habitually came over to Wing One to gather Justin up around this time.

The sets parted company, he and Grant, Ari and her bodyguards, taking their separate ways at least for the evening. They lived next door to each other, met for lessons in this little downstairs office in Wing One, because it was just more comfortable, and because her security didn't want her walking about outside Wing One lately, no matter that Wing One was largely depleted of shops, of restaurants, of diversions—even its lab now mostly gutted of equipment. They kept to their separate apartments and didn't socialize, beyond that.

Teaching her was how he earned a living these days, doing his regular work in psych design two whole days a week, back to back, Thursdays and Fridays, and then five days of afternoon sessions with Ari. His teaching her had been Ari's idea—her insistence, in fact; and that job had its moments of interest, flashes of brilliance, even excitement, when Ari chased some idea through the undergrowth of other opinions, and when, sometimes, she sparked *his* creativity, and opened windows for him into her own esoteric field. That was a reward he couldn't have bought for any price. Some days, many days, Grant sat in on the sessions, and gave his own opinions, and they argued with Ari over coffee and sandwiches—those were the good days.

This hadn't been one of them. Nor had the day before, nor the day before that, not since Yanni had left, now that he added it up. She turned in her lessons, and her notes, and her projects—his briefcase held her current one, which was a huge integration, nearly town-sized: he was supposed to run that for her on the lab computers—another plus: there was no shortage of computer time, not on young Ari's budget. Slip your own projects in whenever you want, she'd told him, and that casual little gift could be worth more than the extravagant 10k a month he drew on salary as the director of a non-existent research wing.

But she hadn't been herself for a week, and Yanni—Yanni, off in Novgorod, seemed to have done something she didn't like.

He didn't like to think about the outside world. Didn't like to think that politics down in Novgorod could ever affect him again. But he was connected to Ari. And it could.

"You're thinking," Grant said. Grant, alpha azi, life companion, lover—Grant knew him. Grant could read him like no other. "You're worried."

"Tell you later," he said. Out in the halls was no place to discuss Ari's business, not even with a friendly power in the Director's office and no more Nyes anywhere. He found himself tired, after the four-hour session—the psychological drag of an upset kid.

Or the fact it was near the end of the week. He hadn't slept well himself, last night, mostly, he realized now, because he'd gotten increasingly worried about the sessions with the kid, and dreaded having to deal with that temper. "I want to drop by the office and pick up a file, get the computer running on this in downtime." He could use his own Education Wing office for an access: no indication on the papers as to whether the combination of sets represented a real town, or just hypotheticals: the work itself was just a listing of Library links and job codes. The result, the only thing that mattered, would drop into the Wing One office computer tomorrow, representing what these personalities would be like in three generations, given that the first generation of the class ones would turn CIT and the second generation of the class twos would be born and reared CIT—by the class ones. It was complex, and it contained, in that fifteen pages of links to manuals, a few noted changes to those psychsets, and of course it included the choice of group ethic. That was Integrations. And Ari ran them in her head. He'd had to *make* her write them down, arguing that the computer didn't read her mind and he wasn't going to write it out for her, thank you, or check them the same way she wrote them—let's be precise, he said; and she'd said, the little minx, run them in your own head: the computer isn't always right.

"Is there time for me to chase down some loose ends of my own?" Grant asked.

"About half an hour. Then dinner out. All right? It's been a long day."

"Fine with me. Not enough time for my business. I'll watch you work."

They shared that office over in Education, their old office, as happened, convenient for the small staff they had—a staff that couldn't get clearance for Wing One, *or* his work with Ari. He couldn't hand Ari's notes to his staff to deal with, for two reasons: one, that anything she produced was classified, and two, because his staff couldn't operate on that level. But staff saw to it that the other things got done, when he was gone most afternoons—Em had gotten the rhythm of their schedule, and kept it going when neither he nor Grant was there; and a couple of beta clericals under Em, who could actually read the prefaces and classify psychsets quite accurately, had the place running like a machine. Things came out of Library, recommendations got printed, results folderized and cataloged, simple requisitions went out, supplies came back. They also handled the routine idiocy from Admin, the inane inquiries like, Please list your monthly case load by origin. State whether resolved or ongoing. It didn't matter if they sat and threw darts for two days—their salary solely depended on his teaching Ari—but the Admin computers didn't know that, because Yanni hadn't ordered technical to fix their classification. Admin computers still added their output into the Education Wing statistics. That could have been an ongoing problem for Wendell Peterson, who was over that Wing. They *didn't* contribute greatly to Wing performance ratings. But Grant kept them in the black, at least. And Jordan did—who never even entered the office.

Downstairs, down again, the two of them took the storm tunnels that crossed the quadrangle underground, a long, dingy concrete passage that offered a longer but warmer walk on a cold April day, when wind exceeded the safe limits of the barriers and brought in contaminants the bots and the pigs would have to track down. The tunnel was crowded today, a popular route, past Admin, between

Admin and Education—they'd recently installed a bank of vending machines down by the intersection, by the water fountains; but those only produced a traffic jam at noon. Right now people were bent on supper, and restaurants.

The route was particularly convenient for them: the storm tunnel exit in the Education Wing delivered them right near their own office door, in the 100's of A corridor, in that sprawling building.

Their office was dark. Em and the staff had properly locked up and gone home on schedule, to residences down in the town—the shuttle buses, a whole new fleet of them, ran a heavy service right at 1610h, the whole fleet lining up at the curb ten minutes after shift change. Em and the staff likely had mentally dumped the day's business and joined the outpouring, blithe and free for their own pursuits of the evening.

Their employers, however, didn't enjoy the luxury of such precise hours—especially not on teaching days.

Justin reached for his keycard, but Grant beat him to it and opened the door—walked in through the foyer that was Em's office, into their own slightly less tidy inner sanctum. Grant disposed his long frame in his own office chair, legs extended at grand leisure, while Justin opened his briefcase and extracted the desired folder. He fed sheets into the reader, which spat them out again. He returned each to the folder in the briefcase, not to mingle them with the piles of paper on the desk.

Fifteen sheets, file done, and the program asked him what program should apply.

He used his keycard again and told it, aloud, "Code Y10, Class alpha through mu. Read to D3, run Integrations. Output results to Base One, code Y10."

"Voiceprint accepted."

For about a second, thanks to his keycard and that spoken code, it hadn't been his own computer talking: that had been Base One itself, in a significantly different tone. It always sounded so human.

Then it was gone. His own computer, with far lower clearances, said, "Done."

"Thanks, computer, endit."

"Well," someone said. It was his own voice. Or nearly

so. He turned, his heart giving a little thump, and saw his father standing in the inner doorway.

"Hey, we're closed for the day." Half a joke. His father wasn't supposed to be here. It took a security clearance to get through that door, in an office that dealt with actively working psychsets *and* one special student's study projects. Jordan Warrick's security clearance was entirely nuked. Gone. Non-existent. And Em would have stalled, held him in the outer office. Nobody being there but them, *they'd* just left the inner door open and the outer door unlocked.

"I figured you were." It wasn't only Jordan who'd come in, it was, of course, his companion Paul as well, whose accesses had also been nuked. Jordan walked all the way through into their inner office and looked around. "My old digs."

It had been. Before the first Ari died.

"You changed the paint," Jordan observed.

Justin was still off-balance. He looked around him, foolishly, remembered it had once been a slightly different shade. Twenty years ago. "I suppose it is different. Still green. I didn't even question it."

"Probably security took the walls apart." Jordan gave a look around him, and Justin snapped the briefcase shut, sealing up the last item exposed. "Probably a whole new set of bugs."

"Possibly," Justin said. He worked with his father in off hours since Jordan's return, in the living room of Jordan's apartment. He brought a different briefcase with him when he did.

Jordan asked him: "What are you working on?"

"Today's a teaching day." He used his handprint to open the safe, and put the briefcase into it.

"Her."

"She's the only student I've got." He shut the door and sealed it, feeling much more comfortable after that door was shut. Grant, meanwhile, had gotten to his feet as Paul came all the way into the office. "I hate to say it, but you know you two are pushing it with security right now."

"What's life worth without a little excitement?" Jordan sat down on Grant's desk edge. "You look tired."

"I am, I think."

"Want to go out for a coffee?"

"I've had way too much coffee today. Bar?"

"Sure," Jordan said. "Got an idea?"

"Abrizio's." It was downstairs in Ed A, it had been there forever, never mind the new decor, and he thought Jordan would be comfortable in his old habitat.

"Great," Jordan said, entirely cheerful, and cast a wistful look around. "A lot's changed. I've been to that bar. I liked the old color. Red. You remember."

"Everything changes." His memory had holes in it, back then. Significant ones. He didn't mention that. He'd shed the briefcase. He picked up one that didn't matter.

"Have you *got* to take that thing?"

"I suppose I don't." He set it back on the floor, and nodded toward the door, anxious to clear the room and lock up before they drew down a set-to with Security.

He didn't quite make it. Three agents were standing outside, ReseuneSec, black-uniformed and somber. Just standing. Watching.

Offer a guilty excuse? Security knew where he'd come from, who'd walked into his office, and by way of the bugs Jordan predicted existed, they'd know exactly where they were going next. He could ignore them. But it wasn't in his constitution to do that.

"Off work," he told them cheerfully, "off to the bar."

"Ser," one said, stony-faced and solemn.

It didn't make him feel any better and it wouldn't stop them from reporting. The report to their headquarters had likely been simultaneous with Jordan's arrival in the office. But it didn't make him feel worse.

"I dropped by, actually, to invite you to dinner," Jordan said as they walked. "Tomorrow night. Paul's cooking."

"Sounds good," Justin said, not mentioning the known fact that he couldn't reciprocate—living where he did. Jordan didn't mention it either.

"That design question you posed Friday," Jordan said, "I think I've got an answer for you."

"I'll be interested." They'd collaborated long-distance while Jordan was over on Planys, a cooperation permitted and not permitted by turns, largely by the whims of the Nyes. Now the papers flew back and forth much faster, and they traded notes on the house system, sometimes hourly, when he was in his Education Wing office.

"I sent you a memo this morning," Jordan said.

"Sorry. I didn't pick up my mail."

"That's all right. You'll get it tomorrow. This is a therapeutic break."

Another turn in the hall. They took the escalator down among a handful of clericals and educators. A scatter of noisy kids, likely residents from upstairs, played tag in the planted garden below the escalator, down among the stone benches. Beyond, on the right side of the mall, a small cluster of neon lights advertised a bakery, a florist, a shoe shop, a casual clothing store, and, farthest in the limited view, Abrizio's Bar and Grill. The little mall was at storm tunnel level: it formed the commercial underpinnings of the Education Wing, a cozy little place, hardly wider than it had to be, frequented at noon mostly by academics, clericals and the occasional tradesman from the adjacent shops, but in the evening, mostly by residents from upstairs—Abrizio's offered a better menu then.

Inside the little bar was dark, neon, and had a reasonable level of music and conversation—one table was left, midway down, and they claimed it, pulled back the worn, still-comfortable chairs that had given up all pretense of authentic wood, and sat down.

Dog-eared menus stood on the table in a cluster of seasoning and condiment bottles. Justin and Grant didn't bother: their regular was a standard choice. Jordan took a perfunctory look. And it wasn't the sort of place where you input your choice with button pushes. An actual waitress—her name was Sonia—came over, asked for orders, and served ice water for starters.

They'd come in just for drinks. Justin and Grant ordered a large plate of chili over chips with real cheese, which was usually supper enough on its own, Jordan agreed, and they talked about integrations and deepsets between chips. It was a slightly high-end conversation for Abrizio's evening crowd, where the more likely conversation was administrative and domestic woes, or the current soccer scores. It was quiet enough for a reasoned argument, at least, and a disposable napkin went the circuit of the table, increasingly blue with the hieroglyphs of psych structure notation—not the sort of item they'd leave behind them, but not the sort of conversation that posed a security problem, either: the items he regularly brought Jordan weren't under security lock. Pleasant evening. Uncommonly pleasant.

"That's interesting," Paul said, regarding Justin's latest insert into the set they described. "Nice."

Jordan snatched the napkin back from Paul. "Ease off. Thought you'd know better. Don't you *dare* take that in."

It was a little feel-good Justin had added, the sort of routine that had once had him going round after round with Yanni. He tinkered with this design—had flown it past Jordan several times without comment. He'd slid it past him again in a moment of mellow curiosity, part of a larger structure he was working on, his own little foray into macrosets. And perhaps it was a due warning: they'd all had, somewhere between the first glass and the chili and salty chips, perhaps just enough vodka to take the edge off their cautions.

"No intention of taking it in," Paul said defensively.

Jordan shook his head. "Worm-ish little bastard. Don't trust it. Whose *is* this crap?"

Justin didn't, personally, agree that it posed that order of problem, or that it was crap. He checked himself short of saying so. The fact was, Jordan was right to check Paul if he had a doubt: being alphas *and* skilled in psych operations, both Paul and Grant were used to taking a small item in on a look-see, sending some little routine all the way to their own deepsets and hauling it out again without ever letting it plant any roots—and producing some good commentary. The only danger lay in something that hit their deepsets and felt good at the time, that tempted even an alpha to hold it, secretly. And it was, in fact, deepsets, that little piece, but he didn't think what he'd handed Jordan was in any sense harmful.

"That's not one of yours," Jordan said.

"Actually, yes." He'd written it. And—perhaps it was a little stinginess, or just that he wasn't quite through refining it yet—he *hadn't* laid that little routine on the table for Ari to sop up and run with, the way she sopped up and used whatever else he gave her. A conversation with her had sparked the idea a few weeks back, off his own notions of reward and gamma tapes, and Grant had thought it was good, but chancy, rule-wise. So he'd put it out for Jordan's comment. Paul hadn't at all flinched.

But Jordan had a contrary opinion. That could be useful.

"This," Jordan said, "is aimed at group dynamics."

"It is," he said, impressed that his father had laid his finger right on it, and added, "macroset, yes. But that's not the important thing."

"You're meddling with deep sets and it's 'not the important part.' I hate to tell you who that sounds like."

The waitress showed up with a bottle and refilled all the glasses while their attention was on the piece of paper. Which was probably, for people parsing pyschsets, one glass too many. Jordan took his forthwith and knocked back a large gulp of it before he returned his close attention to the scrap of napkin.

Justin had a sip of his own, read in that gesture of Jordan's a degree of anger that filled in only one name.

So, well, maybe the kid had been doing a little research in elder Ari's notes—she had them. She'd said she did. And, though it would be a disappointment to him if she'd pulled those items straight from elder Ari and not from her own intellect, he shouldn't be surprised. She had a clerical staff, had an office. She could get any access, God knew. She'd been putting out masses of design work in recent weeks. Certain people in Admin—Yanni in particular— had warned him about Ari One's notes, to be just a little alert for Ari cribbing off her predecessor.

But she'd been arguing with him—and, dammit, she'd argued her points with understanding. There was no mistaking that. They'd had fun with it. And, no, dammit, he didn't think she was cribbing: she was too fast on the response, give or take today's performance. He worked back and forth with the kid. She produced things that were downright elegant—and scarily wide—while he watched her work. He'd listened to that simplicity and simultaneous broad sweep, admired it, and this one was his flight of inspiration, dammit.

But it evidently sounded to Jordan like *his* Ari.

So maybe he had more of the original Ari's notes in that briefcase in the safe than he knew he had . . . God knew what classified programs *that* could dip into. Gehenna was only what this generation knew about. Or—worse thought—one that sent a cold rush through his veins—could he be remembering the original Ari's lessons with him, from way back? Could repressed thoughts have woken up, lately, having, finally, found something in her successor to tie onto?

That was an eetee thought, one he really didn't like. He *didn't* remember the study sessions with the first Ari. Not all of them.

"So you did this?" Jordan asked him bluntly.

"Yes."

"Wide as hell. Feed this to a population with a disposition to take it deep and it'll set hooks. You won't ever get it out."

"It doesn't seem to do any harm. That's what I'm asking you about."

"The *breadth* is the harm. That little routine won't stop. It'll mutate in ways you don't know and the computers can't track."

"Are you sure it will, in the gamma sets?"

"I'm saying it will."

"Where will it intersect? I'll admit I don't know. That's why I brought it to you."

Another slug from the glass. "You don't know, I don't know, she doesn't know. You don't let something loose that mutates as it integrates. That's exactly the kind of thing Ari loosed—where she loosed it. You know that? The damn woman wouldn't listen—she'd just go eetee and say it didn't matter what you thought. She understood it, sorry you don't, it's going operational next week. *Damn* her."

A small silence. Grant quietly retrieved the napkin and pocketed it, conversation over, at least on that topic, that might have grazed oh so close to things security wouldn't want discussed in a neighborhood bar.

"Well, you're likely right about the routine," Justin said, and got a smouldering flash of eye contact from Jordan, a stare that locked, hard. "Probably it's too wide."

"You're *in* it up to your neck," Jordan said. "You're

teaching the brat. Be careful she doesn't teach *you*. Do you know what I mean?"

"That this is an example of it?" Justin said. "I don't think so. It's just a mind-stretch. A thought problem."

"And she's coming up with stuff like this on her own?"

"It's mine, for God's sake. Believe me. But this isn't the place. Let's not discuss it."

"Let's go to our place," Jordan said, "because I've got some things to say."

He didn't want to. That had been three glasses already, counting before and during dinner, and now after, and they were generous glasses. He hadn't taken more than a sip of his third. Jordan tossed off the rest of his and shoved back from the table, then intercepted the waitress and handed her his card.

Justin threw a look at Grant. Grant's face didn't react, but his eyes moved in a quick warning reaction.

"Probably," Justin said when Jordan had paid out, "we really had better get on home. I've got—"

"I have some things to say," Jordan said brusquely, "and I've had alcohol enough to say them."

"Maybe too much."

"Come on," Jordan said, and he could have a fight now, try to corner Paul and get Paul to quiet the situation, if only by handing Jordan enough alcohol to shut him up, maybe even hitting the bar down the row, where the music was too loud for coherent conversation. It had been pleasant until then. It wasn't, now. And Jordan's tolerance with security was already paper-thin, as it was.

He opted for going to Jordan's apartment, exchanging a few words in a venue where they could name names, and then going home, before the naming got too specific. Jordan in this mood would only brood about a cutoff from the bar, and get madder, and there was nothing productive in that, not at all. Jordan was frustrated: he *wasn't* employed any longer, not since his return from Planys. He had nothing to do but sit and read and work on the low-level problems Justin handed him, output which Justin read, remarked on, and passed on to Clinical under his or Grant's name—it gave him a better output on *his* record, and kept Peterson happier than he would have been, but it wasn't doing anything for Jordan's mood or his bank account. Jordan drew a stipend from Yanni's office, the size of which he wouldn't name, but it wasn't large. He had the rent and utilities paid. That was all.

And Justin didn't want another round on that score. Jordan's situation was on hold until the Reseune board met, that was that. Jordan wouldn't get his clinician's certification and his security clearance back until Yanni and Jordan were talking again.

There'd been some sort of blowup right before Yanni headed for Novgorod, and what Jordan had said in that office or what Yanni had said wasn't in his need-to-know, apparently, because neither of them had been willing to talk about it, but it certainly hadn't advanced the cause of Jordan getting his security clearance back.

And it wouldn't be helped by a public scene tonight.

They took the escalator up one, walked over to Education B, where Jordan's apartment was—not a word spoken until they'd gotten inside and into the living room.

Jordan immediately went to the bar, filled four glasses with ice, and poured healthy shots of vodka. Justin frowned and didn't say a thing. He took his when it was offered, and went and obligingly sat down in the conversation pit, with Grant on the other end of the couch; Jordan and Paul took the other side.

"So," Justin said. His plan for a quick exchange and exit was evaporating, but, well, predictably Jordan's anger would probably give way to a complaint about the certification issue, and the clearance issue, which then would go into known territory—not pleasant, but he owed it to his father to sit through another rehearsal of grievances. "What can't we say in the bar?"

"That you're making some bad choices."

"Professionally, or personally?"

"Both."

"They're my choices. Bad or not."

"You bring me these piddling clinicals . . . which you get paid for. In effect, I'm working for you."

"If that's a bother to you, I won't bring them."

"They're all that's keeping me sane." A drink of the vodka. "A damned thin thread, these days. Damn Yanni."

"I hoped you'd give me a reasonable critique on the other set I sent you," Justin said. "I'm waiting for it, in fact." Jordan had had too much vodka to make sense on that topic, Justin was well sure—Jordan had likely forgotten all about it, in the heat of the argument at dinner, but he had questions of his own that Jordan hadn't satisfied. The reward structure in that theta set emanated directly from work he and Jordan shared for years, it was related to the problem he'd handed Jordan in the bar this evening, and he hadn't expected that kind of reaction. Yanni used to heap scorn on his reward concept in the low-level sets, claiming it would produce problems down the generations in an azi-derived population. Yanni had called him a damned fool—until Jordan started working with him, and then Yanni had started listening.

"Piece of crap," Jordan said.

Well, that wasn't what he'd hoped to hear.

"In what regard?"

"In what regard . . . don't give *me* that calm-down routine. Your damn design is out in the ether. Piece of crap, just like that crap you handed me at dinner. Same fucking reason."

"Sorry, then. I won't press you for specifics tonight."

"I'll give them to you with a broad brush, same issue. Same reason. Same damn problem I fought out with Ari. She didn't listen. She implemented. Now I see it in my son. Grant, do you agree with this crap?"

"Ser," Grant said, "insofar as I follow the thread of this argument, I am in agreement with the design, yes."

"But then, you're Ari's design, aren't you?"

"Ser."

"Jordan," Justin said sharply, "don't pull that. You don't believe it, you don't mean it, so just don't touch it. That's your fourth glass."

"You don't see a problem. You think you're fucking brilliant, skipping over any substructure, just go straight for the deepsets: it's the shortcut, everything for the shortcut. And the poor azi you program, pity them—they're not alphas, they're not going to figure that's a leap of flux-thinking logic, no, you're going to have theta minds making a leap from a to zed with no supportive structure, no crosslinks, no work-up in their skill-set level to encourage any critical thought about their actual performance . . ."

"Thetas aren't good at that."

"Don't read me basic lessons! You know damned well you're taking a shortcut."

"I am. Yes. Admittedly. That's the whole purpose."

"And you're going to have a pack of thetas gone eetee with no recourse but Reseune operators to pull them back to sanity . . . *if* they can. A batch of smug, happy, *wrong-headed* workers."

"That's why I come to you." A little bald flattery never hurt. But it was also the truth. "I see you don't think it's a good idea. I respect that. I just expect more specific reasons for your opinion than I'm getting here."

"I don't know why I'd bother. You're getting all your theories from the little darling."

"I'm sorry. I don't think so."

"I damned well know so. You think that's new, that leap of procedures you threw into that last paper? That's Ariane Emory. That's Emory, cut and dried. She'd just wave her hand and say, with the appropriate gesture, 'It will work. It will work.' Hell! That kind of thinking created Gehenna. There's her kind of thinking run amok. She was doing it that far back!"

"But the azi there lived. They weren't expected to. But she expected it of them. She just didn't tell Defense. And what she did worked. The fact there's been other input into the system—that wasn't in program . . ."

"Well, that's the universe for you! Don't you get it? You can't anticipate your little program to run forever in a bubble. Something's going to impact it. Something damned sure *did*, on Gehenna."

"There's got to be a dividing line, between trusting the subject will adapt, and going only by micromanaging little situations, constantly referring back to a Supervisor. We're so damned conservative with the deepsets . . ."

"With reason! Have you ever seen a real eetee case? Has your real-life practice ever gotten the results of one of your damned thought experiments?"

"No. I'm teaching. It's all theory."

"At this point."

"We argue. In point of fact, I know the present Ari would love to hear your objections. She'd be very interested. We could have some good conversations . . . if you were so inclined."

"While she's hot after my son? The hell." The rest of the vodka went down. "Get me another, Paul."

"Jordan," Justin said, as Paul looked dismayed.

"I said get me another. There are things I need to say. I didn't know my geneset could produce a fool."

Paul got up and shot more vodka into the glass. Twice that, Justin thought, if that's what it takes . . . bundle him off to bed and let's end this evening somewhere short of disaster.

"I hate to point out," Justin said as Jordan took the glass, "that's five."

"Have you been alone with her?"

"Are you asking if I've had sex with her?" Justin asked.

"I'm asking if you've been alone with her. Grant, has he ever been alone with her?"

"Ser, I'd rather not enter this conversation."

Grant, damn the situation, wasn't able to lie, not to a man who'd been his Supervisor as well as his CIT father. In some situations he was thorough azi, and too vulnerable for this fight.

"I'm taking Grant home," Justin said, and set the glass on the side table. " 'Til you're sober. Grant, don't answer him. You don't have to answer him."

"Oh, I'll imagine the answer, then. Stay put, Grant! I'm not through."

"*I* am."

"You sit where you are and you listen to me. I'm seeing things in your work—I've been seeing them. I've corrected you. You've changed things right back—"

"Where it matters."

"You've changed things right back in the same vein as that little item you sent me this afternoon. The same thing you shoved in my face at dinner."

"I was uneasy about the concept, I didn't get an answer on the others, just a correction with no note. I wasn't sure why. I was asking your help with a problem, Dad . . .

I'm sorry if it gives you some eetee flashback to your own time . . ."

"Oh, back to my time, is it? What is my time, can you tell me that, son of mine?"

"I didn't mean that."

"Pretty clear what people here think. Twenty years out of the current here, twenty years of a real style change in operations here, Yanni Schwartz losing his mind and putting you with the little bitch to let her pick your bones clean. I don't appreciate that move. I don't care if the spoiled darling did threaten to stop breathing if he didn't."

"Actually, Jordan, I agreed to it. Clear the family name and all."

"Oh. Oh, that's good. I didn't *do* it, dammit! Do you need to hear that?"

"I hear you. I just think it's as well the public—when this goes public—hears it, too. I'd like to see the day—"

"What, the day everything's sweet again? It won't come. You want me to work with you? Quit working with her."

"I can't."

"Can't!"

"Let's put it this way, Dad. I won't. I respect you, I respect you tremendously, but you don't have the right to tell me who I work with. I'm getting something out of this . . ."

"Oh, it's clear you're getting something out of it! And you don't have the right to take *my* theories and hand them on a platter to that little walking memory bank. I had to put up with the last Ari taking my work and putting her name on it and I'm sure as hell not going to see it happen in the second generation."

"I haven't given her your work, except as you've taught me. After that, Dad, in the way things work in the universe, it becomes *mine.*"

"The hell it does."

"It becomes *mine,* Dad, not because I'm regurgitating it verbatim, but because I'm using *my* brain and *everybody else's* input *along with yours* to come up with my own ideas."

"And *her* input, it's very damned clear."

"Because you didn't like a two-line routine I wrote on a

cocktail napkin? I gave you a second instance of a similar routine, because my own leap of logic bothered me and I wanted your reaction on it, but do I get a sensible discussion, on this one or the last two weeks? No. First you ignore it—"

"I didn't ignore it. I corrected it!"

"Twice, without any explanation!"

"I'd think you damned well knew my objection!"

"I'm not reading your mind!"

"So I said something, tonight!"

"In the bar? You didn't say something in any rational way. You went orbital without a launch, just up there, bang! No preface, no sensible discussion, nothing but a fucking emotional reaction, alcohol-fueled, and fluxed to the max. You aren't thinking clearly on this, Dad. If you saw something in my work that triggered a flash of your own—"

"Don't you go patronizing with me!"

"All right, all right. This is it. We're going home."

"Home. Is *that* what you call it?"

"I live in Wing One! I live there, thanks to a time there was a time, thanks to my trying to find out about *your* situation, that I was apt to be arrested, which was damn near a monthly event in my life, and it was getting serious, about then. I'd have been in lockup. That was my choice."

"And then things all changed. All right. Level with me. There was a time they wouldn't trust you. I'm not talking about the little darling. I'm not even talking about Denys. I'm talking about Yanni. They wouldn't trust you. Now they do. Why?"

"Because she told them to. Because Denys Nye is dead, and his apparatus isn't functioning any more. Because Yanni likes me better than Denys did!"

"*Because she told them to.* Because she'd had a chance to work you over, that last time, when Grant was in Planys, and you were here solo, in her reach."

It was too close to the truth. He didn't want to lie about it. "She's a kid, Dad."

"She's a monstrosity. And she got her hands on you when Grant wasn't around. She finished what her predecessor started. Didn't she?"

"Dad . . ."

"I'm not hearing you deny it. Is it true, Grant? Did she do that?"

Silence from that quarter. Grant had prior orders, an instruction from his current Supervisor that outranked anything his first Supervisor could order on that topic.

"I draw my conclusion," Jordan said. "She did. Just you? Or both of you?"

"I have the session tapes," Justin said, braced for the storm. "And nothing happened. She asked me where I stood on certain matters. I satisfied the questions—that I wasn't an assassin. That *you* weren't. And Grant wasn't."

"Let me see the tapes."

Reasonable request, on one level. But not a good idea. That second thought flashed up, fast and hard: Jordan wasn't *any* father—Jordan and he twitched off exactly the same impulses: Jordan took a deep breath and he felt as if he had just breathed. Jordan flared off and his own adrenaline surged, mirror-image. He couldn't help it. He was a PR, Jordan's exact replicate, and the resonances were there, every muscle twitch. It was his face, as he'd never be, because he'd started rejuv at thirty-five and Jordan hadn't until forty-five—but it was close enough. Every lift of a brow, every frown, psychologically connected as they were, to boot, by Jordan's having brought him up as a son—resonated, in a way a natural son wouldn't feel it. They were twins. Identicals. And his father, besides all that, besides the fact that his father's own gut would react to that tape of him lying there, deep-tranked, undergoing questions from Ari's twin—besides all that, his father was a psych operator, and the first time seeing that tape, Jordan might be in shock, but the second and third time through he'd be gathering bits and pieces, tabs, things he could use in a constant, battering attempt to undo everything he'd seen done, to grab hold of parts of his son's soul and jerk—hard. Every damned time anything came up that Jordan didn't like, he'd have a key to his psyche that nobody else would.

"No," he said. "No. Those tapes are private."

"I'll bet they are."

"This was a mistake," Justin said, and this time, in his own moment of temper, reached for the double vodka on the side table and downed it in three gulps, half icemelt, because he was going to need anesthesia to get any sleep tonight. After which he propelled himself to his feet, and Grant got up. " 'Night, Dad."

"Oh, now we run for it. Touched a sore spot, have I?"

"Maybe," Justin said. "But I'm not staying here to have you twist the knife." He got a breath, and one clear thought. "I want to go on working with you. If you want it otherwise, you can have that, but don't answer me tonight."

"Tell me this," Jordan said. "How are the flashbacks?"

He'd been plagued by them for years. Flashes of a couch, elder Ari, the taste of orange and vodka. The smell of it. Not of late. And he flashed on the answer, the thing Jordan was really asking. "Not germane here, Dad."

"They're better, aren't they? Not as many as before you had a session with the younger version. *Was there sex?*"

"Nothing nearly so *entertaining* as the first time," he shot back, referencing the fact Jordan had seen the first tape, and he knew he shouldn't have said that. It was the vodka. Which hadn't been a good idea. He felt an oncoming wave of heat. "Grant, come on. It's not friendly in here. I'm sorry, Dad. I'm sorry for the whole damned thing."

"They're spying on us, you know. This whole conversation will go to her."

"More likely it'll go to Yanni. She doesn't meddle in my business."

"She says."

"She doesn't have to lie. And you've spread enough of my business out for the monitors to see, at whatever level. I've had enough of this argument, Dad. I was glad to see you home. I knew there'd be problems . . ."

"Meaning I wouldn't fall in line with the compacts you've made."

"Meaning everything, Dad, meaning just about everything." He had the impulse to say, Meaning you're frustrated about that license, meaning you're mad about lost time, mad about the current administration, mad that you're still under house arrest. Mad about your whole life. But the vodka hadn't that thorough a grip on him that he should let that fly. He just said. "I love you. Go to bed and sleep it off. Maybe they'll arrest me in the morning because I was stupid enough to let this carry on this far. Maybe not. Things are generally better now."

"Oh, the martyr, my suffering son."

"Have it any way you like. Security is what security is and they'll do any damn thing they like. I'm used to it and they know I'll tell them the plain truth. Hear that, Yanni? So just go to bed, Dad. At least we didn't have this conversation in the bar. But I'm not sure we should have had it at all."

"High time we had it."

"Sure," he said, "if you think so. I didn't have an inkling you were getting that mad about my repeated question. So think about it. And calm down. Come on, Grant."

This time they did make it out the door. He'd bet there was one more glass of vodka poured tonight, if not drunk, before Paul got Jordan into bed. He deeply regretted the one he'd had.

"I'm going to be hung over," he said to Grant.

"Glass of orange, another of water, water every hour, and two aspirin," Grant said. "Sovereign. You were making perfect sense, by the way."

"Sorry. Very sorry."

"You couldn't stop him."

No security had shown up. They took the open air route across the quadrangle to Wing One, and through the doors, and security checked them through and never said a word.

That much had changed since Yanni had taken over. People could be fools these days and not be arrested or interviewed. They might hear from Yanni once he got back, but tonight they made it home all right.

APRIL 22, 2424
2351H

Yanni was up to stuff in Novgorod. Yanni's office wasn't
going to tell her that, but Base One did. Base One found
it real easy to wander where it liked, into communications between Yanni's office and Novgorod, and between
Yanni's office and ReseuneSec; and what Ari heard made
her mad—not a real Mad, so far, but a good one all the
same. Yanni was talking to unusual people, people who'd
been enemies, and probably not making records about it.
That was a watch-it, but she hadn't told Catlin and Florian
about the problem yet, just in case Yanni had a reasonable
explanation.

    Yanni might guess Base One was into his stuff. Prob-
ably he didn't. Denys hadn't known to what extent Base
One had invaded Base Two, or if he'd known, he'd hoped
he'd worked around it, and he'd hoped he was being careful. Or at least he'd hoped to psych *her,* which would have
been the answer to his problem, if she'd been that stupid.
She'd grown up. He'd been one jump too late to stop her.

    She ran through all sorts of records on things Yanni
had done, from way back. She did find that her predecessor had trusted Yanni ahead of the Nyes. That wasn't a
great surprise. Yanni generally told the truth.

    She incidentally found that it was the first Ari who had
given Yanni instructions that if anything happened to her,
she wanted Jane Strassen to be the surrogate.

    And then she looked just a little too deep: Yanni had
had a long conversation with Maman about that, and
Maman had said, Hell, no, what do I want with a baby? I
had one, thanks. See how that turned out. No. Absolutely
not.

    Then Yanni had promised Maman if she did it for

them she could go back to space when the job was done. That she'd have a major directorate somewhere in space, and Maman had said, well, she'd think about it—because Maman really loved being in space. The War was what had made it necessary for Maman to be down on the planet, because it was safer, she found that fact out between the lines, but after the War, Maman had been so important to Reseune, she'd been stuck in an administrative post and hadn't been able to get transferred back up to the station. So for that promise, Maman said maybe she could put up with a few years of inconvenience.

That hurt. That really hurt, and it really bothered her—she didn't cry about it, but the information just bored a sore spot in her heart, until finally she psyched herself and said Maman had changed her mind eventually, that it didn't matter how it had started, she'd finally Gotten her Maman, all unexpected, because Maman had turned out to love her. She wouldn't believe that wasn't so.

Well, it was what you got for getting into people's records and eavesdropping: you caught people saying things you never wanted to hear, and this one, hurtful as it was, taught her that in a major way.

But what she found went on teaching her. She couldn't leave it where she'd left it. She couldn't stop looking at it.

She got into Maman's records, too. She'd never gotten a letter from Maman after Maman had gone away to space, and there were no letters from Maman hidden in the record, but she did find her Maman's report on her when she was five. *She's a handful. But she's bright. God, she's bright. She scares me.*

Ari Senior had also said—this turned up in Maman's letters—Let Strassen choose the second surrogate. And Maman was going to pick Yanni to take over her upbringing after Maman went back to space, but Giraud hadn't allowed that.

That was worth a Mad, too: Giraud had just overridden Maman, being head of Security. He'd sent Maman to space, then ignored her choice, and ended up choosing Denys, as being a relative closer to her as well as actually being a Special himself, without the Senate declaration that said so. Which Yanni wasn't.

No question where Giraud's reasoning lay, however. Giraud hadn't wanted any power edging over into Yanni's hands, and Yanni was the man that would take it and do what he pleased.

And of possible candidates to take her on, Giraud wasn't of the disposition. But Denys had agreed to it. Denys had probably just hated it; but Denys would have done it to get power.

Possibly, too, it was because Denys couldn't stand not knowing how she was developing. Denys had liked puzzles. And she'd been a puzzle to him—at close range. And by the time he was in it, he'd realized that an azi nurse wasn't going to keep her from disrupting his life, nor was domestic staff, nor even his own bodyguard.

The Child has subverted the minder, she read on a certain date, in a frustrated communication to Giraud. *She eluded Seely. She's a monster.*

She liked that one. It echoed Maman, in a Denys tone. She forgot for two seconds that she'd lost one and killed the other. For a fluxed second she was just there again, a little girl in Denys's household, pursuing a Mad about losing Maman, a Mad that had never let her be friendly with Denys and never would.

Or maybe it was just good taste, she thought. She'd picked her enemies, and she'd been pretty accurate so far.

And then, with the thought of Denys, she riffled through the rest of that electronic file, the one that slowly built a case against Denys, finding justification for killing him—

And, still in flux-state, back to Yanni's file, as large as Denys', in Base One.

Was there a connection? Did one temporary authority equal the other? Was Yanni on the level with her?

Denys might have killed her predecessor, and then made it look as if Jordan had done it, so Jordan was exiled for it. Or at least—Giraud had dug up the evidence. Giraud had hated the Warricks with a passion.

But it had been Yanni who had actually brokered the Family deal that got Jordan into Planys, close and protected. There was a lot more security at Planys for several reasons—the military base, the isolation of oceans you couldn't even fly across without decon; the fact that Planys worked on a lot of military projects and every communication that went out of there went through security. If they'd sent Jordan to space for exile, there'd have been ship-calls, people coming and going. Not at Planys.

So it was both a closer arrest, and a safer one—nobody was going to assassinate Jordan inside PlanysLabs, where visitors were so closely tracked. Giraud had been perfectly capable of arranging an accident, wherever else Jordan might have ended up, inside some Reseune facility. Yanni had saved Jordan from that.

Giraud had had power, a great deal of power just after the first Ari had died. And he had used it. A lot. So you could say he'd benefitted from Ari dying, and that was a motive. You could almost suspect him of killing the first Ari.

But in all his communications and even messages to Denys, he'd really been upset by Ari's death. He'd seemed to view it as a tremendous loss to Reseune—worse, a premature one, before they'd gotten the psychogenesis project really organized. They'd taken a whole year getting her started. So for one reason or another, they really hadn't been ready.

And once she'd started looking and sounding like her predecessor, Giraud had warmed up to her, and started doing her favors in a very fond way. She hadn't wanted to like him. But she'd ended up liking him, and still did, even knowing what he'd done to the Warricks.

The hour the first Ari had died, she'd arranged for the first Florian and the first Catlin not to be with her—she'd sent Florian and Catlin each off on an errand. She'd been alone, then. Jordan had come in. The sniffer at least proved that. Jordan admitted they'd had an argument, which no monitor had picked up—again, some device had broken, and nobody knew how. She'd died. But the crime scene had been muddled up because Denys argued they should call in the Moreyville police, not to have it investigated only by ReseuneSec, so as not to have any political accusations of a coverup. And in that process there'd been a lot of people going in and out, which they never should have been allowed to do: that was Yanni's note on the case. The sniffers' evidence was muddled for the same reason there were fingerprints all over—a lot of people used that lab, and a lot of people had been in and out in the immediate furor over Ari's death before the Moreyville investigators ever got there.

Should she take that at face value, as just the confusion of a bad, bad moment in Reseune's history? Maybe. The authority that ran everything had died, and for an hour or so nobody had been running things. Departments were all running at their own admin levels, no coordination, nobody to call or appeal to, until Giraud and Yanni had stepped in.

And Ari sending Florian and Catlin away . . . had she known she'd never see them again? Had she known she was killing them? Had she kept that cold a face and not given anything away to them, who'd have read her the way her Florian and her Catlin could read her? Some people thought the first Ari had killed herself. But she didn't know how the first Ari could have ever gotten that intention past her Florian and Catlin, if they were anything like hers.

She scanned Ari's notes from immediately before she died. She had, a hundred times. She searched administrative comments on Jordan, and *bastard* was about the sum of comments from Giraud and no few others, plus a note that Jordan had found out about Ari having run an intervention on Justin, and that Jordan was madder than hell.

But Ari's records stopped with the lab notes, right at the end of a sentence. Period. Was it significant that Ari had finished her last sentence? She would finish a sentence, herself, even if somebody came in while she was writing. It was just the way she was.

Base One had apparently shut down the instant Ari's death was logged. Base One had gone into an entirely different mode, truncated its wide information-gathering to a single, computer-driven thread, all but shut down—for so many years some people must have thought Denys's base in the house system had actually become Base One, even if it called itself Base Two. But Denys had known better. Denys had gotten her to log onto Base One when she was old enough. And maybe he'd hoped he could get his own access on it. But it hadn't done a lot when Denys was there.

And then Base One had said, *Hello, Ari.* In her predecessor's voice. In her room. She'd gained her secret friend.
Her childhood advisor. Denys had been aware she used
Base One to a certain extent, after that, but his Base continued as the dominantly active one in System. Maybe he
knew Base One would be pegged to her age, and that she
wouldn't be able to use it until she was the right age. But
Base One had always treated her as two years older than
she really was.

Denys had been safe until she'd gotten the keys to open
Base One wide and set it back to work at full stretch, as it
had been in the first Ari's day, assembling and collating
all the log notes from the years it had been asleep—and it
suddenly took priority.

She sped through the mundane records. Being prime
in System, nearly identical with System, Base One left no
footprints where it went. She'd asked it to bring up remarks
in which she or her predecessor or Maman had figured. It
found those. And later, it found Justin's.

She felt abraded, rubbed raw, when she read Denys's
message to Giraud, saying, "Strassen spoiled the little
bitch. Systematically."

Her eyes stung. She backed off, mentally, and just
scanned it—she could read very, very fast—and picked out
keywords that were highlighted in colors. She got vocal records and listened to tone of voice, reserving judgement.
It didn't come out better for Denys or Giraud. She heard
Abban's remarks, that cold, distinct voice that sent chills
through her. Abban had been near the labs when Ari
died.

But Abban had been Giraud's bodyguard in those
years, before Giraud died and Abban joined Seely in
Denys' household.

Curious. Companion azi went in ones. Bodyguards
went in twos. And neither Abban nor Seely had been companion azi, not if you really knew them. They'd been like
Florian and Catlin, products of the training down in Green
Barracks, and deadly dangerous. Giraud had been born,
and seven years later, Denys had been born, and Abban
and Seely had been in the household with Giraud. When
Giraud was sixteen and making his first trip to Novgorod

with his mother, leaving nine-year-old Denys at Reseune, Abban had gone with Giraud, and Seely had stayed with Denys. Which was the way it had been, forever after, when they set up separate domiciles. That was the way it had been until Giraud died.

Had it started out a partnership, Abban with Seely? It wasn't in the manuals, which had been maintained by Giraud's mother, for starters. It would have been Giraud's mother who had failed to record that small detail: she was the expert that had run them, at the start.

A weird arrangement between the brothers—seven years separated in birth, but so, so close lifelong that they were part of each other and neither ever married or had a relationship . . . and a mother who didn't keep complete records of azi under her management, who had, possibly, a secret few pages to those manuals that she didn't enter into the record. For what logical reason?

Some furtive sense of protection of her boys, a layer of security that would always tie them together?

To judge by the rest of the world, Reseune had some real odd family connections, things that weren't ordinary. For one thing, people who ran birthlabs could do pretty much as they pleased—Jordan wanted a Parental Replicate, and the first Ari had encouraged it, and so there was Justin. Ari wanted a tag on Justin, so she created Grant— especially for Justin, and one of a kind.

So Geoffrey Nye had had two sons that were as different as different came, seven years apart and yet as joined as anybody could be who wasn't cloned. They were natural-born, those two—*that* was unusual, in Reseune's administration. They'd had a mother who'd actually lived married to their father, so normal by Novgorod standards you could expect Giraud and Denys to turn out as normal as anybody could ever be. But their mother had been a psych operator, and Denys' Rezner scores had been off the high end of genius. God knew what she'd tried on her own sons, promoting that intellect—she'd wanted Giraud to come up to Denys' level—but she never could turn one into the other. And then she'd died, along with her husband, in a boating accident, and not a common one. The boat had caught fire, out on the Novaya Volga, where you just didn't open the cabin to the outside atmosphere. It had been pretty nasty.

And maybe it was because she was so tired tonight, maybe it was because Yanni was meeting with Corain and Spurlin and Justin was meeting with Jordan, and because she'd found Maman hadn't been in any loving mood when she'd agreed to bring her up, and because Denys, who knew one when he saw one, had called her a monster—all these truths had landed on her in one evening, with dinner being way late and Florian coming into her office and saying, for the third or fourth time, regarding the late dinner, "Sera, you really need more staff."

"Then you pick them!" she said peevishly. *"Do* it. You set the number. You know what's needed better than I do. Just *pick* them, for God's sake."

"Yes, sera," Florian said and went away ever so quietly. That didn't make her feel better at all, but she was still raw-nerved and she didn't want to talk to anybody.

They weren't that badly off with the staff they had, if they'd just had a better cook. There'd been a time this winter when Florian had been making dinner and they'd lived on sandwiches, but they had their little staff, people they'd gotten from random picks, mainly from old Dr. Watts, who'd died, and whose sad little staff needed reassigning; and one good pick out of Amy's dispersed office for a supplies clerk: Callie. Callie had gone into her service as acting majordomo, and she was going to shift back to household supplies when they got somebody trained for the post; Callie didn't like dealing with CITs if she could avoid it. But Callie managed so far. Meanwhile a pastry chef who'd been released by general staff as too emotional for the huge cafeteria kitchens was serving as their general cook, which was why dinner had been late tonight.

It wasn't a staff: it was a collection, and yes, it needed seeing to, and yes, the cook had burned supper two nights in a row the first week they'd had him and last night delayed an entire hour putting together pork sandwiches—provoking Catlin to suggest armed force might hasten dinner—but Ari didn't really care about that at the moment. Florian had looked upset when he left, which only made her feel worse, but she was one jump from breaking something, throwing something, or bursting into tears. The first Ari had hurt her Florian. She never, ever wanted to do that, and right now she was so fluxed she couldn't even go track him down and talk to him.

Yanni, dammit, Yanni. What are you doing to me?

Flux-thinking. The mind skipped, one topic to the next, all of it connected only because one brain held it all in one confused packet before it lay down to sleep and sleep purged the chemicals that had held everything in a forced relationship. Flux-thinking. Skipping between categories. Skipping between emotional states. Linking things that weren't linked and then getting way fluxed because there was an emotional charge left over from something else that wasn't even related.

It was how CITs routinely did things. Azi, which were started on logical, orderly input from the hour of their birth, didn't flux—well, the high ones did, but generally had rather not.

She, being CIT, being more than bright, and having a lot of circuits, was fluxed as hell, and knew it: mixing categories and jumping from one thought to the next in high flux—that was how ideas were born out of nothing. But she so wanted to sleep, and didn't want to take a sleeping pill—there'd been too many pills.

Get some rest, Justin had scolded her. He knew she was taking cataphoric and deepstudying too many hours. He knew she was strung out, but she was trying to watch all of Reseune while Yanni was gone, because she didn't really feel safe with him gone and only ReseuneSec in charge. Hicks, who ran ReseuneSec, hadn't stopped her taking down Denys, but then she'd come in by surprise and gotten control of System. She didn't feel quite comfortable with ReseuneSec now that she'd resigned her takeover, and let Hicks, as Giraud's second-in-command, assume his authority and his office. She didn't know him. She never had known him, except that Giraud had trusted him.

So in this interval while Yanni was gone, just so as not to give anybody any ideas, she'd sealed herself into her apartment with a staff she fairly well could trust, while she ran her own security checks, because she wasn't clear who to trust and who not in any given department. They were names to her, was all, and she didn't know histories, or how they connected to things that had happened.

She was watching things for Yanni, that was what he'd said. Keep an eye on things while I'm gone. And like a silly azi she'd taken it as something she ought to do as a point of responsibility, along with her studies and everything else. She wasn't trusting of Hicks, even if he had stood back and let her deal with Denys. But once she'd gotten into what was going on in Novgorod, all the same, it turned out she'd have done better to keep a closer eye on Yanni himself for the last several months.

A meeting with Spurlin. Dinner with Mikhail Corain, in Yanni's hotel room. And no record kept that she had yet reached via Base One, which meant he hadn't recorded it in Base Two. She wanted Yanni back here. She wanted him back so she could look him in the eyes and see him answer and hear a really good explanation of what business he had having an off-record supper with Ari Senior's old enemy—after an off-record meeting with Defense, which was a bureau that hadn't been that nice to *her* at all.

That didn't make for a good night's sleep, no matter how badly she needed it.

BOOK ONE   Section I   Chapter vii

APRIL 26, 2424
1506H

Keyboarding flowed and went on flowing, a spate of pure creation. The hindbrain could do one thing, recording what the brain had already decided had to happen, while the conscious and unconscious raced ahead, doing what they most liked to do. Occasionally Ari muttered a voice command, like a third hand, to locate a piece of programming and get it in queue, hardly noticing.

She tagged certain things to her just-finished voice recording, then issued another command to autocheck and report on bugs and mandatory halts, a caution, before locking that little bit—and everything ever to be chained to it—firmly into Base One's files.

That was how she wrote program for her successor . . . cautiously. She had put her half-finished creation under a brand new heading, whimsically, as *ariagain*. It was almost ready to go permanent. Electrons ported themselves where they needed to go and changed what needed changing, creating a new, self-defending thread . . . but only in that folder.

It ran and reported clean.

Final button-push. She handed it to Base One for System trial. More electrons checked it through and did whatever Base One did to protect its own programming. She didn't know. She just knew how to make it work. Someday she'd learn what the first Ari had known about System—but someday wasn't this day. She just wanted momentary distraction from Yanni and Giraud and lessons and all of it.

And the little file was only one of a set of files, all linked, all for some day when she would be dead—cheerful thought, but she had to plan for it.

She planned more sessions to follow this particular tape. She was planning, while the fingers, in hindbrain lag-time, handled what she'd thought nanoseconds ago.

On the vid screen at her elbow, a thunderstorm built and broke above the sprawling establishment that was Reseune, thunder that vibrated through the building around her. The tall precip towers that rimmed the cliffs above the river had talked to the weathermakers in orbit, and between them they'd loosed a fair-sized storm, taking the potential that was up there and making the spate of rain happen now rather than later, when the scheduled flight was due.

Just a small convenience. The weathermakers did nothing in this instance but hurry things a few hours and make sure that Yanni Schwartz, inbound from Novgorod, would land meticulously on time.

Reseune was tiny on the surface of the world that was Cyteen—a white dot from the perspective of Cyteen Station, seat of the Union Senate, which dealt with the wide universe. She'd seen her world—well, half of it—well, at least the mid-continental Novaya Volga valley, which was the highway down to Novgorod, to Swigert Bay, and the wide ocean.

Mostly the world outside the human zones was desert. The native life saw to that.

Excepting woolwood forests, which loosed deadly strands human lungs never wanted to meet.

Excepting the mud flats and ocean beaches near human habitation, which frothed with an unwholesome stew of dieoff—you really didn't want to smell it.

Terran stuff had early on gotten into the oceans, a bright idea that the modern generation was working to remediate. Purer Reseune water flowed down to the oceans on this continent these days—gone were the days when raw sewage had run down the river, deliberately loosed into Swigert Bay and outward, killing native life, breeding wildly, and creating that lovely yellow dieoff froth on the beaches.

In the early days, the driving colonial notion of how to manage Cyteen had been changing air and land, ridding the world of native species, creating a new Earth for humankind. Then they'd found that the native life—or part of it—could prolong a human life for decades. Now, the plan was carefully managed enclaves, and in a small program—too small a program, in Ari's view—PlanysLabs and ReseuneLabs alike tried to save what they'd begun too hastily to destroy.

The first Ari had had a lot to do with that change of purpose . . . and the growth of the rejuv industry. Through that, and control of the azi system, she'd built the economic power of Reseune, and, using its dominance in the Bureau of Science, gained immense political power.

Yanni Schwartz wielded that power now, being Proxy Councillor for Science. And down in Novgorod, where the planetary legislature sat, the Bureaus of Science, Defense, Information, and Trade, habitual allies, had all joined with Mikhail Corain's Citizens Bureau to authorize an azi-production lab at Fargone. She'd heard the news. She'd gotten it before the official broadcast. Budget items she'd seen as headed for easy passage, which was what Yanni was *supposed* to be promoting down in the capital, had been quietly dropped from the legislative agenda, none objecting.

She objected. And she was pissed as hell.

Yanni was supposed to persuade the opposition party to pass an expansion of the upriver remediation project. But instead . . . the Council voted on a budget for a new azi lab, on the fringes of space—*alpha*-capable, no less, clear out at Fargone. Reseune didn't let that technology off the planet, and all of a sudden they were moving it out of Cyteen System?

The remediation budget was dead until the next session, and meanwhile how were they going to keep the team of scientists on that project doing something creative? Reseune was going to have to fund their salaries solo, or have them break apart and go onto other projects, momentum lost, knowledge scattered.

Session was over. Yanni was coming home. And she had questions. A lot of them.

Nothing argumentative, she decided. A nice, quiet welcome home. Nothing to let on how much she knew about the secret meetings. If Yanni didn't know how far she was in command of Base One, she didn't want to make it too evident; and if he knew, she didn't want to let ReseuneSec know it.

"Staff memo," she shot out, via house minder. "Yanni. Dinner."

That order flew to staff, and, give or take the emotional fragility of the staff cook, she dismissed dinner preparations from her current list of concerns. Florian and Catlin would see to the invitation and make sure Yanni and dinner arrived in due time . . . if they had to send down to catering.

APRIL 25, 2424
1652H

Yanni Schwartz was on his flight back to Reseune, and
sera, who had been definitely On and angry for the last
several days, wanted to see Proxy Councillor Schwartz, socially, with due courtesies, of course—and immediately—
for dinner.

Florian got the message in the apartment's security station at the same moment Catlin did, at the console next to
him, and they exchanged hardly more than a flicker of the
eyes before Florian turned to make the supper arrange-
ments. He keyed. A message flew to Yanni's Reseune
office, and a small routine—another few keystrokes—
searched Yanni's existing appointments for conflict.

None. Unless Yanni had set something up that wasn't
on his schedule here at Reseune, he hadn't any dinner
appointment.

He had one now, and Yanni's domestic staff had become aware of it in time *not* to prepare dinner for his
homecoming.

Florian fired off a *done*, advised their own skittish
kitchen of formal dinner for two, and resumed work on his
own problem, which had, for the last several days, involved
searching azi profiles of availables for sera's household.

The two of them, Ari's personal bodyguard, were sera's absolute top-level staff. Second in rank were Marco
and Wes, who ran night shift, and protected the household any time he and Catlin were both off premises—they
were older, much older, and canny in the extreme. That
would leave Marco and Wes exactly where they were, their
backup, no matter what others came in—and besides that,
Wes had a special authority, being their on-staff medic.
Corey and Mato ran errands, helped in kitchen and served

as backup security personnel as well as domestics—they had come in from another staff, and their qualifications were excellent. A solitary and harried beta, Callie-BC-3218, majordomo pro tem, ran their domestic staff with tolerable efficiency.

Then there was Gianni, their pro tem cook. Gianni would have entered meltdown had the guests tonight been more than two, but he would likely manage one more serving, given adequate notice, instead of sera's usual changeable schedule.

And, be it noted, in Gianni's defense, he lacked supervisory qualifications—he was not emotionally able to make clear staff assignments. He hated to raise his voice, and, when asked his preferences directly, said he simply wanted to do desserts the way he could really do them and hoped sera would find someone to handle the other things.

Well, they tried. In Callie's place, they needed someone with the security training necessary to back up sera's bodyguard, the ability to order CITs assertively, at need, and—a talent more regularly employed—the *voice* to command respect from Wing One's ReseuneSec officers. Callie BC certainly didn't have the voice. She politely and tentatively suggested rather than ordered. She'd been one of the Carnath household, well qualified in supply; but she hated having to face interpersonal problems. Or deal with CIT emotions.

The household really, desperately *needed* an alpha like Seely, in Florian's own view. They needed one, like Seely, that had the capability to act decisively against anyone, even a born-man who claimed supervisor authority. *That* strength wasn't easily come by. The original Seely had been Denys Nye's majordomo . . . and there was actually a seventeen-year-old azi of that exact geneset-psychset combination available for training, ideal for the job, in Florian's own opinion—if sera would possibly take a direct hand and request him. But—sera had said, a logical leap that confused him, first that there was already a Seely-type being born fairly soon, and secondly she could never abide meeting a Seely-type in the halls.

True, there was that particular individual in the birthlabs, to be paired with another Abban: that was a problem they well understood. But now that the issue had come up, sera declared she wouldn't have AS-10 assigned on the planet, let alone in her household.

Well, it was clearly a decision, one there was certainly no disputing. And absent Seely AS-10, all other alphas of Contractable age were already committed to specific programs from infancy. There were a very few others, older, some of those quite concentrated in their own specialty, none of them socialized for a household.

So they were down to three household candidates *not* quite as good, one a beta, the other two gammas, the highest classification they could find that weren't designated elsewhere—not optimum, but satisfactory, in their estimation. They'd have to mesh smoothly with Gianni and Callie, not get underfoot of sera's security, *and* the majordomo had to know when to turn a situation over to security.

That put it down to the solitary beta, who was at the top end of beta, but under-socialized for the job.

It was frustrating. They were both up to their elbows in lists of tapes studied and certifications given, which sera could have read at a glance. But sera was either in deepstudy or, lately, on her computer, and on a motion-sensitive trigger, so neither of them thought it good to ask sera about it.

There were other experts they could ask: they sat in Wing One, in the heart of ReseuneLabs, where such sources abounded. But that meant exposing the makeup of sera's potential staff to people outside, which they were more than reluctant to do. The manuals of Contracted azi, containing the alterations made in that specific mindset over a lifetime—those were closely guarded, property of that azi and his Supervisor and not available in Library. But for anybody with a Base access above Three—and they were using a small subset of Base One—they could just walk though any unContracted's manual there was.

Scary, already, in their way of thinking. They hadn't known how accessible the unContracteds' manuals were to people in Wing One and Admin. They were supposed to find new people who were safe. They found instead that the ones they already had hadn't been as safe as they hoped. Somebody had been sloppy. And they ought to report that to sera—when she was herself again.

But that wouldn't happen until they had the household running smoothly, and that meant relief in the schedule, freedom for them *and* Marco and Wes to leave the premises and know the apartment would be safe. That meant a good majordomo who wouldn't go limp under pressure.

And that brought it down to five paired beta genesets in the security track. And finding out whether Denys or Giraud had ordered any special features in lower-level, unassigned security was, again, in Florian's estimation, something sera really needed to do, with her expertise. The best they could do was search the database they could reach for all interventions in the training, any decision that indicated a deviation from that geneset's initial program.

They learned a bit, doing it. They learned more than they'd planned to know about where to look and what to watch for. Social tapes, sera had said to Florian, half asleep, in bed. *Just be careful of those. The skill tapes don't tend to cause problems. Social tapes are generally what to watch for.* That was where spurious instructions could get in, at a very general level.

Well, at least the available betas weren't long on social training. And they were beta-smart, meaning they'd take tape fast, and literally, if they had to.

They ran their search from the security office inside sera's apartment, in premises where the first Florian and the first Catlin had been the authority, in an apartment where the first Ari had lived. Two of the wall screens were the weather and the airport schedule—the Yanni matter. Two more monitored the main concourse of Wing One, downstairs, where the number and manner of people out and about the building seemed ordinary. One monitor covered the upstairs, the hall outside. That was vacant, their immediate surrounds.

A bank of other screens, constantly shifting the view, monitored the riverside, the private boat dock and the big wharves where shipments arrived in the town adjunct to Reseune. Cameras swept the town streets, with its usual traffic of azi and CITs on their own business, a bus, some few runabouts whizzing about to the hazard of pedestrians.

Another set of cameras swept the broad fields and pens down in AG, where crops were burgeoning out of winter earth and pigs and chickens lived in long, safe sheds, protected, like all the town and labs, by the ring of tall precip towers that kept the world at bay.

Another screen, to the left of the view of the town, was occupied with the parsing of lines of code, the beta psychset they were currently investigating.

Three screens, on the side console, kept an electronic eye on sera's friend Sam Whitely, at work on the construction site adjacent to—but not yet accessing—Wing One. Sam's azi, Pavel, had a camera clipped to his collar and rarely left Sam for more than a brief errand. That afforded them a good constant view of Sam, who was not the sort to get into trouble in the first place.

The cameras gave them a view of everything and everyone they had to protect . . . a split screen kept an eye on Justin Warrick and his companion Grant ALX-972, in their small office over in Education, where they were spending the day—it was where they were supposed to be on Thursdays.

They *didn't,* however, have one to track Warrick senior—who was on no one's trusted list, and who was the reason they didn't want to present the files they were working on to Justin Warrick for review.

Jordan Warrick. *There* was the problem that disturbed the whole house—and one reason they were anxious to improve sera's general security. They weren't a completely conjoined problem, Justin and Jordan. Jordan and Justin hadn't met face to face since a notable argument some days ago. Jordan had mostly stayed in his own apartment since, and had he attempted to crack a restricted level, the whole of Reseune would have twitched.

As it was, ReseuneSec just logged every keystroke, every request Jordan Warrick made of Library, and passed the collected information on. What the elder Warrick asked to access today were all generally published files two years old, so they raised no alarms. The actual content was for some specialist in Hicks's office—ReseuneSec—to read, because they involved genetic expression, and for that maybe even ReseuneSec would have to ask one of the scientists.

Harmless? Probably. Not definitely, however.

There was also some indication the argument between the Warricks had abated somewhat: Jordan had sent a message to Justin this afternoon asking him to supper. Justin had refused to come. Another message had followed. Jordan had proposed a restaurant. They'd agreed to meet, so ReseuneSec informed them, via sera's standing request for information about such contacts.

And if they passed a memo to sera to tell her that was going on, sera, in her current mood, would tell them back off, that Jordan Warrick was not her concern at the moment.

But then ReseuneSec, Hicks's office, would move in on the meeting all on their own. And sera had told them to protect Justin, had she not?

It was like the other instructions this week—a scheduling problem.

"We could use *both* these sets," Florian said to his partner, regarding the two top candidate pairs. "They could be ready soonest. We could use the extra hands. And one more set than we planned gives us backup to handle a situation at the door. There's that. Sera won't mind the cost."

"Which one should be senior, then?" Catlin asked. "I say BT-384 and GJ-2720."

"Agreed." BT-384 and GJ-2720, at twenty-one, were younger than the other two, in fact—senior was always in terms of genetics, rank, and training, not birth-order. But the BT-384 geneset combined with the 348–3498 psychset in fact did have an older history: five of that geneset-psychset combo had been in the military: their complete records had been difficult to get. But by what they did get, all five priors had died in the Company Wars, two sets in the same action, attempting to rescue the company commander. Gallantly devoted and distinguished for courage under fire.

It would have been more commendable to have gotten themselves and their company commander out alive, in Florian's way of thinking. Still . . .

"Agreed," he said. BT-384 and his partner were both security-trained, beta and gamma in Green Barracks, where gamma was as low as they accepted. Both were older than Florian and Catlin were. GJ-2720, female, was currently engaged in demolitions instruction, in the security wing, which was an asset, and a gamma tended to be steadier than most betas in that application. Demolitions was his own field, and he had a certain bias in favor of GJ-2720.

BT-384, their high-end beta destined for majordomo, was surveillance, trained for a desk job, simple monitoring, but that meant good attention to detail, an asset.

None of their choices had at any time been in direct or traceable contact with Denys Nye, Yanni Schwartz, Giraud Nye, Jordan Warrick, Justin Warrick, or any of their staffs. No one had messed with the standard path in any recorded degree.

BT-384 had a name. It was Theo. GJ-2720 was Jory.

"Take their Contracts?" Catlin asked. "We might as well make a decision."

"We'll order initial tape for Domestic Supervision," he said. That would call Theo BT-384 and his partner Jory to the labs for what they might think was a routine training update. Instead, under a heavier sedation, a deepset tape would reorder their priorities and loyalties and bind them simply to their Contract. They would lose the focus they had, and gain a more general one, the knowledge they were to serve an important domestic situation somewhere, of some sort, together.

That would break their absolute focus on their current general assignment. It was—an azi could well remember—a disturbing and emotional experience. Theo and his partner had been destined for ReseuneSec. But they were about to run a ReseuneLabs household . . . a different world indeed. The walk they would take from the barracks to the labs where they would get their Contract would be a cold walk through absolute non-existence.

It felt so good when the Contract turned out to be the answer to every study, every ambition, every hope of one's life. Even knowing intellectually that the emotion was pre-programmed in an azi, it still jolted everything, still evoked a response of absolute joy.

"Bring them here for all the specific skills tapes?" Catlin said, following his train of thought, as she did, without his quite uttering it. It was best to have that part done here, not exposing any of sera's people to lab personnel.

No need to report the decisions to sera. Sera had told them handle it. They did.

They took Theo BT-384 and Jory GJ-2720 to be in charge of the household, Callie to be under their authority in domestic matters, but in charge of orders and supply, which would please Callie no end. They took the other set, Logan GL-331, with his partner Hiro GH-89, for general staff, under Theo, Jory, and Callie, and then swept up two individual epsilons, Tomas and Spessy, for general cleaning and maintenance service, with a paired couple of thetas, Del and Joyesse, for maids of all work and sera's personal wardrobe.

And most of all—the one find about which they'd had absolutely no doubt—two other betas, a paired set, Wyndham and Haze. Wyndham and Haze, both male, had been destined for a hotel in Novgorod, to run a very high-end restaurant with a VIP security certificate—the CIT master chef intended to retire. The CIT chef and the hotel could wait another year. Sera had just gained one sure prize.

Staff might be a little crowded downstairs, given the number of rooms in the lower half of the apartment given over to storage. The CIT living space of the apartment was very large. Its travertine floors and high-ceilinged rooms had easy room for a hundred CITs at a party. But the staff, all but themselves and Marco and Wes being resident in the downward L of main staff quarters, were going to need more beds than they had. Those had to be ordered.

Training tape would occupy the new staff's leisure time for several weeks. They'd be in deepstudy in their quarters in their off hours during that time, and then they'd emerge to make the place run smoothly.

Especially the front door. Especially the kitchen.

So. Decision made. Die cast. The new staff would go through medical, take their pre-Contracting tape. Contracting itself took a single moment, once that essential groundwork was done. They'd first be taught social behaviors and protocols in lab, nobody but Admin knowing where they were going, and there would be no great fuss here to disturb sera's mood. All sera had to do was agree to it and sign the request.

Once it was done—they could draw a breath, not be working twelve hours on and twelve off, as they were now, as they had done for months, while sera studied day and night, and ran background checks on everyone around her. They didn't disagree with sera's preoccupation with security. They weren't quite sure that the threat to sera's life was entirely past. They'd seen her through childhood. They'd gotten her this far alive.

But the day was coming when sera would need a staff far more complex than they had ever been, and in which they might not be as close to sera, as all-in-all, as they had once been. They saw that coming—though Florian was upset by the prospect. Sera seemed less happy because of the pressure on her, and that defined everything. She'd snapped at him. She'd never done that and not apologized. So they had to take special care of her.

"We should monitor Justin tonight," Florian said abruptly, "or Hicks will. I don't want that."

Catlin said, "I can do it."

"Set it up," Florian said. "I have to make sure Gianni stays on track until dinnertime. Then we'll trade assignments, and I'll go."

The storm passed overhead. On the monitor, a ray of sun hit the tower, in the gray, glistening world outside.

A private plane, glistening white, came in wheels-down for a landing on a puddled runway. The tail emblem, the Infinite Man of ReseuneLaboratories, was distinctive. It was Reseune One.

Yanni was back.

APRIL 25, 2424
1748H

"How was Novgorod?" Ari asked purposely, over the shrimp cocktail. "Quiet?"

"Agreeably so, actually," Yanni said. He had never yet asked the reason for the dinner invitation.

Not uncommon for Yanni. Yanni Schwartz gave very little away, and he'd always accorded the same privilege of reticence to her, since she had been on his good list, or thought she was. He was on rejuv, of course, dyed his hair, was eightyish and looked forty, except that most people that looked forty weren't forty. He wasn't handsome, but he had a strong face. She liked that face. And it made her feel better that he showed up on time and didn't act guilty at all—as if he was going to have a reason to give her. Oh, she so hoped he had a reason. Something in her unknotted just because he'd come in and met her cheerfully, without a flinch.

He'd brought her a trinket from the capital. Giraud used to do that, and this one, when she unwrapped it, looked even to be from the same company as some of Giraud's gifts. It was a desk sitter, a little glass globe with a holo insect that crawled in a circle so long as you set it in the light. He had handed it to her before they sat down at table and she had it by her plate. It kept running, brilliant green armor and serrated jaws, round and round.

The gift-giving urge in Yanni was new. She noted that.

One thing was sure: Yanni had thought about her when he was in Novgorod, and Yanni had never particularly curried favor: he'd always been fair, and expected it in return. Now that he was here, at her table, she could actually quit fluxing and remember Yanni, not the reports she'd found in System. Maybe he *had* brought her the thing just because it tickled his fancy, and made him think of her.

In her opinion, that was the way family ought to be. She'd almost begun to think of him that way. Until this last week.

"I love the bug," she said.

"Beetle," he said. "A Glorious Beetle."

"Well, he is, but is that his name?"

"*Plusiotis gloriosa.* Native to the western hemisphere of Earth."

"He's really that green?"

Yanni took a little advert card from his coat pocket and set it in the middle of the table, between them and facing her. "You can actually get a collection of insects. The butterflies were obviously the big item. But you have one of those, I remembered. I thought you'd rather have the beetle."

She had Giraud's butterfly. They lately had real butterflies in the Conservatory. All sorts of them. But they didn't have a beetle.

"I absolutely love him," she said. It had been ages since she'd spent time in the Conservatory. Reseune sprawled, from the high end, where Wing One sat, down to the town and the fields, and she hadn't been to the Conservatory since—oh, long before the shooting that had brought Denys down, long before the world had come apart. She and Maman used to go there when she was small, to walk the garden paths and see the flowers.

The family that she had once had, had been broken by Denys' order. Yanni's family, too. Scattered by the same set of orders, sacrificed to the Project that was her, sent out to a distant star-station, depriving Yanni of relatives, including stupid Jenna. She wouldn't be surprised if Yanni did resent her. But she hoped he didn't.

Lump-lump-lump, in its endless silent circle.

She dropped her napkin over it, to remove the distraction. Looked Yanni in the eyes—they were brown, direct, hard eyes.

"It doesn't have an off switch," Yanni said. "Except light."

"So there's nothing up I should know about," she said, direct to the point, regarding Novgorod and the legislative session.

"Oh, the Paxers are kicking up the usual fuss, we *didn't* get the remediation increase we wanted, and there's talk about putting an embargo on Earth-origin wood veneers."

So he wasn't going to get to the topic of secret meetings straight off. So neither did she. "It'll only drive up the price. It won't ever stop the demand, will it?"

"It might drive the price far beyond what the average citizen can afford. Take the mass out of mass market. Earth is claiming its woods are a sustainable resource. We're saying they're not, on an interstellar scale, and we're talking about a hundred-year embargo."

"If Alliance doesn't go with it—" she began. She hadn't been interested at all in that, but a brain cell fired, and she couldn't help it.

"Alliance *is* actually going with it."

That rated a lift of the brows, for an item that hadn't been to the forefront of the news at all. The Alliance kept their hands off their own forested world, at Pell, a planet called Downbelow, barred exploitation by vote of the station residents, if not the far-flung ship-communities that were the greatest majority of that government.

So the whole ecosystem of Downbelow was protected from intrusion—because practically speaking there was nobody but Pell Station that would mount an expedition down there. The ecological sensibilities of the Alliance capital, however, had not stopped the Alliance merchanters from buying up luxuries out of Sol System hand over fist, which they were selling, hand over fist, to Union. Since the Alliance sat halfway between Union and Sol, a ban on certain Earth products *couldn't* be be meaningful without Alliance compliance, and she'd have bet Alliance, composed mostly of merchanter families, wouldn't possibly go with it.

Uncommon that Alliance and Union both, former enemies, ended up banning something so prized by the rich. Never mind that they could easily synthesize the product. Never mind that there were very good synthetic veneers, down to the cell structure, if you wanted that. The fact a thing was *real* aroused a certain lust to possess, in certain moneyed circles. People would pay fortunes for what was *real* and Earth-origin. Crazy, in her opinion.

"Well," she said. "So no more wood from Earth?"

"I think it will pass in the Council of Worlds," he said. "A lot of talk, a lot of fire and fury and discussion. The spotlight's on the users of certain products, and no senator wants to be tagged as one of the conspicuously rich consumers. They've exempted historical pieces from the ban. I've objected that we'll see an uncommon glut of relics coming out of Earth. And we get one other quiet little provision—the Hinder Stars Defense Treaty gets moved forward. Talks renewed."

"That's good." It was.

"So," he said, in a changing-the-subject tone, "how are things here?"

And still no mention of the private meetings. "Same as last week. Same as the week before." There was some local news, not as dramatic as the ban on wood veneers. "The new wing has its foundations laid."

"Saw that, as the plane came in. Looking quite impressive back there."

"They're mostly finished with the storm tunnels and accesses now—conduits are going in. *And* they finished the power plant up at the upriver site. Precip stations are about to go online."

Not that much besides a twenty-bed residential bunker and a machine shop stood on that remote site yet. The new building, well upriver, was in the early stages, a lot of raw earth and robots at the moment, superintended by a small azi technical crew and a supervisor, and soon to be occupied by the loneliest and craziest people on Cyteen, linerunners on the automated precip stations.

"Fine," he said. "And how are your studies going?"

"Oh, good enough."

"So—" Archly. "—are we moving researchers in upriver?"

"We're a few months from that."

"I don't think I'd like the climate."

She didn't like the implication of that, not at all. He'd sensed she was stalking him. He'd got her. She was sure her face had reacted in some dismay. As of now, it had a frown, which she immediately purged.

"Oh? And what did you *do,*" she asked, in her best Ari One mode, "in Novgorod?"

"You have to trust me."

And *now* was he going to bring up those secret meetings? "Oh, I do, but I'd really like to know, and you know I'd like to know."

"Well, I agreed with Corain on a compromise. Fargone's hurting for jobs. His constituency *at* Fargone is extremely important to him getting re-elected if he's challenged for the seat. So we put in a new lab wing. We get Centrist Party support on a rider tacked onto that bill, *because* it helps Corain's constituency at Fargone, and, here's the core of it: the Eversnow project gets underway."

"Eversnow!" That hadn't been part of the report.

"Eversnow."

"It's a dead project."

"Not dead. We get a station at Eversnow, a full blown research station *on* Eversnow, and a new lab at Fargone that's very quietly aimed at terraforming, exactly as originally planned on Cyteen—the Centrists' favorite dream—but out there, where it's *not* going to cause us trouble."

Her pulse rate was getting up. Her blink rate would be. And he'd read that in a second. "So we're suddenly friends with the Centrists and we're terraforming Eversnow, of all things. And producing alpha azi at Fargone."

"A few."

"We *have* a lab at Fargone. The Rubin Project was at Fargone."

"Mostly terraforming research . . . a clearing house for what we learn on Eversnow. Ultimately—ultimately azi, yes."

"Alpha production has never left the planet!"

"Our personnel, mind, no release of proprietary secrets. By the time we're bringing any great number of azi into the Eversnow system, we'll be on the planet. Azi production. Full scale by then. You'll be putting together the sets for that population in your lifetime."

The Eversnow deal had been dead as long as the first Ari. And Reseune had allowed a prerogative of exclusivity to lapse, enabling labs that high-end, that capable, to run out at Fargone—with the possibility of somebody outside Reseune staff laying hands on the manuals? Bad enough they'd licensed out military thetas to BucherLabs and had *those* problems to mop up for the next forty years of the first Ari's career—they'd never done anything like *this*.

And terraforming? That was a dead issue.

"None of this is in the news," she said calmly.

"None of it is going to be in the news. It's under deep cover, disguised as that azi lab."

"But, damn it, Yanni." She kept her voice down, kept the whole situation under control, holding the lid on. "I assume you've got a very, very good reason. What happened to the remediation budget?"

"It'll wait a year."

"While we create a terraforming lab out at Fargone?"

"Yes," Yanni said, head-on, "It was the first Ari's project. It got scrapped."

"The first Ari isn't alive now. I am. And I have an opinion. You didn't ask me. Where are my budget items, Yanni?"

"Next year."

"We have two labs full of scientists we're going to have to fund till next year and I'm making a heavy hit on budget as it is!"

"I know that."

"So you could have talked about this. Eversnow, for God's sake! And an alpha lab! What else?"

"We manage the lab, top to bottom. Our personnel run it, no training of local techs to do anything: they'll all be Reseune people, born here, trained here, retiring here, ultimately."

Yanni's voice was so quiet, so reasonable. He wasn't that way with a lot of people. But he knew he'd sneaked this one past her, and he was presenting a case in which she was going to have the say. She'd be in charge when this thing came into full bloom, and Yanni—Yanni would be gone by then, at least gone from Admin, and back in the lab.

That thought settled her heart rate a tick or two. She didn't want that, yet.

And she thought about what he was doing. He'd been meeting with Corain, of all people. Corain didn't meet with Science.

"So," she said, "and Citizens voted for it."

"Jobs," Yanni said. "A lot of jobs. Council knows what it's for. We're just not advertising it for the media yet."

"They know, and they voted for this."

"Everybody but Internal Affairs and State. Two nays. I'm sure you know."

She knew. Corain had gone along. Jobs, Yanni said. Jobs at Fargone. Elder Ari had warned her about unrest in the population—the Citizens Bureau, which Corain represented. Ari had warned her about unhappiness—at Fargone, at Pan-Paris, which wasn't on the expansion routes; both flashpoints. Jobs had been scarce, opportunities scant since the War. Fargone was supposed to be in for major expansion when the military had planned to go ahead with Eversnow; she knew that was the history of it at that star.

And then peace had happened, and the project had stalled—people elsewhere hadn't thought terraforming anything was a good idea; and then the first Ari had died, and it had stayed a dead issue for twenty years.

But the Eversnow collapse *had* had an effect, politically. Fargone Station's independence tilt, voting sometimes with the Expansionists, sometimes with the Centrists, and bargaining hard for its vote, had been a factor in the Defense election that had put Vladislaw Khalid in—her least favorite Bureau head in her own lifetime.

And that unrest, of people feeling trapped and dead-ended, was still out there at Fargone and Pan-Paris, in the electorate of Citizens, in Defense. It spread even through the Science Bureau, out there: the Expansionists had just squeaked through its traditional majority in the last election Science had had.

That was dangerous, even if it was just one star-station. She had an inkling all of a sudden where Yanni was leading with this little surprise, and it wasn't stupid: it was an answer to the kind of problems Yanni had faced in *his* tenure as Proxy Councillor for Science *and* head of the Expansionist Party. Give Fargone a major project, jobs, prosperity—and mutate Fargone's maverick electorate into one more in line with Reseune, who'd be running the project. Setting a whole new population-burst of azi out there, who would, over time, migrate to freedman status at Fargone and then, supposedly, at Eversnow Station, azi who'd teach their own CIT children *their* opinions—

And Corain was going along with it? She felt her week-long Mad cool off just a degree. Defense still had a strong interest in Eversnow. It was going to be a problem to pry their fingers off it, and Yanni was trying to work with them . . . had Yanni thought of that?

"We set up an alpha-capable lab at Fargone," Yanni was saying quietly, and she began to track it, "but the locals are naturally immediately thinking of CIT-use, ordinary CIT births, and that's what they know. Corain hasn't mentioned Eversnow in his own arguments, or at least it hadn't leaked by this morning. But Council has something to gain from this bill. Fargone's going to be the stepping-off point for Eversnow, which will become more and more economically important to Fargone voters and to the Citizens Bureau. But most of all, to us. Not just a new city. A new planet. For us, a whole new genetic resource. A whole new population to birth and set up. Corain's agreeing to cooperate with us on the Hinder Stars Defense Treaty, but we agreed to drop the remediation funding increase for this session, for this project. Seed money. Corain gains jobs and votes and he gets funding without a tax increase. But ultimately we gain everything."

The damned thing was an appalling daisy chain of favors exchanged. She suddenly had a much wider window into the content of the mysterious meetings, and here was Yanni—stolid, just-the-facts Yanni, non-activist through her whole life—advancing an outrageously ambitious Expansionist agenda the first Ari had contemplated and slowed down on, toward the end of her life, as too much, too far.

In Yanni's plan, they acquired not just Eversnow as a base, but the string of stars beyond it; that was the thing. The strand that had been, without Eversnow, unattainable. Defense wanted that: she could see it.

And the Centrists, particularly numerous in the Citizens Bureau, whose whole platform had always been to have Union's power to stay clustered tightly around Cyteen, were suddenly going along with Eversnow? The first Ari had started out supporting terraforming at Cyteen, her mother Olga's project, and then pulled the rug from under that once rejuv manufacture became a vital industry. The Centrists, wanting to expand population, not territory, had been outraged. They'd seen it as a ploy to keep Cyteen mostly desert, carved up into Administrative Territories, notably Reseune's protective reserves, where CITs couldn't get a foothold. They'd been furious and called Eversnow a pie-in-the-sky piece of politics that was going to give Reseune one more protectorate and never would benefit the average CIT.

And now the Centrists, who had been so fundamentally opposed to that project at the edge of space, were suddenly willing to give up their campaign to terraform Cyteen and concentrate on Eversnow.

The universe had changed in a week.

And she didn't know enough. Eversnow had been a problem she'd planned to postpone for decades.

A world locked in a snowball effect. A world without a spring for millions of years—with, however, the strong likelihood that there was still life there, genetically unique, locked in rocks in the sub-basement of a frozen ocean.

In the first Ari's day, with all of humankind busy blowing each other up in the War, the Expansionists and the military had both been hot to seed Eversnow for their own reasons—their hedge on a bet, if the Alliance had hit Cyteen. But Centrists hadn't wanted to spend money there at all, and a few Centrist-leaning scientists had argued they needed to preserve and study that world for a few decades.

Too late, by then. An early Defense Bureau project had already broken the freeze, or begun to break it, artificially, with solar heat, and tipped the balance toward a melt . . . how that had ever turned out, she didn't know in any detail. Earth-origin phytoplankton reportedly bloomed in certain areas, thanks to Defense.

She would not have done that: she would have said a vehement no. It was a living world, and living worlds were precious in the cosmos. Even snowballs. That was what she'd thought in her slight reading of the project—good they gave it up.

But now came politics. And Yanni was getting friendly

with Corain? Establishing a population burst out at Fargone and then at Eversnow, where the Centrists weren't paying attention—

That actually could be smart, she had to admit it. Centrists attracted the violent fringe elements, people like the Paxers and the Abolitionists, whose major agenda had gone from a unilateral peace in the Company Wars on the one hand, and an abolition of all azi production on the other. The Paxers and the Abolitionists had, as a curious side agenda, the terraforming of Cyteen, which they thought would break the power of Reseune, and *that* was how those fringe groups had found an ideological home in the Centrist Party.

But let Corain of Citizen shift the political focus to "jobs for Fargone," and snuggle up to Science, and watch the fringe elements scramble to cope with *that*.

The first Ari had created her, she'd said, to keep watch over her projects—among which was Gehenna, and maybe, yes, she supposed, that could include Eversnow, even if it wasn't, like Gehenna, populated.

So, well, maybe Yanni didn't deserve spacing.

A sudden expansion of Reseune interests out on the fringe of human space—a whole new strand of stars. New frontiers. A commitment to expansion—and to Expansionism, with all it stood for, and all the dangers in the deep unknown . . .

Was *she* ready to open that door to the universe and deal with whatever lay out there? Was *she*, for that matter, going to be as Expansionist in her own career as her predecessor had been? She didn't know. Decisions were coming down on her too early . . . and she was about to be stuck with this one: there were ways for her to undo everything except the dispersal of the Earth genome into an alien, living world.

But Defense, by all reports, had already done that part, even including higher lifeforms.

"I'm not sure, Yanni. I'm still not sure. Tell me why."

"A planet with only microbes to recommend it is interesting, but we have samples."

"All right. Keep going. Why now?"

Yanni took a sip of wine. "Here's the urgency in it. The

War's over; that used to be our cohesive factor, as a nation: we had to stop the Earth Company. So now Union's teetering somewhere between an amalgam of star-stations and a fully formed state, and there's power to be had, power Reseune holds virtually solo. Reseune keeps Union going in a specific direction, keeps a momentum, or God knows what it would do. The Council may govern, but Reseune still makes the rules that govern azi, and azi are still, and for a few centuries more, the source of the population base."

"That's supposed to end."

"Not yet. And this is the reason. As long as we expand into new frontiers, CIT births won't keep up with the need for population; azi go on being born, and Reseune goes on making the rules, the newest population goes on voting our way, and we'll always outvote the Centrists and *keep* them from clustering all our assets around one vulnerable planet. Plus we retain our police power, where azi are concerned, and we remain a clearing-house for information that most of the citizenry doesn't even *want* to know, but which could come back on their heads. We don't know what the future holds, but it's a sure bet the Centrists know less than we do. Earth is out of serious play in human politics for at least a century. It can't even get a consensus together to manage its trade relations, and right now they see us as an endless source of funds and invention, so they don't actually have to solve any of their problems. They sell us their antiquities, their artwork, their unique biologicals, and we make the worst of their politicians drunk with money and importance. The only thing they really badly want, we won't sell them."

That, of course, was rejuv. On a populous planet like Earth, it could be a disaster. And she saw Yanni's point: left with *nobody* to make a decision not to trade in it, it would have happened, and Earth would have collapsed.

"Earth won't move until it's uncomfortable," she murmured, quoting. The rest of what Ari One had said was: *It won't make any decision until at least three of its factions combine.* "So where do you see things going for us all? Another war?"

"Alliance has its own problems, transitioning from a

collection of merchant captains to a government making law for two worlds. It's set Pell off limits. It saw Gehenna as a potential resource, but now they know it's a time bomb. So they came out of the War owning *two* planets they don't want to touch—partly noble ethics. But this is the important part: partly it's the paralysis of not *having* a ReseuneLabs to make informed decisions, and they refuse to ask us what to do with Gehenna *or* Pell. Their R&D was always driven by the likes of LucasCorp's operation, all profit, no long-range planning—ecological disaster in the making. Plus their two planets both have higher life to worry about. Our two worlds *don't*. Right now they can't do anything about what we do."

"But," she said, "Cyteen's biosystem produces rejuv, and we can't jeopardize that by terraforming here. Go over strictly to lab production and it drives up the cost of something everybody has to have for most of their life—so you create a class who can live for a century and a half being young, and separate them from the people who can't afford it."

Staff brought the next course, grilled fish, with citrus. It took a moment. And she was annoyed with staff, who should have waited for a signal. Probably the fish would have seriously overcooked. But she needed a stern talk with staff about interrupting. A very stern talk.

"So," she said, after the obligatory compliments, and several bites further on.

"So," Yanni said, perfectly composed.

"So I'm following everything you're saying, and it makes sense. But why are you personally voting for terra-forming Eversnow this fast? What if there's something as important as rejuv down there? Something we *can't* make in a lab?"

"One reason: Reseune's continued existence, its power to make decisions, aboveboard or in secret, is the core of all Union stability. Without us, Union falls apart. That's not arrogance. That's fact. Right now, Union isn't populous enough to avoid fragmentation. Decisions are being taken. Some really stupid ideas are current in politics, and some damned selfish ones. Reseune is at a low ebb of power, dur-ing my interregnum, so it's perceived—because I'm not an

Emory, a Carnath, or a Nye—not even a Warrick. I'm an unknown, and it's widely perceived I'm merely a footnote, filling time between Denys Nye's control of Reseune—and your taking the office, for which all the Centrists are busy bracing themselves. They perceive me as weak, someone they can get concessions out of—before you come in. But on this one matter, on this, I am passionate. We need the expansion of human space to go on holding the power to make decisions; we need labs to extend our reach to other places, labs, incidentally, out of immediate view of Centrist leadership here on Cyteen . . . but I'm not advertising that feature of the plan. We may still find biologicals we can develop at Eversnow; and the experience will be invaluable; but right now, and in the immediate future, we need the expansion of our loyal voting base, before some short-sighted, over-content business interests on Cyteen Station and in Novgorod break up Reseune and let us fall behind the Alliance. Fatally so. In which case I *guarantee* you there'll be another war. We need to hedge our bets by spreading outward. Concerns for microbes take second place. The way Earth is managing its affairs currently, we may be using your predecessor's genetic Arks to recover what they lose."

"And what if we lose something like rejuv because we rushed in and messed up a place we don't wholly know?"

"We could lose something, yes. But we know what we gain. A power base. And whatever we mess up there, it won't be *us*. The Centrists envision a planet they can live on in billions, like Earth, the great fantasy. They see this project as a foot in the door of that science. We get the Centrists involved *far* outside the understanding of their comfortable power base on Cyteen, and we edge their children closer and closer to our point of view. The Long View . . . in this case, from a standpoint of distance from the center of Union. We get their kids involved in this project. We turn the Centrists into our asset. They go for the profit out there, being people with families they want to support—and we go on as we are, controlling colonization. There are other worlds beyond Eversnow. But we can't reach them without stepping stones. Trade *drives* expansion. Trade drives *us*. And the Treaty of Pell meant our trade pays a price. It may have meant peace, but Alliance is getting fatter on a share of our trade. And some of those merchanters are using the profit to update armaments—the way some of our warships nowadays run a little cargo—of a medical and emergency nature. The Treaty may someday break down on that point. We have to get other options, we have to maintain our economic push that *keeps* us stronger than the Alliance, or see the consequences."

It wasn't a stupid idea. She could see that. And it was a vision. It might be stupid to think Expansionism could go on at the same pace forever, but there was something to it going on for a while: Earth was one planet, one star system, and fragile. Earth had antagonized all its colonies, who held the only safe direction for Earth to expand—Earth now knew it wasn't going to grow without running into intelligence in the other directions, and they only hoped Earth didn't provoke something out in the deep. Alliance was already committed in the direction of Gehenna, but that planet was a problem.

Eversnow would lead Union development further out on another tangent, away from Earth and farther out than the Alliance, down a strand of stars that worked like a river in space. Broaden Union's population base, widen their territory, make them secure, and yes, make sure there were jobs. That had been a poser, but Yanni's plan solved that at a stroke.

Going away from Alliance made them unassailable, militarily: Defense would like that. Folly for Alliance or Earth to attack something that much bigger; and a strong Union, with other resources, wouldn't actually *need* Earth, or even Alliance . . . while a strong Union was a big market, for Earth, and for Alliance. So it could possibly preserve the peace better than standing still.

So was it worth ruining a planet? A snowball, the domain of microbes? It might be.

"So let me ask you one," Yanni said. "This new research post upriver. It seems your own plan's gotten beyond that . . . while I've been in Novgorod. Now we're talking about a major lab expansion—five hundred jobs on this budget request, my office tells me. Requests for extension on use of the excavators. There's nothing there to *mine* up in the hills. No industry likely. But now you're requesting residences. A river port, with coffer dam and shields. *Why* do you need a river port for remediation research?"

"To move supply."

"And? It's seeming a little beyond a bare-bones research post all of a sudden. I'm not complaining, understand. I just want to know what we're suddenly funding up there. What are you up to, young lady?"

She really hadn't been ready to talk about that. But maybe it was time. Secret for secret.

"Actually—a township."

"An adjunct to Reseune? Or a rival?"

"A real township. Like here. Shops. People. Manufacture, eventually. I'm thinking of calling it Strassenberg."

"Strassenberg," Yanni said, sitting back a little. That had been Maman's name, Strassen. "Well, now *there's* an ambitious design for an eighteen-year-old. You're building a new wing on Reseune and in the last three weeks your research lab has mutated into a town. And why, pray, do you think we *need* another township in the world?"

That, like her question about Yanni's programs, was a deeper question. Fair question, considering the funds she'd counted on weren't going to be plentiful, if they now had to fund the remediation. "Two reasons: first the isolation, what I said at the start: a place to put the rest of my uncle's staff where I don't have to deal with them. But I want a lab for *my* decisions. The first Ari created me to carry on *her* work. I'm setting up a place where absolutely all the decisions are mine and all the mindsets are what I choose to be up there, CIT and azi. Give or take my uncle's people, that they'll have to encapsulate, they're *my* research question. I said it was a lab. And it actually is. It's my comparison to what the first Ari did in, say, Gehenna."

Eyebrows lifted. Clearly a city wasn't quite the answer Yanni had expected under the title of a research lab. But it was the truth. There might be a timebomb in the Gehenna mindset, but—a more closely-held secret, and one she wasn't sure the first Ari had ever directly discussed with Yanni—there was possibly one in the Cyteen population itself, simply because the mindsets were what they were, exactly the same mix of psychsets Yanni had been talking about continuing at Eversnow. All but the CITs who'd come down from orbit were Reseune-designed mindsets—the same as Yanni planned to go on using out at Eversnow. The station over their heads had its founding families, a certain aristocracy of CITs, people with citizen-numbers from the origin of the system: the Carnaths, the Nyes, the Emorys, and the Schwartzes, plus a couple of hundred other names that had proliferated through the station—and then a number had settled at Reseune and Novgorod, on the planetary surface, once they'd begun to colonize the planet.

But it had needed a succession of population bursts to build civilization and sustain an economy independent of Earth's economy, independent of the Merchanter's Alliance, from which *they* had seceded by force of arms. A planetary economy needed hands to work, minds to devise, and people to mine resources, consume products, and fill the vacant spots in the outback, dense enough population for viable commerce. In the early days Union had boosted its numbers by birthlabs, by cycling azi into freedmen at an extraordinary rate . . . azi who'd been given their ethics by tape that Reseune had created in the first Ari's mother's time.

And the first Ari had had a very heavy hand on that process, tweaking what her mother Olga Emory had done; and then those azi had become freedmen, and married and had CIT kids, and taught them their values. More, the first Ari had operated increasingly with deep sets, in a style that scared a lot of other psych designers, and *they* didn't read what she'd been doing.

Teaching the kids' kids' generation to carry on, that was what—just like Gehenna. A lab-made ethic was threaded all through the stations in Union's grasp—just exactly what Yanni intended continuing with another surge in azi population in the deep Beyond. The same ethic the first Ari-generated population-burst had installed was buried in the psyches of all those people who took the subways to work and voted in the massive Bureaus of Citizens and Technology. Educated votes counted multiple times, and there were devices in the way the vote happened to keep the decision-making within a Bureau constantly in the hands of people expert in the fields in question, but the fact was, in Union's system, the popular vote, moving in a unified direction, could swing a certain way no matter what the experts wanted.

Count on it: the azi-born were never going to turn on Reseune: the sons and daughters of the azi-born were never going to turn, no matter what the Centrists wanted, or the Expansionists wanted, or the Paxers wanted. Yanni's maneuvers to divide and diminish the Centrists were, she suspected, all unnecessary, if the first Ari was right. There was a worm working in the programs, something that moved and reprogrammed itself to suit the times, and it was damned scary how it worked, and changed, while azi-descended were now out-populating CITs.

But it was not something she was going to discuss in depth with Yanni. The terrible danger of that ethics implant was what the first Ari had died knowing—she'd died haunted by the fact one human couldn't live long enough to see what it was going to do. It was why an Ari Two had to exist—to watch out for glitches in the mindsets she'd installed, at Gehenna, on Cyteen, inside Reseune itself. It was necessarily an untried theory, in those population surges mandated by the War, decommissioned soldiers, workers, colonists in the Gehenna outback: the first Ari had had to adjust them fast, and do it wide, or see it undone and unraveling. A collective azi-descended socio-set could mutate under unforeseen circumstances, creating not just new attitudes, but a whole artificially-setted human population, an integration with a capital I.

The first Ari had not just tweaked the helm of the ship of colonial ambitions, but rewritten the navigational charts. Gehenna was only a part of it.

And her predecessor had kept that secret to herself, until she passed it to her own image and set her onto a very specific course: to be sure the design didn't blow up in the second and third generation of newly-minted CITs . . . because to tell anyone was risking letting *another* worm loose in the population, one of knowing one's fate and trying to second-guess it.

And where *was* the end? What was going to happen to

humanity as a whole, when half the human population in the universe was on a different, human-devised program? Done was done. She had to steer it.

"All right," she said to this man, her own caretaker. Her protector. The man likely empowered by her predecessor to remove her if she ran amok. And she forgave him his sins of secrecy and surrendered a planet to him, because this man, whose use was his independent thinking, thought it was a necessary move. "All right, Yanni, so I'll study up on Eversnow. I should have done before now. The damage, you're right, is already done. The military saw to that. And I'm sure there are benefits I haven't looked at."

"I have a paper for you on that matter," he said. "Whalesong, on Earth."

"Whalesong," she said. The whim of a nostalgic preservationist: the oceans of Eversnow. "They sing."

"I think you'll find it interesting."

A bite of fish.

"You give me my city, Yanni, and I'll give you your planet."

"Precocious child."

"On a completely different topic—I've almost made up my mind this week. I'm pretty sure we're going to clone Denys."

"Are we? Now? Or some time in the next seven years?"

She frowned. That was a question. A big one: how close will we try to stick to program? "Giraud is the one we're going to trust—a little. Without his brother Denys to protect—how do we make a Giraud? So we clone Denys, for him, so Giraud keeps on track. That's my total reasoning in deciding. I was all set to tell you that this evening, when you dropped this Eversnow business in my lap. You said you were leaving the decision up to me. And I was thinking about it a lot while you were gone."

"Denys has no essential value," Yanni paraphrased her, "except to keep Giraud on track."

"No. That's what I changed my mind on. Denys helped create *me*. And if you have to create me again, you'd probably want a Denys to keep the new me in line, because Giraud is too soft."

"You don't think I could fill that position?"

"Uncle Yanni," she said fondly, "you're much too easy on me. You let me get away with everything."

"Hell. Sounds as if you're already making a lot of minor decisions, especially when I'm out of the house."

"Except the Eversnow thing. I wouldn't call that minor."

"It'll be your problem, young lady."

"It'll be your problem until it's pretty well underway. You're staying in office at least two more years. Maybe more."

"Two more years in purgatory. *God,* I hate politics."

"But *please* don't fall down the stairs, Uncle Yanni. You have to be Director. My alternative right now is Justin or Jordan."

It was a joke. Yanni didn't laugh. "Better to install Grant," Yanni muttered.

Probably true. Justin Warrick would hate the job more than Yanni did.

Sacrifice was the situation Yanni was enduring. Never mind he was creating a planet—he *wanted* to be working with azi, which was what he really loved.

"Yanni. Could you do *one* thing more for me?"

"What?" Yanni asked, and an eyebrow lifted. "When you take that tone, I'm on my guard."

She thought: Ari wanted you to bring me up. She'd agree with me. But she wasn't supposed to know that, so she said, "Giraud's going to need a father in a few months. Would you?"

"Good God!"

"You'd be good at it."

"Like hell. Giraud? Good loving God. He'd turn out a serial killer. I'm not good with kids. Especially that one."

"You're good at politics. People promise you things."

"I'm not sure that compliments my intelligence."

"So will you do it?"

A sigh. "I'm already loaded down with Council work and Admin. Where do I find the hours?"

"Who else am I going to get? Dr. Edwards? Giraud's too devious for him."

"You're serious."

"I'm completely serious."

"Well, it's *my* appointment to make," Yanni said. "Unless you want to take over this week."

"No."

"So I'll think about it."

"Seriously?"

"Seriously."

"So tell me about the rest of the session," she said. "I'm sure you were brilliant."

"The rest," he said, "was absolutely, deadly dull. Well, except the bomb scare. Paxers up to their old tricks. Nobody believed they could have gotten anything into the building, but I went back to the hotel and actually got my correspondence done."

Dinner wended happily on to dessert, a chocolate mousse, just a little of it, with a lot less tension. She found herself happy—so happy from relief that her hands shook a little; and she was fluxed. She'd just lost a planet, for God's sake, and she found herself being grateful it wasn't anything that personally threatened her. As for Yanni, he didn't look at all guilty of double-dealing: he looked very tired by then, trying to be sharp, but considering the trip home, the wine, and the rich dessert, he was probably thinking of bed and really hoping she wouldn't try any Working at the moment.

She didn't. She had all of her dessert and said she was tired herself, and yawned. That was no pretense and no Working. "You're the one who's had the long trip," she said, "and look, I'm the one yawning."

"I'm done," he said. "I've got a detailed report for you. I wrote down all the details. Session vids. Dull stuff." He fished in his pocket and laid a capsule down. "All there."

"You're so good," she said warmly. And meant it, this time in gratitude. Even if she was relatively sure the secret meetings wouldn't be in there. She pushed back from the table and Yanni got up and moved her chair for her, gentlemanlike. "Uncle Yanni."

"Don't call me 'uncle.'"

"Grump." She'd found that word in a book recently. It fit Yanni. She put her hands on his shoulders and kissed him on the cheek. "Good night. Go get some rest."

He returned the kiss, casual, but it made a warm feeling. There was no other CIT who had done that, not since Maman had gone away. Uncle Denys certainly hadn't.

And she had lately to think—did he dare try to manipulate her, sweeten his Eversnow maneuver, which he had come here knowing wouldn't be totally to her liking?

But she didn't want to think that. And he *had* brought her a written report, and the session tapes. She just filed the feeling away . . . let it go for a while. There'd be changes. There'd be her administration, after his, but it didn't have to be, yet. He was doing all right: she didn't *like* the Eversnow thing, didn't *like* the new labs, either, but he was being careful about it.

She saw him to the door, his companion Frank joining him there, and Catlin showed up, too.

Yanni left. The door closed. Systems went up again.

"I think he's all right," she announced to Catlin when that door shut.

There was no surprise there, just a nod of agreement. Her security had likely monitored the whole conversation. On the whole, the business with Yanni had gone amazingly well.

Tonight—maybe it was the sheer relief of getting Yanni back, even if she had to bargain a bit of her soul for him— she finally felt as if she could get some sleep.

BOOK ONE   Section I   Chapter x

APRIL 25, 2424
1901H

Fancy restaurant. Columns of light and coherent fog with a rhythmic sea sound in the background, and a holographic beach shimmering in mirrors that reflected, by some optical trick, the diners but not the columns.

It was a place called Jamaica. Justin hadn't been here before. And whatever stipend his father was on, it *didn't,* he was relatively sure, provide for a place like this. Jordan had called up, after a silence of several days—had asked him and Grant to dinner in the apartment; he'd balked, not wanting a renewal of the argument.

He'd suggested a quiet dinner out. Jordan had said he'd call back. And did, with a reservation.

Here.

Jamaica lay on the main level of Admin—that should have warned Jordan about the cost. It lay a short walk from both Education and Wing One, an outdoor walk across the quadrangle or a protected one through the tunnels. Probably his father had seen the convenience—hadn't likely seen the menu.

And the late hour? Because, Jordan had said, it was booked to the hilt at prime hours, which must mean the food was good.

It meant other things, too: that it was one of those Admin watering holes and Jordan was two decades out of touch with the changes in Admin. It had gotten pricier, to say the least. Jordan likely had no idea what he'd booked them into.

"Nice place," Grant observed. "Are you sure he said Jamaica?"

"He's not going to pay for this," Justin said. "Make sure the bill comes to us, will you? I'll keep on the lookout."

Grant immediately took charge and inquired with the maitre d' near the desk. There was quiet conversation, a nod, a credit chit passed, a little bow. The maitre d' moved a little closer to where Justin stood and offered them immediate seating—Jordan hadn't arrived yet—or a seat at the bar if they wanted to wait for their party; but in that same moment Jordan showed up with Paul, and claimed both them and the reservation.

Jordan looked quite professorial tonight in a tweed coat, quiet brown, a little academic for the milieu. Justin wore green, mild sheen, fashionable among the youngish set—which did fit in here. The maitre d' escorted them to their table, saw them seated, and promised them a waiter named Edward.

"Well, and how are you?" Jordan asked, as they settled in at their table, two and two, serving assistants deftly maneuvering china, filling water glasses.

"Oh, fine," Justin said, and the drink waiter showed up extraordinarily quickly for a place like this, crammed as it was with diners. It might be that someone had recognized Grant, whose red hair and vid star looks made him easy to ID. In Grant's company, people he had never met knew him, in every corridor in Reseune.

But it was Jordan Warrick's name on the reservation. So it was very possible it wasn't Grant that had gotten the fast attention. Very possibly it was Reseune Security that had picked their table for them, and bugged it. *That* might get the maitre d's quick attention, too, not to have a foul-up with security reach the ears of the other patrons.

Menus were set in their hands, bound in leather, quite the extravagance, while they eyed each other intermittently like fencers and didn't quite succeed at small talk. There were no prices on the menu. Not one. And Jordan by now knew what they were into, but he hadn't said a thing.

"Did you come across the quadrangle?" Paul asked.

Grant nodded. "Nice evening."

"So did we."

Jordan played the host, scanned the menu, inquired about appetizers, signaling they were going to go the whole route—they settled on the pâté—and didn't say a thing about his line of credit. He was animated, pleasant, cheerful, Jordan's public face, the face Justin had wanted to engage for this first phase of peacemaking. Jordan's card was going to bounce if the maitre d' failed them. And that *wouldn't* help the peace. Justin could foresee the moment, the embarrassment. God, the bill had better come to him. Quietly. Tactfully.

He and Jordan could patch things up. They'd not fought, since he'd grown. They didn't know each other, that was the sad truth. Twenty years of separation from Jordan was a significant time, even in rejuved lives. Jordan had dealt with him in the interim, corresponded with him—not lived in reach of him, that was the problem, and they had to learn about each other all over again. They'd been through the tentative, polite period. A few days ago they'd finally gotten down to honest opinions and somehow, expert as he was in psych, it had just slid inexorably downward.

Which it wouldn't do here. Jordan knew how to play to a crowd. He wasn't going to embarrass himself, even if he was likely to try another tag-you're-it attack. It would be subtle, if it came, reserved . . . unless something really, really jolted him; and they weren't going to mention the name Ari tonight—if Jordan did, he'd stop it cold. He'd stayed away from the past with Jordan these last weeks. He'd broken the rule, pulled the scab off old wounds in their last alcohol-fueled debate, and maybe he had to go on avoiding the topic until Jordan did get his license and his security clearance back and had a few months of be-having himself.

Or maybe they never would be able to discuss that par-ticular subject—Ari, and the night that had changed him. Terrible as the experience had been, long before the argu-ment with Jordan, he'd come to wonder if the first Ari's action hadn't been a rescue. Jordan's path wasn't really what he wanted. He'd been set on being Jordan until that night. That night he'd become somebody else. He wasn't sure who. But he'd become different.

Thank God. Or he'd have agreed with Jordan four nights ago and they'd all lose their licenses. This way—

"Ever eaten here?" Jordan asked him, over the menu.

"No," Justin said. "Never have." And the real question: "You haven't?"

"Random choice. A yen for something different." And still, typical Jordan, not a mention of the absent prices. He'd heard the night's specials and not asked. He main-tained a pleasant expression on his face—also pure Jor-dan. "Planys was a lot of the same thing."

Play along: change the subject: keep it light. "Not many choices there, I'll imagine."

"Five. It got boring in the first month. There were actu-ally six choices when I got there. Two of the restaurants consolidated. One changed the menu, oh, about five years on. The other one never did. One Greek, one Italian, one French, one Colonial, and one you couldn't depend on. That was the excitement. That was our suspense, that fifth restaurant."

It might be humor. Every piece of humor he'd heard from Jordan lately had had a bitter edge. But he dutifully laughed, trying to take it lighter. "Remember Illusions? It's been through most of those choices. Now it's New Era."

"I'm afraid I've missed that delight, so far."

"A lot of expensive spices. The real thing, I understand, imported. Some of them are pretty good. Some of them I'm not so sure about. But the steaks are consistently good."

"We'll have to try it. Anything new."

"We can do that." Justin meanwhile looked through the menu. "Angry Shrimp and Pell Bordeaux," he said. Pell Bordeaux wasn't going to be cheap. "Sounds interesting. I think I'll do that."

"Adventurous," Jordan said, and added, darkly. "You must be rich."

"Well, I secretly thought I'd treat my father."

"I didn't ask you here to soak my son for the tab."

"Let me do it. It's my pleasure."

"They pay you pretty well for what you do."

"I've been where you are. It ends. You'll get back. All the way back. You'll be treating me." Fast change of subject. A cheerier one. "How's it coming with the sets you did? Your own ones, that you were looking at—how they've developed over two, three decades? That's got to be interesting."

"Getting back into it, at least. I need an office."

"Yanni might be agreeable."

"You're rattling around in our old one."

"We have staff," Justin said. His guard was instantly up. . . . God, he hated to be so paranoid. And he didn't want to show it in his expression. But talking to Jordan lately was like walking through broken glass barefoot.

"Nice location. Convenient. And there's room enough."

Guard went way up.

"Not with staff. Sorry, Jordan, that won't work."

"Paul and I haven't gotten all our Planys notes pried out of Security," Jordan said glumly. "Our wardrobe's barely made it through. You can see our splendor this evening. Pretty shabby stuff."

"You're fine."

"Don't suppose you can use your influence with the little darling to speed our stuff along."

"I'll ask, if you like." He was glad "the little darling" was as far as the sarcasm about young Ari went in this venue. The walls had ears and even if they didn't, he didn't like Jordan dragging him into a proxy quarrel with Admin while half the Wing Directors and Agency heads in Reseune sat at the other tables. "Be genteel. Trust me. This time, trust me, and take my word for it. She's not her genemother."

"No?" Jordan feigned surprise. "After all they've done to be sure she *is?*"

The waiter arrived. Mercifully. The dinner wasn't going well and they hadn't even ordered yet.

Justin gave his order. Grant ordered smoked salmon, a likely match for cost, Paul ordered boeuf a la maison and Jordan ordered a modest, all-local caesar salad with blackened chicken.

"Saving room for dessert," Jordan said when Justin frowned at his economy. "I noticed a cheesecake."

"Sounds good," Justin said—not tempted to believe Jordan was through with gestures this evening, no. Not once he'd started. And the waiter departed.

"So I'm going to impose on you," Jordan said. "We need desk space. I'm sure they watch me. I'm sure they watch you. We can consolidate their job. Make them happy."

"I'm telling you we have staff. Five staffers and us in that office. And security won't let you in there."

"So who's important? Your clericals or your father?"

"I'm saying we need the staff. They have work to do."

"Fine. Ask the little dear for space for them. I'm sure she'd find it. After all, she's not stingy like her predecessor."

"Jordan, give it up. You haven't got your clearance. You'll get it. But it's still no, on the office."

"I'm saying I'm going eetee locked into that living room. I can't work in there. Put your spare clericals into our living room if you have to. You're not even there five days a week. Who's using the desks?"

It wasn't an outrageous request—except it was his convenient Integrations computer access, which his staff used, which *he* used, dammit, for Ari's lessons, and his father *didn't* have clearance, or a license. His safe was there. His manuals were there. His projects were there—he didn't keep those in their cubbyhole of a Wing One office.

"You're not happy," Jordan said. *"Sorry."*

"Look, if you want your office back . . ." Yanni wasn't likely to approve Jordan's moving into general office space in the first place, there was that. But he could easier get another office in the Education wing, for them and their staff.

"I would like that. Yes. I mean when I get the license back, for God's sake. We can share. What happened to us working together?"

And his and Grant's work with the G-27, while not under security seal, had some bits in it he felt fairly proprietary about, and, no, dammit, he didn't want another round of security investigations going through his notebooks, or Grant's because Jordan was in there. More to the point, he didn't want his *father* going through his notes and appropriating anything he was working on.

No way in *hell.*

"I just don't see why it's an issue," Jordan said with a wistful little frown. "Apply to move your staff out. I'm sure they'll find a space somewhere."

"It's a little matter of convenience."

"You know there *are* virtual connections—same as being there. Unless, of course, there's some reason you'd rather not."

"You know the reasons I'm a little reluctant. Last Sunday night was a case in point."

"Many fewer drinks in the office."

"Listen, Jordan. My life is going perfectly fine. So could yours be, if you'd just put the brakes on a bit and get along with Yanni. You're home, for God's sake. He knows you didn't—whatever."

"Yanni's a prick."

"Dad. Don't."

"Have you caved in that far?"

He lowered his voice way down and leaned across the table. "And do you have to agitate Admin just to get a reaction? I don't particularly want a reaction, thank you."

"So the little dear *is* something like her predecessor."

Not *sotto voce.* Just normal conversation level, and not cooperating worth a damn. Justin found his pulse rate had gotten up, old familiar sensation. And he didn't like it.

"Well, there you have it, don't you? We're arguing again and I don't think it would work, sharing an office. Look, I've had enough of investigations. I don't want to be in the middle of another one. And get off the notion it's Ari. It's Yanni, and you know you don't want to be in his bad book, but you persist in picking fights."

"Ah. So it's fear for your reputation. But you should be golden. You were quite the hero, overthrowing the Nyes, saving her highness . . ."

"Neither." Jordan was stalking some point, he saw that, and he didn't know why or what. For a top-flight psychset designer, it was downright embarrassing, not to know what was behind his own identical's actions, and *that* hinted at a Working, either verbal or otherwise. Jordan knew him from way back, *owned* most of the buttons, knew his body from inside out, and that was a fact. Sitting here, across the table from Jordan, mirror into mirror with that damned infuriating smile on Jordan's face that his own body knew gut-deep was no smile at all, because it never reached the eyes—*damn,* he knew it. And there was nobody more dangerous to him, if Jordan decided to pull old strings.

Set psych-switches in his own baby boy? Damned right Jordan would have done that, from the cradle up. Ari One had flipped them the other way. Jordan had had twenty years to figure how to get at him past Ari's Working, or worse—and then those questions Sunday night. Had he been alone with Ari? Had Ari done anything further? It very much assumed the character not of an outraged father, but of a psych operator wanting a case history.

And much worse—

Jordan knew how to get at Grant. Grant *had* been under Jordan's supervision, too, in their collective childhood, and if Jordan could get his hands on Grant's updated manual, which was in the computer system in that office, once Jordan got his license back . . .

That thought sent cold chills through him. The very thought, that Grant could be put into that situation—that sent his hand questing after the lately-arrived drink.

Share an office with Jordan? No. Absolutely not. License or no license. And subtlety only wound his own gut in knots. It gave Jordan chance after chance to get to him.

"It's just not going to work," he said. "I'll go to Yanni, if you can't do it without flaring off. I'll talk to him and see if I can get your stuff out of customs and your license hurried along."

"I don't want any damn charity."

"But you damn sure want my office. And I don't want you in there."

"*Your* office?"

"Let's try honesty," he said abruptly. "You want to start the war with Admin up again. I don't. I don't want to subject Grant to it, either. So make your own choices, but—"

"Are you making *your* choices these days?"

"My choice right now is to have my office to myself, to do my work, outside politics—"

"Oh, come now!"

"—to have Grant do his. To enjoy my life . . ."

"Will you? Enjoy it? And *are* you outside politics?"

That did it. He smiled with his father's own false warmth, right back at him, and something ticked over deep in his makeup that could be cold as ice—something he didn't damn well trust, but right now it felt like an asset, not to have himself out of control with this man who had all the buttons. "I don't know, *Dad*. I haven't a clue who's had a go at me or who's reshaped my pysche during Denys Nye's tenure—there are things I don't actually remember. But I'm actually pretty happy these days, and I lately find I haven't any stake in your game, whatever it is."

"You think you haven't."

"I know I haven't. I don't give a damn for what happened twenty years ago and if you plan to live here in Reseune, I really hope you'll just let it all go. So enjoy your dinner. I plan to."

"Justin, Justin, Justin, you really *believe* you're not in it."

"Won't work, Pop. Really won't work." He took a sip of wine. The rich tastes were sharp, solid, complex. Where Jordan wanted to lead him was complicated, too, the wrong end of Jordan's ambitions, whatever they currently were, and he discovered, since the last fight, he truly failed to give a damn, tonight, and decided not to subscribe to Jordan's list of problems.

"You have your own agenda," Jordan said. "You think it's in your practical interests to keep your own counsel. And you don't want to share. I can respect that."

"Thanks for the analysis."

"You're waiting. You plan to have influence in the great someday. Yanni's not any younger and *she's* not old enough, not as old as she needs to be. So you're going to be the stopgap. What kind of position will that put you into? You know, you could parlay your connections into the Directorship, what time the little dear doesn't hold that post herself. Maybe Councillor for Science. And are you ready for that?"

He took another drink of wine, a deliberately small one, thinking: *God, no.* And said: "*You're* scared of her. But not scared enough. Watch it about trying to read me. You could make a mistake. You're locked in what was. And things just may not be the same after twenty years."

"You think I can't read you, down to the fine print? I do, believe me, I do, right down to the fact you're running scared of the little dear, same as you did her predecessor. I know all the twitches."

"I know you owned the geneset first. But genesets are only part of the story. *We* both know that, don't we? But do we both actually believe it? I wonder."

"Oh, programming can do wonders," Jordan said. "And you've been Worked for all those years. How many sessions did you have with Giraud Nye's people, before you had one with little Ari?"

"Arrests, you mean?" He kept his tone light. "Oh, a few. But you were in one long detention, yourself, over on Planys. Do you find that makes a psychological difference? I'd say so."

That actually caught Jordan just a little by surprise. Or maybe it stung, for reasons he hadn't, until now, guessed. "So you won't like having me in your office," Jordan said, flank attack and redirect. "You don't trust me."

"Living the life I've lived, I don't trust anybody. You think they *did* Work you over when you were arrested? Or aren't you sure of that?"

Jordan avoided his eyes. In a psychmaster, that was a devastating flinch. And that avoidance hit him right in the heart, reminding him of his own little sojourns with inter-rogators. Ricochet, he thought, feeling the pain. Damn. And he didn't look at Paul. He hadn't invoked Paul's name, or queried him. Paul wasn't looking at him. But the shots didn't go just at Jordan.

Salads arrived. They ate while Jordan sat and had more wine. They managed small talk, catching up on who was sleeping with whom, who was married, who had procre-ated. One of the many Carnaths had given natural birth to a daughter, opting to skip the birthlabs. It was the talk of the offices. Crazy, no few said.

"There's a certain merit in it," Jordan said. "Think of all the thousands who don't have access to a lab, or don't have it government-subsidized. Fargone. Pan-Paris. All those poor women doing it the hard way . . . those poor childless men with no other recourse. . . ."

Justin didn't often imagine Fargone, or Pan-Paris, way-stations in the dark which touched his personal world very little. He was glad not to have to imagine them, steel worlds orbiting stars whose planets, if any to speak of, were good only for mining. "We're spoiled, I suppose."

"Spoiled as hell," Jordan said, more cheerfully. "Though there's Planys, if you ever want not to be spoiled."

Right back to the bitter edge.

And it didn't pay to go there. "Rather not. Hope never to."

"So how's your apartment? Nice, I'll imagine, being where it is."

"Nice. Yes."

"Bugged. Naturally."

"Naturally."

Main course arrived. Gratefully. Another service of wine. Jordan took a refill. He didn't. Nor did Grant, nor Paul.

"Ever think of moving back to Education?" Jordan asked.

"I think about it."

"You could come and visit me. But I can't get into your restricted little paradise."

"I know. I'm sorry about that. I really am."

"Can't do anything about it, can you?"

"I know it's not going to last."

"Isn't it? Got a date when they're going to stop bugging my apartment? Got a date when I can go into my son's extravagant palace?"

"You know I don't. Maybe, to a large extent, Dad, that depends on you."

"Right next door to the little princess. Convenient for sex. Is that what you do for your keep?"

He said nothing, speared a bite of his dinner, and ate it. The spiced shrimp was curiously tasteless, and he resisted the impulse to lay his fork down and leave. Or have another wine. His pulse rate was up. Jordan always did that to him. And another wine would be deadly. He decided on a redirect, and had another bite of shrimp. "Paul?"

"Ser?"

"Ser, hell. I'm Justin. Remember?"

Paul's face was generally somber. It remained that way—with good cause, tonight. "I remember."

"Grant," Jordan said, and Justin felt his heart kick up another notch. He couldn't help it. And he resented that, resented Jordan having anything to do with Grant these days. "Are you taking good care of my boy? In every respect?"

"No problems, ser." Grant's voice was perfectly light and smooth, not a twitch. "Thank you."

"You came through all the troubles in good shape."

"Absolutely, ser."

"Have you ever needed a supervisor, beyond what you have?"

"Damn it, Jordan, just enjoy your dinner."

"I was just asking. Concerned."

"The hell." Grant's welfare and their relationship and the number of times Grant had needed a supervisor wasn't a topic he wanted opened up. The past wasn't. He didn't want to list the things that had changed his relationship with Grant into a sexual one. He didn't want Jordan's commentary on their existence. They all ate in prickly silence for a space, except that Paul asked how long they should have to wait for Library access, which seemed a fairly minor request.

"I'm sure I don't know," Justin said patiently. "That's

something you might legitimately ask Yanni." He couldn't stop himself from charitable impulses. "Or I can. I will."

"One of ten thousand little nuisances," Jordan said. "I need my own past articles. I don't think I'm going to blow up the laboratories with information I'd find in my own damned articles, would I?"

"We do have an inquiry going in Yanni Schwartz's office," Paul said, "but that's had to wait for him to get back."

"He's back now. This evening. Give him a day to get his feet on the ground. I'm sure he'll give you that access."

"Well, I'm sure I'm not a priority," Jordan said sourly, and shoved his plate back. He'd mostly picked the chicken out of his salad and eaten a little of the green. "In any respect."

Justin decided he was through. Grant was hardly eating. "Shall we order dessert?"

"Out of the mood, thanks."

"Sorry."

"It's sad," Jordan said. "We were one mind, once and long ago. Remember that? We were happy, then."

"I remember you and Ari Emory got into a fight and Grant and I ended up on the short end of it. I'm not looking for a replay, Dad. If you want to pick a fight with Admin, just excuse me out of it this time."

"Why don't you come over for drinks after dinner?" Jordan asked. "Just a quiet family evening."

"Did that, thanks," Justin said. "Had enough to drink tonight, as is, and so have we all. Late supper and I'm going to bed. I've got a meeting in the morning."

"Oh?"

"We're conferring on a psychset," Justin said.

"What stem?"

"Oh, out of the old Reza GLX tree," Justin said, which actually was the truth, and he watched Jordan drink it in and jog a doubtless rusty memory, eyes momentarily innocent, mind working on a problem—*that* was the father he wanted back. If the conversation was going to change direction he might change his mind on dessert.

"Worker set, isn't it?"

"There's a new lab upriver. Or will be. It's quite a project. Research and light manufacture."

"And you're picking the sets that go there?"

"Can't discuss that one. Sorry." He wasn't sure he should have said as much as he had. But it was common knowledge, and the answer he'd given *did* answer Jordan's question.

"And how soon does this new enterprise arise from the wasteland?"

"Awhile yet. They've only built the bunker as is, for the first workers. Precips are mostly built, but not online."

"The little darling's precocious ambition? Or Yanni's?"

"Hers, as far as I know."

"And only eighteen. What are we calling this installation?"

"I don't know."

"But with azi all picked out for it. And what CIT population? Is this where she's sending all the dissidents?"

It wasn't far off the mark, and Jordan Warrick could easily turn up on that list, but he didn't want it to happen and he didn't let his expression change, knowing that was exactly what Jordan was implying.

"I haven't a clue about that."

"Oh, come, you're consulting on the psychsets of the azi component, the things they're supposed to counter. You know damned well what CIT profile the azi will fit around, clear as a footprint."

"Well, if I guessed, I'd be a fool to say, and you didn't sire a fool, Dad, so give it up."

"And she thought of this all on her own."

"You're assuming things I've never said."

The waiter came, offering dessert. "No, thanks," Justin said. "Just the bill."

"Yes, ser," the waiter said, having gotten his instructions, it seemed: the waiter tapped his handheld and called up a bill.

Thank God it was fast. Justin swept his keycard through the offered handheld and keyed a reasonable tip on a monumental charge. He gave it to the waiter, kept a pleasant smile on his own face as he pushed his chair back, and maneuvered himself between Jordan and Grant as they all got up and walked out.

"So where is this place?" Jordan asked, as they passed between the columns on their way out. "The new construction?"

"Not that far upriver."

"Light manufacture? I just wonder what they'll be making up there that we don't have here. Or mining there that we can't get elsewhere." Jordan's face was grim. "Oh, I have the picture, believe me. It's no more manufacture than it is a recreation spot."

"Assumptions are a bitch. They just don't get you to any good outcome."

"Lectures from my son?"

Dead stop. He faced Jordan. "I passed my majority some years ago, Dad. And you know it's damned likely we're bugged. So what in hell are you doing? Trying to piss off Yanni? I tell you, I really don't appreciate being dragged into your quarrel with a kid you never met."

"Are you afraid? Have they made you afraid?"

"The answer is no. No, I'm not afraid. I'm comfortable. I support Yanni. I support Ari, for that matter. I hope she has a long and happy career. And if you'll take *my* advice and just live here, I'm sure you'll get along. If you want a fight for a fight's sake, I'm sure you'll get it from someone. I just don't see the point in it." He walked on, with Grant.

Jordan stayed beside him, Paul just behind. "Too beaten-down. Too little fire. I missed your growing-up."

"Oh, plenty you missed, I assure you. You didn't miss anything good. But that's what we dealt with while you had your own troubles. It's finished. Done is done. If you didn't kill Ari—"

"I didn't. You know it was a frame."

He stopped, beyond the columns, in the public corridor, and faced Jordan. "I reserve judgement. You might have killed her—to protect your investment in me. Or Denys Nye thought she was going to die anyway, and a clone would be manageable, especially in his hands; and you weren't connected to the right people to protect you.

Whatever happened, it didn't work for you. For good or for ill, you missed my growing-up. You missed my times in detention. You missed my being Worked over by security, and you missed Grant's troubles, too, but, you know, we just can't recover those happy days, can we? So let's not try. I'll take your word you were innocent. You'll take mine that I believe you. We'll both get along."

"We'll talk about this tomorrow. In the office."

"Damn it, Dad, you can't come in there. It's a security clearance area and you haven't got one. So keep out!"

Jordan reached into his pocket and held out a card. Justin started to take it, automatically, and when he stalled in sudden apprehension that it had nothing to do with the office or the security clearance issue, Jordan reached out and dropped it into his coat pocket.

He wasn't a kid, to skip out of the way. It was ludicrous. It was also an attack.

"Damn it, Jordan."

"Damn what?"

He'd had earnest hopes when he'd heard Jordan was released and when Jordan made it home to a changed Reseune, that he'd have the father he'd been deprived of during all the Nye years. Everything would be healed and clean and new.

Neither Paul nor Grant said a word to what had just happened. He wanted to take the card out of his pocket, fling it away to be trampled by passers-by, swept up by the cleaning-bots—pounced on by security. He didn't even reach into his pocket to look at it. "I really don't appreciate this, Dad."

"Tomorrow," Jordan said. "See you tomorrow. That's still one of your non-teaching days, isn't it?"

"No," he said. "You're *not* moving in with us."

"Tomorrow," Jordan said again—the way he'd just held his ground in arguments two decades ago. No argument. Just a position from which he wouldn't budge. "That was *my* office."

"Damn it, Jordan."

"My office, I say. Sure you won't come over for an after-dinner drink?"

"Good night," Justin said, and started off in his own

direction, toward the doors. Grant walked beside him, not saying a word until they'd exited the corridor for the outside, and started across the darkened quadrangle.

"You told him no," Grant said. "But he will come ahead tomorrow anyway, won't he?"

"My bet is on it," he said. "And we've got to advise the staff. Lock up the office if we have to. Damn him, Grant, *damn* him. All he has to do to fit in is just do nothing. That's the only requirement, just settle in, don't push any buttons, and let things be." Grant said nothing in reply, and Justin remembered that face, set and angry: Jordan, his elder twin—biologically speaking. Twin psychologically speaking, so far as being raised by his father went. Next best thing to psychogenesis.

Ari's face, too. Elder Ari's face. A glass in his hand. The feeling of being drugged. Sex. And a voice saying—

He couldn't remember what she'd said. To this day, it blacked out at that point. He'd tried not to let his father know what had happened. He'd tried so hard.

But too many had known.

And he'd spent his next years being arrested for the suspicion of thinking. He'd given up his father's head-on attack on life and adopted a stubbornness that laid low, laid modest plans, and just survived into the next Ari's growing up, to become a general annoyance to Denys Nye.

Mirror into mirror, physically, himself with Jordan. But the psychology Jordan knew in his son had been Worked on and Worked over every time they'd arrested him and hauled him in . . .

He suspected they'd tried to bend him, at least.

But cracking any Working the first Ari had done—that wasn't easy. He'd been set on a course. He'd even begun to cling to it, mentally, telling himself from the start that the Nyes could have done the murder themselves, and that they might someday kill him, but they weren't going to crack him, because he was *Ari's* piece of work. What kept him alive, he greatly suspected, was the fact they couldn't tell whether he was somehow essential in the plans Ari had laid down—essential in the construction of her own psychological and physiological clone. The genius that had made Reseune what it was had to be reborn to keep the power Reseune had, which was currently in their hands: and if Justin Warrick was somehow part of it—the Nyes had to keep him alive.

They'd gone into convulsions of policy when their precious clone had found her way to him.

They hadn't known what to do with him after that, except try to make sure he didn't come up with any Working of his own, where it regarded the little girl, who'd become a bigger girl, who'd become a young woman and developed notions her guardians finally couldn't control.

Sex, prominent among them. He'd gotten away from her. He'd known that was worth his life, but the Nyes weren't what scared hell out of him in that regard. What scared him was young Ari herself, the fact that there was no predicting what psychological trigger could go off in that interface, as if whatever the first Ari had done had set a mark on him that wouldn't stay quiet if he ever got involved with child-Ari. It wasn't where he wanted to go. It wasn't who he was supposed to be. His whole being shrieked no and he backed away.

And Jordan came back into his life, now that the Nyes were done, and now that Yanni Schwartz was in charge.

Yanni sat sphinxlike behind his desk, watching all the pieces shift on the board, doubtless wondering whether the piece that was Justin Warrick would gravitate to the troublesome piece that was Jordan, and whether Jordan would gravitate back to his old intention of getting out of Reseune and attacking its policies from the outside. Jordan had had contacts—contacts that had had contacts with the Paxers, the Abolitionists; and he'd had friends at the opposite end of the spectrum, the Defense Bureau, who'd been the first Ari's allies, but who simultaneously wanted to get the upper hand over Reseune. And Jordan had dealt with them . . . back then, dealt with every contact on the planet he could use to break Reseune's power and overthrow the system.

They were all watched, constantly, had been for years, and Yanni reported regularly to an eighteen-year-old girl who would own absolute power over ReseuneLabs whenever she wanted to take it up. Within a decade, the corporation that was creating population and civilization in the farthest reaches of human exploration would come back under the control of a second Ariane Emory.

And a third Ariane, someday. That event was already in the planning stages. Every detail of young Ari's life was being stored up, the way the first Ari's life had been stored.

And come the day, the inevitable day—the question would be ... *which* of the two Aris ought to be born again.

And how many of the people who'd been part and parcel of the second Ari's life had to be recreated, and *which* Ari were those replicates going to have to deal with?

He had a horrid suspicion a storage somewhere now had *his* data, and Grant's programming, and maybe Yanni's. Giraud Nye, who had probably never looked to face such an event, was already less than a year from rebirth. Denys Nye, the shadowy eminence who'd run the labs in the interim years, was still a question mark ... but he'd bet a year's pay which way that decision was going to go. Ari's teenaged emotions were still in the ascendant; but the cold, keen intellect was rising fast.

He didn't know how much of that situation Jordan knew. How did you tell your father you—and therefore he, through you—were destined for immortality, right along with the original Ari, Jordan's onetime partner and life-long rival, all to help her exist again and go on shaping humankind for all eternity?

It wasn't going to make for family tranquility once Jordan got that picture, that was for very damned certain.

And that city young Ari was founding, upriver from ReseuneLabs? Who *was* going to live there, except people that Ari didn't want living under Reseune's roof, or down-river in Novgorod, either, where the government and other troubles resided?

"It should have been a pleasant evening," he remarked, in the chill, deep silence of the deserted quadrangle, the absence, usually, of electronic bugs ... unless somebody was aiming ears specifically at them. And he wouldn't say absolutely that that wasn't the case, given the red flag of Jordan's invitation. "I'd tried to look forward to it." He felt the card in his pocket, a little paper card.

"Tried?" Grant asked.

"He's bitter," Justin said. "I can't blame him for that part of his attitude. Twenty years in exile . . ."

"Against whom should he be bitter?" Grant asked. Judging CIT emotions was not what he was born to do. "You? Does he blame you because you work with young Ari? Is it Yanni he dislikes? Or did I miss the entire point of that discussion?"

"No. You didn't miss it. He blames me for coming out of it on her side. That's one thing."

"They're all dead, all the ones actually responsible for his situation. Yanni's alive. But Yanni didn't send your father away, did he?"

"He didn't, exactly. Or he actually may have, but the deal probably saved Jordan's life. But the fact those responsible are dead now is only one more frustration for him. A slice of his life is gone in those two decades. He could live a hundred years more, on rejuv. But all he sees is the twenty years he lost. And the fact he's been robbed of a fight about it. And what he really wants—what he really wants, between you and me, is no Reseune."

Several more paces in silence. "What would take its place?" Grant asked. "Does he know that?"

"I didn't say it was a reasonable attitude."

"He's as intelligent as either of us."

"That's no guarantee of rationality."

"I've observed that occasionally," Grant said dryly. It was worth a dry laugh, even under the circumstances.

"What I've said still holds," Justin said. "You're not to go anywhere near him without me, and you're not to occupy a room with him or Paul without me, and you're not to take seriously anything he tells you privately, not even if he tells you I'm dying. Just—no matter how finely you dice it—stay away from him."

"He created me. Reseune forever holds my Contract and you're my Supervisor. I know what's right."

"Contract, hell. Protect yourself."

"Protecting myself, I protect you. That's logical, isn't it?"

"Very. I'm glad you see it that way."

"Someone is by the pond," Grant remarked. And it was

true. A shadow stood near the small fishpond ahead of them, where quadrangle walks crossed. Four benches offered seating there, to anybody who wanted to contemplate the water—a pleasant place to sit and think, on a sunny summer day. It was still April, it was long after dark, and the wind was up. Their ordinary coats were barely enough to make a walk to the other wing bearable. And somebody was standing there in the dark, somebody in dark, close-fitting clothing.

The shadow watched the water. It might be a despondent lover, someone wanting solitude. It might have nothing to do with them.

But fear had been a constant, in the Nye years. Fear of arrest. Fear of being tampered with, of having Grant tampered with—Ari was their only protection. And Ari wasn't going out of her Wing lately.

The figure had been intent on the water. Now the head turned. The whole body turned to stand confronting them.

"Ser," the shadow said politely as they met, and recognition revised the shadowed vision into familiar detail, the black elite Security uniform, dark curly hair, light build.

Florian. Ari's personal bodyguard. A youth no older than Ari herself, with absolute power—to arrest. To kill, without a second's warning. And he had that damned card in his pocket.

"Jordan proposes to share your office," Florian said.

"I told him no." Surely Ari's security knew he had. He'd bet his life they'd heard every word of it. And it was better than other alternatives.

"Let him have it. Your materials will go to another office." Florian held out a keycard, offering it.

He took it. He had no choice but take it, in a hand growing chill through. "But our personnel—"

"Sorry, ser, they'll have to find other employment. They aren't cleared for Wing One."

"They're our people."

"No longer."

"And the computers, our files . . . we have notes, handwritten notes—the order they're in—in delicate position. Stacks that can't be disrupted without losing information—

we're not that neat. Things we can't have just anybody
rifling through, for God's sake. It's a mess, but we know
where things are. Things in the safe. Look, if we have to
do this, we can go over there tonight. We need to do this
ourselves . . . we're *willing* to do it ourselves."

"We're aware of the state of your office," Florian said—
dark humor at his expense, he had no idea. "And qualified
personnel will perform the transfer."

"We need to go over there."

"Best you don't, ser, so the persons moving it can do
so with the greatest attention to detail. All the items will
be there in the morning, in their original order, and new
equipment will be in place in your former office by 0500."

"For him. *Bugged* equipment."

"Absolutely."

"He'll think I arranged this. No matter how you explain
it, he'll think I had something to do with this."

"Unfortunate if so, ser, but your notes will be safe, and
your staff will be safe, in other employ, at a priority. They'll
be given employment, no problem. Just not Wing One."

At least they wouldn't miss a paycheck, Em, and the
others. They'd be all right. But they were the ones that
knew his work. They'd been his people.

"No wipe."

"No wipe, ser. Nothing of the sort." This with a slight shift
of the shadowed gaze toward Grant, and back. "We ask you
to accept this arrangement and not attempt to circumvent it
in any fashion. Grant, you're not to go there, either."

"My father won't take this well at all," Justin said. "I'm
afraid he'll be in Yanni's office in the morning."

"We'll advise the Director. It's not your problem, ser."

"I appreciate your concern." The cold of the night had
penetrated his dinner jacket. He felt a shiver coming on.
"I'm freezing, at the moment. Can you tell me—I take it, it
was Ari ordered this?"

"Sera has retired for the evening. We're operating on
our own discretion, on sera's general instruction. We'll inform sera in the morning. You won't need to."

"And where is this new office?"

"Downstairs, ground level, and a right turn from your
apartment. More convenient, and a better office, I believe.

There's room for staff. But it will be Wing One-approved staff."

Yanni Schwartz didn't maintain an office in that high-security territory. He had one, already, a cubbyhole he used for Ari's lessons. Downstairs—those rooms—they had a historic connection with the old Wing One lab, where the first Ari had died. That lab had been decommissioned now. And he didn't know how up to date the offices in that area were, these days, whether they were still tied into System. But Florian said their computers were coming over. They must be.

"Do go on, ser," Florian said. "You're chilled. Good night to you."

"Thank you," he said, and started on his way, Grant attending without a word.

Then he thought of Jordan's card in his pocket, wondered, all in a rush, what sort of trouble he could bring down on Jordan's head; and considered the fact that Florian hadn't asked him for it.

Florian didn't know? Something had slipped past Ari's staff? It had been a surreptitious handoff.

But Reseune Security surely knew. Florian might let him go his way. But someone inside Ari's wing might confront him yet.

Maybe Catlin. Maybe, worse thought, someone he didn't know, out of ReseuneSec, and that was more trouble than he wanted. He'd been fluxed by the office matter. He had an excuse for having forgotten.

But an azi of Florian's bent didn't flux. Not for two seconds running. Florian damned well hadn't forgotten it.

He stopped, turned, reached into his pocket. Pulled out the thin card. "Florian."

Florian had walked the other direction—was a diminished figure in the dark. But he heard, and stopped.

"I'll take it to him," Grant said.

He surrendered it without a word. Grant knew. Grant had seen Jordan's action. Grant knew his reasoning the way Grant knew their situation from the inside out.

Grant crossed the dark distance between them, delivered the card, and walked back again. Florian stood there a moment, until Grant reached him, took the card, then

turned and pursued his way back to Admin, where they
had come from, and maybe on to the Education Wing beyond it, where their office was—or had been.

"Damn," he said when Grant joined him. "Damn it,
Grant."

"Do you know what was on the card?" Grant asked.

"I haven't the faintest. It may be a joke, for all I know. I
don't want to know. Damn him!"

"I intend to evade Jordan's company, in private," Grant
said. "I'm relatively confident I could, even if we shared an
office. But it seems the question is settled for now."

"Settled," Justin found himself saying, and realized
it was impossible the second the word came out of his
mouth. "It isn't settled—not with him. Whatever quarrel
he had with his Ari isn't mine. It wasn't *my* choice to support young Ari against him. But—"

"But?"

"He'll keep it going. And maybe he's justified. Maybe
he's pure and right and just my living here put me on the
other side. I've missed him all these years. But here I
am, living on the other side, in her wing, working in *her*
wing . . ."

"A different Ari. A very different Ari."

"We don't know how different she'll become, as time
passes."

"Even azi," Grant said, "aren't identical."

"But her interests are the same as the first Ari's."

"The people who pursued us are dead."

"And all being reincarnated." He reached the door. And
stopped there, in the wind and the dark, in the last haven
before they went into heavily monitored Wing One. "Maybe
that concept ought to bother me more than it does."

"You think that constitutes Jordan's motive in this?
That he believes she'll eventually become his enemy?"

"I think it's personal. I think it's him against Ari. All
the traits that make her and him. My immortality—if they
do that to us—won't be his. I don't know if he'll see it that
way, but we're *not,* thank God, psychological twins. I'm
myself. I'm the first of myself. The only."

"I understand that," Grant said, who was also the first
and only of his kind . . . so far.

"Thinking about it makes me a little crazy."

"You're *not* crazy. Your actions have been completely logical, given the flux."

"Including giving her security that card? Jordan's going to land in trouble for it, and I set him up for it."

"No. He set *you* up for it. You simply returned the favor."

Cool, clear, utterly reasonable. He shivered in the cold wind. "Sometimes I don't understand him. I just don't understand him. Or I don't want to."

"Your father is intelligent. He *is* capable of staying out of trouble. He simply declines to do that."

"And it's what you always said. CITs have their logic sets installed late. Emotions on the bottom, logic on the top. Sometimes it's a complete bitch-up."

"Apparently."

"I wish I could talk to him. Damn, I wish I could talk to him. Sensibly. Logically. You see how it goes. You saw how it went Sunday night."

A moment passed. "I have a question."

"Ask."

"Should we be physically afraid of him?"

He had to think about that. There was one fair answer, one answer that would protect both of them. "Yes," he said, and slid his apartment keycard into the outside door lock. The door opened, letting them into the foyer for a dozen other id programs to work over. "Maybe we should be."

BOOK ONE   Section I   Chapter xi

APRIL 25, 2424
2039H

Justin and Grant had reached their apartment. The door shut and locked. The light on the console showed green, safe. They were in, and their conversation on the way had been scant, and worried. Tracking had flicked from one station to the next, and surveillance had been hard pressed to keep up with the two parties, homeward bound in opposite directions.

Justin and Grant weren't the problem. Jordan was. And *he*, with Paul, had gone home, too, talking about Library access and his intention of calling Yanni Schwartz in the morning.

Catlin flicked a switch, passing the watch back to the senior ReseuneSec team that watched over Wing One, entry by entry, movement by movement. Florian was on his way back. So was Marco, from Education, having ascertained that Jordan had made no detours.

She and Florian had one paramount interest in their action tonight: protecting Ari, which was to say, keeping certain individuals away from Ari, tracking the activities and interactions of absolutely everyone who even casually crossed into her security zone.

Secondary was protecting Justin. That was sera's explicit and standing order. And third priority was a general and constant surveillance: keeping abreast of a list of individuals outside Reseune whose whereabouts and safety could impact Reseune's operations. ReseuneSec, under Security Director Hicks, had numerous agents solely dedicated to that purpose, and that office informed them of what Hicks deemed necessary to tell them.

But, occasionally crossing Hicks's office—they had their own watch-list of troublesome individuals *inside* Reseune. It wasn't the first time they'd mounted their own surveillance, no matter what Hicks did or didn't do—as tonight, when Hicks had wanted to bug the restaurant; but they had done it themselves, told Hicks to stay out, and fed the information to Hicks as it came available . . . promising that, for Hicks's promise to stand back.

Yanni's coming for dinner in Wing One, for instance, aroused no particular alarms. The Director's contacts, the ones he himself chose, were either clean, or they were obligations he dealt with for ascertainable reasons, even if sera had been angry with him for matters she'd declined to mention to them. Yanni came into Wing One with no large security contingent, and sent no orders to Hicks. But she and Wes had been in position. If sera had indicated Yanni should be detained or otherwise dealt with, it would have

happened, and a very specific code would have flashed to
Florian, triggering yet other actions, as best they could
manage, as fast as they could manage.

But there had been no such outcome. Yanni's companion azi, Frank AF, shadowed Yanni everywhere, as closely
and as obsessively as they followed Ari; Frank was out of
green barracks, like themselves, and while Frank was, like
Yanni, a little reticent on Yanni's personal business, he
was certainly a solid type, and absolutely loyal, not only
to Yanni, but to the entity Yanni served—which was Reseune itself. So Frank was a watch-it, but no great worry.

What clustered around Justin Warrick, however, was a
different matter, and dealing with him was not simple. Justin and Grant had not a single close contact except Yanni
that they *did* trust on that level. It was a constant worry
that those two personally had sera's clearance, residing
right next door. But sera maintained they were important
to her and insisted that they were securely hers—so they
took measures, sera being unavailable for consultation.
They had had to improvise tonight and move fast, and in
such a way that what they did could be amended, if sera
ordered.

That move was underway, via their access to specialized housekeeping over in Admin, which was intended,
perhaps, for Ari's own use. They used it. And it had made
Justin Warrick a special problem, Justin and Grant con-
stituting a pair that were supposed to be free to come and
go as they chose, but who also had to be protected against
certain decidedly unsafe contacts . . . notably, henceforward, Jordan Warrick. Jordan Warrick was number one
on the watch-it list, until sera countermanded that, and by
what they heard tonight, they were right. Right now Jordan Warrick was in the same category with a handful of
azi who had worked closely with Denys and Giraud Nye,
and who ought *not* to be admitted to the administrative
wings.

Jordan Warrick did come and go as he pleased, inside
Admin and Education, and was only restricted in Library
and completely barred from Wing One—a situation which
greatly offended him. Justin thought he'd go straight over
to Yanni in the morning, complaining, and that would be

a disturbance, perhaps provoking an Intervention from Yanni. So things that had happened tonight might grow more complicated in the morning.

They would have to brief sera, once she waked—about the late supper, the meeting, and their preemptive action, and it seemed at least likely she would approve. Sera had previously discussed moving Justin out of convenient range of Jordan. The office Justin and Grant used, previously Jordan's, had never been outstandingly secure: the staff lacked adequate clearance for reasons of inadequate security training—that situation, exposing Justin to hazard, had never been to their liking, and now they had found an excuse to solve the problem. Catlin personally hoped they had solved it in some lasting fashion. And personally hoped, too, that they could manage something to be rid of Jordan Warrick, even if sera had brought him here.

Florian arrived back in the wing: Catlin noted the flash of ID on the readout as the outer door opened and shut. She sat and waited, checking the monitors. So was a ReseuneSec squad down in Main Security watching, on night-shift. Hicks's eyes were technically on the job, but Hicks himself would be abed, his second-in-command Kyle AK probably on duty—and, being azi, Kyle AK would theo-retically be accounting for his decisions to Hicks in the morning. Which would give them time, if sera slept late, to inform sera before their actions began to racket through several systems.

Second flash from the console. Florian had deactivated and reactivated the alarm within System as he entered the apartment.

Soft footsteps outside. Florian arrived in the security office doorway, came in, and disposed himself in a chair, booted feet propped luxuriantly in the neighboring seat. He held up a small card between two fingers.

"What is it?" Catlin had seen the handoff—both handoffs.

"A business card. A contact number in Novgorod." He spun around in the chair, touched a few buttons, put the card in the visual scanner . . . not the reader, sensible cau-tion, for a card with a reader strip. He looked at the screen, punched more buttons, and retrieved the card. "A profes-

sor in Novgorod University. And the card wasn't printed
on any Reseune printer."

"An educator. Jordan works education tape."

"We'll investigate the number on the card—I'm sure
Jordan wants us to. Or wants Hicks to. Maybe Jordan's
trying to lead the investigation astray or get someone else
in trouble."

A Novgorod address, from the hand of a man who had
no recent contacts outside Planys and Reseune.

Justin, too, had not quite promptly turned it over to
sera's security. But there was that connection to Jordan,
a born-man connection, emotional, and difficult to parse.
Catlin afforded him a little latitude for that, but not too
much.

"We aren't likely to understand this," Catlin said. "It
seems unreasonable on Jordan's part. It seems unlikely for
him to have such a thing, unless he received it from someone in Reseune."

"It seems we've moved Justin none too soon. Jordan's
action toward Justin seems to be an aggression."

"Justin knew he was watched. But so did Jordan. Did
Justin forget the card when he met you, do you think, or
did it take him a moment to make up his mind?"

"Surrendering it would betray Jordan," Florian said.
"That may have taken a moment for him to decide."

"But Justin knew he was watched. He knew in advance
he would be stopped."

"He could guess he would be stopped, and the end
would be the same, whether he turned it over to me, or
whether ReseuneSec asked for it. Perhaps he wasn't thinking of that yet. He'd just argued with Jordan."

"Perhaps Jordan wanted him to be stopped, to make
him angry with Admin."

"Possible."

"Neither of them is stupid," Catlin said.

"The same geneset. One won't easily get the better of
the other. But Jordan has lost something tonight. Justin
won't be in his reach. He won't like that. I wonder if this
card is worth it."

"How did Justin seem?"

"You heard the exchange."

"I didn't see Justin's face."

"He expressed distress at disturbance to his work—which I'm sure he knows is being copied. He showed no particular reluctance to be separated from Jordan. He had warned Grant to avoid being alone with Jordan."

"I heard that part. He thought there was a physical danger. To Grant, did he mean, or to him?"

"To Grant, likely. But anything that would harm Grant would harm him. They're partners."

"No choice but get them out tonight," she said with a shake of her head. "Well that we did it. Can Section Three handle the transfer top to bottom? Will they bring it over in time, or do we have to go through Hicks's office?"

"They indicate yes, they will. I put it through as an emergency. I think that's accurate. They'll tell Hicks in the morning, likely. Hicks will get the copies they make in Justin's office. I'm not happy about Hicks's access, but the alternative is much worse. Meanwhile we need to put through Justin's address change. Inside sera's wing he won't be having his files copied again."

"Easily done." She spun her chair about, her fingers flew for a moment, and she sent, registering Justin Warrick's new office address with Yanni's office and incidentally with ReseuneSec.

That handled details that might have inconvenienced Justin in the morning—just to keep him calm in the transfer. For Jordan Warrick's imminent inconvenience, or state of mind in the morning, she had no great concern at all.

One thing did worry her. "Sera's papers are in that safe."

"Not now," Florian said. "Marco took them before Section Three could arrive. They'll be in the office sera uses."

They trusted no one completely, she and Florian . . . and that, on certain levels, meant they *didn't* trust Hicks's office, or Yanni's, to run things, or to hold information that might bear on Ari's security. Their predecessors had failed, by all outside accounts, and died—deservedly so, because they had let their Ari die, and let Denys Nye take over Reseune. They took that event as a personal failure, a fault committed by their genesets, and they were ab-

solutely determined to bétter the record in their tenure.
They were not about to lose *their* Ari to Jordan Warrick—
if it had been Jordan that murdered Ari One, as the public
records officially said had happened . . . though that certainly wasn't the whole story, and sera agreed they had had
every reason to blame Denys Nye's staff for the crime.

It didn't matter. Denys Nye and his personal guard were
dead and past. They guarded against Jordan, knowing he
could have killed the first Ari—that he had wanted to kill
her, that was the salient point. They didn't altogether understand Jordan Warrick: his actions sat deep in a very
complex CIT psychology, a man so brilliant he was a Special, all but immune to the law. Sera said the long exile had
made him angry, and the focus of that anger might be her
existence, which had defined the term of his exile.

For their part, not understanding the man simply meant
being on their guard against him. And they constantly
were.

They didn't understand Justin Warrick, either, though
they knew him better—knew, for instance, that Justin Warrick had initially welcomed his father back to Reseune, and
had disagreements with him. Justin himself had not been
the one to apply for Jordan's release from detention. It had
been, in fact, sera herself who had brought Jordan back
from exile, which brought a very dangerous man back into
a place where he could be more dangerous, in their estimation. But sera had moved fast to get Jordan out of military reach, and out of the reach of any dissident attempt to
contact him. There was a leak in Planys: they knew that.
A leak could turn into an access for all sorts of mischief,
from assassination to rescue: sera had been right.

But letting Jordan stay in Reseune now that things were
tranquil had taken turns into CIT politics: a decision on
sera's part, possibly to avoid upsetting Justin.

Just wait, Ari had said, in discussing the matter. He's
not Justin. It's the same geneset, but the first Ari changed
Justin's psychset. Jordan hated her for that.

Jordan had hated the first Ari well before she'd taken
Justin. That was true, too. Jordan had briefly been the first
Ari's working partner, sharing ideas, sharing power.

Except, sera had said further, that neither of those two

was of a nature to share anything. So the partnership had dissolved into a feud—more bitter on Jordan's side than on Ari's, in terms of overt anger, sera said; but not in terms of who had gotten in the first strike. The first Ari had converted Justin to her own design, appropriated Grant along with him.

Jordan wanted Justin and Grant back—two assets their own Ari very much wanted for herself.

That implied that there would inevitably be trouble in that quarter. And their Ari had chosen to live right beside Justin—kept him in her wing, all except his office staff, which he had clung to, and that was the reason Justin maintained his office over in Education.

Well, as of now, sera's wing had Justin's office, too, and the staff was gone. Now there was no actual reason for Justin ever to leave her highly secure perimeter and cross Jordan's path . . . unless Justin chose to do that, which would be many fewer opportunities, and ones they could watch.

First on the list, they had to be sure Justin was comfortable in his new office, to keep him and sera happy.

And they could expect that Jordan was going to be furious when he found out in the morning that that office was shut and empty—and it could be all his, for what they cared. They had even left a request for Hicks to officially allow Jordan possession of that office, with staff, if he asked, a request it was likely for several reasons might go through. They smoothed things over, not willing to provoke the man by their own action: sera might not approve that.

Catlin keyed a screen up, saw Jordan and Paul standing in the living room of their apartment, Jordan with a drink in hand. There would be a record of that conversation. She could scan it visually faster than she could listen to it.

"They've gotten to him," was the only thing that truly leapt out of the current transcript. She took the reference as applying to Justin, and understood "they" to mean sera and her whole apparatus.

It was true. There was also nothing Jordan could do about it.

There was no reference to the card with the Novgorod number. Florian had set the card on the console and looked at the screen.

"Patil," he said. "Dr. Sandur Patil, University at Novgorod."

Catlin focused in on that. Sharply. "One of Yanni's meetings in Novgorod was with that person. Sera has a list. I have Patil's CIT number. I asked System for a bio."

"Call it."

She located the file.

Professor of Science, but under the Defense Bureau's Secrecy Act. Lecturer in the Franklin Series, whatever that was. Expert in nanistics, and Catlin did know about that. It meant microtags, stable and self-mutating nano-structures. It meant a whole class of contraband for customs, and it was a bioweapon, besides its commercial uses in medicine and manufacture, which she had never looked up, but she sent out a search.

"Nanistics. I'm calling up references."

Florian copied her screen to his console.

Nanistics, the information came back, was a course of study not banned from theoretical research or commercial use on Cyteen's surface and on Cyteen Alpha Station, but all actual experimental work was done out at Beta Station, at the deep end of the solar system. There was a lab at Beta serving both Defense and Science. The science was used on Cyteen, in Reseune, mostly in medical or agricultural research, or in the manufacture of carefully selected exotics, particularly in replication of Earth or Pell goods.

And a cross-search with Patil involved university offerings, lectures, Paxer and Abolitionist attendance. Nanistics and Patil had been a major part of the terraforming project, now canceled: the Preservation Act had excluded certain types of bionanistics from Cyteen surface. Bionanistics and Patil wound through the list.

The inquiry rapidly developed side branches. A lot of them.

Right now the words of interest were clearly nanistics, Patil, Planys, and Warrick, any two of those words in association, and that search had produced one other warning flag:

More information is available from 1381 sources requiring higher base. 142382 sources are in Library behind gateway access. Proceed? Y/N . . .

Base One, sera's base, could cross that threshold. It warned when it was about to go somewhere securitied, and it didn't leave footprints in System. But it would draw a lot of securitied information into their office, and that was worth a little hesitation.

No, Catlin decided. But: "Interesting," Catlin said. "Patil is someone Yanni was talking to. He told sera they were going to terraform a world called Eversnow, and it's not public knowledge. He was talking to Dr. Patil."

And Florian asked: "How did *Jordan* know Yanni was meeting with her?"

BOOK ONE   **Section 2**   **Chapter i**

APRIL 26, 2424
0500H

Giraud and his two companions grew fast this week.

The organs were present—just barely starting to function inside the body cavity, largely visible through transparent skin. Fingers had discernable nails. The yolk sac had gone. Blood functioned to feed the cells.

The babies were mostly head at this point, because brains—very high order brains—were developing fast. Nerves were growing out from the spine. Arms had wrists and elbows. Underdeveloped legs kicked, a function of those newly active nerves. Giraud and his two companions weighed only a quarter of an ounce apiece, but they had some distinction as human.

They were *becoming*, was what. They were becoming what they could be.

Damn. Staff had been busy last night.

Florian had taken direct action, the morning's messages informed Ari while she dressed: Florian had gotten Justin and Grant out of range of Jordan's machinations—well, that was good. She'd been trying to accomplish that for six weeks. There'd been the chance, the very real chance, that Jordan might resort to snatching one or the other—likely Grant—for a few hours of therapy. Her staff had been watching nonstop for just such a move. Now they could all relax a bit.

But the next line of Florian's report suggested otherwise.

A contact number? Yanni's Dr. Patil. Yanni's transcript had included that interview. She'd initially ignored that part of the schedule as probably just one of Yanni's frequent meetings with ranking scientists, and university professors were thick on his usual list. But Patil was clearly a significant name, and Ari *did* know the content of Yanni's talk with her.

And it wasn't the first time she'd heard the name. Dr. Patil had had a set-to with Uncle Denys about a paper last year. Denys had gotten mad. He'd threatened to send Patil to Planys, except Yanni had talked him out of it.

And Jordan handed Justin a card with that name on it?

Damn! was her immediate reaction.

Florian suggested Jordan might want to signal Yanni he knew something about Yanni's business in Novgorod. Or maybe there was some connection with the fight Jordan and Yanni had had before Yanni left . . . which made a certain sense.

Jordan wasn't in official communication with anybody

but Yanni, had no social contact but Justin, and he had no security clearance beyond Library, not all of that, and not even the most basic access to System.

That posed a question.

A possibly scary question.

She keyed a message back to her security, whoever was at the desk: "Find out how Jordan got that card. Do anything that furthers that investigation."

Then she pushed back from the desk and got up.

It was probably safest not to talk to Justin until the immediate irritation of the disarrangement had gone away—he was bound to be adrenaline-high, and that never improved communication, did it?

Yanni, Florian's message had said, was already notified—about the move, at least. Yanni wouldn't object to whatever she did regarding Justin Warrick.

But Yanni *hadn't* heard about this Dr. Patil being linked to a mysterious card Jordan knew they were going to question.

That was a matter worth telling Yanni, and getting his reaction. And since she'd officially read the transcript and it jibed with what she'd gotten from Base One, she could at least take that caution out of her thinking and ask some questions.

If Jordan had found out that Yanni was talking to Patil, how had he known that? He didn't get mail. He had no way to get a business card. Maybe Yanni himself had dropped information, making the move to rattle Jordan out of his cover. In that case she had better find out about it. And the worst thing she could do would be to start giving blind orders to put Florian and Catlin in the middle of it.

She put on her sweater, searched her closet for a pair of pants, herself—she managed her own wardrobe lately.

There was a leak somewhere. Maybe Yanni had arranged it, just to see where information flowed. She didn't like to be caught by surprise.

And she didn't want Justin involved in any investigation of his father. He *wasn't* involved in Jordan's business: she'd stake everything on that. And did.

But she still didn't want to trip up anything Yanni was doing.

Meanwhile Justin was probably mad as hell about being moved, and upset about the business with the card, and probably under-informed, over all. Justin without enough information was going to wonder about it, and wonder, and build his own hypotheses in private, and just stew for hours.

Maybe it was better to send a simple friendly message to Justin, just a deliberately naive welcome-in. Justin wouldn't believe she was innocent of ordering this disruption of his life.

Or he might: this time he had Jordan to blame. She might be able to turn the frustration in that direction.

She lapped her hair into three quarters of a braid and let it go—it would be hanging loose in ten minutes; but she put on makeup, at least, and took care about it.

Grant had to be considerably relieved, this morning, to know they weren't going to be working up close with Jordan daily, where it was oh, so easy for Jordan to get at him. Justin had to be relieved, at least, that Grant wasn't involved. Justin would certainly focus his irritation on Jordan, unless she stepped in the line of fire and created an issue and a target. So any message she sent into that ferment of vexation had to be cautious.

She sat down at the keyboard and tapped into the secure, local net. *It wasn't my order,* she typed, which was the truth. *But I think it's a good idea. He can have the office all to himself. It was bugged anyway.—Ari.*

Justin might think that was funny.

Or maybe he wouldn't.

She sighed.

And typed a postscript: *Justin, don't be upset with me. Phone, if you have a problem with this.*

Not that she was going to back down from what Florian had done. It was only moving the schedule up, regarding the move to her wing for both residency *and* office space. Justin didn't know that, but it was the truth.

She went back to the console and keyed one more message. *Yanni didn't do it either.*

Then she put on her boots and went to gather up Florian and Catlin.

*   *   *

Straight to Yanni's office, over in Admin, before she did anything else, and she did that, with Florian—Catlin was busy with some research. By the time she got there it was 0840h, and Yanni's foyer was already full of problems.

She didn't go through the foyer. She took the side entry, the one Yanni himself used, and Yanni's secretary, Chloe, looked up in startlement.

"Sera?"

"Tell Yanni take a restroom break. I need to talk to him."

"Sera," Chloe said respectfully, and pushed a button on the console. Chloe didn't even talk to Yanni. Yanni came through the door fairly promptly.

And stopped cold.

"I need to talk," Ari said. "Now."

So Yanni immediately opened the door behind Chloe, and went in. Florian walked in, to stand behind her, while she sat down at one end of the conference table—it was a big one—and Yanni did, at the other end.

"A problem?" Yanni asked. "I had a report this morning—that there was some goings-on involving Justin. That you moved him out of the Education Wing altogether, fired his staff, and gave Jordan an office. Is *this* the sudden problem?"

"Jordan is the problem. Jordan wants an office of his own."

"And you apparently gave him one."

"I did, ser," Florian said, behind her. "It was done at my level."

"I stand by it," Ari said, "if it doesn't actually hurt anything. It didn't seem to me it does."

Yanni remained as he was, just looking at her, and thinking—clearly thinking. "Jordan asked me for an office before I left. Evidently he thought he could get away with going around me."

"He didn't ask me. He said he was going to move in on Justin. So Florian moved Justin to my wing."

"Except his staff, ser," Florian said.

"Are you going to talk at me from two different levels?" Yanni asked, looking from her, seated, to Florian, standing.

"Sorry, ser," Florian said.

"If you want Jordan out of that office," Ari said, "you can tell him that. Meanwhile Florian says he had no place to put Justin's staff, but they're good people and Florian promised they'd be taken care of. Admin should hire them."

Yanni was silent a moment. Then nodded. "All right. It can happen. I'll make a note for Chloe."

"Good. Justin will feel a lot better about it."

"Oh, I'm sure he will. And Jordan's got what he wanted . . . this week. Hell if that'll content him for two days. Damn the man!"

"That's not all he did," Ari said. "He dropped a business card into Justin's pocket. Justin didn't like it. He gave it to Florian. I have it in my apartment. It was from a Dr. Sandur Patil."

"Patil."

He didn't say anything but that. Not after a long wait.

So she said, "I brought Jordan here from Planys. It seemed a good idea at the time. I hoped he'd do better than this."

"He's a damn maniac."

"I thought you were his friend."

"With Jordan? Being Jordan's friend requires fireproof gloves."

"So did this Patil figure somehow with why you're mad at him? I've read your transcript. I know who she is. Is Jordan somehow connected with this?"

"Not exactly."

"So what *does* it mean?"

"Let me drop another name," Yanni said. "Thieu. Dr. Raymond Thieu."

It didn't ring any bell. She was genuinely puzzled, and shook her head. "I don't know him."

"Nanotech," Yanni said. "Biologicals. Former head of the Planys remediation project."

So. There. Biological nanisms, living nanomachines, anathema on Cyteen, except under strictest conditions. Patil's expertise. Beta Station was where they worked on that, where you had to have all sorts of clearance to get in, and where nothing could escape. Nanobiology applied in the remediation areas out in the Planys death zones, where Cyteen microbes met Terran ones. But when they loosed something into the biosphere they did it with great, great caution—not the wholesale dumping the terraforming plan had involved; not the extent of what they were likely to do at Eversnow.

"So he's no longer head of that program? Why?"

"Retired. He's lived at Planys since the War was at its height. He's elderly, came from Beta labs, was head of Research in that discipline, taught at the University in Novgorod for two years, moved to Planys when the terraforming project got canceled, managed the remediation program there until he retired, five years ago. Distinguished career, bit of a prick."

"He knows Jordan, I take it."

"They were socially acquainted at Planys. Understand, the Planys lab doesn't have the facilities to have done anything of an anagenetic nature, not in the most esoteric sense." That was the ten-cred word for terraforming, where there was already life. "Let's just say terraforming has been a hot topic behind certain closed doors, including Denys', including the military's, and it's been hot for months. ReseuneSec is currently taking the whole Planys lab apart, and using Jordan's departure as a plausible excuse to look into every nook and cranny of Planys operations— which has made Thieu madder than hell. Thieu and Jordan socialized—only twenty-three primary researchers in the place, off and on, so everybody socializes, you can figure that. But Thieu has retained very close ties to the military at Planys and to the University in Novgorod. Terraforming Cyteen was going to be his big program. He spent decades laying out all the details for his project, right along with Patil—and Council vetoed it just before it launched, then shifted him out to Planys, threw him the sop of an applied project out there, because he was madder than hell and not keeping his mouth shut, frankly. When the nanolabs shifted their focus to remediation, it was mostly to maintain the careers of people who specialized in that field—Defense didn't want to lose them: but it also gave us the chance to get Thieu away from the media."

"Because we stopped terraforming in its tracks," she

said, shaken out of any sort of complacency. "But the military kept the research going. And the crazier Centrists still want it applied here."

"We're giving them Eversnow. But a lot of old business exists out there at Planys. Part of the black projects in the military wing we can't get at, and we don't like, are nanistics of a nature I don't like. Officially the nanistics program slowed to a stop when he retired, no other personnel was brought in out there, and what remediation uses is very carefully regulated, but lately, with the Eversnow matter—it's back, this time in Novgorod. There's an inherent problem with research labs, you know. They contain knowledge you'd like to have just in case your enemies have it, but that you'd just as soon not have on the public market. And when people who know military things retire, they still know things and they have opinions—unless you want to mindwipe a Special, which wouldn't attract too many people into the program."

"So you think he's been talking to people? Including Jordan? It's not Jordan's field."

"Politics is. Jordan's always been a political animal. And we know there's been a leak to Corain."

"One we found," she said. "You think there's more?"

"Oh, I think we brought a major item of it here, with Jordan."

"My fault, you're saying."

"Having him sucked up by the military wouldn't have helped at all."

It wouldn't. She'd prevented that. That was true.

"Thieu arrived at Planys during the War," Yanni said, "quietest retreat he could have. We'd moved a major part of the lab there, in point of fact, because we didn't want to risk a raid on Beta, and that research falling into Alliance hands. The staff moved back to Beta when the War ended—but he'd already gotten on the wrong side of your predecessor in an absolute fury over the cancellation of his programs. So there he was, just quietly aging, still within the Planys labs, not the man he had been, but still—still within the structure, still doing some work on biologicals for Defense, supposedly doing some side work on the rejuv sensitivity issue—he either wasn't allowed to work on the remediation as of two years ago, or he refused to work on it any further: it's not totally clear how that happened, and we're quietly asking at this moment. The man has a temper that doesn't always serve him."

"But he still has his security clearances."

"He still has some clearance—though he carried on correspondence with a few people in the University in Novgorod, not all of whom we were quite comfortable with: people who'd gotten burned in the program cancellation; people who leaned just a little to the Centrist fringes—ReseuneSec found it useful to let it continue, to see where the lines of communication led, granted nothing classified got out. Meanwhile he met Jordan Warrick . . . when *Jordan* moved out there, not, of course, voluntarily. They weren't close for the first ten years, didn't even speak; but in the last few, as Thieu tended toward retirement, they started up a friendship. We can't prove a damned thing, except our quiet in-house inquiry about resurrecting a nanistics project—the Eversnow project, which we didn't say at the time, nor mentioned Patil's name—got Thieu very exercised. *He* breached security, at least within that close community of academics, and contacted a student of his currently teaching in Novgorod, qualified in the field, security clearance, to be sure, but not a contact he was authorized to make."

"Patil."

"Patil. He'd corresponded with her for years, but all those letters were innocuous, two scientists talking about programs, and definitely subject to censors who actually can read in that field. Recall there's a strong Centrist bent in Novgorod University, through the social studies department and into some very shady nooks of the rebel chic. Patil's work has a cult following. She doesn't encourage the radicals. But they get excited when she publishes. When she lectures, they show up at her lecture series. If we revive the old studies for use at Eversnow, I want to be sure it *doesn't* get used here on Cyteen by some lunatic with a lab vial. Let me tell you, with Thieu retired and Patil's whole operation off at Eversnow we're actually safer—barring something coming back by ship. All of which I mention to you just in the case I *should* fall down the stairs and break my neck—"

"Please don't!"

"—in case, I say, I'm telling you verbally. There is that one very untidy and roundabout link to Jordan Warrick that we don't like, the elderly and sometimes erratic Dr. Thieu, who connects with Patil, who's the person we want to use at Eversnow, partly for very political reasons. But while we're going ahead with the Patil nomination, we're also going through the establishment on Planys with a microscope right now on the excuse of investigating Jordan, and it's why we shouldn't roundtrip Jordan right back to Planys at first excuse. If fire and fuel *can* meet, we just want to be very sure the bottles are secure. Once we ship Patil out to Fargone, we'll feel a lot safer."

"But you're saying it's possibly all innocent."

"Patil's a natural candidate for the Eversnow post. But hauling her from the Centrist party to the Expansionist side of the slate is going to mightily annoy some people. It's possible certain factions will be more interested in the politics of it than in the actual science, which is years off. Short-term, it's very likely to be political."

" 'Rethinking the Theory of Long-Period Nanistic Self-direction.' "

"God, where did you run across that?"

"It was going to run in *Scientia* last year. It was pretty thick going, but I read it."

"I should think it was. You and the censors. How did you get it?"

"The Centrists had made a fuss about it, pre-publication, said it proved they could do what they wanted to do on Cyteen without killing the rejuv ecology. Uncle Denys was mad about it. He was threatening to have the editor fired if it ran, so they pulled it. I figured I should give it a look. So she was writing up what she shouldn't have written about?"

"It was an agitation on her part. But a quiet one, the presentation of a theory, not a how-to. The War's over. We could enlist any nanistics expert we want out of Beta, and will—but for various reasons—including the fact she's the darling of the Paxers, the Centrists, and the military, and could get us the votes—she's our pick for the lab going out to Eversnow. It's a dream assignment for her. She may

be the Centrist intellectuals' darling, not that they understand half of what she's about, but she does want to see
her theories put into the field, and *she's* how we got the
two Councillors to shift their vote to support mine, notably Defense and Citizens. And just to draw a line under
the fact of who's in bed with whom, our Jordan's spent the
last eight years having lunch with the professor who taught
Patil."

"He doesn't *have* a Base in System any more. So how
did he know about it? How did he get the card? Maybe
he wanted us to have it. Maybe he's trying to ask a question . . . in his unique way."

"That would be an interesting position," Yanni said.
"Or maybe he just wanted Justin to take exception to the
ensuing investigation."

"To drag Justin into it on his side," Ari said, "but I don't
think he did what Jordan would want him to do."

"Oh, it probably was within his guesswork," Yanni said.
"I assume Jordan expected the card to be confiscated, and
Justin to be involved, and upset, and maybe more amenable to Jordan's arguments. He's psych, not nanistics,
educational psych, at that. I *don't* like the notion he could
have gotten this card from Thieu, and gotten it through
our screening. Security's got to take a look at that. But it's
not much more comfortable a thought that someone here
gave it to him . . . probably with information."

"It has a reader-strip, ser," Florian said. "We didn't put
it into a System-connected reader."

"Probably a *very* good notion," Yanni said. "Damn it!
Damn Jordan to bloody hell."

"I'd rather not if I can avoid it," Ari said. "But Justin is
staying in Wing One."

"Granted," Yanni said. "No question. Good call."

"*You* didn't bring Patil's name up with Jordan, did
you?"

"Hell, no."

"Just asking," she said easily. It remained a possibility,
all the same. But less likely, perhaps.

So Justin was safe. But Jordan definitely wasn't.

APRIL 26, 2424
0855H

Late to bed, late to rise, and not that early to the office.

The morning was definitely off routine, when you had to rack your memory to recall what your own office address was, and it was entirely surreal to walk in and find the set-up pretty much what you remembered—and you hadn't put it there.

Justin had expected boxes. The office was—just moved. Things were on shelves in exactly the same order . . . apparently so, at least. Florian hadn't exaggerated.

"Well," Grant said, at his shoulder, "they were neat."

"Certainly better than some invasions we've had," Justin muttered, and let go a long, long breath. He hadn't known he was that wound up about the move, but he had been. He didn't see a safe. Opening several desk drawers didn't turn up Ari's material. It had gone somewhere, and that bothered him.

"Her stuff isn't here," he said.

"Security will have it," Grant said. "Five against ten, Florian will have gotten it, personally."

"Well, it's not a bad office," Justin said, looking around. It wasn't bad. It was even good, given there was room for the two of them—ample room, but nothing for staff. God knew what Em thought, this morning, arriving to find he had no office and no job.

There was a window. The view from the purported window was fake, but it was a very expensive fake: a screen showed the Novaya Volga from, one supposed, the top of the cliffs, more likely the top of one of the precip towers— he'd never been up there: nobody went there, except the repair and maintenance crews working on the weather system, and most of those were robots.

It was a dizzying image, if one thought about it. It gave an illusion the whole building was forty stories tall, when the brain knew for a fact they were on the ground floor.

"Nice view," Grant said.

"You're such an optimist." Justin ran his hand over the spines of the physical books on the shelf, finding no flaw in the order of them—printout of this and that psychset. He *liked* printout, when it came to review. He marked-up with abandon, and liked things in order, *his* order. The stacks on the desk looked like his stacks. He thumbed through them. They were in a reasonable order. Likely the stacks on Grant's desk were the same.

But he wanted to find something they'd messed up. He checked the drawers. Exact order, exact contents. "I hate it when I don't know what they've done wrong. I'm sure there's something."

"The movers were ReseuneSec, weren't they?" Grant asked. "They're used to not having things look disturbed."

That was worth half a laugh at least.

There was an in-office coffee dispenser sitting on a sideboard. That was new, and good. The machine was loaded and it turned on and functioned at the touch of a button. That was even better.

And the movers had improved on one other thing: the move had organized the supply cabinet contents in a logical, eye-pleasing way, with little colored bins for the various styli and clips and pointer-tags. He surveyed it top to bottom, looking for flaws.

"Color-coded," Justin remarked, giving up his search. "I suppose our mess was too much for them to get here intact. We have all shiny new paper clips."

"Have a cup of coffee." Grant handed him one, an implicit calm-down.

"You know Jordan's going to be beside himself this morning."

"Likely he is," Grant said. "Just about now."

He took a sip. It was better coffee than what they'd had available down the hall in the old office. Much better. It was probably real. "Pricey."

"Free," Grant said.

"Meaning we're entirely on her tab." That didn't improve the taste.

"Do we ever actually run through our wages?" Grant asked.

"We never get a chance to find out, do we? And what about our regular work?" He turned full circle, looked at the walls, the river view, and something beyond vertigo bothered him, something indefinably bothered him and made his shoulders twitch. He walked across the office and back before it dawned on him. "It's backward. It's damned *backward!* The back wall is south. The old office wall faced north."

"Is that going to bother you?"

"It's already bothering me." He was still frustrated. The office had always had its carefully designed clutter—even his every-other-layer stacking was preserved, in the pile on the corner of his desk. The room was white-walled, had a view that cost a month's pay. The desks were new black lacquer, not brown fake wood, scarred from years of use. Their use. It was like that damned black and white bedroom they lived in, that was what. "I want some flowers in here. Some pictures that *don't* move."

"I can order the flowers," Grant said, and added wickedly. "Red?"

"No. Blue. Green. Purple. Anything but red." There was one red pillow, one red flower, in their professionally decorated black, gray, and white quarters.

"Maybe you'd like to pick out the pictures yourself."

That nettled him, too. "Ordering flowers is not your job to do. You're not my—"

"I'm not as afflicted by the decor as you are," Grant said. "It's a born-man problem. You're fluxed. I'm sure I could order flowers in a sane, logical way. Possibly I'd be calm enough to pick out complementary pictures. Clearly—"

"The hell." He found his mood improving, unwanted improvement, even toward laughter. "Oh, hell, blue. Blue would be good. Blues and purples, that sort of thing." The single screen pretending to be a window drew the eye and suggested blue-greens and grays. "Cancel the purple. Blues and quiet greens. That might do it. I'd like that. If you wouldn't mind doing it. I'm not that logical, at the moment."

"I'm sure there's something that'll work," Grant said nicely. "I'll look."

By computer. You could do anything by computer. It would be there in an hour, if they opted for messenger service, and flowers and paintings could get through security, oh, by tomorrow, if security was in a good mood.

It certainly wasn't the way he'd done things in the days when he'd been free, on his own salary and Grant's.

Before the first Ari had gotten her hands on him. Before Jordan had gotten himself in trouble and gotten shipped to the far side of the world.

So Jordan came back, and Ari protected him from his own father . . . meaning she'd finally gotten her way and gotten him all the way into her wing—to do *nothing* in his career, but teach her.

Standing, he flipped on the computer. The screen blinked up.

Three messages from Ari, in the upper righthand corner.

Calamity?

He dropped into the chair, keyed the messages up.

And had to laugh, however ruefully.

"What is it?"

"Ari's postscripts. The first Ari didn't do postscripts. Wouldn't have done a postscript when she was six. Our girl's done two in the same letter. She's worried I'll hit the ceiling. I think she's really worried."

"What does she say?"

"That they're giving the other office to Jordan. That we're better off here. That the old office was bugged, anyway."

That got a laugh from Grant.

Justin keyed off and got up. "Let's go out for lunch."

"Out for lunch? We haven't gotten any work done yet. I'm just into the flowers."

"Lunch. Relaxation. Out of the Wing. Prove we can. But somewhere *less* likely to run into Jordan."

"Jordan is going to be heading for Yanni's office about now. If we stay off that track, we'll miss him."

This time *he* laughed. It made fair sense. Jordan was going to take about five minutes to realize he'd been given the office solo, and bet on it, Jordan wasn't going to be working today, either.

Straight line course for Yanni's office, no question.

Not that Yanni would do anything to make Jordan happier. *Yanni didn't do it,* Ari's final note had said. And she claimed she hadn't done it.

So who had? What other authority was there, ruling his life?

Justin walked over to the desk, picked out the printout he'd been working over. Laid the project-book, open, on his desk, where he would work on it when he got back. "There. We're officially moved in and my desk is officially cluttered, so it's home. God knows what the fallout was from that card Jordan handed me. Opening barrage, in what's going to be some kind of war, I'm afraid. A war for possession of *us*, for starters. For possession of Reseune, I'm very much afraid. Jordan's not going to win anything and I don't think he'll stop until someone stops him. And I don't want that, Grant, damn, I really don't want it." His mood crashed. He leaned on his chair back. "He's headed for a fall."

"You think she'll send him back to Planys?"

Deep down, he actually wished she would, this morning once and for all. And that was so startlingly dark and traitorous a thought that he felt deeply ashamed of himself. Jordan had spent twenty years in comparative privation, shut out of the modern world for a crime his accuser had likely committed; and his own son at least owed him some sympathy for the resultant bitterness, didn't he?

But not when Grant was in danger from that sympathy: Ari had created Grant, Jordan had written some of his first tapes, knew at least his initial keywords and triggers, and if Jordan decided there might be flaws in Grant's loyalty, and wanted to revise things, he could do major damage.

And *hell* if he'd let that happen, not if it meant Jordan going straight back into exile. He shoved back from the chair and picked up his coat.

"Jordan's not making it easy for anybody," he said grimly. "Not for me, not for you, not for two hours running since he's been back."

"Why does he do it?" Grant asked, reaching for his

own coat. "What does an intelligent CIT want out of this situation?"

"Intelligent as he is, I'm afraid intelligence is nowhere in this situation."

"You're angry with him." Halfway into the coat.

Justin settled his own onto his shoulders. "You noticed that."

"Angry enough to take action against him as you did. That seems justified, from my own view."

"I'm angry about being uprooted into an office that's just damned *backward* to what I've been used to for most of my life. I'm angry at being coopted deeper into Ari's wing. I'm angry because I'm going to miss Abrizio's . . ."

"We can walk over there. Nothing's stopping us."

"We could run into *him!*"

"So you want to avoid him permanently?"

"Damn it."

"But not damn *him?*"

"I don't know!"

Grant frowned. "So all across the horizon, very intelligent CITs aren't acting rationally. Young Ari didn't do a thing, Yanni didn't, the elder Warrick makes a stupid move, and the younger doesn't know what he damns, but he doesn't want to talk to his genefather at all. *What* was the card you asked me to give Florian?"

It bordered on funny, it was so stupid. The idiocy of the situation afflicted his already raw sensibilities. At very least, his universe was not on the same track this morning, and he no longer knew where it was going, not an unusual condition in his life, but not one he liked.

"Jordan's likely to be at our favorite lunch haunt on any given day if he's using that office, and I don't want the confrontation. So, for starters, I think we'll walk to the north corridor of Admin for a late breakfast. That won't be on his route." He stared disconsolately at the cabinets, finding everything out of sorts. "They've color-coded the damn supply cabinets. It looks great. But are we going to remember to put the clips back in the red box? Should we have to remember? Does anyone care?"

"At least your father won't be into your notebooks."

"Definitely a point in favor of this place."

"And it *was* originally his office."

It was. It had been. "Let's just get out of here before—"

The desk phone went off. He shot a look at Grant. It rang again. It *was* Jordan's ID. He hesitated toward the door, then looked back.

It went on ringing. He swore, and punched in Speaker.

"Dad?"

"Where in hell are you?" came from the other end. *"What's going on?"*

"They moved us. I think we were bugged."

"You think we were bugged! Bloody hell!" So much for that piece of deliberate naivete. And more quietly, even gently, Jordan added: *"Are you all right?"*

He hadn't expected parental concern. That ploy hadn't even been on the radar. It set him back about a beat or two and almost hurt. Not quite. "We're fine, Dad. We are."

"Where are you?"

"Wing One." Where Jordan couldn't come. Not a hope in hell he'd ever get through her security to have a look around this office. "They moved my office."

And Jordan had to know that the move was for good.

"Are you going to protest this?"

Tell the truth or temporize? Truth was simpler. Kinder, if that mattered. "No, actually."

"No?"

Outrage. Truth, again? Or was it a lie?

Both wrapped together, both truth *and* lie, likely. Jordan wanted his son to rise up and challenge Admin, and challenge Ari's existence. But he didn't really expect it to happen—for reasons Jordan thought he understood better than the rest of the universe. "It won't do a damn bit of good if I do. It's not a bad office here. More room. Certainly more room than four of us and staff jammed into the other one."

"Come to breakfast."

Now a lie was necessary. Absolutely the polite thing. "Things are in a mess here. I've got some unpacking to do. I've got to find some things."

"Supper, then. We'll cook."

It wasn't an invitation. It was a challenge to trust.

Maybe to come talk about that card he no longer had. And he didn't trust Jordan, not at all. He wasn't bringing Grant and himself through Jordan's doors, subject to whatever they were handed to eat and drink, which might have God-knew-what in it. "I can't."

"Arrested?"

"Just detained. I don't know for how long. It'll ease up. It always does."

"Damn it, I'm going to Yanni with this."

So they both went through the motions. The pretense of familial affection. The reality of outrage. "Don't use up your credit with him. This was bound to happen. They're not going to like us working together. You knew that when you pushed it."

"You mean she's *not going to like it."*

"Look, you've got to settle in, start producing again, start your work up . . . let them *see* you haven't lost a beat. That's what's important. Get current with things . . . I understand they're going to give you that office."

"Current!"

"All right, yes, I'm sure that's an issue among the younger researchers." It was, and a painful one, which he used with only the faintest twinge of shame. "Get a new project going. And since you're in that office alone with Paul, there won't be any question what's my work and what's yours."

There was just a little silence on the other side. As if his *son's* work was going to overshadow his, as if, if it was any good, no one would believe he did it. That was going to sting. And he did it deliberately, knowing how instinctively jealous and competitive his father was. Jealousy had been the core issue with Jordan and the first Ari, that Jordan wouldn't be second to her . . . he'd tried to be her equal partner in research, and that hadn't worked, because the first Ari *had* been smarter than Jordan, just like the second. *He* accepted that fact of life, with his Ari. Jordan hadn't ever been able to. He didn't know what he felt at the moment, but it was perilously close to unreasoning anger—which didn't damned well help in a fencing match with his father.

"That's the way it is, is it?" Jordan asked. *"That's the*

concern she has, just so solicitous to have me look good?
Pardon me if I don't buy it."

"I don't either, Jordan, but there's a certain assumption around the labs that you're so many years behind the times, that you can't possiby overcome—"

"The hell! The hell I am! And the hell I can't!"

"It's the next generation, dad. They don't know you. Just produce. They'll learn who you are."

"Who I am? Damned right they will!"

Jordan broke the connection, right there.

Grant lifted a well-controlled eyebrow. "Breakfast?"

BOOK ONE   Section 2   Chapter iv

APRIL 26, 2424
1302H

Message from Hicks, director of Reseune Security, to sera's security: *Consultation urgently needed.*

It might involve the card—if Hicks was running an operation at Yanni's direction, they'd gotten in the middle of it last night, and Hicks was probably quietly furious at their having swept it up.

They could say no. They could hold onto the card and force Yanni to request sera to order them to release it; but a feud with Hicks wasn't profitable. Hicks had agreed when they'd outright insisted on their monitoring the business with Justin and his father, and relaying what they found to him; and the interview seemed, overall, a reasonable request.

"I'll likely be a while," Florian said, while leaving the security station.

"All secure here," Catlin said. "I'll hold things down. It wouldn't be good to annoy ReseuneSec if we don't need to."

"No," he agreed. "It wouldn't."

He took the card with him, carefully protected in an

envelope—its disposition dependent on what he heard from Hicks: maybe he would turn it over, maybe not, and Hicks would not lay hands on him, not if Hicks wanted his career. He headed out, downstairs, out of the wing and over to Admin, to an office that supervised his kind, but not him, not Catlin, and no one else inside sera's apartment.

ReseuneSec was operationally directly responsible to Yanni Schwartz these days. Hicks had succeeded Giraud Nye in the post, and *hadn't* been implicated in Denys' attempt on sera's life—in fact Hicks had stood down, done his best to keep things calm and safe for most of Reseune, and taken neither side, while sera's people and Denys' people shot at each other in the halls of Wing One. So Hicks had kept his job. Yanni said he was a good man, and since they trusted Yanni—so far—they trusted Hicks—so far.

Over to Admin, upstairs to the executive level, down the corridor from Yanni's office. The ReseuneSec offices were a busy place, even at this early hour. The anteroom was full of people in suits, people in uniform. If he had to wait, he had things he could do in the interim.

He went to the desk. "Florian AF, Sera Ariane Emory's bodyguard. The director called."

The receptionist immediately lost the preoccupied look. "Ser. You're expected." He stood up and personally escorted Florian down a carpeted hall straight to the director's office, past cameras and other devices—no matter all the waiting CITs back there.

That was gratifying, on sera's behalf. It made a good impression—so far.

"Florian AF."

A man with dark hair, dark good looks, and a gold bar indicating a colonel's rank, intercepted him and the receptionist both.

Kyle AK. Alpha azi. Hicks' aide.

"Ser." Kyle AK outranked him. And might prevent him, but he would *not* do business with a substitute. He eyed Kyle AK with a certain reserve, just stared at him, at a dead stop, and the receptionist retreated.

"The message was from the Director," Florian said. "I'll *see* the Director."

"To be sure," Kyle AK said smoothly, and opened the

door that said *Adam Hicks, Director, Reseune Security* in gold letters.

He walked in with Kyle AK, facing a silver-haired, square-faced man at a desk.

Suit, not uniform. That was Hicks, CIT, and never trained in green barracks, not an expert in actual practice, only in administration. He'd gotten the services of Kyle AK, a very highly trained alpha, former Fleet service. And it was widely suspected that Kyle AK was and had been the source of no little policy and no few orders in ReseuneSec . . . but it was the born-man who held the office and signed the papers.

"Ser," Florian said. "Florian AF. You called sera's office."

Hicks got up from his chair and offered his hand across the desk, again, proper behavior. "Florian AF. A pleasure. Have a seat."

"Ser," Florian said, placing hands in the back of his belt and continuing to stand, post-handshake, as Hicks sat down: he had reached a decision. "Jordan Warrick surreptitiously passed a calling card with a contact number to Justin Warrick. The younger Warrick volunteered the card to me when I intercepted him on the quadrangle, and made no further comment. I think you'll know that from my report."

"Do you have the card with you?" Hicks asked him.

"Yes. May I have your word, ser, we'll have the benefit of your investigation? This regards a person under sera's authority."

"Agreed. Absolutely agreed."

Florian reached into his jacket front and pulled out the envelope. Hicks took it and laid it on the desk in front of him.

"What do you know about the card?" Hicks asked.

"The number, ser, belongs to a Dr. Sandur Patil, University of Novgorod."

Hicks's face betrayed very little. He was good, in that regard. "Researcher and professor. Did the Director brief you who she is?"

"Scheduled for promotion to a directorship at Fargone. Yes, ser, Director Schwartz said so, in conversation with my principal."

Hicks nodded slowly. "How far did he brief her?"

"Perhaps farther than he briefed you, ser, so I shouldn't go into specifics."

Momentary silence. A perusal by very cold, very opaque eyes. "You know about Eversnow."

"Yes, ser. We do."

"You got this card from the younger Warrick."

"It was given, ser. Volunteered by him."

"He got it from Warrick Senior."

"We observed that he did, ser, unless cards were switched. We didn't search him. Justin Warrick has been honest with us."

"Your personal recommendation on the matter, Florian AF?"

He drew a breath. "We've pulled Justin Warrick into sera's wing, to prevent further contact. That was our immediate action."

"Is he aware of what's on the card?"

"The card was given him without explanation. He wasn't observed reading it. He volunteered it to me, and we ran the address on it. We didn't, however, run the data strip. It seems to us that needs to be done in lab."

"We'll do that," Hicks said, "with precautions."

"Sera will appreciate notification of the contents, whether or not it immediately concerns her security."

Hicks' jaw clamped. He was a man not in the habit of letting go of information without knowing parameters in advance. But slowly he nodded. "We appreciate your turning this over, Florian AF."

"Sera will take action based on the contents, ser. We will keep your office apprised."

"Sit down," Hicks said. "For God's sake, sit down,"

It seemed Hicks had something specific to discuss. Florian moved over to the chair and did sit down, leaned back, and looked at the man on the level. It was a worried look on the other side of the desk. A CIT with what seemed to be a problem.

"What's your opinion on what you've found?" Hicks asked.

"First, that Jordan Warrick may or may not have known what was on the card. Second, Justin had no idea, and was uncomfortable with the possession of it in the circumstances. Third, Dr. Patil may or may not know that her information was traded."

"What, in your opinion, was Warrick's motive?"

"We have no current theory, except to say he wants his son closer to him and we want him farther away. Closer in the metaphysical sense as well as the physical."

"His loyalty, you mean."

"The younger Warrick isn't amenable to his father's past politics. He avoids that topic. He has no political leanings of his own."

"Everyone born a CIT has a political leaning."

"His is definitely not toward the Centrists, then, ser. His beliefs run counter to theirs."

"So you don't think his gift of the card to you was simply because he knew he was watched. Do you think he would have turned it in under other circumstances?"

"*Jordan* Warrick knew they were watched, ser. He's always watched."

"That doesn't answer my question."

"In response to your question, ser, if he hadn't handed it to us last night, he would have likely handed it over sometime today, because he isn't in agreement with his father's gesture. He doesn't favor involvement with clandestine matters. And while he regards his father highly, he will equally well wish to avoid any involvement in his father's actions, where they may cross ReseuneSec. He has had extensive experience with your office, ser, and has no wish to cross your path again."

"What do you think is going on with the elder Warrick?"

"Resentment of past confinement and present limitations. A desire to agitate, possibly to inject new energy into a quiet status quo with Admin. Possibly a third motive. My information is insufficient."

"But your information is current in the case of the younger Warrick. You're quite satisfied that he poses no risk to your principal."

"I am very confident of my estimate of Justin Warrick. We wouldn't allow him in the same room with sera if we were in the least doubtful about his intentions."

"What is your estimate of the Patil situation?"

"I can't possibly estimate, ser, except to ask if it's possible Director Schwartz himself provoked Jordan Warrick to do this. The coincidence is extreme, if there is no causality. Both know Patil, ser Warrick secondhand, as best I know, and Dr. Schwartz has met with her—intended to meet with her at the time he last spoke with Warrick Senior. We know there was an intense argument between ser Warrick and Dr. Schwartz on that occasion, before Dr. Schwartz left for Novgorod. We don't know the content."

"It was an unrecorded conversation," Hicks said. "In that, Florian AF, you and I are in the same situation."

Interesting. And there was one, perhaps one, window to ask into that matter. "Ser. This touches sera's security, considering Justin Warrick was involved, and Justin Warrick and his companion are under her protection. Eversnow was the topic of dinner conversation between Director Schwartz and sera that same evening. An hour later, with no direct contact with anyone we've monitored, Jordan Warrick chose to produce a card with a name on it involving Eversnow, in a way he knew would come to the attention of ReseuneSec and sera's security. Sera went to Director Schwartz regarding the card: Director Schwartz revealed a connection between Eversnow and Patil, and between Warrick and Patil, via a third party. We find this card assumes a threatening character, regarding supposedly secure conversations involving Director Schwartz's activities, and sera's security officially calls your attention to that fact."

A moment of silence. "Meaning, ser?"

"Meaning we will act, ser, if we see a problem to sera's wing or sera's interests, including the safety of present Reseune Administration."

"You're bright. Tell me, Florian AF, what would *you* advise we do about Dr. Patil?"

"Investigate. There's no information yet. The action doesn't seem friendly to her interests. But we don't know with any surety what her interests are."

"Facts: the Director met with Dr. Patil in Novgorod. They discussed her promotion to a division leadership in ReseuneLabs at Fargone, involving a covert Reseune development at Eversnow. Jordan Warrick signals us that he knows Patil. Which he does ... possibly more than secondhand, for all we can discover. You know what she works on."

"Nanistics. Bionanistics of a secret and restricted nature."

"Then you understand the difficulty of turning up information. The military has classified much of her work, classified much of what goes on at Planys. *We* can't get over that wall. And the nature of what she works on— makes a physical search of her premises problematic and dangerous. If she's doing something she oughtn't, or communicating with people she oughtn't, yes, there is a danger."

"I would put forward a suggestion, ser."

"What would that be?"

"Let her leave for the assignment. Then detain her and her baggage once she reaches orbit. That narrows the problem. She'll either attempt to destroy things before she leaves, or take certain things with her."

Hicks' face was habitually unexpressive, lined with years of grim business. An actual smile flickered in the corners of the mouth. "Good. Not, actually, surprising. What other suggestions, Florian AF?"

"Sera's personal security doesn't have the scope or the equipment to take certain steps. You do. We would also be extremely interested to know about any leak of information out of Planys, or into it."

"We've consistently taken steps to find out."

Over a period of time, then, a long-term watch. "From before Jordan Warrick came here?"

A grudging dip of the head.

"Planys staff?" Florian asked. "Operatives inside the University?"

"Not all the specialist agents are as far removed as the stations in orbit. We can deal with a nanistics situation. Clearly we have mutual concerns. And we've come to a point of mutual interest. You're very much what I expected. Alpha. No question."

"Ser?"

"Is your partner outside?"

"She remained with sera. Internal policy."

Hicks nodded slowly. "You insisted on monitoring that dinner at the restaurant. You consider young Warrick yours and you protect his privacy. Understandable. We agreed to that. But we'd like to have *all* the records from that encounter, including anything you know from young Warrick, anything he or his companion may have said in handing you the item."

Hicks had protested their handling it solo. Clearly he'd had his own observers.

"The younger Warrick is in our wing, ser. His safety is at issue as well as sera's. We remain extremely concerned about Warrick senior being here. We remain concerned about any leak of the younger Warrick's activities to Warrick Senior. And might I point out—I doubt Justin Warrick would have been as ready to offer the card to one of your agents." An interesting thought, a troubling scenario. "You'd have had to search him if you'd wanted it. And I'm very sure he wouldn't have liked that. Maybe that was part of Jordan's intention, that Justin get arrested. Jordan didn't know it wasn't ReseuneSec doing the monitoring that night. He expected you. And that would have bounced it to Yanni's office, and then to sera."

"Interesting notion. But he didn't give that card to you when you met. He sent his companion back with it."

"Clearly you don't need my answers."

"Actually we don't, on that one." He tapped the envelope with the card. "This, however, is not in the form of a petty annoyance from Ser Warrick. It's very troublesome."

"You're certain Director Schwartz didn't set it up."

A flat, impenetrable stare. "Not to my knowledge," Hicks said, which Florian took for a warning. It could mean, *Don't ask.* It could mean, *No, Yanni Schwartz didn't inform me of any trap he was setting, and I don't at all like not being informed.* And it could simply mean, *There's a leak somewhere, and I don't like not having clues.*

"Are you sure of your own staff, in Sera Emory's apartment?"

"We're all azi, ser. We're Contracted. A leak there isn't highly likely. Certain of the staff came from general security." That was Wes and Marco. "A few elsewhere, from

sources that passed clearances. Infiltration is possible, but
not likely."

"My point is, we can't work at cross-purposes. You're
eighteen. And there are the two other security agents besides your partner on your staff, am I right?"

"Yes, ser. I am. And there are."

Hicks made a vee of his hands. Looked at him a moment. "Your predecessor was very good. I knew him . . . I
knew him tolerably well, when I was an assistant to Giraud
Nye. We cooperated."

"Yes, ser." Time before he had existed was not emotionally attractive to him. There was no resonance for him
with his predecessor, such as born-men expected to exist.
And this was a Supervisor, who should know that trait.
Florian remained engaged, wary of verbal traps.

"Your predecessor set precedents," Hicks said, "set up
frameworks of cooperation with my predecessor's predecessor, that lasted into Giraud Nye's administration of this
agency, until the first Ariane's death and the birth of her
successor. And I'm about to invoke one of those arrange-
ments. I can place three squads of my people directly under
your authority, as Wing One security, establishing the
same sort of arrangement my predecessor had with *your*
principal's office—two-way information. A very discreet
two-way flow. It's not safe for you to keep us in the dark—
or—it's not *as* safe to have our operations crossing one another at critical moments, and I'd rather prevent that."

Interesting offer. He did know about the prior arrangement. He'd expected to ask for it himself, once sera took
control of Admin. He'd expected to get it without question at that point, whether or not Hicks was still running
ReseuneSec. It was a little surprising to have it offered to
them without asking.

"You're worried about Patil and Warrick," he said to
Hicks, but only the dilation of the eyes betrayed Hicks'
reaction. "There's a leak and you don't know where it is."

"Yes. Frankly, yes. And I'm concerned about Warrick
and Warrick, the latter being inside your perimeters in *the*
most sensitive area of Reseune."

"I'm aware of the protocol that existed before my time.
But name its details, ser, if you would."

"Thirty beta- and gamma-class agents, all dedicated to maintaining your security envelope, at your orders, full access to ReseuneSec information, exactly what the first Ari had ... with an appropriate clerical staff, and an administrative office sited in Wing One. We could assign supervisory protocols to the Director himself. Or to me, personally, if you're satisfied with that arrangement."

"I am aware what specific arrangement the first Ari had with Giraud Nye, ser, and your offer is acceptable if sera is their Supervisor of record."

"Her youth—"

"My partner and I are alphas, ser, and she's *our* Supervisor."

"Technically—"

"In actuality, ser. She has been capable of directing us for a classified length of time, but you may at least conclude it wasn't yesterday."

Hicks regarded him at some length. "You're still eighteen."

"I'm very good at what I do, ser."

That got a smile. The best Supervisors could be like that, able to appreciate an azi's humor. And one had to be wary, not to get sucked in and set too much at ease.

"No buttons available, ser. She has all mine well-catalogued."

The smile persisted. "I'd expect that."

"I add one more qualification: these agents: their Contracts go to her. Specifically."

Not outright refusal, but wariness. "That's *not* what was."

"That chain-of-command may have killed her predecessor. Certainly it was a weakness. My partner and I have studied that arrangement very closely. Their Contracts will be solely to her, ser, or we can't accept. Also, should we find a problem in any mindset, that agent will be directly dismissed and sent to retraining."

Hesitation. "I can understand your reasoning. But you weren't ready to ask for it. You have a lot of responsibilities inside the walls. Yet you don't feel ready to deal with this increase in scope?"

Supervisor's question.

"I personally find no great advantage in declining your offer, ser, under the terms I name. You see a need: you made the offer. Should we decline it, we run risks we both foresee, regarding sera's safety. Should the offer turn out to involve less cooperation than we know we need, we will have to decline it, also for security reasons."

"You think this office has problems?"

"I have some reservations, knowing a leak of information happened somewhere. We know our own staff. We don't know yours, ser. Does the offer stand?"

"It stands."

"She'll require their Contracts and their manuals."

"Pending her approval of this arrangement."

"If I approve here and now, and I do, the deal is done. Sera will agree."

A frown. "Irregular transfer of Contracts."

"My predecessor had similar power. You knew him, you say."

"Your predecessor was very much older when I knew him."

"He's dead now," Florian said. "My partner and I intend to do better than that."

A moment of silence. "Quite," Hicks said. "Quite. Done, then." He turned to the console, entered a program, and a stick popped up. He passed it across the table. "Valid for every individual in the file. You can reach their Contracts and their personal manuals with this clearance. They're yours."

"They're sera's," he amended that. For a born-man, Hicks was very easy to work with—plain, direct, and saying what he meant, at least on the surface. Hicks would have the job fairly securely for the next twenty-odd years—until the next Giraud came of age—if he succeeded in the next few. His office might have problems; so might any office in Reseune, at this point. Sera wasn't in charge. Other, lesser people made decisions.

And within those twenty years of Hicks' office, they were going to face the same threats their predecessors had consistently faced, namely a fair number of people wanting power, or having power and intending to hold onto it. Yanni was intent on holding power on sera's behalf: there was less likely an indication of treachery there, but there were questions, and minds could change, over a decade. The security breach at Planys and Yanni's dealings with Patil were very likely a case of Yanni trying to ferret out the known problems of a prior generation before Ari had to inherit them, rather than a born-man trying for power of his own.

But that was an inquiry he planned to make, via the resources which this expanded staff would give him.

At very least Hicks and Yanni and the rest were on their guard—and motivated. If anything adverse did happen in Reseune in the next twenty years, life expectancy for the chief of ReseuneSec would be commensurately short—likewise the Director's.

Sera's life was at issue. Primarily sera's, most clearly. Any enemy getting power would immediately want a new Ari-clone to work with, or see all Union space thrown into a power struggle. Certain enemies might think they would like that event. But only the most fringe elements—or Alliance agents from outside Union space—could benefit from losing Ari altogether. Domestic enemies, sensibly bent on unified power, would need to have people on-staff at Reseune to make sure there was a third Ariane Emory.

Those were the ones to worry about most acutely: their ambitions were far more local. Some individuals with those well-targeted motives might *be* inside their perimeters, and Jordan was only the visible problem, the most likely focus of trouble.

"A pleasure to cooperate with you, ser," Florian said, and took the datastick, got up and gave a little bow. "If I have the requisite materials in this, I'll handle the other details."

"Done," Hicks said. "And that stick is clean, by the way."

"Of course, ser," Florian said pleasantly, with every intention of passing it through protocols, even considering it came directly from the man who saw to the safety of all Reseune. "We can't say that about the card's data-strip. But we'll look forward to the information."

"Pleasure," Hicks said, and looked as if he meant it.

So that was that. Kyle AK was waiting to show him

out. Florian walked out of that hall, out through a reception area where the number of waiting CITs had nearly doubled.

Elsewhere in the system, in other offices, a number of security-trained azi were about to hear a keyword to disturb them to the depths. They'd be notified of reassignment to new specific operations, with special training.

They'd be excited, anxious at the same time, vulnerable as their professions never let them be for any other reason.

It was his job and Catlin's, and Wes' and Marco's, to settle the new security staff in their duty and handle the logistics. They'd have residency in Wing One: they needed to have it. But, unlike their own hand-picked domestic staff, they'd never come into direct contact with sera, not until he knew them specifically and by experience, and until sera had had a close look at their files.

Patil was a useful first question for them to try their new ReseuneSec access on. The quality of the information that query produced would tell them more about Hicks than about Patil.

Hicks himself might be the more vital question. When people gave things gratis, looking into the origin of the impulse was a good idea.

And when rumor said there was more than one authority inside the office, and that Hicks wasn't the strongest administrator ReseuneSec had ever had—that fact was worth noting.

In the meanwhile, Florian thought, passing the outside door . . . in the meanwhile, and with their own careful examination of what Hicks handed them, ReseuneSec's close cooperation with sera's staff might prove useful.

APRIL 26, 2424
1538H

After brunch was an extended but less than productive day trying to arrange the backwards-feeling office—in which they waited, continually on edge, for another call from Jordan.

Damn it.

But at least their current cases had arrived in the paperwork ported over from the Education Wing.

Justin doggedly slogged away at a routine check of a psych record, a fifteen-year-old azi up at Big Blue who'd had extraordinary scores in work-study, a cheerful looking girl with freckles on her nose and a quite amazing ability to troubleshoot problems in a handful of aging bots. It was a mechanical aptitude that had never manifested in the ThT-382s—possibly because no ThT-382 had been faced with a broken bot and a looming production deadline. Strong ethic to succeed, strong bond with her CIT Supervisor, who was about as old as the bots, and a deadline.

It was a good combination. Create those desires and skills in the ThT-382 path and they had a new training route with a fairly complex technical slant. Reseune liked to keep a strong theta presence in a given genepool, good practical sense, good hand-eye, ability to fix the plumbing before the water rose, as the first Ari used to put it— but more than that, it was a diverse, adaptable geneset. All sorts of things cropped up in the ThT-382s that were good traits in a population. The mechanical ability was a revelation.

Alpha types—mentally top-end and having more delicate psychological needs, in order to function at maximum—found employment mostly inside Reseune, very few outside, until a settlement reached a need for higher-end management, and then only a few, specialized in admin, usually, very few in science, went to that assignment. An alpha closely paired with a born-man Special—the CIT equivalent of an Alpha—those sets were all at Reseune, or at Planys, or at installations like Reseune-Space. His pairing with Grant, Jordan's with Paul—

God, there was one mortal waste in his father's situation. Paul and Jordan hadn't done a damned thing useful in twenty years, and the stagnation had to be killing both of them.

There wasn't a thing he could do about it. Jordan and Paul were sitting over in his office by now, stewing, not getting anything done not only because they were so far behind it was going to take years to catch up, but because Jordan wasn't ready to get started catching up. And Paul, who was totally innocent of anything but loyalty to Jordan, was suffering right along with him.

Maybe, if he *could* find a way to work with Jordan, he could fix the situation, get Jordan moving again on something creative.

And maybe that was at the core of what Jordan wanted—come bring me up to speed, give the old man a hand, put us back where we were . . . before Denys Nye framed me for murder. . . .

The revenge part of it . . . that wasn't going to go away so readily. *That,* he didn't know how to cure.

Jordan had tried working with Ari Emory. That didn't work. Jordan could work with Paul, but Paul didn't work at all while Jordan was emoting, and if Paul was currently trying to deepstudy his own way back to what he himself had been, it was under impossible conditions: Jordan was scattershot at the moment and mad as hell, and Paul was suffering.

Paul was still functioning tolerably well in the crisis—socially speaking. Jordan, being a born-man and a Special, was not that well-organized. Jordan was damned pissed, and intent on everyone around him knowing it, intent on everyone acknowledging he'd been wronged, whatever it was that would satisfy him . . . and by all evidence, nothing ever would satisfy Jordan. His enemies were dead—and reborn—and twenty years of his life were gone. Meanwhile his son, his personal rebirth, had gotten entirely pragmatic about those missing years, and *had* stayed current with his work, and was living under the current Ari Emory's thumb.

That was what was eating Jordan alive.

Well, he couldn't help it. Couldn't change it. He wasn't going to change it at Grant's expense, no matter what kind of pseudo-filial impulses surged in his gut whenever Jordan pulled one of his pity-fests, damn him. No, no, and no, he wasn't going to divert himself and Grant from a comfortable career doing useful work to go join his father in self-destruction. Selfish, maybe. But this version of Ari had a certain hold on him, too, and it wasn't hate.

Memory of the first Ari—even that had had its good spots. One really bad one, but some good ones, too.

Memory of the second—a kid with a gift of guppies, a teenager upset as hell because her first attempt at seduction hadn't at all worked—

The two weren't the same. Opposite ends of the age spectrum, for sure, but they weren't the same.

Isn't that what the whole program is about? Jordan had asked him.

Yes and no. If and maybe. The kid was brilliant. The kid was sopping up deepteach on science at a phenomenal rate. He didn't know precisely at what rate: he supposed Yanni knew, but he didn't. Just—her questions were getting scarily top-level. Her integrations challenged him, *taught* him things in a field he'd not had contact with in years. A little love of guppies hadn't blunted the great genius into uselessness. It might even have unwound some knots and let that phenomenal mind work at full capacity. But you couldn't tell that to Jordan, who was still dealing with his own devil, his own Ari, and couldn't see that anything had changed.

Stop everything he personally was doing, detour for a year or so to rescue Jordan from his twenty-year-gap?

Maybe he *was* a selfish ingrate. Maybe he should spare a couple of years, out of a long life.

And every time he thought about doing it his stomach knotted up.

A couple of years couldn't make Jordan happy. He

could take Jordan off to the wilds up by the new lab they were building and do dedicated deepstudy until he could get Jordan factually up to date, and Grant could meanwhile work on Paul in that isolation—he'd actually thought about it—but what would they have at the end of it? An up-to-date Jordan who was never going to accept Reseune the way it was—who'd given him that card, damn him, knowing they were being watched.

Jordan had done it deliberately, knowing he was going to run his son and Grant straight into an inquiry, if—hell, if!—he'd done it *because* someone in security would have spotted that card—Jordan would have been disappointed if they hadn't.

It was bait, was what. It was Jordan stirring the pot, seeing what would happen—maybe hoping his son would be stopped, harassed, that the card would be confiscated and gone over by security—and so would his son be, which would throw him into a funk where Jordan could psychologically get at him; or maybe bring Grant running, in distress, right into Jordan's hands, or maybe get him severed from Ari's company and put under equal suspicion.

And what was the number? What in hell was Jordan doing? The thing was radioactive. You didn't want to touch it. The room they were in was bugged beyond a doubt.

He couldn't stand it.

He couldn't stand it a moment longer.

"Grant."

Keystrokes stopped. "Mmm?"

"Did you chance to look at that card?"

"It wasn't chance."

Heartbeat bumped. Leave it to Grant. "What was on it?" he asked.

"A number."

"What number?"

"It had the form of a personal number. I recall it. Do you want me to find out?" Grant asked.

"No," he said, and made a sudden decision: he didn't want Grant involved, didn't want to be on record doing anything furtive. "No, *I* will."

He windowed up the message function and shot a query out straight to Ari's security office address. WHAT

WAS ON THE CARD JORDAN GAVE ME? DO YOU
KNOW?

The answer came back fairly quickly. A CONTACT
NUMBER AT THE UNIVERSITY IN NOVGOROD. A
WOMAN NAMED SANDI PATIL. DO YOU KNOW THAT
PERSON?

He typed: NOT A CLUE.

The answer came back, under Ari's household ID,
no further name telling who he was talking to: SENIOR
LECTURER WITH A SPECIALITY IN BIONANISTICS.
THERE IS NO APPARENT CONNECTION WITH JOR-
DAN. WHAT IS YOUR THEORY?

His heart began a series of labored beats, old familiar fear, of a flavor he'd known for all the bad years, the
twenty years when the Nyes had run Reseune. He typed:
IS THIS FLORIAN?

—CATLIN, SER. MY QUESTION?

—I HAVE NO IDEA WHY HE WOULD GIVE ME THAT
NUMBER. I DON'T KNOW THIS WOMAN. I HAVE
NOTHING TO DO WITH HER FIELD. HER FIELD HAS
NOTHING TO DO WITH MY FATHER'S, EITHER, AS
I'M SURE YOU'RE WELL AWARE.

Grant had gotten out of his chair, and leaned over to
see the screen. Set a hand on his shoulder. His heart beat
harder and harder, the old instincts awake and alert.

—WE DON'T KNOW THE REASON OF THIS CON-
TACT, SER, OR OF HIS GIVING IT TO YOU. BUT THE
RESTRICTED MILITARY NATURE OF THE PROFES-
SOR'S RESEARCH URGES CAUTION.

Bionanistics. God. Manufacturing? Genetic machines?
Experimental, self-replicating *life?* Military secrecy?

—I HAVE NO IDEA, he typed. HE'S NEVER MEN-
TIONED ANY SUCH CONTACT TO ME.

—WHAT WOULD YOU HAVE DONE WITH THE
NOTE IF YOU WERE WELL-DISPOSED TO OBEY YOUR
FATHER AT THE TIME?

Thump. Thump-thump. I SUPPOSE I WOULD HAVE
LOOKED UP THE NUMBER. MAYBE I'D HAVE CALLED
THIS PERSON IN NOVGOROD IF I WERE A TOTAL
FOOL AND WANTED TO KNOW WHAT IT MEANT OR
WHERE IT LED. I'M NOT A FOOL. AND I'D HOPE MY

FATHER KNOWS I'M NOT. I'M NOT INTERESTED IN
HIS OLD BUSINESS, WHATEVER IT IS, AND I THINK
HE KNOWS THAT, TOO. He added that last sentence and
felt like a traitor, for reasons not entirely well-defined. He
manipulated azi minds for a living—and his own motiva-
tions eluded him. There *damned* sure wasn't any connection of experience with Jordan left for him, nothing but
an identical biology. CATLIN, I'M ENTIRELY UPSET BY
THIS SITUATION.

—UNDERSTANDABLE,   came   the   answer.   SO
YOU HAVE NO INCLINATION TO PURSUE THE
INFORMATION.

—NONE WHATSOEVER, he answered back.

—BE AWARE THAT INFORMATION OR DEVICES
INVOLVING DR. PATIL COULD PASS IN FORMS VERY
DIFFICULT TO DETECT. TAKE PRECAUTIONS IN ANY
FUTURE DEALINGS WITH YOUR FATHER, WITH THIS
IN MIND.

—I TAKE THE WARNING. THANK YOU.

Catlin signed off. He did. He felt sick. He didn't move.
He felt the pressure of Grant's fingers, and finally got up
from the chair, knowing, damn them all, that everything
he said was being recorded, watched, parsed, combed
through.

"Security's upset. I can't blame them. Nanistics. They
don't want the experimental stuff on a planet . . . particularly the one we happen to live on. Particularly the one the
radicals have wanted to terraform for the last century or
so. Damn. Damn. Damn it, Grant. I don't want any part
of this. What is he doing to me? What does he think he's
doing?"

Grant shook his head slowly, helplessly. "Logic tells me
he wants you involved with him in his situation. Beyond
that—"

It hit like a hammer blow. He could have said it himself ten times, even thought it himself, and not heard it
quite the same way, but from Grant, in that calm, reasoned
way Grant struggled to navigate CIT emotional insanity,
it made utter, reasonable sense. Jordan wasn't azi. Neither
he nor Jordan had, as Grant liked to put it, their logic-set
at the foundation of their reasoning. No. They were born-

men, and born-men grew up by chance, not by tape-study. Emotions ruled their actions, foundational, and inescapable. Flux-thinking at its finest.

Jordan had created him out of his own geneset and Jordan had lost him. Lost him to Ari, who had done things to Jordan's work that Jordan couldn't counter, and the new Ari was coopting him out of Jordan's reach.

"The government didn't kill him for killing Ari," he said aloud, to Grant's worried look. "They could only exile him. So he figures whatever he does, exile's the worst that will ever happen to him. He created me. He wants me back. He's making his best play."

"To get you on the outs with Yanni."

"To get us *all* sent to Planys, where he *ran* his own little world." Things clicked, just clicked, all of a sudden. "It might have been a prison, but he ran it, inside, and Ari ripped him out of it and brought him here to put him under what he sees as close house arrest. He's not grateful for it, not once he got here and saw the way things are: he's damned pissed. He wants me to break with Ari. He wants to create a situation. I don't know who this Patil is, or how Jordan got that number, but Patil isn't really the game . . ."

BOOK ONE   Section 2   Chapter vi

APRIL 26, 2424
1659H

"*. . . it's him. Maybe he hates Patil. Or maybe there's something actually going on, and he doesn't give a damn about it, because they're trying to use him—the old radicals— hell, I don't know how they could have gotten to him, but he won't play anybody else's game. Just his own, always his own, the hell with anybody else.*"

Interesting observation, Ari thought, sitting beside Catlin at the console. The audio clip ran to its conclusion:

"Will you go to Yanni?" Grant had asked.

And Justin: *"I'm going to give Catlin another phone call. I'm not taking this. I'm not taking this from him. He wants us back under suspicion, he wants us arrested, he wants me upset, he'll make himself the martyr, so we both get sent to Planys, back to his private kingdom, and he has years to work on us. . . . Damn it, Grant, you're right."*

"*Did* he call you?" Ari asked, when the clip ended.

"Yes," Catlin said, with a nod. "He did. He said—" She keyed another clip, listened, then made it audible.

". . . he doesn't give a damn about this Dr. Patil. He's after me. He wants to get me at odds with admin and better yet, get us all sent back to Planys, where he has a base."

"Why would he pick Dr. Patil?" recorded-Catlin asked.

"I've no idea. An outside and problematic contact he once had. Somebody he didn't really know and doesn't care about. Maybe somebody he hates. I just don't know."

Catlin stopped the clip.

"Jordan Warrick is a very interesting person," Ari said. "And now Justin's quite angry at him. Jordan's supposed to be good at Working. Very good. I wonder if he intended all he got from Justin."

"Warrick Senior's behavior seems self-destructive," Catlin said.

"Not only *self*-destructive," Ari said. "He'd gladly take us with him. He seems to want things back the way they were before I was born, and he's bound to be frustrated with me."

"There is a solution to this," Catlin said.

Kill him, Catlin meant. It wasn't legal to do, but that certainly wouldn't stop Catlin and Florian, if she ordered it. And very likely Yanni wouldn't let her or them take the consequences for it. There was far too much invested in her. So she could even get away with it, under the law.

But not in Justin's eyes, and the likelihood that Justin would find out sooner or later—oddly enough that was the first Stop the thought ran into. Not the law. *Justin.*

Jordan was just very, very interesting—someone from the first Ari's time, a piece of the puzzle of the first Ari's life and death that had been missing all these years. Everyone had said Jordan was a problem.

He certainly was. A very high-powered problem. He was attempting to Work his son, whatever else this was about, and Justin possibly had it figured out entirely accurately.

It was also clear Jordan Warrick still had secrets. The first Ari had wanted him for a partner: they'd worked together productively for a while, before their personalities clashed. Politics had been part of it—the Centrist Party with their program of stopping further explorations, concentrating Union into a tight, strong knot, so that their longtime rivals over at Pell's Star—the Alliance—had to concentrate there, too. So no one would be expanding. If mankind went on exploring and expanding and trying to outrace each other to likely stars, expanding so fast they had to use birthlabs to multiply fast enough to keep economies going, the Centrists feared that so much use of birthlabs was going to change mankind—

And that was quite true. It was changing the balance in the genome. It had, already, in much more than just the genome. There were differences between them and Alliance and Earth far other than genetic balance.

But psychosociology wasn't the reason why Jordan had aligned with the Centrists. Oh, no. His reason for taking their side was that the first Ari and most of Reseune was Expansionist. The first Ari's whole life's work was Expansionist.

And, not too strange to say, Jordan had taken up corresponding with the Centrists and their more radical branch at about the time the partnership between himself and Ari had broken up . . . so figure that Jordan didn't really believe in the Centrist Party or give a damn about their fears for the future. He'd just used them.

Interesting.

Interesting, interesting.

"We're going to watch him," Ari said. "Yanni's managing this so far. I'm sure you'll tell him there was some sort of a leak, when you think it's right to do."

"Hicks has given us agents to be totally at our disposal," Catlin said. "Thirty, with clericals."

This was news. "Because of Jordan Warrick?"

"Perhaps. Ser Warrick, Dr. Patil, Dr. Thieu, and events unforeseen. We laid down conditions to our working with this staff. Florian is over at the barracks going through their records, analyzing the abilities of what we've been given."

"A permanent gift? From Hicks?"

"Permanent, yes, sera. Much like the protection the first Ari had, high-level ReseuneSec, with accesses, only Florian said we wouldn't take them except if you hold the Contracts, sera."

"The first Ari's guard. They were Contracted to Reseune itself?"

"Not our predecessors. But yes, the others were. Your predecessor never internalized the staff ReseuneSec lent her—she rather used all of ReseuneSec; but we think that may have been a problem, that her security staff *wasn't* wholly hers. We're taking care of that. You need to hold those Contracts."

"To be inside the apartment?" She was a little appalled. "We need domestic staff."

"Those are coming, sera. But we were offered the others. They can have a barracks here, in the wing, an adjunct office with computer ties to ReseuneSec. We're moving out the rest of the records storage and taking over the guest apartment on the first floor. We can cancel everything if it's not a good idea. But there's room for them on the first floor, down by the old lab, and they won't be in the apartment—we wouldn't let them in, until we're very comfortable with them; though I'm sure, when they are Contracted, that they'd like you to be there, sera. If it's all right."

That was a natural thing, an emotional thing. And it would cement the Contract, in that sense. She'd be their Supervisor, the CIT they'd come to in distress or in need—to be remote from them was unacceptable. And she'd told Florian to see to staff. He certainly had. She'd turned them loose to see to things, and they'd done it without making a ripple in her own schedule . . . maybe a bit widely, but—all the same—they had the chance to gain loyal personnel. That wasn't a bad idea.

"Of course," she said. "Of course I will. When are they coming in?"

"Soon. A few days. The domestic staff should get here

first. Florian's checking on their progress while he's down the hill."

"You've been very quiet to be so busy."

"These are things we can do. I hope we've done them well enough."

She'd been completely lost in her work, her deepstudy and her own tracking of problems down in Novgorod, out of touch with domestic issues, so long as her clothes appeared clean and her breakfast and supper arrived mostly on time. She walked about with her head stuffed with population equations and spent her days in the first Ari's population dynamics designs—she'd reached a point, a strange point in such study, when whole disciplines had begun to come into focus, as if the brain had started assembling all the scattered bits of what had been her predecessor's operations two decades ago, and put it all together. She was at that critical point, dammit, on the verge of overload, and she just went there on any stray thought, far, far from the needs of domestic staff. Her head ached—literally ached—from the effort it was to jump between the real world and the first Ari's world, and back again—to try to grasp the underlying reasons for the ethics her predecessor had installed to patch what had already been done at Novgorod—laying down the commandment to work, and the necessity for recreation, and above all the mantra "We are different as our world is different, and our different world is a valuable resource . . ."

Hell, that was dangerous. It was sweeping, it had no exceptions, it was potentially troublesome, and the first Ari had dared embed that in the tape, high and wide, which was the way she worked. Half a million Novgoroders kept voting against terraforming, and, azi-originated as they were, and doggedly devoted to work for validation—they had deep suspicions about CIT-descended Centrists and about proposals for terraforming, and were increasingly inclined in the last ten years to favor red-brown architecture, one might note—the color of Cyteen's outback.

Was that significant?

Was that going to produce a problem integrating into Union ethic as a whole—where her predecessor had done other interesting tweaks in local mindsets?

"Sera?" Catlin asked, and she blinked. That was how she was lately. That was the territory where her own thoughts wandered, and the choice of protective and service staff— essential to her safety—became just part of the overload.

"I think it's likely very fine what you've done." She brought herself to short-focus on it, and try to integrate it into her concept of her household, and how it was all going to work, and Catlin was right to persist in getting an answer out of her. You couldn't make mistakes with azi. You couldn't just Contract them and throw them away.

And it was scary, thinking of all the changes racketing around her.

She had two people in all the world—Florian and Catlin— that she trusted to be competent and devoted to her—an array of people like Sam and Yanni, that she trusted for other fields, but when it came down to it, it was Florian and Catlin who would keep her alive and give her time to pursue those abstracts she chased through the maze of records.

They reported to her. They made choices—in this case, they'd made one that affected the household around her.

And more security. Her life, certainly—maybe Union's survival—depended on her bodyguards' judgement.

"I have no doubt of you," she said briskly to Catlin, totally focused for the moment on the here and now, and Catlin's fair demand for her to back them or not. "Do what you see fit to do. Did Justin stay in the Wing today?"

"Working in his office, since a late breakfast, sera. So is Grant. Perfectly cooperative. Jordan called him; Justin left the office and went to breakfast. There was, however, no contact between them beyond that. Justin and his companion spoke only to the waiters at the restaurant and to each other. And he of course communicated with me. Jordan stayed in his new office with Paul and rearranged things. He found two bugs. It wasn't all."

Ari gave a perfunctory laugh, not whole-hearted, more wistful. "It would be so much nicer if Jordan weren't an enemy. Does Justin like his life, I wonder? Is he mad at me, do you think?"

"Grant is content," Catlin said. The azi, she could judge quite well. The born-man, she didn't attempt.

And that was, of course, a correct answer.

"I wish I could turn things around with Jordan," she said. "I wish I could figure how to Work him. But he's stubborn. And he knows all the tricks." She gave a sigh and got up from the console. Paused, then, looking directly at Catlin, a second time sharply focused on the present, and on Catlin's and Florian's problems. "Sending Jordan back to Planys wouldn't be good, would it, if he has a network there? I'd planned on Strassenburg. But he'll Work the azi there and try to change them, and they're all foundational to that city, and *that* would be a big problem. I could build an ethic around him in that population, but once he's dead, what will that do? He'd be a rock in the stream. Everything would bend around him. Forever."

Catlin shook her head. "I'm sure I don't know any answer, sera."

"Unfortunately I don't, either," she said, and went to her bedroom, and her private bath, and took a headache remedy before she took another deepstudy pill and went back to her bed, leaving everything to them, going back to what she had to do.

There'd been a garden once in legend, a perfect garden. But there'd been a snake in it. The woman hadn't known what to do about him. And every problem of humankind had started from that. The snake had done a Working, about knowledge, and pride, and the woman had gone off her path and taken all her descendants with her.

She had her own snake under close watch. And she couldn't let concern about Jordan disrupt her concentration, not when things were starting to gel, not when her essential job for the next few months was absorbing the sum of several sciences, dosing down with kat so often she could almost go deep-state the way Catlin or Florian could learn, just by thinking hard, and become only the thing she was absorbing, without objection, without question, just wide open to unquestioned knowledge.

You had to trust the tapes, you had to really trust them to dose down that far, or to go that open. You had no resistance when you did that. You had no way to say no. You had no extraneous thoughts. You just recorded, embedded the knowledge as fast as possible, burning it into the brain's pathways, strong, strong, *strong* pathways.

There was only one source of tapes she'd trust like that: the first Ari's tapes, stored in Base One, tapes recording Ari I's thoughts, her opinions on technical questions, her data, her projects, her working life.

If there was any personal prejudice embedded in those records, any Working her predecessor had designed for her beyond the obvious, it was going into her head, too.

If she'd had the choice, if she'd had the leisure, if the world hadn't been as high-pressure as it was, and if the legislature wasn't boiling with important decisions Yanni was trying to handle—if all those things were so, and the world were safer, she'd have taken less of the deepteach drug, she'd have taken longer in her learning, she'd have stayed near enough to the surface to let a little of her conscious mind work on the problems, and see more critically what she personally thought.

But in Denys Nye's fall, Union had gone quietly into crisis, and civilization could make some serious missteps while she lazed her way through, learning at an ordinary pace.

So she took the dose she did, on her off days, and gave up critiquing her predecessor. She wasn't giving up her conscious mind in the long run—she banked on that. She was strong-willed, she was psychologically knowledgeable, she knew the tricks a person used in Working another, and she had a good memory for where and when she'd learned something, right down to the session. If she ran up against an ethical problem, she'd do her own thinking—eventually. She had tags on all of it.

Was it her own thinking, for instance, that had let her matter-of-factly consider Catlin's matter-of-fact offer simply to kill Jordan Warrick? She might have been shocked a few months ago. But maybe not. Denys had been trying to kill her. Ultimately they'd killed him. That was a lesson life had given her.

Was it her own thinking, still, that said doing away with Jordan might still be the better, safer answer, that said there might be a way to do the deed quietly, and that Justin might not stay too long in mourning if she did it very cleverly?

She said no. *She* said no. That was the one mentality in

the transaction she could entirely identify. That was her, saying no, and not clearly knowing whether it was the first Ari's pragmatic sense or her own soft-hearted inexperience behind that answer.

It was scary. Two days ago she'd taken Poo-thing out of his drawer and set him on the dresser, so she could see him from this bed. She'd been too old for him. Now she was old enough to want contact with the childhood years he represented. Poor battered bear. He'd been through a lot. Denys, in the main. But never discount her predecessor's intentions, battering her mind into a pattern she was supposed to follow for all her life.

Was rebellion stupidity? Or was it just her genetics snuggling around the first Ari's precepts, hardheadedness and arrogance trying to find a convenient shape to settle into?

She wanted Florian tonight. She really wanted Florian. But she, and he, had so much work to do . . . so very much work to do . . . things about the household, which kept them all fed, and safe . . . in a Reseune that didn't all want them to stay alive.

The dose began to take hold. Critical thinking ebbed. The machine started up, a gentle repetitive tone, warning the tape was about to start. She had to press a button to get it to go on. She had that much volition left.

Beginning. The Novgorod designs, the overall structure.

Maybe nobody should examine their own world that closely. She'd been out in the world, however briefly. She'd seen the world from the air, seen it from the ground, gone through its corridors and met its violence.

Now she was working directly with the ethics that drove it, examining the ethics set into the azi who had been the foundational citizens. Did she intend to tweak that mix? She could. She could subtly, by sending in other azi into key positions, shift the whole Cyteen electorate.

She could set others at work at Fargone, where Ollie ruled. She knew Ollie's ethical structure. She had a copy of Ollie's personal manual, down to the day he left. She could skim it at high speed, and recognize ordinary structures from special ones. She could design azi to fit around Ollie, no question, the foundations of something special, around one that she'd loved, when she was little. She could make all Fargone Station into Ollie's image.

Ethics were the stop-marks, and the directional choices, in a psych-map. And she knew set after set of the classic ones, the ones from before the first Ari's time, the ones designed by committee.

She knew the ones that had the first Ari's peculiar stamp on them. Like those key sets in Novgorod, and at Gehenna—the people that would rise to the top and become important, the leaders, the movers.

She could replicate that at Strassenburg. She could do something else. Yes, she could.

And *something else* was her choice in building that place.

Surveillance of past projects like Gehenna was her job, the key thing that the first Ari had created her to do. Be the watchdog. Steer the directed populations in a good direction. Understand. Change at need. Know the program, and know how to change it.

Strassenburg would always be closely tied to Reseune, and it would be *hers. Her* chosen genesets, her chosen CITs, her designed psychsets, never part of Novgorod or any of the rest of Cyteen: something new under the sun. The thetas she was about to manage for sheer practice would be the foundation of a site where *her* programs ran, not her predecessor's. Every problem case in Reseune was currently worried that the new facility might serve as a gulag for her opposition—and in fact she *had* thought of creating a little secure lab there, for the likes of Jordan Warrick.

But there was a problem with secure labs, and the Patil incident had demonstrated that, hadn't it, abundantly? Secure labs were full of very bright people, who could be very devious if they wanted to be.

And getting a Special like Jordan involved there would jeopardize the far more important reason for Strassenberg, that the whole town was itself a lab, a control for herself, and for her successor. She wanted to see what *her* designs grew into, isolated from those at Novgorod.

She intended nothing antithetical to Novgorod, unless intolerance for other ideas was a timebomb developing in the first Ari's design.

Within decades, Novgorod would meet something on its beloved planet that wasn't Novgorod, when it had been the only true city in the world for all the world's existence. Novgorod had had some experience in tolerance, tolerating Reseune itself, Reseune's autocracy—even *needing* an Ariane Emory, and voting for her programs.

But would they tolerate diversity when it wasn't *their* brand of diversity?

For the good of the planet, they would have to. Or their idiosyncrasy became a problem that she would have to handle with subsequent population surges.

And what she did carried through generations. That was the point of everything: ultimately it was *people* you were dealing with, people whose psychsets might have been planned like a jigsaw puzzle, groups of the one psychset clicking into place with other groups of another, and tending to bond *and* procreate with individuals of like psychset, so there was a certain persistence of type—*that* was setted-in, too. All part of integrations.

No apparent problems in Novgorod. So far. Even the Abolitionists might be healthy. At least people disagreed with the majority.

So let Novgorod meet something Else. In her time, in her successor's time, let two separate psycharcologies learn each other. That would deliver a poke to the urban organism downriver, to see how it wiggled.

It might also guarantee that her successor would need to exist.

Azi felt a certain pride in the continuance of their type. It was part of their sets. But was it wired into what was basically human?

Curious, curious. She was able to compare herself only against the first Ari. Her successor would at least have a broader field of inquiry in that department.

And perhaps her successor would found yet another colony, just to check things out. She thought if she were that Ari, that thought would certainly occur to her.

But that would complicate the situation long-term, when populations merged and met, as they would when the world grew. Too many variables spoiled the soup, to mix a metaphor.

Forgetting that they were dealing with living, self-willed people spoiled it, too. Too much deepstudy, too much immersion in the theoretical, the give and take only of electrons, not the behavior of whole organisms. The world was more complicated than theory ever yet predicted: that was why she was important. It was her job to see things coming, and figure how to shift the demographics without conflicts. A machine didn't work, mixing in yet one more metaphor, if it was all one homogenous piece. Neither did a city, or a species.

Finding the glitches was her job. Her problem. Man started out analyzing his environment, graduated into understanding his own psyche, graduated, again, into analyzing the behavior of the human species en masse.

That guaranteed employment for several of her kind, didn't it?

BOOK ONE Section 2 Chapter vii

APRIL 27, 2424
0117H

Florian was back from down the hill—late. Exhausted. He fell into bed in the dark, and Catlin rolled over and asked, face to face, brow to brow with him: "So. What's the story? Do we accept these people?"

"I didn't find anyone to object to. I've interviewed them. I've ordered them into a single barracks, two days of special tape. They'll be firmly under our orders and initially operational by, I'd think, the fifteenth of next month."

"Good." She eased an arm around him. She was tired, herself, from hour after hour at the screens, and running up and downstairs seeing to the move. He was tired from a day with Hicks and trekking from one end of Reseune to the other, down to the labs and the barracks, back to the offices, meeting upon meeting with prospective help.

"Has sera asked after me?"

"She knows where you've been all day. She's very busy in her studies, but she approves of what we've done."

"Good." He pulled her close, bestowed a weary kiss on the forehead. She wasn't *that* tired, that that didn't get a reaction. But she stayed tracked, business first. "There was an interesting development on my side today."

"Oh?"

"Justin called me. Called *us*. He wanted to know what was on the card. He wanted to distance himself from that inquiry. But he also wanted to know."

The penalty of interesting information. Florian pushed her back enough to look at her eye to eye. "Curious about the card, is he?"

"Curious and worried. He's conflicted. He wants to know and he doesn't want to know. On my own judgment, I told him about the Novgorod doctor to see what his reaction would be, and also to warn him about the nature of the danger. He didn't know her, not even by name. I ran the clip of his call for sera to hear it."

"Interesting," Florian murmured. "And what did she say?"

"Much the same. She found it interesting."

Hands moved. And stopped. "Do you think sera's going to call me tonight?"

"Definitely she won't," Catlin said. "She skipped supper again and went straight into deepstudy."

"She shouldn't do that."

"I said so, too. She said she'd have a big breakfast in the morning."

"She's pushing herself again. It's not good."

"It's not good," Catlin agreed. "I think she feels we're in danger. I think she suspects something she can't identify, the same as us."

"What's Unusual?" Florian said. It was the old game, the childhood game. Find the change. Find the anomaly. Find the problem.

"Jordan," she answered. "Jordan being in Justin's old office."

"The card." He tossed the list of Unusuals back. "Yanni. This Dr. Patil. The new colony. The new wing. The new township. Am I missing anything?"

"I think," Catlin said, "that the card fits *Jordan*. Jordan wanting Justin to get caught. Justin giving us the card and being angry at Jordan. Justin calling me this afternoon."

"Sera studying late," Florian said, "night after night. She doesn't feel she's ready. Or she's looking for something."

"Yanni coming to dinner, right after his trip to Novgorod. Talking about Eversnow. Which Patil is going to run. Connection."

"Hicks suddenly giving us all this staff. Which he was prepared to do before I walked in. Which meant he could have prepared to do it before the card ever came up—or only *after* he knew about the card he didn't have—yet—until I gave it to him. Does the card show him some specific danger? Or is he trying to plant a spy on us, by giving us this staff?"

"Sera pulling Justin into the Wing," Catlin said. "She didn't even exit the Wing to talk to Yanni. Yanni came here to talk to her—so she's still regarding our warnings—but she pulled Justin inside our perimeters."

"She may be going out of the Wing more often than the last couple of months, if we have this new security staff," Florian said. "That exposes her to danger. Would Hicks want that?"

"We're about to have domestic staff down in prep," Catlin said. "That's an exposure."

"Hicks seemed to relax once he had the card. He seemed more friendly. That's an emotional assessment. He's a born-man. He has authority, despite what we hear about the office. And he is cooperating."

"So what do we conclude?" Catlin asked. "That something's moving, one. Jordan's stirred up, Justin is, Reseune-Sec is, that's two. And we still don't know what Eversnow and Patil have to do with anybody."

"Something's moving," Florian agreed, "and once we have more staff, sooner or later sera's going to be going outside the perimeter we've established."

"We've just got to watch out for her. It's all we can do."

"And follow up on Justin and this card."

"Sera won't like it," Catlin said. "But we have to."

"Justin Warrick is the one piece we *can* move. We have to. Or we have to ask Yanni about Patil and the card, and I don't think he'll tell us the truth."

"Do you think Hicks will tell us the truth, once he has an answer about the card?"

"Emotional assessment. No. Not for free. So I don't want to ask, officially, not while we don't know who talked to Jordan, and why he gave Justin that card."

Catlin heaved a sigh and put her arms around him. He put his around her. They had sex, purely a tension-reliever, mutual release, mutual pleasure. Afterward Catlin said, side by side on the same pillow:

"At least we'll have help on staff."

"We'll have more to do for a while, watching the watchers. Being sure Hicks isn't our problem."

"Good news, if he is being honest. And if his staff is. And we know there's danger outside. But we've been shut in the Wing so long there's risk of sera losing touch with outside. Isolating herself from Reseune—from Novgorod—she can't afford that. She has to go outside sooner or later. That's coming. We just have to be sure of our own staff. That's basic."

"True." He shut his eyes and relaxed with his partner, a long sigh flowing out of him. They could rest, the few hours of someone else's watch—Marco and Wes took the night shift in the Wing One office. Those two, they could trust.

They did know at least Justin Warrick was safer than he had been, thanks to them getting him into a new office.

The question was whether they might have opened another window for an attack on sera, by letting Justin in—and yet another by accepting Hicks's offer. There were very many, very skilled people they were letting into the wing.

Catlin objected to things. Catlin was always suspicious, and Catlin had agreed with him in this. He wished she'd seen a major problem up front . . . because the transition to outside made him very, very uneasy.

MAY 1, 2424
2000H

Eleven weeks, and Giraud, and Abban AB, and Seely AS would each one easily fit in the circle of an adult's thumb and forefinger, and that was after the latest growth spurt. They didn't weigh as much as a lab mouse. But their bones were forming, and their teeth were starting. They had the beginnings of a breathing apparatus, that floor of the rib cage, the diaphragm, which prepared them to draw breath. They were transparent, full of blood vessels, paths for the blood which had definite structure. Their fingers and toes were starting to grow in length. Legs grew longer. And they moved their whole bodies. They stretched, widely, and often, asserting their presence in the world.

MAY 1, 2424
2123H

I'm different than the first Ari, first young Ari, so far as I can figure, in one very major way: it was her Maman who drove her so hard, not Denys Nye, and she never loved her mother. I had Jane Strassen to take care of me, and I loved her very much. I expected to love people. The first Ari didn't. The first Ari was very much solo throughout her life, but I have my friends, and I even liked Giraud Nye at the last—and he protected me, though I don't think I'll ever forgive Denys—my Denys, remember. Don't let my feelings prejudice yours. Maybe your Denys will turn out nicer. Until I meet him, I won't know.

So there are differences. Sometimes I worry about that. I don't know if I've turned out as bright as the first Ari. She was really good with computers and her Florian was, and I'm still not, though I suppose I'll learn, and I know Florian's studying, and he's getting into programming as fast as he has time for. So I'm working very hard to absorb what she knew on a whole lot of fronts at once. I'm studying how Admin works and who's responsible to whom. The thing the first Ari was incredibly good with, psychsets, I study really hard—I've dropped five kilos just from the study this last month, and I can't eat enough to keep up with the weight loss. But the harder I study, the more I just keep seeing a maze of possibilities, when it comes to fixing a psychset onto a geneset—and I'm starting to do that job for real. I'm confident operating at the gamma level, but I know I'm not ready to mess with an alpha's sets. And she was capable of that, at my age, which just amazes me.

Understand, I've mostly met the alphas she setted later in her career—the early ones, the older ones, are either dead or assigned out, admin jobs, that sort of thing— except Ollie, who was with Maman. There was Ollie, and he was pretty remarkable—still is: he's running Fargone Station. Maybe she was just that good, that early. Who knows? Maybe I would be, if Yanni let me have a try at alphas. But I just don't want to mess one up, so I'm not arguing with Yanni on that point. I'm starting my work with simpler sets.

I do worry that being overall happier might have taken something vital off my potential. That's yet to prove. If you never hear this, well, I'm not the model someone wants you to follow. But I think I'm intellectually close to the first Ari, despite some detours, and despite the fact I play off a bit. I'm very close to being up with my studies, at the benchmarks she set for me, so I guess it's all right; and if I think about it I'm exceeding some of them. I did start study early. I tend to forget I'm younger than I'm supposed to be by a few years. And I'm close to being able to make my own decisions in the labs, and I know I'm going to be capable of Admin, though I just haven't got the time even to consider actually taking that on, and I really don't want to. I'm so glad Yanni is running things and I don't have to. And anything that suggests there's any problem with Yanni scares me. There's something right now, just a question about the way he's handling Jordan Warrick, and I want to trust him, but I'd be a fool to say I'm not thinking about it, thinking hard. If I had to step in and control Reseune, it would be a major setback for my studies. And I don't want that, and most of all I don't want to lose Yanni, because so much he does is good. And he could even be right.

It's natural he should keep secrets from me. I haven't let him see all I can do. And maybe I should just call him here and ask him outright what he's done or what he thinks he's doing, but I'm just reluctant to do it while Florian and Catlin are investigating things. I could make everything blow up. And that's no good.

For now, Yanni limits what I do, and that's good. He gets the results of my tests, and he's my outside checkup. He says he wants me to keep focused on study precisely so I don't appear in public and disturb people—especially people down in Novgorod—but I think, too, so I don't scattershot my studies. I can do so many things and I'm interested in so many things I sometimes think I could just fly apart. Strassenburg's a toy, in one sense. In another, it's important for me to set that up early, and you'll see why, if you think about it two seconds. And now I have to think about Reseune itself, and find out who's doing what, and how the lines of power run.

I've been far too happy in the last couple of months to be entirely safe. Isn't that a paradox? And I'm frustrated because there are things I can already see skewing off Ari's plan, and I can't fix them without taking authority over things and potentially making things worse—because I'm not as good yet as she was when she set up the parameters of what I think might be going wrong.

Is being able to see trouble coming normal for an eighteen-year-old? It's not normal for an eighteen-year-old to have the power to do what I can do, that's for sure—and just in the rules that govern Reseune, I can do anything right now but make an unchecked decision in the labs. I know I could remove Jordan Warrick. I could have

him killed and no one would find out. Is that normal for
an eighteen-year-old? It's not supposed to be normal for a
civilized being. But I just have to worry if it's normal for
me. I keep thinking—if I got rid of him I could save Yanni,
if Yanni's involved in anything he shouldn't be.

And the choice not to do it may be a mistake on my part,
but I see real problems down the years if I do remove him.

Jordan Warrick's existence may even be important for
me. He's my enemy. And I need one. I need a good, strong
enemy to gather up the people who wish I didn't exist, so I
can keep an eye on the lot. I just can't get distracted from
the possibility he's not my only enemy.

He wants Justin in his control. He'll fight me for Justin.
That makes me mad every time I think about it.

But Mad doesn't think straight. Mad may be honest, but
it doesn't plan well at all.

So I won't give way to Mad.

And I won't kill him. Or replace Yanni. I really don't
want to do things like that. I wonder who put that reluctance into my pyschset. I'm not sure it was ever in the first
Ari's. But I watch impulses like that. I'm telling myself
there's a logical reason I'm reluctant to take extreme measures, as Florian would call it, but I have to be sure it's
a logic structure, and not air castles. Do you know that
expression, air castles? I found it in a book. It's a city without any foundations, a perfect dream without any feet on
the ground. And you don't see the fact there's no connection between it and solid thinking, because you're looking
at how pretty the towers are, instead of the fact there's no
logic supporting them.

Pretty is good. But survivable is important, when real
people are depending for their lives on your logic. And
people do depend on me. I depend on me. I want to live a
long time.

Soon I will have a security unit that will report directly
to Catlin and Florian, and they'll be able to know if there's
any undercurrent anywhere in the world that I need to
know about. I can trust them to come to me if there's anything peculiar going on, anything out of parameters . . .
even in high places.

They're going to be very busy for the next while. Soon

they'll be getting a whole lot of files on all our current problems. And maybe I'll learn things I don't want to hear once they do start reporting on people I know—I wish I could omit that, but I'll have to deal with it when it happens. This was Hicks's idea, Florian tells me. He's the director of ReseuneSec, the post Giraud used to have. And in my worry about people's loyalty, Hicks is one I've wanted to keep an eye on. Now he sends us a gift. Florian says all the people he's sending are clean, so far as he can tell by the manuals. But I'm going to go over the manuals myself: that's going to be instructive. I have to be sure there's nothing in them I can't rely on, once their Contracts are engaged. Yanni won't let me work above gamma, but these people are higher than that, mostly, and if I make a mistake it could be very bad.

That means, among other things, if we find these people are reliable, I can actually get out of this wing and go places on a regular basis—for the first time since Denys died, with minor exceptions. I'll be able to go wherever I want in Reseune, whenever I want, and I'll be so glad of that. I haven't ridden Horse for months: his trainer is taking care of him. I haven't been out to the pond to see the goldfish. I haven't seen the new construction, just the virtuals. Now maybe I can do all those things. I feel as if I haven't been able to breathe for weeks, and now I almost think I might—and yet I have all these worries about Yanni, and Hicks, and the very people who are supposed to be helping Florian and Catlin—not to mention new staff coming into the apartment . . . those are all delayed while we look through their records and check through the tape they've had.

One thing I'm certainly going to do, so when you accede to power, you won't have to go through what I have, and risk what I've risked. My security office may not outlive me—but I'm going to see to it that a security staff inside ReseuneSec is automatically offered to your Florian and your Catlin when you reach your majority, and that you don't have to fight for it or ask for it or wait until someone offers. I very much suspect Denys ordered Giraud to take the first Ari's security apparatus apart when she died, under the excuse it was dangerous to his power. I don't know what circumstances may apply when you're hearing this. But by the time you're making your first steps into *being an adult in charge, you have to have information and a secure perimeter, and you have to have it fast. I was very lucky to have had Yanni, and not somebody much worse than Denys stepping into control of Reseune, or I might not have survived.*

So as soon as Florian and I can manage Base One the way we need to do, I'll be making the reconstitution automatic, embedding various provisions that won't look like they're working together, the pre-training of certain Contracts, with an instruction that will trigger retraining for personnel on a certain date to be set by your circumstances—meaning they'll turn up in your life when the time is right, and assemble themselves, because I'm going to have a direct hand in the tape they get. It's not going to be apparent even to the directors out at the azi facilities that these people and these programs·have any connection with each other. On a given trigger, they'll assemble, and they'll know what to do.

And your Florian and your Catlin will run that office, so that's the explanation of one mystery for you, which you may have already seen in operation. I hope it's a peaceful transition.

I was lucky to survive my teens, and I don't count on luck even once, let alone twice. Thank me for your safety, which will at least be greater than mine, granted I live long enough. And do the same for your successor, and leave notes for her time. Learn how to program Base One, how to really handle it, and get your Florian to: we're running behind on that. I'm able to do the links that surround the segments I'm recording for you, quite honestly because I'm copying what's there on the files she gave me; and I'm making notes; but it's not integrated, yet. It won't run yet the way Ari I and her Florian made it run because I haven't linked the whole structure in yet, just made a chain of unerasable files, to make sure you get my thoughts appropriate to the age I am now, and that I can't edit them, and I really hope you aren't having to excavate those files the hard way.

My office hasn't gotten anything solid for me yet on the ongoing puzzles we're Working. The questions are all still questions. But at least I'm about to refuse to be confined to the Wing and I intend to start asking questions of my own.

May 2, 2424
1342h

Florian opened the office door, and Ari slipped into the space where two men, one extravagantly red-haired, one common brown, were busy earning a living.

Or at least—they'd been trying to.

"Hello!" she said in her brightest tone, and Grant half-turned and raised an eyebrow. Justin swiveled his chair around, leaned back against its auto-adjust, and crossed a foot over his knee.

"Well," he said. "Is it trouble?"

"Oh, never." There wasn't another chair. It wasn't her scheduled day to be here, and she hadn't been in this office ever, though Justin and Grant had moved in nearly a week ago. These two didn't do patient-consultations, and they no longer had staff, nor any room for them, so there was no available chair for a visitor. She had to stand, and simply leaned back against the wall, until Grant, seeing the situation, surrendered his with a small flourish. "You're so sweet," she said, and patted Grant on the arm. "We've got to get other chairs in here. At least one more."

"I'll arrange that," Grant said, and as Florian rotated past the door frame and out into the corridor, Grant left, too, leaving the two of them alone to talk, herself and Justin.

"I so love the idea of your being in the Wing," she said to him.

"It seems safer," Justin said. "So I take it we're not on the current arrest list."

"Don't joke like that. I'm not Denys. I won't *be* Denys."

"I know you're not. Are we revising the schedule for lessons today, or—"

"We're keeping to schedule. I'm sorry I haven't been here this week. I've been studying."

"I thought we agreed you were going to get some rest."

"Well, it's important. I'm onto something."

"What?"

"What we were talking about. The integrations. But I'll talk about that later. Monday."

"Sure. Good." Justin made a gesture toward the other counter. "Coffee?"

"I wouldn't mind that, thank you." She watched as he got up and poured a cup. Her stomach suddenly said empty. "You wouldn't have a biscuit, would you?"

"As a matter of fact, we do," Justin said, as he opened a packet and laid a tea-biscuit on a paper saucer. And another for good measure. He gave her that saucer with the coffee. "The place came stocked."

"I really hope you like the office."

"I'm getting used to it."

She regarded Justin's first office with deep nostalgia. She remembered slipping by and giving him a gift of guppies. They hadn't lived.

Those days had seemed so much safer. She'd been out and about, unwatched, or she'd had the illusion she'd been unwatched—and never likely was. And he wasn't there anymore.

She washed down a biscuit in two bites and a sip and tried to put the past out of her mind. "Mmm. I had breakfast. But I've been studying a lot and I know I'm getting skinny, and you're right, and I'm reforming. I'm taking on real work this week, just a couple of projects. I've told Labs to let me run checks and I'll actually do a theta design. I'm sure they're going to have someone go over it. But I don't think they'll find mistakes."

"I doubt they will."

A second biscuit went down. That freed a hand to reach into her jacket pocket. "Here." She handed him the data stick she'd brought. "I've looked at it. I want you to."

"What?" Justin looked amused. "You can do that. I've no doubt you can do it."

"Not the theta stuff. These are staff. All sorts of staff. They'll be mine. I want you to look them over and make sure there aren't any bombs."

His face went sober, thoughtful as he picked up the

stick. He gave her a look, like he wanted to ask a question, and maybe thought it wasn't wise to ask it at all.

"I trust you," she said. It wouldn't make him easier in his mind. She read him that well. He'd been through too much with Denys. He'd just had the row with his father and he knew Admin was upset. He was in a state of disturbance and flux, unable to settle, either physically or mentally, and he probably wasn't getting a lot of work done. "I need it really soon."

He nodded somberly and laid the data stick atop the books on his desk. "I'll put it at the top of my list."

"I know about the card," she said, and saw his face suddenly go cold and wary. He wasn't looking at her. Wasn't looking at anything in particular. "I'm sorry you got into it," she said, and he still didn't look at her. "What do *you* think your father's up to?"

"I haven't a clue." He did look her way, and the hard face gave way to the old Justin, the very worried Justin, who had stood off Uncle Denys—confronting *her*, now, as the prevailing threat in his life, *and* his hope of tranquility. "I really haven't."

"You know he's under surveillance. He knows he is. He's mad about it. I'm really sorry, Justin. I'm sorry he did that."

He was upset. And the look was a little less protected, a little more the real Justin, worried, and on his guard. "Do you know what it's about?" he asked her flat out . . . maybe a little ashamed to be asking. She read that. Ashamed of the situation with his father. Ashamed of *having* to ask an outsider to the relationship.

"My staff is trying to find out," she said quietly. "I don't really know what it's about. He's not that easy to read. But I'd say he didn't expect you to keep that card a secret."

"I'm sure of that much," he said.

She wanted to ask—what do *you* want me to do with Jordan? But that wouldn't be fair to ask, and the hurt would outlast the good it would do. Justin would never forgive himself, not inside, if he asked her to send Jordan away. In a technical way, neither of them had had real parents. In an emotional way, they'd both lost the single parent they'd been most attached to. They were alike, on that one emotional sore point. Something had happened, when Jordan handed Justin that card, and they had to patch it up, and try to bring back the even tenor of the lessons, the conferences, the work together. It wasn't going to happen automatically. Jordan had already had that effect—Jordan, and the twitch of security, proving it was still alive.

"I'm trying to protect him from himself," she said. "He's certainly not making it easy."

Score. She saw it in his expression, just the little dilation of the iris. "I appreciate that."

"This Dr. Patil," she said. "I can tell you something about that. We're going to send her to Fargone. She's the authority in her field—she's certainly got the credentials. But we're digging into her associations, all the way back. Just so you know what that was about."

"I'm not sure I want to know more than that."

"Justin, I'm not in charge of Reseune. I won't be, for a while. But you know I direct some decisions. Yanni listens to me."

"I'm sure he does."

"Don't be like that. I'm not your enemy."

"I don't want you to be," he said plainly. "I hope you won't be."

"Jordan wants me to be your enemy."

And his eyes averted, his whole body posture changing, as if he had to re-balance his thinking.

"Does he?" she asked flatly. "Or what do *you* think his motive is?"

Justin didn't say anything for a moment. His hand found the datastick atop the books, picked it up, turned it over. And over. And set it down, not looking at her. "I don't know why you ask my opinion on this," he said, and let a long breath go. "I don't know why you need it."

"I need it," she said. "I do need it."

"No, you don't. You're good. The hell you're working routine theta sets, you're *good.*"

"So are you," she said. "You're *too* good to go along with something even he didn't plan to have work. You know what he's really up to."

"Then I wish *you'd* tell *me* what that is!"

"I just did."

"God." He did turn his face toward her, upset. "Dammit, Ari."

"I'm being honest. *I* want you to be all right. I really do. I don't mind you getting along with Jordan. But he certainly minds your getting along with me. That's what it's about, isn't it? Am I wrong? His battles are all old history. The Centrists lost a lot of their power when we passed the anti-terraforming bills and saved Cyteen's native life. They lost this world to develop. So some not-very-bright people in that party thought they were going to get their way when Ari died. But Giraud didn't let them repeal those laws. Giraud was friendly with Defense and that blocked them. And now there's Yanni, telling them they've got just a little time to make deals before I come in. Eversnow is a poor second choice, but it's what the pro-terraformers have got."

"Eversnow."

"It's a planet out beyond Fargone—"

"I know that."

"Well, Patil's in charge of terraforming it, and that's a secret, so don't tell it. If certain people think they can bring that snowball to life without wrecking it, well, they might, mightn't they, but then, that's not a very Centrist position for Corain's people to be stuck in, a dozen light years from anything civilized, and no longer in the center of anything. It's not their kind of territory. They want cities. They want Earth remade in a temperate world that's central to everything, with all of Union clustered around it, and they want it fast. Well, fast won't happen there. It's going to take a long time, and we'll be changing the Centrists, right along with Eversnow. People that go out there will belong there. Or their children will. That's the way things work."

"You're losing me. Eversnow. Not Fargone."

"Fargone's just a cover."

"I'm not sure I want to know these things. I'm not sure Yanni would be happy with my knowing these things."

"Oh, pretty soon more people inside Reseune are going to know it. We're just not putting it on the news until it launches. That's why security's all stirred up about this card."

"You think Jordan could have had any contact with a

secret some professor in Novgorod is up to? I thought you monitored his phone calls."

"Not any current contact, no, he doesn't have. But then he never cared whether it was Centrists or Expansionists he was supporting, so long as it gave his Ari grief, do you think? She was all his focus. Whatever she wanted, he was against, once that partnership split up. And the fight between them wasn't ever really about Cyteen, or Eversnow, or Alpha or Beta or Fargone or terraforming or any station in the whole universe, for that matter. Reseune was everything. He wanted to leave it, but he didn't, not in his head. And now he's back, but Reseune after Denys isn't the place he remembers. So it's not a happy situation, and he's not dealing well with the changes he finds here. That's what I think."

"That, I'll entirely agree with."

"I can't make him happy. You can't."

Justin heaved a long sigh. "You're right about that." And then looked at her: "You just gave me that information on Patil to track whether or not I'd let it leak."

"I know you won't. You're good on other things I've told you."

A small, sorrowful laugh. "No, I'm not likely to. Lack of opportunity, maybe. I'm not in anyone's social circles. So I take it you're wondering if I'll be crazy and take it to Jordan."

"Florian was right in what he did: you needed to be out of Jordan's reach unless *you* initiate the contact."

Justin muttered something under his breath, and pushed the data stick in a circle, where it lay. "I won't ask you for favors. I know your security requirements. I know they're justified. I won't become a problem to you."

"I couldn't replace you," she said. "I really couldn't."

He gave a short laugh. "Seems that's what we do here, isn't it?"

"Not in my lifetime. I'd miss you terribly. I really would. I've lost a lot of people I relied on."

"Giraud. Denys." That was a gibe. Giraud hadn't been one of his favorite people. Denys wasn't one of hers.

"My mother," she said, matching dark for dark.

Lips tightened, and he didn't look at her when he said, bitterly: "My father."

"Right now," she said soberly, "one of my worst problems is that I can't be absolutely sure that Denys didn't install some feature in the systems that just hasn't gone off yet. Right now security has me completely walled in, same as you, because they can't figure what else to do with me. Same as you. But that's going to change, starting with my getting a security presence that's mine, no one else's. I'll have a much longer reach and a way of knowing what's going on that I don't have now. I'll be able to protect myself if I can trust it. And maybe if I'm safer, it can change things for your father—if he calms down. If you can talk him toward common sense. He took my gift and got off the plane looking for a fight, with Yanni, with me . . ."

"With everyone. No question of that." A small silence, Justin looking hallward, in Grant's general direction, then back. "I'll talk to him, best I can. *When* we talk. I'm not meeting with him until he calms down."

"Tranquilizer in his coffee might be a good idea."

He laughed, shortly. "Coming from someone who could actually do it."

"It wouldn't be real peace." She got up. "You've got work to do, and I'm bothering you. Let me know what you think of those sets as soon as you can. It's a priority. I'll be back for a lesson Monday afternoon."

"Will do," he said, and she walked outside, where Grant and Florian waited, not in conversation.

"I think I'm going to have a small dinner party tonight," she said to Grant, "just Justin and you, Jordan and Paul. What do you think?"

"You may have to send security to bring Jordan."

"Maybe not," she said. Jordan was rather like a bomb with a motion switch: thus far, she'd hesitated to jostle him. If you were going to Work someone you needed a good hook, and a theory had begun to gel. Jordan wanted dominance, wasn't well socialized, had to be the center of attention, but didn't like to be talked at by fools, because there wasn't an ounce of tolerance in him. He couldn't tolerate, say, a cocktail party, or someone who bored him for a minute. But his curiosity suffered in that isolation of his, the engine of that curiosity being a very keen intellect. She'd gotten that much long-distance—that and the fact he was Justin's twin as well as his father . . . Justin had been very much his twin until the first Ari ran an intervention and set a broad streak of insecurity into Justin's pattern: insecurity, a strong sex drive, and self-doubt.

The first two, Jordan certainly had. Self-doubt was the big difference, self-doubt in Justin that constantly put out feelers toward other people, constantly checked the environment and analyzed it, all with a high emotional charge. It hadn't made Justin more brilliant than Jordan, but it had made him much, much more social, much more reachable.

She had the entire record of that encounter. It was hard to deal with. It told her what the first Ari could do: it told her what *she* could turn into. It told her the Ari who'd fought with Jordan had had some of Jordan's characteristics—and tolerance of a rival hadn't been high in the first Ari's own list of qualities. The first Ari had actually tried . . . she'd tried very hard to work with Jordan. But he'd wanted to dominate their partnership and she *absolutely* had wanted to run things, as natural as breathing. What kept bringing the first Ari back, she suspected, what might even have sexually fascinated her, was the fact that she hadn't been able to Work him: that would have kept her mentally engaged with him. The fact she hadn't been about to work *with* him—that was the thorn in the arrangement. The same terrible boredom had afflicted the first Ari: the first Ari had shared that trait of impatience with Jordan, but, unlike Jordan, the first Ari would at times tolerate fools— would analyze them, and use them, sometimes ruthlessly. *Challenge* set her off, challenge that would rouse her out of her boredom—so even that thorn in the arrangement might have been just one more attraction. She met challenge: she provoked it, enjoyed it until it potentially threatened her, and then she absolutely crushed it.

There was an extreme watch-it in that mix, wasn't there?

A very extreme watch-it, for Jordan and for herself . . . because that *challenge* thing stirred something so visceral in her. It did, and she tried to keep the anger in it down. She could tolerate parties. She had friends—Sam, and Amy and Maddy, that she didn't see nearly often enough

these days. She valued people like Justin, who'd disagree
with her. She valued him extremely. She defined *challenge*
as a threat to people she loved. And that was different than
the first Ari, wasn't it? She didn't let a challenge to her as
what she was . . . become personal. Anger was the bad part
of it, and she kept that way back, bottled, stoppered, and
far back on the shelf.

She walked on her way, saying nothing to Florian at
first, knowing Catlin had heard the exchange with Grant,
too, and both her bodyguards knew that what she wanted
was ultimately what would happen, even if her staff didn't
like it. Scary notion, a supper with Justin and Jordan, in
her hitherto off-limits premises. Deliciously, excitingly
scary. Maybe stupid. But she wasn't sure it wasn't smart.

She'd been patient, she'd been so good, but she was close
to freedom, was what, and, out in the wide world, things
were all of a sudden happening that she didn't like. With
that gift of security personnel from ReseuneSec, if they
passed Justin's scrutiny as well as hers and Florian's, she
established a presence inside Reseune Security. And once
she had that, she'd know things; she'd know when it was
safe to go somewhere, and she'd know when she needed to
deal with a situation. She'd be much less reliant on others
filtering what got to her attention . . . like secret meetings
in Novgorod.

Interesting, what she felt. Aggression was part of her
motives: she recognized that when it reared its head, and it
was potent. The challenge impulse. Curiosity. Much more
than Justin was Jordan, she *was* the first Ari. It felt good to
go on the attack in this long waiting. It felt very good.

That was a suspect emotion, too. She was having strong
reactions to this news about more freedom; she was having emotional reactions to the business with the card and
someone having told Jordan about Patil, and at least part
of what Patil was up to.

Endocrine thinking, she said to herself. The first Ari
consistently warned her about that, told her do something
to get rid of it. Sex could work, if it was a passing urge. But
that just touched off more flux-thinking, and sometimes
complicated things worse than before. Rational thought
was the long-term cure for problems.

That was what the first Ari had said, out of Base One.
Steady down. Think.

Florian asked quietly, as they walked: "What are we to
expect tonight, sera?"

"I don't quite know," she said, still wondering if she'd
just done something very unwise. But something to break
the stalemate between Justin and Jordan once and for
all—was that unwise? "Something interesting, at least."

BOOK ONE   Section 3   Chapter iv

MAY 2, 2424
1528H

Maybe, she still thought, she should have been a little less
aggressive, and a little more cautious. Justin wouldn't turn
down her invitation, if his father was going. She was relatively sure of that: he'd be there partly out of unbearable
curiosity, partly to be there to fling himself between his
father and a bullet, so to speak—or literally. Jordan would
be there out of pure curiosity, and because he wanted to
hear what calumnies his son would say about him—she'd
bet on that, even more than she'd bet on Justin.

So she sent an invitation to Jordan that said dinner at
1800h. And one to Justin that said 1830h. Justin would
turn up five minutes early because he worried about being
late. Jordan was guaranteed to be at least a quarter of an
hour late, just to prove he could be. She bet on that, too.

Her staff was not happy with the arrangement. Wes
and Marco were taking the security station, Florian and
Catlin were dining early, to be actually on duty in the dining room. Gianni, their pro tem cook, was in a state, and
dented one of their pots. The unprecedented clang set off
house alarms and scrambled her security to alert.

But she dressed in silvery satin, her current favorite
gown, and her hairdresser did her hair in a modern way,
nothing at all like the first Ari in the portraits. It was her

coming-out, like in the old stories, though not for a ball-
room full of people—just two. She wore her hair upswept,
wore a single diamond, a modest one, and her rings, several,
and had the servers light the candles the very instant Jordan
turned up in the hall—no way could he look at a quarter of
an hour's candle-melt and feel smug in being late.

Marco showed her first guests into the hall and took
their coats . . . precisely at 1816h. Ari met him just outside
the dining room.

"Jordan Warrick," she said in her nicest, warmest tone,
and offered her hand. "I'm so glad you've come. Paul."
That for the quiet, handsome man who shadowed him.

"Ariane." Jordan took her hand, a chilly and unenthusi-
astic grip, and what he was seeing, or remembering in that
moment, there was no telling: certain things weren't in the
first Ari's records, lost, lost except for this man's memory.
"Is my son here?"

"Soon, I'm sure. Would you like a drink?" Service staff
was hovering just inside. And Catlin moved in, very deftly,
to cut Paul off with conversation and steer him aside.

"You always made a good vodka Collins."

"*I* don't." She flashed her brightest grin, and signaled
staff. "I haven't the least idea how. A Collins, Callie. Paul?"
She glanced over her shoulder. "What will you have?"

"Wine, sera, white."

"Wine for me, too. I had my juvie fling with hard liquor.
It does my head no favors. I'm so glad you came, Jordan."

What are you up to? was likely the question he burned
to ask her. He didn't. "Invitations are rare. I'm a little out
of the social circuit these days."

"Well, there hasn't been much social circuit lately, not
since Denys died. It's all been too grim here. Guards everywhere. Locked doors. Minders on high alert. But that's
changing. I'll imagine a lot of things changed."

"Some have. Some haven't."

"Oh, Catlin, do entertain Paul. I'm aching to talk to
Jordan a moment. Jordan, do come into the dining room.
Please." She snagged his arm, moved him, solo, the two
further steps through that doorway. "I'm so curious about
you," she said brightly. He was warm, and smelled like Justin. "There aren't many people in my acquaintance who

really remember from way back, way back when everything was starting up in Reseune."

An eyebrow lifted as she let go his arm. He looked at her, just like Justin. "I'm not that old."

"But you did actually meet my sort-of grandmother."

"I did."

"Was she really the bitch everybody says she was?"

That got a little flare of the pupils, and an immediately suspicious shutdown, no laughter at all. "I never knew her personally. But she was reputed to be that. *And* passed the trait on."

She took that with a silent laugh. And just then Callie showed up with the drinks, damn her timing, but she took hers and let Jordan take his own. "I know about your feud with the first Ari. Two very bright people trying to work together. Two people who each *had* to run things."

That didn't sit totally well. "You could say so."

"She valued you, though, as the most brilliant designer in Reseune, right along with her. She couldn't get along with you, you weren't in the same field, exactly, but she did respect you."

"The hell."

"I have her notes. She also warned me you were pigheaded." Sip of wine. Jordan hadn't touched his Collins. "Is it all right?"

"What?"

"The drink. Did Callie do it right?"

Jordan just looked at her.

"You surely," she said, "can't think I'd pull something as silly as that."

"You did on my son."

Wide eyes. *"What* did I do?"

"You know what your predecessor did."

Lowered lashes, a nod to the correction. "I know what she did. I'm sorry for that."

"Of course you are."

"I don't like what she did, understand. I don't like what happened to you, either. Let me tell you the truth. Uncle Denys thought he was going to make me into his own model. But he didn't. I came out something else, and not liking him much at all, especially for what he did to Justin.

And the way you couldn't work with the first Ari, I *can* work with Justin. I don't ever want it otherwise. I just wish you could be part of that arrangement."

A sardonic smile. "Is that so?"

She drew in a breath. "You're going to see it doesn't work, aren't you?"

"That's your conclusion? You have us bugged, you have my office bugged, you have our apartment bugged, including the bedroom. And that's the best guess you can manage? I'd have thought you understood us inside out."

"Who's Dr. Patil to you?"

Ah. He didn't control that look, not well at all. She'd got him mad, and she got a reaction.

"Friend of a friend. Someone I'd like my son to know, outside the cloistered halls of Reseune. Is that a crime?"

Florian walked into the dining room. That was the arranged cue: Justin was arriving.

She smiled. "Denys would have thought it was a crime. *He* was your enemy. *He* set you up. *He* blamed you and made your son's years here—and mine—more difficult than you know. I doubt Justin's told you the half of it. You should ask him."

The front door opened, a hall away.

"When," Jordan asked, "am I going to get that chance?"

"Not over tonight's dinner, I hope." She put on her warm smile again. "Let's make peace, just for the hour. I can't offer you explanations on everything, but I'd like to see things work themselves out. I'd like to know the things you know about my grandmother. I can't call the first Ari my mother, really, not the way Justin can call you his father. It wasn't, obviously, that kind of relationship."

"Being posthumous, you mean? Have it straight: she had it coming. I didn't kill her, but I'd like to have."

Oh, good shot. Just as Justin and Grant showed up at the dining room door. She smiled at Jordan and laid a hand on his arm.

"You *are* everything I expected. Hello there, Justin, Grant. Delighted you could make it. Would you like a drink?"

"Vodka on ice," Justin said with a worried glance at Jordan. "H'lo, *Dad*."

"You're late," Jordan said.

"Am I?" It was a question whether Justin would come out with his version of the time he'd been told to arrive; but he was a survivor of the secretive Nye years, and he simply said, "I guess so."

"Grant?"

"The same, thank you, sera," Grant said. "Ser. Paul." Paul had come into the room with Catlin. "Good evening."

"Good evening," Jordan said darkly.

"Why don't we sit down?" Ari suggested with a wave at the table. There were flowers, and the lit candles. Staff had done their best on very short notice. She took the host's seat at the end, and let her guests sort things out—Grant and Paul would settle farthest away. There was no endmost seat, just the service cart for the drinks, and that left Justin and Jordan one on a side—Florian and Catlin stayed standing, and Callie, who was being bartender, offered the requested cocktails, and prepared a bottle of wine and another of water, while staff hurried around in the hall beyond—a little unpracticed in formal service, but doing their best.

"How do you like your office?" Jordan asked Justin.

"More convenient to the apartment," Justin answered, stepping neatly around that one.

"And how are you liking being back in your office?" Ari asked, as if she were completely oblivious to the undercurrent. "It won't have changed much, will it?"

"A little barren," Jordan said. "But I'm sure the walls are well-populated."

"Jordan," Justin said under his breath.

"I really don't blame your father for missing you," Ari said. "But it's regulations, Jordan. Justin's on restricted projects. No one's objecting to his being there, or you, but it's the stuff he works with. I don't know if he felt clear to explain that, but that's a fact. You *could* apply for a security clearance."

"There's a waste of time," Jordan muttered. He was at the bottom of his Collins, nursing the last out of the ice. "Let's go back to honesty. There's not going to be a clearance granted. There's already an investigation going on. —You gave her that card, didn't you?"

The last sailed across the table, at Justin, as Callie set the requested vodka down by his hand.

"It was a little obvious, Dad. I don't know what else you expected."

Ari smiled tightly. "Of course it was. And I'm sure it's an inconvenience to Dr. Patil, whoever she is. I'm sure you know that."

"And *I'm* sure," Jordan said, "you know damned well who she is."

"I'm learning," Ari said. "She must have really annoyed you."

Jordan rotated his empty glass, frowning at Justin.

"And why do you assume," Ari asked, "that you're not going to get your clearance back? Don't you want it back? Or is your whole aim to assure you don't? There could certainly be several reasons for that."

"And we aren't even to the first course yet," Justin said. "Can we save this for dessert?"

"It's not my choice," Jordan said.

"Many things are," Ari said, and smiled, and signaled the servers. "But Justin's right. Let's enjoy dinner."

"We may not need dessert," Justin said, as the salad course went down. "Nice."

"Let's love each other for at least three courses," Ari said, smiling at Jordan. "How is your work going, Jordan? I think you and I are about at the same stage—deepstudy until our eyes cross. I'm trying to get started and you're trying to span the gap."

"It's not that big a gap," Jordan said defensively, and had a bite of salad, while service poured the first wine.

"Of course there's a lot I have to learn. Justin's going to cross-check me on my theta sets. Would *you* like to, just to get back in the game?"

Jordan frowned, probably looking for a stinger somewhere in that offer. "Might be interesting."

Curiosity, curiosity. He couldn't turn down actual information, and seeing how she worked, compared to her predecessor, was a question. "Delighted," she said. "I'll be interested in any criticism."

"I'll imagine you're quite precocious."

"I've been told so from the start. I'm really trying to make peace, here. And I really am interested in your input."

"I'll bet you are."

"Dad . . ."

"Oh, I know she is. She still can learn some things. I'm sure she's no more omniscient than the first model. She hasn't gotten as argumentative yet, by half. But that will come, I'm sure."

"It might come earlier if she has to deal with too many disagreeable dinner guests."

"Oh," Jordan said, "are we taking sides now?"

"Neighbors," Ari said with a smile. "Thank you, Justin. But don't worry. Good minds make interesting conversation. And I think Jordan is very interesting."

They made it through the salad, even into the main course, which was pasta and imported sausage, with marinara and real cheese.

"Must say the food's better here than Planys," Jordan said.

"I'll relay the compliment," Ari said. "Thank you. — Were you able to get out of the labs there, Jordan? Did you see anything of the countryside at all?"

"Damn barren," Jordan said in his conversation-stopping way. "No, we weren't offered tours. There weren't even views. One window in the main office, for the secretaries. None for the rest of your favored guests."

"There's no reason for that," Ari said. "There ought to be views. I don't know why there weren't."

"Maybe they thought giving us a view of the landscape would guide us when we made a break for it."

Across desert where there weren't even precip stations. Where the waste of the labs and residences had to be carefully processed, every iota of foreign life eradicated, so it wouldn't destroy the native micro-fauna, and contaminate the other continent. When planes flew between the main continent and Planys, they decontaminated the landing gear and the hulls and sprayed down the inside . . . because they had a world where, unlike old Earth, unlike Pell, there were two distinct ecologies, two landmasses that hadn't drifted close enough to mix for eons, where there were two circulating currents either side of a high oceanic ridge, and where the only thing that flew was vegetative, most of which wouldn't survive in the opposing environment—what floated or swam could get there, but that was all. Massive ankyloderms cruised the subsurface, occasionally making a nuisance of themselves; over here it was the other kind of subsurface creature, the platythere, and both of them turned their feeding-grounds to desert.

"So you never did see an anklyoderm," she said, ignoring the barb.

"Never did," he said.

"I'd like to," she said.

"They don't surface as often as the platytheres," Jordan said. "So I understand. In great detail. The ankyloderm guy there is a complete spacecase. You should have to listen to him on the topic. And we did, interminably. They had a guest lecture program. We were all supposed to get to understand each other. All damn useless."

"Who *did* you associate with?" Ari asked.

The habitual frown went a shade deeper. "You want other targets for your people to investigate?"

"Dr. Thieu?"

"Thieu's a dodderer."

"That's how you got Patil's card, isn't it? Is that the friend you referenced?"

Jordan went as hard as deep ice.

"They corresponded," Paul said, out of the quiet.

"You with Patil?"

"Thieu with Patil," Jordan snapped. "And I'm sure security knows it. Why is everyone in such a flap?"

"Security just hates it when their compartments leak," Ari said. "Especially where it threatens the biosphere. Especially when it'd be so easy for some lunatic to contaminate, say, the Planys reserve. Nanisms could run riot—if they were tailored for it. The Centrists would get their way completely . . . no reason, then, to stop their pet project."

"Not my field," Jordan said with a shrug. "Ask Thieu. Nanisms have nothing to do with me."

"Except the card."

"I thought we were waiting for dessert."

"I think we're ready for dessert," Ari said, laying her fork down. "Are you?"

"I think I've had enough."

"Dad."

"Damn it," Jordan said, banging his fork down and looking straight at Justin. "Pick your side and stay with it."

"Politics doesn't mean a thing to you," Justin said. "You used to say it was all nonsense. Pick your side, you said, and use it for all the use it can be to you."

"Thank you," Jordan said, "for that reminder of basic principles."

"Dessert," Ari said cheerfully, and waved a signal at service. Florian and Catlin hadn't moved from where they stood, facing her, a perfect, black-clad and elegant set, Florian the dark one, Catlin the bright, and neither face ever showing an expression. Dessert came through the door between them, a confection of light pastry and egg cream.

"Looks good," Grant said, as cheerfully—and doubtless wishing he could get himself away from the argument. Things hadn't been said, outright. Yet.

"Coffee, ser?" Callie was back, bearing a silver pot, making the rounds. It was a good, rich coffee, not synthetic, which complimented the egg cream—real egg cream, too. They got the best from the AG unit. Chickens, the one bird allowed onworld, were a definite plus, bred for centuries to be plump, nonseasonal, and flightless.

"Nice," Justin said, after a bite.

"So did that card come from outside," Ari asked, "or was it printed from transmission?"

"Transmission, far as I know," Jordan said. "But I could be wrong. Thieu gave it to me and said contact the woman, give her his regards, old colleagues and all—I told you he's a dodderer. His rejuv is going. He's sometimes on, sometimes not."

Transmission suggested no physical card had gotten to Planys . . . or broken quarantine. Hence nothing more sinister had gotten to Planys, either, or had gotten from Planys to the larger continent. It indicated that Jordan had done what he'd done solely as a means of agitating security *and* his son. She was sure Justin could add that equation. The remaining question was whether the reassuring story was the truth at all.

"I knew damned well I'd make trouble for Patil if I called her," Jordan said, after a bite. "Or if I mentioned her name while I was sure we were bugged. So I just handed the card on to my thoughtful son, who created a hell of a lot of trouble."

"Bugged and watched, Dad. We always are. For our protection, our *legal* protection as well as physical."

"It wasn't that way in my time here. But you've gotten used to it. Adapted, clearly. Nice dessert."

"Thank you," Ari said, taking another, delicate spoonful. So they at least had a story to explain the card, true or half-true or no relation to the truth at all—and truthers were running. They had the card, physically, which had either come, illegally, from Planys, or which had gone, illegally, from Novgorod *to* Planys before coming to them. Contaminants of the sort Patil worked on could use a small, small vector. Protecting the ecosphere was, very unfortunately for the ecosphere, still a political debate. Centrists might not like the idea of wholesale adaptation of the human psyche to other worlds, but they still wanted to obliterate all native life on this one, and being human, wouldn't ultimately stop with one world, no matter what they argued, if they turned out to need something just out of current reach. It wasn't just a debating difference. It was a profoundly different future in that debate.

And Jordan had said to Justin, once in the long ago, choose the side that's useful . . . while the first Ari had said, in her tapes—watch out for Jordan.

"So you don't take any side but your own," Ari said to Jordan. "When everybody else has a theory about what humanity should be, you're completely without opinion."

"I'm not God," Jordan shot back. "And I don't theorize from that vantage. Let events and biology decide."

"That's sort of a Centrist opinion."

A bite. "This week, it is," Jordan said. "Stand by. It'll change."

"You're interesting," Ari said.

"I'm so flattered."

Justin just gave an exasperated sigh and stabbed the pastry.

"I think we should do this from time to time," Ari said. "You're sort of family, you know."

"In what possible sense?" Jordan shot back. "Family, in the sense you've gone to bed with my son?"

"No," Justin said shortly. A muscle jumped in his jaw.

"Denys was my family after he exiled Maman," she said. "Yanni sort of is, now. But I don't know what to do without a disagreeable uncle. So I pick you. You can succeed Denys."

"I'm not honored," Jordan said, and ate the last bite of his dessert.

"You don't have to be *like* Denys, you know."

That got a dark, naked stare, all the way to the bottom. "You little devil," Jordan said. "You little devil."

Got to him. Found a button.

"I'm not," she said. "I'm just Ari. The new model. You were almost partners, you and the first Ari. Justin and I already *are*, at least as much as you two ever were. You're my disagreeable uncle, whether or not you're Denys."

"Denys killed her."

"I'm pretty sure he did," she said. "And he as good as killed you. The question is whether you can recover from that. Maybe you can. We'll see."

"The devil," he said, and drank the last of his coffee. "I think we've had the discussion. I trust I can leave this place."

"Of course you can," she said. "Paul. I'm glad you came." She pushed back from the table. Justin and Grant did. She wondered if they would leave the apartment with Jordan and Paul and walk them to the doors of Wing One, or make a maneuver so as *not* to leave in that company.

"Thank you, sera," Paul said, pro forma. Trust azi manners to try to force a calm over the situation.

"Thank you for the evening," Jordan said with a small, tight smile. "It was very informative."

"It was, very," she said, and offered her hand. "I'm so glad you could come."

"Nothing much better to do." He took her hand briefly, as chill a grip as before, nothing like Justin's. "Good night." And to Justin, a look shot past her to the other door: "I suppose you're staying."

"No," Justin said, "but good night, Jordan."

Letting Jordan walk out with Paul and the door shut, Justin put on his coat very slowly, while Grant waited.

"I needed to know," she said in that artificial pause. Toward Justin and Grant, she felt an impulse of remorse. "I'm terribly sorry. I hoped, not too rationally, that it might go better than this."

"You gave us different arrival times," Justin said. "You set the tone."

"I tried to set it better than it turned out," she said.

"I don't think anything was ever out of control," Justin said darkly, implying, she read it, that things had gone just the way she wanted. She shook her head to that.

"Remember he's somebody the first Ari couldn't Work," she said. "She couldn't handle him, or everything would have gone better than it did. She really did want him to work with her. But he wouldn't share, and she couldn't change him."

That got a thoughtful look, a long and thoughtful look. "I wasn't so hard a target."

"For her? No. You were young. You were as young as I am now."

"I don't think you've had the chance to be," he said, "not that young. Not that stupid. I was, once. At an absolutely emotional pitch, caught between her and him. I don't like that territory. I don't intend to go there again."

"I don't want you to," she said, and kept her hand off his arm, much as the urge was there to touch, to plead, even, for a kinder look. "Justin, I asked you here because I didn't want to meet him and have any question in your mind what we said."

"And because he'd have exploded if I wasn't here. A whole complex of reasons. I get them."

"I hope you get all of them," she said, "because they add up to my doing this because I'd like to stop this upset, and I don't want you ever having to do things like give Florian that card."

He looked at her a long moment. "I'd be as glad not to have to. I'd be as glad to live under a regime where that's not an issue."

"I'm trying. I'm honestly trying. Those sets you're going over—a lot of those *are* my security. Or they're going to be."

"I had an idea they were, from the skill-sets involved."

"Don't give me anybody I can't rely on. Help me set this up right this time."

. "As if you can't read them yourself."

"I do. I have. But I *want* a partner. I want backup. A double-check. I do." This time she did touch him, gently, briefly. "Justin, I need you. Maybe the first Ari didn't need your father as much: she didn't need people. But I do. I want people. I like people. I don't even mind people who argue with me. Jordan's all right, Justin. He really is, or he would be, if he could just stop short of trying to take over."

Justin's expression grew very somber. "You said it. The first Ari couldn't work with him. Are you better than she was?"

"I don't know," she said. "I know I'm not, yet."

"Good night," he said firmly, cutting off any hope of longer conversation. "Good night, Ari."

He was upset with her and with Jordan. She was sorry for that. But she'd had the truthers running, the while, and she had a load of data for Florian and Catlin to sift, before they gave any instructions to the new people.

Questions remained. Doubts didn't. Justin had firmly stepped to her side. He just had to reconnoiter a bit, and settle his stomach about it. He was upset. But he stayed hers.

Jordan—Jordan was still Jordan. That hadn't changed. But she knew him better because of this evening. And that was also very useful.

BOOK ONE   Section 3   Chapter v

MAY 3, 2424
1003H

It was more home than it had been, the new office, with the quasi-window showing a rainy day and blue flowers brightening up the corner. The color-sorted cabinet still grated on the nerves, but the annoyance was fading.

Mostly the phone stayed quiet this morning. And for

that, Justin found himself very grateful, considering the scene last night.

But it worried him. Jordan had more than one way to work on his nerves.

"Coffee?" Grant asked. Grant rose from his own desk to pour a cup. Justin held his out mutely, swivelled his chair around, and received it back when Grant had poured it.

"No phone call," he said.

"Enjoy it," Grant said.

"She's trying to make peace with him. It's not going to work."

"It won't, likely. But that's his choice, isn't it?"

"They've been fair with him," Justin said. "Sometimes I just want to shake sense into him."

"I'm only content he doesn't try his version of that with you," Grant said, and sat down with his own cup. He leaned back, crossed long legs in front of him. "Young sera, however, trusts you. And this, frankly, is a better thing. This is, mind you, a logical judgement. Or I believe it is."

"Believe it is."

"Convincing Jordan of her isn't likely," Grant said. "Young sera remains somewhat flexible."

"No matter if she deviates from what she was born, she can't deviate from what she was born *to*. She's going to *be* what Jordan flatly won't accept, that's the bitter truth. *Any* director of Reseune is in his way, I'm afraid that's the sum of it, and that's what she's going to be. So it's a chimera we're chasing, peace with Jordan. Doesn't exist." He thought of the monitoring and looked at the ceiling. Grant's eyes traveled the same direction, and met his, and he shrugged. "Doesn't matter. I said it last night. I said it all last night."

"We live in a glass box," Grant said with a shrug of his own. "But it's quieter for it."

"If I have any guilt in the world," Justin said soberly, "it's on your account. All the things you could do, and you spend far too much time worrying about my family, my future, my problems."

Grant's brow, generally azi-like, innocent of frowns, acquired one. "If I were burdened with choices, I'd still choose to be where I am. I'm relatively sure of it, given the requisite information."

"What? If someone told you you'd be linked up with the clone of an egotistical problem case in a lifelong feud with a dead woman, you'd jump at the chance?"

"I'd at least find it an interesting proposal," Grant said. "A source of unique experiences."

"God."

"Not all pleasant experiences, true, but I've found no need to run tape at all, not in this whole year. Which indicates I'm perfectly adjusted." Grant gave a violent twitch of his shoulder. "Mostly."

He had to laugh, in spite of it all. "I wish there were tape that could cure me of worrying about the damned son of a bitch."

"Oh, I know there is for me, but there you are, the disadvantages of being a born-man. Just shut down, go peacefully null—"

"You can't do it so well yourself nowadays, you know."

"Curiosity is a plague. Contagious. I can't help it. I want to *know*."

"You're right it's contagious. Jordan's a carrier. God, I wish he'd use good sense. Just—calm down and let it all flow past him. But no. He's got to be in the dead center of the flow, going upstream while he's at it. In some ways I can admire him—" Momentarily he'd all but forgotten about the bugs, twice in five minutes, and consciously, wearily amended it: "—and in others I know he's a lunatic."

"There's nothing wrong with his sanity," Grant said.

"No. There isn't. Everything's perfectly reasonable if you realize he wants to manage Reseune and he thinks second prize doesn't matter. *Why* he wants to—" He tried to make it make sense and simply shrugged. "He doesn't like to be inconvenienced. And *anybody* else's orders are an inconvenience."

Grant laughed softly. "That's one way to look at it."

"God, I want to love him. But he doesn't give a damn. That's the bottom line. I stopped being his project, and he washed his hands of me. Second prize again—isn't good enough for him. Things are perfect or they're garbage. Thank God for you, Grant, or I'd be—God knows what I'd be. Not as good as I am, for damn certain."

"Nor would I," Grant said with a nod of his head, "be anything worthwhile, in that household. I escaped, along with you, and I have just enough born-man ego to be glad of that fact."

"Nothing wrong with your ego," Justin shot back. "Perfectly well-exercised."

"Oh, now—"

A knock at the door—which opened.

Florian.

Face of an angel and inevitably the bearer of bad news. Grant sat still. Justin nodded a welcome.

"I don't suppose you dropped by for coffee."

"No, ser, thank you," Florian said. "I came to ask your help."

"My help."

Florian let the door shut, reached into his jacket pocket, pulled out a small card, and handed it to him. It had a number hand-written. "This is Dr. Patil's number."

"I gave it to you. I don't want it back."

"We understand that. But, purely in an investigative way, we'd like you to call it and simply find out what the reaction is. Are you willing to do that?"

His heart began a thoroughly familiar acceleration of beats. He saw, out of the corner of his eye, Grant set his cup down, as if he was considering entering into the conversation.

"And say what?" he asked, forestalling that, and straightway protested, though he marginally thought he was believed on this point: "I've told you I don't know this woman."

Florian reached in his pocket, drew out a folded piece of paper, and gave it to him.

The printout said: *Your father gave you the number, and you assumed he wanted you to convey his good wishes and Dr. Thieu's.*

Possibly you became curious.

You wish to warn Dr. Patil that there is some concern here because of her relationship with your father. You feel that you can be of use in that matter because of your connections with me.

"This comes from Ari," Justin surmised. "'Me' means Ari."

"You understand that this entire thread of conversation is classified," Florian said. "Sera suggests this line of conversation as an assistance."

"Florian, I can't lie. I'm terrible at lying." Begging off, abjectly, and in front of Grant—was undignified. Embarrassing. But survival, Grant's safety, everything was suddenly at issue. "I can't do this."

"You're a certified Supervisor, ser," Florian said smoothly. "You're not lying if you make these representations to this woman. You're temporarily adjusting her reality, just as you might maneuver one of us for good reasons, to reach a point. If, out of her own reality, she chooses to believe certain things about your motives, that's hardly your fault."

"God, Florian, it's not the same situation. You know it's not."

"I'm sure sera will understand if you refuse. But she urges me to say you could do a great deal for Dr. Patil, should she be innocent of any suspicious action—and for Reseune, since Dr. Patil is scheduled for a very sensitive appointment. On my own judgement, let me inform you of one other matter: Yanni Schwartz, on his return from Novgorod, discussed the resurrrection of the Eversnow project with sera; within the same hour, Jordan left his apartment on his way to dinner at Jamaica, carrying in his pocket the business card of the woman meant to be in charge of the Eversnow project. Jordan gave you that card in full view of surveillance. Does that make sense to you?"

His heart reached max. He looked at Florian and froze inside.

But he had to ask it. Cold and clear. "What's my father up to? Do you know?"

"We don't. We do want to know why that peculiar juxtaposition of events."

Florian was leveling with him: Justin had that sense. That was a situation both reassuring for his own future and as precarious for Jordan's as he could conceive. He didn't know what he'd been dragged into.

"I'm *sure* you want to know," he said to Florian, and picked up his coffee and had a sip to steady his nerves, looking, meanwhile, at Ari's script for a phone call to a woman who might either be, like him, a target, or someone he wished his father had never heard of.

Nanistics, for God's sake. Jordan had nothing to do with nanistics. Jordan had had nothing to do with Abolitionists, either, but had once had phone numbers of people who themselves had ties in such dark places, twenty years ago. Jordan's political contacts had nearly cost him Grant that night. And since that time he had taken nothing at face value, where it regarded Jordan's correspondents.

Grant sat over at his desk, silent, impassive—he glanced in Grant's direction and met Grant's eyes. Expression touched Grant's face, a nod, support for whatever he opted to do . . . when Grant would assuredly suffer right along with him if he made the wrong choice or the wrong move.

Grant was an alpha, and there was a limit to how much information anybody could make him unlearn . . . if anything untoward should happen to his CIT Supervisor. He couldn't forget that.

"Maybe you should take a break," he said to Grant.

Grant shook his head slightly. "I don't think so. You're going to do it, are you?"

"I don't want trouble," he said, "but I don't want trouble from my father, either. Damn him, Grant. Damn him." He had another sip of coffee, a larger one. "Florian, I'll try it. Let me wrap my mind around this note of Ari's."

"Sera trusts you more than any other CIT in Reseune," Florian said quietly. "Her staff *will* protect you, ser. Those are our orders. That's why, of all CITs outside Reseune-Sec, you are the only individual *we* have informed of the connection Director Schwartz has with this set of circumstances; and you're the only person we've told what connection the Eversnow project has with this woman in Novgorod. We trust you understand how important it is that this goes no further and how closely we are tracking vectors of information. Sera hopes Yanni is conducting his own investigation, that it might involve Jordan, and that this could explain the coincidence of your father's possession of this card. Her security assumes no such thing. Be very clear that you hold highly restricted information on several matters. You should deal with it very carefully."

"No question," Justin said. He had compartments in his

head, for things that couldn't get out, mustn't get out. He'd developed those containments, oh, years ago. Grant had the same ability. He'd meet Yanni; he'd not let on. He didn't remotely believe ill of Yanni—but he wouldn't let on.

He read and reread the script, fixing the sequence in his head—trying to concentrate past a rising sense of panic. No side thoughts. Deep-think. Internalize the message.

He glanced at Florian, then picked up the phone and input the number, with the script laid out in front of him.

God, he hoped the woman wasn't in at the moment. He'd just leave a message. He'd say—coherently—

A recording answered. *"This is Dr. Sandi Patil's residence. Input your code."* He cast a troubled glance at Florian, but then the message continued. *"Or record your message and state your business."*

It beeped. He was in the clear. She wasn't in. Thank God. He could get her to call him back, and ask what he wanted, which created a far easier information flow. He could envision that. He knew how he'd handle it.

"This is Justin Warrick, Jordan Warrick's son. I—"

Someone picked up mid-word. *"Patil here."*

It disconcerted him. He scrambled for a recovery. "Justin Warrick, Dr. Patil. My father is Jordan Warrick, in Reseune. He gave me your number, suggested I call you—he's busy going through the lab certifications right now—" Lie. Complete lie. "But he gave me your business card, and I assume he wanted me to call you and pay my respects." He saw Florian nod approval of the tack he was taking. "I'm sure he'd want to convey his own."

"I'd heard Jordan Warrick was back." Dead silence then. He was supposed to say something inventive. Fast. *Possibly you became curious,* the script said.

"I'm sure he'd want to express the same from Dr. Thieu, out at Planys," he said; and decided against the curiosity gambit. "I understand you're a friend of his."

"Former student. Colleague."

"So I understand." The script said: *You wish to warn Dr. Patil that there is some concern here because of her relationship with your father.* And his effort wasn't going well. There was chill, clipped response from Patil—interspersed with equally chill silence. "Look. Let me level with you.

My father's a bit of a hothead. I'm sure you know that.
He's picked a fight with Reseune Admin. Admin's cut off
his contacts for the next couple of weeks. You understand?
I had this number, last thing he gave me before he picked
a fight that's got me worried. I don't know what your relationship was with him, or is, but I know your reputation
is impeccable, and I know he's prone to pick fights that
sometimes have fallout."

"If you'd come to the point, ser."

"I thought I should call, and apologize if my father's
caused you any inconvenience. I hope he hasn't."

*"I don't know your father. I know of him, in common
with most people who remember the last administration.
I'm aware he was at Planys. Dr. Thieu mentioned him as
an acquaintance, that's all. Thank you for your concern,
but it's misplaced."*

"I'm afraid you don't understand."

*"I understand that I'm a very busy woman with no pos-
sible connection to your father's problems. I don't know
how he came by my card or why he gave it to you, but—"*

She was going to hang up. He grabbed for the strongest
word he could think of. "Murder, sera. Murder of Ariane
Emory." And improvised. "He didn't do it. They sent him
to Planys for something he didn't do. I know that for a fact.
He wants the matter reopened, which isn't—isn't exactly
what Reseune would like to see, for various reasons. So I'm
pretty sure they'll be asking Dr. Thieu, probably you—"

*"Look. I have absolutely no knowledge of your father
or his case."*

"I'm sure Dr. Thieu has put you current with it, at
least."

"Not a thing."

"Dr. Patil," *You feel that you can be of use in that matter because of your connections with me.* "Forgive me, but
he gave me this card with your number right before he put
himself at odds with Admin, and I'm sorry if I've been
forward in calling you, but I felt I owed you a warning."

"And I tell you I don't know him."

Time to back off. "I understand." As if, finally, he could
take a hint. "I apologize for the inconvenience. I feel I need
to bring this matter up with Admin, to be on the level with

them—I know young Emory. I know her quite well. Her influence isn't to discount—should you find yourself cross-wise of any investigation. She's mentioned your name. She doesn't want you inconvenienced."

"Where are you calling from?" Sharp tone. Very sharp tone.

"From Reseune. From my office. Which is also my personal number."

A small silence. Then, more quietly: *"I appreciate the advisement. My respects to your connections. Good day, ser."*

Contact abruptly broken. He drew a long, shaky breath, and looked at Grant, and looked at Florian.

"Well-handled, ser," Florian said. "Very well handled."

"I don't know. Maybe I shouldn't have mentioned Ari's name."

"Sera authorized it in her note," Florian said. "The call is recorded, as I'm sure you know. It will go no further than sera's security."

"I appreciate that," he said, feeling his stomach upset. He didn't know who he'd just betrayed. He was sure, at least, it wasn't Ari. That part made him—and Grant—personally safe, as long as he was in Ari's wing.

Outside was another matter.

"Sera's thanks," Florian said, and held out his hand. For a moment Justin had no notion what he wanted. Then he realized the paper with Ari's instructions was on the desk, and he gave it back. Florian folded it and tucked it away.

"The card, ser."

He'd forgotten that. He handed that over, glad not to have it in his possession. Florian pocketed that, too, bowed, with a "Good day, ser, Grant."

And left.

Damn, Justin thought as the door shut. And said it. "Damn, Grant. What did I just do?"

"Assuredly what pleases Ari," Grant said softly. "Which is probably a good idea."

"I'm sure it is," he said, which was a lie: he wasn't sure of anything in the universe at the moment. "I think I just upset Dr. Patil."

"I don't think we're responsible for Dr. Patil," Grant said. "We don't know who she is, or what your father wanted."

"Or what Yanni wants," he said. "Damn it, Grant, *Yanni,* of all people. He can't be moving on his own. I can't imagine him doing that."

"In a wide universe," Grant said, "it's extraordinary that this woman's card arrived on that very evening."

"It's extraordinary," he agreed, staring off into memory, that evening, the foyer at Jamaica, that card going into his pocket. Florian, in the dark, by the pond. Grant walking back to hand it over, because he'd known then that his father had handed him trouble, and challenged him to do something besides coexist with Admin.

Now he'd done something, and not on Jordan's side. Not against him, necessarily, but not on Jordan's side. His father had challenged him. And he'd picked a side. Committed himself, with a phone call.

Committed himself, when he'd given Grant that card to turn over to Florian that night. He was sure of that. He was one step further into the quagmire, and now a second one.

And Florian emphasized—*sera's* security, not ReseuneSec. Why that distinction, he wondered? Was there actually a distinction? Or was there about to be? A schism, in the relations between Ari and the current directorship of Reseune?

"We're Ari's," he said to Grant, still staring into memory, that night, the cold wind. Bright light, and Ari, perched in that chair in his office. And he had to consider where that office was. In it, neck deep, they were—living, now working, in her wing, doing work on, and for, her security. "I suppose we're Ari's. If there was ever any doubt of it in my father's mind, he's forced me—and we are."

MAY 3, 2424
1121H

Major headache, right between the eyes. Deepstudy did
that sometimes—especially on too little food, especially
when it was tape-study on population dynamics, which
wasn't a commercial tape, wasn't paced to be, was just raw
notes and data and conclusions dumped into one's head
under the deepteach drug, so the habitual mind wanted to
add it up and make it make sense and the critical faculties
just weren't answering the phone.

But the too-little-food part was another very good reason for the headache, which was why Ari had scheduled
herself to come out of it at 1115h. She still was on the edge
of the drug—when she was coming out, she'd told domestic staff just not to talk to her or ask her anything or tell
her anything. She was apt to have what they said running
around in her head all day, otherwise, and there was already too much running around in her head, psychsets,
genesets, this population burst, the other burst added to
the Novgorod sets, all of it classified, most all of it done
during the War, with the Defense Bureau nagging her predecessor to do this, do that, psych-design by committee and
with no understanding what they were asking. So the first
Ari had done what she wanted to do because nobody in the
Defense Bureau had the skill to check on what she did.

Her predecessor had, for example, prepped a cadre of
azi to survive if some Alliance ship had taken out Cyteen
Station and dropped a rock on Reseune itself. They were
to get to the weathermaker controls and the precip towers,
hold them if they could, otherwise go for the safety domes,
take over by armed action, and run things, never mind
any plan Defense had laid down. There were some alphas
seeded into Novgorod, just for leaven in the loaf. They'd

have children by now. Children would have CIT numbers,
ultimately indistinguishable from the CITs whose ances-
tors had come down to earth from the station. If the average held true, the children were probably not geniuses. But
she could track them down. A little computer work, carefully shielded, would be interesting—if she had the time
to do that research. She didn't. Her schedule said she was
supposed to be doing math tape this afternoon. And she
sat, muzzy-headed, wishing she could take a day off from
everything on her schedule.

The door to her study opened, quietly. She took a sip of
coffee and looked up at Florian.

"Sera," he said. "He was willing. He did very well. Are
you able to hear the report?"

That was a mental shift. A serious mental shift. Florian
meant Justin. Willing meant Justin had done what they
had talked about last night, she and Florian and Catlin.
And she'd told him to report as soon as she was awake. She
was intensely curious—too wide-focused at the moment,
but curious.

"Did it work?" she asked, shoving population dynamics
and all the equations to the rear. What concerned Justin
worried her, on a personal basis, and she didn't like involving him in operations. "Did you learn anything?"

"Patil claimed not to know Jordan Warrick except
by reputation. But she accepted the younger Warrick's
advisement that he has influence with you. I have the
transcript.—Is this too early, yet, sera?"

She had a second sip of coffee, blinked at the headache
between her eyes, and shook her head. "No. I'll go over it.
I want to. What are the details? How do you read it?"

"He invoked an investigation into your predecessor's
death, as if Jordan was seeking a new inquiry to be opened
into that matter—his innocence established."

She didn't know why. She didn't quite like the sound of
that, granted Justin had had to improvise. Was it because
that issue was riding Justin's subconscious, and that was what
had surfaced in his mind? She was a little surprised, a little
off put. But there was *Jordan's* motive to question. He was a
son of a bitch. But was he *trying* to get Admin's attention?

"Ser Warrick suggested that she and Thieu might be

subjects of investigation because of the card and the connection to the elder Warrick."

Which was even the plain truth, just a large enough dose of it to make it credible.

But the other matter hit her skull and rattled around unpleasantly before heading through her nerves, just an unsettling, undefined malaise. The question of Jordan's innocence. Justin—the cause célèbre in suspicion falling on Jordan . . . a political firestorm if that case got raked over again in the media, taking public attention away from her before she'd had time to settle the image she wanted in public attention.

Deepstudy drug. Damn it.

"I *am* a little muzzy yet. I think I need to cut back the doses. Shouldn't be lasting like this."

"Forgive me, sera. You said—"

"I said tell me when I awoke. And I ought to be awake. I *am* awake. I'm just a little disturbed by the direction he went."

"Dr. Patil was about to end the conversation. He used that matter as a wedge."

"What did she say then?"

"That she had no connection with Warrick Senior. And they concluded politely."

"Someone provided her address to Jordan. Either he handed on a card the full significance of which he didn't know, a total coincidence, or he did know."

"In our opinion, the elder Warrick knew whose number that card was, and that she is currently important."

"Do you think that *is* possibly his motive, that he wants vindication? Florian, *who* actually sent Jordan to Planys?"

"Our indications are it was Yanni."

"That's what my own search turned up. Yanni held the keys. Always. During Denys's tenure. Yanni held the keys to Jordan's sentence. And it was primarily Yanni who protected Justin, when Giraud would have taken a harder line. All these things are true?"

"Our indications are that, yes. But, sera—"

She waited.

"If you're not prepared to talk, sera . . ."

"I'm thinking quite clearly at the moment." What the

drug did, besides diminish the ability to reject a fact, was to lower the bars on partitioned information—make cross-connections easier, if there was a shred of connection possible. It was like momentarily seeing the world from a plane window, disconnected from the land, but seeing all of it, every wrinkle, every canyon, every change of strata, how it all, all, all connected, even if it was too wide to remember once one was back on the ground. "I'm thinking quite clearly at the moment, Florian, thank you. I'm just a little deepstate. I'm sure you understand."

"I do, sera."

"I need to do something." She was aware she was staring straight ahead, her eyes wide open. She knew the look: black centered, unfocused, focused everywhere, and nowhere in the real world. "I like him, Florian. I like Yanni. I really do. But I can't have him running operations he doesn't tell me about."

"Should I take orders from you at this point?"

She was perfectly collected. She slowly moved her head from side to side. "No. You should not. I need about fifteen more minutes to get my head clear, Florian. I need a cold drink. Would you mind going and getting that? That's a request, not an order."

"Are you safe to leave alone, sera?"

"Perfectly safe. I'll sit here and think. I'd like that drink, thank you. Something sugary."

"Fifteen minutes, sera."

She wasn't surprised when, hardly a moment behind Florian's leaving, Catlin quietly opened the door and came in.

"Sit down," Ari said, still not focusing on anything but infinity. "I'm thinking a moment, Catlin. I know you're there."

Catlin subsided into a chair without a word. And Ari stared off into her thoughts.

Yanni. Yanni was a resource, and a problem. What he had done said nothing about his motives in doing it. Yanni had intervened in the past to prevent further assassinations, of the Warricks, in specific.

Yanni said he had concerns about Jordan in her bringing him back, and was searching for involvement in leaks in Planys, which had gotten to Corain and possibly to others, possibly by the same conduit. One man was relieved of his position. That didn't mean there wasn't another.

And possibly Yanni had put challenges in front of Jordan before this to find out how he might react. Possibly he was testing Patil herself, who had at least some connections to Jordan, through Thieu. He talked about putting the woman in charge of a world in its transformation, in the most Centrist-friendly decision Reseune had taken in years: the woman had Centrist backing, a lot of Centrist backing, the same party that had taken up the cause of the Warricks' plight as a case of political persecution—and called it a power grab by the Nyes.

True. It had been exactly that.

But the Centrists had, after Giraud's death, attempted a brief but cuddly relationship with Denys Nye, seeing that Denys was *not,* after all, going to push the Expansionist agenda Giraud had espoused—not because Denys was Centrist, but because Denys Nye was on his own agenda and wouldn't spend a cred on Ariane Emory's projects.

Denys Nye was going to continue the one Project, the cloning of Ariane Emory herself, but he was going to keep it, and her juvenile self, under his thumb for at least a decade . . . the Centrists hadn't minded.

Meanwhile Denys focused entirely on post-War economics, on the complexities of Earth-Alliance-Union trade, and on those agreements, which pleased the Centrists no end. They might not have gotten their terraforming bill passed, but they *had* gotten an administrator of Reseune who was pushing most of their agenda and precious little of Ariane Emory's—just the Project, which guaranteed, so long as Denys Nye had physical guardianship of the Project, that it wasn't going to threaten him . . . in its lifetime.

Yanni'd done the day-to-day administrative part through all of both Nyes' terms, running Personnel, which, in Reseune, was a key post. Denys had been the genius behind the programs; Giraud had kept the lid on dissent and quietly smoothed the bumps in the very short, very defined road Reseune had traveled in the post-War years.

But Giraud and Denys had each been seduced—Giraud by devotion to Denys, and Denys by the one thing that Denys coveted for himself—immortality. Denys and death

hadn't liked each other. If the Child succeeded, it proved
the psychogenesis process was possible. Denys *wanted* the
Project to succeed, at least until he knew the result.

And meanwhile Denys was busy storing all his own data,
and Giraud's, out in that archive. It was very likely that Denys
had double dealt Ariane Emory's plans by killing her; had
double dealt the Centrists by continuing the Project; Denys
had double dealt absolutely everybody, all to keep Denys
Nye alive for another lifespan . . . solipsistic bastard. He'd
attempted to kill her only when she'd succeeded and he had
his result—unfortunately for him, she'd succeeded too well,
too fast, and consequently he'd been the one to die, else he'd
just have blamed her assassination on another Warrick and
started all over again. That would have gained him another
twenty years, during which he could bring up his own successor, another Giraud, who would be duty-bound to bring
up *him,* the all-important center of his universe.

And Yanni? Yanni had kept his hold on power through
both administrations, letting the Nyes run things, mop-
ping up, keeping the Nyes from doing too much damage,
while the Project ran, and she grew . . .

So which side was he on?

Florian came back into the room with the requested
glass of orange and put it in her hand. She drank it, absorbing the sugar hit, still staring elsewhere.

"Yanni's not necessarily pernicious," she said. "He *is*
bent on his own agenda, and he's been very clear about that.
Getting the Eversnow project going . . . that's major. He had
Thieu in safekeeping at Planys. But Thieu's gotten too old;
he's on his way to the grave. So now Yanni needs Patil. He's
saved the Eversnow project. He's gotten it passed. He's saved
the Warricks, kept Justin sane. I'm not so sure he wanted
Jordan out, but he's got him. He probably wants Justin for
his ally. He can't have Justin. Justin is *mine.*"

Blink. The thoughts were trying to shred and go away
in different directions. She held onto the central problem:
Eversnow. "Yanni kept all the first Ari's projects alive, and
he preserved the Warricks, especially Justin. Yanni's still on
her program. Not Denys'. Hers. And that's not necessarily
mine. He's courting the Centrists. He's trying to move them
onto his agenda, and they're buying it, seeing him as Denys'

backup, in the years before *I* take over. If I did take over sooner, it would disturb them a lot. The Paxers would have a fit. They'll go back to the underground, blowing things up again. But they'll do that, whenever I take over."

Florian and Catlin waited, both seated, neither saying a thing to interrupt her.

Blink. More shreds. Tatters. But the structure stayed. "I still like Yanni. I don't want him to die. I just don't want him to do what he's doing. Eversnow is something I wouldn't have done and the more I think about it, the more uneasy I get. Yanni sees the job crisis and a new trade route as important—more so than I do. It takes us further from Alliance, and I'm not sure that's a good thing for humanity at this point." She thought: *Ari set me to watch her projects. Her projects, and this was one. But keeping Union together—keeping humankind from fragmenting: there were already more variables than she could handle—or she wouldn't have created me. It was already a field-too-large problem, just with what we've already created, Novgorod, and Gehenna, and the military azi, and Alliance, and Earth. Then pile Eversnow on top of that, as odd as people could get, learning to survive on a snowball. It's a planet, not just one more star station. Gravity wells breed difference. They don't communicate with the outside.*

There might have been a reason besides elder Ari's health that she let Eversnow drop.

It was hard not to plunge back into deepstate, following that thread. But Florian and Catlin didn't go away. They waited for something more concrete than her worries. "I'm not sure yet," she said. "Who, do you think, does Hicks belong to?"

"Possibly to Yanni," Florian said. "He was Yanni's appointee in the current office. Giraud Nye's second-in-command when Giraud was alive."

"Both, then. But he didn't protect Denys. He just protected Yanni. And he didn't resist me ousting Denys. Possibly Yanni protected me from Hicks."

"Likely," Catlin said. "Hicks and Yanni together would have been a difficult opposition. We met none, once Abban died."

She nodded slowly. "I have to take over," she said, half-numb, and with that wide focus that blanked out the whole room, except them. "I have to take charge. I don't want to, but Hicks's gift isn't enough. I can't let Yanni go on in the direction he's going. I like him, understand. I don't want him hurt. But Eversnow is much too dangerous. Yanni doesn't see things the way I do. He belongs to the first Ari. And he wouldn't like it if I started steering from over his shoulder. He'd rather go back to his labs. He should, now."

"Wait," Florian said, "wait, sera, until we have Hicks' people passed through Justin Warrick's opinion, and installed, and tested. We're not enough to secure your safety, as is."

Sobering thought. Honest thought. People like Yanni had *been* honest, at least honest enough not to make an attempt on her life. On her freedom, however—she'd been advised into seclusion. By Yanni. By the agreement of her own security. Now Hicks offered her either spies—or real power, in the presence of some unnamed threat—or in the progress of something Yanni was up to.

Did Hicks himself have an opinion? A loyalty? Unlike with azi, they couldn't find it in a manual.

"We can wait," she said, "so long as we don't alert anyone to our intentions. I don't want anyone to be killed if we can help it. I want Justin safe. Can we do that?"

"Are you going to tell Sam and Amy?" Catlin asked. "And Maddy?"

The other members of the junior cabal. Her friends, her allies, the kids who'd grown up to take jobs in the real world. She was the only one who hadn't. Who'd had real power, and laid it down for a time. She was still studying, still growing up. There was so, so much yet to grasp, so much to understand.

"I don't know yet," she said. "I may not tell anyone my opinion. Or I may tell *them*." She looked at them, finding the blood moving away from her brain. She felt a little lightheaded, but collected, all the same. "I have a headache, still. I'll be in my room. Go see about these things. Lay plans. Come back to me with a report before you implement anything. Let me know where we are and what we need to do."

"Yes, sera," Florian said. He and Catlin got up and opened the door. They left, and she got up, and walked out of her office and down the short hall to her bedroom, in her section, her own safe section of the safe apartment in the sacrosanctity of Wing One, where—theoretically—she controlled her own security. But ReseuneSec guarded the doors of Wing One. ReseuneSec was in the halls. The old lab was dead. Dead as the first Ari. Equipment mostly removed. The place had become a little shabby—she'd laid other plans, a grandiose plan, a notion of gathering what was hers where it was indisputably safe. That was what that construction was, between Wing One and the cliffs. She intended to live there. With people she loved. Yanni had been part of it.

She shut her bedroom door behind her. Locked it. She felt a Mad coming on, though she wasn't sure yet at what. Maybe at Yanni: she couldn't trust him enough. Maybe at the people outside Reseune, who didn't have the sense to know enough to make themselves safe, and the stupid Paxers who were going to make bombs and kill people because they didn't have any better plan.

She ought to have ReseuneSec track every one of the Paxer leadership before the news got out that she was taking over.

She could have them killed. Every one. She'd have the power to do that. The first Ari had had it. And hadn't done it, when the first Ari had done so much that was just— things she didn't want to think about.

She stood in the middle of her own room and looked around her at a place that was safe. She looked at *her* things, that, if she owned the whole world, still mattered, her chair, her bed, her dresser, and what was in it, things she shouldn't keep.

She walked over to the dresser, picked up Poo-thing, poor, ignored Poo-thing. She smoothed the fur around his button eyes, and rubbed his nose into shape. His sweater was all wrinkled. His fat tummy was still fat, and she straightened his feet a bit, and laid him back in the drawer, making room for him. He went on staring. Poo-thing had no way to blink when she shut the drawer on him and cut out the light.

Shoved it hard the last couple of inches and sat down in her chair and cried. Sobbed, with her face in her hands, trying not to make any sound to bring Florian and Catlin back, or staff, or anybody.

I wanted a childhood, she said to herself over and over. *I really wanted a childhood, just a little one, just a year, is that too much to ask? I only wanted a year, and it's not fair, not fair, not fair! I didn't ask to be born! I didn't ask everybody to hate me! I didn't ask to be anything—I don't want to be, I want to ride Horse when I want, anywhere in town, and not have to worry about people shooting me or trying to run off with me, and I want to have my friends around me and I don't want to lose them, I don't want to get them killed, either, and I don't want Florian and Catlin to have to kill anybody, ever again, but they will.*

I want my Uncle Yanni back. I want Maman not to be dead and Ollie to write me he's coming back, and Valery, and everybody, I want it back the way it was before I grew up . . .

But it's not going to be, is it? It's never going to be. Ollie, maybe. Maybe Valery. They might come, if I can get them all back, all of them.

But they can't find a teary, stupid girl when they do, can they? I can't be stupid, or I'll be dead, and I'll get other people killed.

She blotted her eyes, one after the other, with the back of her hand. Sniffed. Got up and examined a reddened, unlovely face in the mirror, and got a tissue from the bath, all with a raw, unhappy feeling inside.

She didn't quite know the girl that looked back at her, red-eyed, red-nosed, just human. It was the first Ari's girl-face, but it wasn't the face of the portraits.

Second try with the tissue. Her makeup was a mess. She blew her nose, blowing away the evil spirits, Maman had used to say that. Maman would take a cold washcloth and wash her face and tell her cold water and a clear head would made a good start on any problem.

She did that for herself, washed her face, fixed her makeup. Sharp pain had gone to leaden hurt, just a weight remaining where the pain had been. And that was stupid. Selfish. She'd had her childhood just now, all ten minutes of it; and maybe she should take a chance and have just a little freedom before the whole load came down on her, go do those relatively safe things she could get away with doing, just because she could, before it was forevermore too late.

BOOK

TWO

BOOK TWO   Section 1   Chapter i

Giraud Nye and his companions were steadily putting on weight. At twelve weeks, having doubled in size in the last seven days, Giraud massed twenty-eight grams, somewhat less than a generous shot of the whiskey he'd one day love.

He had gotten fists, and fingerprints, and his general body shape was a little more human. He'd been drinking in the tank's biosynthetic amniotic fluid, and routinely pissed it out again—proving his kidneys were starting to work, a process that would never stop, in spite of his future abuses to his body, until he did.

His intestines were growing, and began to fill his abdomen. His nerve cells were proliferating, synapses getting organized enough to react to stimuli, but unaware at any higher level—the nerves had no myelin sheath as yet, and that limited their function considerably. Consciousness was nowhere in the picture. His cells all had other jobs to do, mostly that of dividing like mad, according to the map in their nuclei. If it said cooperate, they cooperated. If it said make skin, they made skin, in its varied layers and detail. If it said make nerves, they made more nerves. There was no higher authority.

BOOK TWO　　　Section I　　　Chapter ii

The clothes that hung at the front of the closet, ready for wear, were appropriate for the house—not a construction site—and Ari delved deeper, on her own quest.

She was going outside. On her own. She was ducking lessons today. She'd warned Justin she would. She hadn't forewarned anybody in ReseuneSec, however, except Florian and Catlin—hadn't sent word to Hicks, pointedly so. They hadn't yet gotten the new Security team—they were still taking tape, but most of all Justin and Grant were still reviewing files, and she didn't have to worry about trusting them yet, so she wouldn't.

Just Florian and Catlin, and a fast move, that nobody would be expecting, well, except Sam Whitely.

It was still a scary venture—the first time to be really out in open country. It was the very first time since they'd shot their way into Wing One that she'd really gone outside.

The makeup was scant, and the clothes she'd picked out had once served for riding—when she'd been able to get to Horse. The weight she'd lost since Denys died meant she could put her fingers in the waist of the once nicely fitting denims. The seat was a little less than fitted, now, but Sam wouldn't care, out on the behind-the-building construction site, out under the cliffs that ringed Reseune. The sweater, at least, was meant to be loose.

Comfortable, and part of her life when Denys had been her protection, and Denys had fussed over her and worried about her breaking her neck—she'd almost believed the old miser had cared, from time to time. On a day like this, she could almost believe something had just occasionally stirred in Denys's wizened little heart.

He'd say, if he were here, Don't be a fool. Stay in.

He'd really say something if he knew the information

Florian and Catlin were gathering up, and the net they were beginning to weave through the Wing, and around people whose whereabouts they needed to know, constantly.

But today she was going out on her own, not because it was policy, but because it was her chance to do it and she could do it and she would do it.

She was really going outside the safe bounds. A risk, and worth every minute of it. And she was going to scare hell out of Hicks' office, and probably Yanni was going to blow up and yell, but she was going to do it anyway . . . just flexing the constraints, just making sure what her freedom of movement was like. She'd make ReseuneSec twitch, and she'd do it again, and someday, on the day she chose, it wouldn't be a lark.

It wasn't as if the new construction wasn't constantly available to Base One in virtuality: she'd seen the new wing grow, day by day. But this, she'd decided, was *the* day. The whole site had, for the first month, been an ugly brown flat of disturbed earth, aswarm with bots twenty-four/seven, following their preprogrammed dig plan, tearing up the landscape and installing lines and conduits—a secret communion between them and the design specs, with rarely a human involved, except to watch it happen. Yanni had given his agreement—*Yanni* knew what it was, but if Yanni had kept his word, nobody but Yanni knew, not even ReseuneSec.

In the second month, human workers had moved in, installing, with robot assistance, a flat barrenness of ground-forms, while still more bots scrambled this way and that on spider-legs, measuring and installing connectors.

Last week, the vertical forms had arrived from upriver, fresh from their use up at Strassenberg, and the site had sudden risen up and up into a confusion of those huge prefab pour-forms and their requisite braces, everything fitted together with a system of bolts and clamps into a configuration that had nothing to do with Strassenberg: the forms were capable of that.

The main pour had been three days ago. This morning the forms had come down at the apex of the wing, and the featureless new walls stood clear and white in the camera-view.

Which was no longer enough for her satisfaction, or Sam's. She hadn't seen her friends in forever. She'd wanted to call Amy and Maddy out—but that was just too much noise.

"Sera." Catlin arrived in the bedroom. "Florian is on his way back with the runabout. We can meet him at the curb."

"Excellent." Enthusiasm tingled through her. She escaped the bedroom, walked briskly, with Catlin just in the lead, down the hall, through the living room, to the front hall, and out the door to the general corridor.

Escape, for sure. She'd dreamed initially, mere cloud-castles, of taking Horse out of pasture, bringing him up to Wing One where he'd never been, and simply riding around the end of the building alone and unexpected, but the runabout Florian quickly suggested in Horse's stead was the practical thing. The safe thing. The thing that wouldn't bring Yanni storming down on Hicks, and Hicks down on the venture midway with a flock of ReseuneSec agents. A car—that was fairly ordinary. Nobody would think a car was a break for a few hours' freedom.

Downstairs. Down another corridor, and toward the glass doors that led to the outside. Florian pulled the runabout into view at the curb just as they passed the inner glass doors of Wing One. Door security in the section, ReseuneSec, caught by surprise, jumped to attention, properly opened the outer doors for them as they arrived, and one of the two guards, doubtless in communication with Florian, went outside quickly to open the passenger-side doors of the runabout, probably thinking they were going down to the labs.

Catlin opted for the front seat, beside Florian—there was a heavy rifle waiting there, and she shifted it to sit down, burdened with her own armament. Ari, carrying not so much as a pocketbook, simply tucked up comfortably in the rear seat, and the instant she had settled and the doors had shut, Florian took off with a snap and an immediate jolt.

Right over the curb near the flower bed and onto the lawn just beyond the building edge—a track not meant to be taken. Florian clearly enjoyed himself in taking them at breakneck speed downslope across the neat grass of the lawn, and, by a sharp right, onto the construction road between Wing One and the river. The landscape bounced crazily. Ari grabbed onto the seat and laughed, wondering what ReseuneSec thought of the maneuver. But no one gave immediate chase, Catlin talked to someone, answering questions, and Ari watched the moving scenery—lazy brown river on the left, the robot-mowed grasses on the right, where the riverside lawn still remained sacrosanct from the passage of the big earthmovers—

Terran, that lawn. Nothing from Cyteen's native life got onto Reseune's territory, except what drifted ashore via the river, and that only touched the shore—and died. Such seeds and fragments of woolwood and other deadly things that somehow got past diversion gates in the river itself met a determined last line of defense down there. Dedicated robot sweepers zapped intrusion to cinder, snifferpigs found anything that took root, and a coffer dam and a high-tech filtration system kept the river water on one side and routed their own runoff back to their own use. All that effort prevented Terran life from getting out any more than they could help nowadays, and most of all it kept lowlevel Cyteen life from getting in.

They passed the dim arc of the coffer dam in the river, and swung around the long side of Wing One. Their course still ran well within the safe perimeter of the precip towers that sat up on the cliffs above their little valley, and on matching cliffs across the wide Novaya Volga. There wasn't any real fear of a perimeter collapse, in these days of triple redundancy in Reseune's atmospheric bubble; but the runabout, designed for the outback, with its six tires and a pressure seal on its doors, was nevertheless well-equipped for that eventuality, with breathing tanks and emergency suits right under the seats: a small yellow sticker advised of that resource, should the sirens sound.

Emergency supplies that might serve in the event of a back country wreck might be just a little redundant for an overset on the construction road, which was their most immediate peril. Florian took evident delight in crossing over the ruts of the big earthmovers' tracks. Ari braced herself between seat and window and craned for a bouncing view

as they swung another right turn around the far end of
Wing One, near her current apartment, which presented
blind walls to the riverside.

The newest part of the construction came into view
through the front glass, walls still shrouded in forms. The
new wing butted right up against the back wall of Wing
One. Eventually there would be a subterranean access at
that contact point, somewhere in that mess of gray pour-
forms. Right now that connection with Wing One was
a maze, a jigsaw of shapes and bolts and supports. And
Wing One would be open for revision, renovation, after all
the chaos since Denys. There would be shops again, and
restaurants, maybe even a new Wing One Lab, convenient
for her use. Someday.

Suddenly, with a veer over rough ground, new foam-
construction hove into view, off-white walls, brilliant
and plain. The new wing as a whole formed a large, two-
storied U, which would join not only Wing One, but attach
to Admin on the other side, giving the new construction
direct access all the way from Wing One to Admin, and incidentally creating considerable interior space for roofed
gardens.

That last part was her idea. Why have a U and not take
advantage of that inner space? Why confine all the flowers
to the distant Botany Wing? They could bring them where
people could enjoy them without a trek way down to the
botany labs. Incorporate them into a roofed-over section
of this wing—

Or why not small nooks of *all* the wings in Reseune,
while they were at it?

Economically extravagant, Yanni had called that notion, and nixed it, while letting her have her flowers in the
new wing. But she thought increased productivity would
pay for it over time, particularly when it increased the
productivity of the best psychtechs, operators, supervisors
and designers in the known universe—which was what
Reseune was.

And she'd said so, and Yanni had said, "When it's on
your watch." And that day, she'd decided, was coming. She
had to think of it calmly, in terms of what she'd do, once
she could—and thanks to the sudden need to use Reseune

funds to keep projects working—all her plans had to be tempered with thoughts of how to pay for things.

Yanni didn't wholly approve what she was doing. She'd put it down to the fact he was old-way, in so many areas, including his support of the first Ari's policies: if it was old, it was good enough until it fell apart—that was what she'd thought was a simple truth, until she'd found out he had an agenda that needed a budget . . . a huge budget, cannibalizing hers.

It was true—even Yanni admitted Reseune needed attention, because there was a lot falling apart. Reseune had started complete bare-bones and in a hurry, when humans first set up a permanent habitat down here—Reseune had come first, even before Novgorod, in any operational sense. So the buildings had all grown in the same white-walled, all-survival style of the early colony, right through her grandmother's time, and the first Ari's. Yanni's generation, previous generations—that architecture was what they knew, and it was getting old, hammered by the storms and repainted and refoamed time after time to patch things.

There *had* once been different ways of building. Elsewhere, Earth existed, as baroque as anyone could wish. Distant Pell Station was growing a forest inside its heart.

So why *shouldn't* Reseune have flowers? A sociological plus, flowers. Not one more huge population-burst to factor in, dug in on an iceball and getting less and less like Reseune, or Gehenna, or the star stations.

A chance to contemplate something fractal, something to take the tension off . . . wasn't a stupid idea, even if it didn't make money in any visible way. *Novgorod* could use some parks, some gardens. It wasn't the frontier any longer. It was the place people lived, and they were getting changed, sociologically, by the walls, and the dynamic of the buildings they'd been living in, and how they fitted together. Gardens focused people into a different mode.

And the inner garden to go in *this* wing was altogether her design. She'd sketched a plan or two for her someday castle, her place with flowers, even before Denys had died. She'd talked about it with Sam Whitely and Maddy Strassen and Amy Carnath in those days—*those days*—as if it wasn't just last year. Just daydreaming, she'd called it.

But on the day she knew she needed urgently to set up in newer, safer spaces, she'd called on Sam, for what he knew—she'd entrusted the whole project to Sam, who was eighteen, the same as she was—Sam, backed by the resources and computer software of two major construction companies and Sam's own gift of getting along with most everybody. He'd stood up for her through Yanni's misgivings, and then Yanni's assigning senior design to the project. Sam hadn't been off-put, and he'd doggedly stuck to their design.

Sam was, depend on it, properly respectful of older engineers, but he'd run the designs through the computers himself, and she'd gotten her tall tower with the slanted walls that the older engineers said weren't cost-effective. He'd had the company architects, he'd assured Yanni, cross-check and criticize structural soundness with their specialized software, new materials said it would stand, safe and strong; and she'd personally bet the architects Sam consulted had found very little fault in what Sam put together. ReseuneSec's labs, their only recourse for the specialized kind of construction that provided systems, had provided some black box areas, just the dimensions and access requirements for electronics that would go in under senior Admin's direction. Those *were* already in: Yanni had had technicians out here on that job before he'd left for Novgorod, all the while keeping the nature of the construction out of public gossip. The virtuals didn't show up on regular vid channels, nobody saw what was going on back here, and it had been going on for months.

Even while the tech designers were still fussing over the details, Sam, with *her* orders behind him, had had the earthmovers running on the basic footprint. Starting with the basic Reseune design had helped Sam speed things along . . . but at the top of the U was her design, Sam's design, inside that footprint. Maddy had gotten a word or two in about the interiors. Amy had contributed her usual cold water bath of cost and common sense, then finally thrown up her hands and said that if Yanni ever agreed to that much expense, she'd be very surprised.

But Sam had gotten his budget, *and* his security-class installers—Yanni had given him the go-ahead for just one spectacular variation on the old theme, at the top of the U—her apartment. And then Yanni, maybe knowing she was going to be mad as hell about what he meant to do in Novgorod, and wanting to give her a toy to distract her, had approved it all and let the companies call in the resources. So their little club, their childhood clique, had found themselves building for real.

Herself, Amy and Sam, Maddy, Florian and Catlin: when they were kids, they'd gotten anywhere and been responsible for all sorts of mischief—outright sabotage of Denys' intention to watch her, for starters. And sometimes they'd just done things for revenge, on a kid's scale, some of them pretty vile.

And today? Today Amy was Admin, born and bred— it was Amy who'd had a good deal to do with cajoling Yanni—it was Amy who'd found justification in the figures she laid on Yanni's desk. Maddy ran an exclusive dress shop, and you'd never think *she* was worth anything in a construction project; but the dress shop was a front. Maddy collected gossip—she *knew* the female elite of Reseune, knew their tastes, their habits, their liaisons, and their figure flaws; and besides that, Maddy had an eye for decor, and design—and understood the use of the gossip she collected: you wanted something out of someone, you wanted a favor, the name of a contact? Maddy had the key.

And Sam—well, Sam built things. Bigger and bigger things were in the future she planned.

So their juvenile fantasy *would* come true. They'd be together again—here, in this wing, when this place they'd all planned was done. Not for the reason they'd all planned—never thinking it was for their safety, just one grand continuation of what they'd dreamed of building for the sheer beauty of it.

When they came in, they'd bring their liaisons, their families, their staffs, everything they needed . . .

And damn it, she'd keep them safe, forever safe, everyone she wanted to protect and *not* have vulnerable to plots and gossip and schemes and outright sabotage once she took the reins. The Centrists and the Paxers and the Abolitionists wouldn't get to the people she loved.

The first Ari—that Ari hadn't had personal weak spots: she'd kept very much alone through her life: Ari Senior hadn't trusted anyone but her Florian and her Catlin. But *she'd* learned how to use allies the way her predecessor never had. She'd confounded Denys, frustrated Denys—finally gotten the better of Denys.

Now she had the better of Yanni and Hicks of Reseune-Sec, who actually knew what this place really was . . .

Inside or outside this new wing, for Yanni?

That all depended. Maybe. Maybe not, depending on how Yanni took it. And how Hicks did. And what this team he was sending her turned out to be.

"Come see," Sam's message yesterday had said. "We'd love it if you could come."

So here they were, driving along beside the white walls, and the whole project becoming more and more real the closer they got, right down to the feathery pour-marks on the new walls, where they'd freed the finished wall from the molds.

All the conduits had gone into the forms before the pour, so she'd learned. The new place had a new sensor system, a new computer installation from the basic wiring up. It had new walls without ten thousand ghosty little luci-filaments running in places that were a real archaeological problem to trace . . . making a security headache for Wing One and most everywhere in Reseune. Systems as arcane as Base One—which had lurked within the lab computers until the day (event-driven, calendar-driven, it was never clear) it assembled itself and made contact—just could not surprise her in the new wing. Base One itself would get in, intact, through a prescribed gateway, and settle itself in, while other Bases would have to stop at that gateway and announce their presence to Base One before touching System inside. She trusted Base One absolutely. She was pretty sure it would do what she asked it to do. She no longer trusted, however, the systems where she lived—she hadn't, from before Denys died. Florian and Catlin had long worried there might be a worm in the works, where Denys and his people had done all the arranging for years. *Giraud* might certainly have done things within Reseune's systems that could spring on them without warning. They'd gotten through the first months post-Denys without disaster—but who knew what event might trigger something untoward? Giraud's rebirth? Denys's rebeginning?

Her own claim on power, when she did make it? She wanted to be in here when she made her move . . . safe, isolated, in control. Yanni ran Base Two at the moment: nobody but an Ari Emory and those she permitted had ever run Base One. But Base Two had been in Denys's hands before that. And having some buried section of Base Two wake up and start actively spying—if Yanni didn't already run those functions—that wouldn't be good, no.

They would be in their new, secure apartment before summer ended: Sam promised it, and she had every confidence that would happen on schedule.

And the building had taken a big stride this morning: the gray, confusing forms that had stood at the end of the U had given way to a section of white angled planes rising stark and beautiful against the sheer natural rock of the cliffs. Florian turned the little car into the rutted and dusty area of what a sign proclaimed as Parking A, among the giant earthmovers, and Sam was waiting for them there, wearing a hard hat and orange overalls no different from any of the azi who worked with him. Sam's square face split with a grin as they got out and walked onto the hard, rutted surface that was his particular domain.

"I hoped the pour would finally draw you out here," Sam said, waving an expansive gesture at the walls. "There you are, people! Home sweet home!"

It was different than anything ever built at Reseune, an extravagant three-story crown at the apex of the new-born Alpha Wing. Her heart beat faster in excitement.

"We'll be done ahead of schedule," Sam said. "No bubbles in the pour. Went like a dream."

That was good to hear. Bubbles in a foam wall were definitely a bad thing, and Sam meant they'd gotten all this foamwork set and hardened without sawing areas out, setting up forms again, and foaming in twice, and no problems with the design. Sam was decidedly happy with his job.

But she wanted to *see*. She wanted to walk inside, and make it real, not just a virtual image she could get on the computer.

"Can we get in there?" she asked.

"Right this way!" Sam led them all toward a gap in the pour, a broad area with rough notched edges. "This is just a workman's door—you won't be able to walk through this wall when you live here: we'll foam it so it's just wall, ever after."

Reseune was like a fortress of sorts, against environmental hazards as much as for any other reason, the only lookout on this exterior side of the building once it was finished would be cameras, no doors or openings of any kind. Her apartment, at the top of the U, jutted out farthest toward the wild and the cliffs, and farthest upward, in its reinforced light-channels. The rest of the U's ground floor would be offices, a few shops, while the upstairs was all going to be very restricted residences: *her* apartment would have its main door on the third floor, the way things were in Wing One second floor. But, unlike Wing One's, her apartment and only her apartment would have an upstairs section above the third floor—that was the height of the crown, up among the angles of the walls. That would be her room, her office, her personal safe place, with Florian and Catlin by her, and their rooms, and all the things they needed, up above the world, almost even with the cliffs.

Right now, the word given out among the CIT workers was that all this construction was new labs. By the time rumor got out that it was going to be a restricted residential area, and hers in particular, the security installations would all be in, and that time was getting very close. By the time Alpha Wing System went on line (and perished immediately as Base One moved in and took over) well, it wouldn't matter any longer, at that point, what anyone knew. They'd be defended. Everyone she loved would be defended, once System came up and Base One ruled Alpha Wing.

Sam led the way inside, over dusty concrete floors littered with foam-construction crumbles and plaster spatters. Sunlight fell in unlikely rectangles and bars from somewhere above—where not all the construction was finished, Ari supposed. Where they walked, first floor, was going to be offices and residences for wing security personnel *other* than her personal bodyguard, and they all would have immaculate security clearance.

Her new apartment, over their heads at the moment, would more than protect her—it would innovate. It would be all angles, and surprises like light, and living things. It would inspire her, and inspire her visitors, with things that had never existed in Reseune. Denys' old apartment, where she had grown up, was a boxy put-together of the ubiquitous Reseune cream-colored walls and recessed lights, just boring, boring, boring—with the same color walls in every room. Oh, it had real imported wood, yes, and all sorts of luxuries like hand-knotted carpet, and bric-a-brac and china. She'd sent the whole lot to storage so that Denys Two, if he one day existed, could have it all intact when he grew up—but, God, that some mentor had to teach a little boy to like that stuffy decor!

And Ari Senior's apartment, where she lived now, had luxury, a lot of it, and it had its graces, but it was all linear, archway into archway, brown travertine and polished floors that would skid with you if you didn't watch the rugs, and it had sat vacant for nearly a decade and a half with Base One gone dormant, an interregnum in which someone very, very clever and skilled—like Abban, like Seely—could have gotten into the place or at the place in some clever way they had never detected, with things as small as a human hair. Illicit surveillance might not have waked up yet, because Yanni might not have full use of Base Two—which might have plunged into partial dormancy itself, awaiting some event to bring it live . . . some event like a young Abban logging onto System.

That wasn't going to disturb her life. Not in Alpha Wing.

"This way," Sam said, and they followed Sam onto a construction lift. It lurched into action and lifted them up and up a narrow dim shaft to the highest level of the building. "This is your front door," Sam said, lifting the safety bar to let them out, and waving them toward a single gap in the white, angled walls around them. Light beyond that door was getting in from somewhere up here. It had to be her design, her sun-shaft somewhere aloft, bouncing light from panel to panel.

Her apartment, this apartment, was going to be a lot of glass, and lights, and living things. *Her* home was going to have fish, a whole wall that was a real tank, not just a projection of virtual fish. They were going to get them all the way from Earth's tropics—well, via the public aquarium at Pell, which was shipping them to Cyteen, which would immediately ship them down to her.

So when you sat in the living room, there would be that living wall to watch on one side, and when you were in the entry hall, there was going to be a waterfall, with real rock going down to a stone floor, with a clever trick, an air wall, Sam's idea, to prevent the spray from getting beyond the rim of the pool.

And upstairs in her office, which was going to be right next to her bedroom, there would be living plants behind glass . . . she'd wanted real birds. She'd had to reconsider that, because anything you imported down to the planet that was ever capable of reproducing had to be clean, with a natural barrier between it and freedom on Cyteen, and had to be considered for the ecology they'd started to restore. The water and the sea were already a mess, that was one thing, and for another, if the tanks ever breached, the fish couldn't walk across the lawn to get to the river. So they were all right.

So no birds. Just fish. But she could do real science with what she kept. She could do so many things . . . she could breed fish and get them to a public aquarium in Novgorod, where people could come and enjoy them, and know something about Earth in the process, and something about living next to an ocean.

And instantly, as they walked beyond the second wall, just short of where the security installation would be, she recognized the recess for the water-pool, just the way she'd drawn it, and saw the straight, bare form for the rock, slanting away and up and up on the left.

Everything was white and dusty from the pour. But a glance all the way up showed a series of white planes, and the sun-shafts and pressurized windows she'd asked for must already be in here, too: real daylight came into the area. There was a balcony above that overlooked it all. There were recesses here and there for the electric lighting that would brighten with a vocal command, once System was in. Beyond, in the open plan dining room, was the section of arched roof for the projection that would show the real sky, just the way it was outside—so when it rained, it would cloud over, and when it was night, there would be stars. She wanted all the contact with the planet she could possibly get, living under the umbrella of the weathermakers and precip towers as they did, and being forbidden windows that really looked out on the world.

It would *feel* open. If it worked, they were going to do the same sky-dome in the big hall of the general public residencies. She was going to fix Reseune. It was going to be a place people wanted to be, before she was done with it. It wouldn't be the same old utilitarian box-shape and domes, not after her.

It was all Sam again. Sam had taken her rough sketches of years and years ago and played with them in his own computer for years. Sam had lately run it all through the big computers and ended up with real measurements that were going to meet regulations and make design sense, and Sam said he was working with architects who were with him and excited about what he was doing. She'd pulled strings with Yanni to get Sam time on systems at night, and Sam had pulled shift and shift. Give him shapes and he could figure the real building down to the joins and conduits. Give him charge of the logistics, and he had a fine grasp of what had to be scheduled when, right down to dealing with the bot programmers and giving clear orders to the azi workers *and* the CITs.

More, Reseune Construction *wanted* him when he was done. They told him he was already official on staff, never mind the regs and his lack of a degree and his age—he'd done his time in tape-study that hadn't been recorded, but they wanted him. The head of architectural design in RC, the same architect she'd aimed at Strassenberg itself, she'd hired to do the job here, too, and asked him to mentor Sam; but within the first month, RC's chief architect had just de facto turned Sam and two of his best people loose to handle everything on-site here while he concentrated on the more esoteric technicalities of the precip towers at Strassenberg.

Fitz Fitzpatrick was the man's name. Florian and Catlin had investigated him top to bottom, the only CIT besides Yanni to be trusted with the knowledge of what was going on here. He was actually an uncle of Amy's; and the relationship between Fitz Fitzpatrick and Sam was absolutely the happiest of all the string-pulling she'd ever done.

And here was the result of it. The planes of the walls evolved one into another as they all walked through. "That's my fish wall!" she exclaimed, spotting the deep recess, delighted, and Sam beamed and blushed a bit.

"The glass is here. That was big. The build for the tank will be among the last. I'll be looking to experts' specs on that."

"I've got the data you want," she said. She was seeing a tank filled with water, where now there was only white. "I want to learn it myself, but I'm going to be Contracting a specialist in salt aquaculture to actually do the running long-term. He'll help you set it up. His name's Chris BCN-3. He was supposed to be on the Beta Station production tanks. He's seventeen, still taking tape, but he's getting info on Earth exotics and he's through enough already to help you, this week if you need him: he's going to be supering all the watery technicals—with a couple of assistants if he turns out to need them."

"Wouldn't hurt at all. I'm anxious to get the pumps arranged. Any of your other staff you'll want to tour through, or consult during the build, you let me know. The kitchens might be an issue."

"Florian and Catlin are on it. They'll get you a list of people we might have come here to walk around at certain stages. Security. Operations. Kitchen, in particular. We're getting staff. They aren't cleared into the house yet."

"A few here might be helpful," Florian said, behind them. "Not many, though. We won't inundate you with advice."

A laser must be running. A burned stench wafted through. Something metal fell, distant, and the impact of something the size of the runabout echoed off the walls.

Sam tapped his hardhat. "Must've dropped a wrench out there. This area's safe. Down the main corridor, they're doing some light work in the ceiling today."

"The supers are all on our list," Catlin said. It was a question, regarding the CITs onsite.

"Always," Sam said, unruffled. "Security never lapses.

They don't even take an inside lunch break: the azi crew is deepset against discussing their work off-duty, so damned enthusiastic I have to make them take breaks—*they* all know what they're doing is unique, and they're excited. So are the rest of us, to tell the truth. Want to see the latest?" He walked them to a serpentine line marked on the floor, which ran to the edge of the living room. "I want to S-curve a meter-deep channel through the flooring. A water channel, clear top, lighted underneath, with rock."

"I love it!" Ari exclaimed. "A river."

"Well, a stream. It'll share its water source with the waterfall, not the tank. Fresh water. Complete loop. There's a submersible pig to clean it and zap the algae."

"Pig." She envisioned the ones that sniffed native life that got onto the grounds.

Sam's eyes danced. They were brown, unpretentious as the rest of him. He so loved knowing something technical that she didn't. "A machine-pig. A cleaner bot. Same as they use for regular water-systems, standard piece of equipment, actually. That's what they call it. It ought to work."

"Pig." She liked that word. It conjured the working pigs that patrolled the grounds and kept them safe. "Do it, if you think it'll work. I like your river, Sam. I love it!"

"It just came to me when I was walking through here. We can have a pump at the top of the loop, right where the waterfall is, keep the water really moving."

"Oh, don't tell me everything! I just want to be astonished when I see it!"

They toured the downstairs bathroom, a modern installation that played a little off the waterfall concept, with sealed stone, but the fixtures were all modern. And there was a second scissor-lift to take them up to the second floor—a scary little step across vacant space, and onto solid foamcrete.

At one end of that hall, beside the as yet rail-less balcony, was Florian and Catlin's suite, which was going to have a gym, and a workshop, and a library of its own. Other staff quarters would be right below it.

"Much more convenient," was Florian's only comment. But their eyes were bright. They were happy and easy with Sam. They always had been.

And then her room, her huge bedroom, with a cozy nook for a bed, and a living-sky ceiling, and a glassed-in area for the divider from her office, where her terrarium would be, and her wardrobe, and *her* bath, which had an in-floor tub, and a mister, and its own little salon, plus a little exercise room of her own ... it was everything, all in one. It was all her imagination wrapped up in a design of white plaster at the moment, and she went out onto the unrailed balcony—Florian and Catlin were there in a heartbeat—but not too far toward the edge, just looking down at all of the living and dining area below.

She might have to take over Reseune early. She might not have the years she wanted.

But she was going to have all her friends, all the people she most wanted. Yanni, too, if she could answer the questions she had. She'd been pent in, feeling like a prisoner in the slow ruin of Wing One. When they finished this, they could start repairs, where the search for bugs had literally ripped walls out—repairs much, much beyond a fresh coat of plaster.

Maybe it was dangerous to think of directing Reseune and still hoping to be as happy as she wanted to be in this castle in the air; but this place was all light and optimism. It cost. But it was where she could keep safe what her existence threatened, make an iron-hard core that wouldn't be vulnerable to threat.

Maybe it was the stupidest, most dangerous thing in the world, to surround herself with the people she was fondest of. The first Ari would have warned her it was, that it was setting herself up to get them killed, or to get herself hurt.

Weak is dead. The first Ari had said that, too.

And the first Ari hadn't *had* anybody she was that fond of, except Florian, except Catlin. The first Ari had told her her own nightmares of guilt ... the discovery she'd enjoyed inflicting pain, and yet did it, when she did it, purely for a reason. The first Ari had warned her, as best she rationally knew how, that the path she was on went further and further into solitude, and into the dark.

She'd had hormones shot into her deliberately to make her mad and had mean things done to make her miserable, all because she was supposed to live the first Ari's life, the way Ari's life, under her own mother, had been one long lab-test, intimately recorded, and full of Ari's mother's orders.

It was just everything, *every* cruel thing justified for the Project, until Denys died and the Project stood on her own two feet.

Well, she *was* on her own two feet, with her own walls rising around her. And she'd always been smart. All it took for her to learn something was for her to get her head in the right mode, and she'd been quick enough to take in what they wanted—once they'd gotten her scattershot mind both mad and focused . . . because Mad was always part of it. She could still be the genius her geneset could make her, without her being as cold as the first Ari—couldn't she? Controlling the Mad was the important thing.

It was what this place was for.

She could love people. Now that she knew the whole scheme, she could try to set things right. Yanni would be here. Most of what Yanni wanted was to get back to his work, his real work. He didn't ever want to run Reseune. He didn't really want to fight her for his big project out on the fringe of space. He'd understand, if she just got his hands off the controls and gave him back his labs.

Sam would live here in the wing, Sam, the one in their group who'd just been so reliable, so sensible, in their growing up, that if Sam hadn't existed, they might have all gone at each other's throats and nothing would ever have worked. Though, when he got through with her wing, Fitzpatrick wanted him up at Strassenberg, which was a big thing for Sam, the height of his childhood ambitions. It would be hard to have him gone that long, but Sam would be her eyes and ears on that site—Sam and the high-level security team Florian and Catlin would pick out to keep him safe. So Sam's apartment would be vacant for a while. Maybe a couple of years.

Maddy and Amy, at least, would be living in the wing with her, right from the start.

And when Sam got back from Strassenberg, all the old gang would be here, all of them. She was going to have Justin, too, though he was twice their age. She had a place for him and Grant, a beautiful apartment, where nobody would ever threaten him again.

There'd been her playmate, Valery. In her mind he was still a little, little boy with a mop of dark hair. He was out at Fargone, like Ollie. Early on she'd sent a letter, inviting them all back this summer, all the exiles, when Alpha Wing was finished. It took six months to get an answer, even; but she had started it, on the last day she'd held absolute control of Reseune, before she'd turned the directorship over to Yanni. She couldn't get Maman back: but Maman's companion Ollie was still alive. He'd had the CIT tape, and he'd become Director out there. She'd asked Ollie to come home, too, but she'd added, as she hadn't in Valery's letter—*only if you want to. There's a place for you here. But if you're happy there, then stay. I remember you and Maman every day. But you do what you most feel you should do, for Maman's sake.* He was azi, or he had been; and *nothing* could shake him from that loyalty and have him be happy, and she knew that.

There was Julia, and Gloria Strassen, who never had liked her when she was little, but she could patch that up. She'd been a baby when Denys had sent them away.

She could set some of Denys' injustices right. And she could use the power she had to protect what her existence jeopardized.

It was scary to think how dead set the first Ari had been against trusting people.

The ones you trust most, the first Ari had said, watch most.

And the ones who'd had their lives torn apart because she was born? They were dangerous because they had a real reason to be mad at her.

But she could try to fix it.

And the first Ari hadn't lived in a prison, not half so much as she did. The first Ari had been absolutely free to run around the halls and go where she wanted and do what she wanted. The first Ari hadn't been afraid of anything. But everybody but Giraud had hated that Ari. She'd begun to realize that, and it was a hard truth to live with.

She was different than that Ari. Some people hated her. But a lot of people loved her. And a lot more people knew they needed her. They'd all protected her so much, so devotedly, they'd made her afraid of people. Most of all, afraid of people.

And that made her mad. And Mad always made her *think*.

And she wasn't like Yanni's beetle, a creature in a bottle, forever going in the same circle, forever the same Ari.

"So sober, Ari," Sam said.

"Thinking," she said, and then thought that she'd used too harsh a tone, too much out of the dark depths of her heart. She set a hand on his shoulder and walked back to safety, Florian and Catlin attending.

Sam led them all back to the scissor-lift, the someday lift shaft, and sent it back down into what would be the central hallway of the whole complex—right where Sam's river would run.

"So?" Sam asked.

"Perfect! It's just *perfect!*"

He grinned, then. Sam was happy. That was all it took. And Sam's pleasure lightened her heart. It always did.

"So," he said, "do you want to pick out colors?"

"Blue," she said. "A blue couch. Just so it's comfortable."

"Cooler white walls, then, for blue."

"Violet and cool white walls. Maybe some quiet blue-greens. Pastel stuff. I want color."

"That should be pretty," he said. "Should be real pretty. Are you moving any of her stuff in?"

She gave a little twitch of the shoulders, a thoughtless flinch. There was what she lived with. There was some in storage. Historic. Some really nice pieces, imports from Earth. Human history.

But human history had started over again on Cyteen. In cities founded, like Novgorod, mostly by azi, and going on into generations of freedmen—what did old Earth mean to them? What could it mean? Human history this lot of humans hadn't replicated, had largely forgotten.

She didn't have as many blank walls in the new place. Not as much room for paintings and sculptures.

And ought she to take those old paintings off her walls and lend them to a museum, or to the University down in Novgorod, and let people study them for what they were and try to figure out what it meant to lay paint on canvas, instead of commands into a computer?

Maybe the old things were important things to know. Maybe somebody should learn how to do it again.

"You're thinking again," Sam said. "Is something the matter?"

"No," she said, and laughed, and laid a hand on Sam's shoulder. "No. I was just wondering whether we ought to teach azi to paint."

"To paint." Sam laughed.

"Pictures. To paint pictures, like the old paintings. I think it might be good for them. Maybe it's good for people. I think maybe I ought to let some of those paintings out, and see what they think."

"They are pretty," Sam said. "I always admired them."

"They're pretty. They're alien as they can be. I can't imagine trees that thick. That's just strange. I think people would be looking at that, the green color, and not at the paint."

"I think you're actually supposed to," Sam said, then. "You're supposed to believe in them, and not the paint."

"That's a point."

"What did you say about my little river? 'I want to be amazed?' I think the paintings are like that."

He never ceased to surprise her. "So what do you think? Should I get into storage? Bring them out?"

He nodded. "I've seen them. Some aren't that pretty. Some are spooky. But you feel something when you look at them."

"Maybe I *should* look at more of them," she said, and found she'd gathered her arms around herself as if she'd met a chill in the air. It wasn't just paintings. It was the first Ari's mind. It was the images the first Ari had seen, lived with, picked out to surround herself with, out of everything she could have had. What even the first Ari might have flinched at, and hidden away.

And instead of building, the first Ari had surrounded herself with things out of old Earth. Priceless things ... spooky things. Things that weren't Cyteen.

Trust Sam to have looked at them, when he was about to build this place. With a heart that had no guilt, no

preconceptions, he'd looked at them, when probing that
deep into the first Ari's stored artwork was something
she'd zealously avoided. She hadn't wanted to meet them.
Hadn't wanted to be surrounded by the first Ari's mind,
swallowed up, drowned in the first Ari's acquisitions. She
wanted some of her own.

But you felt something, Sam said. And Sam was always
in favor of feeling things.

"Hang them all," she said suddenly. "Hang the ones
you like wherever you think they ought to be, in my apartment, in the corridors where people walk."

"Hey, I'm the builder, not the decorator."

"You know them, though. You've seen them. Hang the
really spooky ones in the guest apartments."

He laughed. "Wicked, Ari."

She laughed, too. Laughing took the haunt out of her
predecessor's furnishings and made her think—maybe I
ought to use more of them. I'm saving Denys' stuff, and
Giraud's, to bend their successors' brains into the old
mold.

Maybe—it was a sobering thought—maybe I should
meet her . . . finally. She's the voice of Base One. I've always trusted her voice . . .

So what's to be afraid of, in seeing what she saw, what
she troubled to bring here out of old Earth?

"About the furniture, Sam, *her* stuff. Don't strip her
old apartment, the one I'm in. We'll just lock it up, leave
it as it was, just like Giraud's, just like Denys'. With all
the pictures that hang there." In case they didn't replicate
her, but the first Ari, but she didn't say that to Sam. "But
with what's in storage, if you can use it, never mind my
colors—do it."

"Her taste was a lot of brown and green."

That was true. Along with occasional greens and golds
in the paintings, alien greens, yellowy Earth greens like the
lawn outside, like the plants in the vivarium, when every
green growing thing native to the planet was tinged with
blue and gray, and the ground was red. "Maybe I should do
green and brown in this room, her green, water green. Old
Earth brown. Oh, just make it fit, Sam."

"I told you, I'm no decorator. I'm really not."

"But you knew how to look at the paintings in the warehouse. You'll know what to do with them. Surprise me."

"That's too many surprises, Ari."

"No such thing," she said suddenly, and remembered the first Ari saying, out of Base One, *"There are people who aren't surprised because they don't notice what's surprising in the world and they just never wonder. And there are, much rarer, people who aren't surprised because they always see what's coming. When you're a child, you're surprised by most things. It gets rarer as the years pass. Surprises keep us sane. They set us into new territory. They give us something to think about, when same old things have been the rule. You can go to sleep for years with the same old things. Sleep can eat away at your life. And sleep can be dangerous."*

Not always good things, but maybe—maybe it was good for her to meet some things she hadn't planned.

And paint was cheap . . . until it made a thousand-year-old painting.

"No such thing, Sam. You're king of surprises. You do it all. You pick."

"You're going to hate it!"

"I've never hated anything you've ever done. Don't hold back. Give me the best place you can, with whatever of her stuff fits, and bring all the hidden stuff out where people can see it."

"All right," Sam said, and together they walked out of her apartment and on down the corridor, past scaffolding and into the vicinity of a good deal of cutting and banging—past doors that would belong to people she'd grown up with, and then downstairs by yet another scissor-lift.

There was space for shops, besides the security quarters and wing admin—little hole-in-the wall shops where she and all the people who had a right to be here, and their staffs, could do something she didn't ever get to do in the tight security Reseune had now, and just go shopping—well, at least they could order something to be in one of these shops and go down and look at it before they bought it off catalog: that was *almost* like shopping.

There'd be a nice little snack shop and breakfast place, which would turn into a nice evening restaurant. It would 'cater, too, with special attention to security. That was all planned.

There'd be a men's shop, for Yanni and Frank, and Justin and Grant, and Sam and Pavel, when they got back from Strassenberg, and Amy's Quentin, what time Quentin wasn't, like Florian and Catlin, in uniform. And there'd be a few conference and gathering rooms for anybody that needed them.

They could use one of those conference rooms for displays—for art, she thought suddenly.

"We can have a museum in Alpha Wing," she decided. "We can have our own museum. A little one, for some of the paintings. We can have another over in the Admin Wing, where they'll be safe. I think that's a good thing. Sam, you can do it—"

"A museum?"

"The first Ari knew people who'd seen the world built. They're all dead, now. We're the first generation that doesn't know anything about Cyteen before there were people here. And all their things, if they aren't in archive, are just going away, thrown in the cycler. A virtual museum's a good thing. You can look that up any time you want, but you have to ask for the displays—and you have to know to ask. You need to know what you're looking for in the first place to look something up, and that necessarily slants it, doesn't it?"

"Slants it, too," Sam said, "if somebody picks out what you'll see."

"Someone's always picking for us. But the people who painted those paintings did their own picking about what to paint. You can see the virtuals. You can get any repro you want, if you want to put your hands on it, but if you want to get surprises, that you didn't *ask* to be face to face with, maybe that's the idea. You're right. Maybe I should look at what I don't expect. It's why I decided I want the first Ari's stuff. Maybe it ought to be like that for other people. They need to be surprised. And we need to haul some of the stuff out of the warehouses before it goes into the cyclers and just have it for people to look at. We're the generation that doesn't remember the beginning. Maybe we need to look hard."

Sam stopped still and looked at her a long moment. "Sometimes you don't make thorough sense, but you always seem like you do."

She laughed. Not many people would tell her she babbled. She knew she did. She saw things in her head, saw things she didn't have vocabulary for. The first Ari, people said, had been very spare with words. The first Ari had had ideas in her head, too, which didn't have words. The first Ari didn't habitually let those things out. She, on the other hand, tried to talk to the people she thought would understand. And she babbled thorough nonsense, and amused Sam.

"You see through me," she said to Sam.

"I try to see into your head," Sam said. "You're awake all the time, you know that. You're the most incredibly awake person I know. You want a museum in Admin, sure, you get Yanni Schwartz to agree and give me space, and I'll figure how to do it. I have to go the slow way and look up things like a regular guy, but you'll get your museum."

"I'm not about museums," she said, "I'm not supposed to be, at any rate. It's just a side thought. I have to do so many other things. God, Sam, I'm studying. I'm studying all day long. I'm learning the things I'm supposed to, psych, and design, and genetics, and I spend so long at deepstudy I'm starting to go into deepstate without the damn pills, sometimes so I don't even know I'm doing it. But when I have thoughts that aren't on-topic I have to shed them, I just have to turn them loose and shed them or go crazy, because I haven't got time to do them, and my museum is a thought like that. I had it. I want to get rid of it but I don't want to lose it, and I'm going to be busy, so you do it, Sam."

"Ari." He reached out and gripped her shoulders—a contact Florian and Catlin would allow very few people— and kissed her on the forehead. "Take a break, Ari. Take a day off and take a break."

She sighed, rested her hands on his arms, looked him closely in the eyes. "You're a genius, you know it. You really are."

"That's a laugh." He dropped the contact. "That's the last thing I am."

"I know it when I see it. You are. Always were. Sam,
Take care of yourself. I mean that."

"Is there any special reason you should say that?"

"Selfishness. I need you. I'll always need you. I'll think
of you when I'm studying that wretched population equation till my eyes cross."

Second kiss, this one on the cheek. Like a brother, if
she'd been born with one. She'd never had sex with Sam.
Never would. That wasn't the way they were with each
other. "You just take care of yourself, Ari, hear me? You're
going too hard, again. But what's new about that?"

She was so tired, she felt tears start in her eyes, but she
wouldn't shed them. She laughed, instead. "I'm paying for
this place," she said, "or I will. I'm starting real work. High
time I earn my keep, I say. You'll see."

"Good for you," Sam said and let her go. And he probably did see the dampness of her eyes and had the common
sense not to fuss over it.

It was a rare morning. The bash and clatter of hollow
forms and the whine of cutters was hundreds of workers
and bots busy keeping Sam's promises. She made her own
promises as they walked back to the exit, and the runabout: that by summer and move-in, she was going to be in
a position to take care of Sam.

Pay for it, indeed. Her whole life paid for it.

Just watch, she said to Yanni, in absentia. Just watch.
The first Ari developed most of what we do—what every
lab in the wide universe does. I'm starting where she finished. I've run through the teaching tapes in three months:
everything but this last couple of weeks was basic, and I'm
into her notes, and I'm doing integrations. I'll be working
on gammas soon. Alpha sets before New Year's. Strassenberg population sets by next year. I'll be able. I'll know
what I'm doing, Yanni.

And that's not empty bragging. That's the truth.

MAY 10, 2424
1328H

Information, encouragingly abundant, in Florian's opinion, had begun flowing along new channels. The new security team, and the domestic staff, were finally due to arrive for duty in Wing One. The security team was ready as of now, since ReseuneSec had finished their documentation—but they weren't setting foot in Wing One, and neither were the domestics, until Justin and Grant finished their report, which they said would take longer than they thought.

And there'd been a problem. Justin was waiting on getting general manuals from Library, indefinitely postponed, as they found out, because *Justin's* inquiry had triggered security alerts, and Justin hadn't been aware that lower ReseuneSec levels were investigating his request and stalling it purposefully until the probe had gotten high enough in the ReseuneSec system—namely Hicks' office—to contact sera's office—as the ones with their finger on Justin.

That was a mistake on their own part, as Florian saw it: they should have foreseen that Justin's inquiry might have raised a flag—considering his connections. Sera had called Yanni, Yanni had called Hicks, and Hicks had sent out an order to free those items up, so they'd finally gotten to Justin . . . days late, but ten minutes after sera had found it out.

Catlin had requested a few more rounds of tape-study on protocols for the security group, to keep them busy until Justin could do his work. The new domestic staff, meanwhile, had finished their preparation and passed sera's final scrutiny, and they might be brought in once their manuals cleared—much simpler than the ReseuneSec lot, so, given Justin's prior problems with clearance, Florian called up Hicks' office and made his own personal request, firmly—which got other manuals liberated, to him, at least, who couldn't read them—and who had no permission on file to have them. He took them personally to Justin's office, solving one more bottleneck, and stacking more work on Justin and Grant, who were working extra hours and taking computer time running interface studies among sera's staff. Most household staffs didn't get that degree of lookover, but sera's wasn't the sort that could ever discharge a member and have them easily plugged in elsewhere. There was too much special knowledge: there were too many security issues.

So they delayed that, too, and by now Justin and Grant were running short of sleep.

But today their own promised ReseuneSec authorization clearances had come through, an apparently earnest demonstration of Hicks' good will, a pass alleged to give them access to anything in ReseuneSec files, inside Reseune itself—and to ride ReseuneSec access through any door in the outside world—well, any door ReseuneSec itself could pass.

Any door? They tested their new access, just running through local files . . . not using Base One, but a system-free set of computers they used for handling any outside contact. They could display the second-system content on the same set of screens as Base One, they could keyboard to the alternate system from the same station, or switch back and forth between operating systems in absolute security—Florian was rather proud of that finesse. He'd done a fair amount of set-up, connecting up what would be the new security facility downstairs, so that all of it, the new office and residency as yet unoccupied, and the outpouring of ReseuneSec's version of classified material via their new link, came smoothly into their office via the same secure pipe—a pipe that flowed both ways, but didn't ever breach Base One's isolation.

Everything from those two sources, ReseuneSec and their own upcoming security office, once it had staff, would dump to the system-free computers in their office, to be carefully gone over before *anything* touched a Base One computer. Base One could reach out to it, read-only, would compare what ReseuneSec files contained against what it could find internally, and deliver that daily report, too.

There were, on the daily sheet from ReseuneSec, no current take-down operations anywhere in Reseune.

There was a tolerably serious matter involving stolen meds from a pharmacy . . . case solved. They'd argue that one in court. Base One had interesting information on that: the pilferer was an employee with previous security issues. That would stop.

The list went on, including actionable adultery, minor theft, public nuisance, and other CIT misbehaviors. Azi were rarely involved in any such goings-on, and if they were, the motives tended to be very different.

"Quiet day," Catlin remarked.

Real-time access to ReseuneSec's daily logs provided them a window on a level of ordinary misdeed they hadn't hitherto investigated. It was interesting, to pick up the pulse of the house. The town itself, down the hill, had its own brand of mischief: the drunken theft of a tractor, and the destruction of a piglot fence down in AG—the individual was charged the repairs. There had been minor pilferage in the food production unit, solved with a reprimand.

Far from the focus of their interest. Too much concentration on CIT actions could be, for one thing, stultifying, things over which an azi simply had to shake his head in slight puzzlement, never grasping the nature of the fault—except to say it broke rules by which born-men in responsible jobs and relationships were supposed to abide.

Policing the labs and town was part of the job Reseune-Sec did, generally CIT and azi pairs doing that; but none of these things affected Ari's safety . . . and their very access of these items, using ReseuneSec's access, not Base One, left a trail which might interest Hicks—that was actually desirable, so Hicks would see them using the connection. What was intriguing was not the data, which they could always get via Base One, but the extent of the data which Hicks afforded them, which was a test of Hicks and his staff, not the data.

Reseune's ordinary tenor of domestic life was, in fact, most often quiet—a collection of scientists, administrators, some businessmen, shopkeepers, builders, and

service people all observing the law, give or take their
personal idiosyncrasies—that was the expected daily
event. The largest national upheaval of the afternoon was
an ocean storm that had rolled in on Novgorod and taken
down three coastal precip towers at the river port, surely
a bit of excitement to their south. There was redundancy
for that situation, and three towers lost on a web that size
was by no means a crisis, though a regional collapse of
the shield was certainly newsworthy. The temporary reli-
ance on backup was delaying flights and river cargo out
of Novgorod, and disruption in anything—a bargeload of
supply orders for Reseune and Big Blue, for instance—
could afford an opportunity for dishonest efforts to slip
in and do harm.

It was nicely organized data. Tabular, it was certainly
easier to read than the absolute flood of information Base
One could deliver in a full spate—Base One didn't sort
outstandingly well. Sera said that sorting, in itself, was a
bias, best done in your head, if you scanned well.

They were aware of that, they did scan well, at a speed
nearly up to sera's, and Florian wondered what Reseune-
Sec was hiding from its low-level agencies by providing
them these nicely organized things to look at.

All sorts of things could lie between and behind those
neat tables.

"They think they'll be shipping again by 1800h," Catlin
remarked, from her station.

"1800h," Florian echoed, mildly absent. He was already
chasing down another, much more adventurous track on
their shiny new authorizations, one that took him into
Planys systems: Hicks had noted their interest in the Patil
case and had flagged an item for their attention.

Florian sent the interesting find, a letter, to Catlin's
screen . . . again, something Hicks wanted them to see.

Dr. Raymond Thieu was the sender. The recipient was
Dr. Sandi Patil. The letter was a week old. This and other
items turned up on a simple Base One search of the professor's mailbox. Easy to do, and trackless: ReseuneSec
probes left no footprints except in ReseuneSec itself and
in Base Two, which was Yanni's Base. Base One left none
at all. The Base One search had already turned up nothing

from Patil to Thieu within the last month. The other two
letters, also from Thieu to Patil, were not interesting.

"Apparently a mundane letter, which proves Thieu is
still writing Patil. This comes from Hicks."

"Noted," Catlin said. "She hasn't answered any of them.
She answered prior letters, but not immediately."

It was a chatty letter, advising Dr. Patil to read this
article and that in *Scientia*, offering a little commentary
on the dullness of life at Planys, asking about a dues
renewal—Dr. Thieu complained he couldn't remember
whether or not he had renewed his professional membership in the teaching fraternity, and he asked Patil whether
she had gotten the solicitation for membership yet because
he didn't want to go through the organization office, reason unstated. He also asked whether she happened to have
the recall number of a book, the title of which he couldn't
find on the net . . .

Odd, since the booklist was a basic function of the
scholarly net. Was that some verbal code? Or simply the
truth of an old man's suddenly fading memory?

And Thieu asked, at the end, whether she had heard
from Jordan Warrick. It was probably what had made
Hicks flag it to them.

*. . . He went back to Reseune. He hasn't written yet.
He's probably busy. You ought to call him. You remember
Jordan. Tall, brown hair. Nice manners . . .*

It went on for two more rambling paragraphs about the
too-spicy restaurant fare in Planys and the need for more
variety.

" 'Nice manners,' " Florian quoted wryly.

"It seems mundane enough," Catlin said, "at first
glance."

"One could wonder if Thieu *did* provide that card."

"He complains about losing a library title."

"Let's see what ReseuneSec wants to tell us about the
rest of his correspondence."

Florian searched down the list, flashed thirty-four files
up at once, windowed a few up with a scroll through. Compared that to what Base One had. "Looks complete." Base
One had already been through the lot. Base One had an
interesting little program that could analyze letters for

style. If it found stylistic anomalies in what was certainly from the same hand, it could throw a useful spotlight on verbal code. None found, except the new letter.

But re the issue of Thieu's mental condition—Florian slipped a quiet, trackless Base One inquiry into Planys Medical, and what that pulled up on Thieu indicated Dr. Thieu's rejuv was indeed failing, as Jordan Warrick had described.

"Failing rejuv and mental lapses. This, from Base One. Maybe the request for the book number is real. He may have entered the wrong title in his search."

Catlin, meanwhile, had done a little Base One work on her own, last week: Jordan's Planys records were there, too, sparse, on the medical front. And those results now popped to screen 4. "Contrast with Jordan Warrick. He seems in excellent health. No self-administered drug use or other complaints."

"Note the address," Florian said, flagging the item on the medical record. Jordan's physical address was listed as #18G in Pleiades Residency. And that had just rung a bell, against the address from Thieu's medical records.

#19G. Pleiades Residency.

"Next door neighbors, it seems."

Catlin probed further. "Moved" was the designation that turned up on screen, regarding Jordan's records this week. "Jordan's personal files aren't there, to the ReseuneSec probe. This is interesting. ReseuneSec can't reach them."

The Base One record *didn't* have those same holes in it. "Note. Those files are still there, for Base One—but they're gone, to our supposedly highest-level ReseuneSec inquiry."

"Well," Catlin said. "So either our ReseuneSec clearance isn't quite as high as it might be . . . or somebody's blocked those files from *them*. Yanni could certainly do that."

"I wonder about Jordan's minder notes?" Florian said. "We had those last week."

"Moved." Base One easily found them—a lengthy list of Jordan's goings and comings and the occasional note about a need for coffee or Paul's notes for Jordan about gym schedules. But Thieu's popped right up, along with all Thieu's bioprints, as good as a door key. And Jordan's were still accessible to Base One, which didn't recognize the fake erasures.

"Curious," Florian observed, "gone into the same folder as the rest of Jordan's records. Either Hicks isn't being allowed to access it . . . which would warn him that somebody, notably Yanni, doesn't want him to access those files—or Hicks lied when he said our access would be top level. Oh, this is good, inside Thieu's minder notes, did you note this? Lunch with Jordan, the day Jordan left Planys—Jordan broke that appointment because he was in the air."

"And Jordan detested him?"

Florian scanned the appointments. "Once a week or so—lunch with Jordan. Next door neighbors. Or across the hall." Florian called up a schematic of the residency strip in question. "Actually opposite each other. Certainly looks like a close association."

"Jordan knew we could check," Catlin asked, "but he lied, all the same. He gave that card to Justin. He knew we were watching. And ReseuneSec, which takes orders from Yanni, can't get to these particular files . . . or our new access can't. Another lie?"

"ReseuneSec lying doesn't surprise me too much," Florian said. "And Jordan's hard to understand on every level. Including, very clearly, doing things he knows we'll notice."

"He claimed to dislike Thieu. Called him a dodderer."

"And yet has lunch with him regularly. He and Paul."

"How old is Thieu, actually?" Catlin asked.

Florian keyed back to the medicals, convenient hop on Base One. "Hundred sixty-four." Once rejuv began to lose its effect, it took only a matter of months for a man who looked forty to start looking his actual age, losing the attributes of youth, acquiring ailments, losing faculties—and a hundred sixty-four was definitely in that territory. "If rejuv is failing him, he'll go fast, at that age. I'd think he hasn't doddered long, actually."

"And Jordan was living there for twenty years," Catlin said, "next door to him, unless there's been a recent change of residence, and a very recent change in Thieu's medical status." Click-click-click, from Catlin's console, Jordan's medical records going back and back to 2404. "No. Jordan had that address from the week he arrived. Thieu was there, too, from 2398."

"The information Jordan gave sera is missing some interesting pieces, for sure. Now Thieu dodders. And in his latest letter Thieu jogs Patil's memory about who Jordan is."

"Rejuv failure," Catlin said. "Maybe Thieu's short-term memory *is* going."

"Must be contagious. Forgetfulness seems to have infected Patil, too. She claims no connection with Jordan at all. Yet Thieu, whose memory is going, thinks she'd remember him. I wonder what we could find in *her* letter files."

"Worth noting."

Those records, except what Yanni might have, lay outside Reseune System. "Base One could try to crack University System, but it's not guaranteed to leave no traces," Florian said. "We probably shouldn't try it. We can take what Yanni's got. And his files on Thieu. If Thieu's dying—whether or not Thieu has all his faculties—that might stir somebody to make a move, whatever's going on."

"Thieu couldn't possibly have anticipated Jordan leaving Planys," Catlin said. "Jordan didn't expect security to pull him and Paul out of their office and put them on the plane."

Florian ran further through medical records. "Thieu's doctor records cognitive function definitely suffering. Short-term memory markedly impaired. Long-term recall can be intact for a time."

"So back to his giving Jordan the card—did he have enough faculties left for that?"

"Maybe. Maybe Jordan had it without his knowing. Jordan had access in his apartment. The one thing that *didn't* happen was Thieu knowing Jordan was being released and giving him the card as something to do once he got out, because he didn't know Jordan was leaving. As you say, he couldn't know. That intention was in sera's mind, but not in any record."

"The current letter," Catlin said. "Thieu wants Patil to look up Jordan. He's trying to get them together. Whatever the state of his mind, that's apparently somewhere on his agenda, for some reason."

"And what is Jordan, besides a Special in educational psych design? Very friendly with people in Citizens, in Defense, and people with ties to the Abolitionists."

"We don't know that he knew the nature of the Abolitionist connection," Catlin said.

"He was certainly tapped into the network that moves people and items for the dissidents—some twenty years ago. It doesn't say he's trying to establish such connections again. He can't call outside, anyway. He was barred from mail, to anybody but Justin. He still is. Justin can make a call for him. But Justin didn't. And a restaurant wasn't the place to pass on something Jordan didn't want us to investigate. He was asking for attention."

"A card is a stupid way to keep an address. It's just good for passing it on. If Thieu gave Jordan that card and wanted him to call Patil, Jordan could just have memorized the address and phone number, then simply tossed the card into recycling. He didn't do it in Planys; he didn't do it here. He either slipped it through a security search, or, more likely in that regard, he actually acquired it—or produced it—here."

"And then," Florian said, "he handed that particular card to Justin on a night when he was absolutely certain to be watched. There's certainly a lot here that doesn't make sense. CITs don't make sense. But this one is a real puzzle."

A moment of silence. Then Catlin said: "It's still tempting to think he got the card from Thieu. We're assuming that, because of Thieu's association with Patil. Thieu didn't need to give him a card. It doesn't make sense, except the fact Thieu has been talking about this Dr. Patil for years. Maybe there's been a long term effort, on both sides of the Tethys Sea, to get those two together—for whatever reason."

"It opens up a lot of possibilities."

"It does."

"The old connections," Florian said. "Reestablished. He was a friend of Thieu's. That there was a connection to Patil at Planys doesn't mean there isn't a connection to Thieu or Patil here in Reseune. These are born-men. They have that social dimension. *Knowing* people who know people—those connections matter. Don't they?" Florian swung his chair around. "The card itself can tell us, with luck. I'm betting ReseuneSec has already run the check on the card's chip. Let's see what they found."

He hit keys in quick succession, macros for their clearances, and a search into ReseuneSec files.

Analysis of the problematic card itself was in. It did include its microscopic markers—a very nice precaution from Giraud's time as head of ReseuneSec—which indicated that the office supplies used in the card indeed belonged to PlanysLabs.

"Entirely reasonable for ReseuneSec to assume it was printed in Planys," Florian said. "Planys markers."

"Physically reasonable to assume it. But anyone with Planys card stock could print it, here or there."

An e-card, never manifest as paper, was the common way for CITs to trade addresses, often arriving as an attachment to a sig line, available for print, available to be shot straight into address files if one trusted the sender.

And for office use, it was common to print a card out physically off the signature line of a letter, including even its chip-load, if the computer in question had the chip-write feature. Careful offices tended to prefer physical cards for introductions and follow-up—but they wouldn't routinely slide a card from some random visitor into their systems. Some cards had proved to carry more than ROM. Some could be quite malicious—a little matter some offices in the world had discovered the hard way.

Content, however, was disappointing. It was Patil's academic vita on the card, nothing special. Her bibliography, nothing untoward, in surface appearance. Check of the bibliography against her actual record in file in Yanni's office produced no variances.

"Still possible," he said, "that Jordan could have brought card stock and paper from Planys. Card stock wouldn't necessarily be viewed as contraband."

Catlin clicked keys. "Jordan's file. List of what they *did* find in his luggage."

That went to Florian's second screen.

" 'Paper goods,' " Florian read. "So we can officially wonder what that encompasses."

"Or . . . back to the original assumption," Catlin said, "Thieu gave it to him and Jordan just walked through customs. Sandwiched in with a stack of blank cards, it wouldn't show on a quick and dirty scan. But again, he could have printed it here, himself—if he could find a printer that wasn't micro-tagged. He doesn't have access to one."

"If it came from Planys, Jordan took real pains to get it here and put it in our hands. Yanni said that Thieu was upset with the reactivation of the terraforming project; he'd been an activist scientist, in his day. So was Jordan. That gives Jordan a motive: political. Jordan's old alliance with Centrists. His tendency to play both sides of the game. His anger against sera." He swung back to the second screen. "So what else did security find on him, in the search? Personal notes?"

"Repro'ed and already returned to him. Dense. Scientific." Those had flashed to one screen, at least the initial page, which was overwritten with Jordan's hand notes. There was computer storage. That was huge, encompassing Paul's personal manual, specifically, with all its files internal to the computer . . . nothing reliant on Library. Jordan hadn't had Library access to other manuals. Just that one. Someone must have given him the entire thing, subfolders and all. There were image files. There were more notes, in the peculiar shorthand of design.

"Not beyond sera to decipher. We could ask her if it's significant. Or if there's anything embedded in it. I'm sure Hicks has had to refer the notes to experts. I'm sure Paul's manual would be significant—if sera could find time to look at it."

"Jordan and Paul's computers were returned within the week. His notes came with it. His books. He was complaining two months ago about access to his own past publications. We know the files he's gotten at since he got clearance. Sera might recognize something in that list that we couldn't."

"Interesting thought," Florian said. "Just a second." He called up that list and ran a filter. It took a moment.

"Well," Catlin said.

"Every one of those publications has Ari Senior's articles, as well as some they co-wrote. Not too surprising, since they worked together."

"Interesting, though."

"Topics. . . ." More keys. "Integrations. Nothing at all to do with Patil."

"Nothing to do with Patil at all."

"Integrations was the subject of his quarrel with Justin. And integrations isn't in his field."

"Justin's working in that field. He had a quarrel with that, and with the first Ari's style."

"Could he have picked the fight as part of a diversion?" Florian asked. "Possibly preparing Justin or Grant for some intervention?"

Catlin frowned. "That would be somewhat beyond us. Certainly outside the question of the card."

"Except that Justin became the target of it, after they had a fight about the first Ari's procedures. I don't see a connection, unless he's aiming at something and wants to divert Justin into some scheme of his own. Maybe he really does hate Thieu. Or wants to sabotage Patil, just for spite."

"Or for profit. Profit would be a reason," Catlin said. "A re-contact with old networks. Former alliances. *That* has politics in it. *That's* more like what the records say of Jordan Warrick."

An *action,* not a gesture, something designed to do exactly what it was doing . . . getting Patil delayed in her move to Fargone. Possible.

And someone, probably Base Two, in Yanni's hands, was hiding Jordan's records from Hicks . . . or Hicks was hiding them from sera.

"Well," Florian said, and flicked up the general ReseuneSec Planys office reports on Jordan Warrick. One statistic leapt out. "Jordan received two thousand eight hundred and fourteen security cautions during his tenure at Planys. Persistent note on his file: *Immune. Do Not Interrogate.*"

"That's been the problem all along with him."

"Yanni doesn't want him in the public eye again. Reseune doesn't want the first Ari's murder opened up again.

That was what was going on when Denys went down. We've got the content of the card chip—nothing overt there, if it's not a verbal code; and still no absolute assurance where the card itself was made. They can go after where it's been—testing to destruction if they do. But I think it was made for exactly what it was used for: an introduction, dropped right in front of us."

"From whom?" Catlin asked. "To whom?"

"Let's see what ReseuneSec admits it knows about Patil."

ReseuneSec's top-level surveillance of Patil came up easily, creditably meticulous, and ongoing, in Novgorod, within the University where she taught. Her contacts, back inside ReseuneSec files, were all neatly mapped—including letters, some sixty-three in number, to her old mentor Thieu, and one hundred eighteen from Thieu to Patil, fifty-two of them in the last half year.

"None to Jordan," Catlin said. "None from Jordan. As should be. Several from Yanni to Patil."

"Patil's house sale is pending. Reseune's buying it. This week. Yanni's order. He had some reason. *That* could hurry up her trip to Fargone."

Meanwhile the list of Patil's other possible primary and secondary contacts stretched on and on, listed and identified by ReseuneSec agents in the ReseuneSec files, every class of person from senators and councillors to teaching assistants, radicals, vid personalities, her real estate agent, and the home-repair technician who'd recently fixed her refrigerator. She'd made numerous net calls on the local Fargone site, investigating housing, amenities, facilities, reasonable in someone contemplating a move there. She'd made a few tries at getting into the restricted Fargone ReseuneSpace site, on a long lag to Cyteen Station, which held that site and others available in its months-ago state: data arrived at the speed of ships that picked up that electronic load at Cyteen Station via their black boxes, and delivered that load to somewhere else, and on to Fargone—in a sense, if you sent a message that entered Cyteen Station, it eventually reached every civilized star, and was everywhere at once, until deleted as absolutely irrelevant to the locale where it had ended up. There was no such thing as complete privacy on interstation mail, by the nature of black boxes; and that also went for net data, restricted or not: it got everywhere unless it had a gate restriction that didn't let it flow to any ships but, say, military, or to no ships at all.

A lot of CITs weren't aware of that fact of life, or, being aware, so profoundly took it for granted that they didn't worry about it. Patil's request for information was certainly widespread by now, so if she'd intended any secrecy, that was blown.

Meticulous, vexatious police work filled other pages, agents patiently tracing out the threads of contact and delving into Patil's household garbage, a list of items intended to be recycled, and diverted, some of it interesting, in the list items, including unopened physical mail. ReseuneSec's investigation seemed thorough. It was a fat correspondence folder. The woman didn't open mail that arrived from unknowns: her system routed it to delete, which deleted a lot of files—or appeared to delete them. ReseuneSec had gotten at the mail source, and been into that, with a resultant long list of would-be contacts, some of which were red-flagged.

"Lot of Paxer contact. Lot of complete unknowns," Florian observed.

"She'd be a fool to send messages of any interesting sort to anyone," Catlin said. "She deletes their messages—evidently knows who to delete. Some of them are on the watch list."

Her mailings out to PlanysLabs were all electronic. One mailing was, by title, "Rethinking the Theory of Long-Period Nanistic Self-direction," —the censored *Scientia* article—sent, with indignation, to Thieu, who had been her teacher. Thieu had replied that it was brilliant. She had written back, decrying entrenched War-years thinking and Luddism . . . the commenting agent had flagged that word and supplied a definition. It meant people who were against progress, based on a political movement of 1811 and some years after, against the introduction of weaving machines in pre-space England.

"Patil has a large vocabulary," Florian said wryly, "clearly."

"Why weaving machines?" Catlin wanted to know. But the remark in context seemed metaphorical, not literal.

"I have no idea," Florian muttered. He was already tracing other things, successfully pulling up ReseuneSec files on the ongoing investigation of Jordan's Planys apartment, and the people ReseuneSec had sent into Planys were clearly better than the airport security team haste haste had trusted with the outbound search. Jordan hadn't gotten to go back to his apartment once he'd been notified he was returning to Reseune: agents had packed for him.

While Jordan and Paul, caught in their office, had perversely or purposefully brought *paper* goods—either to camouflage something; or simply because, being a person for whom hand notes and writing were a habit, Jordan had wanted materials he hadn't been sure he'd get easily if he returned to house arrest in Reseune. It might have been innocent. It seemed Jordan Warrick rarely had been innocent—not by that Planys ReseuneSec record.

One thing he knew: sera's security wouldn't have let Jordan fly without a body scan, let alone turning out his pockets. The staff at Planys' airport had searched him for foodstuffs and biological contraband, their usual worry in flights originating from Planys, but nothing more—because, for security reasons, they hadn't been in on the investigation ReseuneSec was making of Jordan's apartment and had no idea at all what they were looking for.

That was a major slip; but sera's orders had been unexpected, and speed had mattered. Not even ReseuneSec at Planys Airport had known why Jordan was being put on a plane, but people were about to die in Reseune, and had already died in Novgorod: it had been just a confused few hours.

The agents at Reseune Airport had naturally confiscated and copied his notes when he landed, but let blank paper pass without, likely, paging through a personal-use handful of blank sheets. Florian made a mental note of his own, that airport security needed more attention to detail, once sera took Reseune.

And it still boiled down to one question: how had Jordan known about the Patil appointment in Novgorod, in security so tight Base One hadn't penetrated it? That took the old fashioned sneaker-net approach. Someone had hand-carried either the card or actual information about the Patil appointment. Either would do.

So. They could certainly politely *ask* Jordan about the card and see if he'd cooperate, but they weren't to that point yet, and clearly there was no use asking a Special any question to which they didn't already know the answer.

So Patil's condo had found a buyer, in Yanni's office, with a possession date on July 20 . . . whether or not Patil knew that was how it had sold. She was currently saying goodbye to the University in a round of parties attended mostly by academics—one such was scheduled this evening. She had sold most of her furnishings, given other items away to friends and charity; was actively arranging storage for all her non-data possessions that she planned to keep, perhaps to ship later. She had no known sexual attachments, no children, no relatives.

She was a scholarly woman with a lot of electronic files, preparing to make a long, state-sponsored and fairly high-mass move to a new life, accompanied by those data files and a fair number of household goods—plus being a CIT, likely a few items of emotional attachment.

"She's teaching two classes currently," Catlin reported, "besides lab courses, and she is maintaining her schedule. I checked other professors. They have more classes. Patil spends a lot of time writing and some time doing correspondence with the military labs out at Beta, which we can't penetrate. No change of pattern there. She does guest lectures, attends bioethics conferences . . ."

"The people she's contacting on Cyteen," Florian murmured, scanning that list, and the commentary ReseuneSec provided, "old acquaintances, former students, but not many."

"The majority may be on Beta, in Beta Labs. Security block, there."

"I'm not going to try to crack that," Florian said. "Not worth it to go after those—yet." He kept reading. "Mmm. Here's a few names on her home system, people ReseuneSec notes for further investigation." He ran a who-is on the few, at ReseuneSec level. "Well. Well. Well. How long have we been at this?"

"Two and a half hours."

"Well, nothing totally new in this. We have some foot-notes here from ReseüneSec. But no mischief attaches directly to Patil, except her lectures attract radicals. Cof-fee," Florian said, and got up and poured a cup from the dispenser. A glance at Catlin drew a nod, and he poured another, then looked at the clock himself. Close to time for shift-change. "I'm going to message Marco and Wes to lie in for another couple of hours. I think we should look through Science Bureau records. Base One can probably get into those."

"Suits me," Catlin said. "Try it. Shall I have Gianni send us sandwiches?"

"I could use one," Florian said, and settled back at his console, pulled out the under-counter return that kept cof-fee off the main desk, and set his cup there. Catlin did whatever she was doing. He worked delicately, probed this, probed that, scanned text without storing it, and didn't get a Base One warning of any unadvertised connections on Yanni's access, no strings attached.

The files had some background of interest. Defense had apparently had a lot to do with Patil's career. Black budget funding had been behind the terraforming labs when they were on Cyteen, specifically at a lab just a little outside Novgorod, a lab later razed in favor of a food production facility. Behind closed Council doors, there'd been an in-tense battle over removal of the nanistics lab out to Beta during the War. Centrists campaigned to keep it at least as close as Cyteen Station, not relegated to the outer system inside a Defense installation. The first Ari had supported the nanistics move to Beta, however, in agreement with Defense, and Centrists had opposed her *and* Defense, at that time, in a rare configuration of political alliances.

Patil, at a hundred and five years of age, had gone out to Beta when Thieu moved down to Cyteen, had subsequently distinguished herself in ways deeply classified, and then Patil herself had been moved back to Central System and onto Cyteen as a safety measure during the darkest days of the War. Patil, Thieu, and a researcher named Ibsen, Pau-line Ibsen, since deceased, age one hundred thirty-six, had all been sent down to Cyteen, three people who had been working on the blackest of black projects—most likely the production of terraforming nanistics, but theoretically only: any lab work was done out at Beta, as a potential and never-used weapon of war.

After the War, Patil *hadn't* gotten promoted back out to Beta. "Articulate, sharp, and gregarious," so the report said, she had "fallen into the social milieu of the University," had found herself a comfortable post and a prosperous side income as a favorite speaker at Centrist and pro-terraforming conferences and meetings.

Clearly her imminent departure into Reseune's employment had stirred up the Centrist community. Some comments had hit the general web, the one that any CIT could access. Some Centrists were pleased at the acceptance of what they called a moderating influence into a Reseune post: others were more concerned about losing Dr. Patil's moderate and respectable voice in Novgorod politics, once she shipped to Fargone, and wondered if it was a means of silencing her voice. None of the reports apparently knew about her relationship to the Eversnow project.

" 'Moderate and reasonable,' they call her," Florian said, having condensed the flow for Catlin. " 'A peace-keeper.' Which might argue that Yanni's move to send Patil to Fargone really isn't the best idea, losing her local influence. The Paxers come to her lectures. She doesn't appear to support their activities."

"Moderation might have been what recommended her to Yanni, however," Catlin said, and they read a while longer.

Then Catlin said: "Read the post under *Gulag*."

Interesting word. They were down to CIT political gossip on the Novgorod city net. Florian looked that word up, before investigating the site Catlin had tossed him.

The Gulag writer was passionately angry, convinced Patil's transfer was a ticket to a Reseune-run oblivion and possible assassination. Well, there might be a grain of truth, not likely in the second.

And there seemed, according to the ReseuneSec note, another conspiracy theory circulating, quoting a Bureau of Defense argument in committee, that it was a move by Reseune to gut the Beta Station lab: one supporter of that viewpoint maintained Patil was still doing Defense work, and could not legally be transferred from a public university into a Reseune-run lab.

"It's not actually the law that she can't be transferred," Catlin commented. "They just make it sound illegal. She's a scientist. Science posts come from Science, even if her post is classified by Defense. She just has a job offer from Science. And if she accepts it, Defense can't claim there's a war reason, because the War Powers Act has lapsed."

Catlin was very much better on law than he was.

But law wasn't the name of the game. "Politics. Politics is all. Both sides are likely pressuring her for loyalty. But she votes in Science, because that's what she is, doesn't she? Check what profession she actually votes in."

A few key-taps, Science Bureau records. "Her voter registration is definitely Science. So she's *not* registered military any more, not since 2406. Defense still runs the lab at Beta, and if she went back out there, she'd properly be voting in Defense again. But if she goes to Fargone and works in the new Reseune set-up, then Defense hasn't got any complaint. They can't claim she knows military secrets, none current, at least. No more than Thieu. So the Gulag writer is wrong in his suppositions."

"And she *wants* to go to Fargone. Otherwise she could easily get legal help from Defense and get transferred to them."

"Which she's not doing. So she does accept going to Fargone. And so do Defense's upper echelons, because they agreed with Yanni. And that will be this Eversnow project, when it starts, and it's likely to be very soon."

"Why did she accept Yanni's offer?" Florian asked. "Why is she agreeing to jump ship to Reseune?" Why was one of his favorite questions, best when asked when things seemed neat and wrapped up. And it seemed to fit, here. Understandable if someone didn't want to be returned to Beta, which was remote and secretive and full of regulations. Fargone was a comfortable station—not the comforts of Cyteen Station, to be sure, but very much better than Beta. There was that. Eversnow, on the other hand, was a frontier. As barren as Big Blue. A bare steel and prefab station. No luxuries. "Novgorod's the height of comfort. She's respected. She has an important job. She doesn't work hard. She's very well paid. She has very many associates who respect her. Why choose to leave?"

Catlin frowned. It was close on CIT territory, asking the unanswerable: the emotionally founded question posing as born-man logic, with *far* too little knowledge of the individual. "Either going to something or from something."

"*To* Reseune's new lab. Or *from* Novgorod. Could there be something in Fargone she wants? Or could there be something in Novgorod she'd like to be away from?"

"The work at Eversnow might attract her."

"Or Novgorod might not be as good for her as it seems. She has the Paxers here. They won't be there. Some of these people at her lectures are politically intense fringe elements. I've got the background summation on people attending. Long, long list." He flashed it over to her. "Some of these people have third-degree contacts under intense watch, indirect links to persons undergoing mindwipe in the hotel bombing that tried to kill *us.*"

"Politics," Catlin said.

"Politics," Florian said, and tagged the whole area for re-reading and absorption. "I'm going to tape this bit—considering how it connects to Yanni, and considering sera's plans—which don't wholly agree with Yanni. It still doesn't answer the timing of the card."

"Give me the tape," Catlin said. "That's a good find. Not the opinion, the names."

For deepstudy, that is: things they needed to absorb completely, names they needed to know and deep-associate with Paxer activity. And with Sandi Patil. So they never forgot them.

It was a luxury he and Catlin had never enjoyed before, to sit atop a pyramid of data, with skilled people doing exactly what they were Contracted to do, people tapped into all of ReseuneSec and going over reports from all that organization did on Cyteen and elsewhere. The Reseune-Sec access didn't lead them to new things, but it organized things in a way different from Base One—and that gave them a window into ReseuneSec thinking.

First it seemed to lead them further and further afield from the item they'd started chasing: Jordan Warrick and the infamous card . . . and then it seemed to lead back again . . . to Yanni's office; and Jordan Warrick. And Patil.

"We need to filter this other, too," Florian said. "The net opinions. Not good to deepstudy it." Deepstudy diminished critical thinking. This was opinion. A lot of opinion, from untrustworthy people. They just needed the names from the Novgorod CIT net, and the suspicions attached to them.

"I don't know where we're going to get the time to do this," Catlin said. "Sera wants to begin prep for moving."

It wasn't convenient, the timing of their complete relocation. Their new staff was delayed. But there was worry on the other side, too, that sera would be less safe if they delayed getting her into a more fortified residence.

"No good complaining," Florian said. "We just have to do this." Patil's data was still flying under his fingers. "We need to understand it. All our lives, we'll need to. These are the Enemy. This is where it starts. The people that may be against sera now are the people that will be against sera all her life. And for now—for now we just watch Base Two very carefully."

BOOK

THREE

JUNE 1, 2424
1528H

Growth proceeded at the same breakneck pace, for Giraud, for Abban, for Seely, at fifteen weeks. They were all without significant defect, and on the path to being male. They took in amniotic fluid, practice and pressure alike expanding the rudimentary structures of their lungs, and Abban was now tallest of the three, a bit heavier—in grams, which was the scale on which they existed.

Giraud's face was broader—hard to see, but it was.

They had human proportions, more or less—their legs were longer than their arms were. Their rudimentary eyes, as yet without an opening in the lids, and not quite on the front of the faces, were growing sensitive to more and less light—a probing beam, into a tank, would get a definite reactive flinch: they didn't *know* they didn't like it, but change in what-was drew response, an instinct to preserve the status quo. It wasn't fight-flight yet, just the beginnings of it.

Details had emerged, tastebuds, which would matter a great deal to Giraud, less so to Abban and Seely. Those appeared, and simultaneously, the ability to sweat—though sweat was not that useful, in the fluid environment, in the rocking safety of artificial wombs. They continued, enveloped by the soft, variable thump of a human heartbeat, steel mother-sound, helping set the rhythm of their bodies. Individuality had asserted itself. Their fingerprints differed, as surely as their DNA. And they were not like each other, not at all.

JUNE 1, 2424
1528H

There's a reason, I think, that the first Ari wasn't kind: not many people were kind to her—they just gave her a lot of privileges, or let her get away with what she wanted to do because they didn't pay attention, and that's not the same. So I don't think Ari quite understood about kindness. But I don't think having had kindness in my life means that I'm less driven to succeed than she was. My brain is as good as hers. I might have just a few different motives—she fought for power and her own protection. I fight to protect the people I love. But she fought, and I fight. That much is the same.

The new wing, Alpha Wing, well—new, in my time, though for you it's not. It's where you live now, unless somebody decides otherwise, or unless you decide otherwise, for security reasons, or just because you don't like my decor any more than I like Denys'. I don't know how long Reseune can add new wings for every one of us that's ever born. But there you are. Or there you will be—I hope somewhat safe and comfortable in your day.

And today I've given the order that will mean my Uncle Denys gets born in due course, seven years from now, or whenever if I'm sure I can compress the schedule a bit: that's a decision Yanni has left to me, but I'll probably stick to the seven years. If I do, it's mostly for Giraud's sake. And I'm going to apologize to you right now about creating Denys, because you'll probably hate him and you'll probably have really good reason. But I'm afraid Giraud is going to be too easygoing, without him. And this time Denys will be the young and ignorant kid, not me. I'm afraid by the time you come along, you'll get the old Denys, the way I did, and I'm sorry for that.

I don't want to change Denys's essential nature—it's

his program—but I'll have to think about that, maybe for quite a few years before I actually order his geneset into the womb. I have plenty of time to get ahead of him. Once you start changing foundational things in our patterns, as you'll be learning, everything after that has to flex, and that's rapidly a field-too-large problem. A very, very big problem. The variables are terrible.

And I don't know how well my upcoming move to a new wing will work. Wing One is historic, and it's important, and if architecture can embody a psychological structure, a lot of what made Reseune is in its walls and its rooms. But I'm trying, at least, to set new patterns, and the new wing is where I'm making my start.

Among first jobs, I want to patch all the things up that my Denys deliberately broke. He sent a lot of people away, people I'd attached to . . . my playmate Valery, and his whole family, even if they were Yanni's relatives. I missed him terribly. And they sent Maman and Ollie out to Fargone, and I couldn't do anything about it. Maybe you've had people vanish from your life, too. I hope not. But if they have, pay attention to what I'm doing now. These people I'm calling home to me may be important to you in your own life, if they all live that long, and if I could substitute Valery for Denys, for your sake, oh, I would do that, so fast. Valery was so kind, so nice, he made me happy as long as I had him for a friend, and they sent him and his mother away precisely because I liked him. And we were only babies, ourselves, well, nearly so. But I never forgot him. That's one piece of justice I'm going to do, first and foremost. I don't know how he's turned out. That's one.

And Ollie. He was an alpha azi when I knew him. He was Maman's companion. Right now he's Director of the labs out at Fargone . . . he's very good at what he does. He's legally a CIT now, and of course he's old, far, far past a hundred, and a long time on rejuv, and he'll do what he wants to. I'd so love to see Ollie again. I'd love to make everything right for him—he'd have grieved so much when Maman died and nobody treated him with any consideration at all, here at Reseune, or out there, at the time. But I won't order him to come, as old as he is, and knowing the trip itself might be hard on him. Fargone was where she died, and for all I know he may be attached to that place, and it's certain he has his work out there, that's very important to Reseune. No matter what I want, I wouldn't want to tear him away from his place there if he doesn't want to come back. And between you and me, I really don't think he will.

And I've given invitations to the others, too, not necessarily to live in Alpha Wing, but maybe they will, if they're nice people. I want them at least to be able to come back to Wing One, where they used to live. Valery's mother was Andrea Schwartz, who is Yanni Schwartz's family, and Yanni couldn't protect her from being exiled: she was out there with Jenna Schwartz, who used to be in charge out there, but she was a fool, and Yanni moved her out. And then there's Julia Strassen, and I know she's still alive: she was Maman's real daughter, and I've written to her, too, to bring her back with Valery and Andrea Schwartz. Maman had agreed to bring me up, because she was a scientist. That meant Julia and her daughter Gloria had to stay away from the apartment and not upset me. Gloria was a brat, but her mother hated me for ruining their lives even if she knew it wasn't really my fault—I was a baby. I think Julia pretty well set up the atmosphere that made Gloria act up whenever they visited. She probably didn't intend to, which I think shows something about Julia. Their going away—I think that would have happened when I got to a certain age anyway; and I'm sure Denys would have sent them away when he sent Maman. But I'm sure it hurt less for Aunt Julia to be mad at me than it did for her to be mad at her own maman, and being mad at me was certainly a lot safer than being mad at Denys Nye at the time. So she was exiled to Fargone, too, and I don't know what Maman thought about it, but I'm not sure she liked Julia or Gloria that much at the last.

So it's time for all those old accounts to be settled, and for me to make amends as best I can—especially to Valery, who never did anything in his life but be my friend without being in the Program.

My maman's real name, you know by now, was Jane Strassen. And she was a brilliant woman, and very dedicated to the Project, but she wasn't ever cold to me the way

Denys was. Maman really loved me and I loved her, which is probably the first place I deviated from the Program— because the first Ari's mother wasn't kind to her at all.

And I'm sure Maman started out loving Julia and Gloria, too, but Gloria certainly wasn't very loveable by the time I remember anything about her, and Julia just looked daggers at me—that's all I can remember about her. Maybe she'll read my invitation and tell me go to hell. I'd honestly be relieved.

Why did Maman get involved in bringing me up, and forget about her own daughter and granddaughter? I found out that Yanni talked her into it and promised her she could get off Cyteen and go back into space where she was from. But at a certain point I think Maman got curious what I'd be like, and maybe she saw things about me that reminded her of the Ari she'd worked with, and deliberately encouraged some things and corrected others. I can't remember that part, and I haven't found all of it in records, but if you can find it, it might be worth looking at, just for your own curiosity—in case it answers some question you have about me. I think Maman had some inkling of protecting me from Denys, or maybe making the Program work better for some altruistic or scientific reason—because I was an experiment, after all, and Maman was a scientist, not somebody just mindlessly plodding along a track.

I remember one day: Maman comparing Gloria to me and finally telling Julia to take Gloria and get out of the apartment . . . Gloria was trying to beat my brains in, that day, so there was a reason, but I can still hear Maman telling Julia to get her daughter out of there, and even then I knew it wasn't the most politic thing she could have said to her daughter. When you live so long—when rejuv lets you go through family after family, the layers get more complicated than nature ever designed us to deal with, I think. The relationships get tangled, adults with kids, this generation's kids with the other one—they sell a lot of books advising people how to get along with polygenerational families and serial partners and rejuv issues. Maybe by your generation it'll all be saner, but rejuv was still a new issue in those days, and people didn't always handle it well. I know Maman's household was likely upset before I even

got there, and my presence just drove Julia over the edge
and made her do things that weren't smart.

And Valery—who wasn't even part of our family—the
Project directors couldn't have me getting attached to a
friend, or have me that happy, so they had to find a way to
get Valery away from me. There just wasn't much of anywhere to send his mother, Andrea, because she was doing
classified work. So off they went to ReseuneSpace at Fargone, where they could be in a sealed research community,
involved with trying to clone another personality. Look up
Rubin, if you're curious.

Denys was probably the one who ordered Valery to go
away—because at a certain point—you understand better
than anyone—it was just time for life to get harder for me.

So for starters, they sent Valery away, and Julia and
Gloria, and then when I was seven, they sent Maman
away. And that was because the first Ari's mother died at
that precise age, and it was time, in the Project, for Jane
Strassen to go away—along with Ollie, which was kind
of Denys, at least, that Ollie went with her . . . but I think
Denys never even thought about that. They just wanted everybody I loved to leave, and Denys took charge of me one
day and told me Maman was gone forever and I had to
move in with him, and that was the way things had to be.

I was upset. I was terribly upset. Everything had been
good, and then it wasn't, and he really hated having a child
around. He made that clear, fast.

Worse, he particularly hated the first Ari. Or at least
what he felt about her was tangled and complicated. If
what I think is right, he may be the one who killed her. Or
his azi did, to protect him from her. And Abban and Seely
are both dead, so nobody can ask them what the truth was,
not that it matters, now, anyway.

I hope, I really do, that you don't have to go through
that kind of separation from people you love. But probably you've already had to, and maybe you hate me as part
of all of it, but likely by now you probably realize why you
had to go through it, so I hope you forgive me along with
the rest of them. I know I might not have survived my coming of age if I hadn't been through the fire.

So maybe the first Ari was right, and if I'd had no

stress on me I'd be like that poor clone of Estelle Bok: I'd guess you still study that case, along with Rubin, or if you don't—do. They gave Bok Two the best of everything, and that genius brain just floundered around with no boundaries, until it went way, way off into miserable territory, and became none too sane. Rubin wasn't a great success, either, or isn't, so far. He's just a pretty good chemist. And his predecessor, with every luxury in the world, committed suicide right in the middle of the program. Didn't that throw my keepers into a fit?

So you are whatever you are, and I am what I became, because they were suddenly hard on me at the right time. The first Ari had had her mother telling her when to breathe in and out, until her life changed suddenly and her mother died and she was just Ari, trying to survive in Reseune and not to have anybody murder her. She suddenly had to fight. So did I. Maybe so do you.

So even at eighteen years old, I'm still sorting out what the Project did to me, and I can say I'm all right and I'm glad I learned to defend myself. But I'm not satisfied with just finding out I'm all right. Now is my time to try to sort out what the Project did to other people—people the Project didn't give a damn if it hurt. Maybe it will work. Maybe it's beyond recovery. But I intend to try.

I hope all those people will find a way to love me after all. It's selfish. But I do hope so. Is that a vulnerability? Maybe. But it's me.

BOOK THREE   Section I   Chapter iii

JUNE 1, 2424
1540H

Ari shoved back from the console. Replayed the last bit. Struck it out, disturbed by what had come out of her in that rambling account, not sure it was good for her successor to hear that much honesty, whether that it was too stupid, that badly written, too naive to say, or whether it revealed too much—it was embarrassing, was what. It revealed a trigger. A touchpoint. That was worth considering. It was just too personal.

But her successor had to know her. It could be life or death. And she recalled that section, reviewed it, then entered the code that made it, with all the other entries, uneraseable.

BOOK THREE   Section I   Chapter iv

JUNE 6, 2424
1657H

It ought to be suppertime, but it wasn't, yet—the new domestic staff was finally arriving. Ari had put on a favorite rose sweater and a nicer pair of pants, plus a little jewelry, anxious to have the new people have the best impression of her and the household.

Catlin and Florian had missed their dinnertime, too—there was never a time she met strangers that they weren't right beside her. Marco and Wes were in the security station, it being their shift as of an hour ago, but the rest of staff was stirring about in the kitchen, getting ready with a nice little party, sandwiches and refreshments for the incomers.

Herself—she was thinking of that pile of sandwiches when the word came that the group had passed building security, presented their ID's, and been logged in. That was about a three-minute process to reach upstairs via the lift, another to reach her apartment.

Deep breath.

And a group of people exited the lift and approached the apartment. Corey was on duty there, with his partner Mato, the two Marco and Wes identicals. They were spit and polish for the occasion.

And, no question, the group on the other side of the

door would be all nerves: they were just Contracted. It was birthdays, weddings, and first jobs all rolled into one bundle and presented to them—and they were Contracted not just to *any* client, mind, but—she could think so without overmuch egotism—to *her*. With all she meant to make *that* mean to them, every advantage, every comfort for her staff. She'd do well for them, and they'd help her run the new place, once they moved over.

She stood in the hallway, hands folded. Corey opened the doors to the newcomers, a handsome lot, mostly male, all wearing the typical azi barracks issue. Her domestics, like Corey and Mato, wore dark blue, her security—like Florian and Catlin, plain black. These wore, at the moment, gray.

The group stopped, shuffled a little, making room for the lot of them in the foyer. They eyed her respectfully.

"I'm Ariane Emory," she said, and that name would resonate off their Contracts, which was much, much more than paper. The whole group bowed, as if one nerve ran through them all. "I expect," she said, "that you're Theo."

"Theo BT-384, sera," the foremost identified himself— a dark, squarefaced man with a cleft in his chin

"Theo, you're our new majordomo."

"Yes," Theo said cheerfully, and drew forward the woman at his side, a thin-boned blonde with fine features. "My partner, Jory."

"Jory will be your direct assistant in your post. Pro tem major domo has been Callie. You'll work with her to get settled in. Callie will be household administration and chief of supply, hereafter, and answer to you, but no other on staff."

Theo bowed. Jory did.

"Very satisfactory," she said. "I'm very pleased with you." Meeting new Contracts, as their Supervisor, she found it was of utmost importance to offer reassurance, confirmation: they were pyschologically exposed, as never in their lives, and so much hung on her expressions and her tone.

"And who is Wyndham?" she asked.

Wyndham stepped to the fore, one of the most anticipated of arrivals, their new cook, with his partner Hiro.

That meant that Gianni, who did excellent desserts, could concentrate on his specialty and give the running of the kitchen over to someone who could orchestrate dinner for eight and take great delight in showing off.

Logan, Haze, Tomas, Spessy: they were general work, domestic and repair. The two remaining women, Del and Joyesse, were solely to attend her personal needs, do her hair, handle her wardrobe, and double-check her appointments and calendar.

And Callie showed up, nodded very respectfully to Theo and Jory when introduced.

"Very well done," Ari said to Callie, because it was important, too, that the original household staff feel appreciated and by no means diminished in the arrival of more specifically trained individuals. "You've all done extremely well, under very trying circumstances. Nothing supplants your respect, and you retain a special place in my regard, for being with me longest and managing everything. I have a special affection for my seniormost staff: I have every confidence in you in this transition. Understand, this arrival frees you of any extraneous duties, and you will repeat this, verbatim, to all the staff: you are needed and much respected."

"Sera," Callie said, and bowed. Her eyes sparkled—that last bit was all keywords, deepset, key to this staff's feelings of accomplishment, resonating specifically off deepsets like an affectionate caress, and Callie was empowered to pass it on. "Shall I guide the new staff, sera?"

"Do," Ari said, letting Callie, for her last time, function as chief of staff. She stood quietly for a moment with Mato and Corey. "Well done," she said to them. "Very well done."

Bows. The spark of pleasure, the little reserve of beta azi very, very secure in their posts and their place in the house. "Sera," Corey said, for the both of them.

Florian and Catlin—no need to reassure them at all. But she smiled at them simply because she *was* happy. It felt like walking a tightrope, selecting new staff, taking Contracts, trying to be sure the incomers, totally vulnerable, felt an instant connection and sense of place. She made eye contact with each and every one, saw their expressions, read them, far easier than reading any CIT in their current state.

"In and safe, sera," Florian said.

She laid a hand on Florian's arm, and on Catlin's, not a calm-down, just gratitude. She felt physically tired, as if she'd given off an energy that outright exhausted her, poured it into those wide-open faces on whom she'd rely for her comfort and her safety.

Or perhaps it was the immediate letdown of having been absolutely On all day, waiting for these people, her people, picking what she'd say, and planning the way she'd ease staff about their arrival—those things, and the plain fact it was suppertime.

Callie's tour would end in the kitchens, Wyndham's new domain, where Gianni had been working on one of his tour de force desserts to impress the new master chef. They'd have supper together, the new staff and old; and meanwhile she found herself ravenous, a good sign. She'd arranged all the staff to be attending the dinner: the fare otherwise was cold cuts and sandwich makings, and that, with two bottles of imported champagne, was waiting for her and her security staff.

Florian and Catlin, too, had worn themselves out trying to be all things and everywhere for months. Now they wouldn't have to turn a hand to make a bed or find a midnight snack. Anything they wanted, at any time, always, would arrive, double-quick. They'd never experienced that situation, not since they were all children together, and they'd had Uncle Denys' staff waiting on them.

"I'm happy," she said, hugging their arms tight. "I'm starved. Let's go have supper."

"Marco and Wes are on duty," Florian said.

"They can have champagne, too," she said. "They can come. It's not as if our enemies will stage a raid."

"When better?" Florian asked soberly, but she squeezed his arm a second time.

"I love you both, but let's take the risk, shall we? Champagne, strawberries, and cold sandwiches. It's a security picnic in the conference room."

They were bound to worry. It was what they did. And in the end, they called in Marco and Wes, cued the conference room screen to display the security station main screen, and had their champagne and strawberries.

It was mostly for their sake, for the staff. They'd taken care of her through so much, and they did things that weren't their duty, doing it.

It was one more step toward that apartment. They'd be crowded for a while, but that wouldn't last long.

Then things began to be Real.

She didn't want to think about that tonight.

There was a baby, she recalled, a boy named Auguste GYX, the first baby she'd ever seen in the labs, the first time she really began to think about what Reseune did, and she'd said to herself a long time ago that she wanted to be sure that baby turned out all right . . . that when his Contract came up, she wanted to take it. And he was something around thirteen, still in training—a gamma, clever at a lot of things. And for some reason, with staff coming in, she thought of him and thought: *I want to know what they're prepping him for. I've got the power to do that now. I can write a set for him. I can take the thirteen years and just bend it in a direction I choose, something I can eventually use, something to put him on staff—not have him shipped off to Novgorod and have him supering in a factory where I'll lose track of him.*

I can work with a gamma set. I'm going to call in his manual tomorrow. I can write a program for him. It'd be nice if he liked fish.

Things had gotten quiet. She looked at four faces, Florian and Catlin, Wes and Marco, all quite sober—their notion of a wild staff party was a glass apiece—all gazing at her, waiting for her to say something—or to really look at them.

"This," she said, "is a point of change. From now on out, we don't depend on Yanni for many things we now ask of him—including my study tape. Wes, tomorrow I want you to walk over to Library and physically pull a manual for me."

It involved printout. "Shall I call it first?" Wes asked, meaning should he call Library and have it prepared for him to pick up.

"No. Ask there and wait for it."

At very least, she didn't want a request on file before she had the GYX general manual in hand—there could well be more than one GYX in progress, and even Wes didn't need to know which GYX she was interested in until she had that particular file in hand. It wouldn't remove it from Library, and anyone interested could still get it, with the sort of clearance, for instance, that Hicks or Yanni had—but once she duped that manual in-house, and began to write changes on that program—she would have her GYX's particular record, and Yanni wouldn't. He could find out what tape they'd run down in labs, but he couldn't find out any oral Working she'd done, and he wasn't good enough, she'd bet on it, to look at the tape list and immediately know what structure she was building or what her GYX was destined to be.

She had the individual manuals on Theo and Jory and the rest. Those came with them. And *those* individuals would see changes very soon that weren't on the lab records. She'd prepare tape of her own creation, and when she was through—they'd be hers, no one else's, ever. That was the way the system worked.

Justin could pass on that, too, but she'd done more than population dynamics in recent weeks. She'd studied set-alteration and deep inhibition as well as integrations. And she'd taken a look at some of the first Ari's set designing, on the Gehenna project.

It wasn't just history of that project she'd been after. She hoped she could spot a deepteach bug in the azi she'd taken in—that she could spot it, correct it, and have that azi absolutely trustable. It wasn't brain surgery. In many cases it was plain language, like what the first Ari had instilled at Gehenna: this is your world. Your world—deeptaught in those azi minds—without any reference to the born-men the military had sent out there deliberately to fail, mess up the planet, and die.

The military had thought they were simply giving Alliance a poison pill, knowing they'd take Gehenna and Union wasn't in position to. But the poison pill the military hadn't counted on, in their own planning, had been letting the first Ariane Emory know that *her* azi were destined to become an embedded, dying and miserably poor popula-

tion on a planet the Alliance was going to claim. Ariane
Emory didn't *do* that sort of thing to *her* azi, no. She gave
them the planet and told them to survive and take care
of it. And survive they did—becoming foreign and odd
in the reckoning of what was human, but they lived. They
succeeded.

The first Ari had, as best she'd ever been able to discover,
given her Florian and Catlin, and Yanni had given her Wes
and Marco, and she'd taken Callie and all the rest.

There were going to be, very soon, some deep-sessions
for certain staff, not for Florian and Catlin. They would be
quiet, refreshing sessions, with some very specific instruction keyed to *their* sets—instruction which could make
them very devoted, or very dangerous, depending on her
skill at intervention.

"You are my first staff," she said, "and the core of my
staff. What you say, I will always hear. And I rely on you
for loyalty and intelligence."

Heads dipped. Eyes fixed on her. Supervisor. They
heard that as they'd hear tape, and they drank it in.

"You are special," she said, "and your decisions matter. The secrets of this house stay in this house. This is
for Marco and Wes: if you have to trust someone and you
have to make a judgement outside this house, trust Justin
Warrick."

Again, solemn nods—just a little resisting flicker from
Florian and Catlin, who'd been excluded from that last sentence. Wes and Marco were absorbing it all—deepstate, as
azi could do without the deepteach drug, as almost now,
she could do: her concentration could go that deep. And
only with their Contracted supervisor would azi accept instruction at that level. She looked at Wes and Marco, saw
their pupils dilated, a sign of deepstate, which said something on its own.

They were hers. About Florian and Catlin, she had no
question at all, never had.

She'd doubted herself at times, which, she thought, was
only healthy to do, but now that she'd begun to focus on
real things, on taking over, she began to think—I have to.
I have no choice, do I? It's life or death. My staff has to be
mine. Especially my security.

JUNE 6, 2424
2122H

She had someone to turn down her bed that night—spooky, at first sight. She wasn't used to that, not since Nelly had left her. She assumed Joyesse had done it, or ordered it. She put on her nightgown—unaided—draped yesterday's clothes over the chair and started to go to bed.

But the computer in her room suddenly showed a unique flasher on an otherwise dark screen, a flasher that lit the adjacent wall red, and her heart picked up its beats.

Not a mail notification that blipped quietly in a corner. *Log On,* it said, across the screen.

She sat down at the counter and did that, no question. And the screen blinked, and became text.

"So you're making a move toward power," Base One said in the first Ari's voice. **"And you wonder how I can guess that. Wonder instead who else can guess it, and act appropriately."**

It wasn't really Base One doing the thinking. It was the first Ari, who'd set certain criteria, and when she met them, things turned up. This one had. And it sent a chill down her back. No good trying to talk to it. It had something to say, and it would say it come hell or high water.

"Correctly identify your allies and your enemies, young Ari. I don't say friends, because that word is misleading and it can deliver you into a serious mistake. Some people you don't like are allies and some people you do like are enemies once you choose a certain course of action, and by now you should understand that."

She did. She had understood it. But Ari Senior put it into words in a particularly cold way that did nothing for the shivers. She wore a thin nightgown in a room cooled for nighttime, and she hugged her arms about herself, because Base One wouldn't stop once it started, wouldn't stop, wouldn't pause, didn't care about her weaknesses or her excuses.

"Rely on Florian and Catlin. No others."

There was Justin. Marco. Wes. But, she thought, Elder Ari didn't know them. But if elder Ari had intended to leave a loophole she would have left it.

"Particularly be cautious about trust. Trust stops reasoning. Look carefully at those you trust. Taking offense stops reasoning, too. You may find a certain person has betrayed you. Limit the offending person so his misdeed cannot possibly repeat itself. Waste no time in regret or sympathy."

I'm about to do that. I'm ahead of you here, older Ari.

"Assume the worst case where it regards those possessing what you intend to take. Assume violent resistence or clever resistence. Assume sabotage. Once you move, move decisively and pitilessly to protect your own allies. If you have pity, bestow it appropriately, on those helping you. Reward compliance and you'll be surrounded by the compliant."

That's not necessarily a good thing, older Ari.

". . . which is not necessarily a good thing, young Ari."

That was spooky. That was just downright *scary.*

"You'll need complete control of ReseuneSec to protect yourself. For the rest, rely on Base One. At need, you can lock anyone out of communication. Your codeword is CannaeCannaeCannae. Input that and the Base you target will only respond to you. You will at that point be able to dispense other codewords, so have them ready, but hand a Base access only to those who are both friends and allies."

Control on a platter. Elder Ari had set it all up for her, the way elder Ari had had Base One assemble itself out of bits and pieces and come alive. She'd triggered something without intending it or even knowing it existed, and possibly it would just roll on like a juggernaut, without her being able to stop it.

She thought: I don't know if I want this. I don't know if I want to lock Yanni out. I'm not ready to do that. Hicks' people—they could start shooting. Hicks is Yanni's man, I'm pretty sure. What am I supposed to do about that?

"Key your receipt of this message so the program is

sure you heard it. It will replay on demand, should you need to review it. I recommend that."

She keyed her login. Said yes to the question. And the screen went dark again, shut down.

She hugged her arms around her and stared at it, feeling the cold go numb, the mind—the mind traveling its own starless space.

Joyesse found her that way some time later, and hovered by her, saying, "Sera? Sera? Are you well?"

She knew it was Joyesse. The surface mind still took account of things, but the deeper thoughts didn't want to be interrupted. She got up, and walked toward the bed, and got in, letting Joyesse draw the covers over her. She shut her eyes, but she wasn't asleep, wouldn't sleep, not while her thoughts were going over the dynamic that was Reseune, and the legislature, and the necessity of appropriating ReseuneSec.

She didn't want to pull the trigger. She didn't *want* to lose Yanni. She didn't *want* to treat Yanni as an enemy, but Hicks had told Florian they were going to have top-level access and either Yanni was hiding things from ReseuneSec, or ReseuneSec was hiding things from them.

And that wasn't good.

Hicks was giving them a gift. Did they trust the thirty agents they were getting?

Assume the worst case where it regards those possessing what you intend to take.

I do have to do something. And something we've done put Base One on alert. It had a trigger tripped. Something I did, or that Florian or Catlin did, tripped it, and that means Yanni may figure it out, too, or Hicks might.

If it wasn't us that tripped the alarm—if Yanni's moved...

It was the middle of the night. She couldn't call Justin. She *shouldn't* call Justin and ask him to hurry in his assessments on the security sets. That wasn't the way to get the best results.

Base One, however, could find out how he was doing. Base One could get into any computer in the Wing.

She got up, grabbed a robe from the closet this time, and said, "Base One, on."

Base One asserted itself in the computer, and turned the terminal on. She sat down. She searched up computers that were active in the Wing and found Justin's office net with no trouble at all. It was listed as secure, probe-proof. That meant nothing to Base One, which ran System in the Wing. She simply had a look into the files, and ran a search for recent files involving betas.

There they were, in a folder labeled *goddess1.*

Goddess, was it? Sarcastic, maybe. Justin could be that. It was certain he had no interest in her *that* way. He'd made that clear when she was, oh, much, much too young. And he was settled with Grant. She'd be a fool to mess with that attachment, a really great fool.

She read the notes on the people Hicks had sent her. Justin had started with the bottom, the gammas. Number one gamma, passed, number two, passed.

She read far beyond that. He had left the betas for last, and was two individuals from finishing, which meant he might be done tomorrow.

"Sera?" From the door. Joyesse again. "Sera, would you like anything?"

"Nothing," she said, and Joyesse went away. Ari delved deeper, deeper into her own understanding of sets, and read Justin's notes, and absorbed his comments, which made *sense.* He saw, clear as clear, where the sets were vulnerable to a command, and noted push-button items that just had to be patched, was all.

Easy to do. She knew the way to do it. People reacted— to expectation of good stimulus, like praise; to fear, linked to imagination—imaginative people feared a wider range of things. And some people had an "off" switch that routed an idea to the analytic faculties, and some—mus, which they didn't birth many of, were like that—you started them on a track and they'd follow it without a second thought. Mus wanted everything to be the same all the time—they were happier when it was like that—unless what they were assigned linked to a desire for an adrenaline rush, which was a whole other problem. . . .

Betas, however, tended to overcheck and hesitate, and reconsider, and given an adrenaline rush, they dithered a second and then acted. These were guards. They had lightning-quick fuses where it came to threat against their Contract holders. But she also had to defuse their "pause" switch where it came to reluctance to report something as yet unresolved.

Report any anomaly to Florian or Catlin immediately, she'd tell them: they'll take the responsibility.

And being azi, the new people would do that, once they took that order deep: they'd *want* that contact with Florian and Catlin—they'd be uneasy and unresolved until they got it, and they'd run to get it.

And if there was some buried contrary instruction in the stack, say, one to report to Hicks or Yanni, something that just somehow hadn't gotten into the records, that command to go to Florian, emphasized with a hard drug punch, would send them into profound emotional conflict—enough to show up, fast, in a very, very upset azi. If you ever feel conflicted, she'd tell them, additionally, report to Florian immediately.

If you can't find a bug in a set, elder Ari's tape had told her, just do something to make the conflict show itself— *make* the subject react, never mind finesse. Present a quandary, contrary to the direction you suspect the bug to react, identify it—and excise it.

So just give me the files, Justin. Quit fretting. I need to get to work, and I need these people. Whatever's been done, if it was done, it's not going to be in any record. That's what we have to worry about.

Justin thought she was still studying the basics—maybe thought she was out of her depth with these security sets; or he was, which was possible: he hadn't really worked with the type before.

She had. From childhood. She knew Florian and Catlin. She looked at the possibilities in a security azi tape . . .

And she suddenly had a picture of how to solve any problem in a security azi set. It was right in the same place in the set that they attached the compulsion. Just conflict it, and get angst in the subject, and then resolve the angst, leaving the subject feeling oh, so much better. In azi, deep set work was so much easier. Deep set stuff didn't need to be unhooked from all sorts of randomly acquired born-man thinking, which ran like a bad cabling job; and it didn't even have to be unhooked from the later instructions: if there were conflicts, they'd show. The azi in question, above delta level, was very likely to report his own conflicts. Azi were so, so elegantly clean. A thought led to very planned places, economical, and ideally unconflicted, everything structured and architectured and efficient.

And she wasn't. God, she wasn't. Her thoughts skipped all over the place. They tunneled, they ran riot through completely extraneous topics, they hopped from one point to another—pity the programmer that tried to solve *her*.

But a beta with a buried directive?

Damn if she couldn't bring *that* to the surface, by exactly such brute-force mechanics as the first Ari said.

And she'd make the tape for the head of her new Security: beta azi he might be, but she could make the instructional tape herself, right to the deep sets, and be sure of him. She'd send Catlin down to barracks, to sit there and personally see he got it.

And when he woke up, he'd know definitely who was in charge and who could cure any angst he felt. *She* could help him. She would be his first recourse, in any case of doubt, because *she* was the highest authority in Reseune, and Reseune was the highest authority on the planet, and an azi who had access to her had access to having his questions answered definitively and absolutely. An azi who obeyed *her* directives was always in the right—as any azi wanted with all his being to be correct. Any delivery of information to anyone other than her chain of command was utterly forbidden; any request from anyone outside her chain of command had to be cleared, and any lingering doubt was utterly overcome by the power she had within Reseune. She owned his Contract, and any azi under that authority could be assured, very assured, that he was psychologically safe following her orders.

She took notes. She took abundant notes on the officer's set, which she had scanned before she sent it to Justin, and for good measure she looked up deepsets for four of the unrelated gamma genotypes with a related program list, for whom the same tape would be quite, quite sufficient. For three others, again program sets related to each other, she could do a minor modification in the directive but it sufficed. For the newly arrived Theo and Jory—a little different approach, but much the same. Physically, they were easy to get at. Intervening with Hicks' incoming security team was logistically a little harder, but Catlin could manage. Catlin would go armed, and if the subjects had a psychotic episode—meaning her rewiring had hit a major or a lethal block—Catlin would deal with it, get the individual sedated, and notify her, specifically, that someone had tried something.

Sorry, Justin: sorry you've had to sweat this, and I know you hate real-time work worse than poison. You don't need to send it to me: I see your notes, and they help me. They show me what I need to do, and it's in the deep sets, not the things they've hung on it.

No wonder it's driving you crazy. It's like a birthday cake, icing all over, decorations here, decorations there, all sorts of programs and routines added on, none of it really showing you what's underneath. We just need to slice right into it, and you're far too kind for that.

I can't afford to be. Maybe later, but not now, not in this.

BOOK THREE   Section I   Chapter vi

JUNE 7, 2424
0821H

Early to the office, early to work, mindful of the extra requests, and there was a note from Ari, time-stamped yesterday at 1701: *Justin: I'm really anxious to have your comments on the sets I gave you. Please hurry.*

Hurry. Hell. He'd already hurried.

Then another one, time stamped this morning at 0131: *'t's not that urgent. Relax.*

Haste makes waste, he messaged back. *But I'm hurrying. I should have something for you this evening. And ﹖hen are you sleeping, anyway?*

"Little sera wants miracles," he said to Grant. "Lunch is going to be in, today."

"No problem," Grant said. "Shoot me what you have."

He shot. Grant took it, and there was silence for an hour, until Grant ran out of coffee.

Grant filled his cup, fuel for the morning.

And into the afternoon.

Grant ordered sandwiches delivered. With cream pastry. Justin devoured his, reading and annotating the while. One set to go, a fairly simple one. He'd been over it twenty times. He'd done all the betas to try to understand the type. He didn't find a handle on it, anywhere, and it wasn't right. It wasn't right, it *wasn't* the level of work that belonged on a Contract she was taking. At first he'd suspected subtlety. Then he'd suspected error. Now he had a different picture. Library censorship. Again.

He said to Grant: "You know what I think? I don't think Library's given us all the records yet. Florian thought he had that cleared up. But I don't think he did."

"It would answer your objection."

"We're two weeks overdue on this. But I'm afraid it's the fact they're security. Ari's going to have to go back to Library one more time on her access. There's something still we haven't gotten."

"It would answer the question," Grant said. "You're right, and after the last round, I wouldn't want to be in the librarian's shoes. You get to write the memo, born-man."

BOOK THREE   Section I   Chapter vii

JUNE 7, 2424
1542H

The azi in question, BR-283, was a nice-looking fellow, Catlin observed that on the monitor, while BR-283, Rafael, was deep asleep—nice face, nice body, dark as Florian—taller than Florian.

But absolutely no attraction here, just an aesthetic note. Rafael BR *wasn't* Florian, and wouldn't be, being a beta—a situation which suited her. Betas took orders. Alphas didn't need orders, just a goal. Sera had explained the situation to her, as much as, in sera's judgement, she needed to know, and prime among sera's instructions was the posited call, every fifteen minutes, while she was on this assignment. She was to beware any food or drink offered by lab staff. She was to disobey any command to leave or submit to detention, herself, but if held, she should not risk injury—just wait for sera to take action . . . within the next fifteen minutes.

That was advisement enough that sera considered these tapes important to give personally to four of the new security team. The situation itself hardly seemed dicey: walk into the labs with the tape—possibly containing the Contract itself—invoke sera's name and sera's order to gain access and order this group to lab, where she personally installed each tape, waving off the assistance of staff.

And it had run for a relatively tedious hour and forty-two minutes, while Rafael BR and the other three of sera's choosing slept with eyes occasionally open, and occasionally reacted, or smiled, or concentrated.

Contracting didn't take long. So what else were the tapes? That wasn't hard to guess. They were probably primary tapes, a slightly amended refresher on the most basic sets. Tapes like that were generally quite pleasant, an hour or so of confirmation, affirmation—a transcendental experience, when a Supervisor offered it to a troubled or stressed azi. In this case it was likely some patch to enable the four to work together under BR-283's direction.

And since sera had the accesses she did, and she'd signed for them and meant to deliver the Contract tape herself, she was perfectly within her rights to order it, and to order that her own staff carry out the request—for BR-283, and for BG-8, BJ-190, and BB-291, the same, even if the four were listed as ReseuneSec. A note might have gone to Hicks, but Hicks hadn't intervened.

The other three were in the adjacent rooms, on the other three active monitors, affording a constant view, two of them on the same tape, one on a third, and all, presumably, experiencing primary tape, blissful and content.

They were also all on the same schedule, the tape very soon to run out, by the individual counters. And after that, they would enjoy a little peaceful sleep. Tedious, but she'd stay until they waked naturally. She'd bring them up the hill herself, the core members of the team Hicks had provided, having passed them through a sieve and having assured they were settled, in advance of the others.

More, sera provided her own tape without a Reseune-Sec indexing sticker on it: they were ReseuneSec personnel, and the lab had taken a momentary issue with that, and had wanted to call the lab supervisor and Hicks about it, but Catlin had stood fast, maintaining that, indeed, sera did hold the Contracts, was a licensed Alpha Supervisor—there were five such in all of Reseune proper . . . six, counting Jordan Warrick—and if a Beta tape issued from an Alpha Supervisor's office, then a Beta Supervisor should accept it and run the tape as requested.

"My principal," Catlin had reminded the man with some firmness, "*is* Ariane Emory."

One could watch the thoughts pass through the Supervisor's eyes—a born-man considering his career options, perhaps. He hadn't been more cheerful after that, but he'd been polite. And he'd let her insert the tapes she'd brought, giving her access to a whole row of lab beds, clearing two other doubtlessly deserving azi who'd been scheduled for the afternoon.

"This is sera's business," Catlin had remarked further, as severely as possible, "and intimately pertains to her household. She will appreciate discretion. Your name is John Elway. Mine is Catlin AC-7892. I will report."

Reading born-men was possible, when they were strongly conflicted. The man just nodded, and likely had *not* made a phone call to higher levels, even yet.

Twitch of BR-283's head. Catlin looked critically at that subject, and let it pass. Possibly he'd just met a small alteration in his program. The dose had been heavy. BR-283 probably could have taken the tape without the drug . . . but he was deep enough that a twitch was unusual.

Twitch became a tic. Jerk of the hands. "Let the tape run," sera had told her. "Let it complete."

The subject sat bolt upright, eyes staring, then vaulted off the couch, right into the wall—a wall that assuredly was not there in BR-283's vision. He rebounded against the couch, fighting for balance.

He was dangerous in this state, dangerous to himself. He hit another wall, hard. His forehead was bleeding.

There was a red button that could call help. Catlin opted not to use it. By the clock, she was due to call base. She touched the com button on her shoulder and said, "Catlin here. There's been a reaction."

The micro receiver in her right ear said, in sera's voice, *"I'm coming."*

The other subjects were getting to the end of their tape sessions *without* hurling themselves off their couches. There was *one* subject huddled on the floor in a fetal tuck in the corner, one subject in the throes of a psychotic episode from the deeptape he'd been given—and that individual happened to be the officer Hicks had put in charge of the unit. Rafael BR-283.

That said something. And John Elway had not come to assess the progress of the session. In a little bit more, John Elway would have visitors to the section, visitors who would not be prevented. She watched the other azi, walked to the one-way glass and looked at BR-283, who had gotten into a corner the camera didn't completely reach. He was bleeding down his face, shaking and rocking. It wasn't a pleasant sight.

It was 1601h, by her watch, when someone came down the hall outside. She drew her sidearm—one never assumed the other side wasn't prepared to shoot—and faced the opaque door.

It opened, and it was sera, with Florian, a very welcome sight, with Wes for reinforcement. John Elway had come in among them, looking upset, and two of his staff attended, just ahead of Wes, but sera didn't seem worried in the least about them, only about the business at hand.

Catlin said, holstering her sidearm, "A reaction, sera, in the unit senior."

"Well," was all sera said, and sera went to the monitors, on which three azi were quiet, likely asleep; and then went to the window of the first room, assessing the situation.

Sera punched that button for communication and said, softly, "Rafael. Rafael."

The subject convulsed, and knotted himself tighter into the corner.

"This is Ariane Emory, your Contract and your Supervisor. I've come to help you. Can you get up?"

Nothing, for a moment. Then a slight response, a leg straightened out of the tuck, folded, knee against the floor.

"This is your Supervisor. Get up, Rafael."

He moved, unfolded his arms, laid hands on the wall, got a knee under him, and tried to get up.

"Are you all right, Rafael?"

"I can't see."

"Yes, you can," sera said, and Rafael turned his head and stared around him.

"Is that better, Rafael?"

A slight nod.

"I'm your Supervisor," sera said, in that calm, calm voice she could use—the tone that made Catlin's own nerves twitch, and brought a silence and quiet from all of the azi present. "I'm your Contract. It's all right. I have a resolution for you. Are you ready to hear it?"

A nod. "Yes."

"What you believed true, was true before this. Now something else is true, and I tell you it's all right. Do you believe me? Do you accept it?"

"I can't," Rafael said.

Whatever someone had laid into him, it was a hard block.

Sera said, slightly more sternly: "Rafael."

"Sera?"

"When I tell you something, it's true. It will always be true. Do you need to see your Contract, to know that?"

"I want to see it," Rafael said.

Very high beta, strong-willed, not easily overcome. Catlin felt it in her own nerves. This azi was Enemy, and resisting, hard.

Sera said, quietly, "Catlin, unlock the door."

"Sera, show him through the window."

"Unlock the door, Catlin. It's all right."

She was alpha, and her resistance was harder to overcome than any beta ever devised. But she had to, if sera insisted. Florian and Wes were right with sera while she moved back to the console to open the door. If the Enemy went berserk, they'd hit him with all they had. But—

"He's security, sera."

"Do it," sera said.

Sera's orders, in that tone, were sera's orders, off her own deep sets, and Catlin moved and did it, watching the subject the while, her heart ticking up another notch as Florian and Wes moved in, right with sera.

"These are your allies," sera said calmly. "And this is your Contract." She took a small reader from her coat pocket, and walked toward the subject, whose leaning against the wall could propel him off it in half a heartbeat, and sera was small and fragile in that reckoning, the subject a head taller, bloody-faced, drenched in sweat, and, at the moment, between loyalties.

Sera calmly held the reader out to him, and he stood away from the wall, took it, and looked at it. Looked for a long time.

It was something, to see one's real Contract, and read the name on it, for the first time. It was identity, and right, and duty, all those things wrapped up in one. It had to have an effect. Just thinking about it had an effect on every azi in the room, and Catlin moved close to the door, tense as drawn wire, ready to defend *her* Contract if Rafael made a sudden move.

"Do you believe," sera asked Rafael quietly, "that I'm your Supervisor?"

Nod. Second nod. The eyes flickered. Rafael was processing things. Hard. He shook badly as he gave the reader back. It could go any direction from here. *Any* direction.

"It's all right," sera said. "You're one of us. You're safe. You're where you belong."

He felt for the wall behind him. Leaned against it.

"It's all right. Come here. Come."

He got his balance. Sera stood there holding out open arms, and that great tall azi came close and let her take his hands. "It's all right," sera said. "You only report to *me*, now and forever. All other claims on you are completely gone. *Erased.* You don't have to do the other thing, do you?"

"No," Rafael said. A huge sigh came out of him, and he said shakily: "I won't." Deep breath. "I don't have to."

Not a lie, Catlin thought. That had been a Conflict. Bad one. Something in that tape had reached out and presented this azi an irresolvable contradiction, thrown him into a box to which only an appropriate Supervisor had the key.

And sera had come and rescued him, that simple.

Catlin found her leg twitching. She was that wired up. But Rafael was sera's now. Safe. She saw the same subtle shift in Florian's stance, and Wes's. Three of them might not have been quick enough, strong enough, to take the man out fast enough, as close as sera had pushed it: they had to talk with her about that. But done was done. It was all right. The other three, down the row, they were sera's, too, peacefully, with no reactions.

This one—this one had been a spy at very least, and sera had found it out.

"You can come up to the Wing with us," sera told Rafael. "So can the other three. You'll make things ready for the rest of your command."

"Yes, sera," Rafael said. He squared himself on his feet. Gave a little bow of the head.

"My name is Florian," Florian said then, "sera's personal security." A nod over his shoulder. "Catlin." And left. "Wes. Wes will walk up the hill with you. Everything will be provided for you in the quarters there, including uniforms. You don't have to bring anything but yourselves. You'll prepare the place for the others when they come."

"Yes," Rafael said. His face had a different look. An azi knew. He was still somewhat in shock, still rattled, the experience having knocked his defenses flat—it was a kind of openness that might never appear in this azi again. Right now he was fragile, entirely, needing protection. When he got where he was going, when he got an official assignment, and knew where he would be and what he was to do, he'd become what he would be, and not until then. Right now he needed help.

"I'll meet you there," sera said, "and give you your orders."

"Yes," he answered her, and nodded. "Yes, sera." The waking mind was in fragments. It needed time and quiet to reassemble its boundaries.

"You can go with Wes," sera said gently. "Go on, now. The others will follow when they wake."

The door was open. Wes took him by the arm, and steered him out, past John Elway, past the other staff. Sweat stood on Elway's face ... fear *for* sera, or fear *of* his situation, Catlin was unsure which, and didn't like that lack of information.

"It's perfectly all right," sera said, pausing for a moment to address the man. "I can take care of him. Catlin will stay here and escort the others up the hill. Are we agreed about that?"

Elway nodded slightly, looking pale. Elway might, Catlin thought, be just a little less conflicted than the azi, but sera was going to run Reseune one day, and born-men in Reseune all knew that. If Elway was supposed to report this, he might decide to be careful what he reported and to whom. He was a very worried born-man.

And maybe it wasn't just Rafael sera had Worked, omitting to give Elway any clear indication what he ought to do and what was safe.

Instead sera simply walked off with Florian, behind Wes and Rafael. Rafael was theirs now, very, very little chance he wasn't.

It was a scary thing to watch. It had been a far scarier moment when sera had walked into that room. But given sera's work, it was very likely it wouldn't be the last time sera personally did a thing like that, no matter how they objected.

And her security just had to be in position, and fast. Very, very fast, Catlin thought. And armed with non-lethals, next time. Sera had surprised her security. It felt wrong to complain about it, but it certainly shouldn't happen twice, and it was their job to take precautions.

There was another matter. Rafael had come from Hicks, at least by previous Contract.

That was worth talking over with Florian and with sera, on an absolutely urgent basis. For right now, Hicks and all his immediate staff were on her Unreliable list.

BOOK THREE   Section 1   Chapter viii

Catlin was back, Ari noted, from the minder link in her office. Florian had escorted *her* back. Wes was still downstairs, helping Rafael and his three settle into their temporary quarters—Marco had been manning the security station solo the while, and Ari let pass a little sigh, now that everybody was back safely.

Four Contracts down, twenty-six more to set, and there was a message on the minder this evening from Justin, informing her that he didn't think Library had given him everything it said it had given them.

No, she noted, at her console, Justin *hadn't* quite caught the problem. But she hadn't either, from a scan of the set—it was there, and you could spend hours and hours looking through the set and the specific individual's list of tapes given, searching and searching for something to make sense of a set of lines in that program . . . all the earmarks of reference to deep set, but nothing in the deep set record that would quite satisfy it. It was like an if-then link, but when you got there, there was nothing listed. Every instruction ever given to that azi was supposed to be recorded in his specific manual—but if it wasn't?

That if-then was just a shape without anything to attach to—a point at which hooks could be set to turn an azi into a spy . . . or assassin, if that was the game; and Justin *had* found something wrong: he just hadn't assumed it wasn't him, so he was still looking for the link.

She sent him a memo that said:

All done. You should have trusted yourself. You were right to keep looking, your delay warned me to keep looking, and Library wasn't lying to us. 'Night, both of you.

Nasty. It *wouldn't* let Justin get a peaceful sleep. He'd

worry about it. He'd reach a right conclusion. And now
after one long, hard stretch of work, he knew what ReseuneSec tape looked like, and he'd found a problem and put
a finger close to it. Not too shabby an accomplishment on
his part, considering she'd been working with security sets
for years.

And what someone had done with Rafael . . . the deep
level at which that compulsion had gone in said *Alpha
Supervisor* in blazing letters. A Beta Supervisor could
marginally have done it, and it was true it hadn't been totally neat, but it had been damned deep and resistent, all
of which argued only that the perpetrator wasn't the *best*
Alpha Supervisor in Reseune. The best? That was, in her
private assessment, beginning to be *her.*

But it left Yanni, Hicks, Jordan Warrick, Justin Warrick. And, postscript, there was also grim old Chi Prang,
the head of Alpha section in the azi labs. Prang *could* have
done it, at someone's orders, or in collusion with someone,
and she didn't know the woman.

Fast computer search said Prang was one hundred
thirty-seven years old and had, yes, worked in that capacity
during the first Ari's regime and Denys' and now Yanni's.
That was a wide range of potential allegiances. Prang had
five assistants, any one of which was provisionally alpha-
licensed, which meant they had the skills, but had to have
Prang's oversight. *That* spread the search wider afield, and
led, very probably, further and further from the culprit,
because subordinates wouldn't have as immediate a motive. So she was wrong about there being just five people.
But the list of original suspects was still the primary list.
Yanni, she was relatively sure, could have done a better
job, Justin wouldn't have done it in the first place, Jordan
hadn't had access, and that . . .

That left the fingerprints of the Director of Reseune-
Sec, Hicks, who had the rating to handle his own assistant,
but who didn't practice on a wider scale—*his* command
was beta, in the main. Very, very few alphas, and those
not socialized into the general society—specialists,
technicals—they'd report their own personal problems to
Hicks, but being purely technicals, they weren't in a position, in their ivory tower, to encounter much angst. That

meant Hicks wouldn't be often in practice. A provisionally
licensed, only-occasional kind of operator wasn't really up
to finesse, unless he'd been shown how to do it, and was
following a sort of recipe.

There were two styles of dealing with azi difficulties.
One was the meticulous route that figured a Supervisor
could make a mistake: you searched and researched the
files until there was a theory, and a treatment: it was a very
soft, very gentle method of going after the problem and fixing it—which didn't always work at optimum, unless you
were as good as Justin; but at least it didn't generally go
badly. If you *were* good, you could eventually lay a finger
on the specific line in the set that was causing the conflict
and change it, with proper annotations on the record. That
was very much Justin.

The other was the brute force method—when you
wanted something and knew the basic architecture of the
set, you could ignore most of the subsequent manual and go
right after the primal sets, gut level. You could do that if you
didn't, ultimately, care about the result long-term, or you
could also do it if you were that good, that you *could* work at
primary level in a subject, and if you had a clear vision how
it could make everything subsequent settle into place.

I'm that good, she thought. She'd taken a chance with
it. Was still taking a chance with it, in the sense that she
now believed Rafael was clear—because she'd set his Contract very tightly, very exclusively on her, as the resolver of
all conflicts, the source of all orders. She'd been brought
up on the first Ari's tapes. She'd been working with two
alpha sets for years; and, being the born-man equivalent
of an alpha, what she read in the manuals resonated at gut
level; and the differences between an alpha and a theta
resonated that way, and, once she got into the manuals,
beta level made sense—the same with gamma, zeta, and
eta—each with their own constellation of needs and satis-
factions. Even for a born-man . . . it made sense.

Why was the key. *Why* individuals did things, even
when they had consistently negative outcomes . . . *why*
people had to do things . . . she'd been asking *that* question of the universe for years. And born-men got the worst
of it, all their lives.

Why did they have to take Maman away?

Why was Denys nice to me sometimes?

Why is Jordan what he is?

Why does Yanni bring me presents?

Who is Hicks working for?

Those were all, all important questions, and she'd fairly well gotten the answer to all but the last one—which might lie somewhere tangled with the cruel thing someone had done to Rafael.

She was very, very thankful Catlin hadn't had to shoot Rafael, or that she herself hadn't broken him down and not been able to fix it.

Typical of the really big problems in the azi world, the fix was actually simple, because the layers were so clean. Born-men—born-men were a muddled mess, as if someone had stirred a layered pudding with a knife. But when an azi was in primary conflict, his earliest, most basic self-protective rule was, "Appeal to a Supervisor." Second was, "The Contract is the ultimate right." And when Rafael had been drugged-down and wide open, she'd laid hands right on the conflict. She'd given him the Contract at the beginning, and that was all right: he'd taken it in, and immediately his reservations had attached, and he'd arranged his safe loophole. And then she'd hit him with the deep set changes, and a reiteration of the Contract, which had torn it all wide open, and set it up for healing.

He'd sleep once he'd carried out her orders to arrange the barracks. He'd work until he dropped, sleep like the dead, and wake up clear and sure of himself and with all his layers in good order.

The compulsion for a dual loyalty had to have been planted way back, from when he was a child; or it had to have been planted fairly near term by someone with the ability to plant it. Which again said Alpha Supervisor.

But say that the compulsion *had* been there for his whole life.

Fingers flew. Base One slithered quietly across departmental lines and nabbed another azi record, this one from a very young trainee designated for ReseuneSec—another B-28, BA-289, to be precise, which meant there were as many as seven more B-28's already out there, somewhere.

It took a computer comparison to wade through that training record, proving it was identical to BR-283's, and a little research to determine that that particular azi, BA-289, had been born and started on that path in 2412, before BR-283 had proved out, so there were three others old enough to be in place somewhere, and, after 283, four more theoretically in the system, younger than 289. You didn't start proliferating a new routine through a geneset like that until you'd proved it out . . . not if you were operating by the book.

Was BR-283 the first of his kind?

Joyesse came in to ask if sera would want supper delayed.

"Ten minutes," she said, because she was close, and she had an idea exactly what she was looking for.

And there they were. One B-28 in ReseuneSpace, up on Beta Station. One in Novgorod, in the ReseuneSec Special Operations office. One, oh, delightful! was in ReseuneSpace on Fargone, in Ollie's service. BR-280, named Regis, an operations agent, had been born in 2373, and had been in service—in her predecessor's service, no less—when she died. The first Ari's security staff had been reassigned—scattered to the edge of space, evidently, when Giraud took over.

Oh, damned right they had scattered them. That staff, if questioned, knew things. And there was no damned reason her predecessor would have created an off-the-books routine in this Regis—who was in *her* security group— unless she hadn't trusted the security group itself. And that was too many layers to be sane, especially when the first Ari could have peeled any of that group like an onion if she had any suspicion.

No. Someone had actually infiltrated Ari's staff. And Denys, putatively, had been the agency of her death— which Giraud had pinned on Jordan—and Yanni had shipped Jordan to Planys to avoid a trial. While the original Florian and Catlin had died, and the security detail had been shipped out, scattered to all points of Union space, not one of them left on Cyteen.

Chin on hand, she contemplated that scenario.

ReseuneSec. An azi that had served the first Ari, now

with Ollie. Other azi, who had never served Ari, at Beta, in Novgorod. And now she got one, in Hicks' goodwill gift to her.

If it were the first Ari's programming, she'd surely have had the finesse to vary the geneset and the psychset of her spies—piece of cake for Ari One. Someone of lesser ability, on the other hand, might have stuck with the first success and built spies like production items . . . then managed to get his favorite number assigned hither and yon.

Maybe the same person had moved BR-280 out, fast, with all the others, after the first Ari's death. To have killed 280 *with* Florian and Catlin might have drawn attention to him and his history, and all the others.

She drew in a slow breath.

Hicks could, if he worked at it, reprogram a beta. But Hicks hadn't been in office, then.

God, this was archaeology. Everything was buried.

First logical query was to be sure the Regis base program was identical to Rafael's, and that all the others were. Base One filched that manual from deep, deep storage— Reseune never erased a manual. Any version of it.

Beyond ten minutes. Joyesse came back, a little diffident.

"I apologize," Ari said. "This isn't finished yet. Tell cook I am so sorry. Another twenty minutes. Staff should have their supper."

Joyesse left. And she let the computer sift through that mountain of material, which took only one of those minutes. It flagged no difference at all.

So BR-280 was the same as 281. That meant the window for that special routine had always been there in that mindset. And possibly that same routine, which *wasn't* in the manual—illegal as hell—had indeed existed in 280. She couldn't lay hands on 280 to find out, not easily. But she'd bet 280 reported to Hicks . . . who hadn't been in charge of ReseuneSec long enough to have set it up that way.

Giraud had been. It had been Giraud's office.

Oh, lay bets on Giraud. *There* was the mind that might have done it. Hicks had only been number two to Giraud. Hicks might not even have known. But he'd very likely

known the special use of the BR-28 series. And he'd seen
to it that one got into her unit.

If that was true, then the Nyes still had tentacles
threaded through ReseuneSec, and, through ReseuneSec,
into all sorts of places. The dead man's hand was still on
the controls. His programs persisted into the next regime,
still on Giraud's orders.

*Thank you, Uncle Giraud. Dear Uncle Giraud. You
could so easily have done it to Rafael and all his kind, and
the labs are still producing them. You'd do that for Denys,
to be sure he got information he wouldn't know how to
chase. You'd do anything for Denys. You set it up so Denys
would get his information even if you weren't there. And
the BR-28s are just the set I know about.*

*I know one thing, at least. You laid traps you neglected
to tell me about. Denys was still alive, and you wouldn't
betray him: I understand that. And I understand Denys
was protecting me. But you ended up putting me in danger
to give Denys that little advantage in keeping power, because you* didn't *tell me there was anything like this buried
in ReseuneSec.*

And that makes me just a little mad, Uncle Giraud.

*So now I know what you did, and what your mindset
is capable of, in your next incarnation, toward my successor . . . all sorts of betrayal, for the one you're protecting.
And I see very well how your own mindset arrived at the
notion of this compulsion to report. You made it your own
mirror. You so liked information. You never trusted any
of your own subordinates. I'll bet you even planted one
on Hicks. On your own second-in-command. I'll bet if I
went over his beta assistants, I'd find one with a block very
much like that. I bet you did some very special work on
that one other azi. And* ten *of the BR-28's?*

Oh, that was wicked, Uncle.

But now I do know.

*And solving Rafael's problem, I know what to do about
you.*

*Denys doesn't need to be born. Just you do. Just you, to
be fixed on me, Uncle, the way you fixed on Denys.*

Denys has just become irrelevant.

Good. That makes me happier. I'm sorry about it, si-

*multaneously, and I wish I didn't have to, but I think we're
both going to be happier in the long run.*

She prepared a letter to Yanni—just in case Yanni had
gotten wind of her activity with her new, Hicks-provided
staff. Yanni might be guilty as sin in the first Ari's death—
at least in the cover-up and blaming Jordan part of it.
Yanni might know *exactly* what Giraud had been up to,
infiltrating ReseuneSec, ReseuneSpace at Fargone and
Beta—and if he did know, and he'd been letting that happen, and not telling her, he was on the verge of becoming
irrelevant, too.

Dear Uncle Yanni, she wrote, with a little pain in her
heart.

*I turned up something. And fixed it, so you know. I think
you should be aware. I leave it to you whether to tell Director Hicks his own staff may have a problem. Be discreet.
You know what your lines of honest communication are.*

Then the stinger:

Please include me in them from now on.

BOOK THREE   Section 2   Chapter i

JUNE 11, 2424
2158H

Giraud's eyes had been changing position slowly. By this
seventeenth week they had moved all the way onto the
front of his face, so he was much more Giraud than he'd
ever been.

He'd gained weight—hadn't kept up with Abban in size,
but was about the same as Seely. He not only twitched to
stimuli this week, his bones had begun to harden out of the
tough cartilage that earlier comprised his skeleton, and his
joints, responding to muscle twitches, had begun to flex
and move in a way they would do for the rest of his life.

He'd also gained a new sense: he had actually heard the
maternal heartbeat that had timed his life . . . he heard it

when a tech dropped a pan: he couldn't tell it was different than taste or smell—every stimulus was the same to him, but he reacted, the way a plant might react. His newly functioning joints moved.

His sense of hearing would grow more acute as time passed, but Seely's would be extraordinary, an asset, in Seely's future profession.

And something else had changed, radically so, for Giraud. He was solo now. His brother Denys' sequence number had been active in the birthlab computer until just last week, a soft scheduling that would have let it go to implementation on any given day. That data and that material had gone back to deep storage, the CIT number dumped from lab files, officially disconnected from Giraud's, so even if he looked, someday, he might find it hard to find his brother until his Base was significantly higher than the lab's.

Denys might yet be born. There was seven years yet to change that back without deviating from program . . . seven years had been the gap between the brothers. But for now that data had quietly slipped deep into storage, with no extant string to pull it out. That would have to be rebuilt.

A subsequent generation might change its mind about connecting Denys to Giraud, having both of that set.

This one wasn't likely to.

BOOK THREE   Section 2   Chapter ii

JUNE 11, 2424
2158H

Living next door to Ari had its moments—one of them being about suppertime, when the hall suddenly flooded with ReseuneSec in uniform, and Justin's plans for dinner out had taken second place to ingrained apprehension. Their door had stayed shut. The mass of black uniforms had, instead, been admitted to young Ari's apartment, all of them at once.

Well, Justin said to himself, that was unnerving. Thirty was the number of Ari's own detail, if the records he'd passed on had been all-inclusive. Had that been thirty? It could be.

And were they safe, for God's sake? Ari had yanked the initiative back from him, unfinished, said it was all right, he and Grant had been right—

Right? There'd been some sort of problem. He knew there was. Grant agreed. And she went ahead anyway.

"She must have done something," Justin commented to Grant, who stood at his shoulder to see the minder's vid image. "She wouldn't have them all in there, if she hadn't. Damn, I still can't find the glitch, and hell if I want to ask her—she's confident enough, as is."

The message she'd sent, taking the project back, still rankled. He'd lost sleep on that work. Lost a major amount of sleep. And he still didn't have an answer, or a real thank you. There had been times, in the last few weeks, when he actually understood his father's feud with the original.

Grant's hand landed on his shoulder. "Doesn't look like a good evening for us to go out," Grant said.

He ran a capture on the security monitor's immediate record. "Entertainment," he said. And dinner out became dinner in.

They popped pizza into the luxury apartment's very fast oven, and opened a respectable wine while they reviewed the tape ... Yes, there were thirty. Thirty who presumably were about to be received and probably instructed inside Ari's fairly capacious living area ... after which they would presumably pour back out into the hall, ready to go on duty.

It was damned certain the thirty, plus the recently acquired domestic staff, weren't by any means going to fit in that apartment's staff quarters. So they had to be living somewhere else in the wing, likely downstairs.

"That's the BR-283," Justin said, regarding the tall one with the officer's silver on his collar. "Classic officer set. Dates from the 2370's. Spooky, how much like Regis he looks."

"Not spooky," Grant said with a little laugh. "It would be spooky if he *didn't*."

"I wonder whatever happened to Regis."

"No knowing," Grant said. The laugh had immediately vanished.

Dark thoughts. A dark time, a time worth forgetting. The crowd in the hall represented a new age. A new beginning. Regis had vanished, along with the rest of the first Ari's staff. No one ever saw them again. Rumor had it her Florian and her Catlin had been terminated. No one knew how many others.

Cheerfulness, for God's sake. The little minx had probably fixed whatever glitch there was in the BR set. Figure *how* she'd fixed it inside several weeks of working the problem . . . that was a question.

"Probably she did exactly what Jordan complained about," he said to Grant, "and went after the deep set on the BR. Fast fix."

"That's one way to get his attention," Grant said. "It would be logical."

"Rough on him."

Grant gave a slow, thoughtful nod. "But it would work. And they're ReseuneSec. Those are odd sets from the beginning."

"Cold as hell's hinges," Justin muttered, with other unpleasant memories, and tried to shake the mood of that black flood in the hall—his hallway as well as hers. He poured a white wine, poured another for Grant, and reran the tape. "That's the BB-19," Justin said, regarding the thin, long-faced azi. "I've worked with another of that set. A bundle of nerves. Good on details. He'll likely be scared to death of Florian and Catlin."

"With probable cause," Grant said, and, with a pizza wedge for a pointer: "That's his counterpoint, I'm betting. BY-10. A lot like the BB-19. A good combination, those two. One's detail, the other tends to macrofocus."

"Males generally get top posts in that house, have you noticed that? Since Florian and Catlin, that's *her* predilection. It was her predecessor's, too. Not a female in the whole lot." Flash on that apartment, that time. He'd been, then, around Ari's age now.

And that night, in the first Ari's apartment ... had there been staff present, besides Florian and Catlin? He couldn't remember it ... didn't want to remember. He was sorry for Florian and Catlin. He really was. It depressed him to think about it.

"And Theo ended up in authority over Jory on the domestic staff," Grant said. "*I* wouldn't have advised that. Jory's brighter. But they'll manage. He'll take advice."

"You know, Ari is far more social than her predecessor," Justin said, envisioning that crowd in Ari's living room—probably being served refreshments and urged to relax—which would make the lot almost comically uncomfortable. No, she actually wouldn't do it. She knew better. She'd do what *would* make them comfortable—like brief them, give them information. Those mindsets would like that far better than teacakes, all things considered. But sociality ... she'd encourage that, far more than those mindsets had ever seen. "She has a strong inclination to go for company. Not with that lot, but in general."

"I've observed," Grant said.

"Right from the start. She visited our office. Whenever she got bored, she went looking for *people*. Cultivated a set of friends. Still does. Denys really didn't like that habit in her. Of course, Denys didn't like people in the first place."

"Neither did the first Ari," Grant said. "Deviation from the model. Maybe an improvement. Maybe not. I can't imagine that the first Ari ever had that bent in early years."

"Our Ari lost Jane Strassen, but she never grew bitter, just took to chasing us. Maybe she's more people-oriented because *she* didn't spend her early years wondering if her dear mother would kill her if she disappointed. That's what they say about Olga Emory."

"A relationship I can't imagine," Grant murmured. "But then, I can't imagine a mother." A tilt of Grant's head. "Just you."

"I don't qualify."

"You absolutely don't. Which suits me fine."

They were lovers. They made no particular fuss over it. It was just who they were. There was nobody they trusted

more than each other, nobody they loved more than each
other. That had been true for years. For a time, in his growing up, if there hadn't been Grant, he wouldn't have been
sane. If there hadn't been him—it was equally sure Grant
wouldn't have been what he was.

And if not for the first Ari's intervention, Grant would
have been Jordan's work, entirely.

And if not for the first Ari's intervention, so, almost undoubtedly, would he.

"I wonder what she's building out there behind the
wing," Justin said hours later, when he and Grant were in
bed, after a long evening and an entertainment vid. The
only light was the clock face on the minder. The security
force had, as predicted, departed after a precise hour and
forty-five minutes. Headed for the lift. Assigned, signed,
and delivered—

And that gave Ari as much protection as any other
agency in Reseune.

"Building behind the wing?" Grant asked, half asleep.
"What brought that up?"

"She's accumulating an army—counting service people, that's a large staff."

"You think?" Grant rolled over and managed a half-
awake interest. "What are you thinking?"

"I think it's not a building to replace the old Wing One
Lab. I think it's a huge extension of this whole wing."

"You can't really see it on the monitors."

"Lot of earthmovers going back and forth, makes the
ground floor shake. A lot of stuff landed down at the dock
and brought up in that direction. It's going to be big. Everybody's saying labs to replace the old one they shut down.
I'm saying—I don't know why Ari wants huge labs attached
to this wing, unless she's setting up to do some work."

"Makes a certain sense she would," Grant said.

"Physical labs? She doesn't need it. She's theory. She's
computers. She doesn't really need that kind of thing. I'll
bet you—mark me—I'll bet a month's pay the lab story is
a blind." He cast a look up at the ceiling in the dark, not
sure they were monitored, never sure they weren't. "Just
a guess."

"So—if it is—does she move out and we stay here?"

"Would she leave her favorite neighbor behind? Dammit, something in me wants to go take back our old digs, with the worn carpet and the balky green fridge, all of it. I miss the place."

"I don't know why. We weren't safe there."

"We were, for a while." He let go a long slow breath, and remembered. "No, I suppose we were just ignorant." He stretched, hands under the pillow, under his head. "Maybe that's what I want to get back to. Blissful ignorance."

"I've found little blissful about ignorance. Besides, it's not in my mindset to tolerate that condition."

"I'm afraid it's not in mine, either, ultimately." Two or three slow breaths. "Too big a staff, even for a palace. She's got staff packed into that apartment. And thirty guards? That's a lot even for Wing One. I think we're witnessing an expansion. She's going to move. Get the whole wing into something that *wasn't* shot all to hell by a handful of her staff. Make sure it can't happen again."

"It's a lot of building. That's certain."

"If she moves us, at least we'll be rid of the decor."

The room . . . if the lights had been on . . . or even when they weren't . . . was a horror of modern decorating, stark white, stark black, and some mitigating grays. Grant avowed he didn't mind it much. But Grant, being azi, lived more in his mind than he did in his physical surroundings. For himself, having grown up attached to textures and physical sensations, it was absolutely appalling. Admittedly it was a place to be safe. It was a place to be monitored by reasonably friendly agencies, and to maintain an absolutely incontrovertible record, capable of proving to any inquisitive authority that they hadn't been up to anything, and couldn't possibly deserve to be arrested. Again.

Warm, soft place to be, however, it was not—only in this bed, with the lights out, with Grant there, safe. Insulated from the world—and Ari. And from whatever she was doing, filling the hall with a godawful lot of Reseune Security.

Making the place echo with boots.

Advancing power. He could hear it coming.

The phone rang.

"Damn." He jumped. He couldn't help it. Nothing good made ever made a phone ring at this hour. He shot an arm out, felt after the phoneset on the nightstand. Didn't find it, and it was still going off. "Minder? Minder, *answer the damn phone!*"

"Complying," the robot voice said; the clock face over on the wall brightened as the room light came up a little. A telltale beside that clock went green, and a new voice came through.

"Ser Warrick?" Female. But not Ari.

"This is Justin Warrick." He never had blocked off calls after midnight. He'd never needed to. But here it was, after midnight. And he didn't even *know* any women outside this wing and Admin. "Who is this?"

"Sandi Patil. Dr. Sandi Patil."

He sat straight up in bed as Grant lay there a heartbeat, then levered himself up on an arm.

"What do you want?" He was rude. He knew it. But so was Patil, calling him out of nowhere at this hour, on business that couldn't be good.

"Are you alone?" Patil asked.

"I'm as alone as I choose to be." He didn't want any part of this. He waved a hand at Grant, mimed recording the conversation, which took a keypush on the console. He got up to do it himself, on the wall panel near the door, but Grant, starting on that side of the bed, beat him to it, and then turned the room lights up full. "Why don't you call my father?"

"I can't reach him. Listen to me. Dr. Thieu is dead."

Dead. Dead wasn't a metaphor. Not from this source, at this hour. And he didn't want to ask, but not getting information could be as bad as hanging up, outright, for the monitoring that went on in this place.

"Dead? How?"

"They're saying heart attack. But I don't believe it. They're monitoring my phone, they're questioning my friends . . ."

"Look, if you deal with my father it's a dead certainty they'll do that, whoever 'they' are . . ."

"Not Reseune," Patil said. "It's not Reseune. They have people inside."

He made a furious gesture at the other wall, in the direction of next door, Ari's apartment. Grant understood, grabbed a robe on his way and left, running, wrapping the robe about him like a bath towel.

"What do you mean?" he asked meanwhile, trying to keep the tone even and the conversation going.

"They've gotten to Dr. Thieu in the heart of Planys, on the other side of the world. They can get to anyone."

"Look, somebody gave me your card, I haven't a clue why, I don't know who 'they' are, and I don't know why you'd be calling me. What are you into, what do you want with my father, and where in hell did you get my number?"

"I got it from Thieu. Look, I'm in the middle of selling my apartment. All my belongings are in boxes, my physical files are in a mess and I can't find anything. I'm supposed to be going up to the station, and now everything's stalled, I don't know why, and I can't get an answer out of the Director's office! Thieu said to talk to your father, now Thieu's just died and I can't reach him, your number works, *you're* on the inside of the agency that's hiring me and now not talking to me, so here you are, Ser Warrick, and welcome to my situation! Can you just go down the hall or wherever you are and tell your father I urgently need to talk to him? There've been people coming through to look at this place I don't like the look of, they say it's sold, but someone arrives today and just walks through, and I didn't know whether to let them in or not. I don't want to deal with this, and someone I don't know phones me to tell me Thieu is dead and hangs up. So what am I supposed to do? When I get hold of Schwartz, he's going to tell me it's all fine, I don't need to worry, and just let them handle everything, but that's what he said the last time. I need to talk to someone who knows what's going on."

"Well, it's not going to be my father. I think you should call Planys Security tonight and ask them what's going on. You get a call in the night and you assume it's even true . . ."

"Oh, it's true. It's true he's dead. I have no doubt of it. I have no doubt I'm targeted and your father is, and Planys Security can't even take care of its own, let alone protect me here. These aren't reasonable people."

He didn't like it. His heart had picked up the old familiar heavy beat. On one hand it felt like a trap. On the other . . . this woman might be *in* one, and in possession of information ReseuneSec was going to want. And if he could stay on the line and get a record down of this little playlet, naming names, it was safer for him and everyone attached to him.

"I don't understand why my father has anything to do with this. And if you want protection, I can get ReseuneSec to go wherever you are—"

"Thieu," she interrupted him, and somewhere in the background there was a noise, a thump, of some sort. "Oh my God," she said. "Warrick, tell them! Tell them!"

"Tell them what?"

"Clavery! The name is Anton Clavery! Just—"

Something thumped. The phone quit. He grabbed his own robe, shoved his arms into the sleeves and headed past the end of the bed, out of the bedroom, taking down the small, useless table next to the door as he headed down the hall. Lights in the living area had come on, where Grant had passed.

He got that far before the front door opened and black-uniformed security came bursting in—Marco and Wes, specifically, night shift, with Grant's conspicuous red head just beyond that tall blot of black uniforms.

"Her phone went dead," he said, out of breath. "I recorded it, as far as it went." In that moment Catlin arrived, in a black tee and workout pants, unarmed, to all appearances, and probably straight from bed, while Marco walked over and took a look at the house minder unit. He didn't know which one to address, or which, Marco or Catlin, was technically in charge. And he had a shaky moment of realizing he, ReseuneSec's main target for years, had been babbling in that call, urging a woman's cooperation with ReseuneSec, anxious to keep himself and Grant safe from whatever damned fool thing Jordan had brought on them in his eternal feud with Admin—and too sure, maybe, that his father *hadn't* had anything to do with whatever was going on in Novgorod. He felt a vague sense of shame about turning coat on his father. But not enough. That collection of ReseuneSec in the hall—that had been Ari, young Ari, taking real power over a segment of that organization that had repeatedly arrested him. And he had urgently to deal with them—for Grant's sake. "Catlin, it was Patil on the phone. Something's wrong. She needs help. Security. Fast. She's saying Thieu was killed. Someone interrupted her on the phone. Apparently violently."

Catlin didn't waste a breath. She had her com unit, and delivered a fast message somewhere that consisted of, "Information on Patil. Code 10. Her residence?" The last was a question aimed at him.

"I think it was," he said. "Residence." Second thought. "Maybe her office. I don't know."

"Residence *and* office," Catlin said into the com. "Stat, find her, wherever she is." She broke the contact. Grant, meanwhile, had gotten past building security at the door, still with the robe held like a towel, and Florian showed up behind him in the bottom half of a workout suit, dark hair in its usual curling disarray.

"Sera's awake," Florian said. "Ser Warrick. Did you call Dr. Patil?"

He shook his head. "She called me, out of nowhere. Said Thieu was dead."

Up went the com unit, same fast contact. Florian said, into it: "PlanysSec, report on status of Dr. Raymond Thieu, researcher, retired."

There was perhaps a brief silence on that contact. Grant made a quiet move toward him. Building security moved to restrain him. Catlin simply lifted a hand, on the phone with someone else, and security stood down, letting Grant through.

He grabbed Grant by the arm, in no mood to have them separately questioned. Gone over. Drugged. Any of those things. "I'm worried about my father," he said to Florian. "She said someone was inside. On the inside."

"Thieu is dead," Florian said. It was a measure of trust that someone of Florian's nature gave a piece of information to an outsider. And Florian immediately thumbed buttons on the com and called someone else. "Guard alert, Jordan Warrick's residence. See to his safety. Report."

"Thanks," Justin said quietly. Two more individuals in security uniform had shown up at the door, and found their way in, people Justin had seen at Ari's door this evening, people with the com rig and armament of personnel on duty. Her people. He stood there. He didn't know what to do. He was in the middle of the mess, as clued in as anyone could be without that vital comlink. Meanwhile Grant, unflapped, dropped half his hold on the robe, calmly sorted out the top of it and put it on, tying it this time.

"Young sera, I believe, is more than awake," Grant said, indicating it wasn't all a case of Catlin and Florian running things at the moment.

"Your father has answered his phone, ser," Florian said, "and agents are on their way to his door."

That was a relief. He hadn't known how much relief. He was scared for Jordan. He didn't know why he was. Jordan hadn't earned it, giving him that card. But he was glad to know Ari's version of ReseuneSec was between Jordan and anything else stupid. He moved quietly over to the sideboard, out of the way, his own foyer and his living room having become security central in the last few moments. Feigning calm, he started to ask Grant to pour them both a vodka and orange, but at just that moment Ari showed up in the foyer, in a nightrobe, and with her dark hair in a pigtail.

"Justin?" she asked.

"It's the card," he said. "It's that damned card. I don't know what's going on. Patil called, for no apparent reason, except she found out Thieu's dead and then something happened when she was calling us. We have *no* idea. Would you like a vodka and orange?"

"I think I'd love one."

"Sera," Catlin said to her, "agents have entered Dr. Patil's residence. They were on watch. They saw no one. But Patil has fallen out her window."

"Fatally."

"Quite fatally, sera. It's twelve stories."

"Oh, this is splendid!"

Grant had gone after the drinks. Justin stood frozen, rethinking what Patil had said last.

"Anton Clavery," he said, then. "She gave that name, before—whatever happened."

"The name is a new one," Catlin remarked.

"We recorded everything, from the start. It's all on the system, fast as Grant could get over and push the button."

"Why would she call you?" Ari asked.

"I haven't the least notion," he began, then: "Hell. Yes, I do. She asked if I could get Jordan down the hall. She had my number, not his. She has—had—no concept of where we live, or the conditions he lives in. She couldn't get through security to phone him."

Catlin lifted a pale eyebrow, that was all. He suddenly wondered if that last statement was even true, or if for some unfathomed reason, Patil had specifically wanted to go through him—and just gave a wave of his hand.

"It's all recorded. It's what she said. I don't know if she was telling the truth. She was upset. I guess she had reason." He wanted to ask if Thieu had died of natural causes, curiosity being as natural to him as breathing; but no, he didn't want to know that. He didn't want to know anything about it.

Grant showed up with three drinks, poured the fast way, from the autobar unit. It was rescue. He presented the first to Ari, and only then it occurred to him that Ariane Emory didn't drink things handed to her by people who'd just occasioned a midnight security alert.

But this Ari did, with only a little lift of her own brow. "Can we sit in your front room? It seems we're all in the way here. It's become ops. I do apologize for that."

"Certainly," he said, and showed her in, past Grant, at the small bar. "Sorry to have waked the whole house."

"Thieu and Patil. What do *you* think?"

Sideways jolt. She was good at that.

And two new thoughts hove onto the horizon, desperate and little likely. "Maybe someone's *trying* to involve my father. Maybe he thought that card somehow involved me in the first place. I don't know what went through his mind."

"Would he be honest with you if you asked?"

Because they couldn't legally use anything but truthers on Jordan, and Jordan could beat those.

"I don't know. He's not speaking to me at the moment. Not since—not since that dinner."

"I think it's a good moment for you to talk to him. I think it's a logical moment."

One thing Ari had was a sense of timing. He could appreciate it—even if he had rather walk barefoot into the wilderness. "I won't go there with Grant."

"Grant won't stay here," Grant said.

"Dammit, Grant."

"I take it I have leave to defend myself."

"Absolutely," Ari said.

"Ari." Justin rounded on her with no hesitation. "If anything happens to him—I will *never* forgive it."

"If anything happens," she said, "Florian will be through that door faster than you can blink."

"And if I go there with *your* entourage, he won't say a thing."

"Try," she said.

Try. He looked at Grant, not at all liking it. He set the drink down, scarcely touched: he was going to need all his mental resources.

"Sorry to desert you," he said, pro forma, and went back down the hall to the bedroom, righted the damaged table. Grant followed him.

"Sorry," Grant said, "but you're no safer in that apartment than I am. Two of us—"

"My own father," he said bitterly. "You know, among born-men, that's actually supposed to count for something."

"Two CITs are dead," Grant said somberly. "And, I repeat, you're not safe."

"Damn," he said, and grabbed random clothes from the closet.

JUNE 12, 2424
0211H

Press of the button. Possibly the minder was set to ignore commotion at this hour. Justin knocked at the door. Forcefully.

"Ser," Florian said, and reached past him with a keycard. The door opened, and Florian pushed the door open, but Justin put out an arm, barring his way.

"My father. Let me handle it alone. Please. There's nothing wrong. Reasonable people are asleep at this hour."

"Call out to him," Florian said, not giving an inch.

"Dad?" he called out. "Jordan?"

Lights came up suddenly, throwing the apartment into brightness—an apartment like the one they'd had, once, much the same design, dining counter, kitchen, living area, all together . . . it evoked nostalgia every time he entered it.

"Go," he said to Florian. "Wait outside. I'll get better answers."

"Block the door open until you're sure," Florian said, and went outside, leaving him, and Grant, Grant's foot blocking the door from automatically shutting.

Paul came out first, in his nightrobe, Paul, looking as well-groomed and civilized as usual. Jordan followed, much the same.

"Dad," he said, "there's an alarm on. You know that card you gave me? Patil's dead. Thieu's dead."

Jordan stood there, raked a hand through his hair, didn't say anything except, "Come in."

Grant drew his foot from the door. It shut. Jordan was on his way to the couch. Paul was on his way to the bar.

"No drinks, thanks," he said, and he and Grant sat down.

"I'll have one," Jordan said. "How did you get in?"

"Florian," he said. Leveling with Jordan was the best policy, if it was something that obvious. "Sorry about that, but if they're killing off people on Thieu's social list, I wanted to be sure you were all right. What in hell's going on?"

He had Jordan at rare disadvantage. And with a clank of glasses and two fast jets from the dispenser behind the bar, Paul was rapidly preparing a distraction.

"Dad."

"Oh, cut the 'Dad,' boy."

"Well, I try. I'm here. Patil called *me* before she died."

"Florian's out there?"

"I figured he wouldn't add to the social setting. Yes, damned right I called security. Dr. Patil was upset. She wanted me to go down the hall and get you. She said she had my number and called me because she couldn't get through to you."

"Nice." Jordan took the drink Paul handed him, had a sip. "So my own appeal couldn't get you through my door, but you don't mind bringing the little dear's guards to burgle my apartment."

"I was concerned for your safety. She was talking about somebody *inside*, Dad. Who would that be?"

"The possibilities are endless. Ari, some CIT—getting an azi past Reseune Supervisors wouldn't be easy, but with inside help, who knows? Are we worried about assassins?"

"I'm worried for your safety. I'm worried for Grant's and Paul's. They didn't ask to get involved in whatever crazy mess you're in. Planys is a small place. Everybody knows everybody. Who would have killed an old man who didn't have long to live anyway?"

"A long list of volunteers," Jordan said, and took a drink of what looked like vodka. "The man was an insufferable egotist."

Justin sat back against the couch, crossed one leg over the other. "I thought you were friends."

"Society there is sparse."

"Come on, Jordan. Tell me. What happened? I know you didn't kill Ari. Everybody knows it. You were bitter, you wanted to strangle Denys, that didn't happen, and you spent nearly twenty years in the company of a doddering old guy with an ego. That, I understand. But if this guy had associates that were getting to him past the security screen at PlanysLabs, where were they? How was Patil involved? Why were you carrying her card around? And why in bloody hell did you dump it on me?"

"So Ari's got you asking her questions, has she?"

"I'm asking my own damn questions. I wouldn't have, if you hadn't shoved that card off on me, and if Patil hadn't called me in the middle of the night a few minutes before someone shoved her out a twelfth-story window—I call *that* involvement. I call that a damned mess, and if you've got any key to Thieu's goings-on at Planys, I want it!"

"What? Afraid your nice career's getting tarnished?"

"I'm afraid my father's trying to tarnish it, thanks. I'm afraid my father's decided to carry on a stupid war with a dead woman and can't figure out what year it is!"

"Justin," Grant said, a calm-down.

Jordan grinned. "Got to you, did I?"

"It's not a damn game!"

"Isn't it? I don't get out much lately. I need some amusement."

"At my expense."

"Any way I can, son, any way I can."

"Oh, poor Jordan. Poor Jordan. I never thought you were a sympathy sponge. But that's what you want. You want me to feel so sorry for you I'll ask you what I can do to help you out. Well, hell!"

"You could ask Florian in for a drink."

"Somehow I don't think he will. He's here to protect us both. And there will be guards. I'll be real damned surprised if there aren't guards dogging you down the halls, after this. So that's what you won with this stupid stunt."

"What stunt? The card? Did I pull the bandage off Reseune's old sores? Maybe they deserve airing."

"Twenty years ago! Normal people don't carry on a feud with a dead woman for twenty years, normal people don't blame her daughter, normal people don't try to get their own sons arrested for a damn joke!"

"You live with her. You never leave her."

"She's just a nice kid. You don't give her a chance. No, you've got to play politics, and *dead* politics, at that. What have the Paxers got, since the War ended? Their war stopped, we've got the peace they wanted, and they're still running around in back halls passing cryptic notes to each other and pasting up posters, what time they're not blowing up children. The Centrists, hell, the *law* won't let them mess up this planet—" Air went rarified. He didn't *do* real-time work, but a woman had died tonight while she was talking to him, and he and Jordan were going to be closely guarded for the rest of their natural lives. So what the hell did it matter if Jordan got a year's jump on what was going to go public anyhow? "You want the truth, Dad? I'm going to breach security right now and give you a name. Eversnow."

"Actually no surprise. I know about your little secret."

"Knew about it when you gave me that damned card?"

"I don't think I want to tell you. Let ReseuneSec figure what to do about it."

"Patil was your source."

Jordan shrugged. "Or not."

"So you know about it. All right. And certain Centrists know, but *that* doesn't make them happy, because they'd have to go off in the deep dark and actually build their new Earth, which means no nice, warm offices and no influence in Novgorod, doesn't it, so some of them aren't as happy as they could be."

"That could be true."

"And then there's the Abolitionists, oh, ask Grant about *them*. They know what's moral for everybody but them. The world is going along pretty much on course, and the War's over, so it's unemployment for radical types ... everybody's too comfortable. They're sending Patil out to handle Eversnow, and now somebody's killed her. You know, but you don't want to say how you know, and that doesn't look damn good, Jordan, it doesn't. You had your little fling with the Paxer element, which damn near got Grant killed ... So what in hell are you involved in this time?"

"Nothing. Absolutely nothing."

"Dad. Talk to me."

"So how do you know?"

"You can figure how I heard about it. From Ari."

"From the little dear. Who keeps you from unemployment until the bills come due and your pretty, safe world blows up in your face. You know what your precious Ari is, son of mine? The same as the first one—a damn self-contained genius with the power to run mindsets on the whole human species. You get all bothered about terraforming a planet we weren't born to, oh, the poor microbes—the damn stupid megafauna that's been turning this planet to desert for twenty million years: we've got to save them so they can go on desertifying the planet. We get all worked up about that, and never mind this one woman is imposing her mental design on the whole human species, dictating the social ratios from one end of space to the other, dictating the attitudes, the thoughts, the philosophies, of every single azi that gets his CIT status and turns into a breeding, proliferating citizen of this planet and everywhere else we reach! Every freedman on every station in Union space is teaching his kids the sacred dogma Ari Emory embedded in their psyches. Every planet we ever occupy and every station in Union space is going to be populated with just the right ratio of brilliant to moderately stupid that Ariane Emory decided is just fine and right for humanity. We don't need a god. We've got one!"

"The Bureau of Defense was the one that landed a colony on Gehenna. The first Ari modified it so as *not* to create a human timebomb."

"Do we know that?" Jordan fired back. "Seems it did pretty well at being a bomb. Alliance is still trying to figure out how to get the locals out of the bushes."

"Good question. I'm sure I don't know what she's thinking and I don't know what your Ari thought. But I'm even more sure the Defense Bureau doesn't know what they're doing from one campaign to the next, and if you want somebody to blame for this mess, Jordan, blame the people you were dealing with when it all went wrong. They wanted a weapon. A poison pill. They didn't care how it got mopped up so long as Alliance had to do it, and now we're not at war with Alliance, and you're right when you ask what do we do now, sterilize the planet? It's not going to happen, Dad. It's what we've got to live with. It's going to be this Ari's problem."

"We've got a whole new branch of the human species out there, thanks to her. What are we going to do with *that*, when it wants off its planet? Is it going to like us? We don't fucking *know*, do we?"

"We'll learn from it. And we'll deal with it."

"Oh, I'm sure we'll learn. And I hope your little dear keeps her hands the hell off it before it gets worse. *That'll* come back to make us sorry, no way it won't."

Deep breath. "So Gehenna worries you. Fine. Meanwhile your precious Centrists want to play god with Cyteen's ecosystem. Populate the world. Turn it into Earth. And Eversnow's not going to be good enough for most of them and now Patil's dead. What do they want, Dad?"

"Well, tonight they haven't got Thieu and they haven't got Patil. I wonder how *that* benefits them. *I* don't think it does."

He shut his mouth. For several seconds. He really didn't want to know the next answer. "So who does it benefit? Do you know?"

"The short answer is, it doesn't benefit *them*. Ergo it wasn't the Centrists who did it."

"A split in the Centrists? Centrists who were willing to have Eversnow be the project—versus those that aren't? Yanni just made a deal with their leadership. I think you know that. I think maybe you've even discussed it with him."

"So let these mythical asymmetrical Centrists all go play at Gehenna. There's a nice lab. It bites back. They can't make it worse than it is."

"You gave me Patil's card, Dad. *What* in hell was I supposed to do with it?"

"Take it to the little dear. What else would an upstanding lad like yourself do, who wants to keep his precious career spotless? Mine's done. What do I care?"

"Your career isn't done. It doesn't need to be done."

"My own son won't work with me! What's left?"

"For God's sake don't try pity, Jordan. I've got my own problems. You want my help, take it, or quit whining!"

Silence on the other side. Jordan spread his arms along

the back of the other couch, feet extended and crossed. "Dear boy. Whining, is it?"

Somehow that posture conveyed threat. Justin became just a shade cautious. "I'd help you, Dad, I would. But everything I try to do for you is a risk. Not from her. From *you*. Every time I try to make a gesture, you slap it down. Every time I try to do anything for you, you do something to make me sorry I even tried."

"Now who's whining?"

"You dodged the question."

"Ask it."

"What was I supposed to do with Patil's card? What were you doing with it? Why involve yourself with her? And why is she dead?"

Jordan sat unmoving for a moment, then leaned forward and took a sip of the vodka. "Shoved her out a window, you say? That would account for it."

"Don't take that tone with me."

"The little dear can't question me under drugs, so you volunteered."

"I'm worried about you, dammit. Cooperate! You're not guilty of anything."

"Thank you," Jordan said, with a salute of the glass. "Thank you. I appreciate that."

"Well, then don't act the part. Tell me what in hell you meant with the card."

"Thieu talked a lot about her. A lot. Brilliant woman. Going to save the Centrist cause. Ad nauseam. *Nothing's* going to save the Centrist cause. Never was a chance of it from the moment they passed the law that put Cyteen off-limits for terraforming—of course, that was *after* we had ReseuneLabs and Novgorod *and* PlanysLabs already down here, not to mention Big Blue—here we were in the middle of a war, and with the no-terraforming law that hampered us protecting ourselves, it got downright dicey trying to keep civilization going down here. But on-world settlements suddenly seemed a good backup in case somebody got a strike in at the station. Military ne-cess-i-ty. So we enacted the Habitation Zones Act—incidentally what I assume the little dear is relying on for this spurt of building I hear she's indulging in upriver. Turns out she's the best ally the Centrists have got. One little slip, one breach of quarantine, and they'll have to designate another big slice of land into the Zones . . . wouldn't *that* be ironic?"

"Do you know some specific threat? Somebody planning—"

"Hell if I know. Construction here. Construction up-river. Accidents happen. So Patil's dead. Thieu's dead. And Thieu wanted me to call Patil, as if I was a total fool. *No,* he didn't give me the card. I didn't even get it there. Turned up in my coat pocket the day I gave it to you."

"How?"

"I don't know. How should I know?"

"How do you think it got there?"

A shrug. "Library, restaurant—breakfast and lunch— I'd been in public places all day. I found it. I figured it for a set-up like the last set-up. I routinely leave my coat on my chair, all right? Paul's usually there. At one point we both went to the salad bar. Possibly I'd left it at a table in Library and we were both off at another station. I do it every day. I don't even know it happened that particular day. I don't keep things in my coat pockets. I don't put my hands there, as a rule. I felt something when I straightened the pocket flap. There was that damned card, like a visit from Thieu. But not. And I didn't the hell like it. So I just returned it to ReseuneSec. I knew it would get there."

"You didn't run it through your computer, did you?"

"No. Am I a fool? I just gave it to you. Maybe your little dear would run it through her computers, if it got to her, precocious little egotist that she is. Maybe it'd just fuck the whole Reseune computer system and I wouldn't be to blame."

"My God, Dad, you're talking like a teenager with a grudge. You don't want to bring down the house computers."

"I'm sure I don't really care." Jordan lifted his glass, second salute. "But she might port the business home to the agency responsible, whoever that is. Can I offer my son a drink?"

"Had some already. I need to be sober, dealing with you."

"Excuses. —Grant?"

"No, ser, thank you."

"At least *you* don't find an excuse."

"No, ser," Grant said, "I don't. And won't. You meant for Justin to be arrested. That would have made Justin mad at Admin, and it could have caused trouble for Thieu and Patil, maybe, but more likely you found a way to get rid of the card right under security's nose, and you did it because they can't ask you how you got it, and you can play games with them. How does that train of logic apply to the facts of the case?"

"Remarkable. You've gotten very deviously CIT, Grant."

"I hope not."

"Certainly you've acquired a great imagination. Very nice. I suppose I have to credit Ari's work in you."

"Dammit, Dad, leave him out of this!"

A little smile, cold as ice. "*You* don't leave him out of this."

"I chose to be here, ser," Grant said calmly. "Forgive me."

"Oh, I forgive you. I forgive my son. I just don't forgive her."

"Is it true?" Justin asked sharply. "Is Grant right? Was it what you were after, getting Thieu investigated? Or nailing whoever gave you that card?"

"Some of both," Jordan said. "I'd no desire to have Thieu foul up my life. It turns up in my pocket, and I can only assume one of two things—either it's some devotee of Thieu's and I'm supposed to use it, or I'm supposed to be caught with it and arrested; so I passed it on in the same generous spirit in which it was given. You—what do you care? You've got the little darling to protect you. You're not going to get in trouble. I had no inclination to call Patil, based on it, and carry on Thieu's social agenda for some third party—if that's all it was. I didn't figure it came from her. Thieu has political contacts, or did, when he was functioning. He always assumed I was what I was sentenced for—assumed I was a poor fellow Centrist, badly done by because I'd murdered Ari. I never disabused him of that notion. It kept him happy, babbling his theories, giving me printouts, all his grand designs for his project that the legislature had axed with the Habitation Zones Act, on and on and on . . . for twenty damned years. After a while, he didn't even take the trouble to be clandestine about it. He just rattled on. And so I was supposed to call Patil. I didn't. So somebody came looking for me to give me a shove. Not my fault."

"Dad, just talk to Yanni. Tell him all this. Talk to him."

"Damn Yanni. You deal with him. I don't have to. The law says I'm off limits to their inquiries. Fine. I was off limits when they sentenced me to that hellhole with that damned fool and the rest of the spacecases. They can come begging, after this. They can damned well give me lab access, access to my work, my license back—They can do *that* if they want anything out of me! Those are my conditions."

Suddenly a handful of things clicked into place, logic, motive. Jordan wasn't a fool. He was a man who'd been in a hard, hard spot when the first Ari died—and if he'd quarreled bitterly with Ariane Emory, he'd been at outright war with the Nyes, particularly Giraud. "I'll present that case," Justin said. "Honestly I will."

"You don't have to," Jordan said, and drank off the melt in his glass. "Her faithful shadow's out there, isn't he, and we're bugged as all hell. They know what I said. They can weigh it for what it's worth or call me a liar."

Justin shrugged. Drew in a breath and took a chance. "I might take that drink, Dad."

"Fix it yourself." Jordan waved his glass toward the bar, toward him. " Fix me another while you're at it."

"I'll do it," Grant said, and got up and took the glass with him.

"Could ask Florian in," Jordan muttered. "Damn spook. He's getting to look like the first Florian. Getting to act like him, too."

"He wouldn't come in," Justin said. He didn't want the excuse of the intrusion. "And he won't drink on duty. But don't be surprised to see Security in your hallway hereafter. They're upset, two murders on opposite sides of the world, no explanations, and both of us are at risk."

"Just one of those little puzzles Security loves, isn't it? And we're two of their favorite subjects."

Grant brought Jordan and him their drinks, and went back to the bar with Paul's empty glass.

"Personally, I'm still glad Security's out there," Justin said, after a first sip. "I don't want to be getting a midnight call about you."

"Oh, just look at us. We're caring about each other. Heartwarming."

Too easy to come back in sarcastic kind. Jordan invited it, tried to turn everything to vinegar. Justin took another sip from his glass. "Mirror into mirror. We're too apt to fight. But let's face it, I have a certain position, one that I fought for in Giraud Nye's time. He didn't like me much. Didn't like you, ergo didn't like me, and I paid for it."

"Sorry." The tone wasn't.

"Not your fault, particularly. The Nyes knew damned well you were innocent. Maybe that's why Giraud distrusted me, expecting the wrath of the wronged, maybe— or just misliking the fact I got close to Ari—her doing, not mine. Ari, outside of being the incarnation you deplore, is a pretty good little kid in her spare time. Always has been. She stood between me and Giraud. I returned the favor, as best I could, with the other Nye, when he decided she had to go—because, believe me, you and I weren't well off during Denys' tenure, and we'd have been worse off, still, if it weren't for that young girl. There's a lot of history, a lot of history you weren't here for, but she kept me alive, and ever since she did in her uncle, she keeps me able to work, keeps Grant safe, and that's a fair debt I owe her. She rescued you, if you don't know it—pulled you out of Planys during the height of the set-to with Denys and got you behind Reseune's internal security. Whatever you think about it, you're alive. So I'm not interested in your feud with her. Sorry. You can't convert me." He took a deep pull at the liquid, felt the previous sips finally hitting his nerves with a deceptive calm. "But I do sympathize with you. It may not have involved getting slammed against the wall by security—not my favorite moments, those—but I do understand the sense of restriction. They sent all the problem cases over to Planys during the War. I don't think it must have been particularly sparkling society, or a particularly happy one."

"They put us under pressure and bugged the place," Jordan said, "and we all knew it. *I* was innocent of what sent me there—in deed, if not in thought. And that put me pretty well on the outs, finally, because everybody but Thieu eventually knew I wasn't guilty—but they courted me for their various causes and tried to put on sympathy for my plight. God, it was a bloody comedy. ReseuneSec should have put me on payroll. I'd go to venues that supposedly weren't bugged. I was damned sure they were. And I talked, and they recorded, and sometimes certain particularly obnoxious people just went away." A small, bitter laugh. "I tell you, I was a valuable resource. ReseuneSec wouldn't have wanted to give me up. But when Giraud Nye died—after that happened, I really watched what I ate and drank. I figured there might be orders floating in the system, maybe posthumous ones from him—maybe current ones from Denys, who knows? I didn't trust it when the little dear declared bygones were bygones and shoved Paul and me onto a plane . . ."

BOOK THREE   Section 2   Chapter iv

JUNE 12, 2424
0321H

"Interesting comment," Florian said somberly, when he and Catlin reviewed the record, with Marco and Wes in the room. "If it's true about the card, possibly someone in ReseuneSec was trying to draw a wrong action out of Warrick. Or maybe it had, as he said, completely different motives, and came from some source that ought not to be inside these walls."

"Pursue it," Catlin said. She looked tired. None of them had gotten a great deal of sleep this night.

But they had gotten Justin and Grant home uncontaminated, at least in the sense of poison and deepteach drugs. Justin and Grant were, by now, sleeping it off, sera herself had managed to get some late sleep, after a two in the morning call to Yanni, and by now Rafael and their outward apparatus, within ReseuneSec, were instructed to haul in information and sort it: security assignments, who was in what hall, in the restaurants in question, everything, not to mention who had access to Thieu, and who had come and gone in Patil's condominium complex.

It was, to all appearances, death by catastrophic heart failure, in Thieu's case—autopsy had yet to determine more specifics. It was even possible it was *natural* death, a body which had ceased to renew itself, arteries and veins and cardiac tissue losing their prolonged youthful character, in the sort of fairly rapid decline that attended rejuv failure. It didn't take much to tip a fragile body off the edge. Somebody might have applied that pressure.

The force, however, that had torn a sealed window out of its mount and sent Sandur Patil ten stories to the roof of an adjacent cooling tower—that was a plainly hostile action, on the shockwave of a grenade hand-launcher. Sniffers, applied within the hour in the corridor and lifts, had turned up molecular evidence that had yet to match up with anyone in files, which meant the perpetrator had either confounded the scene with a puffer, available, some sophisticated ones quite expensively so, in Novgorod's CIT underworld. That, or whoever had so spectacularly done in Patil was a novice with a hitherto clean record, and thus not on file. They could run the sniffer data and get an ID of everybody who'd been near that apartment . . . but on the grounds of the heavy firepower involved, beyond most novices, Florian personally bet on a puffer in use, specifically designed to foil a sniffer and confuse the scene. That was going to take the chemists time to sort out. The launcher, however—that wasn't a short-range weapon. It wasn't the sort of thing a professional took to a quiet assassination. Whoever had done this was making a statement.

In the meanwhile—their whole staff lost sleep.

"No shortage of Paxer talent to produce a bogus card," Wes said. "Somebody could have done it off any letter she sent with her letterhead."

"ReseuneSec calls it clean," Catlin said. "Electronically speaking clean, nanistically clean. No microprint in the typeface, so it was a private printer, but definitely with Planys microtags. That indicates only that the paper was produced to be used in Planys. Not that it was. The printer site could be anywhere."

"And the card was planted eight weeks before two of the principals die," Marco said. "The card was planted on the day the Council voted on a black budget for Eversnow. It could be coincidence: it could be connected, but somebody had all the pieces ready—the file, the card stock, the access to Jordan Warrick."

"News reports," Florian said, "still say publicly only that there's new construction for Fargone. Patil's name wasn't publicly connected with either the real facts or the published cover. But she wasn't at all reticent about the fact that she was taking an appointment with Reseune at Fargone: they didn't forbid her to talk about it, and she talked to colleagues. The University was making adjustments in her teaching schedule for September. It's possible she wasn't totally discreet. All it takes is one slip."

"Defense was still managing her," Wes said, "even if she was publicly switching to Reseune payroll. She remained under Defense rules."

"Seems so," Florian said. "If they'd wanted her silenced, they could have done that with a phone call. So they didn't object at all to the farewell parties, or she didn't listen. Maybe it leaked to the Paxers—maybe through office staff, someone she confided in."

"Defense is in elections," Wes said. "Jacques is in office, Spurlin and Khalid are running. There are two strong factions in Defense. Only Jacques has the say, Spurlin is generally with Jacques; Khalid—Khalid is a problem. What his feelings are on the Eversnow project, we have no idea."

"Somebody certainly silenced Patil for good," Catlin said. "That's one. And also assured she won't take that appointment, which Yanni offered her, which at least half of Defense wanted, which Citizens, Information, and Trade all wanted, and which Reseune was funding. She was evidently the most universally acceptable candidate. Her death doesn't need a card from Planys to threaten Yanni's interests. One who might, on the surface, have motive, is sera herself: it slows a program she doesn't favor. But that's nowhere in question, and we know she didn't."

"Suppose someone inside Reseune opposes Yanni, or Eversnow, or the agreement Yanni made," Florian said. "They could pose a danger. Someone violently opposes Yanni's program."

"A problem," Marco said, "an outsider, can come into Reseune Township on a barge out of Novgorod, with a load of fertilizer. Can live there, if he's good at blending in. There's a lot of people in town that don't need a key-card to survive."

Wes said: "I don't think sera is in imminent danger. Taking out Yanni or Hicks would be a safer move, to stop Eversnow . . . unless they have extraordinary penetration. Sera's become too hard a target."

"And the elder Warrick said he knew about Evers-now," Catlin said. "If that's true, where did he get his information?"

"I remain worried about sera's safety," Marco said. "Certain people might like to have her gone, and War-rick to blame. Again. Even if supporting Jordan Warrick against Reseune Admin is part of the Paxer cause. It's good cover—to support the innocence of the man they've framed."

"Or maybe," Wes said, "they want confusion. Patil's double-crossed them, in their view. They kill her. And they set up something to stir up trouble and make Warrick an issue again—by getting him arrested for his connection to her assassination. But that requires that card be found in his possession, and it wasn't . . . because he wouldn't have it: he'd given it to Justin. He's smart; he saw the chance of something aimed at him. He didn't want to be tagged with it. He got rid of it as fast as he could, in a way that has Re-seuneSec and sera's staff quarreling over it."

"That part makes sense," Florian said. The rest of the world didn't know that sera herself had begun to move on Yanni, and that everything was bound to change soon; and if that leaked and became public, it was going to cause agitation in many quarters. It wasn't even to be mentioned to Wes and Marco, yet. "We've got a safe copy of the code on the card. It didn't contain anything but Patil's academic

vita . . . on the surface, no slink or ferret. Hicks' office has
sent the card over to the experts. They're having their own
go at it, just to see if there's a code in the apparent content.
ReseuneSec has their report coming. I want our own done,
with a copy of the analysis, directly to us."

"I'll let *you* port it to that wing," Catlin said to Florian.
"*You* talk to them."

Florian smiled absently. The dedicated experts, azi,
were odd beyond all reason, monofocused alphas who'd
rather deal with code than eat or sleep or do most anything. A couple of sensible betas sat as directors over the
lot, the human Supervisor, himself a specialist, being almost as eetee as the azi he supervised. "Should have done
before now, anyway." He punched the recording on again.

"I was surprised it was a large plane," Jordan Warrick
said. *"I was surprised we weren't being sent to some even
more remote hellhole. I was surprised when we crossed
the ocean. I was moderately surprised we ended up landing at Reseune. And I was surprised to learn Yanni was
somewhat in charge despite the little darling. Life was just
a chain of surprises that week. I still remain surprised
we're alive. That could always change. We're here. One of
Thieu's connections tried to get me involved with his pet
pupil. I declined. She's dead. He's dead. I'm here, and I'll
be here for the rest of time. I'm not involved, but nobody's
going to believe it. What more can I do?"*

And Justin Warrick: *"Just don't antagonize Admin, for
God's sake, Dad, just settle in, forget the damn card, just
answer any questions they ask—"*

"The hell!"

*"Answer them, dammit! Leave it for Security. Live your
life. Ask Yanni for a few cases, and get busy, high-level,
low-level, it doesn't matter. I'll go to him . . ."*

*"But you haven't done it, have you? I seem to remember
you were going to do that."*

"I've been a little busy. Never mind how. Just—I will."

*"You really don't get the picture, do you? They won't let
me write sets. They're paranoid. And, no, I'm not going to
get any work."*

*"Jordan, don't explode. She'd check them over. If she
passed them, ultimately, they'll be passed."*

"That's not even worth a comment."

"Because you're too fucking proud."

"Because I'm not going to deal with her. I'm not going to her begging."

"Then I will," Justin said. *"She'll get you through this. Nobody's going to pin anything on you. No more frame-ups."*

"Forget it." Rattle of ice in a glass, and a thump, a glass set down. Hard. *"They'll do what they want to anyway."*

"I'll find a way," Justin said.

"Stubbornness," Jordan said, *"runs in the family."*

"So Justin offered sera's help," Catlin said.

It was curious, considering where Justin's loyalties lay. It was worth bringing to sera, who understood born-men infinitely better.

"Sera should definitely hear this," Florian said.

Reaching to her own keyboard, Catlin said, "I'll send the transcript to her queue. She may not like that part."

BOOK THREE   Section 2   Chapter v

JUNE 12, 2424
0602H

Sleep hadn't come early, but Ari was up and dressed before Joyesse had a chance to show up . . . she'd fallen asleep before she'd heard how things had gone, and trusted Catlin to wake her if they'd gone spectacularly badly.

There was a note in System from Catlin. And files for her. *Interesting*, Catlin's note said. There was a flag on a section of note, but she started skimming the file from the top, choosing rapid-audio over script—she wanted the nuances.

And it was interesting, right from the start. Jordan tended to be that.

". . . So my own appeal couldn't get you through my door, but you don't mind bringing the little dear's guards to burgle my apartment."

A little odd to hear oneself snarled at in absentia. She had a pet name. How sweet.

"I was concerned for your safety." That was Justin, a little further from the pickup, talking about Patil, and she slowed the audio down. *"She was talking about somebody inside, Dad. Who would that be?"*

Then: *"How was Patil involved? Why were you carrying her card around? And why in hell did you dump it on me?"*

There was a nice list of questions. She didn't expect answers from Jordan, but it was a good fight, very much the same as at her dining table.

". . . the fact I got close to Ari," Justin fired back at one point. *"Who, outside of being the incarnation you deplore, is a pretty good little kid in her spare time."*

The audio went on. And on. Her heart had begun picking up its beats. Gotten harder and harder. And she got Mad. As Mad as she'd ever been. And that was all she could hear. *A pretty good little kid. A pretty good little kid.* That wasn't Justin putting on an act. That was Justin defending her. *A pretty good little kid.*

Damn him! Damn him!

She shook, she was suddenly so mad. And her breath came short, and her eyes stung, suddenly swimming with tears.

Well, *that* was interesting. She'd just had a heavy hit of adrenaline, and a rush of hormones, and she kept hearing those same five words, over and over, and she wanted to cry. She wanted to cry so badly she burst into sobs and buried her face in her hands. Which was just damned stupid. She wiped her eyes, and kept wiping, smearing tears all over her face, and hiccuping, which just finished it—she hadn't had a tantrum like that since she was three.

God!

The audio had just gone on, far past, and the worst part was, she had to run it back to find her place and hear it again.

Little kid.

Dammit all. She wondered what else she'd hear that would send her over the edge. Or break her heart. She really, really didn't want to go on listening.

But it was what one got for eavesdropping on somebody

else's conversation, and he probably hadn't even thought twice about saying it. That was the problem. He was, face it, older. A lot older. And that was exactly how he saw her. And that was where he was, her Justin, forever out of reach.

She had to hear it to the end. She had to know, about Justin, of all people, what he was thinking and saying. It was her job to know, if she was going to take over Reseune, if she was going to go on trusting him as a major asset.

And it was an interesting reaction. Her heart was still beating hard. She wasn't thinking straight. Jordan was saying important things about where the card could actually have come from and how he'd reacted, and she couldn't analyze anything. They used to shoot her full of hormones so she'd react in certain ways. This was like that. She was still shaken, and still feeling sorry for herself, and actually *jealous* of the first Ari, for having had, just once, a physical chance at Justin. And simultaneously, she was ashamed of that thought; and knew, still, that the first Ari hadn't won Justin's heart. Or she had, but not in the way anybody would want to—she'd taken him, shaken him, and then died, leaving him to suffer the consequences of being under Denys Nye's regime and tangled somewhere in the first Ari's involvement with Jordan. So it had kept him safe, but it had made him a target. Not mentioning what Ari had done to him, deliberately, as an act of policy.

That *had* to be part of Justin's reaction to her ... as long as she was *a pretty good little kid*, he had her in a safe place in his mind. Sex, in Justin, wasn't going to go her way, and she had to face it, was all. No other woman ever seemed to interest him; and she seemed to be *the* female he reacted to, but it wasn't the reaction she wanted—or that at least part of her wanted. When she thought about it logically—or as logically as she could manage—she knew it was one thing to imagine having sex with Justin; but it was a damned scary prospect to contemplate really doing it. It scared him; it scared her. And—the real stinger—it inevitably had a morning after, which just wouldn't be good for either of them.

So maybe she was *the little kid* for now. As they aged, the difference in their ages would get less. He'd be more like Jordan was now, she'd be more like Ari was then—

And it just wouldn't get any better, would it? Forget the thought.

She just had to prevent it all going nova, was all. She couldn't lose him, the way Ari had lost Jordan. That was the important thing.

She wondered what sort of answer she'd get from Jordan, if she asked him if he and the first Ari had ever had sex. She hadn't found it in the records, and she wondered about it. He'd be shocked at the question, she thought, probably disturbed, given that the relationship had gone the way it did—and then he'd twist it around and ask her if she aimed at Justin. Only he'd probably put it more bluntly—to shock her.

If she took the old war with Jordan into the realm of sexual innuendo, it could divert it away from the real issues—sex being, even with people who weren't *kids,* a short-circuit in the logic process.

So she didn't want to ask him, or get into that dialogue, because he wouldn't answer. He didn't have to answer anything, ever, and he used that fact like a weapon, challenging them, outright *challenging* them to break their own law and go after him, because then they'd be what he'd always said they were.

Maybe that was what went on in his head—just a spaghetti code of a thought process that hoped someday he could break them before they broke him . . .

And, dammit, she'd let the recording get away from her again. She remembered the place, sent it back to the precise number, and ran it the third time—this time hearing that *little kid* remark with a lot more logic functioning. It was sad, it was hurtful, but her pulse rate had settled and she had her brain working again.

The recording ran on. There wasn't anything else . . . down to the bit Catlin had flagged.

"Answer them, dammit! Leave it for security. Live your life. Ask Yanni for a few cases, and get busy, high-level, low-level, it doesn't matter. I'll go to him . . ."

"But you haven't done it, have you? I seem to remember you were going to do that."

"I've been a little busy. Never mind how. Just—I will."

"You really don't get the picture, do you? They won't let

*me write sets. They're paranoid. And, no, I'm not going to
get any work."*

"Jordan, *don't explode.* She'd *check them over. If she
passed them, ultimately, they'll be passed."*

"That's not even worth a comment."

"Because you're too fucking proud."

*"Because I'm not going to deal with her. I'm not going
to her begging."*

*"Then I will. She'll get you through this. Nobody's going
to pin anything on you. No more frame-ups."*

Would he ask her? She wasn't sure how she was going to
answer that if Justin did. It would be interesting to critique
one of Jordan's current designs. But if she said one word to
him, Jordan would blow, and that wouldn't help anything.
If he really did, it might poison the atmosphere between
her and Justin, and Jordan was perfectly capable of writing
something she'd have to criticize, just to get that result.

So maybe that wasn't a good idea. Endlessly, Jordan
played the martyr and Justin tried to do something to help
him. Catlin didn't like it, from the viewpoint of her own
profession, and she'd flagged that particular exchange as
worrisome, but that was how those two were, just being
Jordan and Justin, to the hilt. That she'd be upset about
something else in the file—Catlin, dear, loyal Catlin, hadn't
picked that up, didn't feel the least upset herself by Justin's
statement, or remotely think *she* would be upset, or Catlin
would have warned her. It was downright funny—Catlin
just hadn't seen it.

She loved Catlin. And Catlin helped her, finally, get it
all in perspective. Her own reaction was all gauzy wisp,
pure emotion, evaporative on a breeze, and nothing to do
with rationality—unless you started taking your own rattled assessment for solid and factual, and that was a mistake that launched your whole universe into mythology,
especially when it was a love-hate reaction. Catlin dealt
purely in substance, and found real substance in that latter
bit that she herself didn't see as alarming, or at least didn't
see as at all surprising—so she wasn't fluxed by it, just analytical, and that was that, and she could tell herself calmly,
yes, she'd hear the request and she'd think about it and
she'd probably say no. When Justin actually asked her.

It was interesting, however, to hear that first scene as
Catlin, and realize that, if she were Catlin, she just couldn't
be fazed by any assessment of her age—Catlin was just
Catlin, and knew what she could do: any other judgement
was, in Catlin's view, just mistaken.

Catlin did, however, worry about Justin's mental en-
gagement with Jordan's frustration, and possibly the vector it would take, entangling her and trying for sympathy.

And it would involve Justin going right to Yanni's door,
at a sensitive time in her own relations with Yanni. There
was that little question.

That *was* worth a slow rethinking, in Catlin's way of
looking at born-man behavior. In Catlin's view, a born-
man following his emotions was apt to do any damned
thing, not necessarily prudent, or successful, or even in his
own self-interest.

This request certainly wouldn't be in Justin's interest.
That was the thing about *real* self-sacrifice, unlike Jordan's
martyrdom: it knowingly gave away bits of itself, trying to
make the environment saner, and better.

On the other hand, another inquiry about Jordan could,
coming from her, constitute a very interesting probe into
Yanni Schwartz's motives.

She thought about it a moment. And she was surer and
surer about her course of action.

She wrote a note to Justin, and sent it. It said:

*Don't go to Yanni with your father's situation. The Patil
investigation is going to have Yanni's office in an uproar,
ReseuneSec is conducting the investigation, and I don't
want Hicks' office to sweep you and Grant up for questioning. Then I'd have Hicks getting all upset and bothered
because I'd have to go over his head to Yanni to get you
out. I would do it, understand, but that would just complicate things and you still wouldn't get your answer out
of Yanni and I'd have Hicks mad at me, which would just
make matters worse. I have to talk to Yanni anyway. Let
me approach Yanni about Jordan's getting some work to
do. I'd be happy to. I want things to work out, the same as
I know you do. You and Grant just be careful about going
out of the wing, even to restaurants, and don't send Grant
by himself. I don't want trouble with ReseuneSec.*

Justin had a strong tic, where it concerned ReseuneSec. And it wasn't altogether the most honest thing she'd ever written, but its purpose was. And there was *still* the question of who had put Jordan on to Eversnow, and who had dropped that card into his pocket—if they could believe a word of what he'd said.

I won't critique his work, she said at the end of that note. *I won't say a word. I know he'd like me to so he can have a fight. So I'll just pass/fail it. Tell him he'll have to write it well enough to get it past me and I'm going to be hypercritical. Bet he can't do it. Tell him that.*

BOOK THREE   Section 2   Chapter vi

JUNE 13, 2424
0802H

"God," Justin said, and then laughed, outright laughed.

"That's good," Grant said.

"I hope she can convince Yanni," Justin said, and Grant:

"I want to *see* this one."

BOOK THREE   Section 2   Chapter vii

JUNE 13, 2424
2310H

Pajama conference. That was what they'd used to call it, back when the Enemy was Denys, and they did it now that they ruled the Wing and had a force of their own. Florian and Catlin sat on Ari's big bed—Ari in her nightgown and Florian and Catlin in their gym sweats; and Ari tucked her knees up with her arms around her ankles and Florian and Catlin sat cross-legged. They played the oldest Game, Who's the Enemy?

"Paxers are easy," Florian said. "They're always out there."

Ari asked: "But have they got a leader?"

"We have names," Catlin said. "But there's no one single leader that anybody knows."

"Anton Clavery. Is that one?"

"A new name," Catlin said. "Anton Clavery doesn't show on any records. There is no CIT number."

"An alias, then."

"Or a nonperson," Florian said. "Births happen off the record. Particularly Paxer children. And children from the outback don't always get logged in."

That was a small revelation—though not a huge surprise. She saw it could certainly happen, if parents opting for natural birth didn't go to a hospital or register a birth for weeks—or months. Or never got around to it. "They'd have to intend to do this long-term. Motive?"

"Secrecy from the authorities," Florian said. "No registry of DNA, fingerprints, retinals, nothing of the sort. Hard to track a nonperson."

"Hard to find a job, too," Ari said. "How do they manage?"

Catlin hugged her knees up. "They borrow. Their job is being off the records and out of the system. They borrow cards, to ride public transport. People steal for them: they use a stolen card, then dump it before they get caught. They always have jobs. They're employed by clandestine groups. They're greatly prized for employment in some circles."

"Do we have data on the parents of these individuals? Do we try to track pregnant people that don't register a child?" She was instantly interested: a subset of the Paxers likely of other dissident groups. And she'd about bet they were all CIT, not azi, in origin. Azi-descended weren't inclined to plots, and they'd prize that CIT registry for their children; but CITs were inclined to be argumentative. People who'd opted to leave where they were and emigrate to Cyteen hadn't been the happiest where they were, o they'd have stayed. They'd either been hungry for something they didn't have, or they'd been at odds with where they were. Maybe a certain segment was at odds with the status quo again.

"There are names and numbers," Catlin said. "Some are known. It's a felony to fail to register a child—crime against person."

Mark a new element. Novgorod had existed at the outlet of the Novaya Volga since Reseune had existed near its headwaters. Her predecessor's mother, Olga, had seen the first days. So they weren't that many generations into Novgorod's existence. The Paxers had organized around opposition to the War, which had pretty well been going on since before Cyteen existed, in its cold war phase. But malcontents had been there probably since the second batch of people got to Cyteen Station in its pioneer days and complained about some regulation the first batch of colonists had voted on.

It took something, to deny your offspring a number, a normal life—medical care, and schooling, and easy travel, and everything else you could do with a CIT number.

"People groomed just to get past surveillance," she said. "I suppose they're more used than users. I can't see it would be a happy life. But if there was a nonperson who was really, really a black hole in the system, and he was really smart, he could get power, I suppose. If he was really determined, if he had a lot of arms and legs, he could do damage."

"He could," Florian said. "You'd only see the arms and legs. And Anton Clavery doesn't exist. A nonperson is one possibility. A hollow man is the other thing you have to deal with. A dead person anybody can be, if he pays the rent on the identity. Back during the War, there were even a few instances of Alliance agents—stationers. Not spacers, that we never found. The stationers didn't cope well, however,"

"There are a lot of schemes in Novgorod," Catlin said. "Cons and schemes alike."

"One thing Novgorod CITs are in my notes as being," Ari said, "is really good at finding ways around rules. I'm betting CITs descended from azi aren't much inclined to be nonpersons. Or use hollow men. I'm betting that's not in their psychsets. They'll go to birthlabs, mostly, to have their children. They'll get them registered. A CIT number is important to them."

"I certainly don't want one," Catlin said. "But then I don't want to be a CIT."

"You're not setted for it," Ari said, which threw her into thinking about what would in fact happen to them if she died, the way Maman had left Ollie, and she didn't want to think about that. It was one real good reason for her to live a long, protected life, was what. Two people relied on her, absolutely, and this Anton Clavery, whoever he was, whatever he was—threatened more than the Eversnow project. He had brought her really unpleasant questions, like currents running in Novgorod, among the Paxers, and the Rocher Party, the Abolitionists, who absolutely wouldn't understand Catlin's rejection of being a CIT. They'd want to *free* her, depend on it.

"I'm glad I'm not," Catlin said. "Most of the troubles anywhere in the universe are CIT."

"Well, we do have our uses," Ari said, a little more cheerfully.

"So we don't have to do things," Florian said. "You do them."

"Well, right now I wish I could figure how to find a man who doesn't exist."

"We've looked through lab results," Catlin said, "and the rush from the blown window and the blast from the grenade messed up the sniffer, so we don't even have the smell of this person, well, not much, at least, but we're pretty sure it was male: we have a little bit of a scent. He was likely using a masker or a puffer to mess up the sniffers, to boot, but all we really have is Dr. Patil's saying the name before she died. We don't know if she recognized him as breaking in, or if she just thought of him when someone else was about to kill her. The way she said it—'the name is Clavery'—seems to indicate she wanted Justin to remember that name and report it."

"And it was definitively a grenade?" Ari asked.

"Yes. Hand launcher," Catlin said. "They aren't big. They carry farther than a toss can do. Unskilled people can use them the same way they'd use a handgun. Setting it off in a room wasn't really appropriate use for it. But it was probably on a few seconds' delay: that's one advantage of a grenade. That would let the perpetrator get the door shut so he wouldn't get blown out, too."

"Using the launcher in that small a space says this was a novice," Florian said. "Someone that was likely to make a mistake with a grenade, maybe freeze. The launcher—you just preset the delay you want, and pull the trigger. It could have sent the grenade halfway to Admin from here. In that little room, it probably stuck in the wall and then blew up: if it had hit the window, it would actually have done less damage. The door was shut by then: there was blast impact on its inside. The perpetrator was on his way out of there—if he wasn't blown out, too. They tried sniffers outside the room, but he was probably using a puffer, and he was probably moving fast. They went ahead and took sniffer readings in every room on that floor and above and below, but they never found the launcher or the puffer, so that part was clever. Somebody probably took it from him, maybe somebody else took over the puffer as they passed in the hall—that's the lab's theory. If he didn't land on a rooftop somewhere as yet undetected. Possibly the assassin was on building staff. I don't think they're going to find too much that's useful. A lot of things about this are very well-organized."

"That could even mean they meant to give the impression of a novice," Catlin said, "and whoever was running it really wasn't. A grenade like that—it could have taken out the apartment downstairs. It didn't. The owner downstairs was very lucky, or the assassins knew the building design."

"Not nice, all the same," Ari said.

"No," Florian agreed. "Not nice. And Paxers haven't been at all careful about collaterals. No rules."

"If it was Paxers," Catlin said.

"Paxers had the motive," Ari said, "if they thought Patil was betraying their interests or selling out to Reseune. Paxers really don't like us. But you're right: there could be others. And where do you *get* grenades and launchers?"

"Mostly from Defense," Catlin said, "but there's pilferage, mostly at Novgorod docks, and things can be had."

"That needs fixing," she said.

"It's not easy to fix," Florian said, "from what I hear."

"First is to make sure they're not hiring any Paxers dockside," Catlin said, "which has happened."

"That would be top of the list, yes," Ari agreed. It was a wide, confusing world—unlike Reseune. But there were slinks in both, and they hadn't found the one in their own halls, not yet: that there *was* one, potentially—the movement of the card indicated there was.

"Sera," Catlin said, "you have on file a list of all her contacts."

"Yes. Largely Defense, and academics. Academics don't have access to grenade launchers. Unless they're getting them from Paxers."

"Defense is having elections," Florian said. "That's a period of instability."

"Namely?" Catlin said.

"Jacques and Spurlin backed Eversnow, but there's Khalid. I'd expect Defense professionals to be more careful," Florian said, and a little line appeared between his brows. "But the charge *didn't* penetrate the floor. Just blew the pressure out. Does anyone live downstairs? Do we know that? And who are they?"

"I did check about downstairs," Catlin said, "a single man, Shoji Korsa. He was out on emergency assignment with his company. This appears a coincidence. Coincidences have to be proven. He's an executive with Geotech. That company called him to Moreyville. His apartment wasn't damaged, except a mirror broke. The building is being investigated for structural problems."

"Meanwhile we're investigating via the ReseuneSec link," Florian said. "We've kept our inquiry out of Hicks' awareness, sera, except for that. We've done a little, just to keep up the appearance of using his system. Should we ask him directly?"

Ari shook her head. "Not until we talk to Yanni. I imagine he's upset about Patil. But I'd like to know how upset he is. Have you sent Yanni and Hicks the transcripts?"

"Yes," Florian said.

"Good." She'd ordered that, a gesture of good will. She was tired. It had been a long day with the computers, and she'd missed her lesson with Justin. Again. Her eyes were scratchy. Jordan had found out about Eversnow from somebody. And when she thought about things really hard, she got sleepy when she was in this state: that was ideas trying to find their way out of the maze. Regarding Justin. Regarding Paxers. Regarding two murders, one delicate, one a blunt-force mess that might have destabilized an apartment tower. "Let's just go to bed."

"Shall I leave, sera?" Catlin asked.

Leaving her and Florian alone, Catlin meant, which would be good if she had any energy left, but she didn't. She just wanted comfort. And ideas wouldn't happen if there was sex, so it wasn't a good idea on that account, either.

"Stay," she said. Her gown was thin, the room was chilled down for night, on the minder's program, and those in their gym sweats were warm, longtime company. She made a place under the covers for all of them, and they got under, Florian in the middle, and tucked down together, the way they had before they'd ever discovered sex.

She could let her mind go, then, and just think, and she did.

If Patil had recognized Anton Clavery in the person who'd showed up with a grenade launcher, then she'd met him under that name. Novice, Florian and Catlin had said. And *that* would seem to rule out anyone important or anybody military. Unless, Florian and Catlin had said, it was someone trying to leave the scene looking like a novice.

If Patil called out that name in the face of an armed man and her imminent death, she'd tried to send Justin a message regarding someone she counted as a threat, or the source of threats. "They," she'd said. A mysterious "they" had been watching her, scaring her, making her desperate enough to call Justin to try to get through to Jordan.

And why Jordan? Why not ask him to go to Yanni?

Jordan's name had been popularly attached to the dissidents. They'd campaigned to get him released. Thieu had been in favor of terraforming and against the forces that had stopped it, namely the first Ari, Giraud, Yanni, all that generation: Jordan said Thieu had regarded him with sympathy, and courted him, believing he'd murdered Ari.

It wasn't a sweet old man, was it?

Thieu would have wanted *her* dead, likely. Thieu had wanted the planet terraformed, all the ankyloderms and platytheres dead, everything in the oceans—all done; and the first Ari hadn't. The first Ari had been a citizen of the planet, and Olga Emory hadn't influenced her enough—the first Ari had changed her mind and begun to protect it.

Like Gehenna, wasn't it? *This is your world . . .*

Had that had an emotional resonance for Ari One, herself? Take care of it? Defend it? Protect it?

It did with her. *She* wasn't for losing what Cyteen had grown up to have. She'd defend it. And that would put her on the outs with Dr. Raymond Thieu, who'd been sure Jordan Warrick would take his side and admire his work and his intentions.

Maybe that was over-romanticizing it. Maybe that was giving too much credit to Jordan because, bastard that he was, he hadn't liked the man's insistence. Jordan wasn't anybody's follower, he was nobody's disciple. Free-thinker, yes, argumentative son of a bitch, definitely, but not the sort that would sit in the shadows with anybody and connive and scheme . . . just not in his makeup. Not in Justin's. In a certain measure, they had something in common, and damned sure when the first Ari intervened with Justin, it wasn't to make him capable of connivance and subterfuge—she couldn't think of anyone actually worse at it than Justin.

And Justin wanted the world as it was. He wanted to save the native fauna. Jordan wasn't for destroying them so much as he was just for getting off the planet and going away and having all mankind living in space—living a lot like the Alliance folk, in steel worlds, in ships. Maybe with a forest at the heart of Pell, but that was not—not something that was going to be Jordan's first project. He'd be trying to educate kids to be rational beings. That was what he used to do, before he became so angry.

He wasn't Clavery, that was sure. But the two people they could reach who probably knew who that was . . . were both dead.

Clavery could be a nonperson or he could even be a hollow man sort of a nonperson, someone who'd never really existed, only who various people opted to be when they wanted to be somebody else. He could be a construct, a composite.

Even a foreigner. Somebody from Alliance. Somebody bent on mischief that could start the whole War again, and she didn't think that was the case. If Patil had recognized him in her doorway, she'd known who she attached that name to, and she'd wanted it known to Justin and Jordan, as her last living act.

She couldn't get through to Jordan, so she'd called Justin . . .

Couldn't get through to Jordan.

But that was the one she'd wanted. Couldn't get Thieu. So she wanted Jordan, as if he should know, or as if he should be warned.

Tell him about Anton Clavery? Thieu was dead, and that name was at issue, and Patil was terrified for her life? She'd gotten her message out. Not all of it. If she'd done a little less arguing with Justin and a little more saying what she had to say, the world would be safer.

It had been a collected, sensible gesture, in extremity. That at least was admirable. The first Ari would have done that, if she'd had time.

But, damn it, why had the woman had to feel her way with Justin and not just say it out loud?

Whoever hadn't scrupled to kill two Specials was a person they urgently needed to find and deal with.

And which Specials were gone?

Both in nanistics. *Every* Special in nanistics. There were researchers and experts, but the brilliant people, the theorists, were gone.

A bad trade for the universe, she could think: whether she supported the project or not, they'd lost two geniuses in the same field.

It slowed Eversnow *way* down. *There* was a problem for Yanni's program, wasn't it? Yanni had to move fast, and sign some people, replacing Patil, or his project was going to fall through. Deals Yanni had made with Corain and Jacques were now subject to review.

She ought to be happy about that, but she'd promised Yanni not to oppose Yanni's objective.

Maybe somebody thought they'd now gotten the better of Yanni, and reduced his political power.

Somebody might have second thoughts about that move if Yanni turned out not to be in charge, and if they suddenly saw they were dealing with someone who was going to be in authority for a hundred years.

But then—maybe it was the project itself that had stirred this kind of opposition. Maybe it was nudging somebody else's territory. And if someone thought getting rid of Patil and Thieu would stop Reseune from a project Reseune needed—

Well, Yanni needed to talk to her about what was going on, and it had to be very, very soon.

BOOK THREE   Section 2   Chapter viii

JUNE 14, 2424
1802H

Another dinner with Yanni . . . and Yanni had protested, this time. He'd claimed he was too busy, said he had far too many things to do, and she was impinging on the little relaxation he did get.

Dear Yanni, she'd written back, *urgent. Be here at 1800h.* And he was.

He did look tired. She showed him right into the dining room, and Haze personally offered him a drink. "What are we eating?" he asked, sensibly, and Haze suggested an early start on the wine, a white, which Yanni agreed would be fine. So it was a Sauvignon Blanc for both of them.

The first sip went down with a deep sigh. Followed by a second. Yanni wasn't reckless in that regard, not like Jordan in the least. She had one sip, just one, and waited.

"We have a new cook," she said. "I don't know what he's put together, but it should be good."

"Thanks for the transcripts on the Patil case," he said, straight to business.

"No problem," she said, and signaled Haze, who was doing the serving tonight, with Florian entertaining Frank in the conference room, and Catlin on hold for her dinner, just quietly standing in the corner, silent as a statue. Haze brought the appetizers, bacon-wrapped shrimp, and Yanni's disappeared fast, without a comment. She gave a second signal, and salads arrived, delicate greens, with a light vinaigrette.

That started going down, too, as if Yanni were half-starved, and Yanni's wine was at a quarter of the glass left.

"Yanni," she said. "You're worried about something."

"I've got a lot of pieces trying to come unglued," Yanni said, and swallowed a bite. "Sorry. I'm just elsewhere this evening, I'm afraid."

"Who's Anton Clavery?"

"Not a pleasant dinner conversation," Yanni said.

"But this is our window to have this conversation, unless you want to stay for drinks, and I know you're tired. Yanni, I need to know what's going on."

"We don't know. Clavery's nobody. Literally, nobody."

"Nonperson?"

"Something like."

"Did he kill Patil?"

"Behind it, we're pretty sure. Not the hand on the trigger, necessarily, but—"

"Why did he kill Patil?"

"Because . . ." Another bite went down, chased by the rest of the wine. "Because Patil was coming over to Science, or because certain people know about Eversnow, and shouldn't, and that blew up before it ever got to public knowledge."

"Jordan?"

Last bite. She pressed a silent signal, and Haze came in and removed the plates, while Yanni had to think about that question.

Haze refilled Yanni's wine glass. Yanni let it sit.

"Jordan knew about Eversnow," she said. "He said he did. I gave you that transcript, too Did you lie to me, Yanni? I thought you were honest. But maybe you're just good."

Yanni nodded. "When I have to be. Yes, I told him about it. He didn't approve. He hit the ceiling, in fact."

"In your office before you left. *That* was what the fight was really about."

"Young sera, you know quite a lot."

"It was pretty famous, Uncle Yanni. You weren't very quiet. And Jordan is news. So yes, I heard there was a fight. So did everybody in Admin and Ed. Why did you tell him?"

Long silence. And Haze wasn't going to come back in until signaled.

"We're the same generation," Yanni said. "Old associates. I know the way he thinks. He was in on the project at the beginning. I didn't want him to find out later and blow up or go behind my back. I wanted to control how he learned and what he thought and know what his movements were once he knew. And I pretty well got the reaction I thought I'd get, so Jordan didn't surprise me in that respect. He doesn't like it. He said he'd had enough of Thieu, and I was crazy, and terraforming anything was a good way to get biologicals loose we just won't like. Old argument, with Jordan. I said he didn't like planets on principle, and he said they were good for studying, but he'd rather not live there if he had any choice. And he asked me about his transfer to Fargone, old topic. Which I told him was dead. Totally dead. He's not going anywhere in the foreseeable future. He shouted. I shouted. He called me a damned fool. We weren't on record."

"Somebody slipped that card into his pocket, and it turned up, he says, the night you got back from Novgorod, from all this dealing. You didn't do that, did you?"

"No."

"Can I believe that? Did anybody working for you do it? Do I have to pare it down until something finally fits?"

"I have no idea where that came from, or, more to the point, how whoever did it knew Jordan knew—*if* they knew Jordan knew. It's a damned maze. And it wasn't my doing."

"He's connected to Thieu. Thieu didn't know about Eversnow, or did he?"

"Thieu did know something, because we made a request for his Eversnow notes back when we set this up."

"Thieu *had* notes on Eversnow in his files?"

"He doesn't, now. Didn't. We borrowed them and didn't return them. But yes, he was doing some work on that once upon a time. Defense had used his work, in their little version of the Eversnow project. We'd studied it. It's foundational to what we propose to do next."

"Hell, Yanni! That's a little oversight in informing me!"

"It's a worrisome piece of information to leave out, I agree. Doubly so, now."

"I don't suppose Patil phoned Thieu to advise him when she got the appointment. I don't suppose she said the word Eversnow."

"He didn't get a phone call. He did get the advisement back in April that she'd taken a job at ReseuneSpace on Fargone: she sent him a message to that effect. He was not mentally what he had been. But possibly—possibly he did put two and two together. Possibly he knew very well what she was doing, a nanistics Special on the farthest station outward, next to Eversnow. Where he would have gone, if they'd gone ahead with his program."

"And before that he was bedeviling Jordan to contact her. Contact her. As if Jordan *could*. But we have just a slight clue what he wanted Jordan to find out, don't we? If you gave Patil his notes . . . don't you think that explains just a little bit? He had no warning at all that Jordan was actually going to get out of Planys. But he knew Jordan had contacts inside Reseune, that he has a son here. And you just lifted his files and sent them where he couldn't get them, so small wonder he was a little agitated. How long ago?"

"During Denys' tenure. Late last year."

"The man was a Special. It was his life's work. His stuff was disappearing. They were never going to run his work on Cyteen. He knew that better than anybody, if he'd managed the remediation program. And there's the military nanistics program—he worked on that during the War, didn't he?"

"Yes."

"And he *worked* on Eversnow, you snatched his files, and he knew the only planet we own where it's remotely appropriate to use the terraforming data *is* Eversnow. And Patil was moving to Fargone, right next door."

"He was in rejuv failure. The notes were classified. It was perfectly logical we take them, in his retirement. We don't know how much of all that he put together. The rejuv failure was progressing fast. We're talking about a few months, here."

"Does Patil have them in her possession? Were they possibly in her apartment?"

Yanni shook his head. "No. They were sent on to Fargone—copies were. She didn't have them yet."

She let go a short breath. "Thank God for that."

"She didn't have them, and they're in a military courier's black box en route. Nobody can get at them *but* someone with the keyword."

It didn't make her feel that much better. "So Defense has them."

"Can't access them. Not unless they've messed with the black boxes themselves. Don't even talk about getting into those. Elections. The stock market. Public records. There's deeper security on that system than anything else we've got. It'll feed into Fargone Central, totally robotic, and it has a gate-restriction on it. It won't feed out again until someone arrives there with a password. That's the way it works. Those notes will be sealed, until someone authorized shows up there."

"What password? Do you know it? Or who does know it?"

"I won't tell you here. I know it. I hadn't even told Patil. I *will* tell you."

"Do. Please. That's too thin a thread, Yanni. There's security, but that's way too thin a thread. Catlin."

"Sera."

"Paper."

Catlin went to a sideboard, got a single sheet of paper and a pen, and gave them to Yanni. He wrote, and Catlin carried it to her. Alphanumeric, long, and without mnemonics evident. GIIW20280082Y2.

Then 28912HW. And W/18.

She tucked that paper into her decolletage. "Ash before midnight," she said. "Thank you, Yanni."

A nod of his head. Catlin had resumed her place. Likely had already memorized it, in the one glance she'd gotten. Catlin was good at that.

"So do we have a copy here at Reseune?" she asked.

"It's there," he said. "Filed in your archive."

She had to be amused. They hadn't turned it up by accident. It wasn't part of the ordinary Library archive, nor Security's ordinary file, not out there. "What else have you stored in my files?"

"Just things your successor might need. Or you might. Someday."

"Clever."

Yanni gave a little nod, sipped his wine. "Thank you. You're right: somebody might have assumed she had them—but they didn't stay to search the apartment, so they didn't think they were there. They might try to hack her access."

"Or Thieu's. *Thieu's* is the place I'd expect them to go after."

"And he was dying. It was a good idea to get those files entirely out of there. Beyond an erase. They're gone from storage at Planys."

"And they're here. Under my name. And in that ship, outbound. The only copies in the universe."

"The only copies."

"Nothing at Beta."

"Nothing at Beta—at least on our side of the wall. If Defense has a copy, we can't find that."

"So Thieu wants to know what's going on with his files. The man may have been going downhill fast, but he wasn't stupid. Jordan meanwhile didn't want to get involved in his scheme—"

"Jordan was involved in another information flow," Yanni said. "A man named McCabe—"

"Airport maintenance. Giraud told me. A middleman in a contact between Councillor Corain and Jordan."

"A two-way conduit of information. We detained him, of course we did. But we don't know if he's the only one. A leak to and from Novgorod? Absolutely there was. There may have been others. It's possible Thieu didn't need his mental faculties about him to know Patil was going to Eversnow . . . if Corain's contact man wasn't the only font of information in Planys. The fact that the news hasn't broken in wider Paxer circles yet indicates if there is a flow of information we haven't already stopped, it's tightly controlled and it's being careful. We're watching that possibility carefully . . . feeding a little disinformation to see where it turns up. It was one reason I wanted to break that news to Jordan and watch his reaction. I was running truthers. The surprise seemed real . . . so he didn't get the information from Corain's man. But what goes on in Corain's office . . . who knows where they have contacts? You don't blow a good spy for some minor piece of news. You let him sit and wait until there's something worth his being there. And so far nobody's breached security in Corain's office—until—possibly—now. Somebody took out our plans for Eversnow, in one day."

Finally. Finally she had the notion Yanni was leveling with her.

"So," she said, "Thieu wanted to get to Patil—who's the logical recipient of those notes you took from him, one of the only people, maybe, who'll really understand them."

"Understand, there was absolutely nothing illegal in what we did: it's classified material, the man was going downhill medically, we had to protect it. The military sits right there next to Planys, with the capability to 'protect and defend' military interests. They could be across that gap in fifteen minutes flat."

"Eversnow is still their project. Thieu was working for them, but physically inside PlanysLabs. And they didn't have those notes."

"He'd been working with them, still corresponding with them quite extensively—we *don't* have the content of many of those letters. They dropped into the great black hole of Defense Communications. We *assume* they don't have his last notes. If they have their own copy, we don't know. Can't know."

"Didn't his notes go to them, if he was working for them?"

"His work is proprietary to Reseune. They wanted something done, they got the result, not the research. We have *his* side of the exchange with them, not their answers."

"Will Jacques talk?" she asked.

"I may make headway with Spurlin on that front—assuming the election goes his way. Meanwhile, before the election results, I want the project staffed. I have to replace Patil."

"If Khalid *should* get into office . . ."

"Exactly. I'm going to be raiding other nanistics people out of Beta—where Defense is going to be mildly unhappy with me. I'm going to hire people away from *their* programs."

"So you're going full speed ahead. But we're running out of nanistics Specials."

"We're *out* of Specials. I do have five candidates for the Eversnow directorship, backup in case Patil had said no, top of her list of her own choices to go to Fargone. I'm going ahead with the project, all out. Be advised of that."

"I think we pretty well have to, don't we?" she said, because that really was where her thoughts were tending now. "We need to find out what's going on. Not to let our enemies win this. I wasn't for it. But somebody who doesn't like us is *against* it."

"I'm glad you take that position," Yanni said, looking tired. He'd resisted the wine, beyond a sip or two. He picked it up, looked at it. Looked at her. "If I drink this and get indiscreet, are you going to be a priss about it?"

"I'm not," she said. "Never will be. But answer me first, Uncle Yanni. I really, really love you and I so want you to tell me the absolutely honest truth in this. Maybe Jordan's lying to everybody. Maybe he brought that card with him from Thieu for his own reasons. Do you have any inkling that's the case?"

"I just think he knows more than he's saying."

That was a disappointment. She wanted more out of Yanni. She pressed her lips together. And waited.

Yanni said: "You really shouldn't try to run Reseune yet, you know."

Shift of direction. She saw it. She still tracked. "What makes you think about that?"

"Because you're getting very sharp, very fast, and you've gathered a small army."

"Yanni, somebody bugged my new staff, and I'm pretty sure who, and probably you are. I didn't like that."

"It wasn't me," he said.

"Hicks, then," she said. "Independently. I may eventually forgive him for it, but he did it, and he pretty certainly knew he did it. I'm onto it, and I've fixed the problem. Don't mention it to him, though. I'm trusting you to know about it and keep quiet. For your own protection. My people are dangerous to people who'd try to do things like that."

"You remind me of your predecessor."

"Did you like her?"

"Odd question."

"Did you *like* her, Yanni?"

"I did, actually. She was what she was, and she did good in her life, on the average. And let me say right now that if you want me to step down tonight, I will, but I hope you'll reconsider a move like that."

"Why?"

"Because, for one thing, we can get quite a bit of yardage for Reseune's programs if we don't let Corain know you're coming into power sooner than most people think—and I think you are. They'll deal, right now, because they're scared to death of you. Corain is shocked by what happened to Patil—but he's still on board with the Eversnow deal. So are the others. Secondly, we haven't seen the outcome in the Defense election, and maintaining a bit of our flexibility in the face of that outcome is a good thing. Polls have been wrong before."

"And meanwhile there's somebody running around Reseune leaving cards from somebody who's supposed to be under strictest security weeks before she was murdered? And it had Planys markers, Yanni. What's the theory on that, officially?"

"Authenticity," Yanni said with a shrug. "Whoever did it wanted it to smell like Planys, as authentic as possible, and whoever did it went to a small bit of trouble to do that—probably to rattle the walls and see if they could provoke some action. Or maybe it's real and Jordan lied. Maybe an old man with a failing memory and a few weeks

to live really wanted some personal acknowlegment from
somebody about to take over his life's work. It's Planys
paper. It may have been printed almost anywhere *but* on
Reseune office machinery—there's that security feature:
micro-ID in the typeface, if your security hasn't told you.
Which still leaves, as a source, the town, various neighboring towns, and passing rivercraft, not to mention the
airport. The card has all kinds of issues attached, *no*
finger-traces of any kind except the people that we well
know handled it—super-clean."

"So it was real. Or it was somebody knew about the
markers and knew to be careful about the microprint. Did
you search Jordan's apartment?"

"While he was at supper with you, yes. We did. Found
nothing, of course."

"Did you tell him you searched it?"

"No. Nor left any traces he could find, if Hicks was entirely up to his job."

"Yanni, I want you to back off Jordan. Don't make him
mad. Give him work to do. Real work."

"There's a small problem with that."

A pose, a quizzical tilt of the head. "You mean you
don't trust him?"

"I trust he'll do something. He'll sabotage something
just to make us find it. And we're busy."

"Send the results to me. It's good exercise. I'll check
them."

"You have enough to do, yourself. Just keep going with
your lessons."

"Do it, Yanni."

"He'll burst a blood vessel."

"Probably, but I'll check what he does. Who's Clavery?"

Yanni blinked, then shrugged. "Clavery is a name not
in the computers. Ergo a nonperson, a construct, a codeword, or an alias."

"Possibly someone she knew by sight."

"We're running checks on everybody who was ever in
contact with her. But just occasionally, in Novgorod, there
are places where you aren't being logged, and people can
make contact off the record. Restrooms. Subways. Standing on a street. At the theater. If she was ever accosted by

somebody named Clavery it wouldn't be in her apartment
building—not until that night."

"A hollow man?"

Yanni drew a deep breath. And gazed at her directly.
"I'm not even asking where you learned that term. Myself,
I'm strongly betting on Paxer involvement in the murders,
but I'm not a hundred percent certain."

"I'm worried about people running around the halls of
Reseune putting cards in people's pockets. And *no* camera caught them, either?"

"We're working on it. Just say we're working on it. Jordan favors very crowded, dark little restaurants where the
chairs are jammed up together and people are moving all
over the place. We don't have good imaging. Right now
we're investigating a lot of people."

"Jordan's a magnet for blame. You never thought Jordan killed the first Ari, did you?"

Yanni shook his head. Took a drink of wine. "For one
thing, he was in the hall when the electronics went out, and
the system was very selective with what went dead at that
point. —Are we going to starve?"

"Sorry." She silently cued Haze, and said, "Yanni, will
you support me if I do take over?"

"I'd support you, yes."

"What if I'd asked you to drop the Eversnow project?
Would you do that?"

"I wouldn't be at all happy about it."

"But would you do it if I asked it?"

"Actually," Yanni said, "I'd probably go full ahead
until the hour you nuked my accesses, because I believe
in it. And I think you'd be quite wrong. So I'd fight you
on that."

"Good. I like it when somebody tells me the truth. Why
do you think I'm wrong?"

"Because Eversnow solves the employment problem on
Fargone."

"Doesn't help Pan-Paris at all."

"It still solves one critical unemployment problem and
makes Pan-Paris less critical. No, it doesn't help Pan-Paris
and they'll be mad about it and we'll have to find something to give them pretty fast."

"Not on this year's budget."

"We'll let Pan-Paris stew and protest and get jealous of Fargone, and then we'll agree to do something. That makes it evident we're listening."

"You're a total cynic."

He shrugged. "Works. We've got worse potential problems on the horizon. We have an important alliance on this bill: us, Citizens, Defense. We can get Information and Trade in on it, and that's our majority. But Defense is in mid-election and Corain's getting old. He could see himself challenged for the seat in Citizens, and believe me, a lot worse could come out of that huge electorate than Corain. It's diverse. It may be true that if there hadn't been a Corain to hold Citizens together, we'd have to invent one, but in any given year, we could see something nasty develop there. Another reason—*another* reason to pursue a major population burst at Fargone. Population in an area farthest removed from Alliance Space . . . most of them will end up voting in Citizens, supporting, we hope, moderates like Corain."

"All right, let's discuss it. You think that Eversnow is still an asset. I frankly see it having serious problems."

"I think it's a safety factor. If there's another war, Alliance will think twice. If we toss their merchanters out of that route, we can enforce a ban, and we can protect it. It's a *very* narrow corridor."

"No great abundance of jump points in the region?"

"Scarce. Just about what we're developing as destinations, places we'll be able to defend. That's the word from Defense."

That was certainly a point in favor. "How soon is your population burst at Fargone?"

"All right. This is getting to be in your need-to-know, one more reason why it's not good for you and me to have a contest for power this year. There's a station onworld, already. That's all military and classified to the hilt: it's been black-budgeted for decades, since your predecessor's time. We've kept its secrecy because we use its facilities pretty freely, but there've been some issues over the years, too."

"That's how you got the samples! It wasn't a robot. You lied on that, too."

"Well, it was a robot, but we have people down there, as we speak. Very cold, very lonely people, in company with a lot of cold, lonely Defense people, and not an azi in the lot. Defense has been damned worried we'd tamper—so they haven't allowed azi down there. Just a nice little born-man society."

"What are we, for God's sake? At war?"

"During the War, it was a lot friendlier. Lately it's gotten political and full of rules and restrictions. The restrictions on our information-gathering and on our flow of person-nel to and from is one motive on our part. We very much need a Reseune presence down there, an expanding pres-ence in our own facility before the whole planet becomes a military zone where they make the rules."

"Hence Patil's project. Hence this whole thing. Patil's an excuse. Terraforming never was it. It's the population burst. It's a colony, never mind what the rest of the planet is like! They can sit on an iceball. Terraforming's just what you're paying to enlist Corain's people."

"Well, not altogether," Yanni said, "because ultimately, we want that planet, we want to colonize freely there, and we don't want Defense controlling that real estate. Ter-raforming's the excuse we use to get a base of our own down there. Right now Defense has themselves a nice one-thousand-kilometer-wide salt water puddle they're using Beta Labs nanistics people to work with, long-distance, which is no way to run a laboratory. We need to be self-sufficient down there, we need to be on-site and in charge of anything genetic. We're going to need integrations on foundational sets for Eversnow residency and some CIT volunteers pretty quick. We have that in part: *we* have the orbiting station and the military has the onworld base, which gives us the capability to land, and it's kept them moderately cooperative, because they need us for supply—rather than them having to build their own sta-tion. But right now we only have the kernel of a star station in orbit. It needs to grow. Fast. It needs the onworld lab. We keep the military from owning the whole planet, we boot them entirely out of nanistics research, and Union gets a highway to new stars. I've needed *you,* young lady; I've desperately needed you to get up to speed on integra-

tions. We need azi that can face down military CITs and
say no, ser, that's Reseune territory. Keep out."

"You're doubling the size of Union. You're handing us
problems we don't even imagine yet!"

"It's not me that's running that onworld presence. Not
at the moment. The elder Ari died at an inconvenient time
and I couldn't get Giraud to move faster. Not to mention
you ate up a lot of budget, young lady—your new wing,
hell, your budding township's nothing against what you've
already cost Reseune in lab time, in research, set-up. But
we've done our Eversnow research, in budget masked behind the Fargone lab we already have. We've surveyed
stars down that strand. There's no likelihood of sapience
down that route unless it comes a long way to meet us.
Several planeted stars. Resources. Jobs. Habitat. New genetics, at least at Eversnow, not likely much at the gas-balls
and ice moons we'll be dealing with further along. A lot
of advantages. And as you say—prime opportunity for a
major population burst that would solve several problems,
including the Citizens electorate, within the next two to
three decades. That could be of incalculable value."

"Look, I'm sorry for what I cost—"

"Don't be."

"But *I'm* going to argue with you. I'm looking at the
population dynamic that results from this project, not just
down that route, but all over Union. I'm looking at Cyteen
and our own home territory becoming a stagnant backwa-
ter in a few hundred years, if Eversnow works. Because
if it does, the center of gravity of all of Union shifts—
considerably. Political interests, population dynamics,
everything goes out there to what we call the edge of space
right now. And if it doesn't work, we'll have spent a bigger
budget than I ever was, ending up with no viable planet out
there, just one more star station, and twice and three times
the population sitting out at Fargone with no jobs, while
Pan-Paris falls apart out on an unused route and hates us,
maybe for nothing."

"It's going to work. Even at the rate we're going, Eversnow is about twenty years from a tipover point, after which
the melt accelerates and goes on its own. You'll know it in
your lifetime."

"I'm not done, Yanni. I'm also looking at a future in which we lose touch with Alliance, if we shift our center toward Fargone. We're at a point where we stand a small chance of making a lasting peace. Alliance has already gone poking off in another direction themselves, and they've proven that's dangerous. But once Alliance finds out we're expanding in another direction—what are they going to do to expand, but either start putting enclaves on Downbelow, or throwing some colonial effort onto Gehenna, which *is* their one usable planet with one hell of a local problem. —Or they accelerate their push into the Hinder Stars, and get closer to Earth. Not to mention Eversnow moves our center away from the border we share with the Alliance and that lets them take the star stations *we* used to own.."

"Not very profitable ones, except Mariner. I'm afraid I'm not an optimist about the peace with the Alliance lasting through your tenure."

"*I* am. I think we *can* keep the peace if we're sensible and get control of our own people bombing subways and talk to Alliance with some kind of notion how our own politics are going to run for ten years consecutive. You talk about integrations out there. I'm worried about integrations *here*. We have a disease in our own heart, Yanni. We have a serious problem in the Novgorod population, and I'm pretty sure it's not an azi problem, it's probably come down from the station, and I think it's serious. I think it's serious enough that before we start any future population burst of the size you describe, we need to know why we have Paxers, and what drives them. Is it the azi-CIT mix, or is there something about *us?*"

Yanni was silent a moment, thinking about that, and at that moment Haze and Hiro carried dinner in, briskly served. It was chicken with herbs, in a delicate pastry crust, and it smelled good.

"Eat," she said. "It's Cook's first formal dinner. They probably went crazy back there keeping it ready to serve. Don't let it go to waste."

He had a bite. "It's good. This is really good."

Ari looked at Haze and Hiro. "Tell Wyndham so. It really is."

"Thank you, ser, sera," Haze said, pleased, and quietly departed, and the door shut.

Two bites later: "I *can* take over Admin," she said, "when I want to. Don't think Base Two can ever over-power Base One. It just won't happen. That's not a threat, Yanni. It's a warning. Please don't try me. Convince me. I'm willing to listen to your plans. I am listening."

"You find out things already, don't you?" Yanni asked. "You get what you want. You didn't need my clearance. You're as deep into the information as you want to be."

She lifted a shoulder, and had a bite. To get information, sometimes you had to give away a real piece on your side. "Generally," she said, and swallowed, and laid down her knife and fork and looked at him. "Yanni, please don't be against me. I don't *want* to be against you."

"I won't cede you Eversnow. I'll fight you for that. On everything else, I'm with you. But for that, because I believe in it, and I believe I'm right, I'll fight you."

She considered that a moment, on two bites of dinner, then nodded. "All right, Yanni," she said, finally. "I think you're making me a lot of trouble, long term, but I'll think hard about what you're saying. I did promise, and you'll get your onworld base and I'll work your integrations— I'm not up to what you want now, and you're right, I don't know enough to argue. But I'll be there; and I'll back your project until I have a clear reason not to. I promise you. If I have to set my successor on the case, it will run, and we'll take care of those people. But I want you to know I'm worried. My predecessor was murdered. We have people in Reseune we can't trust. We have a lot of people in Novgorod who aren't behaving rationally—you can argue it's rational from their point of view, but not in the mac-rosetted view. Macrosets in that population aren't work-ing the way they're supposed to. People aren't as happy as they're supposed to be, for no damned reason I can figure."

"I'm not sure those people will ever be happy: the planet isn't what their parents were promised it was going to be. They were all going to be rich. It wasn't going to take them a great deal of education to succeed. Now it is. That's just pure human nature, Ari, nothing too arcane."

That was a point. She thought about it. "So it *is* more work than some people want. But that's not all that's going on. Those people, who are persuading other people to build bombs—you can always find somebody out of sorts and desperate: people get themselves into mental messes. But the Paxers are out creating more unhappy people as a matter of policy, because they want power, and they're getting recruits because they're either tapping into some flaw in the macrosets—which is possible. But I have a theory that upsets me more than that."

"What?"

"Maybe they're using Reseune techniques to get the recruits they want. Maybe they're doing things we don't know about."

"The Paxers?"

"Look. We created the science: the military went off on their own tangent thinking they could use it, and we ended up with some spacecases and some real dangerous people. The first Ari's book got published, and all of a sudden we had people trying to run interventions on each other in their living rooms. It's serious, Yanni, don't laugh. What we do is power. And power is what people want. The people operating in their living rooms, they're fools, especially if they do it under therapeutic kat; but remember what the first Ari said about ordinary people understanding Einstein, in this age, and someday they'd understand Bok?"

A bite stayed poised on Yanni's fork. "Meaning we've got a society that thinks they understand what we do."

"I think Ari's book wasn't exactly a trigger. It just warned us that we needed to look at how much people believe they really do understand what we do. *Power* comes from doing what we do, and maybe there have been a few people who are smart enough, but not smart *enough,* if you get what I mean. Ari One and her mother both designed azi sets that worked around that CIT footprint, but what if a handful of CITs have been freelancing for the last few decades, and bringing up bent kids? Look at Giraud and Denys's mother. Look at Olga Emory herself, the things she did to my predecessor. There wasn't a method, back then, there was just this viral idea floating around society that if there was a hyper-efficient way to educate azi, there could also be some process to make a bright CIT kid a genius. And if some people ran the wrong intervention on the wrong kid, they could create what Denys called me."

"What's that?"

"A monster," she said. "A real monster."

"You have a *hell* of an imagination," Yanni said.

"I'm serious, Yanni. Novgorod's lag-timed by rejuv and birthlabs: if they store the genesets, people can have kids into their eighties and hundreds, with birthlabs: and the time the Paxers start blowing things up is during my predecessor's lifetime—that's third-gen. That's where the problems *usually* come out in a bad set."

"That also happened to coincide with the War they were protesting."

"True. But there's no War now, and they're still protesting. They're not real clear *what* they're protesting, except the planet isn't what they want it to be, and they clearly think they can dispense with *us.*"

"Nothing psychotic about that. Humanity did without us for thousands of years. Alliance and Earth, somehow, still do."

"That's not it, though. It's not that they can do without us, it's that somebody wants to *be* us. What if *that's* the viral idea, Yanni? That somebody's always going to *be* us, and that's where the power is situated, and maybe somebody's little kid, or several people's little kids, were turned into something that's angrier about us than the parents were. Maybe that's why they're still protesting a war that's been over for decades, and why it's only gotten worse and crazier. I mean, the first Paxers blew up buildings at odd hours when people weren't likely to be there, and now they're just trying to cause the worst casualties they can. It's accelerated. They're sucking in mental cases their violence created, and giving *them* bombs and sending them out—but you don't think the leaders of this movement are ever going to carry the bombs. They'll sit back pretending to be us, congratulating themselves that they've *become* us."

"So do you see a fix, short of a mass mindwipe of every CIT in Novgorod?"

"I see Paxers proliferating like crazy, once Eversnow goes public. That worries me, Yanni."

"Why would they proliferate?"

"Because it's change. Because it scares the followers. Because change changes the balance of power and that's going to agitate their leaders. Some people won't want the whole terraforming question shunted out to the edge of space: they want it here. Some people won't want it anywhere. Some people will agree with me that it's too much too soon. It's going to be like yeast in a bowl, it's just going to froth up and make a hell of a mess."

"In your theory you could change the national polling hours and they'd bomb subways over it."

"They probably would," Ari said. "It would all become some Reseune plot."

"So there's a monster in the walls. What's his name, Anton Clavery?"

"You're making fun of me."

"Not exactly. Your theory would say the Paxers took out Patil and Thieu. The one's easy, the other's hard. You need sane people to get into Planys and then go insane."

She shook her head. "You need a killer. Money's a motive, too. When you need something delicate done, you hire an expert."

Yanni sat and thought about that a moment. "Nasty theory, young lady."

"It's scary. So's your Eversnow, but I said I'd support it. You know what else worries me in the whole issue? Jordan worries me."

"Regarding the Paxers?"

"*He's* an issue with them. If he's as self-interested as you say, he'll do whatever benefits him. He's the embodiment of the disaffected, the third-gen problem. You can't *make* him care. And he doesn't."

"Interesting analysis."

"Am I right?"

"Jordan's an old issue with the Paxers: they *think* they'd like to see him out in public—they think he'd blast Reseune in the media if he gets his chance, and they'd really love that. He doesn't personally give a rat's ass whether we terraform or don't. And if you want somebody who's got the skill to be a real operator, your bogeyman in the CIT sector, that's Jordan. But—" Yanni said, "there's one thing against it. Jordan *is* entirely for himself. He'd fry the Paxers quicker than he'd fry Reseune. Stupid people bother him. He'd turn on them in a heartbeat, the moment they cross him."

"And he designs azi sets."

"Damned good ones," he said.

"So have you ever worried what he put into them?" she asked. "Back when he was working, and mad at Ari? I say it's *probably* CITs that are the cause. But we had the War, we had the military running interventions on their own azi, who later decommissioned and went civilian, a lot of them in Novgorod. And we had Jordan designing azi sets for decades and decades. I don't think he could have gotten anything past my predecessor, but that may just be my own ego. We never had the handle on military sets I wish we had."

"We had people blowing up subways forty years ago," Yanni said. "Well before Jordan became the ass he is."

"Was there ever a point he wasn't one?"

"You want the truth? He said he was in love with your predecessor," Yanni said. "I don't think he really was. But he may have thought he was, for a complex of reasons involving power, and he was certainly less of an ass before that major blowup."

That was interesting. "So he lied to her. He was interested in romance and power, and she was interested in her projects?"

"I don't think she cared about the sex. It was his mind she wanted. I think he lied to himself, for one of the rare times in his life. Major self-delusion, wrapped up in his self-concept. He was sleeping with Paul while that affair was going on. I told him it wouldn't work. He told me go to hell. A year later he had Justin conceived, born the year after. The Ari affair was on again, off again. They were trying to work together. He suddenly got the notion she was taking his ideas. Sharing didn't work with either of them. That's where it blew up. What happened in the bedroom, I don't know; but the ideas were the issue *he* complained about."

"I can imagine that," she said. "He's very self-protective in that regard."

"So," Yanni said somewhat cheerfully, "it all blew up. I don't think Jordan's the godfather of the Paxers, not even the model of them—he may have done a few designs that could be problematic in Ari's integrations, you could be right about that. She tossed certain of them out and wouldn't let them go to implementation. There was a hell of a fight about it—he called her a goddess-bitch and she said he was a damned lunatic. They traded those words back and forth and had one shouting fight right in Admin offices in front of the secretaries and the visitors. I don't think they slept together after that."

She had to laugh ruefully for a microsecond, and grew sad after, thinking about herself and Justin, and swearing to herself it never would happen to them that way. "What did Paul think about it?"

Yanni looked at the door, as if measuring the distance to the conference room, and said, quietly, "Poor Paul. Always, poor Paul. Paul puts up with him. That's got to be a ferociously strong mindset, Paul's. God knows Jordan's tinkered with it over the years. But Paul loves him."

"That's what Paul gets out of it, at least. Did the first Ari ever try to do anything with him?"

Yanni shook his head emphatically. "No. That would have really torn it worse than what she did with Justin. Paul's where Jordan lives, that's all. Justin just *happened* one year—a project that ran for a couple of decades, and blew up when Ari intervened. Became a permanent reminder of a quarrel he'd had with Ari. That's one way to look at it, on Jordan's scale of things."

"That's sad, too. Justin loves him."

"A lot of people have tried," Yanni said with a second shake of his head. "God knows. If you have an altruistic bent, young lady, take it from me on this one. Don't try kindness, not with him. He's just what he is. Let him be."

"I wish I could Get him, all the same," she said, and set to work at the dish again. "Yanni, Uncle Yanni, you keep being Director for a while. I'll wait. Just don't you be my Jordan, and let's be friends. I'll respect your opinion, you respect mine, and don't hold out on me anymore."

"I'll take a good deep look at your theory on Novgorod," he said.

"Good," she said. "I'll be interested."

"Eversnow," he said, "stays."

"Through anything I can foresee at the moment," she said, wishing otherwise—but it was necessary, right now.

So was keeping her word, if she didn't want to make honest people mad at her. And she had always thought Yanni was honest. "I'll really try to make it work, Yanni."

She signaled for the next course. Gianni had made a really beautiful dessert, showing off, she was sure. It was layered, and oh, so good. Yanni ate his and ended up being persuaded to another half slice, and a little glass of liqueur to top the evening off. She couldn't eat another bite. Her stomach was a little upset by the time she saw Yanni to the door.

But it hadn't gone that badly.

Yanni said he still trusted Hicks. That was a problem.

She didn't anymore, not until Hicks really proved himself.

She could take Hicks out, put someone she really trusted into that post—like Amy Carnath. Amy had the brains and she'd be fair. But she'd absolutely hate running ReseuneSec. Besides, she was only eighteen, same as the rest of them, and that was the problem—in a post like Hicks', history mattered. Yanni knew all sorts of things, just a long, long memory, and so did Hicks, and you didn't just replace a memory like that with a new appointment and hope to have anything like the prior performance in a job involving information.

She could take Admin herself, and put Yanni into Hicks' job, but he'd really hate that, and that wouldn't improve matters.

So they were stuck, temporarily, with Hicks.

The good part was, so far, she still had Yanni. They could work with each other, until things had to be different.

"Hello," Ari said, opening the door to Justin's office, and he spun his chair around.

Grant turned more slowly.

She came in solo. They *had* gotten the extra chair, which they used in her lessons, since they'd folded their other Wing One office into this one, and she turned it around and sat down, primly proper.

"Coffee, sera?" Grant asked.

"Please. Thank you. I need to talk to both of you."

"Is there a problem?" Justin asked.

"Yes and no." She waited until Grant had handed her a cup of coffee in a pretty gilt mug, and just held it in her lap, not to delay or draw this out. "The sets you did that I snatched back. Thank you for that. I came to tell you you were right, there was a problem."

"Which set?"

"The one you delayed on."

Justin gave out a long, long breath.

"That set was tampered with," she said. "I think I've fixed it. I'm sure I've fixed it. Sure enough to have him in charge of my own guard."

"That's very sure," Justin said.

"His name is Rafael," she said, "and now he's under my orders. I think he was under Hicks', and I think Giraud's before that."

"He's too young," Grant said.

"He is, but he's not the first of his number. I think there was some off-record done with his whole type . . . no, I don't just think. I know. There *was*. I'm quitting being the kid as of this week."

Zap.

"I didn't get that out of it," Justin said, frowning, so her bow-shot had gone right past him. "I should have. I assumed. Never assume. You certainly beat me on this one."

She shrugged lightly. "I had a head start. I *know* green barracks programming." With a shift of her glance toward the hall where Catlin waited. "And you wouldn't have that experience. Still, you had something spotted. That's what warned me to look twice. You had your finger pretty well on it."

"What did it do?"

"He conflicted like hell when I took the Contract. He had a nice little reservation built in and I blitzed it. Not as good as an axe code, what I did, but close."

Grant made a face. Grant knew.

"Anyway," she said, "you deserved to know."

"Thanks," Justin said.

"I have it set up with Yanni: Jordan will get to work; I'll check. If he blows up, maybe he and I will eventually have to talk about it. But we'll just see how it goes. Let him calm down first."

"Thank you," Justin said.

"You're still bothered about the BR set."

"It bothers me that I missed it."

"It bothers you. That's why you're good. Besides being Special-level smart."

He laughed silently at that. Didn't say a thing. But self-doubt was major in him.

"I'm sorry I've missed lessons lately," she said.

"I think you're getting beyond them, aren't you?"

"I don't think you're at all through teaching me. I learn all sorts of things. You were spotting that conflict from the microset side of things; I was looking at the large picture, and I fixed it by yanking at the deepsets. You're *kind,* is what. Grant knows what I mean."

"Sera is right," Grant said quietly.

"It's why you want to rehabilitate your father. You're just soft-hearted. I need somebody who teaches me what soft-hearted is."

"I don't know that it's so valuable a commodity these days."

"Because Reseune isn't safe?" she asked. "It isn't. Neither is Planys. Neither is here, granted Jordan got that card the way he says he did. We could have a problem at Planys that we never spotted. We could, here. Something like a Rafael type. Nothing of his geneset is there. One is in Hicks' office, probably with nobody to report to now that Giraud is dead, but I'm going to put a tag on him—I'll know every contact he has."

"Ari," he said, and cast a look up, at the over*head.*

She smiled sadly. "It's only Catlin listening. We know about this office. We have our own protections around it, and if it's leaky, they've gotten past all my bodyguards and nothing is safe. Just figure: there are three hundred fifty-one azi at Planys. And somebody killed Thieu. And somebody killed Patil. I'm betting they got a professional in to take out Patil, somehow, maybe azi, maybe not."

"An azi didn't originate the idea," Grant said.

"I agree with you," Ari said. "An azi didn't. But I'd be interested to hear your thinking on motivation. You're not green barracks."

"I'm house," Grant said. "And I hardly remember when I wasn't. I absorbed my values from tape, from instruction, and from being part of the household."

"That changed," Ari said.

"Ari," Justin said, a warn-off.

"Grant, you don't have to answer me. I'm not being a Supervisor, I'm just curious where your focus is."

"Classified," Justin said.

Grant shrugged. "Not hard to guess it's you, born-man. Ari doesn't scare me."

"I really don't want to," Ari said. "I'm sorry, Grant, but I don't want to ask my own staff, and I want an azi viewpoint on this question. In your psychset, could anybody get you to kill?"

An easy shrug. *"He* could."

"Ari, leave it!"

"I'm not at all conflicted about it," Grant said. "No more than Florian would be, under a hypothetical. I just ran your question through my deepsets and there's no prohibition against it, no great emotional charge to compare with my attachment to your orders, Justin."

"Well, then, shut up, for God's sake! Quit answering her damned questions!"

"I have a strong attachment to questions, too," Grant said with a little tilt of the head, with humor. "Can't resist them, if they're hypothetical. Or I'll think about it all night."

"Don't, if you please."

"Now I'm conflicted," Grant said, "because it's actually an interesting question. You're saying some azi out at Planys murdered Thieu simply because some born-man asked him to."

"Might have. Abban probably murdered the first Ari."

"That's my prime candidate," Justin said. "That's what I believe."

"I don't think I'd botch it, however," Grant said, "if I was asked to do a murder. I'd look up techniques and pick one I knew I could carry out."

"Now I'm angry," Justin said. "It's not damned funny, Ari."

"I know it's not," she said, "and I won't run a calm-down on Grant. That's your job. He's just the closest alpha I could ask who's not Security; and a beta couldn't. I'm sorry, Grant. Justin's concerned about you, and I haven't been entirely nice."

"I'd leave the office," Grant said, "if it weren't an interesting question. And I've thought about it—what I would do. What I *could* do, if someone threatened him. I told myself I could, and would. I actually take a certain comfort in that."

"Same," Justin said, "on this side."

She nodded. "It's nice to have somebody that close," she said. "I do. I'm glad you both do." She took something from her coat pocket, which turned out to be two com units, and she laid them on the nearest table. "Those are exactly the same as Florian's, as Catlin's—a few limitations: they only call Base One, they can only get voice contact if someone calls you back, and if you hit the red button, they're going to bring down the ceiling, so don't use that unless you have to. Just carry them and don't for God's sake lose them. If you see anything suspicious around you, if you want someone to show up quietly and intervene, hit any button but the red one. If you hit the red one, figure you're going to get an armed response. Understood?"

"Understood," Justin said, looking a little mollified.

"I hope you'll never need them," she said, "but I'm carrying my own." She touched the door. "And don't put yourselves in situations. Please."

"Like visiting my father?"

"You'll protect Grant," she said, "and he'll protect you. You do what you want to do."

She left, then.

She'd made Justin mad for a few minutes, and she hadn't wanted to, but she felt better, knowing Grant wasn't limited in Justin's defense. She'd suspected the answer she'd get: but she'd not been entirely sure she'd believe it. Now she did.

And that was good.

BOOK THREE   Section 3   Chapter i

JUNE 26, 2424
1528H

Giraud, at nineteen weeks, had bones instead of cartilege, and those bones shaped a face increasingly distinctive from, say, Abban, or Seely. For all of them it was the same story: arms and legs finally matched in proportion. They made urine: kidneys were working.

Giraud's heart, which one day might betray him, functioned well enough now, on a steady beat. He was just starting to grow the sandy hair that would characterize him in life. His lungs weren't at all developed, so nothing but the artificial womb could sustain him at this point. His lungs lacked their life-giving minor passages, and breathing any substance as rarified as air was impossible for him; but he was already getting vocal cords. His brain wasn't cognitively active, and had nothing like its destined size, but it was acquiring a little organization. Areas of his brain made the most rudimentary start at sensing a touch, tasting, and smelling, though stimuli were much the same right now, and until that organization happened he couldn't differentiate between touch or smell or sound: it was all the same to him, just a stimulus that got on his nerves.

He'd be a little insomniac throughout his adult life—but he'd begun to have periods of quasi-sleep, or at least quiet. That, again, was the brain, organizing. And his nerves, which had lacked a myelin sheath, had begun to acquire it, which would be a process not limited to his stay in the womb. As that coating formed, finer and finer organization would become possible. As yet, it was very basic.

His eyes, completely colorless as yet, had begun moving, simple languid muscle twitch, behind sealed lids.

When he was born he would have a restless blue gaze, noting this, noting that, until those eyes fixed, and then one had better take care, even when he was a little boy.

He was nearly halfway to birth, which was scheduled for November 20.

But right now Giraud didn't see a thing.

BOOK THREE   Section 3   Chapter ii

JULY 1, 2424
0928H

I went to see Giraud today. He's at twenty weeks, and about halfway toward his birthdate. I don't know why I went—or I'm reluctant to admit it, but things in the house have changed so drastically that I just wanted to get him in view again and use my brain about him, not my emotions.

He's just a baby. He's even gotten to look pretty well like a human being, and I halfway felt guilty about stopping Denys. I'm sure someday he'll ask about his brother.

And I worry about what I'll have say to him to explain it. He'll feel a sense of loss, even for something he didn't have.

*It wasn't Giraud who really shaped me, after all: it was
Denys. It was definitely Denys that tried to kill me, and I'm
reasonably sure he killed the first Ari, but I'm still trying to
prove that, and I don't know what the balance is.*

*Do I have to do to them what they did to me? Do I have
to create a mess of an infant's life to create a man to make
a mess of your early life? I'd rather not.*

*And what if I live as long as the first Ari, or longer, and
the Giraud I created gets too old and dies, and they have
to start over with a new baby Giraud right before you're
born? It's all crazy. Making everybody all match is going
to be impossible if they go on replicating people whenever
they die, and so far they're not saving us all up and starting
the oldest first, so it's going to get all scrambled about the
timeline. Giraud might drown in the river before he's forty.
And then where will we be? Again, a total mismatch.*

*It's absolutely crazy—and I'm the one—and you're the
one—the universe has to have continually at work, fast as
we can.*

*So I officially give up trying to make things as exact as
I was. I know it's not possible. I don't think it's altogether
necessary: I hope that it isn't. The medics were going in
blind when they used to take the first Ari's constant tests
and bloodwork and make mine fit her profile in any given
week I was due for a major new tape—shooting me full of
hormones. Now we have me for a test subject, and Dr. Peterson is writing up the work they did, matching my learning with what I was working on, and with what I needed to
be working on. So that will tell us some relevance between
hormonal state, particular tape, and test scores.*

*With Giraud, we know what he studied, and when he
studied it, and we'll still play games with his blood chemistry to make sure he has his brain on line when he studies
certain things, but I don't honestly think it has to be week
by week, and I don't think it has to be that tightly on schedule or sequence: I think the main thing is whether the brain
is going to be totally fluxed and doing freethinking with,
say, art, or whether it's going to be absorbing facts on a
given tape where facts, fast and exact, are what you want.*

*Besides, I'm not going to do to Giraud Two what Gi-
raud One's mother did, which was bear down on Giraud*

hard to be a genius. Denys was, Giraud wasn't, and she couldn't change that. I'm pretty sure she didn't do Denys any good by coddling him: he could be as odd as he liked and she excused it. She was always hard on Giraud. And when she died he took over being hard on himself. That is a key to what he was, and I've got to think about that one in his setup.

I've arranged for Yanni to take Giraud: he hasn't exactly said yes, but I just don't see him refusing at the last moment, and it's just a few months to go. And Yanni didn't say anything when I said I'd backed out of creating Denys. I know he thinks something about it, but he's not easy to read. I've found that out. I don't think he really wants either of them. He knows he's going to get Giraud. But I think he feels something about Denys and I can't get a straightforward answer out of him. He says I know what others don't and I'll make up my own mind.

Well, I still have seven years to talk to Yanni about it. I don't want to have Denys back and forth, but I didn't destroy his geneset. I just sent it back to deep storage.

Maybe it would be a little less crazy if I just threw up my hands and declared everything had to follow program as close as possible, and Denys had to become a thorough bastard and have a maman who was as crazy as the originals' was.

If I admitted that it's entirely nurture, or the lack of it, that wakes up the genes, then everything and anything is justifiable.

But I've gone off my program, marginally, and I'm still pretty good.

And Giraud helped in that: the first Giraud did. He turned downright fatherly with me, warning me, trying to guide me toward survival, even while Denys was probably telling himself if I got too close to taking over too soon, he'd kill me without a qualm. I have to wonder if Giraud picked up on that, and tried to hit some middle ground between Denys killing me and my killing Denys. And instead, Giraud died.

It probably wasn't all sweetness and fatherly feeling on Giraud's part. He'd probably been worried about Denys doing something to foul up everything Resune had worked for, for very selfish reasons. Denys could be selfish like that, if Giraud didn't step in and fix things.

And if I create Denys, Denys could be like that again, if he turned out to be really Denys: utterly disagreeable, and utterly self-centered, lost in his own world. It may be there's something in Denys's brain that made that happen, and it could be genetic, essential to what made him a genius.

Poor Giraud was just Giraud and I don't think a little kindness will really hurt him. His end-of-life change of mind very likely was sincere—I figured that out, trying to plan for a maman for Giraud, and I just can't come up with one. There was that critical a difference between the two brothers.

And Denys, if he had had one strong emotion in his head, wanted him reborn, wanted himself reborn, so, so much—wanted himself, with Giraud. Not because he loved Giraud, I've come to think, because so much about him was sociopathic, but because, to him, Giraud was part of himself, part of his all-important existence. One of the things that drove Denys to try to kill me might have been a fear that, when I took over, I might abort Giraud, in one sense or the other—either physically or psychologically.

And, oh, Denys knew by then he hadn't won any favors of me, and I suppose I should have kept my feelings a little more secret. Denys had wanted Giraud back so desperately.

But Giraud had never been just for Giraud. That was the difference a little love had made, and Giraud might have interpreted their mother's hammering away at him as a kind of love—in his own way, he might have taken it for that. Giraud was, of the two, far more the wild card. Giraud would attach, sooner or later.

If I knew I had a sister who wasn't reproduced, I'd feel deprived, wouldn't I? And knowing it would fester, and turn toxic in the process . . . so maybe I'm wrong. I won't know. I won't know for a few years. I'll see if Giraud asks the question.

A lot of things will change in Reseune. Or maybe I'm deluding myself . . . trying to change some things back to what they were twenty years ago.

My letter's had time to get to Fargone. An answer could

be coming back to me as I write this. Maybe even the people I invited have gotten on a ship and they're coming here. I'll know, before Giraud is born, what the answer is from all those people I wrote to.

We aren't making any progress to speak of on the Patil investigation. They've hauled in some Paxer elements, the usual. The investigation at Planys is slow: there are two CITs from Big Blue, and before that, from Novgorod: they'd been in the University. Hadn't everybody, when Centrists, Abolitionists, and Paxers were the radical chic? They passed a questioning under trank. Patil's still dead, and likely to stay that way—but we have her geneset on file. So never bet on it.

There haven't been any other cards turning up in people's pockets.

We still assume the two events, the card with Patil's name, and Patil being murdered, were connected.

And the rest of it just boils down to a lot of police work, sifting hundreds of records of people who were put into Planys during the War, because of radical connections or Defense-connected projects—wasn't that a brilliant mix? Everybody's background has suspicious connections, because Defense used to shove anybody called "essential to the war effort" into Planys. And then Reseune, in Yanni's time, moved in Jordan, who's not the sort to be quiet or suffer fools.

The same with the University: Expansionist professors and Centrist professors, some that Defense moved down-world for protection, and the ones they taught, and then those that couldn't take the pressured environment and just got jobs out in the city. It's an odd, odd network in the University, not like Reseune at all: most of the professors have contacts in the city, and they live all over, some in the University neighborhood and some clear over in the port area, and it's very hard to track what their contacts are. There's just no information in Novgorod that isn't tangled.

We have too many suspects, not too few. Patil hadn't socialized with the radicals, but they clustered around her.

And Thieu was connected to her and Jordan. And he worked for Defense.

I wish I knew who'd pushed that card on Jordan. It al-

most makes me think Jordan is innocent of involvement. He's innocent of an unusual number of things he was almost involved in. I find that odd enough to constitute a watch-it.

But I'm taking measures to protect everyone I can. And when I set up the new wing, I have to decide who's in, and who's out, the way it was when we were kids.

There's Stef Dietrich. He's been on the outs with us for a long time. He used to be one of us, but he's a troublemaker when it comes to sex, and he can't settle with anybody— people just don't trust him. I don't think I want to bring him in.

There's Amy and Maddy and Sam, them first; Justin and Grant; Yvgenia Wojkowski's in a relationship that won't pass muster: if she asks, I'll tell her that—it won't make her happy, but at least she'll know what her choice is. There's Tommy and Mika Carnath; they're definitely in; there's Stasi Ramirez—she's in; Will Morley: he's all right, but his girlfriend isn't—another Yvgenia case. Pity Yvgenia's boyfriend and Will's girlfriend aren't interested in each other. And there's Dan Peterson—he's got an azi companion, a beta, who's all right: I checked. And there'll be Valery, if he comes home, and there's room for Gloria Strassen, who probably hates me; and Julia, who's Maman's real daughter; but she'll probably tell me go to hell. That's all right: I hope she does and she won't be my responsibility.

I suppose I'm going to move in poor old Patrick Emory. He's not that old, he's just dull and a little odd, but then he's my only living real relative but one, so for once in his life somebody's going to be nice to him. And my aunt . . . God, my Aunt Victoria. She's probably going to refuse to move, but there's room if she wants to. I won't leave her out. Nobody would dare do that. But I hope she'll tell me go to hell, too. She's still offended I exist, and she'd gladly pull the plug on Giraud, never mind Denys. And I think she's immortal.

I hope Valery comes. I so much want to see him.

But there'll be room, too, in that wing, for people that aren't born yet.

You, maybe. I've no idea who'll bring you up. Amy would be one of the best. But that's, I hope, a long, long time from now.

JULY 3, 2424
1405H

There wasn't much to pack, and staff handled most of it.
For herself, Ari just put together a bag that held her essential makeup, her current notebooks, her study tapes,
anything security-sensitive, and Poo-thing—poor raggedy
Poo-thing *couldn't* make the transition to a new life in the
bottom of some box.

She took her bag on her shoulder. She met Florian and
Catlin, who had also packed their personal items—many
of them lethal, she was quite sure, or at least classified, and
this time when they went out to go to the new wing, they
didn't take the runabout. They took the ordinary mid-hall
lift down, the three of them, and walked into the ell that
had always been a dead end, keyed their way through a
door that had only opened this morning, to a reception by
her security—Rafael himself was on duty—and then to a
lift that you had to have a key for.

The lift took them up to the upstairs hall of the new
wing.

And it was marvelous. A gray carpeted floor had a rib-
bon of bright blue rippling down the middle and along the
edges—weaving and interweaving not so much that one
wanted to follow that path, but providing a hint of cheerful
whimsy that she would lay bets was Sam's personal notion,
not Maddy's.

She hadn't seen it in its final preparation. She deliberately hadn't seen it in the month and a half Maddy and
Sam had been doing all the work here. Her paintings—the
first Ari's—stayed where they were, in Ari's apartment, to
wait there until her successor made a decision, and by the
time it was her successor's successor in question, the first
Ari's apartment would probably become irrelevant, to that

centuries-from-now world, its content just scattered where it made sense to go.

But the artwork on the first Ari's walls had been only a fraction of the collection. Paintings in the modern mode were spaced along the walls of this corridor, turning the gray and white expanse into segments you could say belonged to the green painting, or the red one—nothing of the sterile black and gray and white surrounds of Wing One. Alpha Wing, still smelling of paint and plaster and the attendant moisture, was a different world, a profound change from where she'd always lived. Very, very unlike anything Denys would approve.

And the double doors that each gave access to various apartments down the hall—they weren't black, or beige, or one of twenty variations on white: one pair of doors, apartment 10, was red, 9 was blue, and 8 was bright green.

Her own doors, at the end of the hall, were as blue-green as new Cyteen leaves, and when Florian unlocked them, they gave way silently onto her waterfall, bubbling and flowing down a wall that could have been natural rock, and making a soft sound to welcome them.

The miniature brook, lighted underneath the glass, ran right across under the stonework hall floor, and meandered off into the living room. She followed it there, and just stopped and set down her bag, and looked around her and up at the tank, the immense tank that sparkled with ripples and moved with small living fish and shadowed with living rocks and waving sea life. That watery wall reflected off the unbreakable glass that topped the cross-floor river, so that the river underneath her feet was brown rock and flowing fresh water, and when she looked across the room, the glass top of the river reflected the Earth-ocean that was the wall.

The ocean suddenly vanished. It was directional glass, and Florian demonstrated the wall control. "If sera wants to have it plain," Florian said, "it will vanish. The light is still on, on the other side. Sam sent us the instructions."

She looked away, turning slowly. Paintings. Framed colors, on the severe stone walls. The master artisans of Earth.

Part of the living room wall was garden behind glass—

the wall that divided the living room from the dining room turned out transparent, with that kind of glass, just like the other. It could turn opaque at the flick of a switch, making the wall something else, making the dining room or the living room a private, undistracted area at need.

And the living room, even with the furniture, was big enough for several large sets of people to sit and talk at once—in some privacy. The water-sound permeated the space, luxurious, and peaceful. Florian switched both walls back to transparency, and the ocean and the garden were instantly back.

It was everything Sam had promised. It was magical, top to bottom. She'd wanted to be surprised, and she was overwhelmed. Florian and Catlin looked around as she did, their own baggage left in the foyer.

Catlin asked:

"Are you happy with it, sera?"

"Very. Very."

And there was no Sam. She'd thought he might be here to meet her, but he wasn't, which was like him—just to have his work make its own declaration. He'd done it all: everything was going to be fresh, from the dinner plates in the dining room—rose-colored pottery, mostly—to the couches, blue, just as she'd asked, but they turned out a grayed blue that went better with the stonework and the water and the plants behind the glass.

It all just fit, a harmony of sound and color that reached right into the senses. It was hers, in a way no place she had ever been had been hers. Maddy had helped do this. So had Amy, in the organizational sense, finding all the pieces Sam wanted. They'd given her this wonderful place, and she loved them. And Yanni was going to talk about the cost, but she'd told them—do it with their own places. Do it everywhere. Make it right.

She was happy, she decided. Really, really happy. She'd been so scared it wouldn't feel right to her, and it wouldn't *be* home.

But it was. It was home even when she'd never been here before.

BOOK THREE   Section 3   Chapter iv

Through with work for the day. Dinner over at Antonio's, one of their older haunts, over in the main wing, and home again, or that was the direction they were going, in Justin's intentions—himself and Grant, homeward bound for an entertainment vid they'd looked forward to, and with every intention of spending a quiet evening with absolutely nothing pressing to do.

But the door security at Wing One said, as they came through into the Wing: "Just a moment, ser. There's a message for you."

Message from whom was the instant question. Jordan or Yanni were the two fast guesses.

It turned out to be a note which the guard called up on his handheld with a few button-pushes, and it started out, *"Justin, don't be mad."*

That was Ari. He didn't even need to read the next line to be sure it was going to be something he wouldn't like, a bad surprise about Jordan, or—

"Your stuff has all been moved. Most of it, anyway, and the rest will be by the time you get back. Don't worry about a thing. If you want anything else from the apartment that didn't get transferred, you can get it—just ask security.

"Go down to the storm tunnels the usual way, go to your left, to where there used to be a dead end, in C corridor. There's a big door there today. To get to the new wing, just use your regular keycard and walk through the doors. Security on the other side will let you in, give you your new keycards, and tell you where to go. I really hope you like it. Love, Ari."

Love? *Love?* was it?

And *moved?*

"Thank you," he said to the guard.

"You're welcome, ser."

They walked on. He reached the point of decision, at the corner by the lift, and said, "I suppose there's no real reason to go to our apartment, is there?"

"I suppose the vid will show up eventually," Grant said. "It probably got switched over to the new system anyway."

"We'd better try the route," Justin said. "Find out what we're into."

They took the lift down to the tunnels. C corridor had always had a nook in it. They'd seen it on a fairly frequent basis since they'd come to Wing One. Two days ago he'd swear it had still had a nook in it.

Today it had a clean new doorway with a card slot and no labeling whatsoever except: ID AND KEYCARD REQUIRED.

He shoved his card in. The door opened. They went through. Another guard, in the glass-enclosed foyer, sat at a desk. The guard said pleasantly, "Justin Warrick, Grant ALX. Your keys. Your apartment is upstairs on the third floor, number 2. Your office will be on the first floor, number 28. Take the lift."

"My keycard," he said, and the guard returned it.

"Use the new card in the lift, ser."

"Right," he said, and he and Grant went into the lift. Grant hit 3, and they rose fast.

"With authority," Grant commented. And the door let them out into a corridor with gray carpet—gray carpet, with a ripple of blue threading down its length. Abstract pictures hung at intervals, each one a bright color that played off the last one.

The place smelled of paint and plaster. And they walked. It was ghostly quiet. Deserted.

"Are we the only ones here, I wonder?" he asked.

"Not a sound," Grant said.

"I can understand the suddenness," he said. "Her security requirements. But, God . . ."

"It is certainly a surprise," Grant said.

On the analogy of other moves, it would likely be thorough . . . and might include the rented vid. If there was a vending chit forgotten at the bottom of a drawer, he had

every confidence that it was going to be swept up, installed
in a neat box of "we don't know where this goes" items,
but it would be there. Anything that seemed like personal
property was likely going with them.

It wouldn't, however—a stray and irritated thought,
from experience—include the electronic list in the minder,
all his phone numbers and addresses. He remembered the
color-coded office supplies.

And his minder file was precisely the sort of thing a
security operation was going to peel out and go over with
a microscope before they gave it back to him—but if he
asked nicely they *might* stream it onto the new minder, in
the new place, for his convenience.

That prospect annoyed him, in advance of the event,
no matter that there wasn't a thing in it he cared if they
knew.

"They've moved our office again," Grant commented.

"And, damn it all, we just got the pictures hung!"

"They might move them, too," Grant said. "Or not.
Maybe they've provided some."

High-handed security touched off old twitches, no
question, visions of little rooms and endless questions.

But this Ari was not the enemy, and she was keeping
herself alive, and presumably taking care of those she
deemed close to her. It was just one more step toward a life
that, nervous as it made him, wasn't going to be the quiet
life he'd tried to make for himself and Grant. It wasn't
going to be inconspicuous, or safe—probably he lacked all
power to do any damned thing in his career henceforward
but serve as her backup, checker, and sounding board, but
hell, he wasn't ambitious. He'd survived this far. That had,
all along, been the name of the game. Never mind the job
classification. Never mind personal aspirations. Just stay
alive.

They walked. Doors on the left and right, very widely
spaced. "Big apartments," he said to Grant. There was
number 10, 8, 6—all evens in this hall. And a corner.

Number 1, a blue-green door, occupied an enormous
stretch of hall, and right across from it—

"Number 2," Grant said.

There was a red door on the right, number 4, then, oc-

cupying the middle, number 2, a bright green one, and
beyond that, finishing that corridor before another bend,
gold number 3 and blue number 5.

"Right across from her," he said tentatively. "Who are
3, 4 and 5, I wonder?"

"I have no notion," Grant said, and used his new keycard on the door. It shot open.

The lights came on, brightened overhead, a high-
ceilinged corridor with the illusion of mid-afternoon sky
overhead—it drew the eye up, in total startlement, made
one think, nervously, that it was a skylight.

But it went on brightening. There was the sound of
water splashing, somewhere. And down the hall, beneath
it—statuary, and pictures, old ones, classic ones.

Living room at the left. New furniture. Medium green
couch. Abstract carpet pattern in rust browns. Classy.
Goldtone metal edge on the coffee table in front of it. Big
wall sculpture in brass and rust brown enamel, an explosion of angles. He just stood there, half-blocking Grant's
entry, until he realized that fact and walked all the way
in.

Dining room, beyond that, in brass and glass, tiled floor
like stone. A stream of water ran noisily down one wall,
with a splashing sound that carried into the living room
and the foyer.

"My God," he said.

"Rather pleasant place," Grant said.

"We can't possibly earn this much," he said.

"It seems we do now," Grant said. "And I'm sure, for
whatever reason, we're worth it to someone."

He drew a breath, headed back through the apartment
to the bedroom.

Correction: bedrooms. There were three, one green,
one rust and reds, one blue. And an office or study, in
lighter green.

"What in hell are we supposed to do here?" Justin
asked, turning from one bedroom to the other, in the hall.
"Is it multiple choice?"

"This must be the main one," Grant said, and walked
into the largest-looking bedroom, the blue one.

Justin followed. Beyond was a bathroom beyond the

size a public gym might need. Sunken tub. Shower. Exercise equipment. He didn't even go in. He just turned full circle, saw a bed in a mirrored nook, mirrored ceiling.

"Good God." He was embarrassed.

Grant walked over and touched the switches by the bed. Room lights went down. Water ripple made the whole area look underwater.

"Dramatic," Grant said.

It was. Grant stood bathed in that light. He was still moderately appalled, as Grant apparently hit another switch. It became firelight, playing games on the bed, and in the mirrors on either hand.

Third was flashing neon. A blare of music.

Grant cut it off, startled, and, after two tries, went back to firelight. It was an interesting aesthetic effect. It might be, if nerves could quit insisting the building might be afire.

"I think she means well," Grant said.

"I can't imagine where they got this thing," he said. "God, what does she think we are?"

He walked midroom, where there was a bureau. A vase of fresh flowers of mixed colors sat propping a note card.

Dear Justin, it read, *I hope you like it. I hope it's not too gaudy, but you'd said all along you wanted color. You're safe here. Staff will do cleaning once a day, or oftener if you need them: you don't have to maintain anything, or cook if you don't want to. The minder has the call button. Wing staff will clean for you: they're all going to be high security. And there's going to be a restaurant downstairs on 1 sometime next week, so they'll cater for you, at any hour: I wouldn't presume to install domestic staff for you, but if you and Grant decide you need some, and Wing staff isn't enough, you only have to ask. Guards assigned specifically to Apartment 2 security are Mark BM-18 and Gerry BG-22—they're general Alpha Wing security, but they're two you passed on, and if there's a general emergency, their first priority is you and Grant, so know who they are, and they'll just look out for you in general. Your accesses are a subset of Base One, officially now, registered that way, so you don't have to pretend to be Callie or Theo any more. All Library is open to you, and any security situation in*

*the Wing will be at least as transparent to you as to any of
my staff except my bodyguard, if you just query Base One,
so if you ever get worried you or Grant can access it immediately from any handheld anywhere in Reseune. I know
you're careful with codes.*

*Have I ever mentioned you and Grant kept me honest
when I was a kid? You still do. You never flattered me,
never lied to me. Please talk to me first if you ever have a
problem. That means you'll never cross up something I'm
doing. Meanwhile I just feel safer and more comfortable if
you're across the hall. I don't know why that is, but it's so.*

*The minder is primed with all the Alpha Wing service
numbers as well as all your old ones. You can go anywhere
you ever went. Just guard those keycards with your lives.*

*Grant, keep him out of trouble. I love you both so
much. And I'll be so happy if you like this place, but you
can change anything you want to change, anything at all.*

Ari.

He walked back, sat down on the side of the bed. Just
sat, and looked up at Grant, thinking—they'd never get
back to their plain, ordinary apartment, their little place
where they'd been alternately safe and scared as hell.

This place wasn't the ongoing penance of the posh
black and white apartment. It was comfortable. Extravagant beyond belief.

"It's nice," Grant said.

"God, if that music cycles on in the middle of the night,"
he said, "I'll teleport."

"Well," Grant said, "there's probably a manual somewhere in System. We can look. Maybe we can change the
programming."

Justin gave a rueful laugh. And looked around him soberly then, all but overwhelmed.

"Why are we possibly this important to her?"

"You're asking the azi, born-man."

"It's just—every ratchet up the scale, we're increasingly
in the target zone, if anything ever goes wrong."

"I think that's always been a given, from way back.
Hasn't it?"

"I suppose it was. Is. Will be."

"It's probably very wise to put us behind her security

wall. You'd easily be a target, if someone aimed at her. And I think, if you want my opinion, she'd be a different Ari if she lost you. I think she knows that very well."

"I don't know why," he said.

"I do," Grant said, "but I'm not going to tell you."

"You're a help."

"She absolutely trusts you, and considering who you are, that's probably quite a scary situation for her."

"I don't have to be here for that. We had our arrangement. She can trust me anywhere."

"You're a vulnerability. She's sealing up her armor."

That, he saw. He could all but hear the clanks of doors shutting. Figuratively.

She was growing up. The place was a fortress. Total security, her own guard . . .

"She's preparing to take Reseune," he said. "She's preparing not to be caught the way Denys was." He recalled the paintings outside—different from anything that had hung anywhere—uncertain they were art, or just for color, but they had an effect. They dragged the eye from one to the next, took hold and led, one to the next.

He remembered that night in Ari Senior's apartment, when he'd had an injudicious drink and found himself changed, yanked sideways, away from Jordan, in ways he still couldn't overcome. That hallway. The paintings on Ari's walls.

He'd admired one. A painting of trees that weren't woolwood. He'd been terrified of his situation, fascinated by the intricate, fine-scale art. Set off balance by the luxury.

Overload. That was what he was getting, in this place. Wild angles. Water. Art that went sideways and splashed wild color, vastly different from anything in Wing One—anything he'd ever seen. But it was an Ari kind of thing, the paintings. It played psychological games. They were stark. Potent. Expensive.

"She's becoming Ari," he said. "We're seeing it now. This may be the beta version, but this is power, not just wealth. This wing isn't just decorated. If somebody did it for her, they know her. They painted *her* in this place. This is power. This just hits you in the gut."

"In some ways," Grant said, "she's alpha azi—but with

an emotional dimension I certainly don't understand."
Grant's eyes traveled up and around. "Then I see this
place. The ceilings, way off scale. The way colors hit you.
The waterfall in the living room—" His voice trailed off.
Justin made the little caution sign. If they'd been bugged
before, they were surely bugged now. "The waterfall is
CIT. Pure CIT. But it's pleasant."

"The sky arch in the foyer. Like being outside. That's
a psychological difference, isn't it?" He took the warning,
took a deep breath. "Maybe a big difference in our Ari.
Who knows?"

"I'm sure we're going to find out," Grant said.

"Are you all right here?" Grant asked him then, quietly. "Are you all right with this?"

Sometimes Grant functioned as *his* Supervisor. He did
a mental check. "I think so," he said. It didn't feel like
home. It wouldn't, for a while. "We had apartment design
A, apartment design B, and C. And pick one of three, over
in Ed. This is certainly something else, isn't it?"

"It's not black and white," Grant said.

"You know what bothers me here? The black and white
place was a place where we stayed. This one—this one
just gets right under your skin, doesn't it? I like the colors.
Like the look. She read me. Read both of us, didn't she?
She did, or somebody sure did."

"I'm not that difficult," Grant said.

"That's what you think," he said, and thought about
their growing up together, and thought about Jordan, who
never, ever could get in here to see where his son lived.

Jordan. Step by step, he won't like this, he won't live
with it, he's going to blow, sooner or later.

He's doing those sets knowing she's going to check
them, and there'll be something wrong, because he'll find
out about this place, and it'll eat him alive. He doesn't like
unknowns. Doesn't like anything that's been happening.
And when she does take over—

"What are you thinking?" Grant asked.

"That Jordan's going to be pissed about this
arrangement."

"We can't fix it."

"May be. But I'm a stupid, emotional born-man and I

want to fix it. And he's a damned fool. He's writing those sets. He'll foul them in some particularly subtle way to try her. Just to try her. And if she bounces them back with no comment, he'll just try again."

"At least he has a focus," Grant said, and that was true.

"I don't think she's shown anybody yet what she can do," he said absently. "I don't think she knows herself what she can do. Jordan's going to try the limits. Hell, maybe it's good for both of them."

"Maybe," Grant said.

"All those other numbers up and down the hall. And this is the third floor. Who else has she targeted, do you think? Who else decorates her universe?"

"Amy Carnath," Grant said. "Sam Whitely. Probably Madelaine Strassen. —Maybe Yanni."

"The kids. Yanni. And us. Oh, that's going to be a well-matched social set."

"Yanni won't want to move from where he is," Grant said. "Yanni always seems to like things to stay the way they are."

"Yanni'll hit the roof if he gets home and she's moved *him*. If he gets it. If he doesn't get in on this—Yanni could be on his way back to the labs. God knows. I honestly hope not. He doesn't deserve that kind of dealing."

Upheaval in the whole world could be going on and they wouldn't know. Except Ari had said they could know anything if they just asked. It didn't seem that easy from here.

He got up off the bed and opened a closet. Their own plain clothing hung there, mostly brown, casual, out of place, looking lonely, a little worn and tired outside the offices they'd worked in.

What did they do for a living now? Where did they go from here? They had a new office downstairs, near, he supposed, a restaurant that was going to exist next week.

Where did they sit in the evening, in a living room with running water and no vid that he'd spotted with any casual glance?

What did they have in the fridge?

Probably what they'd had in it before, a saner thought

informed him. The automations were probably loaded. He remembered the coffee dispenser in the Wing One office.

That would be good. Now they just had to find the damned kitchen.

BOOK THREE   Section 3   Chapter v

JULY 3, 2424
1728H

Just cocktails, Ari had said, inviting the new residents for the evening reception in her apartment, and she knew if Sam and Justin and Grant were there it wasn't going to be a wild evening, certainly not in the sense that the youngers had used to have wild evenings. They were all grown up now. They had outside interests. It was just a quiet drink shared among new neighbors, canapes and not even a very late evening.

And it went well. Amy showed up with Quentin—*they* were a couple, everyone knew it, even if Quentin hung out with Grant and Sam's Pavel and Yanni's decidedly older Frank. Maddy's Samara stood out like a fashion doll in that company; well, but so did Maddy, who'd arrived in a *very* pricy azure blue bodysuit with just the tiniest hint of white sparkle-lights running at cuffs and collar. Maddy looked fabulous. Amy wore a nice black suit with an electric blue blouse, shocking and stylish contrast to her companion, Quentin, in his black uniform—bet that Maddy had had something to do with that, too. Patrick Emory showed up—he looked fairly cheerful, for cousin Patrick. He'd already spilled a drink on his coat, and had two more, and was getting a little loud, but he was family, and Ari felt responsible for him, not to leave him outside the way everyone had, even the first Ari. He had worked in Admin, in records, just quietly, forever, the same job, every day, and he did pretty well, by all she knew, though he had no relationships and never seemed to get any enjoyment out of life. His obsession was vids, and he would talk about them if you wanted to; and he always came to family parties.

Aunt Victoria Strassen hadn't moved in: Aunt Vickie had her apartment over in Residential A. She sent a precisely written, neatly folded note that informed her niece that she appreciated the offer, but that she preferred her current residence and her old neighbors, and sent along a little box, which she called a housewarming gift. For Aunt Victoria, that was very, very considerate. It proved to contain a small carved plaque, which said, between sprigs of carved leaves, *Family Matters*. Probably Aunt Vickie had taken a bit of effort picking that out, to mean absolutely anything one wanted it to—particularly whatever Aunt Vickie meant, which might not be entirely polite, considering Vickie's opinion of her origins. But Ari had Spessy hang it on the inner wall of the dining room, where it nearly matched the stone.

Justin and Grant showed up in brown knit and tweed—it set off Grant's red hair and did absolutely nothing good for Justin. Set Maddy on him, was Ari's wicked thought.

But she held back. She thought probably she'd pushed Justin just a little too far all in one day as it was, and figured if he'd wanted to stand out in the crowd, he might really have picked something other than that medium-beige sweater and Harris tweed coat.

Truth was, he didn't look particularly happy in being here, and mostly, nursing one drink, and surrounded by people twenty years younger than he was, he stayed close to Yanni, who himself stayed close to the cluster of azi—social, all of that lot of azi, more even than Florian and Catlin. The olders seemed more comfortable there, and with each other.

As for Florian and Catlin, both of *them* stayed on the fringe of the azi group, cheerful enough, but *not* indulging in wine at all this evening, she'd noted that, not even with these people who were her dearest friends in all the world. She saw absolutely no reason in present company that they couldn't or shouldn't relax, but they didn't let go, not for a heartbeat. They'd worked so hard, so long, they'd gotten her here safely, they'd gotten her friends here, and there wasn't anything wrong tonight—was there?

Was there something afoot that she didn't know?

She almost went and asked them. But she was the hostess, and she had a very conscientious serving staff trying to manage a new arrangement, a new kitchen, and new premises, and trying not to ask questions of her. That was her situation to watch, her current level of crisis being an upset and lost azi maid standing there idle.

"Joyesse," she said, "you've done very well setting up. Would you mind serving canapes? Go to Wyndham. He'll like your help."

Joyesse took off. Happy again. All her younger friends were happy—Sam, with his girlfriend at his side, and with Pavel hovering close to him, was telling one of his stories, talking about the build. Justin and Yanni were talking about something—probably lab business. Or Jordan, their mutual problem. And she wasn't going to think about Jordan tonight.

The fish wall was an absolute success. Everyone admired it. Even the azi serving kept looking up at it, or around at it, in moments of utter, unguarded distraction, eyes taking in this and that detail. Amy naturally wanted to know the names of all the fish and everything that waved or moved or crawled in that tank—because Amy's place had a similar tank, but round, a cylinder in the middle of her living room, and her aquarium specialist would serve Amy's place, too. Amy knew fish, but she'd never dealt with salt water, and she was fascinated, happy and excited—for Amy. Maddy—Maddy got a waterfall, with orchids. Sam got a river all through his apartment, with a little pond under a glass floor in the rec room; and Yanni got a big vivarium, with lots of little skinks, which were lizards; and plants and flowers—Yanni said it was a damned waste of money. That was Yanni. He was most probably nervous about actually enjoying it.

She hadn't asked Stef Dietrich to move in, so there, for someone double-dealing in relationships from the time he was a kid. She'd arranged a very good job at Viking for Stef, he'd live like a prince on a Reseune salary on that mining station, and that was that for him, who'd tried to break hearts in the group . . . and never had changed his ways.

There were Dan and Mischa Peterson, each with a significant other; there was Stasi Morley-Ramirez, who'd grown up taller than any of them—she just towered; she was going into airport admin, and had a beta azi assistant she'd gotten on her own. She'd grown much more serious than she'd used to be, and that was very, very serious; but she unbent and laughed with Dan and Mischa, like old times.

And there were Mika and Tommy Carnath, each with their own place, both single, so that would have to be watched: they got terrarium gardens and sky-roofs. There was Dan Peterson and Will Morely with under-floor ponds—Will had a relationship going with Peterson's sister Judith, and she was all right: she was a Gamma Supervisor, and had a clean record, and they were almost engaged.

There were no children in the entire lot. That was going to change, this November.

God, she thought, Giraud. Giraud was going to be fascinated by the skinks.

And that would actually work very well. Giraud had so loved little microcosms. He'd visit here, with the fishes. With Sam's river. He'd be all over the place. If she were a kid again, in this place, she'd have it all mapped out, and she'd be everywhere.

Sam kept company with his significant other, Maria. She looked very nice in a white lace-edged skirt—was a little tanned, a little freckled, a little on the well-fed side, and was very anxious, clinging close to Sam and thus far speaking to no one without being spoken to. But it was *nice* to have somebody find a relationship who wasn't a security problem, and if Sam liked her, she had to have special qualities. Give Maria plenty of latitude—because it was, in a very major way, Sam's evening, and he deserved to be absolutely happy. Ari found the chance to say so, in the way of welcoming everyone officially.

"This is all Sam's doing, all this place. He's worked so hard. How do you like the new wing?"

That was a set-up question. Of course they all had to say yes, and Sam blushed, and looked at Maria, and Maria looked at him with a little blush of her own, adoring, so sweet it was acutely embarrassing.

At least she didn't need to single Maria out for a special

introduction: most present knew Maria, and Sam took care to introduce her to anyone else in range, even Patrick, who hastily wiped crumbs from his fingers—on his coat—and extended a hand. "This is Maria Wilkins-Teague," Sam said, beaming. "She's from the AG wing. This is Patrick Emory. He's Sera Ariane Emory's cousin."

Wilkins-Teague. Freckles and curious mixed-color eyes, mostly green. Ari had only rarely met the name of Teague, more often the Wilkinses. Definitely not one of the Families of Reseune, not at all common names in the CIT lists, which repeated a great deal. But Maria had never even had a security reprimand, not from her very outdoor childhood. And she didn't wipe her fingers on her skirt.

Sam made his way across the room to pay his respects officially, did so: "Ari, you know Maria."

"Of course," she said. "So glad you'll be a neighbor, Maria." And Maria blushed brighter than Sam and said, softly, with, God help her, a kind of little curtsey. "Thank you, sera. Thank you so much."

"My pleasure," she'd said. "Anyone Sam likes is all right. I'd be jealous if Sam wasn't my brother. You've got a good one in him."

"I know I have," Maria said, and hesitated over an offered tray of pricey imported cheese and crackers while Sam asked Ari matter-of-factly how the tank plumbing and water system was working.

"Fine," Ari said. "Absolutely not a glitch." Which showed where Sam's mind was today, besides Maria. He was looking around, up and down, seeing all the forms and the conduits and the works of the place, and he just wanted everything he'd done to work right, all the switches and all the plumbing.

She loved him tremendously for that. And Maria had finally taken a peppery piece from the tray and now looked as if the taste wasn't at all what she wanted. Ari pretended not to notice, and Sam, with finesse, simply took it in his big hand and ate it on his way, hooking Maria's arm, as it proved, to show Maria the workings of the electronic glass, which switched on and off in the next moments.

Ari wended her own way over to the olders. "How do you find your apartments?" she asked in general.

"Big," Yanni said, in Yanni's way. "My furniture's kind of swallowed up."

"But is it all right?"

"Nice," was Yanni's answer. "The garden's infested with fast little things. They ate one of the bugs. I take it they take care of themselves. Where does the shit go? Or are we supposed to clean it?"

She was amused. "There'll be maintenance, Yanni. Trust me."

"You don't need my beetle, now, do you?"

She kissed him on the cheek. "It's in my study," she said, "holding down my important papers, right along with Giraud's butterfly. And I will never, never in my life think he's superfluous."

"Go on with you," Yanni said. "Carry on this way and there'll be talk."

She laughed, moved on, and snagged Justin's arm next—in such a happy mood she went up on tiptoe and kissed Justin's cheek, next. "You're a dear," she said. Justin had tried to turn, but she held fast.

"A dear, am I? That old?"

"Not nearly too old," she said, and caught Grant's arm on the other side, and walked them both to the waterfall hall, where there was a bit more room, and the sunset sky overhead. "I absolutely meant what I wrote in the note. I want my lessons. I need them, understand, I really desperately need them right now."

"Is my father behaving himself?"

The designs Jordan was doing, Justin meant. "He's dropped a bug in. Naturally. It went back. Naturally. I'm sure he'll clean that out and add another one." It was funny, and it wasn't. She didn't kiss Grant. She hugged his arm hard. "You take care of each other, hear me? It may be chancy in the next few years. I proved who I was in court, but a court ruling is one thing. By the time certain people figure out that I really am what the law says I am, I'm going to be in charge. I'm in charge of this wing, in a way I wasn't ever, in Wing One. And this wing is coming alive, tonight. Reseune is going to know Base One is active again, not just tiptoeing around the edges. It can snatch control. It can lock out any other Base, just the way it did.

I laid it down for a while, so far as people know, but it's up and running full bore now. And as of tonight, Yanni's still Director, but every operation in Reseune, down to the electronics on the precip towers, and the off–ons in the birth labs, they're all reachable, if I want to reach them. It's been true all along—I think you've suspected so. But now everybody in Reseune will know it. They'll know it in the town tomorrow and I give it twenty-four more hours before it's all over Novgorod and Planys." She hugged Justin's arm. "Your father will know it, right along with everybody else, and he's likely to be upset, but I don't want to upset him. I'm glad I'm working with him. It gives him an outlet for his frustration. Is that all right with you?"

"Fine," was Justin's answer, very proper, very quiet, and never quite looking at her.

"Justin, you're not mad at me. Please say you're not upset."

He didn't answer glibly, or at once. "Truthers running?"

"No," she said. He looked at her then, quite soberly.

"I'm not upset. It's a beautiful apartment. More than we earn, by a long shot. I just hope we won't get a hell of a bill one of these days . . . in the physical or the metaphysical sense."

"No," she said. "You never will. Not that I have any control over. You paid it. All those years, you certainly paid for it. What you'll do in future will pay for it. Don't doubt that."

"I want to design sets," he said. "I'm a designer. That's what I trained to be. I like doing that."

"No doubt of it," she said. "You and Grant—both. You're going to do pretty well what you want to do. Teach me for another year. Maybe two. There are projects coming. Things on the drawing board that mean I need your advice. What you do—what you do is going to matter in the universe. And you're *not* going to be wondering when the next security panic comes through. If it does, they'll be protecting *you.*"

"That would certainly be a novelty," Justin said.

"No question of that," Grant said.

"You've got what I gave you."

"Yes," Justin said, touching his coat pocket. "Does everybody have them?"

"No," she said, the truth. "Do you like the apartment?"

"It's not black and white," Justin said, humor restored, and that made her happy.

"Lessons on Monday next?"

"Lessons Monday next. We still have to search up our office."

Humor definitely back. She grinned and hugged his arm and Grant's, and slipped free, happy, finally, because everybody was all right. For once, everybody was.

Then Florian turned up in her path, with a very businesslike look. "Sera," Florian said.

Catlin was there, too.

And the happiness took a dive. Instantly. Florian's eyes traveled further down the hall, where it became private, in front of the security office, and she went there with him.

Florian said, "Sera, there was a bombing at Strassenberg."

"At *Strassenberg*." She was utterly floored. "What damage?"

"The precip tower's down."

"Damn." It didn't make sense. Strassenberg wasn't a place anybody went. Yet. Except for the construction crew, the transport people, and a handful of sniffer pigs and handlers. "Anybody hurt?"

"Reports are still coming in," Catlin said. "A perimeter alarm went off. ReseuneSec reports the alarm triggered was between the port and the barracks. Somebody attempted approach. They thought it was a platythere: they scrambled to deal with that. Then the tower came down."

"No need to disturb the party, sera," Florian said, "at this point. There is a general shutdown of perimeters, a search in progress, but it's believed they got in by river, overland, not by using the port. ReseuneSec's placed Reseune and Reseune Township on yellow alert; they have river patrols out, looking for the landing site. They're diverting flights to Moreyville."

Strassenberg was several hundred klicks upriver, still in Reseune Administrative Territory. It was a long stretch of river to try to find anything human-sized—even a small boat. Reseune itself, on yellow alert, sat isolated in the midst of a no-fly zone, surrounded by hundreds of kilometers of unbreathable atmosphere and antagonistic flora and fauna. The Novaya Volga ran along its shore; it had an airport. Those were the two most likely approaches for trouble to take. Overland was too much work. But—

She saw, down the hall, Yanni and Frank, in process of leaving.

She went that way. Yanni delayed for her at the front door, by the waterfall.

"I heard," she said. "Yanni, can I help?"

"I'll handle it," Yanni said. "Just carry on. We're not going to make a big thing of it. Natural gas explosion. That's what we'll say."

"It wasn't, though."

"Whole damn truckful of explosives by the look of it. You carry on, you and your young people. This is going to take some sorting out."

"Go," she said, and by this time cousin Patrick had shown up, tucking a napkin full of something into his coat pocket, one more piece of Admin on his way.

"Ari," Patrick said, with a little bow, and then he followed Yanni and Frank out, alone—they didn't wait for him.

"Searches are in progress," Florian said, "there and here. We're under a mild alert, nothing that should bother the guests."

You didn't get into Reseune by water that easily these days. The bots zapped anything small; they reported anything big. The big machines that channeled the wild part of the river—they didn't let things in easily, either. *Somebody* had gotten to Strassenberg a short distance overland, she'd bet on it. There was legitimate shipping that got close enough to it. You landed, and there were no barriers on the river shore yet, nothing like Reseune.

"Why?" she asked, the big why, but she wasn't surprised when Florian and Catlin both shrugged an I-don't-know.

"We're hoping to find out, sera."

"Understood," she said, and thought, *damn*. She knew she had a worried, unhappy expression on her face, and tried to amend it as she walked out into the living room, but maybe Yanni and Patrick hadn't been too discreet in their departure: heads turned. Conversation, already at a low ebb, died.

"We've got a problem," she said. "Tower blown upriver at the new construction, definitely hostile action, but that stays under this roof. We don't know why or what. We're under a mild security alert here: if you're going anywhere else this evening, use the storm tunnels."

"Damn," Amy said. Just, "Damn." And conversation stayed dead for a moment.

"Well," Ari folded her arms and looked at the rest of her guests. "So we're stuck here. Anybody want to follow this on the System?"

"Is somebody possibly on the grounds?" Maddy asked.

"Unknown, sera," Catlin said. "But this wing is secure. Also secure: Admin, Ed, Labs A, B, C, and D. Search of Residencies A and B proceeding. Search of grounds proceeding, cascading alert. All AG notified."

"Slow," Ari muttered. She'd had time to hold converse, and they were just now closing up AG? "They can move faster than that."

Storm sirens blew. Finally. They advised anyone out to get under cover, into the storm tunnels. Lethals might be patrolling the grounds: the little weedzappers, which already had a camera function, turned suddenly nasty and helping defenses target any response. It wouldn't be a time to be walking around out there.

"Well," Maddy said with a nervous little laugh. "I'll stay in the Wing tonight. Champagne, anyone?"

There were takers, most of the party, and staff moved about seeing to it.

"It's just become a dinner party," Ari said. "In case any of you had planned on elsewhere after this: we'll be serving something, and serving late. Joyesse, go tell Wyndham so."

"Yes, sera," Joyesse said.

"Catlin, tell Wes put the security screens up."

"Yes," Catlin said. Florian was in the hall, checking something, probably conversing with Wes and Marco, maybe communicating with Rafael and company.

The fish tank went opaque, dark blue. Then the other wall came alive with images, some with sunset darkening to night, showing the downed tower from a perspective below the cliffs, some with numbers, and one showing the view from a bot scurrying at turf level across Reseune grounds.

"Ari." Justin came up at her elbow. "My father. I'd like permission to leave."

Above all else she didn't want Justin running around in the dark with the whole complex under alert. *No* was the reflexive answer.

But she couldn't hold on to him. Or she'd lose him. She understood that.

"I'm going to be a spacecase until you get back. You've got Mark and Gerry with you. Get your father on the phone. Be sure he's all right before you go anywhere. Security may have moved: Mark and Gerry can pull rank."

"I—" he started to protest, but the security comment quieted any objection.

"Thank you," Grant said, and the two of them went for the door, while she advised Marco to have Mark and Gerry meet them somewhere before the security desk.

Amy drifted over to her side, champagne glass in hand. "Something up with Jordan?"

"Not in play," she said to one of her oldest co-conspirators. "Whatever's going on, if it's Paxers, or if it's not, Jordan's a piece worth pinning down. Justin's just going to tell him we care."

Amy nodded, took a slow sip of champagne. Quentin was over with Florian and Catlin, getting information, watching the screens, which weren't apt to change much this far into the emergency. Just the little robot skittering along in the dark, gone to night-vision.

From Novgorod to Moreyville, even in Big Blue and faroff Planys, that scene was playing. The world was on alert.

Wonder if they knew, Ari asked herself. Wonder if this is specially for me. Another housewarming gift.

That implied a certain knowledge of the inner workings of Reseune—where the fact of so many relocations into Alpha Wing had, in fact, created quite a stir, and quite a lot of gossip.

The storm sirens still blew. Not a physical storm in the offing—but a storm, all the same.

JULY 3, 2424
1934H

Two security were in the lower hall, black-uniformed, rattling with full kit, including seldom-worn helmets, and on
an intercept. It didn't make quiet company, but they were
earnest types—Mark and Gerry, their names were. They
hadn't had time to introduce themselves formally—two
lanky, tall azi, a lot alike: Mark, a serious fellow and Gerry
a little less so: Justin actually recalled their files; but both
were deadly serious at the moment.

"Ser," they called him, and they said "ser," to Grant,
too, keeping their pace with no effort at all.

"We're going to Ed," Justin said. "My father lives there.
I want to be sure he's all right, considering what's going
on." He had his ordinary pocket com. He punched the
fast-response buttons as they exited the lift toward the security station, and let it ring.

And ring.

"Brilliant," he said to Grant. "He's not home and he's
not answering."

"Probably out at dinner," Grant said.

"Ten thousand-odd people are probably caught out
at dinner." They reached the desk and Justin showed his
keycard. "Sera's direct permission," he said. "Out to Ed,
personal."

"Yes, ser," the guard said. "Stay to the tunnels."

"Absolutely." They went out the door, into the familiar
storm-tunnel level of Wing One, and took an immediate
left, Mark and Gerry rattling along behind. The sirens were
intermittent now, as they were during a storm. The main
corridor as they came out of Wing One and into the area of
Admin was full of traffic, people generally in a fair hurry,
one direction and the other, most trending the same direc-

tion they were going, which led, as the rim of a great box, through the Ed tunnels and over to the Residencies and the Labs. Anybody from the Township was going to have a long wait for buses or a long hike, via the Labs, to the second tier of storm tunnels and shelters . . . and there were people with children, one upset lost child—the father came and swept the lost boy up out of the bewildering traffic just as they came in range: the father and his partner had four others in their group, and tried to urge them to more speed.

"It's all right," Justin said as he came up with the harried father. "It's a precautionary alert. No rush."

Others heard, shouted out, "What's going on?" and Justin yelled, "Precautionary alert. Damage upriver is all."

He didn't know if he made a dent in the distress, but a little further on, just as they were leaving Admin, Yanni's voice came over the general address:

"This is Director Schwartz. The alert is downgraded to level three. Those with indoor business are advised to pursue it with attention to level three cautions. Repeat . . ."

That calmed things, afterward. People caught their breath and quit trying to buck the flow. People began to walk normally, and to talk, and to ask questions, particularly of Gerry and Mark, who just said, repeatedly, "We're on duty, ser. We can't stop."

Justin made another try on the com. "Dad? Answer, dammit."

And a second one, after the next intersection. He wasn't used to this much exercise. His legs were burning. "Dad? Come on, answer."

"What in hell's going on?" the question came.

"Where are you?"

"Abrizio's."

"Right below you. Coming up." He was vastly relieved. And he had two large, heavily armed azi in tow, who weren't going to help his father's nerves at all. "Mark, Gerry, you're on my tab. Just go in, after us, order soft drinks and sandwiches, sit, and have dinner until Grant and I leave."

"Ser," Gerry said, "we're on duty."

"This *is* your duty, to look inconspicuous and not have my father create a public furor, which is bound to cause me and sera trouble. Just do it. You're doing personal security at the moment: my rules apply."

"Yes, ser," came back, from both, and meanwhile they reached the escalator and rode it up, this time, to the concourse level of Education.

"He's going to notice them," Grant said. "They won't stay that far back."

"I'm sure he will."

They had Abrizio's in sight: yellow lights were flashing, lending an unwholesome look to the area, but people were moving about in a fair simulation of calm. He and Grant lengthened stride, got a little ahead of Mark and Gerry as they reached the door, came in and advanced a few paces to try to spot Jordan. Things had gotten quiet, just as Paul stood up to make clear where they were. Paul's eyes were averted to something behind them, and Justin didn't look: the silhouettes of two helmeted ReseuneSec agents appearing in the doorway, blinking with ready-lights, could generally put a pall on conversation, or stimulate it, and both happened.

They had Paul and Jordan in view, however, and wended their way through the clutter of tables to take the vacant two seats.

"You're being followed," Jordan remarked as Justin sat down.

"The whole damn place is under alert," Justin said. There was a half-eaten order of chips and cheese with peppers. It was one of Abrizio's better offerings. He took a chip with cheese. "Just came from supper and a party. Not real hungry."

"The same," Grant said.

"Party," Jordan said.

"Social evening. The new wing's open. We've moved again. We didn't plan to."

"And you just got lonesome for our company," Jordan said.

"Drop the barbs. I got worried. There's been an explosion at the upriver construction. We don't know if there's anything going on here, but since you draw trouble the way I did, I borrowed a couple of Ari's guards and came looking."

"An attack on the construction. Interesting. And a couple of Ari's guards in attendance. I should be flattered."

"It's nothing. It's probably just an accident, hit a gas pocket in a dieoff area, something like that. Methane. Blew a new precip tower to bits. Security's on alert, nonetheless. They're not letting anybody onto the grounds."

"We heard the announcement," Jordan said glumly.

At least Mark and Gerry had taken off the helmets and the lights on their gear didn't show. The waitress was over there. They were making their order, likely soft drinks. Maybe sandwiches.

"Well, I was going to call you. We'd just had one thing after the other. We took an early supper, headed home from the restaurant to find out we'd been moved—my number hasn't changed, neither has Grant's. Office, the whole thing. Then we had a note on the minder we were due at a reception not that long after, so we didn't actually change for that. Just went. Had a few drinks, so I'm at max. I was going to call you in the morning . . ."

"We just heard the warning sound," Jordan said, "and there hadn't been any advisement they were going to make weather, so we figured it must be a natural storm. Guess not. Methane, eh?"

Sometimes the web of lies he told Jordan just overloaded. Sometimes, if things were ever going to be different, there had to be a dose of truth. "Fact is," he said, lowering his voice, "it probably wasn't. Somebody apparently blew up the tower up at the new construction."

"Somebody?"

"The usual suspicion goes to the Paxers. But that would be major for them, a real break with habit."

"Logistics." Jordan had leaned forward, and Paul had too, both of them, just taking it in, and for the first time in a long time, there was no bitter edge. "How in hell did they get through?"

"They needed river transport," Justin said. "They had to get either upriver past Reseune or downriver."

"Out of Svetlansk," Jordan said, "maybe. Downriver saves fuel."

"Not much civilization up there," Paul said, "or wasn't—last we knew."

"Mining, shipping, plenty of opportunity to lay hands on explosives. Unless things have changed."

"Not much to stop them going ashore at the new construction," Justin said. "No filtration equipment like here. No weir. No bots. All they'd need to do would be get a boat somewhere, load it with something—go ashore in suits, get out again."

"So what," Jordan asked with sudden sharp focus, "would anybody at Svetlansk have against whatever's going on at this new construction?"

And how much to tell Jordan? How many secrets to dance around? He'd gotten a response with the truth, a real change of disposition out of Jordan. He could make Ari mad. But Ari said she wanted to help Jordan. And was *that* the truth?

"Jordan," he said, "I'm going to tell you something I don't want to go beyond you and Paul. The new construction is another township in the works. Name of Strassenberg."

"Strassenberg." Jordan gave a short, bitter laugh. "My God. She's building a *city.*"

But he kept his voice down when he said it.

"Dad, I'm about as close to Ari as I can get. And that's likely to be a permanent arrangement." Jordan drew back a little at that, and Justin brought his hand down on Jordan's, pinning it. "Just listen to me. Permanent arrangement. It's where I live. I'm not her lover. I'm her teacher. And I'm not inclined to say no."

"Clearly it pays well."

"I want to do it, Dad. I get things out of the arrangement . . ."

"Oh, I'll bet you do."

"Listen to me! She's damned smart, is that a surprise? But I get access to the first Ari's notes, so you should know money isn't the game. Neither is sex." Jordan tried to move the hand and he held it, hard. "Listen. Talk to me about this. I want you to understand me, just once. I'm learning. I missed a hell of a lot during the bad years. Same as you. I'm getting a break, and I'm taking it. I don't think that's such a bad deal."

"Count your change. That's all I'll say."

"She'll use some of the things I know, yes. But meanwhile I get input in what's going on in the world, I get some policy input, and that's important. I get to have a say."

"Sure. As long as you agree with her you'll have a major say. Wake up."

"I'll have to see how it plays out. I won't know. But I'm not locking myself away from the chance."

"You look pretty well locked away to me. You don't get a say in who you can let in the door—do you?"

"Dad. Eventually, yes. This isn't the time . . ."

"Bullshit." Jordan jerked his hand free. "Paul. Have you had enough?"

"We'll walk you back," Justin said.

"The hell. With those two over there? The hell you will. Paul. Come on." He stood up. Looked down at Justin. "You're rich. You pay the bill."

"Sit down. Please."

"No, thanks."

Jordan headed for the door, Paul in his wake.

Justin got up. Grant did. "Grant," Justin asked him, "pay the bill."

"We don't split up," Grant said. "If you go after him, we go."

"Grant, just for God's sake, take care of it." He shoved through the narrow gap between two occupied chairs and started to leave, and Grant did, both of them heading for the door, but Jordan and Paul were already outside.

"Hey!" a female voice yelled.

They knew the waitress. Justin stopped, half-turned to show his face in the dim ambient light. "Justin Warrick, Greta, just put it on my tab. All of it." He could see their guards on their feet and starting out. He turned, hardly having stopped moving, and got out the door.

A presence at the side caught his eye—two ReseuneSec agents and Jordan and Paul up against the frontage of the bar—familiar sight, but not familiar with his father and Paul involved.

"Hey!" Justin said, and immediately faced a drawn stunner. He raised his hands to show them vacant. Grant did.

And about that time two more on their side came out of the bar.

Guns came next.

"For God's sake!" Justin exclaimed. "We're on the same side!"

"Interfering in an arrest," one of the outside guards said.

"On what grounds?" Jordan shot back.

Justin, hands still lifted, siad, "Dad, just shut up!"

"Both of you, up against the wall."

"Don't move!" That, from one of their own pair. "Don't anybody move. They're under our watch."

"Where's your orders?" one of the others asked. "Who are you?"

"Mark BM, special assignment, Alpha Wing."

"There isn't any Alpha Wing."

"There is," Justin said, "as of today."

"Shut up," the agent advised him. "Get over there."

"Ser Warrick isn't moving," Mark said. "Special assignment, Ariane Emory's personal guard, Alpha Wing. Ser Warrick. Stand away from the wall."

"Don't move!"

"Call—" Justin began to suggest, and flinched and shut up when he heard the hum of a stunner.

"We will shoot if you fire that." That was the other voice from his side. "Gerry GB, Alpha Wing. Call your headquarters."

Justin stood still. Grant did. They'd drawn a crowd. "Hell of a fix," he said, and remembered what he had in his pocket. And he didn't dare reach for it. He found occasion to lower his hands a degree. In case.

"Stand still!"

"This is a warning," Gerry said. "We are authorized. Call your headquarters."

"Better do it," Justin muttered. "Director Hicks is going to be damned mad if you and her security start shooting at each other. Let me get my com and I'll call Yanni Schwartz if you want to take the chance."

"I'm calling HQ," the other agent said.

"I want to know," Jordan said, "on what charges we're being arrested."

"Shut up, Dad."

"I want to know!" Jordan said sharply.

"Because there's an alert out on you. Detain and hold for HQ."

"And I want to know who gave that order," Justin said. "Was it Hicks? I want to see badges, and authorization."

"Stay put."

"I'll find out," Justin said, seeing he was gaining ground. "You can bet I will, and if I can't, Emory's bodyguard will."

There was a brief exchange on the com. Justin couldn't hear the other side of it, but he heard, "We've found Warrick, ser, in company with his son and two azi—"

"Grant ALX," Grant supplied, "and Paul AP."

"Grant and Paul," the other agent said, and began making signs to his partner, who took a step back. "No. Not actually in detention, ser." Handsign for "back way off." "We've got a pair in uniform with lethals claiming to be bodyguard from Alpha Wing. Claiming they've got jurisdiction." Moment of silence. "Yes, ser. Understood, ser. Thank you, ser. —We're to back off," he said to his partner. "Apologies. You're free to go."

"The hell!" Jordan shouted.

"Jordan," Justin said, and quietly went and got Jordan by the arm. "Just come with me." Jordan's cheek was red—contact with the ornate frontage, likely, not a voluntary contact. "Paul. Let's just go."

Jordan wiped at his cheek and looked at his hand, and looked venom at the two agents, only slightly less so at Mark and Gerry.

"It's all right, Dad. We're going now. Grant, Paul, can you go back in there and settle the tab? Mark, go with them, will you?"

"Yes, ser," Mark said. And the other two agents, nameless, went on down the mall. Not unreported. There'd been badge numbers, and Justin would bet Grant remembered. Not counting the report Mark and Gerry might file.

"It's going to bruise," Justin said, still holding Jordan's arm, and Jordan shook him off.

"I'm fine."

"Sure you are. Thank God they really were ReseuneSec."

Jordan gave him a stark stare. "Any reason to expect anything else wandering around the mall?"

There wasn't. But there could be. "You attract cards, remember?"

"No fucking way to run things," Jordan said. "Damn!"

"Glad I came after you," Justin said.

"Why did you?"

"Just generally worried," he said. "Worried about your safety." The com wasn't the only thing he had in his pocket. He felt in his pants pocket and found the old key-card. "I can't bring you into Alpha Wing. But I can get you into Wing One. If there's anything else afoot—that'll stop some things."

"Since when, Wing One?"

"Since it's mostly vacant, since we have a perfectly good apartment there we still have keys to. You'll have to go out for meals—I recommend the Admin section. I don't know if there'll be sheets, but there's a bed and I know they left the furniture. Tonight, with things going crazy like this—I just want you to go there, Dad. Come on. You know you're curious."

"I know that Wing pretty damned well. I know her apartment—pretty damned well."

"She's not in it. She's in Alpha Wing now. Security there's still tight, however."

"Well, it's tight here! You saw what came of it."

"If I tell Wing One Security you belong there for a while, I don't think anybody's going to bother you. Dad, just do me the favor. Please. I'm begging you. For Paul's sake. Don't mess around with this. You're on somebody's list, and some stupid order got fired off when the alert went out, maybe an accident, maybe an accident somebody just let happen, but I don't want you running the risk. Bruises heal. A stunner's not damned funny." He pulled the key-card out. Offered it. "Yours, until I get this sorted out."

"You get us in there," Jordan said with a shadow of that sour quirk he could take on, "and Security doesn't nail us twice in the process . . . and I'll be very interested to see how it plays with her highness."

"I'll talk to her."

"So nice to have a son who has pull."

"Come on," he said. Paul and Grant came out of the bar, mission accomplished, he trusted, and he caught Grant's eye and then turned to Mark and Gerry. "You understand what I'm doing. I'm moving my father and his companion into Wing One, our apartment there, where they'll be safe. I want you to advise your command we're doing it, tell them what's happened, and say my father would appreciate it if he has sheets, towels, and a bar setup."

"Yes, ser," Gerry said.

He'd tossed the last in. Gerry seemed in no wise fazed by the order. He motioned Jordan on toward the down escalator.

"We haven't got a change of clothes," Jordan said.

"Welcome to my ever-changing world," Justin said, and turned his head toward Mark. "Mark, my father's had no chance to pack anything. Can you arrange him and Paul to have clothes, personal kit, that sort of thing?"

"We're going to get turned back at the door," Jordan predicted.

But they didn't. The Alpha Wing keycard got them right through, and the ever-present Wing One security guards said, "Justin Warrick, ser. We have orders from Alpha Wing. Go on up."

They rode the lift to their old apartment. Silence aboard, just the thump of the car on its tracks. They got out into a hall as brightly lit as ever, right by their door. "Go ahead," Justin said to Jordan as they reached the keyslot. "You've got the key."

Jordan put it in. Opened the door. Their living room, their couch. And a small tray of canapes, and another of vodka and glasses.

"That wasn't sitting here all day," Jordan said.

"That's from the party, pretty clearly," Justin said. He walked over and turned on the autobar. "Still stocked. Good they brought the glasses."

"Clearly they've got a key to this place," Jordan said.

"There's no place they can't get, actually," Justin said, and took a look into the bedroom. "Sheets and towels. I imagine your clothes will arrive shortly."

"Fast service," Jordan said.

"She approves," Justin said, fixing Jordan with a level stare. "Or you wouldn't get the canapes."

Jordan didn't say a thing. Just walked back into the hall, had a look at the bedroom, and walked back again. "You're right. Black and white and grey. A psychotic's dream."

"The bed's not bad," he said. "Pretty comfortable, actually."

"What's the rent?" Jordan said. "Your immortal soul?"

"Call it caretaking. Ari's moved. We've moved. They're going to be renovating all over the Wing, what I hear; but this place can wait." He gave a nod toward the adjoining wall. "That was her apartment. Which I suppose you know. We're across one major wall and a security gate, but not that far away. Assuming you want to stay here."

"Is there ice?" Jordan asked.

"The bar says there's ice."

"Then we'll stay," Jordan said, sitting down on the couch. "Paul, all right with you?"

"Fine," Paul said, and in passing, shot a look of gratitude Justin's way, just that.

Justin nodded. Looked at Grant, then, and at Mark and Gerry, before glancing back at Jordan. Paul had gone to the bar, was preparing a drink. "Lunch tomorrow, Dad?"

"I can't afford those fancy places over in Admin."

"My treat. Just shut up about it. You get those designs done and you'll have income again."

"They could fucking pay me while I'm working."

"Look, there's a perfectly good office in there. Not like working in your living room. Computer connections probably work." It was a thought. He didn't know if they'd gotten that equipment out, and he went back specifically to look. Everything of that sort was stripped. "Your stuff's coming in," he reported, coming back into the living room. "Plenty of room for it. I'll talk to Ari about permanency here."

"The place is psychotic."

"You've got colored towels. Colored sheets. It's not psychotic. I'm going to ask for a guard to be put down here. Contact with housekeeping." He put his hand on the door switch, prepared to leave. "Glad you're here," he said. "Don't let anybody from housekeeping in until you get the guards out there."

"Oh, thanks," Jordan said. Paul put the drink into his hand. He lifted it, silent salute.

"And lay off that stuff," Justin snapped, and hit the door switch and left.

BOOK THREE   Section 3   Chapter vii

JULY 4, 2424
0251H

The party ended, late, with all youngers in attendance, those who *didn't* have responsibility for the safety of Reseune. Sam made a few calls to check on Fitz and crew, being sure that personnel had gotten out unscathed at Strassenberg—and Ari just keyed into Base One in her office and searched up details Sam couldn't get.

ReseuneSec had sent a plane up there with senior officers, they'd landed at the airstrip, and they were trying to track whoever had gotten up on the cliffs with that much explosive. Boats were searching the shore for any sign of landings.

About time they got some bots on the site, guarding the area, Ari said to herself, but they cost, and she was going to have to convince Yanni they'd be cheaper than rebuilding that tower.

And the messages came flooding in.

From Yanni: *"We've had an armed confrontation with your guard in the middle of the Education Wing mall. I have enough on my plate without the Warricks at it."*

From ReseuneSec: *"To: Sera Ariane Emory, Director, Alpha Wing*

"From: Office of Adam Hicks, Director, Reseune Security.

"Posted by: Kyle AK-36, duty officer: automated system.

"This is to notify you that staff under your supervision has violated:

"*Code 2871–82, section three: Resisting arrest.*

"*Code 2281–91, section one: Interfering with Reseune Security officers in the performance of their duty.*

"*Code 2281–91, section two: Inciting others to interfere with Reseune Security officers in the performance of their duty.*

"*Code 291–1, section two: Involvement of azi in the commission of a crime . . .*"

It went on for a list of twenty-one items.

It made Rafael's note compulsory reading: "*To: Sera Ariane Emory, Director, Alpha Wing*

"*From: Rafael BR-283, Commanding Officer, Alpha Wing Security*

"*Officers Mark BM and Gerry BG accompanied Justin Warrick to Abrizio's Bar and Grill in the Education Wing where, pursuant to the orders of Justin Warrick, they disengaged but observed. Justin Warrick engaged Jordan Warrick in private conversation at another table. Jordan Warrick left the bar and was placed under arrest outside by officers BY-210 and BO-8 of Reseune Security. Justin Warrick objected. Reseune Security threatened him with a stunner, while applying restraint to Jordan Warrick. Alpha Wing officer Mark BM then drew a lethal and instructed Reseune Security to stand down . . .*"

Oh, even better. She skipped to Justin's message.

"*Ari, forgive me. I lost my head. It wasn't Jordan's fault . . .*"

It went on to say, "*On my own discretion, I told Jordan the nature of the upriver construction and the incident there. His reaction was sympathetic, and despite the public locale, the ambient noise was as good as a silencer, so I am relatively confident no one overheard. Conversation kept to a quiet level until Jordan left the bar with Paul, whereupon they were arrested by ReseuneSec personnel outside the bar. Grant and I followed, an argument ensued, and Mark and Gerry intervened to abort the arrest of all of us. I think Mark and Gerry will report more details.*

"*You know that I put Jordan into our old apartment. I apologize. If you want to talk about this incident I'm available at any hour. I very much regret the inconvenience.*"

There was even one from Jordan Warrick: "*I don't*

know if this will get to you, but it's a nice place. Thanks for the tray."

She wrote back. To Yanni: *"Sorry about that. There was a communications problem. I'll communicate with Hicks and straighten it out. Keep me current with what you find out on the other matter. If you need me, call."*

To Adam Hicks: *"We had a problem tonight. Jordan Warrick should be subject to observation, not arrest during general curfew, unless, as per any other CIT, he violates the law. Justin Warrick is not to receive any reprimand for his actions of last night. All charges are to be dropped. Jordan Warrick is now resident in Wing One and has received rights of access there."*

To Rafael: *"Your personnel acted as they ought. Please stress that they should contact ReseuneSec Command offices and cite my authority to defuse any further such situations, so long as Alpha Wing personnel are safe, and that should remain the priority. Under no circumstances is any Alpha Wing resident to be arrested on any charge without clearance from me."*

To Justin: *"I knew it was going to be interesting when you left the party. I'm glad you're all right and it's all right what you did. That information is due for release soon anyway, before the news obsesses about it. Jordan is safer where you put him, and I don't think I could have persuaded him to go there. Congratulations on that part. Please write Hicks and Yanni a meaningful apology and say you were following my orders."*

And, not least to Jordan, who'd actually initiated an exchange with her: *"You and Paul are welcome. You can contact the Office of Domestic Services, Alpha Wing—the minder will have the number; and arrange a pair of betas, set of your choosing, to serve as domestic staff, if you like. Justin and Grant never opted to have anyone live in: that was their choice, but they relied somewhat on my staff. Now that I'm removed from that area, you probably will find it easier to have someone to take care of the day-to-day operations. It is, however, entirely your choice. I hope you like the place."*

Last was a mundane detail, an order to the ODS to allow exactly that, to send the bill to her office, and to allow Jordan Warrick, whose request would otherwise ring bells all the way to Yanni's office, to come and go on his own.

She leaned back, then, still in her evening finery, and got up, called Joyesse to get her out of the blouse and hang things in the 'fresher. She slipped on a gown and told Joyesse, "Call Florian."

For some nights there was no other solution.

She lay there abed, waiting, hands behind her head and thinking, with some amusement, that she'd probably issued the order for Jordan's free pass only marginally ahead of Jordan's first provocation of security in that wing.

And thinking, with much less humor, that the world was a little darker tonight, now that somebody had decided to bomb a tower on something *she* was building. It hadn't hurt anybody. But it had done financial damage. It was Reseune property. More, it was her project.

Maybe whoever had done it had known it was a special night for her. Was that too paranoid to imagine?

First the two nanistics Specials, mightily inconveniencing Yanni's plans; and now this, a setback in hers . . .

The Paxers usually expressed themselves harmlessly in graffiti, or, not harmlessly, in subway incidents in Novgorod. They didn't challenge Reseune directly.

Maybe that had just changed.

It might actually be an improvement. If they got out in the open, where security could lay hands on them . . .

Florian showed up in the doorway.

"I'm not at all in a bad mood," she said. "I'm actually fairly cheerful, all things considered. You don't mind my calling you, do you?"

"Not at all," he said. Which he always said, but he always seemed to mean it. And he was just what she needed at the moment: a major distraction.

BOOK THREE Section 4 Chapter i

Twenty-two weeks, and Giraud was growing a pancreas—not so dramatic as a heart, or lungs, but it meant he would be ever after able to digest food, to produce insulin and deal with sugars, and proteins . . . and thereby regulate his body chemistry. Not as dramatic as a heart, not as romantic, but just as life-essential, and very, very important to a man who'd value good health and enjoy his table as much as Giraud would.

He had gotten a bit fuzzy, meanwhile: body hair had started. His skin was too big for him: he was wrinkled as dried fruit, but he actually had gotten lips, and had tooth buds—they'd be squarish teeth when they finally came in, the two center ones a bit prominent—but those wouldn't be needed for months and months yet. The bones were still growing, and teeth now got their share of calcium and other nutrients.

He and his companions were getting much more complex.

BOOK THREE Section 4 Chapter ii

Disappointing, the lack of progress on the Patil case and the Thieu business. Ari had a small soiree for at least some of the youngers—Yanni and Justin were at dinner elsewhere, Sam had gone off to Strassenberg: she'd urged

him to be very, very careful, and she'd diverted two of her
own security to go up there with him and make sure neither Sam nor Pavel did anything rash. Maria had stayed
here—barracks living was no place for Maria, Sam said,
and she'd take care of the place.

But Maria would have been lost in a council of war, so
she didn't get the dinner invitation tonight. Sam would
have come, however, and they missed him.

Tommy and Mischa and Mika came. Yevgenia
Wojkowski, who had lost no time dumping the boyfriend
who had jeopardized her chance to stay with the group . . .
she was there. Will Morley arrived, and of course Amy
and Maddy: they had a simple supper and drinks after, and
they sat under the fish wall, which cast a rippling light on
everything, and tried to absorb the complex detail Catlin and Florian told them in the general what's-going-on
briefing.

Namely: Rafael's lot had turned up a list of twenty contacts Patil had had with shady connections; nobody yet
knew anything but rumor on Anton Clavery—but Reseune-
neSec was still digging—and the Thieu autopsy was still·
doubtful as to murder, but on circumstantial grounds the
death was just too connected to the Patil murder to be
anything but.

"Meaning they're good," Catlin concluded regarding
the perpetrators, "and that means they're not amateurs."

"Or it means they meant to kill Thieu the hard way,"
Florian said, "and ended up just stressing him to death.
But there are no marks, no bruises, except the livor mortis
that happens when a body—"

"Ugh," Maddy said, and waved the information away.
"We don't need that much detail."

"Blown out a window is nicer?" Mischa said. "Twelve
stories down to a cooling tower?"

"Nasty," Tommy said. "So we know they weren't
squeamish."

"That's not highly helpful," Amy said. "As if you're
going to commit a murder and squeamishness matters?"

"It does probably add into the 'not amateur' theory,"
Florian said.

"Getting into Planys also does that," Amy said.

"And the tower at Strassenberg," Will said. "Which is organization."

"Considerable logistics," Florian said. "ReseuneSec lab's traced the explosives to a mining company at Svetlansk. That's no surprise. The mode of delivery is uncertain: no boats are reported missing from Svetlansk, none scheduled to be in the vicinity on that day."

"But the explosives might have been planted earlier," Catlin said, "and detonated by timer or remote. Proximity-detonation would have been possible, but it's not really logical to do it that way, and it doesn't seem they did."

The site was an inconvenient remove and an inconvenient height above the Strassenberg complex.

"One other thing of note," Catlin said. "We also *did* have a boat out and in motion at that time. It came from Moreyville, visited Svetlansk, and came back."

"Long trip," 'Stasi said.

"Especially long if they came from Moreyville, past Strassenberg—" Ari said.

"Upcurrent," Yevgenia supplied.

"And," Ari said, "didn't refuel at Reseune docks."

That got attention from the rest. "Big gas tank," Mika said. "Did somebody do that?"

"Yes," Florian said. "ReseuneSec is wondering about fuel drops along the way. The boat was in fact on its way back from Svetlansk when the tower blew. Rafael is trying to check currents and times. Downriver's naturally faster. The time could work. It's a large boat, a rental, which makes it more suspicious. It's easy to piggyback in more fuel tanks without altering the boat."

"So they didn't want to refuel at Reseune so we wouldn't have records?" Maddy said.

"Something like," Ari said. "That's the lead we're following, at least, the best we've got."

"A link, who knows—from Novgorod to Morleyville, past us, to Svetlansk, for people wanting to blow up the tower," Tommy said. "At least they didn't get help here at Reseune."

"Who was aboard?" Mischa asked. "Can we tell?"

"The rental was made by one Sera Penny Esker."

"Never heard that name on any list," Amy said.

"None of us have," Ari said. "It searches to an Esker line resident in Novgorod, some employed by Novgorod Transport, Penny Esker being currently employed by the public library, data archive department."

"Where Patil used to lecture."

"Former student?" Tommy asked.

"Way out of her field. No University connections, not on any of the watch-it lists, but they wouldn't use somebody who flashed red lights. Penny Esker seems to be a nobody, so far as criminal records, which is the sort, if you were up to no good, that you'd prefer to use, especially to rent boats. Florian says, and I agree, she wouldn't have been on the boat."

"Why did they do it at all, though?" Amy asked. "Blow up a tower? Paxer nonsense?"

"Maybe," Ari said. "Maybe something about the site leaked—but that sort of incident doesn't do the Paxers any good. They'd want some sort of media coup, blowing up something of mine, coupled with revealing I'm some sort of junior megalomaniac out founding towns at random, building secret laboratories and siphoning money out of Reseune to do it. They want publicity. They want public dislike of me, in particular. What the bombers actually got out of this business was my attention, and a slowdown of about two weeks in the Strassenberg build."

"It could scare people, though," Tommy said. "It could scare Fitz Fitzpatrick. It could be aimed at him and his company."

The man in charge of the construction company, the man Sam was up there working for. She nodded, not liking that version of it, but it was indeed possible.

"Did we do anybody out of a contract they wanted?" Amy asked. "Fourstar was closest bidder besides Fitzpatrick."

"Worth checking," Catlin said, "since Fourstar is working next door to us in Wing One. They've already passed a security check, but a second one wouldn't hurt."

"Investigate Svetlansk Mining and the rest of the Svetlansk operations that handle explosives," Ari said. "How many companies are working up there?"

"Four," Catlin said.

"Probably we won't find anything blinking on and off with colored lights," Ari said. "But if we continue asking questions, individual by individual, something may turn up."

"Have we got any investigative people up on scene?" Mischa asked. "I know Sam is, but—"

"That's the other thing," Amy said. "Sam *is* up there and he's at risk if this gets more serious than it is."

"ReseuneSec's going to be investigating," Ari said, "already is, but that all lands on Hicks's desk, and it's clumsy, and it's slow, and it's damned useless if we need three layers of authorizations to stop a boat on the river. We do have Sam's bodyguard: this is what doesn't get out. He's got non-uniformed security with him. The two I sent with him aren't trained as engineers. They're taking tape on construction, but that's not what they really do. So, yes, we do have our own investigation onsite. The problem is— they aren't to leave Sam to go chase anything; and I don't want Sam anywhere near a problem."

"I'm glad they're with him, though," Maddy said.

"I have a question," Tommy said. "Are we sending ReseuneSec all this info we're gathering?"

"Not," Ari said, "until they give us better results than they have in the last two weeks."

"You don't have confidence in Hicks," Amy said.

Ari shook her head. "I don't know if it's malfeasance," she said, "but it's not total competence. This is what bothers me: Uncle Giraud was a demanding sort. Hicks is making mistakes: jumping on Justin was one. We're not getting things he promised us. We know we're not. So, no, I'm not trusting him."

"But Yanni's all right," Maddy said.

"I think Yanni's all right," Ari said. "But, so you know, yes, we're running down all the civil police reports and university police reports on the Patil case. We're having a little trouble getting at Planys. Thieu's had a lot of tendrils that go under Defense doors, and we can't get everything we'd like from there."

"Same trouble in Novgorod?" Amy asked.

"To a certain extent," Ari said. "Patil's ties to Citizens and Defense are a problem, where it comes to access. The fact Patil was actually registered in Science opens up a lot of files to us that we otherwise couldn't get. But most of her scientific research is classified, and not just anybody can get at it. Yanni being Proxy Councillor, he technically can. He's got a lot; I've got that; I've asked for more—and if he gets it, I can get it. But what we've gotten so far is a complete disappointment. I hoped I'd find keywords and names that might be useful, but there's nothing. A lot of correspondence with Councillor Corain—we can get her side of it, and it's nothing startling. She complained significantly about crazies at her lectures this last winter. One letter to the Dean of Science asked that enrollment in her courses not be available in virtuality—it already wasn't— and that enrollment be interview-only, with a background check, and no auditing her classes, which they did implement for the next session . . . that was before she agreed to take the job on Fargone. I tried to get the actual interview lists, of people she'd enrolled, but that wasn't available. Corain could get it, and I might write to him, or get Yanni to, but I don't think it's too likely the people we're after would be in any way up to her coursework."

"Sounds as if she was worried, at least," Will said.

"Well, she was being made an icon for the Paxers," Maddy said. "I don't blame her. But her restricting who got to her classes didn't help her much, did it?"

"Anything on that name?" Mika asked.

"On Anton Clavery?" Ari said. "Almost a hundred percent it's a pseudonym, maybe a shared identity. And here's another place we don't have all we want from Hicks. We know there's undercover work going on, and Yanni's dragging his feet about getting Hicks to divulge what's out there."

"Undercover?" Mischa asked.

"Infiltrating the Paxers," Ari said, "but that's a deep secret, supposedly. There's no report I've been able to ferret out. Hicks has it stored somewhere, and I'm wondering if it's in a disconnected computer. I'm going to corner Yanni on it and insist. What generally bothers me, since the big bang at Strassenberg, is that there's nothing wrong in Novgorod. The Paxers have been uncharacteristically quiet for the last two weeks. Likewise the Rocher crowd. Just silent. When something that disorganized suddenly does—or doesn't do something—all together, that's worrisome. Somebody may have pushed a button. And we didn't think anybody had that much control."

"Anton Clavery," Tommy said.

Mischa dug an elbow in his side, saying: "You're making a bogeyman."

"Maybe we've got one," Ari said, and the little flurry of laughter died. "I just don't like any signs of coordination in that lot."

"Who could get them all to face the same direction?" Amy asked. "*How* could they do it?"

"Fear," Catlin said. "A few might die. The rest would understand."

The whole gathering got quiet for a breath or two. Catlin dealt in things like that, in a level of seriousness that had never quite gotten to the group, not even when they'd brought down Denys.

"There's reason to think some have died," Ari said. "People have accidents in Novgorod. That statistic's always there. But the number of crazy letters on certain boards we monitor has fallen right off. It's just a silence. That's all we can finger. And I want information out of Yanni, and I'm hesitant to press for it, because I don't want alarms to go off in any system watching *me*. So I'm not making a great fuss. And, no, I'm not easy about Sam being where he is, but I have a code arranged that will bring him back fast, if we have to." She sighed and leaned back in her chair, ankles crossed. "I don't want to move yet. I don't want to until I have enough information. I don't want to call Sam back on a just-in-case, because it's important what he's doing. It's his job with Fitzpatrick that's at issue here."

"All the same, somebody killed the first Ari," Amy said grimly, "and we're not going to lose the second."

"I appreciate that vote," Ari said with a little laugh.

"Was it Denys that did it?" Amy asked, and that didn't deserve a laugh. "Did we get them all? Or do we have to worry about Hicks and Yanni now?"

"I hope not," she said, "but I think about it. I do think about it."

"What matters," Catlin said, "isn't all who. It's why. Does the *why* still exist?"

There was another small silence.

"Power," Amy said. "It was about power. The question is on what scale. Jordan wanting out. Or Denys wanting in."

It was a little creepy, sitting and listening to your best friends figuring who'd want to kill you. "There's a long list," Ari said. "Power's one. Revenge, in her case, maybe. But no, I don't count it solved. I'm quite sure Jordan didn't do it."

"You moved him into Wing One."

"Justin did, actually. And Jordan's behaving himself pretty well. He wrote a tape-set that's driving me crazy, because I think there *isn't* a bug in it. I'm sure he's laughing. And if there is and I just fail to find it—" She let her voice trail off and gave a shrug. "Better in Wing One, which is watched, than over in Ed with all the traffic. Construction's starting in Wing One. Remodeling all over the Wing. It's not going to be very active for the next year. But by the time we're through, it'll be up to the standard we hope to set. So, for that matter, will Strassenberg. Every place we build, we do it right the first time."

"Are we sure about that company?" Will asked.

"Fourstar, which is doing Wing One? They got a good contract and don't have to live in bunkers. Soft job, comparatively. They shouldn't be discontent. But we'll just have a deeper look, as Catlin says."

"So are you going to go after remodeling Ed, next?"

"It's not as bad as Wing One," Ari said, and shifted in her seat, thinking, I won't have that much time, that much budget. "We're going to have to earn our way into the next major project, though."

"We cost a lot," Mika said. "A whole lot. This place is incredible."

"You earn it," Ari said. "You're important. Whatever you're doing, you see things, you hear things, you say things. Just never, never forget you're tied to me, more conspicuously than ever in your lives. Be careful. Just be very, very careful about getting into situations, going places alone . . . that's the price you pay for this place. Don't be alone down at the docks, down in the town, down where the security is just a little less. Let my staff know where you'll be, when you'll be: just a convenience for Florian and Catlin, Wes and Marco. They track you, in case you've never noticed."

"Who'd care," Yevgenia laughed, "if I went to my hairdresser?"

"We know you're there, though," Ari said soberly. "And if you didn't show up, we'd know. You'd get a call. If you didn't answer it, someone would come looking. I don't say it'll always be like this, but it will for a while. Expect it. Expect nerves to be pretty taut."

"Is there a reason we should know?" Maddy asked.

"Just—politics," Ari said. "The Council election's about to come down to the wire . . . they're going to read the results probably on the twenty-fifth. We think Spurlin's got it, but if Khalid should win, that's a problem. Two different philosophies in the military. Khalid's not that careful about observing registration when he goes after information—sees no reason he shouldn't be able to inquire into Science, or Citizens, or just anybody he doesn't like. Particularly Science. Don't get me started on Khalid."

"But Spurlin's got it."

"Safely so, we think. He'd have carried Fargone by a big majority, no question, *after* the new Reseune build at Fargone passed in Council: all those jobs going there, and Spurlin was supporting Jacques voting for it in Council while Khalid was up on the station and not really doing much of anything. Unfortunately the vote was already in progress on Fargone before much of that news had gotten there . . . unfortunate timing, but we're hearing there was some favorable impact during the last two days of the balloting. Whether any large number of military was excited enough to go in and change their vote before the deadline, I don't know, but we think the news did help Spurlin."

"But is there that much military at Fargone?" Mischa asked, and Tommy dug an elbow back this time.

"The whole big hospital installation," Tommy said. "Which I bet is big enough."

"It's a classified major lot of votes, say—partly because it's supporting an operation out at Eversnow. Trust me, it is large."

Eyes flickered, simultaneous registry of a tidbit of information on the existing universe.

"The whole military base out there," Amy said. "Too covert to vote?"

"So far," Ari said. "They can't admit they exist. So they can't vote."

"You know, when Eversnow goes into official operation," Amy said, "that's going to take nearly two years to get a vote through."

"Going to matter who's Proxy Councillor-designate when that happens," Ari said. "It already does, but it's going to matter a lot more. I like that argument. I'll use it on Yanni the next time we have a fight about Eversnow. If humankind goes stringing off down Yanni's route to new stars, we're going to have elections that last a lifetime. God! That's more entertainment than the universe needs."

"Just cross our fingers about Khalid," Amy said. "I certainly hope you're right."

"I hope I am, too," she said. And meant it. Passionately.

BOOK THREE   Section 4   Chapter iii

JULY 18, 2424
1829H

"The office all right?" Jordan had asked, for openers.

"Fine," Justin had said guardedly.

And all through dinner they hadn't talked politics, for once. Jordan talked about psychsets. They, Jordan, Grant, Paul and Justin, talked for two hours about design and sets and things that would bore the adjacent tables in Farrell's to unconsciousness.

It was the best evening they'd had since Jordan had come home.

And it didn't end in a fight. They walked back via the open air, in balmy night temperatures, walked into Wing One, which lately smelled of paint and plaster, and continued the conversation for a moment in front of the lift, which they hadn't called.

"Last night you'll be buying dinner," Jordan said. "I'm applying to go on salary."

"Seriously?" That wasn't the right word. Justin tried to find one, and didn't.

"I'd expect better than that."

"Excellent news," Grant supplied.

"I'm taking refresher tape," Jordan said. "I'm trusting not to be mindbent. So far so good."

"I can't tell you how glad I am to hear it," Justin said. "Dad, that's great."

"All I have to get," Jordan said, "is your little dear's approval."

That wasn't so great.

"You don't think I can."

"What have you sent her? Dad, this isn't some game, is it?"

"Why in hell would you think it's a game? I don't think it's a game."

"Dad." He stopped himself, held up a hand. "I'm glad. All right."

"Good," Jordan said, and punched the lift call button. "You can talk her into it."

"Dad, either your designs will, or I can't."

"Oh, I'm sure of my design. I'm very sure of it. How sure are you?"

"Dammit. Just one evening—just one evening can we manage not to have a quarrel—"

The car arrived. Opened. Jordan stepped in. So did Paul. "Want to come upstairs and explain why you won't back it?"

"I will, dammit. I have to read it first."

"Those two statements are contradictory," Jordan said. "Make up your mind, can't you?"

Jordan had let the button go. The doors shut. The car left, upward bound, and their way was back to the U and the Alpha Wing gateway.

"Damn," Justin said.

"He has improved, however," Grant said. And they walked in silence.

Which lasted until they'd gone through security and ridden their lift up to their floor in Alpha Wing.

It lasted until they reached their own front door, across from hers, and reached their bedroom, and started getting ready for bed.

"Damn, damn, and damn," Justin said. "*Why* is he like that?"

"You're the closest to his psychset," Grant said, "at foundational level, at least."

"Not lately. Ari works the deep sets, doesn't she?"

"Maybe he's trying to find out what she did," Grant said. "Sounds like a probe to me."

"Meaning he's redirected his plan, not his objectives, and he's *still* a bastard."

"Meaning, perhaps, he wants to know if that indefinable born-man flux still bends in the directions he understands in you. He knows you don't like conflict. That's *very* different than he is. And, forgive me, he doesn't believe the impulse doesn't exist in you. He's fishing for it."

"Don't like conflict. Hell, I hated it when I was ten!"

"True," Grant said. "And *you* grew up with a man who has to have it. What's that going to do to an impressionable young mind?"

"Make my life hell."

"Do you want my opinion?"

"Definitely."

"Jordan had you born; he started out trying for psychogenesis. And when you got out of the cradle and onto two feet, he came face to face with his genes—his looks—his temper, which he doesn't control well. You two used to scare hell out of me . . . when we were seven. You had his temper. He had his temper. And when we were seven he gave you *me,* and you had to hold it in, because I got upset, and he told you so. Nasty little trick, that was. As I faintly understand the rules of born-man combat—that was fairly underhanded. It assured he could always win a fight. And we know he has one other quirk: he likes to fight, but he has to win all the fights, or he's going to be very unhappy. I can just go null. I did, if you recall, at certain times."

"I remember."

"Impossible for his replicate, however."

"I'd try to calm him down, to get you out of it."

"So it wasn't just Ari had a go at remodeling the Warrick psyche. He'd already blinked at creating his own double. He couldn't take the arguments. You were seven. And he just had to win, didn't he, or burst a blood vessel?"

It was certainly a point. He gazed at Grant, who had a momentarily earnest look, saw at least what made a certain grim sense.

"He ties you in knots," Grant said. "And you remain the one that can return the favor . . . if you ever would, but you never let that shoe drop. In the meanwhile, he ran afoul of another man who didn't like to lose."

"Giraud."

"Who hated him. And what the Nyes did to him was make him afraid for Paul."

He stared off across the room, seeing—seeing Giraud, and one of those small nasty rooms. Terror, when he didn't know where Grant was.

"You think he's lying about starting work again?"

"He may try. He may be trying. Or he may be trying something else. You're the great unanswered question to him. More than she is. He thinks he knows what *she* is; and he's likely wrong; and the fact he might actually see that is going to frustrate him more, because he can't prove what he thinks is true, is actually true. You completely frustrate him. You're supposed to *be* him, never mind he took the one step, reining in your very nicely adrenalized temper, that assured you *never* would be him. It's always amazed me how intelligent born-men, designers, can flux that far, that they can do something they know absolutely flies in the face of the result they want to get, and never expect it not to work out the way they want. If I designed an azi set like that, what would you tell me?"

"That it's a conflict."

"Beyond a simple conflict, born-man. It's a roaring great deep set/psychset mismatch."

He heaved a breath, found himself mentally shying away from the concept of going after Jordan with the same energy Jordan used on him—because, dammit, he knew that would be a blowup to end all blowups. "It's beyond a simple conflict. It's that two Jordans can't occupy the same space. Neither could two Aris. Psychogenesis works if one of the participants is dead."

"Please don't go that far."

"You're saying it's irresolvable."

"That the temper is there. That you either defuse it so it doesn't bother you at all, or you and he will continue to go at each other over the most minor of differences."

"That's grim."

"I, however, have faith in you," Grant said. "You're *better* than he is and you have no need to prove it to him. Just don't let him suspect it, is all. He's competitive, if you've missed that."

"But how can I *live* with him?"

"That," Grant said, "is going to be a lasting problem."

He didn't sleep well. He lay staring at the water-rippled ceiling, trying to find some null point in the fractal patterns, but his mind was awake and racing.

He laid out mental patterns for a living. He cured azi problems, when something had gone wrong. He'd never cured his own, which was that gut-deep knot that happened when he got into an argument. He'd always assumed, assumed, because that was the watershed point of his life, that the first Ari had set that into him, a flinch away from anger.

But Grant had handed him a key, a memory that hadn't been that significant, until he recalled—past the towering dark of that night in Ari's apartment—that Jordan *had* told him that, the day he gave him Grant for his own responsibility.

Responsibility.

Hostage. With the very proper advice that he couldn't let his temper go again, not with Grant.

Possibly Jordan had given him that responsibility completely cold-bloodedly, seeing it as a way to win the argument with a matching temper, which had been, admittedly, out of control: Jordan reined it in for Paul. He had to for Grant. It was symmetrical, wasn't it?

God, he thought. There was a saying in Reseune, that a designer with himself for a patient was a damned fool. There was a reason there was a psych overseeing psych operators. There was another saying among designers, to the effect that CITs were a guaranteed bitch-up. He'd had Jordan's temper. He'd traded it for a gut-deep knot; and Jordan didn't get mad at Paul—Jordan just made Paul suffer the effects of Jordan's getting mad at everybody else—of Jordan's getting mad at himself, very possibly, but mostly just battering himself against anything that opposed him. No compromise with the universe. Jordan was a Special, a certified genius at what he did, but Jordan had reached a point with a seven-year-old where he'd couldn't win the fight. So he'd just shut it down.

And Ari, with her own very active temper, had gotten hold of that situation and jerked it sideways . . . with much more cold calculation, and more accuracy, maybe, than Jordan had been capable of using. He'd had a brain. His ideas had been fairly well out-there: Jordan had a habit of getting impatient with his what-ifs and shutting them down, hard. Damned nonsense, was what Jordan called his ideas. Ari had called them interesting.'

He squeezed his eyes shut, trying to control the immediate visuals. Trying to shut Ari down and get Jordan in some kind of perspective, as not a bad man—just a hard-headed one who'd tried to steer him into a Jordan-esque path.

And God knew what Jordan's own upbringing had been—a father brusque, emotionally shut down, very much on facts as he interpreted them to be: he had gotten that impression, at least, of the man who was, in a sense, his real father, since he was Jordan's: mother—there had been, obviously, since Jordan himself wasn't a clone: but nobody that had stayed; maybe nobody who'd even been there: people who died in the early days—sometimes left legacies in lab. Ended up being the gene donors for the foundational azi lines. Jordan's mother could have been cells in a dish, for all the record he'd ever laid hands on.

Didn't make him unhappy, in the sense that he'd always been just as content to be like Grant, who was fairly perfect, in his eyes, both motherless and fatherless. He'd always been content to be Jordan's Parental Replicate. But it was a question, whether if there'd been another influence in Jordan's growing up, if Jordan would have grown up with a little doubt that one truth covered everything in the universe.

Jordan got the law from his father; Jordan tried to replicate *himself*, that was the damned key. Jordan hadn't

started with the concept of a kid who'd have his own
notions—Jordan had tried to trim off any bits that didn't
match him . . . had fixed him on Grant, the way he'd fixed
on Paul, only in that household there'd been room for only
one personality, and nobody could argue with it.

CIT. Designer. And thorough bitch-up. No question.
Ari could stand him off temper for temper. But she hadn't
been able to work with him.

She'd conned him, was what. She'd conned Jordan
into the whole concept of a psychological replicate, then
snatched the result and did a job on it.

He lay there, totally null for a moment, asking if it really hurt as much as it once had. Thinking that—if not for
Ari—he'd have made Grant into Paul.

Which couldn't happen, because Grant wasn't Paul.
And she'd gotten Jordan to accept Grant, because it was
so damned hard to *get* an alpha companion, and the labs
had had only one—that she'd created, knowing right then
and there what should have been so, so clear to Jordan—
that Grant wasn't Paul. Grant wasn't compliant. Grant was
a fine, fine piece of work, who had taken his own path and
already begun to drag a young born-man sideways. Jordan
might have laid down Grant's early programs, but not his
absolute earliest, preverbal ones; and beyond that—Grant
had just—self-directed. Psychologically, endocrine level
and all, stable as they came, and an intellect that might
well get beyond him.

Ari's best. Ari's near-last project, right along with the
design that would replicate herself. Thank God for Grant.
Thank Ari.

He just had to think what to do about Jordan.

And maybe he had to be a damned fool, and do a bit
of work on himself, try to unwire that clenched-up anger,
and figure out where to send the adrenaline rush Jordan
provoked in him. Just thinking about it set him off. And
set him to work.

Calm down, first. Take the energy out of it. Find a place
to put it. Don't shut it down. That makes the knot. Find a
place to use it.

Create. Think. There's energy in flux. There's creative
potential in things that don't match.

Grant turned over. "Are you still awake?"

"Thinking," he said.

"Thinking good things or bad things?"

"I'm working on that," he said. "I'm not going to let Jordan bring himself down. How long has it been since Paul took tape, I wonder?"

"Probably not in a long while." Grant set a hand on his shoulder. "Justin. Mess with Paul and you're taking a very large chance. He's not stable. And you're not his Supervisor."

He shook his head. "I'm not. And he won't trust me. But Paul's storing tension the way a battery stores power. Paul's not right. So Jordan's not right. Jordan's Worked Paul. But the conditions Jordan imagines to exist, don't, so the world he's made Paul live in—doesn't exist. And Paul sees it. I think Paul sees it, and doesn't know how to fix it."

Grant considered that a moment. "That could be."

"You have a sense of him."

"I have an azi's sense of him, which I think is accurate. Storing tension, very much so. But the wrong Intervention could do damage. Might lead to shutdown."

Grant had been there. Grant had been through that. It was Grant's own watershed experience, more so even than the sojourn with the Abolitionists.

"It's a plan, at least. Jordan's wound tight, protecting Paul. But he's only adding to the tension. There's a hell of a lot wrong in that relationship. They're wound up together. I don't know where to take hold of it. I don't know I should, until the chance happens, until I know what Paul's mental state is."

"I can't read him well enough," Grant said. "The other night, the first night they were in the black and white apartment, Paul was dipping in and out of shutdown, just skimming it. Creating his own calm-down."

He remembered it. He'd taken it for overload—max stress, even on an alpha. Listening. But Grant intimated Paul hadn't been listening, hadn't been processing, hadn't been recording, at certain intervals.

"That's information," he said. "Watch him. Watch him. See what you can figure."

"I will," Grant said. "Just—be careful with him."

"I will," he said.

He didn't know if he could do anything, that was the thing. Real-time work froze him up. I was a problem that Jordan might have given him, right along with the genes. The stress of it might even be Jordan's problem, which Paul had absorbed. It was a damn interlock.

But he had to try. And, God, if Jordan caught him at it—

Hell didn't half describe it. He *wasn't* as important to Jordan as Paul was. He'd accepted that fairly unemotionally, since, in point of fact, Jordan wasn't as vital to him as Grant was, and he knew which he'd choose.

Maybe he ought to—choose, that was. Go to Ari, tell her it wasn't working, couldn't work. Put Jordan back in Planys, give him something to do there, let him and Paul live their lives.

But he couldn't do it. That was the hell of it. He was like Jordan, stubborn on an issue, and he had to try.

BOOK THREE   Section 4   Chapter iv

JULY 20, 2424
1722H

The item alert was blinking on the screen, and Ari clicked it.

Mail alert, it said . . . some sender she'd specifically tagged to trigger the alert flasher, and that was a very, very short list.

She clicked again.

And her breath quickened. Cyteen Station in the sender line, Fargone Station as home address, via the merchanter *Candide,* docking in the last two minutes—a ship's black box had just dumped its contents to Cyteen Station in orbit over their heads, and a longed-for letter, at least one letter, had flown down the datastream to Reseune. Via protocols established in Alpha Wing, a reply to *her* letter opened the gateway, straight to Base One.

Click. *Three* letters. One from Oliver AOX Strassen. Ollie was still alive.

One from Valery Schwartz. Her heart danced.

One from Gloria Strassen. That wasn't so welcome. But she'd had to write to Gloria and to Julia just to be fair.

Discipline. Ollie outranked everybody. She read his letter first.

Dearest Ari, it said. Nobody called her dearest, but Ollie did. *I received your invitation and very sympathetically understand the frame of mind in which you sent it, I do think. I remember you as Jane's daughter, and with the utmost affection. But I must decline your kindness on several accounts.*

First and most of all, Fargone is home, now. It was Jane's home and mine, my best memories are here, and I have responsibilities that fill my time very usefully—ultimately useful to you, I hope.

Second, if things are going well for you, your direction is no longer Jane Strassen's, but Director Emory's, and you will be more comfortable in that role if I am not close by to prompt you to be that little girl again. I know you will be as intelligent as the great Dr. Emory, I hope you will be at least as wise, and I hope you will be good, but the meeting cannot satisfy me, or you. If I were still azi, that statement of logic would cause me no pain; but since I have become CIT, it has to pain us both. Let us remember those days as happy as they were, and keep that happiness in our mutual past, unchanged.

I must add one other matter: I know you have invited the Schwartzes and the Strassens to Reseune. I hesitate to be so blunt, but use caution. Jane's relatives have been outspokenly bitter about their forced residency on Fargone: Valery Schwartz has grown up in close association with the Strassens. His mother is deceased, eleven years ago: a drug overdose which is inexplicable as an accident. Young Schwartz may or may not elect to accept your invitation: he is known here in the art community and has a reputation in deeptape experientials—an art which I have only lightly sampled, given my own character and origins. I am ad-

vised there are psychological considerations to prolonged exposure to these arts. Please use caution. I enclose files, in hopes you are surrounded by competent security—you surely must be, and I hope I know by whom.

Ollie had never met Florian and Catlin. He couldn't have. Except the originals.

I do hope you are well, dear Ari. I hope the very best for you. I knew about love before I ever had the final tape, and I have been a very lucky man, to have loved Jane and to have loved you, as still I do.

It hurt. It stung her eyes, that last. She did understand why he said no. She expected a refusal from him, for many of the reasons he'd just given. But not—not quite that she was, in one sense, just an episode of his life, and that he'd valued a life where she just hadn't been.

And she wasn't too surprised about Gloria, who had been a brat, and who was still probably a petulant brat. And Julia—Julia was the one who'd had real reason to hate her, for displacing her and her baby and getting them both exiled to Fargone. That Julia had hated her and talked against her was no surprise, and not even unfair, in the balance of things. Ollie was just worried about her, was all, because he still loved her. It wasn't as if Julia Strassen was going to launch some interstellar conspiracy against Reseune.

But the business about Valery's mother, and Valery growing up with Gloria, of all people—that was just upsetting. She'd never heard that Valery's mother had died. And he'd become an artist, of all things. She'd never guessed that, either. She'd never searched him up on the web, not wanting to go down that path and go longing after someone she couldn't get back, and she'd never imagined he was halfway famous. It was the first she'd ever heard of who he'd become . . . and you needed clearance and funds to do a Universal Search, which Florian and Catlin hadn't had when she'd sent those letters. She hadn't asked Yanni, who could have done it—Valery was Yanni's nephew, sort of, but so far as she knew, Yanni hadn't ever bothered searching his niece up. Yanni had never said, for that matter, how he felt about having his relatives sent off to Fargone, all to bring Ariane Emory up in a bubble free of Valery Schwartz.

Had Yanni resented it?

Had he—God!—even *suggested* their exile, the way he probably had suggested sending Jordan to PlanysLabs?

That was a disturbing thought. She had no window into the time when Denys and Giraud had run Reseune along with Yanni Schwartz, and critical decisions had been made—first to put her with Jane Strassen, and then to take her Maman away; and to let her play with Valery; and then to send Valery away . . .

Had Yanni consented? Been participant? Instigator?

Yanni'd never said. Never, ever said. And he'd known she'd written to Valery.

Hadn't he? She thought he'd known. She hadn't taken any measures for secrecy from him.

It could have been a mistake, her visiting the past and sending for people who'd had separate lives for decades.

It could really have been a bad, bad mistake—that cold, clammy thought crept through her.

She'd intended to open Gloria's letter next, saving the good news, from Valery, for last. Ollie's return hadn't worked out. But she stuck to the plan. She clicked Gloria's letter.

Dear Ariane, it began, on a first name basis, when to her memory, Gloria had been a screaming, red-faced hellion, three years younger than she was. That made Gloria around—fifteen, now. Which was too young for Valery. So there. *Maman says if I want to visit I can. So I will. Maman has decided she's coming with me to keep me out of trouble. I don't remember Reseune, so this should be interesting, and Maman says . . .*

Hell if Julia was Maman. That was Jane Strassen's name. *Her* word. But that was the way Gloria put it.

. . . Maman says if we come it's only because it's round trip and we can get home again. So we hope you don't mind if we just stay a few months.

Gloria was uncommonly direct. Ari-like in her bluntness, not too diplomatic, but then she'd never been convinced either Julia or Gloria had anything like Jane Strassen's intellect. Tact or graciousness just were not in her expectations of Gloria.

There was a thought . . . the first time it had ever dawned

on her, though she'd had the notion that Julia just wasn't
that smart. And Jane had been. And Gloria had been a
little squalling lump.

Maman hadn't started out wanting her. Maman had
had Julia, counted that enough. But they'd handed Jane
Strassen a kid who *was* on her level, plus some, namely
her . . . and Jane Strassen had accepted her for one reason,
and been hooked into the most important study project in
her long career. She'd taken her in, taken to her, shoved
her own biological offspring and her own grandchild off—
partly because she'd had to, because Julia kept being a fool
and pushing the issue, and insisting on pushing it . . . which
was how Julia had gotten a not-roundtrip ticket for herself
and Gloria to Fargone.

So it was true. Maman had loved her. Not Julia.

Then Maman—Jane Strassen—had gone out to Fargone to live, to spend her last days with Ollie, and Julia
and Gloria. Maman had been very old, and knew she
didn't have that long: Julia was the child of her last good
decades, tank-born; and Maman had gone out there to
live, and spent those few final years—how?

Had Maman ever warmed at all to Julia and Gloria?

How had Ollie fit in, and had Ollie protected Maman,
the way he'd always protected Maman, from untoward
incidents? Ollie would have done that; Ollie would have
stood them off at the door.

And Ollie had ended up Director of ReseuneSpace,
with all the power to handle anything Julia Strassen could
ever think up, that was what. That was *justice*.

Oh, there were questions she should have asked.

Oh, there were questions she definitely should have.

*So I suppose we owe you thank you for the tickets and
we'll see you as soon as we tie up a few things here. I've
never been on a ship before. Maman said it's nothing
much, but I'm excited.*

Best thing she'd ever heard about Gloria.

Deep breath. She punched the button on Valery's
letter.

It exploded on the screen; became white light, a black
blot that ran everywhere and left an impression on the
eyes, a red, lingering glow. It hurt.

The glow had the shape of a face when she shut her eyes. She thought it looked male, but she wasn't sure. It was a furious, murderous face.

God, how had Base One let *that* through?

On her damned e-trail, that was how, her blanket permission for any letter answering her letter. *There* was a warning, a cold, chilling warning. Her sig had power to crack the electronic gates of Base One, on which the security of all Reseune, hell, all *Union* rested. And she had to be more careful, hereafter.

A letter had turned up in the wake of the image, an ordinary letter. *Dear Ari,* it said. With that hellish face still blinking faintly red in her vision.

Dear Ari, hell! If that damned thing had brought anything pernicious in with it . . .

Base security search, she told Base One. *Focus: Candide packet in Base One, all activity, all files.*

Base One set about its business. The letter remained.

I wondered if you remembered. Clearly you do. Thanks for the offer. It presents me a mild dilemma. I have a reputation here in the art world, and your offer would both bring new opportunities and take me out of an area where I have considerable commercial value. I do have to consider, however, that your patronage is no small matter, and if I could be assured of creative freedom and your patronage during my establishment at Reseune, or in Novgorod, your support of my work would be invaluable.

Not a shred of soft sentiment. *Creative freedom. Patronage* during his *establishment . . .*

She let a slow breath go. Temper had gotten up, since the fright. Adrenaline helped nothing.

So I will be arriving for an exploratory visit and hope to renew old acquaintances.

Oh, to be sure. Sit in the damned sandbox and I'll lend you my shovel, Valery. Damn your presumption. My *patronage!* Bloody *hell* if I'll be used!

At first blush, she was just mad, damned mad, as Justin would put it. And then just generally upset.

Was that *thing,* that grinning devil gone to black in her vision—was *that* the experiential artform? Was *that* what Valery was now?

And connected to Gloria?

It *wasn't* who she'd thought she was inviting back to Reseune, to do justice for, and about.

They'd had lives out there, at a place that wasn't quite real to her. All these years of her life and theirs had gone by, and Ollie might be the same, and maybe Julia was, but they weren't, not Gloria and not Valery, and in directions she hadn't anticipated. She'd made a mistake.

But ships took months in passage—her letters to them had taken months in passage; their replies had taken months coming back, and by the time the reply got to her—her three invitees were already on a ship on the way here.

Damn!

BOOK THREE   Section 4   Chapter v

JULY 22, 2424
0834H

It was a luxurious office. It had the view from the cliffs on a windowlike screen—Justin liked it; Grant liked it. They were glad it was a feature. There was a little guppy tank in the corner—they'd had to laugh about that. It made this move, the last move, they hoped, a little more thoughtful. And their wall had a seascape, a strange thing to contemplate, sunlight through a breaking wave, vastly different colors than the yellow froth and desolate sands of Novgorod's shoreline—which nobody wanted to visit.

"It's from Earth," Grant had surmised.

It could even have been Novgorod's shore, when they first landed. Getting back to that would take the native microlife eating all the terrestrial microlife—and native life had a chance of doing that, now. In their own lifetime, one really good thing Denys had done was join Moreyville and Novgorod in cleaning up the Novaya Volga, building the coffer-dam and the treatment plant—probably it had taken the form of a deal, but Reseune stayed cleaner, and the river did, each in their own way. Some things did get better. He liked to think of the picture that way. Grant said he liked it.

So he could say yes, they loved it, when Ari asked the question. "Very nice."

She wanted her lessons, as she called it, which consisted now of their working over sets. And she brought him things, her designs, her questions—good questions, that, if there were no Jordan anywhere on the horizon, would have kept him happily working for days.

As it was—

"Ari," he said, when she arrived for her lesson today, and settled in with them, supplied with coffee and a morning cookie, and the tranquility of the room notwithstanding, his heart was beating overtime, doubt about what he wanted to do, doubt about how she'd take it—doubt about what sort of mess he was opening up to her.

But he couldn't get what he wanted on his own. And he knew everything it could provoke, if it got back to Jordan, and everything it could provoke if Ari got too interested in it.

"Ari, I want a particular manual. Say it's an actual current personal manual. It was once confiscated in security, in a computer. Can you get it?"

She held the coffee mug like a little kid with a cocoa, in both hands, and brought it down when he asked that question.

"We're not talking about my getting Grant's."

"No," he said. In point of fact, he was sure she had that.

"Paul's?" she asked, straight to the mark, in a very limited range of likely manuals he'd be interested in, and he nodded.

"I can crack his storage," she said. "No question. I haven't, lately. I *have* the manual."

Chilling confession. Honest, absolutely honest with him. He *hadn't* expected the last, and realized he should have expected it. Probably ReseuneSec had its own supposedly current copy. Yanni had. Hell, there must be half a dozen copies floating about various offices.

"It's mostly done in hand-notes," he said carefully. "I'd be surprised if not."

"Not surprisingly," she said, "I've skimmed it. A lot of cryptic notes, a personal code."

"Not surprisingly," he agreed.

She didn't ask the obvious question. She was being very good. *His* Ari . . . was being very good. And had several questions, likely, questions that would set her on her own quiet search.

"We're worried about Paul," he said. "Grant is worried about Paul."

She looked from him to Grant. Grant said; "I'll let Justin do the talking."

"I want a copy of the manual," Justin said, "and I want Jordan and Paul not to know it."

"You'll have it ten minutes after I get home. Now, if you really want it."

"It's possible I can read his notes," he said, feeling ashamed of himself the whole way, going behind Jordan's back, offering to open up a system that might reveal other things. "I used to be able to." If he gave her the translation of the notes, and she might demand them—it would be a Rosetta stone for the rest, for anything he'd encoded. Total key, to anything ReseuneSec currently couldn't read. And he *didn't* want to know the rest, and he didn't want to betray Jordan, and he *wanted* to ask the best mind of this age and the last one what he could do to fix what was the matter with Paul—but doing that would open up everything to her. Not just the manual. All the notes. All Jordan's work.

And Jordan was hellishly protective of his ideas, his work—and her getting her hands on Paul—it was Jordan's nightmare.

"I'm going to ask you for it," he said to her, "and let me see if I can read it. And I'm going to ask you—not to ask me for the shorthand he uses."

A little silence ensued. Ari thought about it, and had another sip of coffee, one-handed, this time, the other hand idle, elbow on chair arm . . . an attitude so, so like the first Ari that it chilled.

Eyes flicked up to his, and broke contact, self-protective, keeping thoughts private, as she nodded. "All right."

"Ari, it's not that I don't trust you. It's what I owe *him*."

"I won't ask you another question," she said. "And you know that's hard for me."

"If I can't make sense of it," he said, "I may come back to you."

"You're good," she said, and oh, those eyes flickered like the activity-LEDs on a processor. She was. Processing. "If you do need me, ask. But it's all yours."

"You're a—"

"Justin, if you say 'good kid,' all bets are off."

"A good human being," he amended that, unspoken. "You are."

"I like that." She smiled somberly. "I take that one. Grant, am I a good human being?"

"You're a fine sample of the born-man sort," Grant said, not too somberly. "Or you seem so to me. It's beyond me to critique, beyond that."

She smiled. The moment passed. She finished off the cooling coffee, and rotated her chair and poured herself another cup. "It's a two-cup morning. I've been so damn busy with the move I haven't got a thing done on the last set. I read the last of it this morning. But I've got one I want you to look at."

"It wouldn't be Jordan's, would it?" Justin asked.

She had her sip. "Actually, it is. He told you about it?"

"He mentioned it. I was going to ask, actually."

"So we're doing a Jordan morning," she said, and pulled out a convenient keyboard and touched the voice button, called the file, which was beta, and correspondingly large. "That's it. Shall I store to Projects?"

"Do it," Justin said. "Do you have some particular questions?"

"I don't," she said. "It's a management tape, the type's capable of an accurate memory and a strong work ethic. It's just typical Jordan: I've looked at his work, at least skimmed through several, and it's not old stuff—it's using the modern interlinks, using them very appropriately. It's a nice nested set of calls that play off secondary sets, don't conflict with deep sets . . . I'm not finding a—"

Com went off. A worried look crossed her face.

"Not supposed to—" she began, which meant it was her Urgent list, the handful of people who could call her at any hour, and about that time there was a knock at the office door.

Grant started to get up. But Florian came on through.

"Sera," Florian said, and the buzz from Ari's com continued. "Sera."

"Report," she said, and Florian said,

"Spurlin is dead."

Ari froze just a heartbeat, then located the phone, thumbed it on and said: "Ari."

"Sera." It was Catlin's voice.

"Florian told me. Details?"

"Found by the maid this morning," Catlin's voice came through. *"Cause of death uncertain. Last contact yesterday night by the night staff at his residence. That's all that's known currently. Possible natural causes."*

"Possibly not," Ari said. Her face was just a little pale. "I'm coming home," she said.

Spurlin. Candidate in Defense. Khalid's opposition. The one the polls said was in the lead by a wide margin. It wasn't good news.

"Justin, I'm sorry," Ari said, and set down a mostly full cup of coffee and snatched up her jacket.

She left with Florian, leaving Jordan's file up on the computer. Justin shut it down, and looked at Grant.

"This is bad," he said, and tried to think what the constitution said about a candidate dying after the vote was taken. "If he wins—does it go to his Proxy-designate? Or what?"

"Don't ask me, born-man. It's your system. I certainly hope it has an answer."

"I don't even know if he's got a Proxy-designate. *God,* I don't want that bastard in. This is one time I wish the Nine were elected by general ballot." He turned to the console, keyed Voice, said, "Search: Constitutional law: elections: Council of the Nine: candidate death."

The computer didn't take long. It flashed up a lengthy piece of legal language.

"Search in document: if an elected candidate dies; second condition: before official announcement of results of election: question: who succeeds?"

The computer took about a heartbeat. The answer flashed up:

1.) Current office-holder may hold office for entirety of vacated term.

2.) Current office-holder [a] may appoint Proxy Councillor [b], service of [b] to run concurrent with [a]'s term of office.

3) Current office-holder [a] may leave office at end of [a]'s previously elected term, in which case the runner-up [b] in the election may succeed to office and serve for the two-year term.

4) In the case of death of all candidates and the incumbent, the office settles on the Secretary of the Bureau, to run for the elected term.

5) Announcement of results irrelevant. Delivery of all precinct results to Cyteen Station data storage constitutes valid election. Exception: conditions of war or natural disaster preventing the transmission of or timely arrival of precinct results to Cyteen Station will, after one month, disallow those precincts from the result tally. The tally of results at Cyteen Station will proceed on that date and results will be official as of 0001h on the expiration of the deadline for receipt of ballots. Exception: a quorum of precincts [66%] must arrive by one month after the expected date. Failure of a quorum of precincts to report by one month after the expected date will invalidate the election, in which case current officeholders will continue in office as if re-elected.

Precedents: no dates, no instances available.

"It says," Justin began.

"I have it," Grant said grimly. "A first in Union history, it seems."

"Jacques is all prepared to resign," Justin said. "But the proxy can only be valid if he stays in office."

"Is that actually a problem?" Grant asked.

"I don't know," Justin said. "It's certainly better than the alternative."

A light flashed on the screen. Ari. He keyed it. It wasn't a message. It was the arrival of the manual he'd requested. The universe was tottering, peace and war possibly at issue, and she remembered his document. He understood

that mind. She probably didn't even strongly register doing
it—it was just on her agenda and it went, probably with
three and four other things and the staff requests, because
that mind was clearing chaff, fast, not for an emergency
response, but for a policy consideration.

Call to Yanni was next. He'd bet on it.

BOOK THREE   Section 4   Chapter vi

JULY 22, 2424
0911H

"Yanni?" Ari said.

"I have the report," Yanni's answer came back to her.
Yanni was already in his office, ordinary day begun. It
wasn't an ordinary day.

"Natural causes?"

"Still in question."

"I'm questioning it. This isn't good."

"Understatement," Yanni said. "Listen, I've got a call
in to Jacques. Hicks has people on the way to Jacques,
who's still at home."

"Have we had contact with him?"

"He knows."

"Thank God he's alive. Keep him that way."

"We're working on that. I'm ordering up Reseune
One."

She drew a deep breath. "Yanni, what you need to do
you can do from here."

"Impossible."

"Not impossible."

"Appearances, Ari. I have to get to the capital. There's
no question of it."

"I want agents with Lynch. Fast."

"I'm ahead of you on that one. Hicks has got a team
headed for his office, too. They'll do all driving, all transport, all meals."

"*Hicks.* Yanni, I'm not that confident in Hicks. He makes mistakes."

"It happens to all of us."

"I'm saying I don't trust him, Yanni! If we lose Lynch, you lose the proxy, and we revert, God, where *do* we revert? The Secretary for Science?"

"That would be it," Yanni said, "who would immediately reappoint me Proxy Councillor and I'd be back in. I'm damned hard to get rid of, so don't worry too much."

"Not if you're not in Novgorod, I don't need to worry too much, and I don't want you to go."

"The man could have had a heart attack."

"And you know he didn't. Yanni, I can't lose you. I *can't.* You want me trying to figure things out day to day and running everything into the ground. You're risking too much. Easier to send *me,* for God's sake. I'm duplicatable. Your knowledge isn't in databanks."

"Bad joke, young lady, and you're not going. I need to talk directly to Jacques and to Corain *and* to Lynch: there's no substitute in virtuality for a face-to-face. You know *that* or you don't know anything."

"Don't read me lessons, Yanni Schwartz. And don't be a damned fool. You know what I *can* do if you push me, and I'll do it!"

"Don't be a child. And that *is* being a child, Ari."

"Fine. You're not going."

"Ari, do I have to come there and have this out?"

"Don't bother. Reseune One isn't going to budge off the strip, so you might as well release your call on it. How is it going to look if you go flying in there to consult with the election results not even read yet? We may have to deal with Khalid. Let's not start it off with a media show and get caught in statements before we even know what the man died of. And let's *not* be caught negotiating with Corain before the man is buried. Or shot into the sun. Or whatever he wants done with him."

"Fine. And when they read the results, and it's Spurlin, then what do you think we're going to do? I've got to talk to Jacques, and I can't call him here to do it, because we can't have him step down. The man has a lucrative job lined up, he wants it, we bent his arm and *got* him that job to get him out of the post, and now he's got the offer, he wants it. He wants to be rich and comfortable and safe, and the man who's supposed to replace him just fucking died, pardon my language, but he *died,* he may have been murdered, and that's not going to dispose an old man ready to retire to stand his ground."

"This is Defense! He's a Marine officer!"

"He did his fighting mostly behind a desk, if you recall."

"Well, I *don't* personally recall the whole War, and you do, and that's just one of the reasons why I need you not-dead at the moment, Yanni. Call Jacques: tell him hold pat. Get them to hold the job for him. If anybody killed Spurlin, it'd look really peculiar if Jacques drops dead next, so he's safe. Tell him that. Maybe that will encourage him."

A silence on the other end. "I'm not sure it's quite illegal to bribe Jacques with a job, but it's not the sort of thing we want on the news, Ari."

"Well? We already have, haven't we, to get him not to run again? So now we change our minds and we bribe him to keep it until somebody besides Khalid can organize another challenge. Send Frank to tell him so. Frank doesn't get the attention you do."

"I'm not sending Frank."

"Why not? Because it's *dangerous?*"

"Ari, you're taking up my time and I've got business to do."

"That plane's not moving. Think of other ways to do it." She hung up on him. And immediately used Base One to put an executive hold on Reseune One, and to forbid fueling.

Then she put in a call to Amy and Maddy, and told them individually, but they'd already gotten the news, Amy had called Maddy, Amy and Maddy were both taking the morning off and stood ready to come back home. So did Tommy Carnath, Maddy said, who'd told Mischa, and most everybody else must be getting it on the news by now. Sam—Sam was still out on site. "Come here," she told Maddy. "Bring everybody."

And she called Rafael, and briefed him, with orders

to stand by. Florian and Catlin were more than briefed: they were in the security station with Wes and Marco, pulling up Novgorod data as fast as they could and monitoring police reports, which was all they could get out of Defense. Military Police were investigating, standing off the Novgorod authorities, Military Police currently under Councillor Jacques' direction . . . *that* was a damned uneasy arrangement. But there was one other investigative authority, and that was the Council of the Nine itself, with its Office of Inquiry, which *could* cross jurisdictional lines, and which reported straight to the Council.

She called Hicks. Personally. "We've heard the news," she said straight off to Hicks. "We want every whisper out of that situation, as fast as you get it. Route it to my security office. No matter if it's raw."

"I understand you, sera," Hicks said. "You'll have it as fast as we can produce it. Councillor Jacques has requested a Council inquiry, seconded by Councillor Lynch."

Lynch hadn't made a move in months—notoriously didn't act, deferring consistently to his Proxy, namely Yanni, who was Councillor in all but name: but Lynch had waked up this morning and made an actual motion to get at the facts, fast, and locally.

"Lynch is probably scared," she said disingenuously. "I'll imagine Yanni is moving to protect him."

"He is, sera," Hicks said.

"Yanni is in charge," she said. "I'm holding Reseune One ready, but it's staying grounded. Security concerns. Protect Yanni. He's not looking at his own safety. I'm looking at it for him."

"We're in agreement," Hicks said. "I'll trust if you hear anything, I'll get that advisement."

"I trust I'll hear it from you fastest," she said, and let him figure out what *that* meant, whether it was a compliment or an order. "Thank you, ser. I'll let you get on it."

She broke the contact. Sat staring at the police report. The Novgorod Police had the body; the Bureau of Defense wanted it; the Office of Inquiry demanded it be sent to the University, its usual recourse for scientific questions, and it was going on two hours since a frightened housemaid had found the body. By the minute, evidence was being lost.

At least the Bureau of Defense wasn't investigating it as an internal matter, and the Office of Inquiry was going to win. Nobody trumped them; and currently they'd sent a hearse to the District Coroner's office to collect Spurlin's remains. The COI had also put a lock on the potential crime scene, and taken steps to secure all computer records and recent communications. She drew part of that from the news and part fom the Office of Inquiry itself, which she could get to by passive inquiry, just riding Yanni's authority. She didn't lodge any requests. She just read.

And frowned at the screen, and asked herself what in hell they were going to do about it if something happened to Lynch, or worse, Jacques.

"Sera," Florian said from the doorway of her office. "The COI has taken physical custody of the body. They'll be at the University inside half an hour. They've assembled a team of experts."

"This is just bad," she said. "This is bad, Florian."

"Catlin would say there's a solution for it, sera."

"What? Go to the station and assassinate Khalid? And then somebody else comes after us?"

"We have no idea regarding that, sera."

"Come here." Her tone had been sharp. She regretted it. It was loss of control, but she felt less safe than she had felt a certain number of days ago. People died. Every time things reached a point of decision, people died, and everybody shifted places. Denys. That was her fault. His own fault. But Patil, and Thieu, upset Yanni's plans for things, and now Spurlin? Everything Yanni had put together was getting hammered by successive events, and the Eversnow business wasn't even underway yet.

Worse, much worse, it began to raise a specter of who-benefitted, and that answer was beginning to shape up in a very ugly fashion.

Florian came close. She got up from her desk and hugged him, took his face between her hands and saw slight puzzlement. "I'm not criticizing," she said. "Doing that *is* a possibility, a real one, if anything should happen to Yanni. If I take over, they'll be after me, and I don't trust that man."

"We think they already are after you," Florian said.

"They surely plan for contingencies. And, more than a contingency, you're a certainty, sera. You're a hundred-percent certainty unless someone stops you. And we won't permit that. None of us will permit that."

She certainly was a target. The first Ari had been. And it was the same thing she'd said to Yanni: she didn't remember the War. She didn't remember the Treaty of Pell. She just read about it. The fine textures of history just went away, the fabric lost its tensions and shredded until it didn't make thorough sense any more, and nobody knew now what the deeper part of the issues had been, except what they'd recorded during the actual negotiations.

But how could anybody of her generation pull all those hours of recorded history up, and listen to all of it, and understand it? You'd have to live all the hours of all those negotiations, and all the simultaneous other hours of every other record, and you still wouldn't get the gestalt of having grown up in it. You knew more, viewing it from the perspective of another generation, because the hidden things came out, but you knew less, too, because the context that made it all make sense had gone away. The first Ari had been somebody's target, and she'd died, but how could you know why she'd died without being there, and only Yanni and Jordan, of the people still living, had been real close to the facts . . .

And if Abban had done it, *how* had Abban gotten the notion? Abban was Giraud's shadow, not Denys'. And Giraud had mourned the first Ari. He'd loved her, she *knew* Giraud had loved the first Ari, so how had Abban possibly been the instrument of the other brother's policy?

"Sera?" Florian said in a hushed voice, and touched her hair, and looked at her the way she looked at him, only with more awareness than she'd had in the last few seconds. She felt half paralyzed, the way she felt when the brain started working and working and working, pulling things togther from one side of flux and the other, nothing matching . . . nothing making sense.

The first Ari died. Her Florian and Catlin died. Maman died. Giraud died. Denys died. Abban died. Seely died.

Thieu died. Patil died. Now Spurlin. Seven were killed by violence. Three had been old. And now there was Spurlin. The odds were definitely not with natural causes, when power passed from hand to hand.

"A lot of people have died," she said to Florian. "A lot of people. You can't count Denys and Abban and Seely. That was us pushing back when they pushed us. But your predecessors and mine . . . *why* would Abban be taking Denys' orders, if it was Abban that did it?"

"If Denys ran tape on him," Florian said. "If somebody good set it up. Denys had a lot of opportunity."

"Was he the only one who could?" she asked. Her hands had fallen to his shoulders. He was a safe haven, Florian was. "Who could get to him, else? Track that."

Fabric of history, all decayed, all the evidence, evaporating with every stray gust from a vent. The rime ice melted. The body went to the sun. People went on dying around the hinge-points of power. It had gone on a long, long time. Before any time she remembered, certainly.

"What priority?" Florian asked her. His hands were at her waist. He'd become a young man. He'd become what he was designed to be and he asked an important question: in the crisis of the moment, with Spurlin dead and Jacques' decisions in doubt and Lynch possibly next on somebody's list—what priority, the investigation of three twenty-year-old murders?

Absolute priority. It was the environment of her life. It was the reason she existed. Because she existed, all the others had died: her doing, or others' doing, because of her.

Some few were still alive, still in power, in various places. Some of them she trusted. And that could be deadly.

"High," she said. "See if it was investigated, that first. Then see how *well* it was investigated."

"We'll do that," Florian said.

She kissed him, not for any good reason, except it fuzzed the brain for a moment, and it felt good, and she wanted to feel good for a moment. She wanted to lie to her senses for a moment and say they were all safe.

But it wasn't true. The kiss was over and she sent him off to Catlin and Wes and Marco, and knew he'd do both—keep up with what was going on and investigate old history, both, if he and Catlin had to give up sleep.

They weren't safe. And the next few days were going to

be hard ones. Dangerous. She wasn't ready to take over. Yanni'd told her that. But events weren't going to wait for her. People were pushing, already, to get places and do things before she could possibly interfere and change the rules. People might die, in that push.

She couldn't prevent it. That was the point.

So far, she couldn't prevent it.

BOOK THREE   Section 5   Chapter i

JULY 24, 2424
0821H

Giraud and Seely and Abban all reached their twenty-third week. They swallowed ... their lungs developed more passageways, and blood vessels, which would one day soon be useful: the proximity of these structures to each other would ultimately make it possible to breathe. Right now they drew their oxygen through the bioplasm of the artificial womb itself. And it rocked, and moved, and occasionally received sounds, internally generated, which made muscles twitch. By now, the brains sent faint light stimuli to a particular center, and sound to another. Nothing was overload. Everything was even keel.

They each weighed about half a kilo, and looked human. Seely weighed a few grams more than Giraud, and was a few centimeters taller. Abban was larger, and weighed six grams more than Giraud. Proportionately, he always would be larger. But Giraud would overtake both in girth, and Seely in weight, before he was fifty.

They moved, they turned. They had their own agendas, based somewhat on what the womb was doing. But something different had happened. The two wombs that contained azi were active at scheduled times. The one that contained a CIT was completely random. Chaos was a part of Giraud's life now. Order had begun to assert itself in the other two. And that would always be true.

JULY 25, 2424
1931H

Probably every vid in Reseune that wasn't in a child's room was tuned to the Novgorod news channel. That was probably true up on Cyteen Station.

This election mattered—immensely: the balance of power between parties was at stake. And nobody knew the results yet. The computers were counting and recounting and running complex check routines.

Justin and Grant occupied themselves with a manual, at home, over pizza—the downstairs restaurant, named Seasons, had done mostly deliveries tonight, very likely. Ari was closeted with her staff across the hall. Justin had seen the deliveryman with a trolley full of other orders, mostly pizza, with one address designation on it, and that was Amy's apartment . . . so he had the notion a lot of people were there.

Yanni—Yanni wasn't home, or if he was, he was quiet about it. More likely he was in his office; and if Ari wasn't with her young friends for something this important, it was because Ari was busy and planned to be busy, whatever happened.

Himself, he just read through a great deal of Jordan's notes, exactly replicated: he'd already read the basic program. So had Grant. And he couldn't concentrate worth a damn, with the clock now thirty-three minutes past the anticipated hour of the announcement of results. So he skimmed ahead, looking for the last and next to last note Jordan had made on that manual. Sequence of note was determined by the outline of programming itself. But Jordan's handwriting had changed over twenty years, and he knew the way it had changed. It wasn't that hard to find the latest ones.

"Page 183.23," he said to Grant, a little troubled by what he saw.

Grant flipped pages, settled.

A little line appeared between Grant's brows.

The station had been playing old tape of Spurlin, discussing Gorodin's term as Proxy, Gorodin's death—natural causes, that; then commentators discussing Spurlin's suspicious death and the fact the special team at the University Hospital hadn't published a cause of death—discussing Khalid's last administration, familiar stuff to anybody who hadn't been living in the outback for the last ten years—including the famous argument with young Ari—over and over and over. They'd turned the audio way down.

But the breaking news flasher went on, and Justin said, "Minder, sound."

Audio came up. *"The five minute alert has been given. We are five minutes away from hearing the results of . . ."*

BOOK THREE　　　Section 5　　　Chapter iii

JULY 25, 2424
1940H

". . . the Bureau of Defense election," the vid said, and the web didn't get the results or relay them any faster—just the timelag between Cyteen Station, where the counting was done, and Novgorod, where the news station resided. Base One, directly receiving the satellite, was a fraction faster than the news station.

Microdifference, in the scheme of things. Ari forced herself to have a sip of water and waited as the minute counter ran. Florian and Catlin, Marco and Wes, and Theo and Jory all watched the big screen. Nobody said anything.

She had contingencies in mind. She hadn't said what they were, because she didn't want even her most intimate staff knowing what she'd do in certain instances, in case that what-she'd-do changed someday, putting staff at disadvantage.

Second sip of water.

The seconds ticked down. Two minutes and fewer.

She put a call through to Amy's apartment, where all the gang was. "Amy? Ari here."

Amy answered, nearly instantly. *"Ari?"*

"Listening, I take it. If it's Spurlin I'll send champagne down there. If it's Khalid—you're on your own. In either case—I'm going to be busy for a bit. Hang on."

"We're with you," Amy said.

Twenty-one seconds. Fifteen. Ten. Five.

The flasher came up, computer-generated, the actual tally of votes, and the result.

Spurlin by 65 percent.

"We elected the dead man," she said, and let go a breath as her staff visibly relaxed and as cheers erupted in Amy's apartment. "Just a second." She punched in Yanni's office while the gang celebrated. "Yanni."

"Told you," Yanni said.

"I told *you*," she said. "Go have a party. I have my own to go to."

"Not a tear for poor old Spurlin."

"What for? We got his revenge for him. Just carry on what we're doing."

The autopsy had come in. Delicate death. A scarcely detectible drug, administered in the morning coffee. Murder. Council hadn't wanted to announce that before the election. Now it was going to break, and occupy the news.

". . . incumbent Councillor Jacques," the news channel was saying, introducing its next speaker, and the staff paid absolutely silent attention.

"Jacques is on," she said to Yanni. "Let him finish. Then go get some sleep."

"I'll wait to hear all of it," Yanni said, and was silent while Jacques said . . .

"The Bureau of Defense mourns the passing of elected Councillor Spurlin, in which sentiment I know I am joined by candidate Vladislaw Khalid. The constitution provides that if a candidate for a Council seat dies between the clos-

ing of the polls and the reading of results, the incumbent Councillor for that bureau may, at his discretion, remain in office for the next term. I am opting to remain as Councillor for Defense. I will at a future date name a Proxy Councillor . . ."

Ari frowned. "Yanni."

"I heard."

". . . as I see fit. Let us all join in paying tribute to a man . . ."

And so on.

"Did he agree? Is he still going to name Bigelow?"

"I don't know what game he's playing," Yanni said. *"I'm going to find out, but, dammit, this isn't something for phone calls. Release the damned plane."*

Jacques, if Spurlin won posthumously, was supposed to have immediately named Gorodin's long-time aide, Vice Admiral Tanya Bigelow, as Proxy Councillor for Defense. All Jacques had to do then was warm that chair until they could organize another election, and Khalid, defeated, had to wait two years. It had all been handled.

Jacques had just gone sideways.

"Ari?"

"Khalid got to him," she said. "Khalid got to him. God, this isn't looking like Paxer business, Yanni. This *isn't.*"

"I've got to get down there," Yanni said. *"I'm taking plenty of security, but I have to get there. I have to talk to Jacques directly. Dammit, Ari, either take over right now, or don't. Don't try to steer from the passenger seat."*

She didn't want to agree. She saw the situation, however, just the same as Yanni. And he was right this time. Jacques was under threat, or he'd been paid off, and she'd guess the former.

"Yanni, I'll clear the flight. Protect Lynch. Above all, take care of yourself."

Florian and Catlin had come over to her, where she sat with the mini, linked into the minder. They had a much quieter manner than a few moments ago. Marco and Wes joined them, just stood and waited.

"Yanni's going to Novgorod," she said, "to talk to Jacques. Someone's gotten to him. Maybe Yanni can supply enough security to give him a little backbone. Khalid's people killed Spurlin, I'll bet on it. All of a sudden I'm wondering about Patil and Thieu."

"Khalid is still up on the station," Catlin said.

"And out of reach. Out of our reach. But he has fingers down here. We need to know where, and into what. We need to know why Jacques changed his mind. Yanni's going to ask that question personally. He's relying on *Hicks's* men to protect him. I'm not liking this. I'm not liking this at all."

"We'll keep informed," Florian said.

"Inform me," she said, "at any hour of the day or night. If anything happens to Yanni, under Hicks's protection—" She thought about it, about the danger of a man with that many keys to the systems . . . when the source of the danger might lie well within the impenetrable heart of another Bureau. "Get ready to take Hicks down, dead or alive, I'm imposing no conditions. Just don't risk yourselves. Remember I can axe his accesses. If I hear anything untoward out of Novgorod, Hicks is gone."

"Understood," Catlin said, and then: "Sera?"

She looked up at Catlin.

"We know Hicks used to accompany Director Giraud to Novgorod. There were many meetings with Defense in Gorodin's administration and in Khalid's. He went a few days ago. For Yanni."

Bureau heads met. Their representatives met. Hicks had indeed gone there a few days ago, talking to Jacques, carrying Yanni's offer to Jacques; it went on all the time.

"Sera?" Florian asked, in her long silence.

"Jacques is going to name Khalid as Proxy Councillor. He may be hoping we'll raise the bet and bid him back. But we have to be able to guarantee his life. That executive position doesn't help him at all if he's dead. Or if his family is. Estranged daughter?"

Catlin whipped out her handheld. She said, memory refresher, "Solo. No minor dependents. No relationships since 2421. Uncontested division of household. Estranged daughter, grandchild, great-grandchildren, affiliated with former partner, not genetically related to Jacques."

Solo fit a pattern, of people who made it to directorships and Council seats. Including Yanni. "Whereabouts of next-ofs and former partner: Novgorod."

"Novgorod," Catlin confirmed.

"Too available. Relay that info to Yanni, not to Hicks. *Tell* Yanni we're not relaying it to Hicks." Yanni would say to her, What do you expect me to do about it, without Hicks? "Tell him he's got to get some meaningful security around Jacques's family and friends. And Jacques. And damn it, it'll look like hell if we pull ReseuneSec in to guard him. Tell Yanni that Spurlin was murdered: that's proof enough. Let the OCI request *State* to get agents in to guard Jacques, and our bloc will back him in Council for doing it. *And* tell Yanni I say keep Hicks in the dark on the whole move."

"Yes, sera," Florian said, and got on the phone. She heard him talking to Yanni's office manager, Chloe. "Sera's orders. Urgent message for Yanni."

Yanni was going to spit if she kept interfering and nagging him step by step, but she was about two jumps short of voicing the code to override Base Two as it was, and blood was rushing through her veins, pushing her to do something, take action, go *with* Yanni to Novgorod. She'd crippled Khalid politically before: her appearance would remind audiences all over Cyteen and Union how that had played out.

But that wasn't highly prudent to do. Something about all their eggs in one basket and *not* declaring war on Khalid until they'd gotten Jacques back in line.

Damn Jacques for not following the script. But Jacques sat in the middle of the Defense Tower, where there were abundant holdovers from the Khalid regime, people who could deliver a message. It didn't matter that Khalid was on the station. His agents were clearly in Novgorod.

Tell Yanni I'll be there if I have to, she almost added, but she bit her tongue on it. Yanni was the one who'd been dealing with Jacques, Yanni had made the deals with Jacques *and* Corain, and she hoped she hadn't enabled this mess by refusing to let Yanni fly down there the day Spurlin died and start running from one to the other making sure the deals he'd made held. He hadn't accused her in that regard. But there could be some connection.

There could equally well have been a bad outcome to her *letting* Yanni go there too soon and check into the hotel across the park from the hotel that had blown up and caught fire the month Denys died. There were crazy people in Novgorod. Worse, there was something very, very high-level behind Spurlin's death, and maybe behind the rest of it, and Eversnow—God knew what it had to do with anything, but it was a question.

She folded the mini and set it aside on the couch, knowing it would turn up again on her desk the minute she left the room. She decided she'd call the gang down. Tell them bring the pizza with them: her place was focused down on staff, on a minimal dinner and Cook's service for all the staff she had staying up and taking care of business.

So she did that. Or she told Theo to do it, and told Jory leave the computer: she might need it.

What she needed at the moment Florian was too busy to provide. And she didn't want anybody else. Not the way she was now. She found herself pacing, looked down at Sam's river underneath her feet, glowing with light, the rest of Sam's river reflecting the blue fish wall, reminding her of a tranquility that didn't exist in the world.

So Jacques had the reins in his hands and wasn't going to do what he'd promised Reseune he'd do—retreat quietly as Lynch had done and leave a Proxy in charge of Defense; draw his salary for two years and then go take his nice posh executive post. They'd had it all set up for Jacques, a do-nothing Councillor, to do nothing another two years and still know his job was waiting for him. And Hicks had flown down there to get that agreement. Well, *that* hadn't gone outstandingly well, had it?

Maybe Jacques just wanted Yanni to come down there in person and hold his hand through the process. Maybe he wanted face-to-face assurance. She doubted that was the game.

She paced. She walked up to the fish wall and watched the fish. She'd gotten rather fond of the little pearly jawfish—that was their real name: *opistognathus aurifrons*, or golden-brow—that made their home in the substrate, right by a rock. They came half-out to see her, tails still in their burrow. They were white, with a blueish opal look to their fins, pale yellow head. Little jewels. Their world was on that side of the glass, hers on this one; and this evening their world was running much more smoothly than hers.

The big Achilles tang came sweeping past, black, orange-detailed, and elegant, *acanthurus achilles.* The jawfish dived into their burrows, and the Achilles, ominous shadow, went on to terrify the rabbitfish, who dreaded everything.

Small wars. Small problems. Everlasting, between species that had been conducting their same business and having the same quarrels since the last ice flowed on Earth.

The more intelligent of old Earth's species weren't doing much better, locally.

A small commotion drew Theo and Jory to the front door, and they admitted Amy and Maddy, Tommy with a stack of pizza containers, and the rest of the gang.

"Are we doing anything yet?" Amy asked in the same cheerful tone she'd used on pranks and schemes against Denys, not so many years ago. It was incongruous. It filled her with an irrational sense of capability. *Are we doing anything yet?*

But they weren't within striking distance of this problem. Just Yanni was. And it was a two-way strike potential.

"Yanni's going. I cleared Reseune One to fuel. He'll probably go tonight."

"He will, sera," Florian said. "He's called for a car. Ten of ReseuneSec's higher officers are going with him."

"Backgrounds," she said. "Tell Rafael do it."

"Yes, sera," Florian said, and went off to the foyer to do it quietly.

Meanwhile Tommy was laying out the pizza containers on available tables, and Mischa opened them one after the other. The smell wafted through the living room.

"Catlin," she said, "tell kitchen we'd like some wine." She'd have one. She'd earned it. But no other, not tonight. "Call Justin. Tell him and Grant come across. We're having an election party."

"But Jacques didn't name Bigelow," Amy said.

"That's why Yanni's on his way to Novgorod," she said, and shopped among pizzas, finding her favorite, bacon and basil. She took a slice in her fingers. "Jacques has weasled."

"Is that a word?"

"An old word for a slinky little mammal. He's weasled. We don't know if somebody's gotten to him, or if he's just waiting for Yanni to show up in person and ask him nicely. If he does something like name Khalid—he's been gotten to."

"Somebody can file on him in two months," Tommy said. Tommy had probably looked it up.

"They can," Ari said, "and somebody's bound to, Bigelow on one side, and Khalid on the other, and we go another seven months trying to get somebody elected who's competent. Don't talk to me about Khalid. I'm eating."

Wine showed up from the hallway, at one end. And Justin and Grant showed up at the door, at the other.

"Pizza," she said. "Drinks. Call for what you want."

Justin didn't ask a question, but he looked a little cautious. So did Grant.

"It wasn't all good," Amy said under her breath. "Jacques was supposed to name Admiral Bigelow Proxy, and didn't, and Yanni's going to Novgorod."

Justin had looked Amy's way.

"It's not totally good," Ari said. "But we've still got Jacques, and Yanni's going there, with a guard we hope he can rely on, to call in a non-military guard, I hope, to keep Jacques safe. Choose your pizza. It's still warm. We're not celebrating yet, but we're not panicking. Spurlin was murdered."

Justin had been picking up a piece of pizza, sausage and cheese. He let it lie.

"Have your pizza," she said. "Just letting you know it's dangerous out there."

"Had that idea," he said, and took the pizza anyway. Haze offered him a tray, white wine and red. He chose red, and had the pizza in one hand and the drink in the other. Grant had gone for cheese on cheese, and white, and settled on a settee near the fish wall, his long legs a little tucked, given the height of the seat.

"I called you here," Ari said to Justin, "because you're on the inside, same as everybody else. Because if I pull

Hicks out of his job, and I may, I may put *you* in as head of ReseuneSec."

"Don't even joke about it," he said, the wineglass in one hand, the pizza, frozen, in the other. "No. Lock me up, but keep me out of *that* job."

"I think you'd actually be good at it."

"Realtime work, remember?"

"You just arrest them. You don't cure them."

"I don't want to arrest anybody," Justin said. "Ari, you're joking. Tell me you're joking."

"I'm joking," she said; but she wasn't—she had a short, short list of candidates she'd trust for the time it took to fill the job permanently. "Your other choice is Yanni's job."

"No," he said, fast.

"If anything should happen," she said. "But it won't, if I can help it. That's why you're here. You'd do it, wouldn't you, a week or two, if you really had to?"

He stood looking at her with the ridiculous pizza and the wineglass, and finally went and laid the pizza piece back with the nearest pizza.

"Ari, if you're anywhere close to serious, I'm asking you, pick just about anybody else in Reseune. Amy, over there, damned near *ran* Reseune for the duration of the last—"

"I trust you," she said, "beyond most people over the age of eighteen. And if things go wrong, I'll owe you and Grant a very, very big apology for all of it, because things will go to absolute hell and you're going to get swept up in the fallout. Right now, Base One recognizes Yanni as my guardian if I should die. He's responsible for getting me back. And Base One recognizes you as second in line to run Reseune and to do exactly that."

"No," he said earnestly. "Ari, no. I'm not remotely qualified."

"Who is?" she asked. "Who has a thorough knowledge of the system when it's going badly, and when it's going right? I could appoint Wojkowski, or Peterson, or Edwards, but they're none of them up to saying no to the right people."

"I'm not outstandingly good at saying no, either. Look at how far it's got me. I spent more time being arrested than anybody else in Reseune."

"That's not your sole qualification. You're qualified to bring *me* up if you had to. You'd be qualified to bring up *Giraud* if anything happens to Yanni in the next few weeks—at least long enough to find somebody to be as non-fit as the first Giraud's mother. Tell me you will. Or tell me who's going to do the job. You'd have Amy, you'd have Maddy—she does a lot more than look nice and run a dress shop: believe that. You'd have Sam. He's hands-on, but he's brilliant at what he does. Florian, Catlin—you'd take care of them. You'd see they were safe . . . they'd see you were . . ."

He opened his left arm of a sudden, wrapped it around her gently and hugged her against his shoulder. He smelled good. He was warm, he was stronger than you'd ever think, and he held her the way nobody ever had who was older, nobody but Ollie, a long, long time ago. She didn't cry, though if she weren't so hyped to fight, she might have, and he didn't make a scene of it, he just walked her aside from everybody else, over toward the garden-glass of the dining room, and let her go, and said, facing her, "If I'm all, Ari. If I'm absolutely all there is, I'll do it. I wouldn't be near good at it. I'd be looking for advice, wherever it came from. But I'd keep your people safe, with everything I could put together, and I wouldn't waste any time getting your next edition into the tank and going, fast as I could. My father—my father I know is a question. But he wouldn't be, in this. If it came down to it—I'd be there, long as it took for your own people to get their feet on the ground."

"We don't *know* things about history, Justin. We don't know how things happened. We just know where things are now."

"That's pretty well the condition of everybody born, isn't it? Except you, being what you are—"

"And you're *Jordan's* replicate, so you know things you wouldn't, if you were Amy, or Sam, or Maddy. You *know* things. You were part of that world, the way it was."

"I know things."

"So you're the best I could choose. And I'll give you a verbal code, which will only work in your voiceprint, and only if my CIT number has gone inactive in the system.

Just say my name three times. Just say *AriAriAri*. And Base One is yours. Even if Yanni's Base Two is still active. I trust you, more than Yanni. And if anything happens to me, you take possession of this apartment, and all my staff, and every defense this place has. And you bring my friends in until it's safe."

"Don't get killed. *Please* don't get killed."

He did care. He did. And that mattered. She was in the mode she'd been in when they'd come after Uncle Denys—close to that. But she could be amused, just a little, and moved to put a hand on his shoulder. "So you don't have to run Reseune? There's a major difference between you and your father. You really love the work, the puzzles in it; you tolerate me because I bring you puzzles."

His brows knit, just a little offense, not much. "You're a little better than a puzzle, young sera. Just a little."

"And you're a little better than a puzzle-solver. A lot better, in fact." She pressed her fingers into his arm. "I've been in love with you since forever. So far I've been mostly good. And you know that, too."

"Don't even open that door."

"My name is Ari. Not kid. Not young sera. I wish you'd use it."

"And you know you *are* young sera, to most everybody."

She tilted her head to look up at him, right in the eyes, pursed her lips slightly and shook her head, ever so slightly. "I'm *Ariane,*" she said. "That covers everything people say I am. You're only half a replicate. Thank God. I'm pretty damned close to the original. Don't worry about me. Just don't let anybody get in a hit behind my back. I want you safe while I'm gone."

"*You're* not going with Yanni."

"Yanni will have already left by now—or be on the verge of it. I'm going to be busy. And I'd like to give you Amy, but she's going to Novgorod. She's real quiet. The media let her alone. She'll find out things. She'll have Quentin with her, and he'll be out of uniform. All very quiet. Just a business trip. Give me a kiss. I'm collecting them, storage for the next few days."

He did, just a kiss on the cheek. She'd wondered what he'd do if she asked.

That he could do that, that smoothly, that collectedly, said worlds about his mental state.

She left him, then, to go talk to Amy.

"Sure," Amy said. "When?"

"See if Yanni *can* infuse some backbone into Jacques and get Khalid shut out. I'm worried, all things considered, that that won't be enough."

"If Khalid's involved in Spurlin's murder . . ."

"Likely it won't stop other things from happening. That's what's got me worried: if Yanni succeeds, Yanni's in imminent danger."

"Jacques is in trouble, in either case," Amy said.

"He's a dead man, either walking around for a while, or cold before nightfall. But we can only protect him if he agrees with us and puts Bigelow in the line of fire—if that's what's going on. This is dangerous, Amy. You should understand that. I'm not sure Patil and Thieu aren't linked into this, and that means Yanni is a *major* target."

"I'm in the fish breeding business. It's about your tank. I'm staying in the Wilcox, third floor—fast to reach ground level; and Quentin's my secretary. You want some blennies."

"You've got it," she said. "Bore anybody who asks. If you're absolutely sure you're overheard, you and Quentin start arguing about calcium supplements and temperature stability in the bar."

Amy laughed. Then: "Understood," Amy said, with a little pat on her arm, and went to talk to Quentin.

A plane took off. Ari caught the sound, above the water-sound of the room. That would probably be Yanni.

Good luck, she wished him. Good luck.

Please stay alive, Yanni.

JULY 26, 2424
0828H

"Ser." Rafael met Florian in the foyer of the little office, opened the back hall door, and showed him right through.

An item had turned up. That was what Rafael's message had said, and when Florian went into Rafael's office a very anxious young woman leapt up and bowed that slight degree ReseuneSec protocol taught. She was no older than the rest of them, just old enough for assignment. Her uniform tag said CARLY BC-18, and she was dark-skinned, broad-faced, wide-shouldered. She clutched half a ream of physical printout to her chest as if it were state secrets.

Which, given that Rafael was investigating staff backgrounds, it might be.

"This is Carly BC, ser. Records."

"Ser," Carly said.

Florian took the available conference chair. Carly settled on the edge of her seat and held her printout on her knees.

"So what do you have, Carly BC?"

"Ser, Giraud Nye's contacts, systematized; the azi in question. Also Giraud Nye's aides and seconds, their whereabouts, their contacts. I have the computer file." She touched her breast pocket.

"Tell me what you learned," Florian said. He expected a little nervousness. Carly BC was new, straight from the barracks. First real assignment.

And Carly had, first off, a shorter document, within the cover of the first. She pulled it out and handed it over, a set of graphs and schematics. Trips to Novgorod. Time spent in Novgorod. Meetings with Defense. Persons involved. Giraud. Abban. Gorodin, deceased Councillor.

Regime change. Giraud, Abban, Hicks. Khalid. Jacques. Spurlin. Jacques, just recently.

He looked up at Rafael. "You've seen this?"

"I've skimmed it, yes, ser."

"Specific data on Hicks. Carly BC."

"Ser."

"Can you pull that out?"

Carly opened the printout on her lap and frantically turned pages. "It's here, ser." Large, dark eyes fixed on his. "I broke out stats on each individual involved. Nye, Abban AB, Hicks, Gorodin, Khalid, Jacques, Spurlin. . . ."

"Give me the data file," Florian said, and held out his hand. Carly BC opened her pocket and handed it to him immediately, a finger marking her place in the printout.

Branches. Branch led to branch, led to branch. One person connected to another. It didn't always produce valid theory, but the investigative AI tended to err on the side of the smallest connection, once it launched.

"Well done, Carly BC."

"Thank you, ser."

The threads all wove back and forth. *That* was the pattern. Never expect that it was going to connect up too tightly. Defense was massive.

"Visits by Abban to Hicks," he said. "Do you have that stat?"

"A lot, ser. I can find it." She started to resort to the printout again.

"That's good, Carly BC. No, don't bother. If it's searchable, it's in here, isn't it?"

"Yes, ser."

"I think we're through with Carly BC's report," Florian said quietly. "Thank you, Carly BC."

"Ser." She looked uncertain. Then started to get up.

"I'll take the report," Florian said. And took it, and Carly received a nod from Rafael and left.

Florian looked at Rafael, at the azi who'd been primed to report to Hicks.

"How are you now, Rafael BR?" he asked. "Are you with us on this?"

"My Contract is to sera," Rafael said firmly.

"No lingering troubles."

"None, ser."

Florian looked at him a long time, and Rafael gazed back, level and long.

"Take precautions," Florian said. "The ferret she sent may have rung bells in certain offices. It shouldn't. But sometimes we aren't as clean as we hope to be. Assume we're not. That's safest."

"Yes, ser," Rafael said faintly.

"Assume nothing," Florian said. "Expect anything. At any time."

"Yes, ser."

Florian pocketed the datastrip, took the printout in hand, and left what ought to be the securest office in the securest wing in Reseune.

He went upstairs to sera's apartment, to the security station in the front hall, and laid the printout on the desk by Catlin's elbow.

"Sera Amy is safely in the hotel," Catlin said. "Third floor, as she wanted."

"Hicks accompanied Giraud to Defense very many times," he said, "and was Giraud's go-between there, as sera remembered. Sometimes Abban was with him. Yanni is, by comparision, a stranger in that tower."

"The military have their own psychs," Catlin said.

He nodded. "I think this has to go to sera," he said. "I think we need her opinion on this."

BOOK THREE   Section 5   Chapter v

JULY 26, 2424
0929H

"Yanni's not meeting with Jacques today," was the gist of Amy's report. It was Friday, Jacques ought to be available, Spurlin's funeral was on the vid, and Jacques was notably absent.

Which wasn't good. Ari didn't acknowledge receipt of

the message from Amy. There wasn't anything to say. She did message Yanni, saying, "How are you doing, Uncle Yanni?"

And Yanni shot back, *"As well as can be expected. Funerals depress me."*

"We're all fine," she wrote. "Don't worry about things."

That was about five minutes before Florian came through the door and told her they were not fine.

"Sera," he said. "We have specific data. Abban and Hicks were both Giraud's special envoys to Defense tower, during all recent administrations, including Khalid and Gorodin, and sometimes they were there over eight hours at a stretch. Two: Hicks is a provisional Alpha Supervisor. He has an alpha assistant, Kyle AK, and he's provisionally certified for that azi; the certificate was obtained in the last year of Giraud's tenure. He was in Giraud's office as deputy director for fifteen years. He had a key. He could have accessed any manual. As an Alpha Supervisor, he could have used any manual in that office . . ."

"Oh, this is good, Florian."

"You know born-men, sera. But we know access. He had access."

"He certainly did. Access to Abban. Probably to Seely. Access to Yanni's office, right now, while he's in Novgorod. Every *time* he's been in Novgorod. Damn it! Florian, do *you* think Abban would have betrayed Giraud? Killed, contrary to Giraud's wishes?"

That drew a rapid blink of Florian's eyes. A rapid assessment. "Sera, no, I don't."

"Abban was upset as hell when Giraud died. Denys took him in. But Abban *stayed* upset. Denys didn't do anything to help him. Or Denys couldn't. That's what I think. And maybe Abban continually supplied Denys with what somebody wanted Denys to know. Or think. Denys was only half paranoid—until Giraud died, and Abban moved in."

"Were we mistaken to kill Denys, sera?"

"No," she said definitively, and then amended that: "I don't think so. I don't think there was anything to save, once Giraud died. He'd have killed us."

"I believe he would have, sera. I know Seely would have."

"Seely was always Abban's partner . . . out in green barracks. The way you and Catlin are partners."

"He probably was that, yes, sera. It makes sense that he was."

"But it's not in his manual, nor is it in Seely's. That's just damned odd. A subsequent generation wouldn't guess that relationship—not based on that manual. A spy wouldn't. It was just in their heads. And Giraud's. And whoever really, really knew them. Bring me a cup of coffee, Florian. Call Catlin. We need to talk about this."

"Yes, sera."

She didn't need the coffee, so much as the time. When they were there, Florian or Catlin, she had a range of possibilities that might be *too* wide, too drastic.

Call Yanni home, now, urgently? That might protect Yanni—assuming Yanni wasn't aiding and abetting.

Hicks. With access to alpha-level personal manuals in Giraud's office. Giraud had been a real Alpha Supervisor. On the record Denys had an alpha license. But Seely and Abban both, once they'd been solely in Denys' care, hadn't had expert handling. They'd both given her cold chills, but it had always been true, Giraud was the one who'd have had those manuals, Giraud was the person that could make the world make sense to Abban, and to Seely. . . . and when he'd died, Denys couldn't handle them.

Giraud, dammit, should have found it out if somebody had gotten to Abban. He'd known Abban that well. He'd *lived* with him that closely. How did anybody get to Abban and Giraud not know it?

But *everybody'd* been upset for weeks after the first Ari had died. Giraud more than most. Giraud hadn't been at his best . . . Giraud had been emoting, leaning on Abban, not the other way around. And Abban had taken care of Giraud. An alpha could. An alpha could end up being the support for his CIT—even if it meant hiding a truth, and lying, and not getting caught at it. That was the hell of working with alphas. Given the collapse of the CIT they relied on, they so, so easily ended up doing all the navigation on a map they didn't wholly understand, and satisfying their

internal conditions by the nearest available substitute—
the satisfaction of coping well, and rescuing their CIT, and
keeping him going. You *couldn't* have an emotional meltdown and stay in charge, not with an Abban type.

Abban might have killed the first Ari—but working
with the security sets as she had, she knew—she knew in a
way she hadn't been able to accept—that scary as Abban
was, Abban hadn't been doing the steering. Abban hadn't
been to blame. And she'd gotten over it when she'd made
up her mind that she wouldn't abort Giraud, and more
particularly wouldn't abort the Abban and Seely Denys
had made to keep him company.

Pyramids in the desert. The immortality of the ancients,
the burial with worldly goods, with attendants, with all the
panoply of kings. Offerings to the dead, for the rebirth.
She'd had that thought, when she'd first known Denys had
activated all three genesets.

All *three*. Even while Abban and Seely were still
alive—they'd been reconceived. Were weeks along, when
Denys and Abban and Seely had died.

The sarcophagus and the womb-tank.

She gave a little shiver. Knew *exactly* the same decision
had attended her birth, and Florian's, and Catlin's, though
they'd all been dead.

Who'd given the order to terminate Florian and Catlin?
Not likely Denys. *Giraud*.

Full-circle, now. Absolutely full-circle.

*Hicks betrayed you, Uncle. Betrayed all of you. Jordan
had been conniving with Defense. He was going to break
it all open and bring Reseune down—but that wouldn't
have served Defense. If there'd been no Reseune in those
years, Defense would have been desperate to have one.
So Defense just wanted to control Reseune, not bring it
down. They already had their man inside Reseune—and
they wrote their own script, not Jordan's. They knew about
the psychogenesis project. They knew it, probably, from
Jordan, who'd tried it with Justin, and Jordan would have
warned them not to go along with it—warned anybody
who'd listen, if they'd asked.*

*But the warnings wouldn't mean a thing to Defense.
They just saw a way to have a re-start on Ari Emory, a*

quieter, merely potential Ari Emory, who wouldn't bother them for years, while Reseune kept their contracts, Reseune did the work for Defense, gave them what they wanted . . .

But, damn! who just authorized Defense to move in on Planys? Who authorized that military base built right next to our labs?

She leaned over the computer and posed the question:

2404. The year the first Ari died. The year Jordan Warrick became the man in the iron mask, the prisoner at Planys.

The military moves in, to keep him quiet. Cooperates— aids and abets—in keeping Ari's so-called killer and *their agreed ally in Reseune . . . away from any communication with the outside world.*

Wasn't that a window on their real set of priorities?

The first Ari safely dead. The second in planning.

Jordan . . . silenced.

Their installation set up at Planys, with Giraud's consent.

And their own man, Hicks, or Abban, with easy, constant access to Giraud's office.

But there was a problem with that line of reasoning.

Hicks himself had been a victim.

Somebody *put a Rafael type in Hicks's office—and Hicks—or somebody—put an identical into my security organization.*

So whose were they to start with?

Hicks didn't have the wherewithal—didn't have the knowledge to create them. He had the authority to order it done. But how did he get it past Giraud?

And how old is that set? When was the first one setted?

2373. *Fifty-one years ago.*

Fifty-one years ago. On the first Ari's staff. An azi named Regis. And who *could have done that?*

How to excavate that much history? Who'd been in a position to do that in those days?

Jordan? Not old enough. Giraud himself . . . when he first started Operating. He could have. She'd been down this track before, but mostly *Not old enough* kept coming round and round and round, troubling any conclusion aiming at the people she'd *like* to blame. Chi Prang, head

of alpha azi—holding that position a long, long time . . .
that was the best candidate to have created someone to
infiltrate the first Ari's staff.

But why? Whose? Chi Prang had never done a thing on
record but do her job.

Shoot off a letter to Chi Prang and just *ask*; did you infiltrate the first Ari's staff, and Hicks' staff, and now mine?
It just didn't make sense. And it kept coming down to . . .

One who had been alive, and in office a hell of a long
time. One who played his own side of the board, consistently, and generally not too quietly.

In between the outbursts, you tended to forget.

Yanni. Yanni was what he was, one of the best.

Not necessarily a bad set of motives. But worth questioning.

Maybe Hicks had somehow figured out there was a
double agent in his office—one he daren't touch. But he
could bestow the same gift elsewhere. As Giraud had been
doing. Spying on the station. Spying on the military.

Two games had been going simultaneously. The military moving in on Planys, and getting a hold on Hicks; and
Hicks knowing his own Director, Giraud, was spying on
him, but Hicks moving very carefully to get at manuals in
that office, so Giraud hadn't known.

Hell. There was one contrary possibility in that
scenario.

"Sera." Catlin came in. Florian was right there with the
coffee—three coffees. Florian knew her.

"Sit down," she said. "Wait. I'm thinking."

She hit the keyboard again. Pulled up Hicks's age as
102. Not that old. But old *enough* fifty years ago. He'd
taken his alpha certs when he'd acquired his assistant,
who'd been from Giraud's office—

—AK-36, Kyle, *alpha,* for God's sake . . . military alpha.

She stared at the history on the screen.

Could she be so blind? Contracted first at eighteen to
the military, military intelligence, no information available, reverted to Reseune, assigned to ReseuneSec after
restructuring. The law said—decommissioned alphas had
to come home to Reseune. This one had come to the most
natural home for his abilities. Straight from the War, year

of the Treaty of Pell being 2353, to Reseune, with the de-commissioning of his unit in 2358.

Put into labs at Reseune for retraining. The routine was supposed to require the axe code, partial wipe, re-Contracting. She looked for that specific date, that specific session.

Didn't turn up until 2362.

God.

Who hadn't given the code early on? Why not?

Somebody wanting to debrief Kyle AK-36, and learn what he'd been into, and what he'd done for the military? Somebody who thought they'd just ask questions and mine him for all kinds of information—somebody who was an expert interrogator—and who might have reason to suspect the military?

Somebody who wouldn't leave traces and records in the system? Base One could do that. Up to a certain limit, Base Two or Three could do it.

The first Ari could do that. So could Yanni. So could Giraud. So could Jane Strassen and Wendy Peterson, in those days . . . when the relationship with Defense, in the last days of the War, with the whole Gehenna situation, had been going quietly unpleasant.

AK-36 himself had specialized in security. And he was alpha. He was one of those the military had used to analyze azi behaviors, to actually serve as Supervisors, before Reseune had pitched a fit about the practice and demanded that mentally damaged azi be taken out of action and returned to Reseune, no matter the inconvenience to the military. In 2350 Ari had gotten that measure through Council and snatched back azi who were routinely being mentally and physically patched together and sent back into combat. She'd had a famous row with Admiral Azov. But she'd won, which had outraged the military and set the stage for years of uneasy relations between Science and Defense . . . so long as Azov was in office.

And Kyle AK-36 had been with the military for a number of years after the Treaty of Pell. Served in a classified function from which there were no records accessible. Then in 2358, by law, all remaining alpha and beta azi had come back to Reseune. Reseune, namely Giraud, must

have tried to unravel him for four more years after that,
learning things, maybe, maybe just trying to understand
what his history really was. It was worth looking for those
sessions, of which there was no readily available record.
That period had ended in 2362.

After the axe-code that ended his Contract to the military, Kyle AK-36 had been with Giraud, a skilled psych
operator, skilled interrogator, trusted aide until—around
2404, when Ari died, Giraud had passed the ReseuneSec
office to Adam Hicks . . . and passed Kyle along with it, as
the one, maybe, to keep the office on an even keel under
a much weaker administrator . . . and who could keep on
reporting to Giraud.

And who *had* ordered production on the Rafael types
from the outset, in those years between 2358 and 2404?
Search failed. But one of them had ended up in Ari's
household. And another in Hicks's staff.

Who'd *setted* the other B-28's? *No signature.* That
could mean Ari herself. It could mean anybody down
to Giraud . . . or somebody working for him. Once AK-
36 had finally had the axe code and become, allegedly, a
Reseune azi, he'd been Giraud's specialist assistant, between 2362 and 2404. The axe code, designed to revoke
a Contract—could be a wide-ranging wipe, but wasn't, if
the azi was well setted. Ideally it just reset the Contract to
None and erased specific areas of knowledge and belief,
an organized amnesia. You wanted an azi to know things
he could later completely forget: you linked them to the
axe code. But the military theoretically couldn't do that on
his level—because they theoretically didn't have military
Supervisors at his level.

An axe code was rough, emotionally rough, physiologi-
cally rough on an azi. And without operators like AK-36
to manage it, the military couldn't do that anymore, and
when AK-36 was sent home, he certainly couldn't do it for
himself, could he?

So he'd have held the last secrets the military hadn't
erased. And he'd have waited, waited four years for somebody to do it for him. Giraud didn't even try to do it—for
several years of a miserable limbo, and finally did, maybe
with help from Prang.

Nice safe azi after that. So Giraud must have thought. An alpha, recovered from the military, and so helpful that Giraud had him doing things he'd used to do, skilled things. She'd bet on it.

Or maybe Prang hadn't been in on the actual operation . . . because of Giraud's own paranoia. She wouldn't be allowed that much window into security psychsets.

Did the creation of the B-28's fit into Kyle AK's term of service? One of them had arrived on the first Ari's staff, young, good-looking—the first Ari liked good-looking young men, no fault, as her successor saw it.

And that one, Regis, had arrived, oh, some two decades on. So had the one in what was, at the time, Giraud's office, in ReseuneSec. And others, elsewhere.

Not Giraud's doing. Kyle's. Reporting to *him,* just conceivably; or, in the case of those outside Reseune, reporting to anybody who had the key.

Oh, Uncle. You created me a hell of a mess. Was AK-36 actually doing all the work with alphas that I forever was a little surprised you could really do?

And when the B-28 went into your own staff, and the other into Ari's, was it AK-36 who was running him? Or was it you, ordering all of it?

Spying on Ari. Spying on your own staff. On people outside Reseune, out at Beta, up on Alpha Station. That would be like you. And you left ReseuneSec, and left the B-28, and AK-36 was still running him. AK-36 was probably still reporting to you—just to keep you happy.

Maybe for the same reason, you let AK-36 go with Hicks every time he went to Novgorod, every time he visited Defense, just the silent presence, your nice, trustable azi who remembered things like a human recorder.

And of course he was all yours, all the time, all yours.

Did you run the axe code without *Prang's help? Maybe you did. And it didn't damned well work, Uncle, and you didn't spot it—because you weren't that good and you shouldn't have been operating like that on an alpha. Terrible thing, vanity. Your mother wanted to make you a genius. Maybe it still stung—that you weren't all that good, never mind the license.*

Who killed my predecessor? You did. You didn't ever

*plan it. You didn't want it to happen. You really loved her.
But it didn't take Abban going to Novgorod to have his
head restructured. You could have been as careful as you
liked where Abban was when you were visiting Defense—
but you weren't so careful where AK-36 was, or what he
was doing at home, were you?*

*Defense planted Kyle on you. A Trojan horse. An axe
code that didn't work, possibly because they'd messed with
it, or possibly because they'd just forged the personal manual . . . and everything in it was right* except *that code. Is
it possible—is it remotely possible you didn't crosscheck
that manual with the original set, or look up that axe code
in archive? That would have been unconscionably care-
less, Uncle. Maybe you did everything right, and somewhere in the military system they messed with that code
and somehow kept him sane.*

*With you, he had total office access, access to Abban's
personal manual, probably Seely's, too, since I'll bet
you were supervising Seely; definitely to as much kat as
he needed, on any day of the week. Abban might have
made one mistake in his life, just one mistake, and taken
a cup of coffee in the lunchroom. Easy at certain hours to
have a little seclusion—and if AK-36 was really good, he
wouldn't have conflicted Abban at all, would he, or taken
too long to do the job? Nothing you could spot. Just one
hell of a deep initial dose, reassurance, need to contact him
again regarding a problem. Then verbal work. Everything
couched in benefitting Giraud. Doing good. Giraud being
secretly threatened by spies inside the office . . . Abban
could help. Abban could protect him. Abban could get
Seely's manual. They could go on protecting Giraud if
they just worked together.*

*Who else, besides you and Denys, could operate Base
Two with authority? Abban. Abban could tiptoe through
System with not a trace left. Azi could be created. Setted.
Records forged without a trace. Any of those things. When
Hicks took over, and when Hicks went with Giraud to
Novgorod, AK-36 went with Hicks—and ultimately got
more specific instructions, didn't he?*

*AK-36's still in Hicks's office, the whole reason Hicks
has a provisional alpha certificate. AK-36 is 122 years old.*

Kinder if we killed him. A hundred and twenty-two is old to be given an axe code. Real old. And especially if the military messed with it and put a block in that we'll have to break.

If we give it, he could die on the table. Then we lose all he might know.

It won't be pretty, what needs to be done. We can try to be kind.

But we have to move on it, don't we?

God, all that, all that, because the first Ari pissed off Defense . . . was that it? She'd gotten power enough to start calling the shots, not just with azi—with a lot of the things where Reseune cooperated with Defense. The terraforming of Cyteen she got voted down. The Eversnow business, that Yanni's agreed to provided we get a base down there, which for some reason maybe they really, really don't want . . . check that item at first convenience.

Ari was powerful in Council, and she'd gotten Trade and Information on her side, and there was no real way Citizens was going to set up a Bloc with Defense: they're not natural allies. So she was getting passed just about anything she wanted passed; she was creating the Arks; she was negotiating with Earth at times when State couldn't even get a message through . . .

And Jordan . . . Jordan made a deal with them. He wanted to bring Reseune down, but it wasn't Reseune they wanted to bring down at all: it was Ari. They'd found out she was dying. They'd found out about the psychogenesis project, and they weren't appalled about Ari being reborn—they were interested. Her genius was an asset to Union. But her political power was hurting them. They made their deal with Jordan to get more information— they were using him all the way. And they got the notion they could have a tame Reseune, under a more amenable leadership, and still have an Ari, who could go on being born, and dying, unless the system really, really needed her brain again . . . while tamer people ran Reseune and didn't have her power in the legislature, and Defense got its way again.

But here I am growing up, and I'm not easy to get at, and oh, they'd like to run me. They'd like to. But they can't do

*that, where I am. I've fortified myself inside Alpha Wing.
I've controlled all access. I've gotten my own azi staff, my
own circle of CIT advisors. I trust very, very few people,
and some people can't get close to me anymore. Rafael was
their best try, and I have him.*

So who are "they"?

Who's the Enemy?

*It wasn't Gorodin. I don't think it ever was Gorodin.
Maybe it wasn't even Azov, though I never knew him—
maybe it was some force inside Defense that we never even
saw. Not Jacques, who's just a chair-warmer, and more a
symptom of how Defense can't come up with leaders, past
its own internal politics.*

*And then there was Spurlin—he was clearly on some-
body's bad list. He put his head up: he nearly got into control of Defense. And now he's dead.*

*Say there's two factions in Defense, at least. And one of
them is the side Spurlin was on, which is pro-Reseune; and
moderate; and then there's Khalid and his backers.*

*Khalid didn't like it when I took him on when I was
a little kid. I nearly finished him in politics. The head of
Intelligence wasn't used to public appearances—and he
looked the fool. But now he's back. And he won't be my
friend. He'll have the notion, I'm pretty sure, that Reseune
won't be his to manage if I take over, and I'm very, very
close to doing that. It's personal, for him. It's emotional;
and he is an emotional man—he showed that, back when
I Got him. And he's fast running out of time to stop me
from growing up and taking over—it could be weeks, or
a couple of years. It could be next week, and he and his
know it. All of a sudden they're thinking they've bargained
with the devil, like the old story, and it's not looking like
such a good deal for them.*

*That's where Khalid's getting his support, isn't it? He
doesn't have enough support on his own or he'd have won
the election, but there are people inside Defense who see
me coming up fast, and they're worried all of a sudden.
The rank and file of Defense, the electorate, they went for
somebody who hadn't gotten embarrassed by a fourteen-
year-old on national vid— And Giraud warned me about
that at the time, that I might be sorry. But I was right. I may*

*have kept Khalid from being elected again. The electorate
went for Spurlin; and another defeat would about do for
Khalid permanently—so Khalid and everybody invested
in him has no way to get back in without using some really
unorthodox methods.*

*Like murder. They'd already done that, inside Reseune,
to take out my predecessor. What's one more? What's two
murders, and three more?*

*There's this Anton Clavery business. Patil dying. Thieu
dying. They both had Defense Bureau work, lots of contacts, so they were easy to get to—and then Patil was joining Reseune, and at the same time Yanni was demanding to
set a Reseune base down on Eversnow, right down next to
their military base. Somebody in Defense possibly didn't
like that.*

*We've been thinking about Anton Clavery as a Paxer.
Paxers have been our noisiest problem. But did the Paxers
blow up the tower at Strassenberg? There are those that
could blow something up, a lot, lot easier.*

*Attacking Strassenberg doesn't make sense as a politi-
cal move, except to expose what I'm doing, except to divert
our attention to what isn't their real objective.*

*It's me they really want dead. And they'll take down
Reseune's power one piece at a time, anything to slow me
down. You can only do so many murders without leaving
evidence. So they have to ration those. Just peel away the
really critical pieces.*

*But I'm not playing their game. And when I do move
against Defense, I'll have to move fast, and be ready for
anything. They're not going to let Jacques name the Proxy
we want: they'll kill him, or they'll force him to name Khalid; and then Jacques will die, and Khalid, who couldn't get
in by a fair election, will be Councillor, just plain Councillor, in complete charge of the military.*

*A man named Machiavelli once said something like . . .
commit all your atrocities early. Your enemies will lie low,
knowing what you* can *do, and the rest of the people will
forgive you when you turn out to do good things . . .*

Florian had set a cup of coffee by her hand. The two of
them sat, sipping theirs, waiting.

She picked up the cup, took a sip. Wondered where all

of her people were at the moment. But she couldn't move them. Someone would notice.

Just one. "Florian."

"Sera?"

"Go down to Justin's office. Tell him and Grant to go home. Tell him he's in charge of Alpha Wing for the next while. Gerry and Mark will be under his orders. Then come back here. Catlin."

"Sera."

"Go down to Rafael's office, and tell him I want him and his best twenty, no helmets, light body armor. Lethals in reserve. Non-lethals up front. Wait for me there." She had a last sip of the coffee and put the cup down. "Body armor for me, too. Lay out one of your outfits for me before we go, Catlin."

A slight hesitation. Then: "Yes, sera."

She opened a drawer, took out the mini, waked it up. Things went in a sequence. She wasn't particularly scared, not even mad, at the moment. She just found her awareness stretched wide, trying to see everything, imagine everything, think of everything, and not to drop a single piece in the process.

BOOK THREE   Section 5   Chapter vi

JULY 26, 2424
1102H

Knock at the office door. And it opened before either of them could acknowledge it. Justin shut the manual with some deliberation, saw Florian standing there—it could just as well have been Ari. Grant had the same manual under consideration, and quietly slipped it onto a neat stack of others.

"Ser," Florian said. "Sera requests you go home immediately. Mark and Gerry will be in contact soon from AlphaSec."

"Is something wrong?" Stupid question. Justin got up, picked up his coat. When Florian asked in that mode, it was urgent.

"You will be, officially, ser, in administrative control of Alpha Wing. Use Base One access. Mark and Gerry will be your links to AlphaSec. They will be reliable."

"They're damned *young*," he said, feeling a rise of panic, the scatter of thoughts informing him, *My God, it wasn't academic. She's doing it.*

Florian, who was only months older than Mark and Gerry, *and* the azi in charge of AlphaSec, said, "They'll take their orders from you, ser. You may also draw on Marco and Wes, in sera's apartment. Sera counts on you. Come with me."

Grant came, he did. They both headed to the lift, under Florian's protection. Down the hall, where AlphaSec had its offices, there was traffic, a few black-uniformed officers entering as a group, more of them headed that direction.

Damn, he thought, asking himself what he would do, what he *could* do but lie low, himself and Grant.

Jordan, was the competing thought. He couldn't protect Jordan.

"I'm concerned for my father," he said to Florian.

"He has security in place, ser," Florian said. "They *are* ours."

BOOK THREE   Section 5   Chapter vii

JULY 26, 2424
1128H

Units of two and three went out—walked out of Alpha Wing, into Wing One. One such went to the end of the building and walked across the quadrangle to Admin's curbside door. Another went via the storm tunnels. Another went to Admin via the as-yet separate second-level connection out of Alpha Wing.

That one met up with the unit from the storm tunnels and came up together. Other units were moving. One went to Yanni's office, and into Chloe's office, unasked. More showed up outside ReseuneSec, all with a businesslike manner.

Ari stopped, with Florian and Catlin, at the Reseune-Sec door. Catlin's regular winter coat was a little large on her, very heavy, and not with fabric: it impeded her fingers getting at the mini in her pocket, but she pulled it out, flipped it open, keyed Voice, said: "CannaeCannaeCannae," and "GoAlpha," and toggled off.

"Now," she said, and Catlin quietly opened the door.

Midmorning and the ReseuneSec office was full of people, security and otherwise, with business to conduct.

"The office is closed for an hour," Ari said quietly, loudly enough to be heard, especially as voices died away. "Please leave and come back later. Please remember your places." People didn't like to feel pushed. The fact some clericals might know her, and some might know Florian and Catlin, started a few to their feet without a word, those anxious to reach the door.

She said to the receptionist, who had punched keys, "It won't work, probably. I'm afraid not much will for a bit, so we'd like to minimize that time and get things running again. Let Catlin help."

"I can't," the receptionist began, his face somewhat ashen, and by now the room was filling with AlphaSec personnel and emptying of people to see Director Hicks.

Hicks, in fact, would find his own door locked, as people would be locked in rooms all up and down the corridors. He might have found a weapon. But that was all right. They had non-lethals to take care of that.

"You're no longer working for Director Hicks. My name is Ariane Emory. These are AlphaSec personnel, and *I'm* now the Director of ReseuneSec. Kindly get up and go have a seat over there. Catlin will handle your desk, thank you very much."

The man moved, and AlphaSec moved him to a chair and put him into it as Catlin assumed the desk and appropriated the keyboard.

"Gas masks," Rafael said, and Ari put her mask on, as

everyone did, including Catlin, hardly missing a keystroke.
The reception area door suffered, as AlphaSec didn't even
wait for the niceties of the keyboard, or the chance of a
lethal guarding that access on a mechanical trigger. They
got past that door and set down two bots, which raced back
inside at ankle level, very fast.

The masks didn't even hint of the smell of smoke, or
gas, but they were stifling, all the same, both an inconvenience and a protective anonymity. Ari pressed hers close
to her face, kept out of the way and let AlphaSec do what
they knew how to do, with systems they knew far better,
while Florian and Catlin, armed with lethals, stayed right
by her. She could see a little ways down the inside hall, and
saw two of her teams stopped at an intersection of halls,
braced and ready to fire. Where the bots were, she couldn't
tell.

The general com stream was scary. Beta and gamma azi
wouldn't give up a fight, not by their nature. They needed
to be taken down, and that went on. Occasionally there
was a burst of fire, and the quieter hiss-thump of non-
lethals. Wes was their best medic, but Wes wasn't here.
Jay was qualified, and Jay was up there in the halls somewhere, with two calls on his attention, two of their own
down, how bad wasn't apparent. None of the opposition
needed Jay's intervention, which meant her people were
doing exactly what they were supposed to do, and taking
people down, fast.

Director Hicks wasn't the most essential target. She'd
decided that. Kyle AK-36 was; and Base One said Kyle
was in the offices this morning, and so was Hicks. Kyle AK
was smart, he was independent-thinking, and as the attack
came down he would probably take command back there,
if he hadn't delegated and scrambled for an exit. All these
years, Hicks might have thought he was Kyle's utmost priority. But he wasn't. Right now, she'd bet, in contrast to the
way she had Florian and Catlin with her, Hicks was sitting
in his office with the door locked and immoveable, finding
himself all alone, and nobody defending him. Base Two
and Three, Yanni's bases, were both completely down,
and that meant ordinary doors didn't work automatically
anywhere in Admin. Base One was in charge of things

Base Two had commanded, and if Base One said open a door, it opened, whether or not it then blew up because it was booby-trapped. Base One had retreated behind the gateway of Alpha Wing, and possibly somebody clever in ReseuneSec had thought maybe they could barrier it in there and not let it out, but that wouldn't work. Base One was always a moving target. And right now Base Two and Three weren't awake, just flat weren't awake.

They'd had schematics of ReseuneSec. Knew exactly where the emergency exits were, and where they led. They knew where the switches were. If there was any doubt, Marco and Wes ran ops from Alpha Wing, with the schematic in front of them, and the eye-screen Rafael had on a contact lens showed him where he was in a completely schematic view, a kind of split-level awareness Florian likewise had, and Catlin, so they knew where their people were.

Standard. Florian had said, before they left the apartment, that ReseuneSec was supposed to have some stuff to try to scramble that, but it wasn't going to work without Base Two.

"Live capture, beta target," came over the com stream, and Ari let go a long, long breath, but she didn't let up watching and listening. They'd just arrested Hicks, meaning his office door was open by now. A second later they heard, *"Exit A! Coming your way!"*

A mass of people flooded into the corridor she could see—Ari wasn't ready for it. Florian flattened her to the carpet, made her hit her head so stars exploded in her eyes and things went black for a second; and fire banged out, and the hiss-thump of non-lethals simultaneous with it, right over their heads. Florian's weight went off her as if he'd levitated, and she twisted around to see Catlin come over the desk and two others of her men hurl themselves at a man who was already through the door, but down and not fighting. One of hers was on the floor, trying to hold the man down, with blood pouring down his own arm.

"Easy!" Florian yelled, falling on the now inert target, and was after something in his sleeve-pocket. Florian used something with a stab downward, after which the man convulsed, twitching uncontrollably, and Catlin got a bracelet on him, nasty thing. He convulsed a second time. Tried to get up. Catlin flattened him with a second pulse from the bracelet.

Ari supposed it was safe then. She sat up where she was. Florian had gotten up off the man, then diverted himself to get their own wounded flat onto the floor, and to get at another item in his jacket pocket. "Get Jay," she heard as Florian applied a tourniquet. "Bad one."

Things were quieting elsewhere, however. Quiet prevailed in the hall. Jay came running down the hall toward them with his kit, and relieved Florian of his job of keeping blood in the wounded man. Jay's moves were sure and involved things in a kit he had, quickly applied. And Florian sat against the wall with his knees drawn up, breathing through his mouth, and sweating a little, while Catlin, who hadn't raised a sweat, slowly got up and let two others sit on their prisoner.

"Suicide by non-lethals." Catlin's voice came simultaneously from her and from the com in Ari's ear. *"Rarely works. We got Kyle AK, Alpha Leader. We need a team to wrap him up and keep him from going null on us. We won't leave sera. We need some help here."*

It was no time for her to be sitting on the floor watching, Ari decided. She ignored her headache and swung a knee around, got it under her and got up, using the reception desk for leverage.

She sucked in a breath, went around the desk to the console, and found the switch-set for A, B, C, and Master. A maze of switches. Blinked. Her eyes were hazing, blurring and watering.

Hell with that. She took out her mini, keyed Voice, and said, "Base One, access: Admin One: access: public address. On. This is Ariane Emory." She heard her voice echo through the halls beyond, as it would everywhere else in Reseune. "Alpha Leader, I confirm Catlin's order, at your immediate convenience." Damn, her head hurt. It wasn't quite the way she'd planned to take over. But it was better than the alternative. "ReseuneSec personnel, wherever you are, Adam Hicks has been relieved of command. I am in charge of ReseuneSec and I am acting Director of Reseune. All ReseuneSec personnel, continue ordinary duties. Citizens and azi, wherever located, you are safe. Certain services have been temporarily disrupted. None of these disruptions jeopardizes environmental integrity. Services will be restored, I hope within the hour. Will an ambulance please come to the Admin Wing? We need ambulance service—"

Florian got eye contact and held up four fingers.

"We have four casualties in need of ambulance transport," she said.

Catlin was talking on the com, and it made a jumble in her hearing. Catlin was requesting something of Marco and Wes, but it was coded and she didn't follow it.

"All Wings except Admin, Wing One, and Alpha Wing may proceed about routine business," she said. "ReseuneSec requests all persons currently in Admin, One, and Alpha remain where you are and do not make private calls. We estimate this condition will remain for about an hour. Wait for an all-clear before venturing into the halls. Thank you."

BOOK THREE   Section 5   Chapter viii

JULY 26, 2424
1201H

"She's done it," Justin said to Grant. They'd gone to the dining room of their apartment to have a cup of coffee and do a little work on the manual . . . but they hadn't gotten any work done. The minder had had the communication stream from Ari's apartment, which carried the background of what was going on in Admin, and the last announcement had come over the minder loud and clear—probably in every minder and every PA outlet *and* the vid channels. *That* general warning system, intended for major storms or an environmental breach, hadn't cut on since . . .

. . . Since Ari had taken Denys out.

"She's done it," Grant said quietly. "And four people are going to hospital. No word about the dead."

"Not so bad a casualty list for a revolution, though, as revolutions go," Justin said, feeling shaky. He was thinking about Jordan, hoping he was all right. But Ari had said not to use communications for a while. So he had another sip of coffee and a bite of buttered toast.

"Worried?" Grant asked him.

"Worried that it's not just Reseune she's taking. That it's Yanni's job at stake. That this takeover in ReseuneSec means trouble that goes under all sorts of doors, just—everywhere. Everything. Including questions as to how a candidate for a Council seat just happens to drop dead."

"Not just happens," Grant said. "It's on the news, now. Definitely assassination. High tech assassination."

"I'll bet Khalid had rather it wasn't on the news," Justin said. So Ari that suddenly, after what she'd said on election night—good God, just *last* night—had risen up this morning, taken out Hicks, and taken over ReseuneSec.

And the sum total of everything set tottering sent a little cold chill wafting across his nerves. It wasn't that he mourned the fall of the current administration of ReseuneSec, which had slammed him into more than one wall and shot him full of drugs . . . he didn't exactly mourn for Hicks' fate, whatever it was, since Hicks had been Giraud's aide in those days, and Hicks' orders had been at least at fault in the incident in recent memory. ReseuneSec had always had an uneasy feeling about its workings, and he wasn't sorry.

He was, however, upset about Ari's involvement in it . . . for one thing, he didn't want *his* Ari involved in killing people. Denys—that had been a case of self-defense, and her guard had done it. He wasn't sure what this was, or how many cold-blooded decisions would need to be made, how many extra-legal ones, and he'd have wished, if it was going to be done, that Yanni had. He wasn't sure whether the fact that Ari had moved in Yanni's stead was cold-blooded policy choice, or that Hicks was just too dangerous a man to Ari's interests, and might oppose her takeover . . . and she hadn't included Yanni in the action because, who knew? maybe she didn't trust him.

If that was so, Yanni might not have too much time left to hold power.

He and Grant were nominally in charge of Alpha Wing, her base of operations. They were trusted. They were also a target, if young sera made a misstep. And trust could shift in a heartbeat.

She'd talked about going to Novgorod. About sending Amy ahead of her. Exposing herself to the same kind of hazard that had already taken out a newly elected Councillor of Defense. She'd be risking everything, and she hadn't been able to trust ReseuneSec, who was currently protecting Yanni, and protecting everyone and everything else Reseune called secure, in the solar system, in distant starstations. Did she still intend to fly down to the capital?

And do what? Get Lynch, of Science, to appoint *her* Proxy Councillor, when she was barely old enough to vote?

Get in front of the media and start another war of words with Vladislaw Khalid—who probably had just had his rival assassinated?

What did she have for assets? Her bodyguard, two of them eighteen and the other two, thank God, at least senior security, former instructors, but it was the eighteen-year-olds who ran things. Besides that she had a handful of teenagers, a household staff and thirty ReseuneSec agents, not *one* of whom was much over teen-aged themselves.

What had she said at the party? That there was almost nobody to remember the history, nobody alive who knew how it had been, and why things had happened, and why choices had gone the way they had? Everybody else but Yanni and them—and Jordan—and a handful of the old hands—everybody else from high up in the old regime was dead, except a handful at the Wing Director level, who didn't know the darker secrets. She'd reached the new age and the old structures weren't there for her to lay hands on. Just Yanni, of all the old power-holders, that she had to rely on.

Flaw in the first Ari's plan. Or its brilliance. From his position, storing his own share of the old knowledge, he didn't know which.

Damned sure her enemies in the wider world were going

to notice that something had changed inside Reseune. Give them a few hours, and they'd notice. Orders were going to go out to ReseuneSec units around the world and in near and far orbit and outbound on starships.

New director. New voice. New policy.

God, he hoped she'd thought of the smaller details.

BOOK THREE   Section 5   Chapter ix

JULY 26, 2424
1208H

Couldn't get the daily reports out of Chloe. Couldn't communicate. Yanni had even tried the airport, and Frank— at the moment *Frank* couldn't be found, because Frank had gone downstairs to check on a ReseuneSec glitchup and now *they* couldn't communicate. The com had lost its codes, or they weren't working.

That was downright worrisome. It was so worrisome Yanni had taken out the briefcase that accompanied him everywhere, opened it up, and found *it* was dead, not a single light showing.

That tore it. He'd tried the ordinary room phone, in the failure of every single high-end piece of electronics he owned, equipment that should have been able to call in armed intervention, and now couldn't. He was down to trying to remember his own office phone number.

And when he was sure he had, *that* call didn't go through. There was just a stupid robot informing him, as if he couldn't guess, that the call had failed.

There were several things that could explain it. One was that Reseune had fallen off the face of the planet.

The other was that an eighteen-year-old with the opinion she *could* run things had taken it into her head to try and just nuked everything that depended on Base Two and Three: the list of what specifically it would nuke was extensive.

He tried the general Reseune phone system, and when
that failed, he tried the last useful number he remembered,
from the fact he had a boat and occasionally, before the
world had gone crazy, *had* taken a few days off and used it.
The number got the general river port operator.

"This is Yanni Schwartz," he said to the man on duty.
"This is Director Yanni Schwartz calling from Novgorod.
Is Reseune experiencing a communications problem?"

*"Admin's all shut down, ser. Wing One, Admin, Alpha
Wing. All shut down."*

Damn.

"Can you find anybody to run up the hill—physically,
can somebody just take a car up there and find out what's
going on?"

It was embarrassing. It was downright fucking embarrassing. He was exposed as hell: *any* casual monitoring by
the hotel staff, let alone Defense experts, could pick up the
call he was making, and he had *finally,* just before things
had gone to hell, tracked down Councillor Jacques. Jacques
hadn't been answering any of his calls, though at least his
office had been answering the phone . . . and consistently
saying Jacques was out of the office, and no, they had no
word yet when he would return. Could they know the nature of the business so the Councillor might call back?

"Ser, I'm working a barge in at the moment." Port ops
was automated to the hilt. There were numbers for every
craft on the river these days, and there weren't an outstanding lot of personnel down there. The port operator
just contacted barges on the river to tell them which channel to use, and relayed calls if they wanted to phone someone. It wasn't likely any barge was going to ground itself
on a bar in the next ten minutes.

"Just tell the the barge to hold position or go round
again, and you go get somebody to run up there. What's
your name?"

"Anthony GA-219, ser."

Azi. He hadn't been sure; but he was instantly more
comfortable, knowing exactly the way to communicate.
"Anthony. This is the Director of Reseune speaking, and
I *will* remember when I get back to Reseune. Do it. You're
perfectly within your duty to do this: go find someone to

check up the hill and report back. Their phones are out.
I'll keep the line open."

That took eleven agonizing minutes. Meanwhile Frank
came in safe and sound with the astonishing news that no,
he couldn't fix the ReseuneSec glitch and that now, yes,
indeed, their own communications weren't working.

"I think we're possibly out of a job," Yanni told Frank
calmly. "But I want to be sure she's all right, the backstab-
bing little rat."

"Are we angry about it?" Frank asked solemnly.

"About being hung out to dry publicly, yes, we're angry.
I really don't want to have to explain this to the evening
news." He had the receiver in hand. He heard Anthony
GA come back on. "Yes?"

*"Patrick GP has gone up the hill on your errand, ser.
But they're saying he won't get in. There's been an an-
nouncement that everybody but Wing One and Alpha
Wing and Admin should go about their business. Sera
Ariane Emory says she's the Director of Reseune Security,
and she's acting Director of Reseune. Is that right, ser?"*

He drew a deep breath. *"Thank* you, Anthony GA. It's
locally right. Will you personally try to get a message to the
Director of Reseune Security that Yanni Schwartz wants
to talk to her on an urgent basis? Thank you. Thank you
very much." He hung up and muttered, "Could have fucking told me that in the first place. So why hasn't she—"

His phone went off. He grabbed it.

"Uncle Yanni?"

"Well?" he snapped.

"Sorry about that," Ari said. *"I couldn't warn you. I had
a little trouble with Hicks. Is Frank with you right now?"*

"Yes."

*"Hicks's azi Kyle? Defense Bureau. He's a Defense Bu-
reau plant, is that the right word? It's possible he messed
with Abban and Seely, a long time ago. I'm kind of sure
Frank's all right. I think you have real reason to know he
is. Are you sure of him?"*

Damn the brat!

"I know. Yes, I'm damned sure! And I'm absolutely
sure you've had your fingers into my computer, where I'd
rather you stayed out of, young lady."

*"I checked just to be sure you were safe, inside. But
there's really good reason to think you could be in danger
from outside, Uncle Yanni. I'd really like you to just come
home. Fast. Defense is going to find out what I just did real
soon, if they don't already know. I'm sure they're going to
be monitoring as close as Moreyville, and they'll know."*

"Well, that's fine. I've finally gotten hold of Jacques and
we're just about scheduled to talk—I'm not about to come
home."

"Yanni—"

"No, I'm telling you. And don't you contemplate coming down here. I know there's a risk, I have that figured out
for myself, young lady; just don't pile another one on top of
it by your coming down here."

*"Then don't you go anywhere outside the hotel. You
make Jacques come to you. I think your security's all right.
I ran a fast check on everybody you've got. You know
about the B-28's."*

"I left Raul home, thank you."

*"Good. That's good. You understand what I'm worried
about."*

"I understand. I understand a lot of things, and I can be
trusted with a little advance warning. Do you mind turning my access back on, young lady?"

*"I'm terribly sorry about that. It's back on now. It's how
I'm talking to you. We just had to be sure we didn't have
anybody loose in the network that we couldn't lay hands
on."*

"All agents accounted for?"

*"All accounted for. I have Hicks and Kyle AK both in
custody. We're just going to ask some questions. Particularly of Kyle."*

"I've got a question. Am I going back to lab work, am
I going for a long vacation in your new township, or am I
somehow supposed to finish my job down here without any
further interruption?"

*"I'm just acting Director, here in the labs. You're still
Director. Besides, you're still Proxy Councillor. I can't
change that. Only Lynch can. But I'm just really worried
that their blowing up the tower—"*

"Yes?"

"Catlin thinks it could have been a signal to anybody inside Reseune to take certain measures. Maybe I just took care of that when I got Kyle. And I haven't been easy to get at, where I'm living. Maybe I didn't, though. Just take care of yourself."

"Do me a favor. Go a little easy on Hicks."

"Because he's a friend of yours? Or because you think he's innocent?"

"If he's not innocent he's not a friend of mine. You can tell him that. Tell him I said cooperate with you or I'll break his neck."

"I will. You're recorded and I'll use that. Take real good care of yourself. Your ReseuneSec guard is going to get the news in about five minutes because I'm going to tell them, since I'm their Director. Are any of them with you in the room?"

"No," he said.

"Good," she said. *"Just in case. If any of them leave the hotel, just let them leave. You're not safe to investigate and don't risk the status quo trying to stop anything of that sort. I already know enough answers that I can deal with anybody who's going to go over to the other side. Just whatever you do, don't go into the Defense Bureau to meet anybody. Meet whoever you meet outside, or at best over in Science, but I don't like you traveling through the streets, and be very, very careful who you let through. Make them all come to you. Be a complete bastard."*

"That's not hard," he said. "Just you watch yourself, young lady. Trust the old wolf to watch his own back."

"Love you, Yanni."

"Love you, too," he said, and thumbed the connection dead.

"Is it all right?" Frank asked anxiously.

He looked over at Frank, very sure the girl had been into his files, very sure Base One could do it; and she now knew something only he and the first Ari had known for well over a century. Frank was AF-997. Nearly an original, off the same genetic tree as her Florian, not at all far removed. And that *wasn't* the number Frank had in every other record in Reseune. Damned sure it would be hard for anybody to get to Frank without knowing his real name, and that said something about how detailed young Ari had gotten about her research. He felt a little exposed, knowing she knew that secret.

But at least he wasn't scheduled for a long semi-retirement out at Strassenberg, and she'd just made him an exception in the revision of Reseune authority.

Him, and Frank. When a whole lot else *hadn't* been what it was supposed to be—*he'd* let something major get past him, and he was beyond upset, and embarrassed about the fact: he felt sick at his stomach, felt the years reel back and saw a dozen scenes replay, with a certain different knowledge about a certain azi. He stared out the window at the sandstone and concrete towers of Novgorod, at the gray mirror of the polluted harbor, and the barges that connected Novgorod to the upriver—so, so much that had grown up since the War. So much that had changed.

Kyle? Kyle was *old* history. Kyle had been there for nearly—God—he'd come on staff in '62 in the last century and lived twenty-four more years this side of the century mark, most of it with Giraud. Six decades. Six decades with Giraud, and then Hicks, leaking God knew what to whoever was running him.

Military agent. Giraud had kept him answering questions on military operations for a few years after his return from service in Defense. He remembered a supper meeting in '62, Giraud saying he was finally going to run the axe code, reclaim Kyle to active service.

Giraud had done that. He remembered Giraud saying it had gone pretty much as he expected, that Kyle hadn't lost any memory, or didn't think he had. No conflicts. No problems. Just like the thirty-odd other alphas they'd recovered from Defense after the War ended . . . most of them specialists, technicals who didn't mentally visit the here and now often enough to be a real problem to re-Contract. Some had died.

But Kyle. Kyle had been a psych operator, a military interrogator. Kyle had been on Admiral Azov's staff, first.

Azov. Damn him. The bastard chiefly responsible for the mess on Gehenna. Azov had, later on, conspired with Jordan—had worked against Reseune, in those days. The first Ari had stung him, stung him badly. Azov and Ari hadn't been friendly once certain things started coming to light, particularly the handling of azi in the armed forces, and Azov hadn't lived to find out what else Ari had done to him, at Gehenna.

Meanwhile Gorodin had come, friendly to Science, supposedly a whole new post-War age in the relations of Science and Defense.

But Gorodin had never thrown the off-switch on Kyle or let Ari in on their nasty little secret. Secretary Lu, who'd served as Proxy Councillor for Gorodin, had never told them. Friend of theirs. Close friend of Giraud's, most of the time.

And the military had still been collecting information hand over fist—learning everything that crossed Giraud's desk.

They must have known the first Ari's business, as much of it as she'd trusted Giraud with—which would easily be the whole psychogenesis project, most likely everything involving the feud with Jordan: and, oh, Defense had been able to snag *Jordan,* hadn't they, just at the right time? Nice piece of psychology, that. Offer Jordan the out he wanted, the transfer to Fargone, right when the relationship had gotten desperate—and then when Ari'd gone for Justin—

That had been a delicious piece of news. And they'd used it. Defense had been all eager to talk to Jordan. If Ari had *ever* questioned Kyle herself, *ever* gotten into Giraud's records, *ever* done that—oh, but Ari had been fully occupied with Jordan as the center of her problems in that last year of her life. She didn't regard Giraud's psych abilities all that highly, but she knew he was loyal and good at what he did.

And then she'd died.

And after Gorodin? If Kyle had still belonged to Defense and still been reporting to them, he'd been, oh, likely highly active during Khalid's short term.

His inside information hadn't saved Khalid from walking right into it with young Ari. Maybe Khalid had ignored the intelligence he'd gotten, hadn't believed the kid was what she was. He'd found it out—in public, on national vid networks.

Darker thought, still, had Khalid ever really turned

loose of Kyle once he'd begun to receive information from
him?

Intelligence, for God's sake. Khalid had been chief of
Intelligence before he ever ran for the Council seat.

He'd been managing Kyle's sort—oh, from way back.
Possibly—

Possibly Kyle hadn't ever reported to Gorodin at all.
Maybe not even to Azov. They might not have known what
Khalid's source was, except that Khalid had good information. Azov had died of old age. Lu had. Then Gorodin.
Defense had been nominally the ally of Science, most of
the time, except the brief stint under Khalid. Jacques—
Science had urged Jacques into office to succeed Khalid,
when Gorodin had gone into rejuv failure; they'd managed
to sway Spurlin . . . now assassinated.

Along with two people connected to the Eversnow
project; them, and the Defense candidate who'd agreed to
support it and who'd urged Jacques to vote for it.

Watch out, Ari said, for his own life, at present, in
Novgorod.

Khalid. Chief of Intelligence, from the darkest years of
the War, a young and ambitious officer in those days, not
so old now, when most of that generation were dead. And
it was entirely conceivable that his sudden rise in Defense
had been precisely because of the quality of the information he had on the inner workings of Science.

"Kyle's not ours," Yanni said quietly to Frank, and
turned from that gray, misty vista. "He never has been.
Kyle's still Defense. Did you ever see that coming?"

Frank looked at him, just stared in shock. "He never
gave a hint. He'd honestly paired with Hicks. It felt that
way. It always did, from way back."

"Could that part be real, even if he was Defense?"

"Could be," Frank said.

"It's going to hit Hicks in the gut," Yanni said. "He said
Kyle was like a brother. Relied on him. Trusted him for
years."

"I can't imagine," Frank said. "It's got to have torn Kyle
up, too. He was different, around Hicks. He cared. Cared
about the people in his command. That's bad, if that's true.
That's real bad."

"Defense must have kept getting reports from him. He can't have liked it." A thought occurred to him. Giraud's office. Hicks'. Access to files. Dossiers. A lot of things. Ari had died, and Giraud had taken the Directorship and increasingly turned ReseuneSec over to Hicks.

That was where Kyle had transferred over, and Kyle had attached to Hicks in a way he never quite had to Giraud. Hicks relied on Kyle as a personal aide, in a way he'd never served with Giraud, who'd had Abban. Giraud had let Hicks handle Kyle, let him have Kyle's Contract finally, even finagled a provisional alpha certificate for Hicks explicitly to allow him to work with Kyle, because the pairing had seemed to work so well.

Ari'd died . . . and it wasn't suicide. He'd never liked the suicide notion. Too much had been left unfinished.

If it hadn't been Jordan, it had been Abban. Basic question of opportunity.

Giraud wouldn't have ordered it. Without Giraud, Abban wouldn't have done it—that part of the equation had never made sense to him. But it had never made sense, either, that Jordan had done it. Abban was the one with capability *and* opportunity.

Abban had been upset. Giraud had been upset. Upset had been contagious in the halls in those days after Ari had died. The whole universe had been in upheaval, and for several months after Ari had died, Giraud had been on a hair trigger and so had Abban. You didn't question Giraud in those days. Secretaries had run scared and Denys himself had said, "Don't talk to him. He doesn't want to talk."

In days when they'd had the vital job of getting the psychogenesis project going and they'd desperately *needed* to talk . . . Giraud hadn't been outstandingly well-composed.

Settling into the new job, he'd thought. And mourning a woman he'd greatly regarded. Giraud had been loyal to Ari, he'd stake his life on that.

So Abban couldn't have done it—could he?

But if Abban had done something that hurt Giraud—there was a little reason for upset in that household, wasn't there? Abban's own origins were in green barracks, never shipped out, never left Reseune: *he* had no questionable background. He'd been with Giraud from childhood. Giraud had changed offices; taken Abban with him into Admin; Hicks had already taken over Kyle.

Everything changed when Ari died. He saw it like a chessboard, all the pieces suddenly, massively, shifted on the board: white had castled-up, and young Ari had been a mote in a womb-tank for a whole, mostly peaceful nine months. Once that had happened, Giraud had settled—as if the universe was right again.

"What are you thinking?" Frank asked him finally.

"That Abban never could have killed Ari," he said, "no more than Jordan could. Unless."

"Unless," Frank said.

"Unless he believed it was in Giraud's interest," he said. "Maybe somebody told him that. And then, in the aftermath, maybe he knew it wasn't as true as he thought it was—at least in the immediate effects. Giraud's upset would have been hard for him to take. A very, very upsetting thing."

"He was an alpha," Frank said. "He could put himself back together."

"And he had a rationale. Giraud was walking wounded. But he'd protected Giraud from some unspecified danger. Now he had to take care of Giraud. So he did that, didn't he? But nobody ever took care of Abban. Abban couldn't tell Giraud what he'd done. And the week Giraud died he went into Denys's care, and nobody ever took care of Abban."

Frank looked upset. They'd known one another, Frank and Abban, worked together. They'd remarked, oh, more than once, how it was a damned lie that Denys was capable of handling Seely, let alone Abban, when Abban came over to him. They both knew about Denys' alpha certificate, which was fake as they came. Abban had needed immediate help when Giraud died, and Denys—Denys had gotten notions in his head about staying in power and nobody touched Abban.

He'd sent Abban after Ari, and Abban was already messed up. "Killing the same woman twice," he said to Frank, "and the first having been a mistake, that's got to have rung clear to his deep sets. Nasty, nasty piece of business."

"Nobody ever felt sorry for Abban," Frank said. "But he wasn't right, then. He really wasn't right when he did that." A moment later Frank said: "All those years with Denys—Seely wasn't in that good shape, either."

"More than that," Yanni said, "if Giraud didn't order Abban to kill Ari—Abban wouldn't go out on his own. He had orders. And if they weren't from Giraud, maybe they weren't from Denys, either. That notion's always bothered me. Denys wasn't *able* to order that, not while Giraud was alive. That order came from somewhere else . . . a decision that Ari had been around long enough. Knowledge that she was already dying. That it would only shorten her life a year . . . and *not* let her finish arranging things herself. It would throw the decisions all to Giraud."

"Kyle," Frank said.

"Kyle, and the ones directing him," Yanni said. "Defense. She'd yanked Jordan out of negotiations with them and brought him home, she was working just maybe too close to sensitive areas, on the verge of finding out just who'd been exacerbating Jordan's discontent—setting him up, if you want my opinion, to land on the radical side of things. He'd been corresponding with the Paxers. With the Abolitionists, as it turned out, though I think it came as a shock to him when he found it out. And Ari took measures to be sure Justin didn't go down his father's route. I think she was on the track of something that could have become very uncomfortable for Kyle's managers . . . I think they knew she was close to dealing with it. And Hicks went on meeting with Defense; and Kyle was right with him."

"Kyle got his instructions there," Frank said.

"Exactly. Tell me. Would *you* take instruction from another azi?"

"I don't know," Frank said. "I can say I wouldn't, but if the keys were there . . . who could say he wouldn't."

"And Abban was Giraud's," Yanni said. "And Kyle was, at the time. Totally inside the walls. Damn, that's a nasty scenario."

"In a way, Ari caught it," Frank said. "It took the next Ari to do it. Suppose there was something in the first Ari's notes—suppose the first Ari put her onto it? Or did she figure it out?"

Yanni thought about it, thought about the way things had been going, and slowly shook his head. "I think if the first Ari had known, she'd have moved on Kyle faster than you could blink and she'd have had Giraud's help doing it. I think our little Ari has come up with this one on her own. Damned clever of her. There's only one thing *wrong* with her scenario."

"That being?"

"She's just told Defense she knows what their game is. She just stopped it." Yanni looked toward the gray view again, the towers beside the sea, the towers that were Science, and Defense, Trade, and State. The other five—Citizens, Information, Industry, Internal Affairs and Finance—were just out of view. So was the tower that consituted the capitol itself, Cyteen's Senate Building, and the tower that held the Council of Nine, the Senate, and if the dividing wall were folded back, the Council of Worlds.

He could call down the heavens. If he wanted to let havoc loose, he could gather all his evidence of assassination and espionage and take it to the Nine and lay it before the Council of Worlds—but Ari was right: it was getting dangerous. As things stood, it was a major risk for him just to take a car to the airport, and he wasn't sure he'd survive to get there. It was a risk to go to Science, a risk for Jacques to come here. Damn the girl, she'd upset the whole government at a critical moment, maybe because it seemed to the kid like a good move—

Or maybe because she wasn't the little girl any longer. She might be doing everything precisely to get a jump ahead of the opposition because she had reason to think there was diminishing time to do it. What had she said, that the explosion might have been a signal, to those who knew, that it was time to move?

Other things were moving, all right. And maybe he and Frank had just become two more pieces on the board, white bishop and white knight, say, out there to tempt the opponent into doing something. She'd tried to tell him get their asses home. He'd ignored her warning, confident in the moment he'd done it.

Maybe he *should* get himself and Frank to the airport, and go home, this evening, while they could, settle in and let the youngster run the place.

Or maybe the old bishop had a few moves in him. He and Frank had been at this a long, long time, and he wasn't out of resources yet.

Khalid? He wouldn't concede the board to that bastard, not while he had room to maneuver.

"If we don't get Jacques out of there," Frank said, "his lifespan is limited."

"Jacques is due at Science in two hours and I think we should go there now, just in case anybody's timing our departure. If we're in the target, let's not make it too easy for them."

BOOK THREE   Section 5   Chapter x

JULY 26, 2424
1620H

The security hold was officially off. The halls were totally quiet, except for Patrick Emory on his way home from work. A ghostly hush prevailed throughout Alpha Wing. They met him, Justin and Grant did, on the gray, blue-wave carpet, and Patrick just looked nervous and tired after what had been, to anyone's reckoning, a hell of a day.

"How's Wing One?" Justin asked him, knowing Patrick would have come that way.

"Quiet," Patrick said, "just normal. Except the construction hasn't started back up."

"Good," Justin said, and they passed each other, on their individual business. They picked up Mark and Gerry downstairs. Mark and Gerry wanted to know when they left the Wing, and they played by the rules and didn't make them have to scramble when exit security stalled them: Mark and Gerry met them at the lift, they were all pleasant to each other—

"Hope we didn't mess up your supper," Justin said.

"No, ser," Gerry said, "we had a sandwich. Thanks for the warning."

"Glad to oblige," he said. "Sorry you have to tag us."

"Our duty, ser," Mark said, which it was.

They passed the exit desk, took the lift up to familiar territory: the two Ari had set to watch Jordan's vicinity were on duty there—had a desk, today, for greater comfort, and disguised themselves as ordinary hall security. Mark and Gerry were going to have to stand, at least for a few moments.

"Our intent is to go out to supper," Justin said to their two guards, "but that depends. We could send out; we could just eat in. Don't worry about it. Just stay at ease."

"Yes, ser," the answer was. They clearly didn't mind. After the rest of today, with, as they heard from Wes, some of their number in hospital and otherwise patched up, Mark and Gerry had had a quiet day.

Grant rang the minder. "Grant ALX," he said, "and Justin Warrick. We're looking to take you both to dinner."

No answer, immediately. Then the door opened and let them in.

Jordan was on the couch, looking asleep, give or take the glass beside him. Paul had gotten up, and looked worried.

"Is everything all right?" Paul asked.

"Fine," Justin said, and let the door shut. "Wake up, Dad. Dinner."

No response.

"He's had a few," Paul said.

Well, it wasn't dinner out, Justin thought, and went and shook Jordan, who didn't respond, just moved away from him.

"I'm sorry," Paul said.

"Not your problem," Justin said. He walked over to the autobar, looked at the levels in the supply, leaned on his elbows on the counter and thought, Damn.

"If I can fix you something, ser," Paul said.

Justin shot a look at Grant, and Grant stared back, then gave a nod.

"You sit down," Justin said then, "and let Grant get you something."

"I've had enough, ser, already."

"When was lunch?"

Paul looked a little taken aback, looked at the clock on the minder, and failed to answer promptly.

"Breakfast?" Justin asked, while Grant proceeded about his business at the bar.

"We had breakfast," Paul said.

"He knows what happened," Justin said.

"He followed it, as much as we knew. The vid came on a while ago, said it was the all-clear. Do we trust that?"

"We trust that," Justin said. "Young Ari's fine. She's running ReseuneSec, and between you and me, we're a bit safer this afternoon than we were this morning."

"I hope so, ser."

"I know we are." He watched Grant hand Paul a glass of something clear, water, or vodka, not immediately evident.

"Drink this," Grant said. "Paul."

Paul took it. Paul was the soul of politeness and quiet.

"Paul," Justin said, "sit down. Please. We want to talk to you."

"I don't want to talk, ser. I'm sorry Jordan isn't able to go to dinner. I think it would probably be a good idea if you went on without us. Please."

"Sit down," Justin said, and sat down, himself, on the end of the couch. "Sit down, Paul. I want to ask you something. It's all right. Sit down."

Paul had known them both since childhood. And he did, slowly, sit down.

"My father's put a hell of a load on you," Justin said. "I don't want to. I want to ask you, honestly, how are you doing?"

"Perfectly well, ser."

"I'm not ser. I'm Justin. Remember. It's just Justin and Grant. The way we always were. You used to keep us in line. You'd tell us when we were just a little over the edge. Didn't you?"

"I did," Paul said.

"Well, you can tell us now if we are. I don't want to push you. But I'm pretty good at what I do. So's Grant. And we all know Jordan's got a problem."

Jordan moved. Not coherently. He settled again, and Paul looked back.

"He's all right," Paul said. "It was a hard day."

"He didn't take it well, what happened today."

"I know you say it's all right," Paul said, "but we don't think so."

Justin nodded. "I understand that. I respect it. I'll tell you, though, I don't like what I see."

"I'm sorry, ser."

"Because you can't stop him? It's not your responsibility to stop him, Paul. I don't know how you could. He'll do what he wants to."

"It was just a hard day."

"Every day's a hard day," Grant said. "It's not your responsibility to stop him. Who's the Supervisor?"

Paul made a lame gesture in Jordan's direction.

"So when did you last ask him for help?" Justin said.

A shrug.

"You don't, do you? Or you do, but you don't make it clear to him. When's the last time you did?"

"I don't know. This is private, Justin, I'm sorry. It's between him and me."

"It was December 21, 2405."

Paul just looked at him, appalled.

"Wasn't it?"

"Maybe. I don't know." Paul started to get up. Grant reached out and put a hand on his shoulder.

"Listen to him, Paul."

"The year after you got to Planys. What had you so upset, then?"

"I don't know. I don't remember."

"Dad took care of it then. He handled it. He hasn't handled damned much since. What changed?"

"I don't—I don't know. The isolation. The frustration. Things."

"Paul," Justin said, "you know I know what I'm doing. You know I'm family. I'd never do anything to hurt you, or Jordan."

"I—"

"I wouldn't, Paul. I swear I wouldn't. But nineteen

years, Paul. Nineteen years without any consideration of your own situation—that's not fair, Paul."

"I'm fine."

"Prove it to me. I've got your manual. I've read it. Let me take the load off a while."

Paul shook his head.

"You know better," Grant said. "A Supervisor is telling you you've got a problem. And you know you've got a problem. And you know you can't help him until you get help of your own, Paul. Listen to Justin. One pill. Just take a dose, and relax, and let go for a bit."

"Jordan won't trust me."

"Jordan will cope with it," Justin said. "At a certain point, Jordan is a born-man problem, and I'm his son, and he's my problem. Take the pill, Paul. Just take it, and let's go back to the bedroom and you can take tape. Your proper tape, nothing wrong with it, nothing more than you've ever had. You haven't had it in a long, long time. Please do it, Paul. Fifteen minutes. So you can help him. Grant needs you. I do. He does. Just take care of yourself this time. Quit self-doctoring."

Paul looked at him a long, long moment, muscles tight in his jaw, and on the verge of quivering.

"Just the original tape," Paul said. "Nothing but that."

"You'll know it," Justin said. "Have you got the dose here?"

Paul shook his head.

"Didn't think so," Justin said, and took out his own pill case, and offered Paul one. "Just take it down."

Paul took it, and put it in his mouth, and started to chase it with the glass. "Not water," he said.

"Won't hurt you," Justin said. "It'll just hit faster."

Paul took a large gulp, and set the glass down, got up and headed for the bedroom.

Justin shot a look at Grant. Grant didn't flinch.

"Tape unit," Justin said. "That'll take the data."

Grant nodded, looking grim.

It wasn't an honest thing, what they were doing. It wasn't fair, it was going to make Jordan furious, and it was going, possibly, to save Paul from the misery he was in. He

had the datastick, the condensed tape; and he had the tape
unit he'd used himself—no question it was up to the job.
All he had to do was feed it in: the data conversion would
take about five minutes.

"You watch Jordan," he said. "Give me a short hour."

"You're going to do the whole thing?" Grant asked.
"Both steps?"

"Second," he said. They'd talked about starting with
a quiet imperative, show up, come to us. But given what
was happening in the world, and how Jordan was taking
it, their access to Paul wasn't certain any longer—wouldn't
be as available again, on any relaxed terms. "He may
never speak to me again," he said somberly, meaning Jordan. Maybe Paul. "He may not. But, damn it, if I can't help
him, I can at least do something for Paul, who can."

Grant reached out, pressed his shoulder, said, quietly,
"I'll give you warning. I'll keep Jordan out of it."

"Real-time work," he said, with his hand on the bedroom door. "I *hate* it."

"You're good at it," Grant said. "You've always been
good at it."

"*We're* good at it," he said. "I hope we're good
enough."

He went into the bedroom. Paul was standing there, by
the bed.

"Just sit down," he said. Paul would be getting muzzy
in a bit, and he'd hit him with a born-man dose, which was
hard, for an azi who didn't entirely need it, to take in tape.
"I want to explain this."

"That would be welcome," Paul said, and did sit down,
on the edge of the bed. "Why have you got my manual?
Did Jordan give it to you?"

"Because we knew something was wrong," he said.
"And no, he didn't. I found it. I looked at it. I suppose you
have."

Paul shook his head. "Didn't. He hid it, when we came
across. They had it—for a while. But we got it back. I hope
it's still all right."

"If it isn't," Justin said, "I can fix it. Paul, I *can* fix it.
I love you. You're family. I won't let anything happen to
you. I won't. Believe that."

"Have to," Paul said glumly. "I'm full of pills."

Justin pulled out the case again. Took out another. "I want you to take this one."

"Too much."

"Do it, Paul. Just do it."

Paul's critical faculty was diminishing by the second. He hesitated, which was how strong he was; but after a moment's insistence, he took it, and swallowed it dry. One pill of that dosage was heavy enough. Two was a sledge-hammer, and after a moment Paul lay down on the bed and just stared at the ceiling.

Justin set about it, then, activated the tape function on the minder, fed the stick in, let it process, took the stick back.

"I'm getting a little glazed," Paul said. "Justin, boy, you had better be truthful."

"I am, Paul." Echoes, from decades ago. Two boys who'd ducked past the minder and gotten down to the arcade in the mall. Paul had asked them—asked them if they'd lied to him.

"No," they'd both said. He'd taught Grant to lie. Useful, in the occupation they'd undertaken, in the times they'd lived in. "I won't lie to you, Paul. How's Jordan been? Will you tell me the truth?"

"Hell," Paul said on a sigh, a hollow voice. "Just hell."

"I got that idea," he said. "But it won't be, after this. You just listen to the tape, Paul, and I'll have something to say to you in a bit."

He pushed the button. He let it run. It took about a quarter hour, and it was nothing but Paul's exact tape, the same that Paul had had from his earliest boyhood years, simple things, simple principles, simplest instructions. Back to utter basics.

Down to deep sets.

He watched the time run. He saw all the tension go from Paul's face, as if he'd shed years; and he kept very, very still, and didn't interfere until the light flashed, indicating the program run, completed.

Then he said, brushing Paul's hair back off his forehead, very, very gently, "Paul AP."

"Yes," Paul said.

He said, then, the one patch, the one bit of deep set work he and Grant had put together: "Jordan has all the responsibility for you, Paul AP, and he is your Supervisor. Love Jordan, and believe in your own capability. Be honest toward him in everything. Relax, now. Remember to be happy."

Paul let go a long breath. And the slight frown smoothed out, and became what he hadn't seen on Paul's face in years—a slight smile.

"Good," he said, while Paul was still receptive. "You're very good, Paul. You always were."

He'd winged it, on the last. It was reckless. It was stupid. It was love for his second father, too much to keep quiet. And having been stupid, he drew back very quietly and opened the door and just let Paul sleep it off.

He walked into what had been their living room, and saw Jordan still sleeping it off. He sat down beside Grant, and said, "It went all right."

"Suppose we ought to just go?" Grant said. "I think we ought to."

He thought about it. Thought about Paul lying in there, completely unprotected. Shook his head. "Jordan wouldn't hurt him, but—"

The name was enough. Jordan stirred, put up a hand between him and a specific light, then went back to sleep for a bit.

They didn't say anything, or move, for a good while. The minder clock marked the passing minutes.

"About forty-five minutes," he said softly to Grant, "and he'll be safe."

Hell of a thing. He'd never thought in his life that he'd be sitting guard between his father and Paul. Which only proved things had gotten very, very bad.

And one thought said he should stay and face Jordan when he woke up, and tell him what he'd done; and another said it had been, quite obviously, a bad day in Jordan's calendar, and that Jordan wouldn't be in a receptive mood.

But he didn't want to lie. He'd lied enough for the day. He didn't feel easy about it—far from it. He wasn't even sure he'd done well enough for Paul, and wanted to sit long enough for Paul not only to transit into natural sleep, but to wake up. Hell, Jordan didn't know; Jordan wouldn't remember. He could tell Jordan they'd agreed to it while he was blind, stupid drunk and Jordan couldn't prove it . . . damn it.

"Probably time," Grant said softly.

"I'll look in on Paul," Justin said. "Just be sure he's all right."

He got up very quietly, went back to the bedroom and opened the door in silence, saw Paul had turned on his side, his favorite way to sleep, and pillowed his head on his arm, and looked comfortable enough. He shut the door then and came back to the living room as Grant got up.

"What are you doing here?" Jordan asked.

"Been here a while," Justin said.

"Damn," Jordan said. "So you're still walking around. Princess' pets."

"In charge of Alpha Wing, actually, so we go pretty much where we please, which is the way things are, today. Hicks isn't in charge any more. I can't say I'm too sorry."

"Hicks," Jordan said, and raked a hand through his hair and winced. "God."

"Dad," Justin said, and Grant laid a hand on his arm, pressure toward the door.

"How long have you been here?"

"An hour or so. Dad, I want to talk to you."

Grant took hold of his arm, hard, and he shut up.

"Justin was worried about you," Grant said. "Thought we'd go to dinner."

"We can go to dinner," Jordan said, "if they're not shooting people on sight. Paul?"

"We can cook something here," Justin said. "Or call out."

"No reason we can't go out."

"There's a good one," Justin said. "You're sleeping it off, and so is Paul, for two different reasons."

"What's that?" Jordan asked, frowning at him.

"Paul's taken tape," Justin said. "Just his regular tape."

"The hell!"

"His regular tape, Dad, which I have access to, and have had, for some time, and while you're busy trying to kill yourself, Paul's been the forgotten element in this transaction." He had the datastick in his pocket. He laid it on the counter. "This has the primary file. I've installed it in the minder, for his convenience."

"Damn it!" Jordan came up off the couch and hit the corner of it.

"Watch your step," Justin said.

"Damn you, you damned conniving, ass-kissing bastard!" Jordan made it past the couch and Grant shoved, sent Justin back and turned toward Jordan as Jordan swung.

Grant went down, knocking into Justin, and Justin caught him short of the floor—Grant wasn't out, just shocked, and started trying to get up again while Jordan loomed over both of them.

"Get the hell back!" Justin yelled at Jordan, and hauled, helping Grant up, and Grant grabbed him.

"That's entirely enough," Grant snapped, and spun him back toward the door.

"It's not enough," Justin said, and stood his ground. "Jordan, you self-centered bastard, you listen to me. You let Paul come out of it on his own, you keep your mouth shut until you know how he is, and if he isn't all right, you call me and I'll come."

"Did she organize this?"

"She? Did *she* organize this? What do you think, that I can't run basic tape on somebody I've known since the day I was born? Or maybe it's harder than I think. Clearly you were having trouble doing it . . ."

"Justin," Grant said, and got an arm around his ribs and hauled.

"No, Grant, he's wanting a fight. For all I know he'll go in there and start in on Paul, drunk as he is. For all I know that's what he *has* done!"

"You watch your damned mouth! Get out of here! Get out of here and don't let me see you again, don't let me ever see you!"

"What, you're going to avoid mirrors from now on? I'm *you,* damn you, Jordan: that's what you had me born to be, isn't it? The newer, better *you?*"

"On your best day you aren't, you little bastard! You're her piece of work, you're back in bed with her—"

"Forget your favorite obsession! You knew that territory before I ever got to it, you knew it, you connived your
way into it, maybe you were even, God help you, in love
with something other than having your own way. Maybe
you can remember that. Maybe you can remember what
it's like to care about somebody besides yourself. *Paul*
might appreciate it!"

"You shut up about Paul! You let him the fuck alone,
damn you!"

"Good!" he said. *"Finally! Thank you!"* and he gave
way and let Grant drag him the rest of the way to the door.

And out it.

At which point they stood there in front of the security
desk, and Mark and Gerry straightened up properly, as the
door shut.

Justin drew in a deep breath, and looked up at Grant,
who nursed a cut lip. "Is the tooth all right?"

"I'm sure it's very solid," Grant said. "I apologize. I sincerely apologize."

"What for? For taking the punch?" He was all but vi-
brating with anger, but he had no one around him who
wasn't azi, and absolutely didn't deserve what he was feeling at the moment, a combination of the desire to break
something and a conviction trying to surface, that what
he'd just done and said hadn't been the right thing—damn
it. Damn it all, he'd set Jordan off, and not to Paul's good.
"I should go back in there."

"You absolutely should *not*," Grant said. "He'll do
many things, but he won't hurt Paul."

"What do you mean he won't hurt Paul? He's done
nothing *but* hurt Paul."

"Trust yourself. Trust Paul to handle it. Let it be."

They had four witnesses who hadn't asked to be witnesses,
and who looked entirely confused and slightly upset.

"It's all right," Justin said, obliged to say it, being the
only born-man in the hallway, and supposedly rational. "It
was a born-man argument, over with. No one was hurt."

"It *is* all right," Grant said to the guards, who probably saw Grant as the sane and offended party, who had a
bloody lip. "We'll go to dinner now."

"Are you going to be able to eat?" Justin asked, re-

morse and a decent shame finally making it to the surface.
And he was still shaking with anger. "I don't think I have
much appetite."

"Fruit ice," Grant suggested. "That might do for a sore
jaw."

He was tempted to say a bar would do better, but not
after his quarrel with Jordan. "Fruit ice," he agreed, and
they took the lift down and bought ices for Mark and
Gerry while they were at it, over in Ed, where the best ice
parlors were.

Everything was normal. Kids ran and played. Two preoccupied lovers walked along the mall, under the willows.
The ice parlor had a vid, and it flashed, ominously enough,
with the News logo.

Justin took a hard draw of the shaved lime ice, just
watched. They had the transcript crawl on. It said:

*Councillor of Information Catherine Lao has been
taken to the hospital this evening with chest pains . . .*

He nudged Grant, but Grant was already watching,
solemn-faced.

*The Councillor's sudden crisis came in a late committee
meeting. She has been in failing health for several months.
The Proxy Councillor for Information, Adlai Edgerton,
has not been available for comment.*

*Meanwhile the crisis continues in Defense, as the in-
cumbent Councillor for Defense has continued to postpone any announcement of a Proxy appointment; and has
been closeted with the Proxy Councillor for Science in a
session closed to the news media.*

*Meanwhile the state of affairs in Reseune seems to have
normalized, with a declaration by Reseune Administration that, while Yanni Schwartz, current Proxy Councillor
for Science, remains as Administrator of Reseune, Ariane
Emory, aged eighteen, has formally assumed administrative control of ReseuneSec . . .*

"So they know," Justin said.

"Lao being sick, that's no news."

"That's the sort of thing they say before somebody
turns up dead," Justin said.

"And Edgerton's gone quiet." Grant shook his head and
took another draw on the lime. "It's not sounding good."

"It's sounding like we could have a new Councillor for Information before long," Justin said. "It's what Ari said, we're losing too many that have a grasp of what went on."

"Ignore it," Grant said. "It's over our heads. We don't have an opinion. Keep it that way."

"I do," he said. "That's the hell of it. I can't advise her. If she asked me what to do, I wouldn't know the least thing to tell her. And she put me in charge, more's the pity."

"I'm not sure Yanni knows what to do at this point," Grant said. "Cheer up."

"Why?"

"I don't know why," Grant said. "I just know it's what I said, over our heads. We can't stop it. We can't do a damned thing, except—"

"Except wait for Jordan to blow?"

"That, yes."

"He's not speaking to me. Remember?"

"I give it seven days."

"I don't know why. He has a very good memory."

"He's something we can take care of," Grant said, "so he *doesn't* land in young Ari's new security office . . . and neither do we. We stay out of *there,* and we're doing the best we can be expected to do."

"And we keep Alpha Wing from revolt," he said, feeling a little lighter-hearted. "At least that's not going to happen."

"Won't," Grant said. "But we can double-check that the services are going to work, if we do get another shut-down."

He nodded. It was a practical thing to do, a Grant kind of thing to do. He'd interfered outside Alpha Wing for what he promised himself was the last time, the only time. If Jordan wanted to talk to him hereafter, he'd talk; but if Jordan wanted not to, well, maybe in a quieter world and with Paul better off, he might have options that didn't exist with the current state of affairs. Time cured some things.

It hurt. It hurt a fair bit that Grant had taken the shot for him, but that was a revelation in itself. Maybe it would penetrate Jordan's hard head, that that was exactly what Paul had done. Jordan's perfectly run little hell had just gotten revised, for good or for ill. And what was Jordan going to do about it? Suggest to Paul that he go on absorbing guilt and responsibility, the way things had been?

He didn't think Jordan would do that, not when it came to putting it into words. And maybe if Jordan read the manual he'd annotated for twenty years, read it in the light of what he and Grant had just done to fix it, there was a remote chance Jordan would even see it for himself.

BOOK THREE Section 5 Chapter xi

JULY 27, 2424
0403H

"So you want to know about the military," the first Ari said, out of Base One. **"Are you having trouble with Defense?"**

"Yes," Ari said.

"So did I," the voice said, which was more and more like her voice, or vice versa. **"I particularly had trouble with Azov, who was a bastard of the first order. But you probably don't want to hear about Azov. Is your question about Azov?"**

She was tempted. But it was the small hours of the morning, and her head hurt so, and she didn't have the time. "No," she said.

"Is your question about defense projects or about the Bureau of Defense? You can give a keyword now. The program will find it."

"Military azi."

"Military azi, as in the azi who served in the armed forces."

"Yes."

"Question?"

"An alpha azi named Kyle AK-36."

"Giraud's assistant. Correct?"

"I need to take him down. I need to deprogram Kyle AK-36. I need advice."

A small pause. Her heart picked up its beats, apprehension that the first Ari might not have any advice to give about the man who'd gotten through her defenses.

"This program can locate files on Kyle AK-36. Proceeding."

"Could Defense have reprogrammed Kyle AK-36 while he was in the military? I have reason to believe Kyle AK-36's mindset no longer corresponds to his personal manual. His axe code failed."

Another long pause. Longer than the first.

A mechanical voice, different than Ari One's, said: *"Base One is prepared to open file on Kyle AK-36."* Then a synthetic female voice said: *"Axe code failure. Causes: 1. Incorrect manual. 2. Block installed. 3. Psychset conflict. Choose one."*

"1, 2, and 3. Pyschset conflict. Report."

"Psychset conflict: axe code failure. Three cases on record."

"Print case files to local computer."

"In process."

"1. Incorrect manual, re Kyle AK-36. Check and report." She had a sip of coffee. She didn't think it was the cause, either. Kyle had functioned well enough to be in Admin, in both a military and a civilian operation. A conflict tended to show. Running on an incorrect manual—showed.

"Manual on file corresponds with original manual."

"Block, re Kyle AK-36. Check and report."

A much faster answer. *"Information incomplete. Base One cannot access information from Defense secure system. Further attempts may leave trace."*

"Thank you, Base One. No further attempt. Method of removing a Defense-installed block."

A long pause. *"Case record follows."*

"Physical print, Base One."

"Printing. Transcript is three hundred and two pages."

Her head hurt even thinking about it. But the print began shooting into the tray.

"Base One, Giraud failed to detect Defense Bureau block on AK-36 when he used an axe code. Method of concealment of block: check and report."

"Base One has no record of Giraud failure."

"Well, he did fail, dammit." She dropped her head into her hands. "Base One, did Ari ever successfully deal with a Defense Bureau block? If yes, did Giraud ever access that file?"

"First question: yes. Second question: Giraud's Base insufficient to access Base One record."

Well, *there* was an answer. And he hadn't gone to Ari. He hadn't admitted failure. He might not have recognize it. Faced with dealing with an alpha, he hadn't opened up his files and Denys' to Ari's close scrutiny, especially counting that Denys' certificate was a damned lie. His secrecy would have been compromised if he'd let Ari into the manuals he had. Open one, all might have been of interest. Wasn't that like Giraud, too?

"Note for Giraud Two: dealing with failure. Tell Base One. Dammit."

"Recorded."

She thought a few beats, while the printout flipped into the tray. "Base One, did Ari ever successfully deal with a Defense Bureau block in an alpha subject?"

"Yes."

"Print case file."

"Printing. Transcript is three hundred and two pages."

"Is that the same file currently printing?"

"Yes."

Damned stupid computer. "Cancel second print. Continue."

Same case. At least there were only three hundred two pages to read before she slept.

Catherine Lao was in the hospital with a coronary, a real one, and diminishing liver function. It was likely the tail end of rejuv. Nobody could locate her Proxy, who was either dead in Swigert Bay or hiding out under an assumed name, trying not to be dead, and it was getting chancy whether Yanni could muster the usual closely knit bloc of Reseune-friendly votes on Council. Yanni could call the Council of Worlds into session—but that got into regional fights and vote trading between stations and Bureaus and it was just a whole other headache. They didn't want to go to that, and get Pan-Paris at odds again with Fargone . . . God, no. Yanni had done his job. Catherine Lao was asking Yanni to come to the hospital, and Ari'd told Yanni no, don't go, just come home, but was he going to listen?

She couldn't swear to it—because if Yanni *was* going to call a Council of Worlds, it was more politic to do it from Novgorod; and because Jacques hadn't gotten right onto the evening news and made Tanya Bigelow his Proxy Councillor . . .

God, it was a mess. And she, meanwhile, was wasting time trying to figure out who'd been responsible for killing her predecessor twenty years ago, which wasn't relevant, and trying to make sure Yanni had good information, which was; and most of all trying to find out if Kyle AK had gotten some signal for some other kind of mayhem, beyond murdering her . . . which could relate to what he'd been into twenty years ago, when somebody, maybe the same people that wanted Khalid in office, had been politicking behind closed doors in the Defense Bureau, dealing with Jordan with one hand and arranging her predecessor's murder with the other.

She took a headache remedy. She wasn't supposed to. She'd do better going to the hospital herself, or just asking Wes to look her over, but her pupils looked the same size in the mirror, and she didn't want to upset Florian by admitting he'd cracked her head that hard. So she just took the headache remedy and then threw up, and took another, with less water, which stayed down.

It might not be smart. But it was what she had to do. Scan the files she had to absorb, make sure they were safe, and then have a long stint with deepstudy.

BOOK THREE   Section 5   Chapter xii

Aug 2, 2424
0548h

Breakfast on a sunny morning in Novgorod . . . they'd been down to granola bars and coffee they made themselves, things from random vending machines, since they'd stopped trusting the hotel kitchens.

But after days of short commons, Quentin AQ, the Carnath girl's Quentin, had showed up with a case of dried fruit, another of oatmeal, four cases of bottled water, five kilos of ground coffee, a case of orange drink, a commercial carton of real eggs, fifteen loaves of bread, a case of precooked bacon, five bottles of vodka, and a large carton of irradiated sandwiches that wouldn't go bad for the next decade. *That* lot was a gift for which Yanni and Frank marked Amy Carnath down for future brilliance. They'd sent ReseuneSec down to the hotel kitchens to confiscate a portable grill, a room refrigerator, plates, silverware, and detergent, and ran their own kitchens in the diplomatic suite. A man named Bert BB-7 and his partner took instruction from Frank on elementary cooking, managed not to overcook the eggs, which the Carnath girl had offered to resupply on call; and they'd three times hosted Jacques, damn him, who showed up with two aides and a lengthening list of concerns, the last over a supper meeting of grilled sandwiches, salted chips, and wine Jacques brought, while he and his staff stuck to the vodka.

In the first three meetings it had gone moderately well: Jacques wasn't sure of Bigelow and said there was some concern because the station Defense people weren't happy with her, and they wanted to propose another candidate, a Tommy Kwesi, who'd been out at Beta . . . who would be here in a week.

"We can't have this dragging on another week," Yanni had objected, and then after two days of arguing for him, Jacques revealed that Khalid was landing within the hour in Novgorod, and that Khalid absolutely refused to accept either Bigelow or Kwesi.

"He didn't *win* the election," Yanni had said to that, and Jacques had ducked his direct gaze, and said they had to have consensus within the Bureau, because without it there were some officers who were going to take the matter to the judiciary, and the rest of Defense didn't want that precedent.

Then the stinger, from Jacques: "There's a contingent pushing Albert Dean."

He'd said: "Dean's a damned fool." Dean was the one who'd consistently voted with Khalid's allies on appropriations, trying to get increased military spending at Mariner and Pan-Paris, which played well politically on the stations that wanted the construction, but infringed on treaties in more ways than they could count. "He's playing politics, he's been playing politics, while we've spent the last thirty years trying to build trust on that border—the only damn border we've got, and he wants to go turning up the heat on it! You want to see two years of absolute stalemate in Council—no. We can't work with him."

"I don't think, in the long run, that what Science can work with is the ultimate criterion for the Proxy I choose."

"No," he'd said flatly, "it isn't. It is, however, what the rest of Council can work with. Dean may play well with the Council of Worlds, but they don't originate the budget, and you can't get a majority to back his program."

"So he's safe," Jacques said with a shrug. "Dean talks. He makes his listeners happy. Nothing of his program ever gets done."

"And your Bureau goes on with its internal business, stirring the pot constantly."

"Some say Science is far too monolithic. Far too one-sided."

"It has advantages, having some sort of consensus. We don't live in a friendly universe, but nothing's helped by provoking our trade partners—and talk provokes, even if the program doesn't pass. It *keeps* us from progress in negotiations."

"Their trade goes on their ships through our territory. So does ours."

"That's the way State wrote the Treaty. If you want to change it, debate it in Council. Don't set up a program guaranteed to rip the peace apart by degrees, dammit, Councillor. Khalid didn't win the election, not by a long shot. You have *no need* to accommodate him."

Jacques had had another wine. He had another vodka. They'd settled it down. But he didn't think the last meeting with Jacques had gone at all well. Dean wasn't much better than Khalid, except that Dean was so damned abrasive he'd alienated half those who might have been his allies. And Khalid back on the planet was not good news.

"See if we can come up with a third choice," Yanni suggested at the last. "I'll give up pushing Bigelow. You suggested Dean because you know what I think."

"Science isn't my only consideration," Jacques said.

"It's the old coalition. It's the one that's got things done. You think you can work with Trade? I don't think so. Trade suffers from the same split that's in Defense. One way one time, another way the next issue. You can deal with us."

That was the way they'd parted company yesterday.

Today, in the small hours when dayshift and nightshift were trading places in the twenty-four hour city, his own staff had gotten to Mikhail Corain, and Corain, Frank said, was on his way up. Bert was making a decent breakfast, toast and eggs, orange and coffee.

Corain showed, quietly arrived, and surrendered his gray overcoat to Frank—it wasn't quite a hand-shaking meeting: Yanni didn't expect it, and in Council there was meaning to such events; but Corain very readily took his place at the small dining table, and took the coffee Frank poured for him.

"You're still in charge?" Corain asked him.

"Pretty firmly so," Yanni said. The news had settled down on the matter of Ari's takeover. "It's an internal matter. I doubt she'll hold the office too long. The tower blowing—that's on Hicks' watch. That's an issue. Paxers are an issue. Lao's an issue. Nothing caps the Defense mess."

"Murder," Corain said over his coffee cup.

"Bureau warfare," Yanni said. "Khalid. We have *no* doubt. And we have intelligence that's as good as Defense's."

"We have our constituency," Corain said, "and rumor, which is running in the same direction—and our constituency doesn't like it."

"I don't blame them," Yanni said.

"Do we have a consensus with Jacques?"

"We have an agreement for one more meeting. He's pushing Dean."

"Good God."

"We may get Kwesi."

"There's worse," Corain said, and Frank began to serve

breakfast, and they ate, Corain without comment about the irregularity of the affair. Bert *wasn't* a class one chef.

"You're keeping out of the media," Corain said finally, "but I'll tell you, there's a nervous mood. Lao's on her deathbed. Guards at her door. I was over to see her. She wasn't awake. Harad's worried. You're shut in your hotel and haven't given interviews. Jacques shows up and goes right back into the Defense Bureau, doesn't give interviews either. Media's camped out there."

"You're right about the level of security," Yanni said. "I'm not going the way Spurlin went. I'm watching what I eat, and I know where this came from."

"I'm a family man. I don't like this. I don't like this level of goings-on. What in hell have we come to?"

"Bad times, I'm afraid, if Council doesn't do something about Defense. I'm afraid Jacques is going. I'm very afraid he's not going to live past naming a Proxy."

"You've got Lynch guarded to the max."

"Absolutely. I like being just Proxy. I don't want to hold the seat solo."

"It's crazy."

Yanni finished his eggs, had the orange drink in three gulps, set his forearms on the table edge, and stared at Corain.

"It's a damned ridiculous way to conduct Council business, sitting here in a hotel room, cooking on a hot plate, and both of us worrying about dying of what we might eat down in the class one restaurant downstairs. It's slipped up on us. Half a year ago we wouldn't have believed it could get this ridiculous. And two weeks from now God knows how ridiculous it's going to get. Somebody's blown up a precip tower. That's more than a building. That's environmental stability. That has a psychological message, doesn't it? Today it's the Council huddled together worried about their physical safety. What's it going to be come New Year's, if the man who assassinated his rival gets into office, and Lao's dead—"

"And I'm up for election," Corain said. "Grisham's filed for the seat."

"Oh, *there's* a nice moderate voice. On stable ground, you could blow him out, no question. If you're forced into hiding, like this, because he's got, say, Paxer backing, and it's gotten dangerous—that fool could get into office. And where'd we be?"

"I think about quitting. Quite honestly, I think about my family. I think about their safety."

"Don't we all?" Yanni said somberly. "Don't we all, Mikhail Corain? I have family. I have Frank. I have a daughter. She's a fool, but I have a daughter. An ex. People I'd like to see live their lives."

"You've got a lot better security than other departments. You've got a damned army."

"We try to use it responsibly," he said wryly. "Right now I hope it'll be useful."

"While it's in shambles," Corain said, "back home."

"I wouldn't call it shambles," Yanni said. "I'd call it some serious questioning as to why we didn't see things coming. But not too much time in hindsight, right now. I'm more interested in seeing my old friends stay in office and stay alive."

"Old friends, is it?"

"You. Lao. Harad. De Franco. Chavez."

"Harogo," Corain said. Internal Affairs was no friend of Science, but was, of Citizens.

"And Harogo," Yanni said, lifting his coffee mug in salute. "Honest, if against us. In this age, it's damned sure worth respect. Bogdanovitch—and son—the same." That was State's Proxy. He drank and set the cup down. "Mikhail, if you think you have imminent reason to worry, get the family on separate planes and get them up to Reseune Airport. There's lodging for them, safety, no question. Security we can't provide here."

"You're serious."

"You and I may be sitting in a bunker before this is over. I'm dead serious. The offer's open to you, too."

"That'd look like hell, wouldn't it?"

"It might, but the offer stands. If you think it's a choice between resigning or sending your family up there, send them."

"What the hell are we going to do?"

"Get the Office of Inquiry to speed it up. Brace ourselves. I think Jacques is going to crumple. We'll get somebody we don't want. Lao—can't even *find* her Proxy, what time she's conscious. Edgerton's either hiding or dead. You, and I, and Edgerton if we can find him . . . Harad will go with us."

"Harogo," Corain said. "Five of the Nine, right there."

"If we have unanimity minus one, we can refuse to seat whoever Jacques names."

"It's never happened."

"It can happen. That's the point. We can refuse to seat whoever they name. We can force them to another election. And another. We can take them *out* of the political process."

"And into something altogether unthinkable," Corain said. "My God, Schwartz."

"Exactly. They think we'll fold. We don't fold. If we do, there's *already* been a coup. What more are we afraid of?"

Corain sat and stared at him, and finally rotated his coffee mug full circle, handle back to his hand.

"Unanimity minus one," Corain said.

"We can do it. No debate, no reasoning, just a straightforward vote: the part where we all vote to seat the new Councillor, and everybody goes to lunch? This time we vote no."

"We can't find Edgerton," Corain said. "Lao may be dead tomorrow. If we lose her—we devolve down to the Secretary of Information, with the Proxy in doubt and Edgerton missing. If we call a vote and fail the majority, because somebody doesn't show—that's all it takes. Spurlin being murdered—that's just real fresh in memory."

"They mean it to be. They mean us to be afraid. They mean us to play by rules they're not even going to worry about. We're worried about unanimous votes and legalities. The man who ordered Spurlin killed wasn't worried about the legalities. He won't be when he plans his next move. He's already over the line. And I could be killed, and you could, Lao's terribly vulnerable. Pretty soon we've got a Council full of shiny new Proxies without a clue who to trust, and a strong, strong likelihood that just one of them will fold and let him take the seat."

"And Edgerton . . ."

"As long as Lao's alive, she can name another Proxy," he said. "As long as the media can come and go, that word can get out, and she can take the Proxy back and name somebody we *can* find. Mark my word, media access may not last, if Khalid decides to shut it down. There won't be media at all where the bodies really start to fall. Lay odds on it."

Corain nodded. "I think we've found a mutual issue. I'll get to Affairs and State; Finance; I'll talk to Finance, too. Or get Affairs to do it."

"De Franco, Harad, Lao," Yanni said. "I can get them in."

Corain sat there a moment. "You're the one who has the clandestine organization to move on him. If it came to that."

"We can't penetrate Defense," Yanni said. "We could try. But on Cyteen, we'd be sitting here in the rubble, *hoping* Alliance would be disposed to pull us out. And Defense has warships out there. We don't begin to counter that. Alliance could; would, pretty damned fast; and then what have we got? Not much. Another war. One where the lines would be very, very different than they've ever been. You want the nightmare, Mikhail Corain, *that's* the nightmare. And that's the universe Khalid wouldn't mind having back, the one where he had his real power. He was head of Intelligence. He ran the secrets. *Agents provocateurs*. He knows damned well how to get a situation going, where to hit, who to bribe, who to eliminate, and when. He's in his element, in this. But to have the respect and influence he wants, he needs to get into *ours*. That's where we have to draw the line. We don't let him get legitimacy, or we have *nothing*."

Corain nodded. Bit his lip. "All right. This is how. I'll call on Harogo, get Harogo to get to Chavez, down the chain. I can't say how fast. I can't say I can *find* Harogo without some trial and error, and that's not going to be quiet."

"We may not be back in touch until the vote. Just do it with interviews. That's enough. Watch the vid. I promise you'll see me. More coffee?"

Aug 5, 2424
0122h

Deepstudy and more deepstudy, until the here and now buzzed about her ears—Ari had an orange drink and an iced muffin to fill the space in her stomach and to shoot some sugar into her veins. The headache had faded in favor of a knot on her skull that she mostly felt when she brushed her hair, and she wore it loose, because the usual knot and pin hurt that spot.

Catlin and Florian didn't say a thing, just kept staff at bay, communicated with Rafael, who physically occupied the desk down in ReseuneSec—Rafael actually had had tape about how it all worked, and it was invaluable. Hicks' receptionist knew who was supposed to be where; Hicks' secretary knew what was supposed to be filed, and Rafael just kept people moving, and saw to it that surveillance watched where it was supposed to and that information was directed where it needed to go. Chloe in Yanni's office actually called to ask if she'd heard anything about Yanni, who hadn't reported; and Rafael was able to say with some confidence that Yanni periodically sent an all-okay signal, but didn't give them details.

That said, more than most things, how things were in Novgorod. Amy wrote a log and put it into her Reseune account, and it was full of information, like a news report on the city, but Amy didn't mention Yanni, except to give the codewords "totally in love" referring to a dessert at the hotel. It didn't have a thing to do with desserts: it said she was safe so far and being useful. She also used the code "I'm trying to get information from the shipper," which meant she was trying to get something out of Yanni, and hadn't, and then, "I'm not even thinking about a shopping trip right now. I'm talking to the University about a blenny

breeding setup and I'm going to be looking at warehouses
so we can take advantage of supplies and the shipping network in the city. It's salt water out there, nothing usable,
without a lot of treatment, but if we set up there, and run
a real strict filtration, well, just say it's going to take a lot
of work." That roughly translated to: "I can't do anything
about getting Yanni out at the moment. I'm reconnoiter-
ing. I'm not finding a lot I can do, but we're being careful
and we don't expect this to be easy."

She'd had a decade of practice reading Amy's deliberate blithe nonsense. She read it well enough that Amy
could freehand phrases and she'd catch most of it. It wasn't
worse than she thought; it wasn't better, and Yanni was
being obstinate—was that a surprise?

Meanwhile she knew AK-36 in intimate detail. She
knew everything on record in his manual, at least, and the
first Ari said: **"A block isn't constructed out of thin air, or
off some recipe. It's made out of the deepest fears and the
strongest determination of the subject. The subject helps
you construct a block. He may help you unravel one if
you can gain his cooperation on some point stronger than
the block itself. Finding such an item is unlikely, but not
impossible."**

And then Ari said: **"Knowing the history of the individual is key, being able to correctly identify the sensitive points and particularly the most primal areas of the
mindset.**

**"At the point of fracture the psychological stress may well
trigger the fight-flight response to an extreme degree."**

She knew that.

She asked Base One, in a variation on a question a
dozen times posed: "Who in Reseune, living, has ever
dealt professionally with AK-36?"

"Adam Hicks," the inevitable answer came back, the
same as always. It omitted Giraud. He was dead. And
a long, long string of azi, some CITs who wouldn't have
dealt with him in the offices.

Useless.

She changed the question. She said: "Who in Reseune,
living, holding an alpha certificate, has ever dealt professionally with AK-36?"

It said, solemnly, after *"Adam Hicks," "Ariane Emory."* Stupid program. Base One occasionally, in some applications, had trouble sorting her out from her predecessor, or figuring out that the first Ari was dead, but then, it was true, too: she did fit the qualifications.

It went on with Petros Ivanov, medical . . . anybody who'd been in the hospital might have run into Petros. Chi Prang, alpha psych down in the labs, again, logical, from when Giraud had been running things.

And then Base One startled hell out of her: *"Jordan Warrick."*

She filed that for thought and changed the question: "Who outside Reseune, living, has ever dealt professionally with AK-36?"

The answer came back: *"Yanni Schwartz. Frank AF."* It listed a long string of azi. *"Numerous persons outside Base One tracking: no data available."*

"Big help," she muttered to Base One, peevishly. Yanni and Frank were clearly *not* in Reseune at the moment. Yanni would have been a help. But Chi Prang, alpha supervisor down in the labs, was old, but not that old. Wendy Peterson wasn't involved. Edwards was too young. Jordan Warrick was too young to have had a hand in the creation of a mindset 122 years old. She was eighteen and she had a real piece of archaeology on her hands, in AK-36.

"Base One, year of birth for Jordan Warrick."

"2358."

"Base One, year of birth for AK-36." But she knew it before Base One answered: calculated it for herself.

"2298."

God, the last of the sublight ships hadn't run their course when AK-36 came into the world. Union had been just a collection of dissidents with a planet and a space station. The birthlabs and azi production were still in setup when AK-36 had come out of them, and he'd gotten swept up into the military, because the fact Cyteen existed had just tipped the human species over into war. Kyle was old the way Ollie was old. His memory—

His memory must go way, way back. Jordan had been a baby himself when Kyle had first come back to Reseune after serving in the military. Jordan had grown up while

Kyle was assisting Giraud. Kyle had been part of the scenery for whole lifetimes of people who themselves had actually died of rejuv failure and old age.

He'd still put up a hell of a fight for an old, old azi, and it was a wonder Florian hadn't killed him when he'd had to shoot him full of paralytic. Suicide by non-lethals, Catlin had said, and explained later that it was possible if you got hit the wrong way, or by more than one of them at once. And that was still an old, old, azi who'd taken all that to keep him down.

Tough as they came. Clever. Devious.

She said, "Base One, Alpha Detention."

And when one of the agents on duty there answered, she responded: "Get a blood and tissue sample from AK-36 and take it to Dr. Petros Ivanov in Hospital Admin. Say I want a compete workup, identity match, total, and I want it run on all AK-3's ever to come out of the labs, and I want a strict chain of custody on those samples."

That was going to take time. Chemistry took time. They didn't *have* that much time, but it was a test overdue, if they were going to try to crack what Kyle *had* done, and pin down who had had him do it.

She put in a call to Justin, meanwhile.

"Ari?"

"Can you possibly call your father and set up both of you working on a file I'd like analyzed? I really need to ask you two some questions."

A moment of silence on the other end. Long silence. Justin said, quietly, *"I don't think I can talk him into anything at the moment. I'm sorry. I take it this isn't part of the lessons."*

"It's not. It's pretty important."

"I think—I don't know. He's not speaking to me. I don't think he'll even open the door to me at the moment. You might actually get more out of him."

That bad? she thought. "Is he speaking to Grant?"

"I don't think so, honestly. He tossed us both out."

"Well," she said. "Thanks. Thanks all the same. Would you and Grant look over some files for me? I'm going to shoot it over to you. I really need it. I need it fast."

"Sure. I'd be glad to."

She sent AK-36's basic manual over, sent over AK-36's personal manual with it, which had Giraud's annotations, and Hicks' marks.

She called Chi Prang, and had her run an analysis.

And she thought a moment, and then she did a little file manipulation, recast the date, created a new timestamp, and called up Jordan.

"Jordan? Jordan, this is Ari. I have a problem."

Long, long wait.

"This is Paul AP, sera. Jordan's—Jordan's in the shower at the moment. Can I help?"

"Actually, yes. I'm going to send a file over. I want your opinion on it. Both of you, if Jordan wouldn't mind. It's a set with a problem. I'd really like an analysis."

"You can send it over, sera, of course. I'll advise him when he gets out of the shower."

"It's an alpha file. We've had a criminal act. It's fairly urgent. Thank you so much, Paul."

Name was erased. Date was erased. It was all couched as current work. Which it certainly was . . . in the emergency sense.

She leaned back in the chair, wishing the processes of chemistry ran a little faster or that the processes of politics ran a little slower.

A lot slower.

"Sera," Catlin said. She had her handheld, but she stooped, picked up the wand from the table and popped the main display over to the news channel.

Councillor Jacques was on camera. Jacques of Defense.

"After much deliberation," Jacques said, *"and thought."* The man had an unfortunate delivery. He never sounded altogether bright. *"—I have reached a decision on the Proxy appointment, bearing in mind a sensitivity toward the Spurlin family, friends, and supporters, to whom we extend our most profound and heartfelt condolences . . ."*

Get on with it, for God's sake!

". . . but we are constrained by considerations of the welfare of the nation to make an appointment representing the will of the electorate as expressed in the recent election. I am therefore retaining the seat, but will appoint as Proxy Councillor Vladislaw—"

"Good loving God!"

"—*Khalid, who will serve starting immediately. This decision has been reached after, of course, considerable*—"

"Cut it off," she said to Catlin. The headache was back. And Catlin just stood there, seeming sure there would be some order to come. "I wish I could think of something," she said to Catlin. "Thank you. Thank you for turning that on. I wanted to hear it. The man's a fool."

"He will likely die very soon," Catlin said, the same assessment she'd reached, even contemplating it. "Khalid will succeed him. Am I right about the law?"

"Khalid's got some hold on him," she said. "Yes. You're right about it. And he'll last just long enough for the media attention to cool down about Spurlin, or until he objects to something Khalid does. Monitor Rafael. See if he's getting any news from ReseuneSec in Novgorod or elsewhere."

"Yes, sera," Catlin said, set the wand on the table, and was off like a shot. Florian would be likewise engaged, might already be hauling in information via ReseuneSec— was probably doing that from the apartment security station: Wes and Marco were, she hoped, getting their rest: it was going to be a long twenty-four, thirty-six hours.

They'd just lost Defense as an ally and gained a bitter enemy. Yanni was still in Novgorod, so was Amy: they'd at least be aware what had just happened.

Meanwhile, having found out what she knew about their internal problem, she was, herself, stalled out and making *no* progress on the ReseuneSec situation, and didn't know if they had a greater threat inside Reseune or out. They'd taken in thirty-odd alphas in the batch they'd recovered from the military. Most of them were retired, now, only ten, counting Kyle, still serving, and all others of those were in esoteric fields, unsocialized—so concentrated on their specialities it was likely immaterial to them what planet they were on or whether the rest of the human species existed.

Worth investigating, when she had time.

Spurlin dead. Lao dying. Lao's Proxy still missing. And Yanni had had a meeting with Corain, which gave her a better opinion of Corain than she'd ever had. But at the moment, Council was not in session, couldn't go into session until three Councillors showed up in the Council chamber and formally called for a session to occur: it wouldn't be legitimate to do business until five showed up, and the numbers available to show up were getting scant.

That news feed would have gone all over Reseune, down to the town and the port. It would have gone just about everywhere.

And should she get on the air immediately after and tell everybody it was all right?

That would be a lie. It wasn't all right. Anybody above the age of eight had to have figured that out; but all right, it was a psych question: people wanted to hear from the people they trusted to make decisions, and right now, that had to be her.

She decided, however, not to go to the media at large. A full-blown media event, down at the airport, the usual venue for such press conferences, wouldn't help Yanni in his situation; and her appearance, and a declaration of challenge, might push Khalid just one step farther than she liked at the moment.

She had, however, to figure what she said and how she appeared might leak out.

So she brushed her hair, put it up in the skewered twist she lately favored, even if it hurt like hell. She put on a little rouge, put on a blue, high-collared jacket over the black jersey tee she was wearing, zipped it up and took a seat at the desk that had the vid camera.

She punched in. "Base One. Activate Channel One, override Channels Two through Two Hundred."

"Done," Base One said. Her own image appeared on the screen in front of her, but she didn't look at that. She looked into the camera, somber, but perfectly relaxed, the way she'd practiced that expression.

"This is an informative bulletin. This is Ari Emory, acting Director of Reseune. You may have noted the outcome of the Defense Proxy appointment. I am in communication with Director Schwartz in Novgorod, and I'll be working with him during this period, opening communication with the new Proxy Councillor for Defense. We aren't sure how long this process will take. Let me state we are both appreciative of the response of Reseune CITs and azi to the recent domestic upheaval—which I am glad to say is fairly well along in process of resolution. We request that everyone keep on doing as you have been doing, conducting business as usual, but we also suggest that places of public assembly review their emergency procedures and be sure that storm tunnel accesses are clearly lighted and in good working order.

"Bear in mind that we are now in August, approaching the fall storms, so this is the semi-annual announcement in that regard. What is not routine is the incident upriver, and what happened recently in a security breach. Please bear in mind that should an area evacuation emergency occur during an otherwise routine weather alert, all residents and workers should not risk outside exposure. Use the tunnels, not the outside exits, to reach a secure area, and tend away from any area of disturbance, as you will be advised to do. Sequence flashers will indicate appropriate direction. Please review these procedures with your employees and with members of your family, and arrange several meeting places as contingencies in case one is unavailable. This in no way signals a cause of imminent danger. We have dealt with and arrested the known problem. We have no immediate reason to anticipate another such alert, but we will be in a state of heightened awareness until that matter has been investigated to a conclusion. Until Director Schwartz returns to assess the situation, I am erring on the side of caution and placing Reseune on a moderate level of alert. Thank you."

BOOK THREE   Section 5   Chapter xiv

AUG 7, 2424
1300H

"Ser," Ari said politely, visiting Adam Hicks, who'd spent the last number of days in a very restricted part of Alpha Wing—

Behind the Alpha Wing security office, in fact.

It wasn't a bad little suite Hicks occupied: there was a

dining table, there was a comfortable chair, there was a wide selection of books available via reader. There was a bed, and unlimited access to crossword puzzles—Tommy's idea. Hicks had been a cooperative inmate. He kept the place neat, the bed made. He could send out for coffee and food as desired, and the restaurant passed things to his guards. There was a used disposable cup waiting on a small table by the door—that was the only disorder in the place.

"Sera," Hicks said with a little nod. And as she took a seat at his dining table, Florian and Catlin arranged themselves, both standing, nearby. Hicks quietly took a seat at that table within the corner, opposite her, insulated from Florian and Catlin—she marked that.

She had her handheld in her coat pocket. She took it out, set it on the table facing Hicks, and played the short bit from Yanni: *"If he's not innocent he's not a friend of mine. You can tell him that. Tell him I said cooperate with you or I'll break his neck."*

Hicks's brows lifted. Drew down again as his stare locked with hers.

"That's Yanni's opinion," she said mildly, repossessing the unit. She dropped it into her jacket pocket. "For the record, I'm increasingly sorry for the roughness in the takeover. Yanni tells me you're to be trusted. So I'm very sorry for the confusion, and I'm sorry I had to take the measures I did, but I had reason for concern. I don't know if you know: I'm assuming you don't: Kyle was our target."

"Kyle?"

"I'm sorry to say, his axe code never did work: he's been reporting to Defense for years. For about six decades, in fact, going way back into Giraud's administration."

Hicks looked numbly shocked. Shook his head. "I can't accept that. That's just not so. You're wrong."

"Giraud got you your provisional precisely so you could have a legal partnership with him. I take it this represents a strong friendship."

"Is he all right?"

"He's fine, or as fine as he can be, considering the contradictions he's carrying inside, which I suspect involves a real attachment to you. He's on a suicide watch. We're worried about that."

"God. This is complete nonsense."

"I'm sorry it's not."

"It's a damn trick!"

"Not that, either. He got past Giraud, he got past the first Ari, for that matter: she relied on Giraud and she shouldn't have, in his case. She was busy at the time. It's very likely that Kyle was the agent in turning Abban. It's at least certain he was reporting to Defense every time you were in the building. I am very, extremely sorry for the situation."

"I don't believe this!"

"I do believe," she said quietly, "that you honestly don't believe it."

"I don't."

"This isn't about fault. The fact is, very likely Defense, or someone in Defense, ordered my predecessor murdered, and that Kyle was how it happened."

"No."

"Jordan didn't do it. Abban may have, but would Giraud order it? I don't think so. I don't think you thought so, at the time."

"Warrick—"

"That was Giraud's bias. He was dead sure it was Jordan who'd done it, by some means or another. And he was wrong. It was Abban. We thought Denys might have accessed Abban to do it, but here's the stinger: Denys' certificate was a fake. He couldn't do it. That leaves Giraud, who I don't think had the motive. And it leaves Kyle. I don't say Kyle had a personal choice in the matter, understand. And we could solve his situation in one sense by packaging him up and sending him off to Defense to finish his career there. But he knows a lot that we'd rather Defense didn't get the rest of. And I'm not sure they'd be kind to him, no matter how well he's served them—because I'm not sure all of Defense is behind what he did, and I don't think some of Defense would like him to answer questions."

"You're not making sense."

"There's a lot of vulnerability he could have created. I'm sure Defense now has the building plans for much of Reseune, and we're going to have to do some major revisions. Worse, I'm sure they've got some keys; and codes,

anything Kyle could reach; so Base Two is going to have
to change some codes. That makes a very messy situation,
since Yanni is still off in Novgorod, and I can't get him new
codes that easily: so if I don't change how you access Base
Two, I expose him to problems, and if I do, it's another
kind of risk, of his not being able to handle all the programs he might need to. I appreciate that it's not exactly
your problem at the moment, but it is a problem, and I
know you're a friend of Yanni's. At least he thinks you are.
He's in serious danger, where he is. Spurlin's dead; you do
know that. We think Jacques will be soon. Lao's in hospital. We're having a real crisis in the Council."

"What are you saying?"

"Khalid's got Defense again. Jacques just named him
Proxy."

Hicks' face didn't react much; but he just seemed to wilt
a bit, physically.

Ari said: "You've dealt with Khalid."

"I have."

"Did you like him?"

A slight shake of the head. Hicks looked a little pale,
lips tightly compressed. "Didn't."

"What kind of feeling did he give you?"

"That's subjective. It doesn't matter."

"I think you may record impressions a lot better than
you think you do. How did Kyle react to him?"

"Kyle was just business, that's all. I didn't like Khalid. It
wasn't my job to judge him, just negotiate with the man."

"Did Khalid ever propose anything you thought
unethical?"

Hicks shook his head.

"Possibly Kyle told him in advance what you'd agree to.
And what you wouldn't."

Eyes dilated. Contracted. Dilated again.

"That's a damned fish."

"It must have been particularly hard to negotiate with
him. I hope you'll think about that issue. Try to recall specific incidences where he seemed to know exactly how far
you'd go. It may help us dealing with this man. It seems
we're going to have to, unfortunately."

"I'll think about it." Hicks didn't look cooperative,

quite the opposite; but he was retreating a little, accepting some arguments, or acting as if he did. He was actually very smart on a beta level. He wouldn't buy any whole package. He knew tricks, and he kept things in reserve, and he knew she was Working him to get hooks on an azi he regarded as a brother.

"You know I'm going to have to do something with Kyle," she said. "*I* will—because, unfortunately, I'm about the best Alpha Super alive right now, and I'm only eighteen."

He just stared at her.

"So," she said, "I'm not as good as I'd like to be. And I don't feel as confident as I'd like. I've got a lot of my predecessor's techniques—I've studied. I'll try. I want to do it the best, the safest way possible."

"How many people did you just kill, shooting up my office?"

"Nobody's dead. None of yours needed more than on-site medical. One of mine's still in hospital. Kyle's not hurt at all, beyond a few bruises. He just got a dose of a non-lethal and went out."

Hicks absorbed that, seeming guardedly relieved.

"Yanni says he wants you back in charge of Reseune-Sec," she said, "and I'm not going to argue with that, personally, if we can get Kyle straightened out." *That* brought a sharper attention. "And I'll tell you why I agree with Yanni. Reseune is running shorter and shorter of people with an actual memory of what happened back in our beginnings. Kind of odd to think of, but I have that kind of memory—just sort-of. Just enough to know how much really valuable detail is still going to go away with administrators like you, like Yanni. Kyle's age makes him very valuable, if we can just get him back—get him to the state you believed he was."

No response to that. No challenge, either.

She said: "Absolutely if that axe code never did take, he's been conflicted. He's probably been very painfully conflicted over certain things he's done, which he probably tries not to think about too often. He's worked it out, saying to himself he never hurt Giraud, never hurts you, not in his self-adjusted view of the universe. Everything's for the ultimate good. He's been doing what Defense asks, being a good soldier while he's in Defense; and then he can go home to Reseune and follow a program that will ultimately make the world run better. He's comfortable again, since Denys died, because Yanni's been making the Novgorod trips, and he'll never have to go to Defense again."

"Fantasy. The code took. He's not guilty. He is what he's always been. You want the man who murdered your predecessor, look at the man you brought back from Planys."

"If you're right and it is true, we'll find it out in the process, and we *won't* stress Kyle at all; if I'm right, there will be stress. There'll be a block; and we'll have to go after it before we can apply the axe code and get him back."

"He's not young, for any of this."

"And you're worried I'll botch it. But you're really, extremely worried it could possibly be true."

"I'm worried an eighteen-year-old kid is going to start messing with his psychsets and upsetting him, and he's not young."

"Would you like to be there?"

"I wouldn't *like* to be there. But I want to be there, yes."

"He's very strong, considering—he put up a hell of a physical fight. But you're quite right: if there is a block, this is going to hit his endocrine system like a hammer, and at his age, it could have an impact on rejuv. So what my studies tell me is that he should have complete medical support. Everything to safeguard him. But mostly, you should be there. He's your companion. You *are* his Supervisor, at least one of his Supervisors, though I'm betting there's another in Defense. I hope he'll respond to you. And I do want him to come through this all right, not just because I want the truth from him."

"*You're* saying he's guilty of everything in the book. That he killed your predecessor. What reason do you have to want him to be all right?"

"*You* don't think it'd be his fault, do you? I don't either."

"If it were true in the first place," he said, "no, it's not his fault."

"I'm calling in Chi Prang. And Justin Warrick."

"Oh, that's a help."

"You know you're not his favorite human being, no more than Giraud was. But I know Justin as well as I know anybody outside my personal staff; and he's very good. He's professional. He'd never hold a grudge against an azi. And you should also know I'm consulting Jordan. Jordan's mad at me, no question. He's probably mad at you and at Kyle. But I don't think that would ever extend to his work on a case."

"Then you're a fool."

"I don't think so," she said. "Jordan's actually written an important paper on this kind of operation—what they learned about blocks, both creating and undoing. I read it. He's probably the best authority on it of anyone still alive."

"I'm saying he has a grudge, and he's the man who'd hold it. I'm saying I knew your predecessor, and she was a bitch. She'd lie with a straight face, when it suited."

"Most people will," she said quietly, "in a good cause. But she was exactly what you say, sometimes. And I won't say I haven't had a little trouble unwiring my own feelings about Abban. It got personal, about him. It never should have, because my feelings misled me. I've asked myself how I feel about Kyle, because I don't think I could work if I were ambivalent on this. So I tell myself he's been in a hell of a position for a long, long time, and I wish for a lot of reasons that Giraud hadn't made a mistake in handling him. I wish Giraud had told Ari he had a potential problem, instead of testing his own ability to handle it. But Giraud didn't want Ari to start paying attention to his psych operations, and particularly to Denys, whose certificate to run Seely was an outright lie—and Giraud had run the certification . . . I found that little detail. *You* had no reason to think Kyle had a problem, since you got him from Giraud. *Kyle* couldn't tell you; and you weren't going to spot it—being a provisional Super—but frankly, I know you're better than Denys. Denys wasn't really doing any direct Supering until Giraud died; and then he was handling both Abban and Seely and you could just watch the stress pile up on both of them. I saw it. I didn't know at the time what I was seeing—particularly in Abban. I learned a lot from that. Is Kyle happy?"

"I think he has been."

"Particularly in recent years?"

"Maybe."

"I've asked that of people he worked with, your office people—other azi who've worked with him. He used to be tense, with Giraud; calmed down, after Giraud died and he shifted over to you. Tight-focused on his job. Zealous. All good things. He'd laugh."

"He can," Hicks said . . . feeling better, perhaps, with the implied positives.

"Abban couldn't," she said, fast, like a knife cut. "So you're better than Denys. You're a lot better than Denys. Reports say you're real good with the betas. So I think you know that you're the one that can help him—or really hurt him. And he'll be safer if you're there. Let him focus on you. And stay steady. Stay absolutely steady."

Hicks' face was quite, quite pale. He kept gnawing at his lip. "What happens if you do find a block?"

"It's usually very simple. It's usually just like at beta or gamma level, something hooked right to the deep sets. We give him a lot of kat, we convince him to let it go, and we give the axe code, because we want to redo everything fast. He'll need a Contract very quickly. That's you, if you want to take it on. That would be the easy thing."

"A block—" Hicks said, "can stop a heart."

"I know it can," she said. "And we'll support him, with everything we have available, the best in Reseune. I'm not blithely optimistic on this. I know the danger to him. It's why I want you there. I know, whatever your opinion of me, you'll support *him*."

"I will," Hicks said.

"Good," she said. And rested her arms on the table. "There's one other, unrelated matter I want to ask you about."

Immediately defensive. Suspicious. Very justifiably so.

"Anton Clavery," she said. "What do you know about that name?"

"We don't," he said. "We've investigated, connected it to the Paxers. But that's all."

"So you haven't solved that one."

Hicks shook his head, relaxing a little, deciding, maybe, that it was a change of topics. "Why Patil used that name, she died knowing. We've been all through her affairs. And we have nothing to show for it."

"She knew one other thing we don't," she said. "She knew what Defense knew about the project she was going to work on. She knew all sorts of things Defense knows, and we don't. It could have to do with what Defense is doing. I was just curious." She got up and offered her hand.

Hicks took it with a peculiar look, as if wondering if there had been a connection between the two topics after all; and maybe after an hour or two he'd begin to see there was. His hand was cold. Probably it would be good to have Wes have a look at him, just in case. If they lost Hicks, they lost Kyle, almost certainly, and she didn't want to lose either one: Hicks, for Yanni's sake, and Kyle, because if they lost him, they'd likely never know what he'd done and what he knew and what he could say . . . or if he'd been contacted recently, with new orders.

So she did what she could with what she could reach.

Meanwhile Kyle, besides being on a suicide watch, was pretty deeply under, for as long as they thought it safe or good, and she wasn't going to trouble him with an inquiry he'd only have to resist. The less apprehension he carried into the session the better, and the greater the chance they could keep him from crisis.

Put him and Hicks on ice for the duration and concentrate only on Novgorod? She thought about that, about her whole list of priorities. She thought about going down to the capital in person—which would draw media attention, maybe draw other things, but it would get attention—planetwide and up in orbit.

She thought about how the first Ari had let Reseune matters slide, and trusted Giraud to handle what he was certified to handle, when she went up to Novgorod—her mistake, her very big mistake, a long time ago. And that was the bottom line: Ari had trusted Giraud to handle what Giraud said he could handle, a simple matter for somebody with that level of certification—if Giraud hadn't been dealing with the best Reseune could turn out, with the bollixed-up pyschtech Defense could manage: exactly the kind of thing that *could* fool somebody who, being a by-the-book operator himself, only expected what was in the books.

So, faced with a choice of going to Novgorod before she had the requisite years behind her, she trusted Yanni not to make a mistake—with something not simple, either. Sometimes you just had to let things go in the hands of people who were expert at what they did. Yanni had been talking to Council for years. He knew them. He knew his contacts.

Meanwhile she had to figure out what a spy inside Reseune could have told Defense, and what kind of an organization their enemies had been building, from the War years when Reseune and Defense had had a tight, tight relationship.

Jordan, she thought . . . when Ari yanked back the azi from the combat zones, they'd been dealing with the old Contracts, and undoing what had been done and undone around the time of the War. Jordan, a junior in the labs in those days, must have heard the first Ari fight her battles with Defense . . . and when Ari was old, and he was in his prime, he'd gone to Defense with an offer to betray Reseune. Defense, who already had a man inside, had double-crossed him—why?

Because they weren't interested in what Jordan had offered them. They'd heard what he said and drew some other conclusion. Hadn't they? Jordan hadn't proposed murdering Ari. Had he?

One thing seemed evident: Jordan had written that paper. He'd at least met the problem of the military sets, post-War, and analyzed the security measures Defense had set into its azi soldiers, a self-destruct if captured, in some instances—Defense work cobbled into Reseune's clean psychsets. Involving Jordan was a risk—to Kyle AK, mentally; to Justin, emotionally; in all respects, to himself—and to Reseune, if he was still bent on revenge.

But if you wanted to dig up the things that lay buried in Reseune, Jordan Warrick was one who knew, and who'd been in a position to know. Yanni, who also knew, was in Novgorod, out of reach. There was Ivanov. There was

Wendy Peterson. Neither of them had been involved in the labs the way Jordan had.

It might be a big mistake. If he said yes instantly, it was time to worry.

But he might also be their best asset.

BOOK THREE   Section 5   Chapter xv

Aug 9, 2424
0808h

Prang was her first visit. Chi Prang, Alpha Supervisor, another of the old hands, met her with a notion of what the case was about: Ari had told her that in a letter sent along with the file; and Prang didn't have much encouragement. Prang said if she had ever been notified the code had had any questionable outcome she would have taken AK-36 in immediately. She said that she had, yesterday evening, checked records that Giraud had sent and the notation was simply that AK-36 had had the code administered, that he was "doing well," and that he was under Giraud's Supervision.

Giraud had, Prang added, maintained an ironclad and prickly secrecy about his department, his operations, and his personnel: she recalled he had had arguments with the first Ari on that topic.

The first Ari, Ari thought to herself, hearing that, had isolated herself, had set everybody at distance, didn't read the people she was living with as well or as impartially as she read everybody else she dealt with.

Read a stranger? Absolutely. Instantly.

Read a group of people? Easily.

Read the Nyes? Not well enough. The first Ari had grown up with them; been a child with them. Of *course* she knew them. If you stared at a thing a long time, after a while you weren't really seeing it. Your mind started being busy, and you knew what you were staring at hadn't moved, but maybe you didn't see every detail. You didn't notice when it blinked or its eyes dilated. You didn't know when it changed its mind. You didn't notice when loyalty to something else had gotten to the surface and started to move its thoughts in another direction. You didn't notice that, the older Giraud got, maybe, the more Giraud was being run by his younger brother—who was the real Special, as Ari knew, and brilliant in azi psych, but who wasn't a damned good Supervisor. Do this for me. Do that. Don't let them know. Don't let them inquire. Giraud, fix it for me. Giraud, keep them out. Giraud, she's dangerous. She'll be rid of us . . .

Major blind spot. Giraud loved her: not many had, but Giraud had, and of course she could trust Giraud's motives.

Put *that* in the notes to her successor: mind her own relationships.

Like Justin. Like Amy. Like Yanni. It was scary. It was one thing to say the first Ari should have done it; it was another, to think of doing it with Florian, with Catlin, Justin, and Amy . . .

"He won't come through it," Prang said bluntly, regarding their chances of dealing with Kyle at this point. "He won't likely survive it."

"Is the block likely in the deep sets?" she asked. "Did Defense have anybody that could do it that way?"

"The fact that they didn't have anybody who could," Prang said solemnly, "doesn't mean they didn't try. They had a high failure rate. There were azi we never saw again. Killed in combat. Always killed in combat. Alphas, no less."

"How many were lost?"

"Twelve. None that belonged in combat. None psychologically fit for it. They didn't want *us* enabling combat in an alpha. They wanted their career officers to run them, not have an azi taking combat command. They were clear on that score. Ari—your predecessor—worked to get them all back, and it took the turning point in the War and a slowdown in our production to bend them."

"Betas lost?"

"I don't recall the numbers. High hundreds. Gammas. God. Near four thousand."

That made her mad . . . mad, and she thought she'd lie

awake tonight thinking about it. That attitude in Defense, and then Prang's little shrug, as if—what could we do? What could anyone do?

She'd spent a very little time with Prang, which put her on the edge of furious.

Then she wanted to go ask Jordan about what *he* remembered, but that wasn't going to work, if she went in on a frontal assault.

So she went to Justin's office instead—went just with Florian, and asked him and Grant if they'd reached any results in the case she'd given them.

Justin said, "I can't tell you where any block is. I can tell you, if I were good, where I'd put it, if I were working on the psychset in the original manual. Grant agrees."

She sat down by them and let them show her, just where; and it was where she thought.

But then she asked, "What if you were a total fool? If you weren't that good, and you just wanted to go ahead anyway, and you weren't that smart?"

They both frowned, even Grant, who rarely did. And then Grant said, "If you were a fool, maybe," and searched the file and showed where you could put it in the secondary sets, and it made sense to her—secondaries was where ethics went, and they played off the deep sets, but they were shifty things, and interrelated, and they mutated considerably over a lifetime. It was *why* azi went back time and again for refresher tape.

Ethics . . . and emotional needs.

"Could be," Justin said, and added: "Kyle was a cold bastard, whenever I had to deal with him. I can't say my opinion's entirely clinical. I've tried to get past that. I've asked myself if it was partially null-state, on his part. And it could have been. I could have misinterpreted it."

"You mean when you were arrested."

"He was there, during some unpleasant sessions. I knew him. I can't say I know him lately—I can't say I can do an impartial assessment on him, at all. Except—the azi this original manual should have produced—would have had some emotional reaction. He didn't. That's why I say, subjectively, it could have been a partial shutdown."

"He could have done that," Grant said. "Justin and I

have talked about it. We think it's not just that the axe code didn't take. He's self-adjusted, possibly even to the point of being his own reason the axe code didn't take. He's been running internal adjustments, whatever situation he's in. If he takes tape, which I'm sure a provisional Supervisor would want him to do, he takes it surface-level, absorbs it as a behavioral guide. It steadies him down, re-teaches him what his responses ought to be in order to fool everybody. He has an emotional capability: that's currently completely engaged with his Supervisor. He gets pleasure out of doing the best he can, but he probably knows how messed up he really is. He knows, constantly, that he's lying to the one he's attached to, except when he's dealing with his Supervisor in Defense, whoever that is—and whether it's been the same person all along, or whether that's changed, he'll be loyal, and emotionally engaged, and if what they ask him to do throws his deep sets into confusion, his actions will still be clear, even through the conflict. I've studied the military sets. Actions are the real loyalty. That's the mantra way deep in what they used to set. Do what you're told."

She could see it, in what Grant pointed out, the ethic to follow instructions and do no harm until one could get to a Supervisor, the sort of thing you'd set in for somebody who had to survive where Supervisors weren't going to be as close as the nearest office. It was a beta kind of setting. Grant was more complex on that issue. Florian—

Florian, right beside her, was capable of intense argument: you had to know how to get him to do what he didn't want to, and you had to make it clear to him it really was an order.

And then he'd do anything. Absolutely anything. Catlin would do it even faster, and not need advice and sympathy after; Florian did.

So what sort was AK-36?

By all she'd read, he'd have been a Catlin sort. Point him at an enemy. He was setted for headquarters security, and that was what he'd been intended to be, in the purest form of his psychset.

But somebody had done something with the secondaries, and he had become, to all intents and purposes, self-steering ever since, and they'd flung him into Supering combat betas and other alphas. Surviving. Trying to comply with his deep sets. Everybody did. Even born-men did that, in their own chaotic way.

Ask Florian? There was a level at which she didn't mess with her security's working mindsets. Theory was a designer question, and she wasn't as good yet as she would be. It was, more specifically, a Grant kind of question, if you were going to ask an alpha.

It was a Justin or a Jordan kind of question, if you were going to ask a designer.

She left, thinking about it, and she went into the security office and, in a small conference room with Florian, she called Jordan.

"It's Ari," she said. "Do you have a moment, ser?"

No answer, for a long time. Florian had been standing, and in the quiet and the privacy, sat down opposite her, signing, He's there.

"Jordan? I really need to talk to you. Please answer."

"Please? There's a foreign word. Do I recognize that?"

"I need your help. Would you mind if I dropped by?"

"Oh, now this is familiar. 'Would you mind?' Try telling the truth and see if I mind!"

"Are we talking about the manual I sent you?"

"I haven't got time for games."

"I want your opinion, ser. I *need* your opinion. You're one of the few who might know, and I urgently want to talk to you about that manual."

"Go to hell and take my son with you."

"That's not very nice."

Laughter from the other end. *"Fuck you!"*

Florian's face went dangerous. She held up a hand. "Do I take it, ser, that you recognize the case?"

"What is this, a fucking test? I told you, I'm too old for games."

"Old enough to remember what everybody else has forgotten. I thought you were. I wasn't sure. Now I know for certain I want you in on this."

"On what? This isn't a modern design. This is old history. This is old history, from before I was born, let alone working."

"You're good. You just proved that. And I still want you on this case."

"The hell! It's a damned trick, and I'm not going with it!"

He broke the contact.

Florian looked at her, questioning, perhaps, whether they were about to do something.

"I can't force his opinion out of him," she said. "Not in any useful way. But he *knew* what he was looking at. It made him mad that I didn't tell him who it was."

"Many things make Jordan mad," Florian said. "He's not that much like Justin, is he?"

It was a good question. She knew things that could make Justin mad. She'd done some of them. But the one that would Get him, above all else, was something happening to Grant; and the one that would Get him, just him, personally—

—if he were in Jordan's place—

He'd know he'd put his companion in a hell of a place with his actions opposing Ari, that was one; and he'd be damned upset in his career if he was on the outs with Ari.

It was an interesting thought, too, what Jordan would have been, if he'd been lovers with the first Ari long-term. But that had gone very, very wrong—not because Jordan hadn't ever loved Ari, she was fairly sure of that, and not because Ari hadn't likely loved him. What Jordan wanted was being partners with her, learning things, doing things, having that. It wouldn't have mattered, if he were Justin, whose name was on a published paper; or whether he got official credit; but it had mattered very, very much to Jordan, because—

Switch personae dramatis again—because Jordan was driven, all his life, to be number one, the best, the one who ran things—

And he wasn't the best. In his view, Ari had turned on him. But she'd seen a danger in him. Seen how thoroughly one hell of a sex drive overlying a god-complex had blinded what otherwise really was a great mind . . .

She'd fixed it in the next generation, hadn't she?

This is it. This is all there is. This is all there'll ever be.

All there is.

He'd been seventeen, Justin had, and that had to have hurt, because Jordan had always taught him not to trust Ari; but Justin's own ambition to be the best had driven him to Ari; and afterward—

Afterward he'd had that mantra echoing in his skull, and Grant was the one he could trust, forever after, the way Jordan trusted Paul. Justin had come, finally, to a point he could like her. Just—*like* her; and that was a long, long way for that mindset to come.

She'd met Justin on the same territory, hadn't she? She'd been half afraid of him. And then targeted him for her first adult conquest. And shied off again, bluff called. He'd been scared of her. Grant had been willing to fling himself between. But that had been a dose of ice water, and she'd thought about it later and thought—thank God they hadn't. Wouldn't that have made a mess of things?

Liking was good enough.

Jordan hadn't been that lucky. Neither had the first Ari.

I've found two of your mistakes, she thought, addressing the first Ari. One was ever sleeping with Jordan; the other was letting Giraud run and never just having the fight it would have taken and looking into his competency to do what he was certified to do.

You knew about Denys, didn't you? Knew damned well he was a genius, and knew Giraud was *almost* bright enough to handle things. Giraud really *was* an Alpha Supervisor. He just wasn't the best one on the planet. When an alpha gets messed up, it's a question of who *can* unwind the tangle he can make of his sets, and that's probably just very, very few, even among those with the license, isn't it? It's hard for me to judge—because I'm good; it was probably hard for you to judge. I wonder how often you ever ran into Kyle, or if you ever looked twice at him.

She looked at Florian, pocketed the com, reached across the table, and laid her hand on his, a little calm-down.

"I'm not worried about Jordan," she said. "I'll Get him. I'll Get him and not lose Justin in the process. They've had a fight about something. But we'll fix it."

"We're worried about Defense," Florian said somberly. "Sera, we don't have resources there."

"We don't," she said, "but we're smarter."

"They have weapons *and* numbers."

Here and now, Florian meant. Here and now didn't always figure when she set her thoughts ranging; but trust Florian to pull her back to the real world. Defense, she thought, was her enemy, and consequently all Reseune was in danger. Defense was, in the terms of their childhood game, the Enemy, and Vladislaw Khalid . . . was its modern face.

What have they got? was one thing to ask.

And it was always, always smart to ask—How does what we did play out in their eyes? What do they *think* we did?

Overthrowing Denys . . . who had agreements with them.

Bringing Jordan back.

Bringing *Jordan* back, where Jordan, if he weren't Jordan, might have been moved to tell her things. A lot of things. Jordan had been *dealing* with Defense before Kyle turned Abban into a weapon aimed at the first Ari.

She'd assumed Jordan was innocent. But if there was one person inside Reseune *besides* Ari in those days who could have run a timebomb like Kyle, it *was* Jordan. Giraud damned sure couldn't, and Prang didn't think she could crack what Defense had done and an alpha had worked over for decades . . .

Jordan had taken one look at that pysch manual and exploded . . . not because there was anything in it of what Defense had done, but possibly because he knew exactly what Kyle was, and where he had been, if not where he was now.

"Sera?" Florian asked. The real world. The immediate threat.

"We've got to take measures to defend Reseune," she said. "We can't assume we're safe from physical attack. And not just me. Everybody. The labs. Everything. We don't know how crazy things can get."

"Good," Florian said, the way he'd used to say when they'd laid plans in the storm shelters. "That's *good.*"

They went up to her office then. They called in Catlin, and Wes and Marco, and they said maybe they should talk to green barracks as well as the ReseuneSec senior officers—who weren't happy about having a very young azi like Rafael down there in charge of them; but, Catlin said, after Wes and Marco, old green barracks instructors, had gone down and explained there was a danger, and that Rafael BR was under expert advice and orders, then ReseuneSec's seniors had been a lot happier.

There were cases spilling over to Alpha Wing's attention, a fight between two CITs at the port, over a lover in the town. It was the sort of thing Hicks had used to handle, and that Ari would have gladly given him back; but they couldn't trust him yet with communications, and Rafael had no idea what to do with CIT fools who were themselves warehouse managers and assistant managers.

So she wrote a letter to the offenders: *All of Reseune is in danger right now and Director Schwartz is trying to straighten things out in the capital. You have violated a number of community laws, and if Director Hicks were in charge at the moment you might both be doing community service for months. It's stupid to fight when it's the other person's choice which of you she sleeps with, or neither. A ReseuneSec officer will ask her how she wants things to be. Her word will be final. If I read any of your names again on reports, including hers, regarding this matter, you'll be in front of a judge and this as well as the next offense will go to trial. Sincerely, Ariane Emory.*

It put her in a fighting mood, and she wrote another letter to all department heads: *Regarding the recent call to review atmosphere breach procedures with all employees and all persons under your charge: we will be conducting unannounced drills. Conditions in Novgorod and recent sabotage upriver have made this review imperative. Places of public assembly, likewise review your procedures and be prepared. We cannot be sure the first call will not be a real emergency.*

She was just out of deepstudy the next morning when she received, via Yanni's Chloe, an exasperated message from the birthlabs:

We hope that Administration is aware that we risk losing work in progress due to security drills. We wish to be made an exception in all except an actual emergency.

She considered it, looked up the rules, considered lives

at stake and wrote, to the labs: *Actual emergency is by regulation announced as such. Labs will conduct unannounced internal drills once daily in lieu of ReseuneSec drills.—Ariane Emory.*

She wasn't in a good mood about that. She wasn't in a good mood today about a number of things, and her head was muzzy from the deepteach drug, which probably argued she shouldn't be writing to departments. She asked Florian, via com, "Has Yanni checked in? Has Amy?" and being told that neither had, she keyed up the night's news. It was the fourteenth of August. And Lao was at death's door.

That continued: Lao was rumored to be on life support, which could cover almost anything. Her Proxy was still missing. Other Councillors had declined interviews. The mayor of Novgorod had declined an interview, except that he had canceled all police and fire service leaves. The news services reported panic buying of foodstuffs and water. Parents were keeping children from youth activities.

Rafael reported, from ReseuneSec, that there had been two robberies overnight in Novgorod, four muggings, one hundred eighteen incidents of public intoxication, fourteen resolved cases of missing persons, one that hadn't been resolved, some cases of panic buying of foodstuffs, a break-in and looting at a liquor dealer's, and a case of vandalism in the subway, where someone had painted *Free Jordan Warrick* on a subway car. The latter had gone through ten stations without being reported, and three more stations before the car had been taken out of service for cleaning.

Rafael said that older officers called it an uncommonly quiet night. Her own experience, slight as it was, said the night's activities were usually ten times that, except in a few categories.

"People are afraid," she reported back to Rafael. She put that in her population dynamics equations and it came out very simply, that the azi-born weren't causing any trouble they could avoid and that the CIT-born were worried and expressing it in liquor consumption.

She twisted her hair up, skewered it, asked herself if she could bear deepstudying Ari One's notes on military psych one more time, and thought she'd done it enough.

Com went off. She punched in.

"*Sera*." Catlin. "*The scheduled 0800 flight from Novgorod has taken off an hour late. It will land here rather than Moreyville. We're not getting a passenger list, sera. ReseuneSec has taken notice. We are insisting. They're just saying they have a Council order.*"

It could land at either airport. It had the extra stop if there were passengers with a Reseune destination. Council order. Yanni might be aboard.

Possibly Amy, on Yanni's ticket.

Somebody was coming in, or some message was. And the airplane wasn't talking to security.

"I may be going down to the airport," she said to Joyesse and Del, and went to her room and put on a light blouse and a beige suit—media lived down at the Reseune airport, the ones with clearance to be here; and if it was a wave of more media coming in she was prepared to be exercised about it.

Nerves. She got the reports from Catlin, told Catlin to advise her when it was within half an hour of landing.

When it was on approach, Catlin and Florian showed up in full kit, reported a car would meet them at the side exit of Alpha Wing, which was right by Wing Security—an exit which didn't even, to this day, have a road connected to it.

She went downstairs. Florian and Catlin were talking to ReseuneSec; and there was no use speculating. If it was Yanni coming in, he didn't want his presence on the plane advertised, and there could be very, very good reason for that.

She saw the plane coming in as they came the last bit down to the shoreline road, down beyond the first AG barns, saw it touch and roll to a stop. Novgorod Air, it said on the side. Not Reseune One, which was sitting idle at Novgorod under round the clock guard; not even ReseuneAir, which was *also* sitting idle: its fleet consisted of one of the three planes here, one at Novgorod, one at Moreyville, and they were all idle, lacking ordinary traffic this week.

"Sera," Florian said then. "It's not Yanni aboard, nor Amy. Two passengers show the name Corain."

Aug 14, 2424
1122h

They kept the media away, used the restricted arrival lounge, and the handful of passengers that debarked and walked to that area were an older woman—Emily Latu, ReseuneAir security informed Florian, and Florian relayed it: Emily Latu, wife of Mikhail Corain, her adult children Rebecca Latu, Rebecca's spouse Andrew Gaines, and three children; and Alexander Corain, spouse Morag Westfall, and babe in arms.

It was beyond a disappointment. It was ominous. Ari stood looking at the arrivals with a chill about her heart, then bestirred herself to walk toward Latu, as Florian indicated her to be, and to offer her hand. "Sera. Welcome to Reseune. I'm Ariane Emory."

"Sera Emory." Latu looked to be on the brink of tears. "My husband wanted us to come here. Councillor Schwartz said we'd be safe here."

"You're very welcome. Is your husband all right?"

"Yes," Latu said, "yes."

"And Yanni Schwartz?"

"As far as I know, he is. Lao's dying. Nobody can find her Proxy. Defense is walled up in their Bureau, and it's just scary. It's scary in the city. My husband—my husband sent this."

Latu offered a datastick. Ari took it, gave it to Catlin.

"He doesn't want publicity about your being here," she said. "Is that so?"

"He said—he said go ahead and talk to the media once we're safe. That they're trying to call Council into session. Without the Information Proxy, they haven't got a special measures quorum. They're hoping to get hold of Edgerton. Everybody says he's in the city—that Trade actually knows where he is."

That was hopeful news, actually. There were legal maneuvers. Yanni was still trying that.

"What is the information you gave me?"

"My husband—my husband has a message for the city. For everybody. If you can get it out."

"I'll see what I can do," she said. Not knowing what Corain had said, she wasn't going to run Corain's family past the media, not yet, not now. She said to Catlin, "Get cars for them. Get them up to Wing One, our old apartment."

"Yes," Catlin said, and talked to ReseuneSec.

It wasn't the arrival she wanted. And when she played for herself, on her handheld, what Corain had sent, it took on a far, far more ominous character.

"This is Mikhail Corain, Councillor for Citizens, addressing you not from the Council chamber or from anywhere I wish to disclose at the moment. The murder of one Councillor of Defense and the disappearance of another has left no doubt of the intent of persons inside Defense to stage a coup and takeover of civilian government. Citizens of Union, your Council still exists. We have not given up our lawfully elected posts in favor of murderers and conspirators, nor will we step aside. We call on the Defense electorate to reject all orders from Vladislaw Khalid. Citizens calls for the arrest and detention of Vladislaw Khalid and for the immediate declaration of legitimate elections in the Bureau of Defense. Khalid's acts are void of authority and Citizens calls on Khalid to vacate the premises of Defense and submit to arrest."

It wasn't a great speech. But it was, given the arrival of Corain's family, an earnest one. She sent it out over the public address in Reseune itself, for starters. That, for all the department heads that had lately objected to the drills.

And she sent a copy to the media waiting at the airport. The plane had taken off, on its way to Moreyville before it returned to Novgorod.

But Mikhail Corain's speech was headed for Novgorod much, much faster.

And she hoped to God she was doing the right thing—and that Corain and Yanni both were braced for the fall-out from it: it was a declaration of civil war.

Sitting on it, however, even for a matter of hours—*that* could have consequences, too.

The Enemy wasn't likely standing still, not if things were so bad the Council was sending relatives to safety.

BOOK THREE   Section 5   Chapter xvii

AUG 14, 2424
1301H

"Khalid's acts are void of authority and Citizens calls on Khalid to vacate the premises of Defense and submit to arrest."

"They got there," Yanni muttered to Frank. "Thank God. Time to move."

Frank used the house phone to talk to their guard, which occupied the downstairs of the hotel, simple signal, verbal code. The hotel was down to five other guests, two women who were visiting a relative in the city, and a family from Novgorod who'd suffered an apartment fire, and was keeping very, very quiet under the circumstances. Four businessmen, three from Svetlansk and another from Big Blue, had checked out this morning to catch the flight, the first in two days, that had gone up toward Moreyville and Reseune. Amy Carnath had reported her hotel mostly vacant, and the news said barges were stacking up in the port because dock and warehouse workers weren't showing up and there was no room to offload. Local groceries reported shortages, while food piled up on barges that couldn't find a berth.

That was the condition of the city, as bad a mess as it had ever been during the War: there were rumors, constantly denied in news reports, of Paxer sabotage directed at the precip towers that defended the city, and workers consequently reported sick rather than go into large exposed areas like the docks and warehouses, construction and transport. Companies temporarily shut down operations rather than pay the few workers that did show, and in some families, credit was running short. The city ombudsman had launched a court inquiry as to whether companies would owe back pay, and the city mayor had threatened arrest and confiscation in any shop jacking up prices for necessities like food, water, and medicines.

It was a damned mess, was what, and it was getting worse. Yanni put on his coat over a tee that covered a bulletproof vest, Frank wearing the same protection under his, and carrying the critical briefcase. They met their exterior guard outside, picked up two more at the lift—the two at the hotel room door would stay there to make sure the room stayed secure—and they took the lift down to pick up four more guards at the lot occupying the lobby. They numbered more than before. The ones from ReseuneSec offices across town had come over, and the hotel was an armed camp—in case. Reseune promised the hotel that it would pick up the tab—and that kept management happy about ReseuneSec filling hotel rooms and supervising in the kitchens—the Carnath girl and her azi were, he hoped, on that plane that had carried Corain's family. He didn't want the kid involved any deeper, not today, and the last thing they needed was those two getting swept up in some operation—or worse—and needing him to get them out.

The ReseuneSec locals had a car—several cars—and the hotel airport bus. They used the bus for a decoy and transport for the other guards, and Yanni got into a car with two others and a lot of guns. Frank got into the seat beside him, and they started off with a speed more apt for Reseune's lonely portside road than a Novgorod street. They whipped onto Central, and sped along about a kilometer toward the white tower that sprawled onto a block off Central, then squealed around a turn and up to the emergency entrance of the hospital, where the hotel bus met them.

No wasted time. Frank opened the door, got out as armed guards formed up, and Yanni got out. A handful of hospital security stood at the door, and locked it in apprehension, but unlocked it after a moment when Yanni took out his wallet and showed his Council insignia through the glass.

"Catherine Lao's room," he said when they stood in

the emergency room lobby. "Take us there. Now. Council business."

The guards clearly weren't used to making executive decisions, but one of them led the way down the hall and talked on his com while he was doing it. He said, protesting, "Ser, she's in Intensive Care. She's not doing well."

"I know that," Yanni said. "If she's got a pulse, I need to see her. Fast. The longer I'm here, the more likely there's going to be a disturbance to the other patients. Let's move, shall we?"

"Ser," the guard said, and got them all to a large lift, and up to the third floor. Then a double door and a desk where a nurse posed a more formidable barrier.

"Yanni Schwartz," Yanni said, showing the wallet badge. "Council business for Councillor Lao."

"She's on life support, ser."

"Can she be made conscious?"

"A doctor has to order that."

"Find one and do it. Now. Council order."

The nurse didn't look happy in the least. She cast sideward glances as she talked on the com, and stopped the conversation with a commanding gesture downward, meaning the guns. Yanni made a small gesture of his own, and they lowered. The nurse answered something to whoever was on the com, and then shut down the connection.

"This way, ser. Just you."

"And my aide," Yanni said, meaning Frank. The nurse scowled, but they went through the double doors together, and the visible guns stayed in the foyer.

The room held more machines than human presence. Lao seemed lost among them, a human face, an arm, a white sheet. She'd grown incredibly old, since he'd last seen her, so shrunken and pale it was shocking. The nurse made adjustments on the panel, and after a moment, Lao's dark eyes opened a slit, black as space, all the eye that was visible. Tension touched the forehead, lines of pain.

"That's Yanni," Lao murmured.

"Kate." He came closer and set his hand on hers, which was cold as ice. "Kate, we're in a hell of a mess. Khalid's got the Proxy, Jacques has disappeared, not seen in weeks, Edgerton's missing . . ."

"Addy's missing?"

"Could be dead, for what we know. We need to call a special quorum. The planet's in a mess. We need a new Proxy for Information. I've got the document. You just have to give us a name and sign it."

The white brow knit. Hard. "Damn, Yanni. I'm not focusing well."

"Just a name, Kate. And a signature." Frank had the document, folded, in his coat pocket. Yanni took it, and a pen, and moved the recorder off the desk to get a flat surface.

"Carris?" she asked.

"Not been seen."

The frown stayed. Lao had the pen in her fingers, and lost it. He steadied it.

"Can't see the damn line."

"Here." He showed her where. "Just sign it, Kate. Just sign it."

She signed, carefully, most of her ordinary signature before it trailed off.

"I can fill in the blank," he said. "Who do you want for proxy? Recorder's running. Say it, and I'll fill it in."

"Ariane Emory," she said.

"Kate, it's 2424. Kate?"

She wasn't listening. She wasn't hearing anything. The lines on the machines had all stopped.

"White Rabbit," Yanni said, on com, the car speeding back through the streets, and when he heard Mikhail's voice. "White Rabbit, how's it going?"

"Affirmative. Affirmative. We've got him. Come ahead."

The call cut out. Fast. His heart did a little flutter.

He looked at Frank. "They got him," he said. Meaning Edgerton. Chavez of Finance had told Harogo of Internal Affairs that he knew where Edgerton was, and they'd just made contact . . . which meant they might not need to file that questionable paper. Edgerton was going to show in the Council chambers for about five minutes, which was what they needed. Lao had appointed a dead woman to take Edgerton's place, but they'd, thank God,. located

Edgerton's hidey-hole somewhere in the city, Chavez had just worked a miracle, and Yanni told the driver, "Council Hall."

The car veered. The airport bus, caught by surprise, caught up with them three intersections on, and trailed both escort cars.

They crossed the river on Council Bridge, and the administrative tower, closest to the river of all the various bureau office towers, loomed up closer and closer.

The portico showed ominously vacant, compared to the usual press of media vans and reporters. Nobody was there but one lonely media stakeout with her cameraman, them and a small number of Council aides, with another car giving up its occupants as a third car and the airport bus came squealing up the drive, and more security bailed out.

Guns came out. "Easy," Yanni said. The other car was Mamud Chavez, and Yanni went to meet him, and go with him through the doors. "Mamud." He offered his hand as they passed the doors and came under the scrutiny of Council security. Chavez, ordinarily not his ally, took the handshake with uncommon sincerity.

"Good to see you," Chavez said, the statement itself an earthquake in Council relations. "Corain went to the back entry."

"Good," he said. He stayed worried as they reached the lift, and gathered their bodyguard in, both of them. It shot them up to the Council level, and let them out into a vacant hallway.

Frank opened the door for them. Yanni and Chavez walked into the Hall of the Nine itself, and immediately he saw Corain and Tien, of Industry. That was four of the five they needed for a simple quorum, four of the eight they needed for the vote they intended.

"Harogo's on his way up," Corain said. "Harad's coming."

Five. And six. Harad, State, had been a cliffhanger: he'd been an ally of Gorodin's, in Defense; and it hadn't been certain where he came down—he hadn't liked Jacques or Spurlin.

They tended toward their seats. Took them, in the arc that constituted an official seating. There was no Council clerk. They passed a sheet of paper down, signed their names, and fed it into the automated slot that immortalized it, irretrievable, a statement of their presence here, on this day, to do Council business.

Five more minutes. Harogo came in, Internal Affairs, frail, and surrounded by his own security, from Fargone Station. Two more minutes, and they had word from Corain's watch at the back entry that Harad was in the building, and then Ludmilla deFranco arrived downstairs.

One more needed. Yanni looked at the clock. Seventeen minutes. The longer they sat, the more vulnerable they became.

Eight. Harad came in, walked to the fore of the desk.

"He didn't make his appointment," Harad said, as agitated as Yanni ever remembered him. "I have no word."

He. Meaning Edgerton.

"Damn," Corain said. "Damn it."

"It's not safe to stay here," Chavez said. "We risk getting pinned here."

"Five more minutes," Yanni said.

Harad came up to his seat. DeFranco came in, conferred quietly with Harad, took her seat. And they waited.

Frank talked on com with someone, probably downstairs. Frank walked over to him, leaned near his chair. "There's a military presence at the hotel. And another squad at Councillor Lynch's condominium."

"We can't do this," Harogo said. Harogo sat next to him. "We need to move. We've failed the quorum."

"We can get the eight we need," Yanni said. "Lao's dead. But she named another proxy." He got up and slipped the paper into the slot. "Ariane Emory."

No restriction on the ability of a Councillor to appoint a Proxy. No restriction even of age. None of bureau registration. In the wild early days of chancey transport, *anybody* with credentials could carry a vote into the Council on behalf of an absent Councillor.

"Irregular!" Harogo said.

"Legal," Corain said.

"We can't vote here without our eighth," Yanni said. "I call Council. Reseune Administrative Territories, on the twelfth of September."

"Second that," Corain said.

"Those opposed?" Harogo said, and then wrote on the screen under his hands, and filed it. "Each of us has declared a Proxy. In case."

"Go," Yanni said, and got up from his seat. He alone *couldn't* file a Proxy: only Lynch, Councillor for Science, could do that, and Lynch was holed up in his residence, too old and too timid for what was afoot. He couldn't lay all the blame for their situation to Edgerton's lack of nerve: for all he knew, there was trouble hot on Edgerton's trail. Or Edgerton was dead.

He gathered up Frank, then caught Mikhail Corain at the side of the door. "Thanks."

"Done as much as I can," Corain said, and in the lowest possible tones. *"Did* she sign it?"

"I've got the recording," Yanni said. "Or Frank has it. It's legal. Stay low and stay safe."

Out the door then, downstairs as fast as they could gather a lift-load of Councillors, aides, and security. In the lower hall they separated, headed for the north doors and the south portico.

ReseuneSec held the doors.

BOOK THREE   Section 5   Chapter xviii

AUGUST 20, 2424
1438H

Nearly a week since the broadcast, and Ari had long since taken pity on the reporters camped out at the airport and physically cut off from their news organizations, their families, their means of being elsewhere—she comped meals, laundry service, delivered unlimited vid entertainment, and ordered the restaurant there to vary its menu daily and be open twenty-four hours, the little airport bar to open at 2000h and stay til 2400h nightly.

She'd also sent down two ReseuneSec agents to help

out at the bar, and to gather up any tidbits of information and rumor that came in by various links that didn't belong to Reseune.

There *were* rumors down there, no question. Broadcast news continually said Lao was alive. Rumor at the bar said she was artificially sustained for legal reasons. The broadcast news said Council had met but Khalid had not shown up, nor had the Proxy for Information, and Council had adjourned quickly. Rumor said Edgerton was in hiding somewhere in the city and that he and Council were under direct threat of the military.

On August 20, Amy called—finally, and reported that Yanni had taken over the hotel he was in, that Corain was living there, too, and that she and Quentin had moved in for safety, because her hotel had been used for a barracks. She also said that yesterday there'd been a breakdown in the subway that added to problems in the city. People said it was Paxer activity, but mostly it was just rumors— anything that broke was automatically Paxers.

Meanwhile, Amy said, Khalid was threatening to put the city under martial law; but without the Council he knew he couldn't do that, so he was trying to locate Council members, and that military had been searching hotels, including her former one, and trying to bully Councillors into showing up when *he* called Council. It was certain Khalid knew where Yanni and Corain were, but hadn't made a move on them or searched their hotel. He hadn't found enough of the other Councillors to get eight of the Nine—and without them, he couldn't declare martial law, couldn't convene the Council of Worlds, and couldn't do a lot of things, legally, so there was no point in his raiding the hotel where two Councillors definitely and publicly were.

That was the sum of Amy's report, except to ask how they were, and Ari said they were all fine.

But late on August 23, a barge came up from Moreyville, and fourteen people got off at Reseune docks, fourteen very tired, dirty, and hungry people, among them Ludmilla deFranco, far less than the immaculate person she ordinarily was. Her blonde hair was dyed dark, her customary couturier dress traded for a dockworker's blues.

All the same, a spark of triumph glistened in deFranco's eyes when Ari came down to the docks to meet her.

"A pleasure," deFranco said, and startled her and Florian with an unexpected embrace. "God, you look like her, don't you?"

"I should," Ari said, but she didn't actually mind the hug: she was just startled by it. "I'm glad you're safe. Did you come up all the way by barge?"

"To Moreyville by plane," DeFranco said. "Then the barge." DeFranco had to be past her hundreds, and it was still a long, hard pull, deFranco and this crowd of people, some of whom must be younger relatives. "Has Yanni been in touch? You're Lao's Proxy."

"How?" she asked.

"Filed and legal," deFranco said, and sank onto a convenient counter edge. "Yanni got it from Lao in person. Filed it in chambers, all of us to witness. You're the new Proxy for Information. Council's to meet here on the twelfth of September."

"Here. On the twelfth. Why are they waiting that long?"

"There's preparation to make. Contacts. People to be felt out . . . some of them inside Defense. Those still there are working that angle, making contacts as best they can, pulling every string they've got—of which I don't have enough left to matter. I'm getting too old for this, nearly as old as Lao, and she's dead. We're in a war, sera. We're in an outright war for control of the government. Khalid can't call Council to get a declaration of martial law: he needs eight Councillors, and I, my dear, and now you, are sitting here preventing that from happening, no matter how he threatens us. He can haul in every Councillor left in Novgorod and without us, he won't have sufficient votes either to get seated or to declare martial law."

"And if he comes here?"

"There's a practical limit to what he can order the military at large to do. Individual units, individual arrests, yes, he's got his people. But he can't move divisions. Not what it would take to get in here. Some things he doesn't dare order, because he *isn't* seated."

Yet, Ari thought, chilled by the thought. What Khalid would and wouldn't dare once he had enough power and

legitimacy was another matter—but she didn't say that.
DeFranco, an old ally of her predecessor, deserved accommodation in Wing One, too, along with her relatives or
staff or whoever they were. "I'm very sorry we're so tight
on space," she said. "It's not adequate. But we can settle
you up the hill. Close to Mikhail Corain's family."

"It will be absolutely adequate," deFranco said, "if we
can all get warm showers and beds that don't bob up and
down. Beds with sheets. That would be wonderful."

"Come with me," she said, and gave orders and personally took them all back up the hill on the bus, giving other
orders via Florian and Catlin on com. "We're going to have
visitors," she said, "the whole Council, eventually, maybe
their families and relations. More worrisome, we may have
the military making a move on us. Tell Wes to go down to
the green barracks. He's going to be liaison down there
for the next few days. Tell ReseuneSec to put the bots on a
hair trigger. Tell Tommy—hell, tell Tommy do something
about the logistics in Wing One. We can't put part of these
people in luxury and part of them in rooms with scaffolding. They're Councillors. They need beds, sheets, towels,
ID, and a charge tab for the restaurants, everything you
can think of."

Tommy acknowledged. That would happen and she
didn't have to worry about it. She did have to worry about
Yanni—Yanni was still in Novgorod risking his neck. So
was the rest of the Council. And Amy. And there wasn't a
thing she could do for them—except keep the media down
at the airport as informed as she could; so she sent the
reporters a message: there would be a news conference at
1800h sharp, and she'd be down there to fill them in on the
arrivals from Novgorod and what they'd had to say.

She chose to host the media at the airport. That meant
keeping them happy—in all senses. They were an asset.
They were also apt, as Catlin put it, to become an issue
with the opposition—possibly a target, if certain forces
decided they didn't like the news reports coming out of
Reseune. And there were a great many innocent people at
risk if that happened. Khalid couldn't order large units . . .
didn't dare: that was what deFranco assured her. But the
military at large could be lied to. Khalid, with unopposed

control of the Bureau, firm control of Intelligence, and sole control of the military information network could tell them anything—if he controlled all the sources of information. And she had one of those sources. She had one and she had to protect it and use it to keep Khalid from shading the truth. The rest of the military *had* to learn what Khalid was doing.

There were storm tunnels under the town. There were, for that matter, defenses on the cliffs, near the precip towers. Khalid had shown what he could do up at Strassenberg. He'd launched that maybe to signal something—but it signaled them, too, to take precautions.

She reached her desk and said, "Base One. Defense of the precip towers. Specifics."

Base One delivered information. She mined it at deeper and deeper levels and stored the result. She called Catlin in and then called Rafael.

"Review this," she said. "You and Florian both. Rafael, you too. See what they've got, what we've got. Tell me how bad it could get."

She didn't have people tapped into the military, to know what they had. From orbit—Defense had everything, including warships. They could turn Reseune into a smoking ruin if they wanted to, and nothing could stop it, no shelter withstand it. But deFranco said Khalid didn't dare . . . politically speaking. DeFranco believed some people wouldn't take his orders.

Bet on it? She didn't dare. Not with all they had at risk.

And finally—pause for breath in a day in which she'd skipped lunch, and now remembered she hadn't had breakfast—she ordered up a sandwich and a tea, and sat there thinking, and thinking—about Amy, up there in the middle of something Amy didn't understand and was having to learn fast; and Yanni, trying to use the influence he did have, to keep Khalid from taking the whole board . . . Khalid was a man who'd use what he had, but, possibly, Khalid's asset *and* theirs, he was too smart and too cautious to try to use everything. He'd move what he could rely on. That was Intelligence, maybe isolate special operations, some elements of the Fleet . . . the latter especially if he could con them.

She didn't truly understand the inner workings of Defense, or how they made decisions, or who had the ultimate say in the various services. She'd heard the first Ari's advice. But it was limited, and dated. And current politics mattered inside that Bureau, but she didn't have good ins into its workings.

Giraud had been upset when she'd gone after Khalid.

Maybe she had, in some way, brought this on. She'd certainly made an enemy that day.

Maybe. Nothing proved Khalid was more of an enemy than he'd ever been, just that Khalid, for some reason, was moving before he had full support inside his own Bureau—that argued he was in a hurry for some reason. Mainly Khalid hadn't *won* the election. That would have given him a tougher position. And people still defied him. Corain had outright called on elements of Defense to defy him.

Right now, deFranco might be right. She hoped so.

God, she'd done everything she could think to do, and if she hyped up on stayawakes to try to keep thinking, she'd be increasingly crazier, especially after all the deepstudy she'd done on the AK-36 case. It was time to let bodily chemistry do what it had to do for a few hours. It was time to get some rest. If they were lucky, they had a few days before Khalid got really upset or really desperate.

There *was* Hicks, who'd dealt with Defense. She could let him loose, dust him off, reinstate him, give him a chance to be a hero, and hope that resentment didn't make him a highly irrational personal enemy.

There was Yanni, whom she couldn't reach. There was deFranco, whom she could. DeFranco—if she knew how to read deFranco—was a resource she could use freely; except it was one without a crosscheck: she either believed deFranco's assessment wholesale or she didn't. She could ask department heads like Wendy Peterson and John Edwards, and Ivanov, who'd at least been around as long as Yanni.

But people that really knew what had been going on with Defense, long-term—that was Hicks; and Kyle, who wasn't on Reseune's side at the moment.

And . . . there was Jordan Warrick.

She ought to go to bed. She ought to fall in and go to sleep and stay there pending the next alarm. But the brain was going to stay active.

And she had enough energy left to get up, leave the apartment, and walk across the hall—Catlin and Florian were both on errands, she didn't even alert Theo or Jory, and it was one of a few times in her life she'd left where she lived without one or the other of them.

She knocked at Justin's door. And Justin answered it.

"Ari." Eyes flicked to the hall. The missing escort.

"I need Jordan," she said. "I need to talk to him. I need what he knows. I need you to go with me. Khalid's not attacking us yet, but the whole Council's coming here on the twelfth, deFranco's just come in for refuge, and there's Kyle downstairs, who I'm afraid I'll kill if I try to deal with him. I don't even know if it will do any good, but it's what we *can* do, while we're sitting here being a target. I want to know what Jordan knows. I want his help with the case I handed both of you."

Grant had showed up, at Justin's shoulder.

Justin started to say something. And then seemed to change his mind. "Come in," he said somberly. "I'll get my coat."

"You said he's not speaking to you."

"You're likely to get the door opened. I want to be there to give him an alternate target. Where's Florian and Catlin?"

"On an errand," she said, and that had echoes, way, way back, to the day her predecessor had died. "I can get your Mark and Gerry to come. It'll be all right. Your father's not the danger. I think—I don't know—possibly—possibly Kyle AK is supposed to come after *me*."

"God."

"It's dead serious, Justin. That's why I wanted you both on it."

"And what I read says he's able to kill, if you want the short summation." He pulled his coat on. Grant did the same, and Grant took his pocket com and called the downstairs security office, by the sound of it. "Gerry BG," he said, "Mark. Meet us downstairs."

She'd been too tired to function. She'd planned to talk

to Jordan in the morning. Maybe. If she could talk Justin into it. But now that Justin was in motion, she thought—just do it. Just do it the best way possible, and she went with them, down the hall, down the lift, thinking, How odd, just to walk with somebody, in a safe building. How odd, to trust two people that aren't staff, that don't have all safe connections—because Jordan really wasn't safe.

She did take out her pocket com and call Theo. "If my security asks, I'm with Justin and Grant. I'm going downstairs and over to Wing One. It's quiet, all's well, no problems."

She wasn't totally surprised when, as they picked up Mark and Gerry, Jory showed up from the lift, out of breath, and added herself to the group; and before they'd reached the security desk at the exit, Florian showed up from the other direction, sweating a little, but perfectly composed.

Then she felt guilty, and touched Florian's shoulder, and said, "It wasn't going to be this long or this far." He was as tired as she was. And it hadn't been fair.

"Yes, sera," he said, a little out of breath. And they went on through to Wing One, herself, Florian, Justin, Grant, Mark and Gerry, and Jory, all of them into the dim storm tunnel of Wing One, and into the lift, and up again.

"Let me," Ari said, and went and pressed the button at Jordan's door. "Ser. Jordan Warrick."

There was some delay about it. Then the door opened. Paul was there.

"He says he's going to take a shower, sera, I'm sorry. Justin—" Seeing Justin and Grant just behind her, and the security, he hesitated.

"He can wait about the shower," Justin said. "Paul. Now."

"Come in, sera," Paul said, and she walked in and all of them walked in. It might not be the best thing to do. It likely wasn't. But she wasn't going to tell Florian to stay outside. Ari felt his presence right at her back. And Jory's. Mark and Gerry were there, the whole lot of them.

They waited. Paul came back again, and this time Jordan walked out, in his bathrobe.

"So?" Jordan said.

"That file I sent you," Ari said. "I know you've got an opinion."

Jordan drew himself up and folded his arms, staring at her. "This isn't the way I do consultation. Try tomorrow. Without them."

"You read the file. You recognized it."

"I recognize the type." His voice was edged with anger. But restrained, and he shot a glance past her, full of fury. Then back. "What, did you think I wouldn't?"

"That set's older than I am by a bit." She cast a nod over her shoulder. "Older than Justin is, or Grant. They've never worked with the military sets. But you have."

"I studied the mess the War sent us back. We all did. As I'm sure you know, since you get into every damned thing you like."

"If I had everything you know, I wouldn't have to ask. You worked with the Defense sets."

"As a student. You're talking about ancient history."

"You consulted with them. You talked with them. You wrote one very good paper."

"Several."

She thought about the next question. Florian and Jory were there, if anything untoward happened. Mark and Gerry were. She didn't think Justin would side with Jordan if he went for her.

She said, "Did you know an azi named Kyle, who worked with Giraud?"

Brows lifted slightly. "Alpha. Is that who this file is about?"

"Yes. Did you think he'd been axed?"

A little delay. She wasn't dealing with the son of a bitch Jordan, the opaque stare. Calculation was quick and sharp. "You're saying he *wasn't*. He's still alive?"

"He was, according to records, a Fleet Alpha Supervisor. And no, the code didn't take. After which he had access to Abban, among others Giraud had in his office. He was still working for Defense. Defense was talking to you about breaking with Reseune. Ari found out and pulled you home. Defense knew that my existence was a possibility—knew that from you *and* from Giraud's office. Knew that Ari didn't have that long anyway. *You* were there with a grudge that was proveable. Perfect vector for suspicion. Giraud had been in Novgorod, talking with Defense. So had Abban. So had Kyle, just one of the aides."

"Bloody hell. This is a fucking setup. Get out of here." He waved an arm toward Justin. "Get *him* out of here. Get away from me!"

"No," Paul said, from over by the bar counter. *"No."*

"The *hell*," Jordan said, and turned and walked out of the room.

Paul still stood there, facing them, Paul immaculately dressed, very steady. "Sera," he said, "Justin, Grant." A little dip of the head. "Jordan and I need to talk. We are *going* to talk. If you'd please call him in the morning."

There was something changed in that equation. She didn't know what. But Justin said, "Good. —Ari, he *will."*

Jordan came back around the doorjamb, stood there, arms folded.

"You're not welcome here, boy. As for *you*—" He looked straight at Ari. "You think Kyle murdered Ari?"

"I'm fairly sure there's a connection between him, Abban, and that event, yes. All that's in the past. What we've got *now* is the possibility, the very real possibility of a military operation directed at Reseune, and people getting killed."

"Notably you."

"And a lot of innocent people who haven't the least idea they're in danger. You won't be safe here if Defense launches something. You know far too much. *Defense* was perfectly content while you were shut up inside Planys. You never heard them complaining about your being yanked away from Novgorod and going home with Ari that session. You never heard them arguing that it was some political set-up when you got blamed for Ari's murder. No. And Yanni didn't send you to Fargone for exile for one very good reason: because you wouldn't have lasted the week there."

"You're saying *Kyle* killed her."

"Was behind Abban doing it. But Defense did it. Let you take the blame. And while Denys and Giraud were in charge, Defense was real easy for them to get along with, if nothing else, because they didn't push the way Ari did.

The same day I took on Denys, *I* hauled your ass out of Planys to keep anybody from Denys' staff from doing you in; and I think that same day some faction inside the Defense Bureau got very, very upset that you'd arrived here at Reseune proper, and worse upset by the chance you might finally be talking to me. I don't know what Yanni knows. I don't know if he knows all of it, or just suspects and never could prove it. But I think he knew you were in danger back then, and he saved your life . . . if nothing else, he intervened more than once to put your son on a safer course and to keep him out of Denys' path. So I don't think he was ever against you—the same way he didn't argue against my bringing you back here. So you've had friends all along. *None* of them are in Defense."

He'd drawn up just a little. His face had gone white, just white. The anger was still there. But he might be thinking. Better yet, he might be listening.

"Nice theory," he said.

"I wasn't there," she said. "I haven't any way to know any of this. No record shows it. I just watch where the pieces moved, and who moved them. And I draw my conclusions."

He made an impatient gesture. "You want my help? You want—what?"

"I want your help with Kyle, I want your help cracking the block that's keeping him on the Defense rolls. My doing it's probably going to kill him and get no information, because I haven't had the experience. I need your *help*, ser. I need your expertise, and I need you to help me find out what else Defense has got inside our walls, before they get desperate enough to do something—like kill me, yes. About now, they'd like to see another Ari, who'll get to grow up until *she* starts asking questions, and maybe die again. Always keeping the power together, keeping Reseune together, dying before she gets to be a threat, reborn just to keep the power together—and let Reseune stay under caretakers they can deal with. Well, I'm not ready to die, ser. I don't intend to. But I don't think that's what Khalid's playing for at the moment. His actions have been too high, too wide. He's going for a Council that will give him martial law. Control over all of Cyteen. And us."

"Where's Yanni?"

"Still in Novgorod. Hicks is under arrest and we're on shaky ground with ReseuneSec. The department heads are all mad at me because I'm insisting on security drills and upsetting their routine. Somebody murdered Patil, somebody murdered Thieu, they probably had you on their list to make sure that what you knew didn't get out—but didn't want to stir up the old murder case and get questions asked. They were doing just fine as things were—until you came back here. They lost the election and they murdered Spurlin before he could take office in Defense—never mind they hadn't read the results yet: they had the polls. They could work math. And they moved. That's a faction at work. Somebody blew up a tower upriver, and it wasn't the Paxers. It was a diversion of our energies. Or a signal to somebody. Lao's dead. Khalid's trying to force martial law. He's getting very frustrated by now, because Council can't muster a special decrees quorum if it wanted to, and I don't know at what hour he's going to get tired of reporters down at our airport sending out bulletins about Councillors' families taking shelter *here,* which is what's happening. Pretty soon he'll figure out he's got to do something about the reporters, and me, and maybe you. I'm due down at the airport in a few hours to talk to them so Councillors in Novgorod know their families *are* safe, and more to the point, so Khalid can't lie to his own Bureau about what's going on here. But if we make a mistake here at Reseune, the whole of Union is in for Khalid in charge of the government, and that's not going to be good, so, no, ser, Yanni isn't here, I'm doing the best I can with not too many people left alive who know what's going on or even what it's about, and I need you to tell me what your deal was with Defense, because you're the cause the Paxers have taken up, while they're bombing subways, and because you're the one the first Ari hauled home because you'd been dealing with Defense. And you'll notice Defense moved fairly fast once you came home to Reseune."

"My *deal* with Defense was to get me the hell out of Reseune."

"They *did* that part of it," Justin muttered, and drew a black scowl from Jordan.

Then that stare snapped back to her. "If Kyle was theirs, I never knew it. I absolutely never knew it."

"Who were you dealing with in that Bureau? Was Khalid any part of that group?"

"You want me to come clean? Then I'll tell you my conditions. My name cleared. *Cleared.* Freedom to leave. Freedom to write and say what I want—*anything.* And I'll tell you about Khalid. Yes, I *know* Khalid. There are questions I've got, too, with this azi you've got, *plenty* of them."

"We've got a few days," she said, "maybe a few days to figure out how to get through to him. And I want *both* of you working on this."

"The hell," Jordan said. "He can stay out of it."

"Jordan and I will talk about it," Paul said quietly.

Curiously, then, Jordan glanced aside, didn't look at any of them, shrugged, and walked back into the inner apartment.

"In the morning," Paul said to them. "We'll talk."

Family, she thought. Family more complicated, in its way, than her dealings with Denys. But it was somehow functioning. She had the feeling something was moving. Maybe it was something Jordan had finally believed. Maybe there'd been some other change in the atmosphere. Paul. Paul had never said a word before. And now Paul had an opinion.

And Justin had asked about Paul's manual. Hadn't he? She'd been distracted. *Now* she knew what the latest fight was about.

She walked with Justin and Grant back to Alpha Wing and back to their mutual parting, all their security in attendance, and didn't say anything but, "Thank you, Justin. Thank you, Grant. Try to work with him. Please."

"I intend to," Justin said. "I fully intend to." After which he and Grant went inside.

She went into her own place, with Jory, with Florian, and felt like asking for a vodka, but she still had to go down to the airport. She still had to talk to the reporters.

She went into her office. Only Florian went that far with her.

She turned then, and looked at him.

"Please don't do that again," he said.

"It wasn't fair of me. I thought I was saving you having to run back here. I didn't intend to go farther than Justin's apartment. Then it seemed safe. I think it was."

"It scared us," Florian said. Very few things did, but she saw that that was very much the truth.

"The first Ari made that mistake," she said. "I've asked too much, sent you this way and that, asked you and Catlin to do more than you ever ought to have to. I won't send you apart from me again."

"We're not tired," Florian said. He didn't lie often. He didn't do it particularly well, no more than Justin ever did.

"I love you," she said, and hugged his shoulder, which was solid and sure as he was. She rested her head against it for a moment. He put his hand on her head, and stood there.

A long, long time. Until she grew tired of standing.

BOOK THREE　　　Section 5　　　Chapter xix

August 24, 2424
1421h

"... we will continue to support the Council as elected by the people of Union, and we will continue to provide for family and relatives of the Council who have appealed to us for a safe haven, this in the wake of the murder of one elected Councillor and threats against families of living ones. Two Councillors are with us at Reseune.

"We support the people of Novgorod in resisting the threats of those elements who create civil unrest and we call on them to use their creative energy to sustain the city and its services. Those of you who hold public service jobs, count them of extreme importance and consider your duty critical to the safety of all citizens. Those of you who have sworn or Contracted to defend Union, support the Council in its determination to uphold the law.

"The Council has designated a date for assembly and

*will act. We call on all citizens and azi to support the Coun-
cil in the face of bullying and threat of bodily harm. We
call on the loyal armed services of Union to support the
Council and to refuse unlawful orders. We call on every
citizen to document every act of intimidation, every unlawful demand on the rights of the public, with numbers
and vid records where you can secure them safely. These
unlawful acts will come to trial and the people of Novgorod
will have their day in court.*

"Long live the Union."

The little minx, Yanni thought, and shut down the vid.
She was that. She'd just appealed to Khalid's own Bureau.
She hadn't told the whens and wheres of the Council plan,
just that Reseune sheltered two Councillors' families, a
Councillor and a Proxy Councillor . . . she didn't mention
that one of the two was herself.

And if Khalid didn't currently know where Edgerton was, any more than they did, she'd just clouded the
issue . . . and maybe thrown off that search.

"Sounded good to me," Frank said.

They sat in a hotel they now shared with Corain, Amy
Carnath, and Quentin. They knew damned well the plainclothes watchers across the street weren't civilian police,
and the hotel employees were down to a few—

"Go home," Yanni had told the manager, personally.
"Dismiss your staff. Those who stay to maintain the systems will get triple pay: Reseune will see to it if I survive
to get back to my office. Those who stay on duty, the same.
But it's no longer safe. Go home."

Seven of the staff, including the manager and assistant
manager, the head custodian, two of his people, one sous-
chef, and the head of housekeeping, had stayed on, and
they kept things running . . . making them more comfortable than they might have been.

Sit still, and wait. That was what they had to do right
now. ReseuneSec had a handful of plainclothes agents
throughout the city that made quiet visits to watched
areas, and that made tight transmission to receivers here
and there, data-squeal that made it quick and thorough.
The latter was Frank's expertise more than his. He didn't
set it up or critique it: he just knew how to receive it.

And one message had come in which in no way heartened him.

It said, *Trying to make contact with Lynch. Not answering last two days. Will continue effort pending outcome of other inquiry. M.*

State, Defense, and the city government had police powers, and so, by a trick of history, did Reseune Administrative Territory and its adjunct at Planys. Reseune, with its ability to police azi welfare in every factory and office in Union, had an investigative and enforcement organization in some respects as extensive as that of Defense and the city government.

And Reseune used it . . . not the way Defense did, with obvious intimidation standing on the curb out there in the rain, no. With a little more finesse, Yanni hoped. Finesse might never have been his strong suit inside Reseune, but out here, with armed Fleet agents with drawn guns scaring hell out of the sous-chef when he took a look into the alley, he tried not to offend the people they hoped to contact. He sent quiet queries to certain Defense contacts in other services, and hoped for answers—like the removal of surveillance from his curb.

He didn't reply to the message from M. He just absorbed it and every other tidbit of information that came wafting in. He had dinner scheduled with young Amy, her Quentin, Frank, and Mikhail Corain. They maintained at least some of the comforts of home.

And deFranco had made it safely to Reseune. Chavez and his family were somewhere en route, granted he'd gotten through to the airport. Tien would go there next, solo: his family were safe on remote Viking. Harad, State, commanding another security apparatus, independent of Defense, would be the next to last to leave the capital.

He had the short straw. His people were armed and spread throughout the city—in plain clothes. He hoped to hell the agents that had scared the chef had been vastly exceeding their orders. But they were prepared to fight their way to the airport if they had to.

August 27, 2424
1430h

Hicks had had a heavy dose of trank—he wasn't happy
that the Warricks, father and son, with Grant and Paul,
were involved in Kyle's case at all; but he was a little
glazed, and sat having a little fruit juice during prep, eye-
ing them all the while with distrust. Chi Prang was there,
with her assistant. Ivanov took the medical end of things,
with two psych nurses, a cardiovascular surgeon and her
two surgical nurses on call. Supportive machinery was in
the room—it was Ivanov's suggestion, and Ari took the
advice, even if it crowded the immediate area.

The Admin clinic couldn't remotely handle an operation of this complexity, so they set up in the hospital's A
wing, a real surgery, with specialized monitors brought
up from the psych labs, plus the other options, if that was
what it took. It had needed two days to set it up.

Today finally involved Hicks. And the rest of them.
And the monitors. And Kyle.

Kyle, for his peace of mind, didn't know a thing about
it—he arrived tranked out, though he seemed robust
enough, once the monitors started telling what they knew.
They lit up, one miniaturized bank after another.

"We're being careful," Ari said to Hicks, who looked
increasingly anxious as the moments went on and the
monitors came up. "You'll be right by him when he starts
to wake up. Just keep him calm—you can touch him, but
only say, 'I'm here.' Say your name and say, 'I'm here.'
Nothing else outside the script."

"I understand you," Hicks said. He was, at the moment,
scared as all hell, determined not to get thrown out of the
operation, Ari thought. But that wouldn't happen. That
would be the worst thing for Kyle AK: if they lost Hicks'

active participation, they might lose Kyle, or lose him, mentally, for good and all. If Hicks folded, they'd have to put Kyle back under, fast.

She went over to the rest of her group, who were going through the procedures book and script, a physical print-out, with notes. Florian and Catlin attended her and kept to the background; Mark and Gerry were there with Justin and Grant—they weren't short of security if they encountered a problem, but at the moment security meant four more bodies in not much space for the operators, just behind the heart-lung apparatus.

Jordan was team leader: Jordan and Prang had worked together before, Jordan had said they were the two who'd actually done this kind of intervention once and a long time ago, and he bluntly wanted to be in charge. There wasn't to be any freehand, just carefully planned branches: if Kyle did this, then that; if Kyle branched in another direction, something else. All possible paths were mapped, all with more care than any operation Ari had ever read; Prang had come into the conferences, and she and Jordan had laid down the increasingly complex map, with Ari's participation and Justin's, and they'd done it in three marathon meetings—fascinating, under any other circumstances. Fascinating, too, when Jordan was on business, talking about this branch and the other, and what the trigger might be. He was fast in his decisions, and focused only on the problem. The one point where he and Prang differed was about where the block actually sat, and exactly where a not-very-adept military operator had put in something and just told Kyle to protect it.

"Here," Jordan had said, and pointed to the same area Grant had indicated, down in the secondaries—but then he'd linked it to a second item. Kyle had programming from back in the first days of the azi participation in the War—a routine about defending what his Contract-holder set him to defend. That was fine, Ari thought, but to an alpha that *defend* went metaphysical real fast, and they didn't do that kind of thing: that had stood out, to her eyes. She found that kind of generality in the programming at four other points she could see, things they didn't *do* with alphas or even betas nowadays, because things *had* gone wrong. She had those circled on her own copy, and Justin and Grant both had tagged them as inappropriate from the start. Old-style programming. Old as the azi in question.

Kyle being, himself, an Alpha Supervisor by the military's make-do procedures of the day, had considerably reworked his own programming by the time Defense sent him back to Reseune as a spy . . . that clearly had happened.

Prang had said, regarding the initials on the file: "IC. Carnath, maybe."

"Huh," Jordan snorted. "That's Charles. Ivan Charles, not Carnath."

"Him," Prang had said, and when Ari asked who Ivan Charles was, Prang said simply: "He worked on the military sets."

But Jordan had said: "Emory Senior used to take his crappy work and just shove it through. It made money. They were turning out azi by the hundreds, same type, same geneset. You could have a whole damn company the officers couldn't tell apart, no attempt to do a sociology set on the unit, you just shoved them out the door and they went out to some godforsaken operation and died by the hundreds; and then they'd patch up the survivors out there on the lines and send them back to the War. Emory Senior had some damned idiot staff writing broad-based tape back during the War. Defense wanted to control everything, every damned subclause and dot, a routine to do this, a routine to do that—the client wanted certain things, they got them."

Ari had been a little offended at that assessment. Then she realized Emory Senior, in that context, meant *Olga* Emory.

Way, way back, then.

"Certificates weren't specific either," Prang had said. "The higher-end operators handled both the betas and the alphas, and there wasn't any certification in the sense we use now."

"We're not teaching a damned history lesson," Jordan had said. "Kyle's alpha. He got a crap initial set. They all did."

"He was supposed to serve in headquarters," Prang had said, "no nearer the front than Alpha Station."

"His military record is nowhere in file and we don't know where the hell he was," Jordan had said. "We weren't around for Olga's goings-on. We assume what we have to assume. But we're *not* assuming when we say he's kill-capable. The axe code didn't take, did it? That means, alpha or not, he came back to us with it, and nobody could have installed it on him in ReseuneSec unless the axe code worked. But *somebody* did it. That meant he was near the lines, and *my* guess is he got crap-work patched in to shape him up to work in a combat zone. Sure, Defense swore they didn't ever do that. But they swore to a lot of things that were a flat lie."

"Why," Ari had asked—and she hadn't wanted to interrupt the train of thought, but it was an important question, "why, if he got back to Reseune in '62, why didn't the first Ari ever look at him? Why didn't she catch it?"

Prang had said. "I checked the timeline. Your predecessor had resigned the directorship to take up the Council seat. Yanni was taking over the Directorate. Giraud was running Security. Those two didn't see eye to eye. Giraud handled his department; and Giraud got Kyle. Ari wasn't even at Reseune when that was going on. She came back and Kyle was Giraud's ongoing pet datasource."

"Giraud was a damned fool," Jordan had said. "Ari had gotten Defense to turn over every alpha they had and most of them were over in technical. But this one—this special one—I'm betting he was handling azi line troops, and if he was, it's a damn certainty he got beta tape and got shoved out *there* to patch them up, because they didn't ever ship betas back to some nice safe hospital ship. *We* never sent out any alphas suited for combat. So what else do you think they did, to get alphas that could take the hammering, on the lines? Beta tape. Next most applicable, and they had a pile of it."

It had been hours. Hours of Prang and Jordan arguing, and then Justin arguing with Jordan: "You don't have to touch the tertiary sets at all. If he's self-modified, they're irrelevant."

"What are we suggesting?" Jordan had snapped. "Go straight after the deep sets?"

"I'm saying it's linked back to that secondary you named, and at least . . ."

"Oh, let's just do deep sets and go for an early lunch."

Justin hadn't flared. He'd said, as calm as Grant: "One sharp stress and a calm-down."

"You'll kill him. That thing in tertiary will have a trap on it like you haven't seen. And remember he's built off it for decades. It's got all sorts of embellishments hung on it."

"We do have him supported," Ivanov said.

The talk had gone way deep into medical jargon at that point, and Ari had just sat with her chin on her fist, fascinated, and listened to four of the best there'd ever been going at it line by line—Prang was clearly out-classed; Grant and Paul got into it, and Justin stuck to his argument that they needed to do a preliminary fix in the secondaries.

Then she said, after listening to all of it, and flipping back through the lines of programming, the *original* lines of programming, that Kyle had started with: "The self-defense ethic. That's where."

Jordan had given her a sharp, hard look.

"Support it," she'd said, "don't attack it. That's part of his original deep set."

"Who said attack it?" Jordan had said peevishly.

She said: "We support the deep set, right where this beta tape's taken hold. We say an enemy's gotten inside his defenses, and we know it's beta, and he has to find this enemy for us. So he'll identify that tape and shove it outside his safe perimeter. If you're right, he's wired everything off that start—so he's the safest one to unwire it. Isn't he? He trusts Hicks. If we get Hicks to say he has to get ID on the beta section, can't he do it? Convince him it doesn't belong. And then we tell him to erase the intruder—so he just starts taking out the secondary level, unwiring the combat ethic the block relies on. Doesn't he? *Everything* the military's done is going to be based on the tape they put in. They aren't us. They can't *work* on secondary, and the tape they know best is the tape they put in."

It had at least gotten their attention, and made a silence, and made Jordan frown at her.

"Maybe," Jordan had said. "Dangerous as hell."

"She's got a point," Justin had said.

"She's been studying fucking *Emory.*"

"You know I have," she'd said calmly. "For more than half my life."

Prang had just kept her mouth shut, but Paul had said, echoing Justin, "She has a point. Avoiding fighting it out down on tertiary would be safer, because tertiary may be a lower charge, but it's just that much wider. Whatever they did creating that block just spreads out into territory he knows and we can't map. And maybe, if he can ID the tape, we've got it on file. Maybe they didn't risk anything they'd written or modded and it will turn out to be Reseune tape."

Jordan hadn't said anything about it for the rest of the session, not until the next meeting, when he'd said, "All right, Ari Junior, Justin, Grant. Elaborate. How are you preventing a breakdown if we go into this operation with the happy theory they didn't write their own beta routine—and maybe didn't even write their own block?"

"We ask Dr. Ivanov to keep the physiology stable," Ari said. "Just keep shooting him full of the same feel-good juice the compliance ethic, which we're triggering, naturally manufactures; and we just let Hicks argue him into erasing the beta tape."

"Too risky," Jordan had said then. "I want this man to live to *talk.*"

"So do the rest of us," Ari had said, as gently, as reasonably as she could, even when she wanted to jerk Jordan sideways. "Honestly, Jordan."

And she said it before Justin, drawing a deep breath to argue, could say anything.

"Well, let's look at it," Jordan had said, then, in the same reasonable way, and with a dark glance at Justin, who kept his mouth shut. "How fast can Library cough up a tape, if we can ID it?"

They'd kept from each other's throats today. They got Hicks calm, and instructed: "We're going at this in a way that will protect him from stress," she'd said to Hicks at the outset, "and we're not going to lose him. We have an idea what the problem is. But to make our fix work, we have to have *you* do it."

That had gotten Hicks' attention. He'd been angry, he'd been scared, he'd figured out she was dead serious, and he'd listened to the program.

"You can do it," she told him now, in the room with Kyle, and she laid an encouraging hand on his back. "Just go sit down by him, take his hand, tell him you're here. Ivanov will give you specific signals, and have the script on the monitor. We're here, we're all here if we have to improvise. We don't want to. But if we do, those lines will be in red, so you'll know. You're high beta. We trust you to know how to do what you need to. For his sake. That's all we're asking of you."

They drew far off from Hicks and Kyle, who lay on a white-sheeted table, under restraint for his protection and theirs. There was lighting in Kyle's area, none in the observation post—just the soft light from the vid screen and the readouts. Ivanov was right at hand with Kyle, with the same readouts, and Hicks—Hicks sat on a tall stool and set his hand on Kyle's shoulder, talking to him, just giving him legitimate reassurances, while the machines, flashing with lights, scrubbed the trank out of Kyle's bloodstream and fed in a mild dose of kat.

Kyle came awake slightly. "Weak," he complained.

"You're fine," Hicks said. "Kyle, are you hearing me all right?"

"Yes," Kyle said. "Where are we?"

"Stronger dose," Jordan said to Ivanov sharply, through his earpiece.

Ari thought she would have waited for Hicks to calm him down, but that was all right: Hicks had deviated just a hair off the permissions they'd given him, they were taking Kyle right under again, and it wasn't going to hurt him: it was just going to prevent him taking closer notice of his surroundings. He'd hear. He'd see. For the first half hour they'd just run his base sets, primer tape, from way, way back in his childhood. They had a list of what his intermediate base had been, and of what the military had had access to, therefore what they might have illicitly used. Their best guess was a conversion of beta tape from the best of the marine units, something to instill aggression into the alpha that had to be patching them up and advising them,

doing the work a Reseune-trained born-man should hav
been doing.

They didn't dare take their guesswork for granted, no
until they had their theory confirmed—or not, in which cas
they had to abort and hope they could patch their way out.

"We found a mistake in your sets," Hicks said gentl
at one point, right down the script. "Kyle, you haven't fe
altogether right for some time, and we've found the cause
Somebody gave you wrong tape. It's beta. It was when yo
were in service, on the lines. Do you remember gettin
tape then? I'm your Supervisor. I can ask this. Did you ge
tape when you were on the lines?"

Kyle's brow contracted. "Sometimes."

"They gave it more than once?"

"More than once."

"You know who I am. I'm Adam. I'm your Superviso
Someone once gave you a beta tape. What was the num
ber? Where does it start? Can you find it for me?"

"Viking. October 13 shiptime, 2320, *US Amity*."

"Keep going. Find it."

A long pause. Then: "Tape sequence B14–2818–6."

Jordan nodded sharply in Ari's direction.

She spun around to the console keyboard, called Bas
One, and made a fast key entry—deep in tape archive
no question. The number enabled retrieval; retrieval en
abled an exact excision of what had gone in; and Base On
pulled it out past gateways that would have hidden it fror
any ordinary search.

Let him sleep, Jordan sent to Ivanov, then. They hadn
been at it thirty minutes, and they dropped the subjec
back into kat-induced limbo.

But this time they had substance to go on. They had a four
dational tape in a sequence that Kyle himself had cobble
into an alpha level routine. They had one piece of a jigsaw c
accommodation; but it was a piece with the design on it.

"Hicks, come in on this one," she said, and that didn
please Jordan, but Hicks was qualified on beta, he'd mad
a good go at handling an alpha, and he had the glimmerin
of a hope of understanding the issue as well as the specifi
azi they were trying to fix.

He sat with them in an adjacent conference room, an

Jordan flipped through what he'd pulled up. They went over it independently. It was short, simple. It gave a line soldier permission to kill without conscience where ordered by the Bureau.

"Conflict," she said. "The minute he takes it out, he's got conflict with other programming."

Jordan nodded. "Insert an exception: he may remember killing or arranging killing in the past. This is gone now. It was a temporary condition. He's not guilty."

Hicks looked sharply at Jordan, and Jordan didn't even look his way. Jordan was as clinical, as detached as an Alpha Supervisor had to be . . . even when he was talking about the specific crime he'd been sentenced for. Not guilty. No karma.

"He'll attach to Hicks for any future permissions," Paul said, and Jordan nodded again and inserted a line.

Ari found her arms tightly folded, as if there'd been a chill. Florian was close by. Catlin was. They'd know what Jordan was doing. Their own alpha tape enabled killing. Readily. They were hair-trigger, both knowing what personal issues Jordan was dealing with, what a dangerous thing Paul was saying, with that "Attach to Hicks."

But Hicks was ReseuneSec. He was, at least by his provisional certificate, entitled to have that responsibility.

"You're the Supervisor," Jordan said then, looking straight at Hicks, and said it in his best clinical voice.

"Agreed," Hicks said. Hicks had arrested Jordan, in the long ago. Helped send him to Planys. He'd arrested Justin, multiple times.

Jordan gazed at him a moment, then nodded, quietly still, deathly quiet in the room.

"Say," Ari said, "he also has to respect the authority of Reseune Directors. That won't conflict."

"Good idea," Prang said, and that went in.

"Then we're go with it," Jordan said. "We go with heavy at and unwind it."

Jordan got up. They all did. They went back to the room, where, for Kyle AK, time had stood still.

Now time started up again with the specific beta tape, and they played it under instructions, relayed via Hicks, to erase it, step by step, from memory.

Reaction. Slow, at first, but Kyle was alpha: cross-referencing told him in the first instant he was going to be in trouble.

"Deeper," Jordan said, and Ivanov frowned, and deepened the kat.

Kyle was calmer, then. "Come on, Kyle," Hicks said. "It's Adam. I'm here. Listen to me."

Lines on the monitors had spiked all over the place. They sank abruptly. Ticked way up. And down again. That much kat was a risk.

It took two hours and forty-five minutes to get him stable. And while Ivanov was working, word came from the airport that Councillor Chavez had just come in, with two aides. With her mind strongly elsewhere, but with the assurance nothing was going to happen soon up at the hospital, Ari made the trip down to welcome the Councillor officially, to see him up to Wing One, and for him to meet with deFranco in a conference room and deliver the news from Novgorod as of three days ago. It wasn't much news, but it wasn't good: military police were patrolling the streets of Novgorod, to the exclusion of Novgorod police.

With *no* declaration of martial law. That was definite, too... because Reseune sheltered the requisite Councillors.

It was suppertime in the outside world; but her stomach was on a different schedule. She entrusted the two Councillors to a good catered supper ordered up from Jamaica and took herself and Catlin and Florian back to the hospital as fast as she decently could. She had a sandwich from the hospital cafeteria—Catlin got it for her—and then settled in to catch up and hear the report from Ivanov, who'd finally gotten the subject calmed down and stable: Ivanov had had to give *Hicks* medical help: rapid heartbeat.

"I can't give Hicks much more help without putting him to bed," Ivanov said. "He's not young, any more than the subject is."

"We either leave Kyle in limbo for the night and se he doesn't dream," Justin said, "or we go after the bloc tonight. Stress continues on both of them—even—"

"Go for it," Jordan said, "if young sera's through takin her own sweet—"

Paul's hand landed on Jordan's shoulder, pressed hard, though Paul didn't say a thing.

"We need her concentration *here*," Jordan said, "dammit. This isn't a picnic."

"You've got it," she said. "I don't blame you. You've got it. No complaints, no objections."

"Let's just go, then," Justin said, and Grant got up, and Justin did.

Hicks, asleep on a cot, took a little rousing. "At this point," Jordan said, "you don't have to do anything. Just talk to him occasionally. Tell him what we tell you. Verbatim."

Hicks nodded. They took their positions. They'd unraveled the kill-capability. Now they went after the block. Hicks' job was to let him progress gently, find the block, figure what symbolized it, and encourage Kyle to set it in a neutral position.

And Kyle seized.

Machines ticked on, took over, cleaned out the adrenaline surge, supplied a gentler cocktail, and got Kyle breathing on his own again.

It was past midnight, into the next day.

Justin leaned over the mike, "Tell him reset. It's all right."

Jordan said: "Tell him—tell him to open the door."

Hicks did. Kyle's face contracted, then relaxed. His breath went out, and came in again.

"Tell him: reset," Jordan said then.

"Reset," Hicks said, and Jordan let go a long breath and said, softly, gently, into the mike: "It's usually a door, in some sense or other. You'll want to put that into his manual. It isn't broken. He's keyed on you now: we're not going to have to break it. Tell him he can clean up, put things to rights. It's all right. He can trust what comes in if you say he can. Get him to agree."

Hicks did that, quietly rephrasing.

Kyle lay there, breathing deeply. His face was quiet, seeming to have acquired lines. He had fluids going in and coming out. He had machines doing a lot of the work for him, while he just lay there and breathed on his own, and blinked from time to time. But the storm on the monitors had decidedly quietened.

"Get him to say your name," Jordan said.

"It's me," Hicks said then. "You know me. You know my name."

"Adam," Kyle mumbled. "Adam Hicks."

"Run the code," Jordan said then, sharply. "Straight into the Contract."

"You'll—" Hicks started to protest angrily, and shut himself down, lips bitten to a thin line.

Jordan said, "Go." And Ari thought so, too. She looked at Justin. Justin said, "Code."

Fast as they could, before stress piled up. "Code in," Paul said, and sent it through with the push of a button. Kyle sucked in a breath as if he'd fallen into icewater. The monitors spiked up, a jagged mountain range of crisis. Then Kyle let the breath go.

Contract tape followed immediately. *"You have an assignment,"* it routinely began. *"You have a place. You are wanted . . ."*

Kyle went on breathing. The lines of stress evened out to a steady tick. Strengthened.

Giraud couldn't have done this one, Ari thought to herself. No way in hell. That beta tape was ancient history. It had taken Base One to haul it out of storage. It was tape that didn't belong to any azi living . . . now that they'd pried it out of Kyle AK.

They got up from their small table, then, moving quietly, while Ivanov checked and took notes. Jordan moved closer to their patient. Ari did, out of curiosity to see, besides the monitors, how he was doing.

Then Jordan leaned over Kyle, very close, and said, fast, before anyone could stop him: "Who was your Supervisor before Adam Hicks?"

Contraction of the brows. Ari tensed. Kyle's eyes flew open. He was still deeply under.

"Arbero," Kyle said. "Captain Vincente Arbero."

"Did you ever put Abban under kat?"

Kyle opened his mouth to answer, but no sound came out. Hicks grabbed Jordan's shoulder and shoved him back, and Florian had moved in. Florian restrained Jordan gently, just put himself in the way, while Catlin faced Hicks.

"Yes," Ari heard Kyle say in the interim, and she touched his pallid face gently and said, "You're forgiven. It's all right now. You can rest a bit and wake up later. Adam Hicks won't leave you. Remember Vincente Arbero. But never listen to him again."

She looked toward Hicks, who was still furious, then toward Jordan. "That's on the record," she said. "It's on the record, Jordan, and all of us know it. It was recorded."

Jordan wasn't fighting against Florian, who wasn't touching him now: he looked on the edge of a collapse, himself. Justin had moved in close, and laid a hand on Jordan's shoulder.

"Let's go," Justin said. "Let's go back next door, let him sleep it off. We did it, Dad. It's done. Everybody heard."

"*I* did it," Jordan snapped, jerked his shoulder aside, and looked at Ari. "So what do you propose to do about it?"

"What I promised I'd do," she said. "Let's go next door. Come on. We need to talk. Now. Come on. Everybody."

They went to the conference room, then—a window on the outer hall, one on the operating room itself. Petros Ivanov had gotten Hicks back to one of the consoles, to a table chair with a back on it, was talking to him, probably medical advice. A nurse had come in.

Jordan didn't say a word, meanwhile, didn't sit down. He just stood there, against the wall of the conference room, staring at the windowed view, arms folded, not talking.

"Arbero," Catlin said, quietly, having consulted her handheld. "Not on the Defense rolls. No CIT number."

"That's two," Ari said. She was disappointed, deeply disappointed, but a thought began sliding sideways in her mind, just out of one compartment and into another. Anton Clavery. Vincente Arbero. Every CIT has a CIT number. But *are* there people in Defense that don't? We've been assuming the radical underground, Paxers, Rocher party, everything but somebody in uniform. Kyle's given us a name that doesn't exist. And, under deep kat, he *says* this person was in Defense with a high rank."

Jordan had unfolded his arms. Justin and Grant sat looking at her. So did Mark and Gerry, Florian and Catlin, who weren't going to talk, not in front of the rest.

"Florian," she said. "Catlin. What are you thinking?"

"That CITs in other places are supposed to have numbers," Florian said. "But we can't get into Defense to find out if the rules are different there."

"If they made hollow men," Catlin said, "they'd have all sorts of resources to do that. People died in the War. Some die in training. And they'd be hard to track. Hollow men with all sorts of identities available."

"We assumed a whole Bureau is going to observe the law," she said. "We *assume* if they were breaking the law somebody would talk about it."

"Well, somebody didn't," Jordan said, "until he went under deep kat." A muscle jumped in Jordan's jaw. "Khalid runs Intelligence. Covert operations. I said I'd met him. Bastard. Thorough arrogant bastard. Asked *me* questions I declined to answer. The man collects bits and pieces on everybody. Gets real pissed when you don't react when he gives you that look. I didn't know who he was at the time I found out, the second meeting. People tried to hint to me you didn't cross him. I probably went down in his book as a potential problem. Maybe it had something to do with their decision, the way they handled my case . . . they didn't have a handle on me; they wanted more information and wouldn't give it to them, if you want the bloody truth. You all *assumed* I told them any damned thing they wanted to hear, and I didn't. I told them what Ari was doing—*there* was a dark little history, nasty little secrets left over from the War, the azi designs that didn't work, that she put down and wouldn't give me fucking access to try to fix them . . . you want to know where you can get any human material you want? Ask about *her* deals with Defense, as what kind of spies *she* could create that never would have a CIT number . . ." He drew breath, waved a hand. Said in a quiet voice: "It doesn't matter. If they exist, we can get at them."

"An honest Defense Councillor could," she said.

"Naive," Jordan said.

"You say Khalid did it, ultimately. We'll never attach things to him. If we take it to the media and can't prove it, ultimately that's a problem, because he'll deny it, and we've damaged our credibility with everybody. I'm n that naive, ser, to try to prove anything yet. I'm thinking what we can do now to get him stopped."

"Well, first you find an honest Defense representative and then you get his electorate to put your honest Councilor in. *Spurlin* wasn't likely it—just somebody who wouldn't kiss ass with Khalid, which is why he's dead and you're probably right: you're a target, I am, everybody who's heard this is, and we're fooling ourselves if we think having a Council meeting on the quadrangle out there is going to make Defense run for cover. You're thinking he'll observe civilized limits. He's already out of civilized limits."

"It's a problem," Ari said.

"It's a problem," Jordan echoed her nastily. "Damned right it's a problem. So I'm innocent. The world's going to hell anyway and a Council vote isn't going to fix it."

"I may need you again," she said. It was scary, being told by a very bright Special that he was out of answers, and that there was no fix for the problem. It was particularly scary, because at the moment she didn't see a fix, either, and whatever was wrong inside Defense had been going on for sixty years. Their problem had had a lot of time to build an infrastructure in that Bureau. "Go get some rest. Thank you, especially, Jordan. Thank you for doing this."

"The hell," he muttered. "You go prove I'm innocent. Get me my license back."

"We should get on back to the Wing," Justin said. "We're all exhausted."

Jordan didn't move.

"You'll get your not-guilty," Ari said.

"Promises, promises."

She stood up, leaned on a chair back with both hands. "We'll figure things out," she said. "Yanni will get back, I'll hold a vote, and we'll see what the Council actually can do."

"Hold a vote. Hell." Jordan shoved away from the wall and walked out.

Paul lingered a moment, looking distressed.

"It's all right," she said to Paul. "He could be right, you know. But I hope not. Good night, Paul. Tell him good night. —Justin, Grant, Sera Prang . . . Justin, you can—"

The overhead lights flashed.

Then the storm siren sounded.

"There's no weather," Ari said, and then thought o
the pile of papers and manuals in the surgery, at that back
table. "The records. Kyle."

"Our territory," Prang said. "We have enough help. I'l
help Petros with the patient. *Go!* Get *her* downstairs!"

"Damn," Ari said, and by then Florian had her one arn
and Catlin had the other, and Prang was headed for th
surgery.

"I'll get the manuals," Justin said, and he and Gran
headed out of the room, headed the same direction, Marl
and Gerry close behind them, while the siren howled.

"Sera, come on," Florian said, and she surrendered
She had to. Florian and Catlin pulled her out into the ha
and down the nearest stairs.

They were on the next flight down when somethin
screamed overhead, the walls rattled and the groun
heaved up, like a blanket toss.

BOOK THREE   Section 6   Chapter

August 27, 2424
1927h

Giraud blinked, flinched, moved wildly, first at an unpre
edented jolt, then at the abrupt cessation of everything
his world.

Then the rocking and the sounds started up again, r
ular as the heartbeat that ruled it, and he, and Abban, a
Seely, all slowly settled and relaxed. They all had son
thing approaching a memory for the first real event th
had ever experienced, knit together for the first time
one experience, at one specific age. They couldn't def
it. But they had all been in the same situation.

They were too old, however, to be seriously incon
nienced by a glitch. They each weighed about a kilo—s

none of them carrying the weight they needed for that unruly world that had just intruded. They were adding neurons as fast as they could grow them. Their brains were organizing so one day they would be able to remember things. They were packing on body fat, storing it up, not anticipating any other such disturbance, though hormones had surged and they remained unsettled for some unthought reason.

They didn't plan. They didn't anticipate. They just did things their DNA told them to do, and right now, with all the nutrients they could get, they just filled out their skins and grew eyelashes, because their DNA said it was time to do that.

BOOK THREE   Section 6   Chapter ii

AUGUST 27, 2424
2011H

The drills in underpopulated Alpha Wing hadn't remotely conveyed the urgency of a populated area or the fear in a gathered crowd who'd felt that shock. They'd possibly had a tower fall. That was the image Justin framed in his mind: one of the big precip towers on the cliff must have come down, and of all disasters in his life, of all things that had ever happened to him and Grant—that imagination was the worst: atmospheric breach. Death, if you got caught outside.

Traffic in the tunnels had slowed to a general milling movement . . . slowed, and slowed, until they reached a concourse where people, now in one of the most reinforced areas of the system, generally stood about waiting for information, speculating grimly on what had blown up, talking about the inadequacy of the recent drills, wondering about the whereabouts of relatives and cursing the overloaded communications system, which had flatly shut down all non-official accounts.

Mark and Gerry had kept up with them. They all four
had briefcases full of classified papers and the manual
they'd rescued—they'd managed that coherent task, amid
everything else. But they didn't know what had happened
up on the surface, nobody else did, so they made their way
generally toward Alpha Wing, with hundreds of other people caught out at restaurants, in residences, working night
shift. And, Justin thought, he might get through on Base
One, on his handheld, but he didn't want to make himself
a target of questions from everybody else who was missing
a relative. They didn't have a place where they could do it
in any privacy.

"Can you gather anything?" he asked Gerry, pausing to
let those two overtake them. "Is your com working?"

"Just ops and tracking, ser," Gerry said. "They aren't
saying, except there's an emergency channel, and our
group's not authorized on it while we're detached, ser. Sera's security, sera's security is saying just stay—"

Then a familiar young voice said, over the general address: *"This is Ariane Emory, in ReseuneSec Admin. Defenses have brought down a device on the grounds. There's
no significant damage to Reseune facilities, just a hole in
the ground where it hit. Please stay in the tunnels until an
all-clear, but it looks as if we're all right for the moment.
Section doors will now open, but they may close again if
there should be another alarm, so be alert. Upper doors
will remain shut for a while yet, so you can't get back home
yet anyway. Don't cross a section line once the lights start
blinking: observe the drills and remember: everybody stop
moving if the lights flash red. We'll provide further information as we get it. No one is to go outside except authorized agents at the moment. Thank you."*

Everybody broke out in conversation at once, voices
with an undertone of alarm, frustration, and some relief.

"Let's get home," Justin said, and they weren't the only
ones. A waft of cooler air came through: that was the
opening of the section doors that would let them leave the
concourse. There began to be a general drift in the crowd,
mostly toward the right hand tunnel.

Their own way lay left, and it was thinner traffic over
there, a little faster progress. They lost no time clearing

the concourse, and entering the cross-corridor that would take them over to the Wing One tunnels.

Much less traffic once they were going that direciton, which was to be expected, so much of Wing One being under construction, but once they got to the Wing One concourse, there were faces Justin didn't immediately recognize, and that was entirely surreal: people standing around in the generally dim light the tunnels afforded— two Justin recognized from news reports as guests in the wing, both standing near the stairs, talking with, of all people, his father and Paul.

He could hardly ignore it. "Jordan," Justin said, as they joined the group in passing. "Councillors." A nod to Councillor deFranco, Councillor Chavez.

"My son Justin Warrick," Jordan introduced him. "And Grant ALX."

"Sera. Ser." Justin set down the briefcase and offered a hand in courtesy. Grant did the same. "An honor."

"I'd say it's a pleasure," deFranco said, "except for the circumstances."

"Khalid, damn him," Chavez said. "Taking this little business up a notch. Probably aiming at the airport. Maybe at the media people. Or us. This is getting damned serious."

"A crazy universe," Jordan said, and put a hand on Justin's shoulder, just a little unfriendly pressure of the fingers that said he was, at the moment, as welcome as the plague. "Here we are expecting the rest of the Council, and Vladislaw Khalid casts an early vote. I don't think it's going to win him friends."

"I've got to get back to Alpha Wing," Justin said.

"You aren't going anywhere until they open the upstairs doors," Jordan said.

"I've got a responsibility next door. And twenty kilos of records to stow. I'll at least get through to the tunnel."

"My talented son," Jordan said, and let him go.

He went. He picked up his briefcase, gathered up Grant and Mark and Gerry without a word and went on into the ook that separated Alpha Wing. "Try the key," he asked Grant, not even looking back, and to his vast relief it did work, and let them through, out of Jordan's vicinity.

It let them through at least as far as the guard station and two others of Mark's and Gerry's unit.

"Can I possibly get upstairs?" he asked.

"Keycard will actually override, ser," one said, "but it's advised you stay below. We don't know that that's the last that will come in. Best to go into the safety tunnel, ser. Anyone you're looking for is probably there."

Nothing sensible to do, then, but go aside, down the ramp to the deeper fortification, where, in fact, everyone else had gone. There was a bank of chairs, a galley, an auxiliary command post, quite a few of Ari's staff out and about. Maddy Strassen, Tommy and Mika—they were there. Wes and Marco were busy at the command post. . . .

"We're all right," Justin said to Mark and Gerry, and walked into the command post alcove to set down the heavy briefcase. "Wes, Marco: these belong to Ari."

"Thank you, ser," Wes said.

"What have we got out there?"

Monitors were active. There was a large one above the console. Wes moved a hand, and that one went live.

It didn't make sense for a moment . . . a floodlit area in the dark, beside a white strip that appeared to be part of a road. A lot of twisted metal, lit against the night.

"That's the airport road," Grant murmured.

Then the scale made sense: the twisted metal—a small plane, maybe; but large enough to make a hell of a hole. It was surreal, the crater and that wreckage beside the main road, right near the streetlight—it was tilted; outraged bots were scurrying along the perimeter, never coming closer. A handful of hazard-suited figures were out there in the shadows.

That it hadn't hit any building when it had come down had been, Justin thought, their supreme good luck.

That crater was—dammit—right near the hospital.

"What is it?" he asked. "What was it?"

"Missile," Wes said, and Marco: "Seems to be out o Svetlansk. There's a Defense base up there."

"God," he said. "They're crazy."

And then he thought that Mark and Gerry might hav had training that enabled them to accept explosions a part of the environment, but that Grant certainly hadn't. Justin took hold of Grant's arm. "Are you all right with this?" he asked.

"I'm not sure I ever quite expected things falling on the grounds," Grant said in his best attempt at levity. "I think I'm doing all right. It's like being shot at, isn't it?"

"I think it's a little worse than that," he said. It *was* worse, for everybody. "Come on. Leave the briefcases here. Mark, Gerry, you're on your own."

He walked with Grant just outside the alcove, and ran into Maddy. "Any news?" Maddy asked.

"Not much, except it may be a missile," he said quietly. "Is there coffee?"

"In the galley. Staff will get it. Sandwiches if you want them."

"Thanks," he said. His stomach didn't want food. But a drink of something hot was more attractive. He and Grant walked on toward the galley—didn't even get close, before one of Ari's staff—Del, it was—presented them a choice of juices and sweet rolls.

Juice, he decided. Grant took one, too, and they went and had a seat at the galley tables, which had been let down from the wall. There was a news monitor nearby, people talking into the camera, a low, steady sound.

"I think they wanted to take a tower down," he said, "just like upriver. They wanted to scare us."

"Well, they've certainly done that," Grant said over a sip of juice. "What are the chances of another one, I wonder?"

"I don't know," he said, which was the truth.

"Reseune defenses will get it," a young voice said, and Tommy Carnath arrived with his sister, settling near them, likewise with juice. "If they come near the towers and they're not aircraft, they'll knock them down."

Not saying what they'll fall on, Justin thought unhappily, but, considering Grant, he kept that observation to himself.

"Attention." The vid changed abruptly. Ari was suddenly on camera, not with the news, but somewhere else, somewhere office-like. *"We've identified the object as an 82 air to ground missile, serial number 38298, which did*

detonate conventional explosives. It came from the military base at Svetlansk. It fell in the green space between the airport and the warehouses, and it's no longer a threat. We have the following statement:

"Reseune asks why any Defense installation on Cyteen is in possession of such armament and what enemy they anticipate to exist on this planet. Reseune asks who authorized its import and storage. Reseune asks who targeted it at a sovereign Administrative Territory, where only Union civilians are present.

"Reseune calls on the Council Office of Inquiry to ask these questions where appropriate and to relay their findings to the Council of Nine and the Council of Worlds. The citizens of Reseune call on patriotic members of the Bureau of Defense to consider this event and act immediately to prevent another such attack on the constitution and the rights of the people of Union.

"We will interrupt tonight with bulletins only if necessary. Security doors will open at this point. Please proceed to your destinations and remain alert in the event we are not done with alarms. Thank you."

Justin finished his drink, put a hand on Grant's shoulder, and said, "Well, what do you want to do? Stay here, or go up?"

"I leave that to the wisdom of born-men," Grant said and gave him a look that said he really wished he could "Do you think there'll be another?"

"No way to know. I think if they know where that came from, they'll be watching. We'll get an alert."

"Well, I suppose it's more comfortable upstairs," Grant said.

So they went. So did the rest, except part of Ari's staff who might intend to keep the tunnel facilities active—in case.

Ari herself was over in Admin, now, Justin had no personal doubt, probably in ReseuneSec or up in Yanni's office; and she'd put him in charge of Alpha Wing, a charge he took seriously. A little phone inquiry, once they'd got ten into their own apartment, proved Yevgenia Wojkowski was over in Admin; so was Patrick Emory. Sam Whitely was upriver, in his own hot spot, and Amy Carnath was in Novgorod, which was probably the worst place in the world to be at the moment. He checked on Stasi, Dan, and Will, who all returned com calls after the system had opened up again.

So he knew, at least, where all his Alpha Wing residents were. The Security office downstairs, where Mark and Gerry had gone, reported some members out on the grounds assessing damage and reporting to Ari, the rest accounted for as well.

So everybody was safe. Everybody he was remotely in charge of was accounted for; and those in charge of him were over in Admin, making contact with somebody, he hoped, who could at least have the decency to claim it was an accidental launch. A lie, at least, would be more welcome than a direct challenge.

Or maybe some fool had vastly exceeded orders.

Vid, coming from the news channels now, showed people, black figures, out by the impact site, under the streetlight. The bots were still scurrying around, probably held from intervening on the site until the investigation was done. A call over to hospital reached Ivanov himself, who said their patient was doing well and Hicks had opted to stay with him.

"A good idea," Grant said. And made an executive decision and turned off the vid, which was only repeating, endlessly, all that it had.

Justin sat there a moment staring at the screen, just shaken. He wanted things to be right, and safe, and in good order. And dammit, the people in charge of the world weren't acting sane, except Ari, except a handful of Councillors who were a long way from the halls of power down in Novgorod—sharing the shelters with Reseune's citizens, was what, as helpless as the rest of them.

He took out his own com and called Jordan's apartment, then, reaching a point of resolution to make up at least one point of discord in the world. It rang through, and Grant set a vodka under his hand. He took a sip of it, feeling at least a little calmer, hoping Jordan was. "Dad? Just checking on you. Are you all right over there?"

"Doing fine," Jordan said. "I'm in the process of sending a letter to young sera's office. I want it in writing. I'm clear. Absolved. I want it for the court. And I want my damned back *pay.*"

He didn't know what he thought about the last. But he didn't say so. Leave it to Jordan to think of that . . . but then . . .

"Well, good you're all right, Dad. We're back. We're fine. 'Night."

" 'Night," Jordan said flatly, and Justin shut down the connection.

Dammit, he and Grant sat where they sat, knowing that if Defense had its way, Ari would be dead and God knew how long they'd live—but in Jordan's way of thinking, Defense was only one among many obstacles to Jordan having his way, just one more annoying entity he'd dealt with in his life, one more power that didn't give a damn for the rules.

So what if Defense fired a missile at them? Fine. It missed. Jordan wanted what he was due.

Maybe he was tired. Maybe it was just bone-deep exhaustion hammering the last sense out of him, but after all their work over recent days, there ought to have been some sense of winning the round—getting Jordan vindicated—something.

He wished to hell Jordan had some soft, sentimental reaction in his soul, some sort of gratitude for being part of the team effort with Ari, something he could take away with him tonight and feel good about.

But back *pay,* with a bloody great hole in the lawn, and no guarantee there wouldn't be another hole in a significant building before morning, or the whole damned environmental envelope ruptured, AG in ruins, everything contaminated, as far as Reseune's land ran?

Jordan was going to ask Ari for his back pay?

He had another sip of the vodka, he called Jordan back, and when Jordan answered, he said, "You're welcome, Dad. On behalf of myself, and Grant, and Ari, you're just fucking *welcome.*"

And hung up.

BOOK THREE Section 6 Chapter iii

Vid worked intermittently. It came on—it went off. They had audio, at times, Yanni and Frank did, when they didn't have image on the vid; and they kept it constantly on, a low static hiss for hours of the night, their tie to the outside world.

There was a report of a broadcast that had reached some parts of the network—reports of a missile strike that had come in at Reseune. The Carnath girl had made a try at finding out, young Quentin had risked his neck, and more particularly, his lungs, trying to rig an antenna to get something in from some more distant station that wasn't being interfered with, and they'd still learned nothing more than that.

A storm had come in, unmoderated by the towers—rain had lashed the windows for hours, and they'd lost their watchers for a while, which tempted one to make a move, but Yanni nixed it, on the part of any of their security.

It still spat rain, an outside sound which confused itself with static noise from the vid, but Yanni waked with the distinct impression the static had somehow become words, and then he was sure it had. He came out of the bedroom into the sitting room to a white flicker of visual static. In that light, Frank was sitting on the edge of the chair.

Yanni didn't ask. He took an adjacent chair and listened. In fitful reception from somewhere, maybe even from the Science tower, it was Ari's voice, saying they were unharmed, despite a missile strike designed to hit the reporters at the airport. *"They missed us,"* she said, saying nothing about Reseune's defenses. And then a reporter, Yanni was relatively certain, said they were all unharmed, and that Reseune had taken measures to protect them. She must be down at the airport.

At this hour of the night.

Static took over again. They had a few bandit stations that operated intermittently and from non-fixed points in the crisis, this and that Bureau, maybe—God knew what. They didn't use call signs.

"We don't know," Yanni muttered, "how much of this the opposition intends we get. I don't entirely trust the transmission."

Frank nodded agreement. They were both short of sleep. There was constant harassment, maneuvering of agents around the building, communications that came and went. They hadn't heard from Lynch, and were supposed to have heard: at the moment Yanni didn't know whether he was still Proxy Councillor or Councillor for Science, whether Lynch was still alive or as dead as Spurlin and probably Jacques and probably Lao by now, give or take the mechanical support that reportedly sustained her.

They'd done all they could. They'd sent messages. Bogdanovitch, son of the late Councillor for State, and Proxy for the current one, Harad, had headed upriver by air. Then Harad himself had gone, or was supposed to have gone a few hours ago, last but him and Corain, holed up here in the hotel; young Bogdanovitch carried Corain's Proxy as well—illegal, but Bogdanovitch didn't need to show both, they hoped to God, just one of them. The document was signed. The name had yet to be filled in. Could be anybody. Corain's wife. One of his kids. And they hoped not to get to that.

A pass by the window showed a sheet of water, nothing of the watchers at the curb. Tempting. Too tempting.

Easy to assume they could make a break for it. He hoped Harad had made it. He'd wanted to get Lynch on a plane sometime today, let him get to Reseune, because—never mind that Lynch hadn't voted in the office for years—the point was that Lynch *could* vote, if he got to the rest of the Council ... and if Lynch just quietly disappeared, and dropped off the face of the planet, the Proxy for Science couldn't name another proxy. It didn't actually say he *couldn't.* But there was that pernicious clause ... *and other powers not specifically named are reserved to the Council in special quorum.*

Which was what it took to seat a new member, too. Eight of the Nine.

Now *there* was a gaping great logical defect in a fairly new consitution, wasn't it? The founders had been optimists.

So the meeting was supposed to happen on September 12. But the hours were fast slipping away in which they could still do something—faster still, if Khalid had dared fire a missile at Reseune Airport. Planes weren't that safe. Boats on the river wouldn't be, if the renegade Proxy Councillor for Defense had given orders to prevent them moving . . . not to mention it was a long river with lonely spots where nobody observed what happened. Barge traffic was still snarled, with all its concomitant problems, but it was starting to move. A number of enterprising citizens had gotten together and cleared a warehouse by taking foodstuffs and distributing them to all comers; so there was room to offload an incoming barge or two, barges had gone out yesterday; but things were getting increasingly desperate in the city, and the mayor was ordering the police to take action to get dockworkers to the docks, failing which he threatened to hire any applicant to take the jobs.

That wasn't going to be popular with the dockworkers.

Fact was, a city could only take so much disorder before things began to break; and patience was the first thing to go.

A rap came at his door. Frank got up from the chair, and drew a gun that was very rarely in evidence. Yanni went to the door, flicked on the outside vid, and opened it fast: it was Amy Carnath and Quentin behind her.

"Ser," the girl said, "Quentin thinks we should move. They're not out there."

"Trap," Frank said.

"When is it going to be better?" Amy asked, which was a good question, in Yanni's estimation. "We go over to the hotel behind us. Frank and Quentin get the cars, and two other cars go out front, while they go around the block, and we go straight over the bridge; and then we all just go hard as we can for the airport."

"Planes aren't safe," Yanni said. "They're shooting missiles lately."

"Boats are slower," she said. She was a gawky kid. She'd begun to grow into the lanky, large-eyed height; but at the moment she looked her youth, scared, but willing to try any damned thing, possibly because she didn't adequately imagine failing. "Quentin and I will do it: we'll get the car to the front, if you and Frank can get Councillor Corain to the curb."

"Hell," he said. "I've got files to wipe. I'm not ready for this."

"She has a point," Frank said suddenly. "Make a feint toward State. Two cars that way. Two more toward Lynch. One car gets us all to the airport."

"We only have four cars," Yanni said. "And the hotel bus."

"Wouldn't use it at the moment," Frank said. "Or the cars they know. We take the executive car from the next building's garage. Safer."

"You're agreeing with this," Yanni said.

"The missile strike," Frank said, "argues they're fast losing their inhibitions. They're feeling omnipotent—that, or something's made them desperate."

Yanni cast a glance at the Carnath girl, said, "Stand there," and went to the bedroom and threw on what he'd been wearing, casuals, two tees under a sweater. His coat was going to be no protection against the chill. When the weather got like this upriver, they headed for the storm tunnels. To do what they proposed to do, they'd have to hold their breath and make a dash for it through open space in the alley, trusting the downpour to wash noxious life down the gutters, this far in among city towers: building connected to building by overhangs spanning some of the alley, but it was sloppy and cold out there.

He came back to the main room and started putting on the coat. "Frank, what do we do?"

"Five minutes for me to brief Jack and Carl, you get Corain out of bed, and get downstairs."

"Got it," he said.

"Quentin, you take the south stairs. Meet you at the back door."

"Yes, ser," Quentin said.

"Then go," Frank said, and it was just that fast. They

were into it. Launched. Yanni looked at his watch, then walked over, picked up the briefcase, and laid a hand on young Amy's shoulder.

"Here," he said to her, getting her attention. "*You* take the official briefcase."

He had a gun in his own jacket pocket, courtesy of ReseuneSec. He didn't plan to use it; he never in his life planned to draw it, but he made sure it was there, all the same.

He heard a quiet flurry exiting the room adjacent, where ReseuneSec was camped. Whatever orders Frank had given them, they were moving.

Three minutes. Frank and Quentin would be heading for the stairs.

Two minutes.

One. Their guards had left, somewhere. There wasn't a sound, anywhere near.

"You stay with me," he told Amy, and waited the precise last seconds before he opened the door.

They headed out, then. Himself and the kid, out to rouse out Mikhail Corain, if their security moving into position hadn't triggered Armageddon.

It hadn't. At least that.

They made it down to Corain's door, rapped softly, then louder, and there was a soft stir inside. Yanni stood against the door, trying to look casual.

"Mikhail," he said. "Mikhail, it's Yanni. Open up."

Corain opened the door. Had on only underwear and the shirt he'd slept in. His hair stood on end. He turned an appalled look at young Carnath, and started to excuse himself.

"We're going," Yanni said, catching Corain's arm. "Get dressed. Now."

Corain just nodded, looked anxiously at Amy Carnath, then grabbed his pants off the fat armchair and pulled them on. "Shoes," he said, searching.

"Here," Amy said, and he found them and grabbed his coat. Nothing else. Absolutely nothing else but the coat.

Down the hall, then, over blue, figured carpet, to the emergency stairs, the same Frank would have used. Hadn't moved this fast—

Hadn't moved this fast, Yanni thought uneasily, since

the day Ari had died. Since he'd gotten the advisement, and he'd known every plan he and Ari had ever made was upended, thrown into jeopardy.

Everything since, he'd improvised. Like this, like their escape. Granted they made it.

There was a man unconscious, at the bottom of the landing. He might be dead. He wasn't hotel staff. He wasn't theirs. He was wearing a rain-spattered coat.

"God," Corain said. Young Carnath didn't say a thing, just stepped gingerly over the fallen man's leg, and held onto the briefcase.

BOOK THREE   Section 6   Chapter iv

SEPTEMBER 4, 2424
0821H

The late Councillor Bogdanovitch's son, his sister, and Councillor Harad had made it into Reseune Airport together, in an otherwise empty commercial plane out of Moreyville, and took up residence, young Bogdanovitch and his sister in vacant apartments in the Ed wing, Councillor Harad occupying Jordan's old apartment.

And beyond that, on following days, things settled back to quiet, much too quiet, in Ari's estimation. Hicks had transited from close confinement to medical leave, and Ari had assigned a licensed nurse to be living-in, to be sure neither Kyle nor Hicks himself had rejuv issues—if you got supportive treatment fast, so Ivanov had said, you could sometimes prevent a rejuv collapse, so it was important to keep them both under observation while Kyle tried to get his mental bearings and settle down after the shock he'd had.

Not least—the nurse had a qualification in psych, and kept an eye out for that kind of problem, too. But Kyle couldn't be questioned as yet. He wasn't up to it: they had that from the nurse.

Jordan sent a nice letter saying back pay for the last two decades would be greatly appreciated. Ari wrote back saying there might be tax implications he might want to consider regarding a lump sum payment, but she'd start the procedures and pass it on to Yanni when he got there . . .

Yanni. Yanni was her overwhelming worry. Harad had said Yanni was supposed to have left close behind him, and now it was three days after Harad had arrived, with no Yanni, no word from Amy, who should still be in Novgorod. She'd never understood the phrase worried sick.

Now she did.

The last she'd heard, Amy and Quentin had been in Yanni's and Corain's hotel, and they'd been watched. Nearly under house arrest. She hoped for word from Lynch, of Science, in lieu of Yanni, maybe relaying some word or instruction from Yanni; but that didn't come. What had come, via Harad and Bogdanovitch, was the news that Yanni had arranged a diversionary move toward Lynch, but that the crew who'd attempted it had swung back to the hotel with three cars cutting them off from that route.

And that was that—three days since Harad and young Bogdanovitch had been here, safe, and there was no Yanni, no Corain, no Amy, not a ripple out of Reseune-Sec in Novgorod, and Amy didn't answer Maddy's discreet personal call.

The situation sent her back to Base One to make sure she understood the constitutional scenario if there was a near-majority vote and there should be a Council seat vacated by disaster.

Dicey was what it seemed to her: there was a procedure by which the remaining Councillors could unanimously declare a Bureau seat could not be filled within the likely span of an emergency—but the sticky point was that "remaining Councillors" had to include Khalid, who naturally wouldn't vote to unseat himself . . . except he hadn't gotten seated, not officially, and needed a majority of living Councillors to *be* seated.

That was an interesting point of law, but it was also a real kink in the situation for Khalid. He'd alienated everybody. He was on a collision course with constitutional law—and that wasn't a major point with most CITs, who didn't understand it; but it was a nasty situation for Khalid on the one hand and for the constitution on the other.

You could think it's just a document, she wrote to her successor, in the small hours of the morning, *but it's more. It represents a real point of consensus we haven't got now, and a lot of people were willing to give up things they wanted so they could get that agreement. It was a point in human history where all of Union agreed to a set of priorities, and now we'll either prove that agreement still binds everybody, or we'll prove somebody with enough guns can run everything at any given moment; and that means no peace, even for them.*

I never got excited about studying law—until we are a few missile launches away from not having any law at all.

We've got to get that consensus back. That means we've got to be able to tell people the constitution still works, and make them believe it. That's why the forms matter. People have to see things done by the rules. We've got to make people feel safe again and make them believe that compromises are going to be binding.

Unfortunately people in Khalid's own Bureau haven't done anything to stop him.

His Bureau was taking his orders—or, at least, took them far enough to launch that missile. There hasn't been another. Maybe that means that's all they had, or all they can get to.

Maybe it means it even shocked people in Defense.

It should have. I hope it did.

She put in a once-a-day meeting with the reporters at the airport, who said the broadcasts were having a lot of trouble getting out at Novgorod and they weren't sure about Planys; but they were still getting out intermittently there and fairly consistently in other places: people were sending bits all over the net, and Defense was trying to block it, but Defense couldn't stop what other Bureaus ran. So that was doing some good.

She tried to improve her sleep patterns; she still found herself awake at night and napping on her arms on her desk, after being up at 0500h. She finally took to her proper bed in the thought that if she could sleep at all, at any time, she ought to, no matter what else was going on

in the world, and no matter how worried she was about
Yanni. But she wouldn't take a sleeping pill.

She'd just about gotten to that nowhere state, all the
same, when Florian's voice said, "Sera. Sera, forgive me,
but there's a report Defense has just moved in on Planys.
They've shut down all communication. We terminated
accesses."

Damn, she thought.

But she wasn't wholly surprised.

And she had no doubt they'd be after whatever they
could get, Library, all of it—but they hadn't likely gotten
anything. System had taken measures, that fast. They had it
set up for Planys, for particular operations inside Reseune,
for Strassenberg, for ReseuneSec offices in Novgorod: one
System-level irregularity, and System needed to be reset
from Reseune Admin. One code, out of Base One, and it
nuked accesses at any other given base until codes were
reset.

That had happened, probably at the first probe they
made into System. She was ahead of them that far.

She shoved herself up on one arm, and the other, and
found the edge of the bed, raking hair out of her eyes and
trying simultaneously to ask herself if there was any other
thing she needed to think of, if they'd just lost Planys.

There wasn't anything to do, was there? They'd known
they could lose it, that fast, because a Defense installation
was snuggled up against it, and Defense installations had
guns and a lot of electronics, and they'd probably spent
years preparing themselves to crack System.

That part hadn't worked. She felt good about that.

"Tell Admin," she said, and Florian called Catlin on
com and told her to tell Chloe, while Ari was pulling on
her boots. "Tell the Councillors," she added. That was a
new priority on their notification list, but they kept the
Council, such as it was, as informed as Admin, where it regarded moves by Defense. "I'll be over there. I'll go talk to
the reporters. I'll take calls from anybody on the 'notify'
list." She took a twist in her hair and jammed the skewer in
slantwise. Which hurt, but she was in a hurry.

Joyesse showed up. "Coat," Ari said. "Please." And:
"Florian? How did they do it?"

"There were already Defense personnel inside the labs. Fifty more Defense personnel arrived about midnight local. They took armed possession of the administrative offices and that was that: most people go offshift at 1600."

"Anyone hurt?"

"ReseuneSec in uniform were roughed up," Florian said as they entered the hall. Joyesse brought the coat and Ari turned and slipped it on. "That's the last information we have. It may have gotten worse, but they have their standing orders." Go to plainclothes, offer no resistence, destroy any records you can: those were the instructions. "Physical records they've undoubtedly got, undoubtedly some manuals. And the prior codes. They'll be going over those with every expert they have, looking for some forgotten app they can still get into. They won't find one."

"Good. Then that's gone by the book." They reached the front door and Theo let them out.

"Catlin is talking with Chloe in Admin," Florian said, and then pressed the com into his ear, intent on something for an instant. He suddenly stopped walking—and nothing distracted Florian. She stopped, there in the hall, among the paintings.

"Sera," he said, "there's a plane requesting a landing."

Her heart leapt up in hope.

"It's *Defense*, sera." Florian was still listening. "General Awei, Klaus Awei, requesting permission to land, courier jet. Air Traffic Control requests Admin advice."

"Permission granted," she said. There was little else they could do: let automated defenses kick in and start something, or let that plane land. Military courier. If it landed instead of shooting, Defense was talking, and talking—that, she could do something with, even if it delivered a threat. "How far off?"

"How far off?" Florian asked ATC, having relayed her prior instruction; and he reported: "Fifteen minutes, sera."

"Get a bus."

"Sera, it's dangerous."

"The airport has tunnels, if they're lying." Her pulse had kicked up, a level of aggression she had to watch in herself, and question her own decisions. "If they're going to talk, I'll talk to them."

"Yes, sera," he said, and started relaying that information to Catlin and then to the Transport Office, which ran the buses.

BOOK THREE   Section 6   Chapter v

SEPTEMBER 8, 2424
0932H

The bus had gotten to the Wing One doors by the time they met Catlin there—Catlin carrying a rifle/launcher and Florian with only a small pistol. The two exchanged nods, a signal of some kind, the bus door opened, and Ari started to board. Florian interposed an arm between her and the door, saying, "The plane is coming in now, sera. Wait a moment."

She stopped, and stood beside the bus, looking where Florian and Catlin looked. In a moment she saw a black dot in the east, across the river, coming in on the course most planes from Novgorod used.

"Landing to the north," Catlin said as it banked, and it followed that route, rapidly becoming a distinct, swept-winged shape.

"Gear down," Florian noted in some relief, and leapt up to the bus deck in two strides. Ari climbed up, Catlin behind her.

"Field gate," Ari said before she'd done more than grasp a seat back for support. "Onto the field to meet it. Go!"

The driver said, "Yes, sera," and the bus hummed forward and gathered speed down the drive.

They veered onto the airport road, and Ari didn't bother sitting down; neither did Catlin or Florian, and the bus wasted no time, heading down to the airport road, past where the crater in the lawn had been . . . work crews had righted the damaged lamp, earthmovers and bots had

restored the area and put back sod, so there was very little but the seams in the new sod to say where the missile
had been. The warehouses nearby, which had taken some
damage, were getting new facing: those panels were a little
brighter than the rest. Reseune didn't admit its wounds. It
fixed things, fast, all back to normal . . . on her orders, for
morale. On principle.

And if Khalid had something to say, and sent some
messenger to deliver threats, she'd hear what he had to say.
The media could hear it, as far as she was concerned. And
it could equally well hear her answer.

"The media can come out to the landing area if they
want to," she said. "This isn't going to be off the record,
whatever it is. We're not playing that game."

"Sera," Catlin said, "you know this bus is no cover
against what they have."

"Reseune itself isn't cover against what they have." If
they killed her, if they meant to kill her, it was for one reason: to get a new Reseune administration in charge of a
new infant Ari—she sincerely believed it; and to get that,
if it was war, Khalid would peel back layers of Reseune
until they got what they wanted, with missile after missile,
with a landing on that broad, bot-defended shore, and killing anybody in their path.

She couldn't win a war only on defense. Not against all
the hardware Defense commanded.

She got one com call from Councillor deFranco as the
bus was passing the gate—likely the landing was being
carried on Reseune's operations channel, not kept secret
from the population; and she had someone else simultaneously trying to call her, probably Chavez or Harad.
Either Florian or Catlin could have taken that call, but
it wasn't the moment to distract them from their contact
with ReseuneSec.

"It's a General Klaus Awei," she said to deFranco.

"Awei." DeFranco sounded surprised. "He *hasn't been
Khalid's.*"

In a bleak landscape, *that* was interesting information.
"I'm there," she said, because the plane was stopped, and
opening up, and their bus was pulling into its vicinity.

"Call the others, sera. Tell them follow this on the news. I'm there. Got to go."

She thumbed off, pocketed the com, grabbed the seat back for balance as the bus braked. Florian and Catlin were right with her as she handed her way to the bus steps, with the black, foreign shape of the military craft in the right side windows.

At the same moment she stepped down onto the ground, someone was exiting the still pinging plane, one man, then a second, both in plain flight gear. She walked ahead, closing the gap, taking a look at Marine General Awei—white-haired man in the lead, to judge by the collar, lean and not looking like a desk-sitter. He probably had piloted his way in. The man behind him was of lesser rank, carrying nothing but a sidearm and, a good sign, not touching that. Florian and Catlin were right behind her.

Meanwhile the media had exited the flat-roofed terminal, a moderate distance away—she was conscious of that onrushing and disorderly humanity in the tail of her eye, but her attention was all for the general, his face, his expressions. His body language exuded dignity, reserve, assessing her, assessing Florian and Catlin ... not sure, possibly, exactly who she was—or maybe not sure there weren't snipers on the terminal roof.

She walked up and held out her hand with absolute assurance. "Ariane Emory," she said. "General Awei, is it?"

"Sera Emory." A reciprocal gesture, a large, calloused hand that enveloped hers. The man towered over her, over Florian *and* Catlin. He was like a living wall, and his hand was warm and strong, force matching her force, no more than that, a sign of basic good sense. "I'm here for the three branches of the service that *don't* support Admiral Khalid."

Several things immediately occurred to her: that the Fleet had run Defense since the founding of Union: that Fleet leadership had produced Azov, Gorodin, Jacques, Spurlin, and Khalid, none of whom had been straightforward in their dealings with Science; and that if another branch of the armed services should seize power in that

Bureau, it might upend every entrenched structure inside Defense-as-it-was. A veritable earthquake.

That had value.

Disorder, however, and professional revenge-taking posed another kind of hazard.

"General," she said warmly, and by now the media had gotten close, and cameras were going. "You're certainly welcome. We just had a missile come close to our hospital."

"No more of those," Awei said. "A force is in Svetlansk as we speak."

That could be good news. Or not. "Admiral Khalid has taken Planys Labs," she said bluntly, "as of this hour."

"And he's *there,*" Awei fired right back. "And not in Novgorod. My service holds the port, the airport, the broadcast stations, *and* the power grid in the capital."

Not hollow wares, then. Bad news out of Planys, but this man had deliberately landed himself where Council was, where the media was . . . claiming *he* had Novgorod. And, effectively, he *hoped* to have Reseune . . . at least in the political sense.

"Then you're here to talk to Council," she said. *She* wouldn't fall into that pit, negotiating in front of cameras, worse, being seen to usurp what Council needed to be involved in. "Urgently so, I'll imagine. Florian. Catlin. Advise Admin; buses up the hill; tell the Councillors. Let's go into the terminal, General, if you please; it's a more comfortable premises."

"My pleasure," Awei said, and Ari aimed him and his aide and her own two right through the ranks of the media.

There were immediate questions, and cameras. One question was: "How many troops do you have, General?" Which not even a fool would answer truthfully. And: "Are you officially challenging Khalid for the seat?"

Awei stopped right there and turned a calm stare on the cameras—no fool at all, Ari thought. *Nobody* who'd be maneuvered by questions like that was fit to hold office. This man was laying his life on the line to take control, and he was smart. Maybe he was a man who wouldn't be at all safe as an ally—if the constitution didn't make the Bureaus equal, and impose iron-clad quorum requirements among the Nine.

And *still* watch Defense, she thought, both glad and suspicious of a new presence in the game. And she thought, too, in a sub-basement of her mind: *Let him take on Khalid. Whether he lives or dies trying, we benefit.*

Awei said, in that deep, even voice, addressing the media:

"We demand that the Admiral produce Councillor Jacques, alive. We demand that Admiral Khalid answer specific questions from his own service, regarding the murder of Councillor Spurlin. One dead, one disappeared Councillor for Defense—that needs answers. We're not hearing them, and we remind everyone Admiral Khalid has not yet been seated in Council."

That was about as blunt as it got. Awei was trying a maneuver, and making his own bid for power—doing it on Reseune soil, no less. It was certainly a nervy try; it went clear to the heart of Defense, for certain. She approved of everything she heard, and her blood moved just a little faster.

"Reseune agrees with that demand," she said sharply, and cameras refocused on her on the instant. "As of this hour, Admiral Khalid's forces have intruded into Planys-Labs, onto Reseune territory. Records in Planys, as of this morning, are no longer secure, or safe. Within recent months, two senior Reseune personnel are dead under questionable circumstances, one of them at Planys, one at Novgorod. Furthermore, we've reinvestigated the charges against Jordan Warrick. We know he was falsely blamed for the death of my predecessor, and we question whether certain records pertinent to that case will exist past this evening, in the hands of Admiral Khalid's forces." *There* was a capper, without claiming anything specific. Let the media digest *that* one, if Awei thought he could use Reseune Airport for his own stage and not pay rent, even as a friendly. "At the moment Defense has no Councillor and no Proxy Councillor seated among the Nine; and Reseune is extremely interested in what you have to say, General."

Kingmaker he might intend to be, silver-haired veteran clearly on old-fashioned rejuv. He might be backed by a sizeable and formidable division of the service—and maybe he meant to be king, himself, disregarding the constitution as freely as Khalid.

On the other hand, Awei was here. Vice Admiral Tanya Bigelow, the candidate for Defense Proxy that Reseune had backed, hadn't taken the initiative to get up here—if Bigelow was still alive or able to move. That was a fact worth noticing. For proof of any considerable opposition to Khalid's takeover, they had nothing but one plane and a Marine general who had yet to demonstrate what, exactly, he commanded. And if Yanni showed up in the interim, backing Bigelow or some other candidate in Defense, *there* was a potential embarrassment.

But she couldn't wait to consult anybody, and there was suddenly a momentum going, where the media was concerned. Khalid had troops inside Planys, which the media couldn't get visuals on; and Reseune had had a missile launched at them out of Svetlansk—which they had been able to get on camera for the whole immediate universe to see: guess which was more impressed on public awareness. Now this man came screaming in out of the blue with a challenge and an offer; and she could prime the media and shove things into motion—if nothing else, throw a momentary obstacle into Khalid's hitherto cascading rush to power.

Kingmaker in Defense, Awei might be—or not. History was full of actions like Awei's, and some of them died, and some of them fell, soon after.

The smart ones didn't try to use anybody smarter than they were. Let him figure in the next few hours that that was what he had just met. She could support him . . . if Klaus Awei was smart enough to figure who'd just settled the mantle of legitimacy about *his* shoulders in front of the media, and whose support could make his survival in his bid just a little more likely than any other claimant. She read people pretty damned well—and Klaus Awei, for all his larger-than-life presence, already knew he was taking a chance. He'd known exactly where media exposure and significant images could be had: and if he was telling the truth, he had control of the Novgorod vid apparatus, which meant word would get out much wider than it had been.

He hadn't established himself in Novgorod and tempted *Council* into coming back to the capital and appealing to him for rescue, which argued good manners—or suggested his base might be small and fragile down there, if it existed at all. Or it could argue he wasn't going to go for political process at all: he was a military man, commanding an organization that moved fast: forces already in Svetlansk, he'd said, while he was here, taking the publicly political option.

He had a real chance, if Council backed him—and if media simultaneously got the word out.

"What's this about Jordan Warrick?" a reporter yelled then, and Ari turned, slowly, solemnly, with the cameras all going, and all other questions silent. "What about Jordan Warrick?" the reporter repeated, exactly the side issue she'd wanted.

"A covert operation wanted my predecessor *dead,*" she said. "Now the same people would like to see *me* dead . . . along with a lot of other people that stand in their way. The general has come here, I gather, driven by conscience—and if it's not proper for Reseune to say how Defense should manage its internal business, I can at least say I'm in favor of protecting the independence of the Bureaus, with respect for other Bureaus' territory *and* property, and the right of *all* Union citizens, to elect a candidate in their Bureau and see that candidate *live* to take office."

That created three and four more questions, about on the level of: Are you talking about Spurlin, young sera? Then, more important, a question she wanted: Have you had any word from the Councillor for Science?

"I *hope* for it," she shot back and, seeing the good general was not accustomed to the shouted-questions kind of news conference, which was absolutely her element, she made a gesture of invitation toward the terminal. "The Councillors are on their way down, or they'll be in touch fairly soon. Wait and we'll give you a news conference." And to Awei alone: "General, there's a private conference room, and I imagine you and your companion would appreciate a cup of coffee, at the least."

"Coffee," Awei said. It had become a steady march toward the terminal doors: Florian and Catlin's presence meant questioners didn't get that close, or press up against them: the reporters that had covered Reseune for years had long since understood that about ReseuneSec and azi bodyguards. They knew the distance, knew it to an exactitude and kept it, shoving each other rather than infringing on that imaginary line that triggered armed reaction from security.

At the doors, she called back to them almost cheerfully, and with real affection: she knew no few of them, had known them for years: "Give me about an hour. I'll talk to you. I promise!"

It took half an hour for Council to get down to the airport—deFranco and Chavez were the first to arrive, in no more than ten minutes, if that. Ludmilla deFranco met them in the conference room, quite forthrightly shook Awei's hand, and asked about conditions in Novgorod; Chavez started to pour himself a cup of coffee and didn't get to carry it back to the table himself. Airport hospitality staff arrived in the room with a far more elaborate and finer coffee service than what the machine provided. They swept recyclable cups aside, poured coffee into fine china, and saw the general and the Councillors seated at the conference table with a full choice of cream, sweetener, sugar, spice, and wafers; the same for her, who sat at the far end of the table, and the same for the general's aide, who stayed standing, but who did take a cup of coffee.

"We have order in Novgorod," Awei had said, in answer to the former question . . . which might be an hour by hour situation, Ari thought, knowing the conditions that had kept Yanni and Amy pinned down; and she didn't know where they were. They could have gotten loose, could be somewhere in military hands . . . of either side.

Asking Awei, however, was asking a large predator for help, opened bidding for that help, and she wasn't sure she wanted to do that at this point.

"What *is* your position, General," deFranco asked briskly stirring spice into her coffee, "since, as Councillor Corain said in his report, *nothing* at this point will induce the Council to seat Admiral Khalid?"

"That's not a concern," Awei said.

Encouraging, Ari thought, but letting the hearer fill in the blanks. She didn't let her eyes dart, didn't give visual cues what she thought, any more than she could help. She signaled to Catlin and said, very quietly, as Catlin moved close: "Report on the general," and then listened to Awei and deFranco exchange several more questions.

"What is the situation at Novgorod," deFranco asked, then, "besides orderly?"

"We're trying to get citizens back to work, which means safety down on the docks and safety for transport moving through the city—in some neighborhoods, that's a problem. We're getting a little resistence from Fleet MP's assigned to the docks and elsewhere; we're negotiating that at higher levels. A Council directive would go a long way toward improving that situation. Which brings us to the specifics: I have a short list of resolutions that we'd like to see passed."

We. Always the undefined "we." Ari wished deFranco would eventually ask who "we" was. She didn't want to do it.

Councillor Harogo and Councillor Tien showed up at the door at that point, with four ReseuneSec agents for an escort, three men and a woman who likewise took up station with Florian and Catlin. Ari stood up. The others did. There were more handshakes, more exchanges, politeness with very little substance in the questions. Lastly Harad came in, State, looking cautious, but willing to welcome the general.

Coffee, all around, except Harad: tea for him, with cream and sweetener. Awei's aide, who was listening to something, much as Florian and Catlin were doing, moved close to Awei and said something Ari was sure ReseuneSec would manage to pick up: she couldn't hear it. It might just be an advisement to the general that someone was monitoring. It could be business going on elsewhere in the world.

"We have a quorum for ordinary business at this point," Harad said. "Shall I chair?"

"Seconded," deFranco murmured; it wasn't strict protocols, in Ari's estimation, but nobody objected. Harad asked, "Who's recording?"

"I'm sure Reseune is," Tien said wryly, "and probably the good general, but I'll keep notes, for the record."

"Those present," Harad said, and they proceeded to an informal roll call—leaving out Information, a fact which Ari noted, and didn't take in the least as a slight. Where Council's quorum stood, the five for ordinary business, and the eight for special business—that was something Harad didn't give away for free. They mustered the basic five without her, and she didn't say a thing, just sat with her chin on her hand, and trusted records were being kept.

"We'll dispense with the reading of the last session's business," Harad said, and proceeded on to the general's list, first being a Council resolution on the situation on Novgorod docks, requesting the Fleet's military police to withdraw to quarters; a second resolution giving General Awei provisional authority to arrest and detain inside the city of Novgorod; a third, Council condemnation of the missile attack on Reseune.

Nice politics. Ari made a note, signaled Florian, and said, "Give this to deFranco," and Florian quietly walked to the other end of the table and did that.

It suggested a fourth Council resolution, condemning the intrusion of Defense personnel into Reseune Administrative Territory property at Planys, and requiring the release of all arrested personnel and surrender of all confiscated materials.

It took very little arguing of specific language, and, her little test, and probably something at least deFranco noted, the general quite readily supported it.

So it joined the list up for consideration.

Then came a fifth prospective Council action, on Awei's list, a grant of authority to Awei, with powers of arrest and detention, to investigate the death of Councillor-elect Spurlin and the disappearance of current Councillor Jacques. It was a simple Council directive, but, Chavez noted, operationally unprecedented in scope. They had, Harad said, the Office of Inquiry doing the same.

Damn it, Ari thought, pass it. Don't hang us up on territoriality. But she kept her mouth shut.

It hadn't made it onto the list yet. Then Ludmilla de-

Franco moved for a twenty-minute recess. That, Ari had learned, was where Council intended to do some off the record maneuvering.

"Sera." Catlin came to Ari's elbow as Council collectively took a restroom break. Catlin delivered a set of printout, with her standard request, a summation sheet on top. It was ReseuneSec's answer to her question on Awei. He had not served in combat, had served at Gehenna during the Alliance-Union investigation—interesting; had managed the Fargone Hospital facility, which was only partially a hospital, and had more to do with the Defense base at Eversnow—*there* was a major caution, considering Defense might have killed her predecessor in an as-yet unproven relationship to that project.

Awei could be, she thought uneasily, a worse problem than Khalid, if Awei was deeply embedded in the coverup of military activity on that iceball.

She asked herself whether it was a good idea or not to let Awei know she knew certain things—until they'd gotten maximum good out of Awei. She'd watched the man across the table, watched his eyes, and she had at least some confidence she was reading him consistently: that was one thing in his favor.

But he was also old in his business, knew how to keep his face quiet, and clearly, to her observation at the moment, knew how to talk to Councillors who came at him with sharp questions: no fool, not in the least.

She'd have about the first instant to read past that considerable skill at not being read, if she broached her topic with him.

If she didn't, they could possibly *have* Awei and his service running Defense in fairly short order, unless they first used him to get rid of Khalid and then appointed Bigelow, out of the Fleet, to do things as they'd always been done. Council was certainly capable of doing that, and if Bigelow was more energetic than she'd yet showed, who knew? She might turn up as Councillor for Defense and Awei might be assigned back to Eversnow.

He didn't command all the strings that could be pulled. Council hadn't been prepared for the blow that had come against it—an outright campaign of assassination and brute force. Defense had those weapons to use. They could still have one sticky mess on their hands.

But she was still the kid. The observer in this meeting. Awei had had a taste of her style out by the plane. But he might not be totally on his guard against a question coming from her.

It had better be a good one. A really good one.

She decided on another cup of coffee, and, the serving staff having come back, now that they were in recess, she moved up close to the general, who was standing by the window having his own cup refilled.

"General," she said pleasantly, and got his attention. *"Who* in Defense ordered my predecessor killed?"

Fast change in the eyes. Muscle twitch. As good as a truther unless there'd been a psych plant to prevent a reaction. Did he really want to answer that question? He wasn't at all sure.

"I don't know," he said, "but an investigation might be in order."

He wasn't lying. But he also kept some thought in reserve.

"Easy to accuse Khalid," she said. "Possibly it would even be accurate."

"He couldn't originate the order, young sera."

A little surprising, that answer. Accurate. Maybe trying to shift her eyes higher up . . . maybe to Gorodin. But there was more than one way to originate an order, she thought. First, if you were head of Intelligence, you supplied the information behind it and that made the conclusion obvious. Interesting choice of answers, and she didn't detect guilt in the man, just impatience with her, an awareness of everything going on in the room, in which he thought he had much more at stake, and, still, something still in reserve.

"You're hiding something," she said, and *that* got a reaction, quick as an explosion—in the tiny muscles of the iris, in the momentary glitch in the neck.

"You're a very interesting young woman, Sera Emory."

"What do you *not* have, that you don't want to let us know about?"

He didn't get caught this time. He smiled in a very controlled, patronizing way. "I never met your predecessor. Was she this full of questions?"

"Something major," she answered her own question. "You lack something, and that makes you think you may lose this fight. You're making your move as early as you can and as late as you dare. For one thing, you don't control the Fleet, and the Fleet has been in power since Union began. You don't think you can pry their hands off that power. You have to worry about assassination, for another thing . . ." She was watching his eyes as she ran through that shopping list, and saw reactions that said she was getting closer. "And you have about twenty-four hours to make your bid good, which is why you came here looking for Council backing, because all the people currently backing you are going to be in a lot of trouble, real soon, if you don't gain momentum fast, and you care about that. Good. That makes me feel better."

He looked at her in some disquiet. "And do you have a conclusion to this observation, sera? Or is it a fortune-telling act?"

"Oh, it's not that hard to say: you came here to get a Council directive, which will make you look a lot more legitimate, you know there's not a special quorum here, but you *do* know there's an ordinary quorum, which is enough for a directive. You'd probably like a Council resolution to say definitively that there's no way in hell they'll seat Khalid, and they might do that, but I don't think it would look good politically. I'd advise not, if you have that in mind. Better you act as Council's enforcement, then let Council get together, vacate the Defense seat and appoint a pro tem . . . assuming Jacques is dead, which seems fairly likely; or in Khalid's hands, as insurance, in which case Jacques can be gotten out alive, and he could appoint *you* as proxy—he'll do what he's told to do. Am I following this correctly? You've got your troops, you've got a few important people hanging back, waiting to see how this goes, and whether or not you can outmaneuver Khalid, who's just taken the other continent this morning because he's having to jump fast and you caught him a little by surprise. His being there makes logistics a lot more difficult for you to get at him, but you're after Svetlansk, where possibly you can keep him defending."

A slow, grim honesty arrived in those same eyes. "Say Svetlansk won't be a problem. Planys, however, is. He's shifted certain of his assets across the water. He has time, there. He can politic with the station over our heads. Two warships up there, if you want the truth."

"Reseune *has* assets across the water," she said. "I can *get* you precise recon at any time you want it. It'll be a snapshot, so only ask for it once, but I can deliver it."

He was still for a moment—more than silent: still, controlled, wary. Then his eyes flicked aside, beyond her, about where Florian and Catlin would be standing.

"Numbers before this morning would be very useful, sera," he said then. "Placement of forces likewise."

"Catlin," she said, knowing Catlin and Florian had heard every word, "provide the general with that information."

"Yes, sera," Catlin said.

The clock, meanwhile, had reached straight up, and their twenty-minute recess was done. While she'd occupied the general, Councillors had been discussing, intensely, and now took their seats with a grim look.

Ari went up the table before deFranco, caught her for a moment for a quiet word before she took her seat: "I think he's here without wider support in Defense, except his own branch. He's looking for legitimacy. He's got forces actively moving in or on Svetlansk. The directives he's got will give him momentum . . . *might* sway elements of the Fleet, but I didn't get that from him, and I don't think he's remotely counting on it. Call on him to support the Council by armed force where needful. Call on all the armed services to support the Council and defend its premises."

That happened to be Reseune—and they were in extraordinary danger at the moment, with that plane sitting on its runway, and unproven actions going on in Svetlansk.

DeFranco nodded, walked over, and spoke intensely to Harad, who then spoke at some length to Harogo.

And Harogo, once they were seated, made the motion to consider an amendment to the last-proposed directive.

They passed the Council directive. The added portion read: *support the Council, defend its premises and protect the premises of all Bureaus, cities, institutions and territories, by force of arms where need be.*

Awei drew in a large breath, then—satisfied, it seemed.

"Sera," Florian said. He'd left the room during the last of the session. He had a printout in hand, and handed it to her. "The Planys report."

It was a single page. It gave a breakdown of Defense numbers at the airport, numbers inside Planys.

"That's of this morning, sera, at the point we shut System down."

"Good," she said. "As far as we know, System remains intact?"

"Likely it does."

It was earnest of what they could get, when they needed it. She went to the general, who was taking leave of the Councillors, and handed him the paper. "Numbers and locations of non-Reseune individuals the hour of the take-over. You get Khalid to defend his airport, and his base, and let us know when you need it, ser."

Awei looked past Ari, directly at Catlin and Florian, whose faces wouldn't give him a thing.

And back to her, maybe wanting to know a lot more, wondering if he had credit enough to ask it.

"Right before the shutdown," she said. "Best information we've got."

"Sera, Reseune has air cover while I'm here. But best you get your people and essential operations underground over the next number of hours. We can't defend against what may happen on the station."

Up where the weathermakers were. Where the atmospheric controls were, and the bulk of the power generation.

Not to mention hostile action from ships that might be in port.

She had the picture. Awei turned to the several Councillors, who wished him well.

So did she, and said so, before they took it to the media, outside, and provided the literal text of the resolutions.

The resolutions were going onto the airwaves.

The whole world was about to know for certain the Council was behind Klaus Awei's actions, past and future.

BOOK THREE   Section 6   Chapter vi

The first message Justin got said, simply, as a flasher on the corner of the screen of his office computer: *Wing Directors: red alert is in progress.*

The second, popping up in quick succession, and overlaying it, said: *Justin, you're in charge of Alpha Wing. Call ReseuneSec if you have to find me.*

Meanwhile their office vid, up on the wall, had started rerunning the short news conference, on a split screen with the general's plane taking off.

It didn't take much imagination to know it was no drill, some threat was imminent, and that meant prepare to head for the tunnels.

"Better shut down the office," Justin said, feeling a little queasy. "Damn, we're not getting much outstanding work done, at this rate."

"Better pack for this one," Grant said. "Trigger the warning on the List?"

"You know, I *hate* getting used to this. Yes, fire it off. Our neighbors know the drill better than we do." He tried to think of what he should pack, what it would take to keep his sanity if it came to several days in the tunnels, and, with no functioning sense of priorities, he gathered up current notes on a non-classified set. "Take a case or two with you, or we'll both go crazy."

"Game, batteries, and motion charger, check," Grant said. "Still in the briefcase from the last time. I hate getting used to it, too—just as a useful check on my sensibilities. I distinctly recall being told to appeal to my Supervisor if *I* feel stress coming on."

"Do you?" Justin asked soberly, turning to look at him.

Grant rudely shoved him into motion. "It's a condition of life, lately. Move. I want to get upstairs and pack some necessities this time. Let's be practical about this."

Mark and Gerry showed up in the open doorway: word had spread.

"Ser," Gerry said, "An alert's in progress."

"We know. Thanks. Get on the com," Justin said, settling his coat on, "call everybody in the Wing and tell them this is a real alert, if they have any doubt of it. All staff to go to the tunnels, prepare for a stay. When you've done that, supply yourselves out of your office for at least a three-day stay and report to the storm tunnel."

"Yes, ser," Mark said, and the two of them went off at fair speed—which left them time to get upstairs in good order and pack a bag between them.

Grant looked a little overwhelmed as they were leaving—again. He cast a look around the room, as if memorizing it, and then looked at Justin with a little sigh as if to say he was ready for most anything.

Grant was Justin's overriding thought. Grant's stability, he didn't question. It was a sensible worry whether they could both get through the next few days alive. He didn't know everything they were up against, but the thought of the station in orbit deciding just to flip the switch and shut down the towers until Reseune gave up, or Defense landing troops on their very close-in river shore, troops to break into the tunnels and force their way in—

That wasn't a prospect he wanted to contemplate. They were Warricks, Grant no less than he was. No question they'd be targets along with Jordan. They always had been. And there wasn't a damned thing he personally could do about it, but have a short mental list of one bolt hole after another if it got to that.

Planys wasn't theirs this morning. That news had mixed with the news of the landing; and he wasn't the only one who'd be upset with that news. He phoned Jordan on his way down from their apartment. "Dad," he said, when only the message function answered his call, "take this one very seriously. Paul, take care. Both of you."

They ended up with the lift all to themselves.

Back to the tunnel he'd gotten to know—all the comforts, as far as sieges went.

And settled in to wait.

The galley served modest sandwiches, which Ari's staff said would be available at any time. They had coffee and fruit tea. Tommy and Mika Carnath arrived, exhausted and short of breath, from across the complex, and said they'd been held up a while, getting back, because they'd had to walk all the way around from the labs: they weren't letting people traverse the open spaces, and they were too young to rate a seat on the trams. Yevgenia Wojkowski arrived, and said she'd been delayed by a phone call from a cousin in Novgorod asking what had happened, but she had just told her to watch the news. Maddy Strassen came in with her companion Samara, and settled in. The news services, broadcasting in Novgorod, and visible on the general monitor, showed, intermittent with rebroadcasts of the Council news conference and the general's plane taking off, tranquil views of the city, a small amount of traffic moving on the roads, subways running, mostly empty, on a sunny day.

It was reassuring to know the city was functioning. It showed barges backed up for days on the river, and then showed one barge leaving, which was promising.

"We have news, ser," Mark said, coming over to him. "Svetlansk Airport has had several aircraft disabled."

"So something's going on up there," Grant commented, after. "The general was telling the truth in that much."

"We can hope so," Justin said. There were a handful of places of any size in the civilized world, and Svetlansk had always seemed as remote as another world. Since the missile event, it hadn't seemed that remote. It didn't at the moment.

An hour later there was an interruption on the vid to say that there was going to be a three-hour shutdown of the just-opened Port of Novgorod, due to security concerns. That *wasn't* good news.

Then Ari called in, just on general address. *"This is Ariane Emory. We haven't gotten much news, except there's been a ground attack on Svetlansk Airport, damag-*

ing several Fleet aircraft. We're getting two planes in fairly continual pattern between us and Novgorod, which we think is their origin. We have absolutely nothing reported off the coast in the direction of Planys and hope to keep it that way . . ."

BOOK THREE Section 6 Chapter vii

Sept 8, 2424
1538h

". . . There's a small situation at the port in Novgorod that seems to be a labor issue. Waiting is all we can do at this point. We're limiting our own communications for security reasons. I'll be back in touch when there's news."

Ari shut the mike down. There was a small firefight going on up in Svetlansk, as best they could figure, and since that had started, they weren't getting any satellite images out of Cyteen Alpha Station—disturbing as it might be. Images continued uninterrupted from remote Beta, and she hoped it was Alpha making a declaration of neutrality in the immediate situation, and nothing worse, like Alpha taking sides, or Alpha engaged in its own struggle against elements of the Fleet up there.

Catlin and Florian, meanwhile, had joined several of ReseuneSec's seniors in organizing a defense of Reseune, framed in several contingencies: an invasion from water, from the air, the very low probability of anyone moving in by land after an air landing—getting down off the cliffs wouldn't be easy. And an assault from air or space, in which case they tucked low and defense became *her* job as long as their communications held out, which meant, among other things, keeping a handful of unruly media people under cover.

Defense was not something on which the first Ari had an outstanding lot to say: a search after similar incidents turned up nothing but a few boatloads of Abolitionists bent on kidnapping azi to "free" them, lunatic venture . . . nothing like having a missile threat to contend with. They hadn't guarded the boat launch in those days. They hadn't built the coffer dam, the lock system, and the filtration until Giraud and Denys took over. It turned out being defensive, in plans her security was making, but it had been ecological in origin, pushed by the company working remediation in Swigert Bay.

Meanwhile they had planes patrolling the skies, but suddenly had very little information regarding air traffic—the station supplied most of that kind of information. And that provided a major screen for anybody doing anything.

She made a try at contacting Alpha Station, ordinarily a matter of picking up the phone. It took a considerable wait, on a line that should have gone straight through to Station Admin.

It still did, finally, at least as far as a live Assistant Stationmaster. "This is Ariane Emory, at Reseune. We're not receiving air traffic information. For all we know nobody in the world is receiving information. We have a rogue Fleet officer in Planys, possibly with missiles under his direction, aimed at the population of Novgorod. Are you willing to take the responsibility when this situation goes to the national court with criminal charges, ser?"

"Let me get the Stationmaster," the reply came back, and five minutes more of waiting and she had the Alpha Stationmaster. Emil Erikssen was his name, and she effectively repeated what she had just said to the Assistant Stationmaster, including the bit about personal responsibility and criminal charges. "We have no way of sounding an alarm if we get another missile fired at us. We *had* a missile land within 800 meters of our hospital and 15 meters off a public thoroughfare, ser. Whatever's going on up there, the ordinary citizens of this planet and the Council rely on *you* for services that mean life and death. Don't give us promises."

"We are supporting the atmospherics systems and the power grid," the answer came back. *"Fleet assets have just been destroyed or compromised. We are not providing general positional information to enable counterattacks until we have contact with Council."*

"We appreciate your position, but if you want the Council, ser, you just stay connected." She punched buttons on her pocket com, and rang Ludmilla deFranco. "Sera. I have the Alpha Stationmaster. He needs a Council resolution before he'll provide the global net."

"Let me talk to him," deFranco said, and she punched more buttons, and got four more Councillors. *"We are sitting in shelters here,"* deFranco said in some heat, *"having already had one missile fired at us by a fool, and if you want a directive, ser, you'll have it."*

"This is Harad, of State," Councillor Harad broke in. *"The directive already exists, Alpha Station, in our recent instruction to General Awei to defend the Council. Facimile transmission follows. We direct you turn on current global positional and traffic data. We'll get you a specific directive on both orders inside five minutes if you have any doubt."*

There was a lengthy delay on the other side.

Catlin came to her desk, leaned over, com pressed firmly into her ear, and said, "Geosats are transmitting again."

They had eyes.

That had gone all right, hadn't it? Pity they couldn't have been selective—but the system wasn't set up that way. Alpha could shut down satellites from transmission. But once they did transmit—anybody could use the information.

And about forty seconds later, the airport called Reseune Admin: *"We have regained image."* Likewise at the port.

The outage had lasted about thirty minutes, from the initial action at Svetlansk to the restoration of geosat transmission.

Fleet property had gotten damaged at Svetlansk, no word about personnel. They'd howled in indignation, more than likely.

So had the planet immediately involved . . . howled, now, and there'd be some consideration of the measures Alpha Station had taken, if she had anything to say about it. There *hadn't* been civilian planes in the air when ATC's long vision went out, but there could have been. There *hadn't,* however, been guidance for more missiles for a bit, either. So it was a toss-up. She couldn't say the Alpha Stationmaster had been wrong; and he couldn't be in a comfortable position, watching his government come apart, down on the planet, and two halves of Defense starting shooting at each other. They'd gotten into it step by step: for Alpha Station, there'd been a succession of small startling shocks, mostly in the last week.

So Alpha Station had wanted it stopped. She could understand that. Maybe Khalid would be beseiging his own sources up on station, urging Fleet authorities up there to shut the geosats down again to protect his operations at Planys. And maybe Fleet would start agitating on his behalf, or even issuing threats, but Alpha was a power, too, a de facto sovereign state like Reseune Territories, and Khalid couldn't trump a Council directive.

Had him, she did.

She shoved back from the console in the Admin storm tunnels, and spun about to find Florian in the doorway, Florian with a decided grin on his face.

"Yanni," Florian said, "and Councillor Corain, Amy, and Frank, and Quentin AQ. They're down at the port."

Her heart leapt up. "In Novgorod?"

"No, sera. At *our* port, the riverside. Rafael's sending a bus."

"Are we sure?" she asked.

"Yes, sera!"

She spun the chair about again, and this time punched in every Councillor they had resident. They were immediate on the answer, Harad, deFranco, Chavez, Tien, and, last, Harogo. She said, "Yanni and Mikhael Corain have just arrived at the port. Would you like to meet them in Admin?"

"Finally!" Harad said, and Chavez: *"About damned time."*

SEPT 8, 2424
1621H

Directive control stayed in Ari's pocket—literally—via her
com, which she kept on, with Admin connected, continually. Florian and Catlin were linked into Rafael's operation,
specifically to senior ReseuneSec officers; and to Wes and
Marco, who were doing the same, out of Alpha Wing Ops;
she was linked to Admin, namely Chloe, and the department heads, who'd gotten the heads-up from Chloe via Yanni's office. "Call Councillor Corain's family," she told Chloe,
afterthought, but one she didn't want to omit. "Tell them
Corain is coming in, but tell them stay to the tunnels."

Immediately after, she headed upstairs and down the
long lower hall in Admin, in close company with Florian
and Catlin and two of the regular ReseuneSec personnel.

The Councillors, starting from storm tunnels in Wing
One and Ed, reported themselves headed over via the
cross tunnels, with their aides—they might come upstairs,
if they insisted: nobody was going to argue protocols with
Harad or deFranco, or even Corain's wife. All Ari's attention was focussed on having Yanni and Corain and Amy
across that open space and down in the tunnels as fast as
they could get them there, and she listened to the infre-
quent information from Admin, hoping not to hear warnings, hoping the moderate communications traffic hadn't
helped the opposition.

The bus at least was wasting no time . . . two buses, it became evident as she reached the locked doors—one bus veer-
ing off to Ed, one coming up toward them. "One is a decoy,"
Florian said, and Catlin meanwhile called Rafael, signaling
the physical lock to be taken off the Admin front doors and
left off until she sent word they had the party inside.

Florian swung a door open. The bus came up under the

portico, squealed to a hard stop, and its door flew open.
Quentin exited instantly and held up his hands for Amy,
who flung herself off the bus. Frank came next, with the
briefcase, and held out a hand to steady Yanni coming
down; and the third and last CIT was Mikhail Corain,
looking to be on his last legs—all of them freshly scrubbed,
wearing work blues, still damp from decon and reeking of
potent disinfectant.

"Inside," Florian said. "Inside, quickly, ser."

"Amy, Yanni," Ari said, and embraced Amy with one
arm and Yanni with the other. "Where have you been?"

"In a shipping container," Yanni said. "Hard on old
bones, I'll tell you."

"You took a barge all the way up?"

"Only thing we could get to," Amy said. "And it got
stalled. We're safe. Hid out in sealed cargo, shipped for
Reseune."

"She bought candy bars," Yanni said, "and water before
we tried it. *She*, bright young woman, had credit chits for
the vending machines on the docks: card use, and they'd
have found us." Frank had an arm around him, and Frank
didn't look much better. The guards they'd brought moved
to provide support, one to Yanni, one to Mikhail Corain.
Young Quentin AQ lent a shoulder to Frank, who looked
about ready to collapse in his tracks, but who wasn't surrendering the briefcase.

"We got boarded," Amy said. "And stalled forever
while they searched things. But they didn't get down to
our container."

"We've got a medic downstairs," Ari said, trying to
move them on, get the whole party back down to safety.
They had a whole clinic: it was part of Admin's storm
season routine, to handle decon, or anything else needful, and right now it was five water-deprived, underweight
refugees. And she wanted them moved, before a dozen
reporters dug in down at the airport managed to get the
news out; she started moving Amy along, her arm about
her. It was, by the layout of the older buildings, a fair walk
back—not to create a people-jam near the building entry
in the event of an alert: that had been the theory . . . but it
made it a lengthy hike.

The lift had made a trip down and back, meanwhile, and brought up Mikhail Corain's wife and two Reseune-Sec officers. The lady gave a little cry and rushed to embrace her husband.

"In, ser, in, quickly," Catlin said briskly, and got them in; the rest of them found room; and the lift dropped down again, a far reach to the tunnels—Catlin keyed off the security stop, and it took them straight on down.

Doors opened. More security met them, more of Ser Corain's excited family, observing enough of the security line to let them exit the lift before they closed around him. Councillors were right behind—Harad, Tien, deFranco, Harogo and Chavez, all there to see with their own eyes.

"Medical," Ari said, and Florian called them. Yanni had stumbled on the way down the upstairs hall. Corain had family to buoy him up; Yanni just slumped a little, home and safe, and Ari caught his hand and found it cold.

"Yanni," she said. "Hold on. Medics are bringing a stretcher."

"No damned way," Yanni said. "Didn't come here to be carried down the damned hall. Harad! How's the vote stand?"

"Special quorum," Harad said, and came and put a light hand on Yanni's shoulder. "Proxy, man. We haven't seen Lynch."

"Ari's already taken," Yanni said hoarsely. "If I fall over, if I fall over—" Deep breath. "Justin Warrick's my Proxy."

"Is he here?" Harad asked.

Ari said: "Alpha Wing. I can get him."

"I'm *not* falling over," Yanni snapped. "Have we got our quorum? Mikhail, dammit, get yourself over here! First business, move to seat Ariane Emory as Councillor for Information, Catherine Lao being deceased. We can do it here in the hallway."

"Second," deFranco said.

"Moved and seconded to seat Ariane Emory for Information," Harad said. "Are we recording this?"

"We have a record going," Chavez said.

"Voice vote," Harad said, and the Councillors called it out, over the confused buzz of the curious and the office workers from Admin, who'd come to see the commotion. "Science, aye." "Industry, aye." "Finance, aye." "Transportation, aye." "Trade, aye." "Internal affairs, aye." "Citizens, aye." That, a hoarse voice from Mikhail Corain. And lastly, deep and strong: "State, aye. The Council of the Nine welcomes the new Councillor for Information and invites her, officially if figuratively, to take her seat. So ordered, this date, the eighth of September, the year 2424."

"Move to seat Vladislaw Khalid, Proxy Councillor for Defense," deFranco said.

"Second," Yanni said, "for purposes of the vote. Science votes nay."

"Industry, nay." "Finance, nay." Transportation, nay." "Trade, nay." "Internal affairs, nay."

There was a brief pause. A gap. "Information, nay," Ari said, and immediately after: "Citizens, nay," from Mikhail Corain, and then Harad: "State votes nay. The motion fails. Council will not seat the candidate, and calls on Defense to name a new Proxy. In the absence and presumed death of the Councillor for Defense, the Council calls on the Secretary for the Bureau of Defense to assume the office of Proxy until such time as a duly elected Councillor for Defense may register a Proxy for the consideration of the Council of the Nine. So ordered, this date, the eighth of September, the year 2424. In absence of the appointed Proxy for the Bureau of Defense, the chair of the Council of the Nine declares the Defense seat vacant pending elections in that Bureau, and calls for nominations to be placed before the electorate, none dissenting? So ordered, this date, the eighth of September, the year 2424. The chair moves for the declaration of martial law."

"Second," Harogo said. "Move for declaration of unanimity, all seated members being present."

"Second," deFranco said.

"Any opposed?" Harad asked, and read the date. Then: "Chair moves to appoint Marine General Klaus Awei as provisional commander of all Union armed forces, to restore order and return control to civil authorities within forty-eight hours."

"Second," deFranco said, and Yanni said, in a hoarse

whisper, "Science votes aye," before his knees buckled and he began to slip toward the floor. Frank made a grab for him. Ari did. The two ReseuneSec azi were more effective, kept his head from hitting the floor, picked him up, and carried him.

The medics that had come up to the area and stopped were equally fast, sliding a gurney into the area. Yanni was on his way to the clinic without ever hitting the ground, and Ari glanced in that direction and toward the Council chair, and knew where the Proxy for Information had to be . . . it had cost too much, already, even to wonder. The vote went on. She cast her vote for Information, and the vote went past her, and concluded with the Chairman's reading of the date.

"Are we done, ser?" she asked Harad.

"Move to adjourn," Harad said.

"Move to adjourn," she said.

"Second," deFranco said.

"None opposing, we stand adjourned," Harad said; and meanwhile Tien had taken hold of Mikhail Corain's arm. Tien said: "We'd better get him down there, too."

Frank had already gone, staying with Yanni all the way. Ari slipped her arm through Amy's, locked fingers with hers, and stayed to catch Harad as Councillors and family members began to move in various directions. "Copy of that vote, to the airport, ser? Can Reseune help?"

"We need urgently to transmit the file," Harad said. "Transmission to secure storage, Hall of the Nine, transmit to the media, replication far and fast: official transmission, all Bureau offices, city and district offices, station offices, ships in space . . ." It was official litany, the places that record had to go. She didn't have it memorized, but she said, "Ops can do that, ser. If you go with Catlin, she'll assist."

"Yes, sera," Catlin said, and went off with the Council Chairman, through a throng of the curious and the concerned. Florian stayed right by Ari's side.

Sept 8, 2424
1715h

Pocket com went off. Jordan, Justin thought; but it wasn't.

"Justin?" Ari said. *"Just so you know, Yanni's back."*

"That's great news," he said. He was glad. He was very glad, and he thumbed the com over to speaker so Grant could hear. It immediately got Mark and Gerry's attention, and Maddy Strassen's, with, *"Just so you know, too, you're Proxy Councillor for Science."*

"You're not serious." Stupid thing to say to Ari, in the depths of a storm tunnel. "You are serious."

"Entirely serious," she said, *"and Yanni's in the clinic, with dehydration and exhaustion, they're telling me, and the Council's just voted to unseat Khalid and given a Marine general the go-ahead to go after him, just so you're up to the moment on what's going on."*

"Why me?" he asked. It was all good news—if it didn't get another missile aimed at them. "Why not you?"

"Because I'm Councillor for Information," she said. *"Yanni and Frank and Councillor Corain are all in the clinic; so are Amy and Quentin, but she's a lot better than they are, and Quentin's doing fine. Yanni just fell over. The doctors don't know yet what's going on with him."* A pause for breath. *"It's going to be a dicey few hours, Justin. It is. But we got the vote through. We're transmitting it. Any minute they'll know it at the port, and they'll know it in Novgorod, and up at Alpha and over in Planys, more's the point. That's where we don't know what's going to happen. I don't know what the base over there might have to defend itself, but we're just hoping it doesn't have long-range stuff, so just batten down and hope along with the rest of us. If Council reconvenes you're going to have to get over here on the run. Are you all right there?"*

"Fine," he said. "We're all fine."

"Good," she said. *"Good. Take care. Florian says keep your heads down. All of you."*

"Proxy Councillor," Grant said in amazement.

"It gives me another reason to wish Yanni well," he said, and looked around him at a set of young, so *very* young faces, even the ReseuneSec agents, dismayed to realize every one of them was looking at him the way he'd always looked at Yanni.

BOOK THREE   Section 6   Chapter x

SEPT 8, 2424
1927H

A long, long silence prevailed in communications . . . with the airport, with the city, with the Bureaus, and with the station overhead . . . not to mention the two aircraft that laced the skies, zigging and zagging, occasionally going down to one plane as one aircraft landed down at Novgorod Airport. Those two planes didn't talk to Reseune ATC and it didn't seem a politic time to be trying to pry into the Defense system. Ari just took what she had, which was a fair amount of knowledge she *could* reach.

She wasn't alone in ReseuneSec Ops: Amy had come back to sit in the little room, and regale her quietly with an account of how they *had* dodged people trying to track them from the hotel, and taken out toward the docks instead. They'd walked the last bit, Amy said, so as not to leave their stolen car too obviously close to the barge they'd picked.

"They were moving out a few barges. This stack of containers was ready to load on. It was construction stuff, for Reseune," Amy said, sipping juice by tiny, tiny degrees, and with a monitor patch taped to her wrist. "So Frank got us into a container, got the door to stay shut while they loaded us on, way down deep in the hold, and later on, when we were running out of air, Quentin shot three holes in the plastic and we used one of Yanni's tees for a filter. The medics don't think we got any contamination, being down deep, but they shot us full of stuff, in case. And we *didn't* know Defense people would stop us once we got underway, and start searching the barge and all. They did, about halfway up the river, but they didn't get to the bottom containers, maybe because they expected us to leave a trail for the sniffers, walking aboard, I'm not sure. But we'd come on with the loading machinery. You look look awfully tired, Ari. When did *you* sleep?"

"I'm not sure I remember what that is," she said. She liked hearing Amy's voice near at hand. She wanted to hear from Sam, and they hadn't; she wanted to hear from Awei that his forces weren't losing, wherever they were, and the silence around that operation was thorough.

She was supposed to talk to the media—her security wouldn't let her go down to the airport, but they were going to bring three representives up to Admin for the first time to hear a report—and she didn't know where she was going to get the strength to sound as if the momentum of the Council action was still going.

Yanni was back, and Yanni was doing all right, but they weren't telling him about all the problems. She had Harad and deFranco to make decisions about the outside world, but meanwhile she had to figure whether to try to make contact with Strassenberg or just let them lie low; and whether to let techs go up to the babies in the wombs or just leave them on auto. She'd decided in the positive on that and told them to just be ready to dive for cover. The skies had stayed quiet.

Keywork. She thought better that way. No verbals. Idiom crept in, imprecise. Even the Base One AI wasn't entirely safe, not when it came to sequencing orders. She did it.

Amy fell silent, just watching, maybe interpreting. Amy was all right. She'd been there since childhood, almost the first. Amy didn't know all the tools she had under hand nowadays. Amy could use Base One's functions, but nobody could quite *use* Base One, except her, except Florian and Catlin, and anybody she let have just one little tag end of a command that Base One could execute.

Execute was a dangerous word. A meaningful word.

She stacked up commands, things to cascade once the first button was pushed—knowing if she got it wrong, she'd expose Reseune agents over in Planys, and elsewhere. The whole Planys-base ReseuneSec organization was out there for her to use. She could access everything about the agents there, names, numbers, experience, rank, and how deeply embedded.

Maybe she should bring up the first Ari. Maybe she should give her a chance to argue with her plan. But she knew the keywords. She knew what Ari had told her. **Politics matters. Perception matters. Assassination breeds assassination. War breeds war.**

And after all the philosophy: **If you have any choice, don't be perceived to have struck first.**

In going after Reseune, Khalid had given her everything she needed.

She pushed a button. She stored the orders, left them waiting in System on this side of the ocean. When the pipeline opened, it would open wide, and the chain would cascade in nanoseconds.

An hour later Catlin and Florian both lifted their heads from the console. "Awei is calling," Florian said. "He says—now is the time, sera. He needs the data."

The sequence was prepared. The orders were prepared. They'd probably lose System in Planys once the intruders retaliated. They'd very possibly lose a dozen personnel.

Execute.

The order went out. Spanned the ocean. Touched off quiet alerts first, PlanysLabs staff to take cover—or take action, if they were linked into System; and certain azi staff stayed potentially linked in, if they could.

System in Planys came all the way up. Took a snapshot. Locked doors. Located faces. Fired that information off to Reseune and Awei, and sounded the intrusion alert in Planys' hallways—just to create maximum confusion.

Ari sat with chin on fist, looking at Planys' readouts. A few went out, quickly extinguished. But the room where a major part of System actually sat was deeply buried, difficult to find. That was what Base One said about it . . .

Planys System was a lot like Base One. It moved. It created power-out conditions. It turned out lights. It locked and unlocked doors for a handful of agents whose faces the Planys System knew, individuals who could go like ghosts where they needed to go.

Meanwhile it produced maps for the general, and located vehicles, aircraft, personnel whose faces *weren't* known to System.

The intruders figured out they were in trouble. Some eyes went out. Some stayed.

Florian and Catlin handled communications as needed. Amy hovered close, watching, in total silence.

They had found the Enemy.

BOOK THREE   Section 6   Chapter xi

SEPT 9, 2424
1303H

It wasn't where Justin had planned to be, not at all where he wanted to be. The Council convened in a session open to the media, down at Reseune Airport—at the farthest remove from Reseune Admin they could manage, as he understood the intent: appearances. But things were still all on end, and though Councillor Corain had managed to get out of his hospital bed and show up for the session, using a chair for the most part, Yanni was having a heart replacement, and was in no shape to take the Science seat. Ari was holding the Information seat—had been beseiged by reporters: it was their Bureau she represented, and Catherine Lao's death was officially reported in Novgorod: yes, she said, she hoped to attend the funeral; so did all the Council.

Justin had his own share: did he count his appointment permanent, did he believe Yanni would resume the seat?—"I certainly look forward to that, ser," he said, and having found one question he actually could answer, he felt a sort of calm settle over him like a blanket. Standing near the table that served as the official desk, he looked toward Grant, over by the door, caught his eye, and then realized that that was Paul, who'd just arrived by Grant, right next to young Sam Whitely, who'd just come in to meet Ari right before the session started.

And if Paul was here—

Jordan came into the room, quietly, wearing the usual ugly tweed coat, stood there in camouflage . . . come to see his son take a Council post, or to see his old enemy's replicate take her place on Council; or come to raise hell, Justin had no idea. At the moment Jordan exchanged a quiet word with Paul, and Paul with Grant.

Tap of the gavel. Time to settle. Ari had told him he shouldn't sit yet: he had to *be* seated, by a vote. The Nine—eight, this afternoon, Ari among them, took their places, and Harad rapped the gavel—possibly even the real gavel—three times.

"Council is in session," Harad said. "First item of business is to seat Justin Warrick as Proxy for Science. Does someone want to make the motion?"

"Moved," Ari said.

"Seconded." From Mikhail Corain. *That* constellation of agreements was a new one. Even a novice on Council knew that.

"All in favor. All opposed. None objecting, record a unanimous vote, Defense being absent this afternoon, no proxy in attendance." The gavel banged. "*Second* item of business. The Councillor for Information is deceased, as of 0300h this morning. The Proxy for Information succeeds automatically to the seat." Bang of the gavel. "*Third* item of business. The Proxy Councillor for Defense is deceased . . ."

A strong murmur broke out among the reporters, and the gavel went down again, twice.

"At 0211h on this date, Admiral Vladislaw Khalid was discovered dead in a hallway of PlanysLabs, along with four of his aides. A force of Marines acting directly under the command of General Klaus Awei landed at adjacent Pierce Field and Fleet Command at 0131h this morning, and General Awei is en route to Planys, pursuant to Council directives. General Awei will take personal command of operations at and near Pierce, pursuant to the Council Directive of the eighth of September, 2424."

Understatement, Justin thought. It had been messy, what happened at PlanysLabs: they'd gotten the images. And nobody officially knew who had shot Khalid, but Ari had told him privately it had been ReseuneSec, and they didn't want any investigation, so Science should stand with her if there was any suggestion of it.

"There being no Councillor present for Defense, the Chair of the Council moves a resolution that if Councillor Jacques does not personally and within twenty-four hours make contact with Council, Council will deem that the seat for Defense is vacant and that the Secretary for Defense, Hariman Leontide, will serve pending elections in that Bureau. The Chair has received notice from General Awei's office that he has begun a filing for that seat. We will accordingly be holding elections for Defense."

That was a lengthy process. Notice of filing had to reach all stations, a matter of months; and then anyone at those stations also filing had to communicate that news to reach all stations, for everybody's consideration. Three months for campaigning, and the months of voting . . . not only for Defense, but also for Citizens. Corain was assuredly going to file to keep his seat, and the man who'd filed against him would have a hard time out-campaigning the long-serving Councillor who'd opposed Khalid in Novgorod, stowed away in a cargo container, and left a hospital bed to be here for today's public session in front of the cameras. The opposition wasn't going to top that one.

And there'd be elections in Information: Ari wanted to appoint another Proxy, and said she had in mind one of the senior reporters who'd been covering Reseune all her life; that man would then file for the seat—file for it, and win, if they were lucky. Reseune had had a lifelong ally in Catherine Lao, and without Lao—they needed an ally, to keep the balance on Council what it was.

Himself, he just hoped Yanni would get through recovery all right.

He caught Grant's eye, while business proceeded. Didn't quite look at Jordan, didn't want to give him any encouragement, or start anything.

But Jordan had showed up. To see his son sit where he had wanted to be. Justin was convinced of it.

November 24, 2424.
0745h

The tanks changed, contracted, tilted—*pushed* their contents out onto soft foam.

Abban AB and Seely AS came gently into the world within seconds of each other—were severed from the umbilicals, caught up in azi arms, encouraged to draw their first breaths, again, within seconds of each other.

They were wrapped in soft blankets, hugged in living arms, carried, separately to cradles, which, sealed, would speak to them reassuringly and insulate them from all shocks, all stress, on their way to the creches. They were not scheduled to meet for years. And then the records would see they did.

Giraud slid down into the tray—slid onto foam, a startling sensation, and once the nurses had gotten him free of the umbilical, and gotten him breathing, Nelly wiped him vigorously and hugged him.

She was older, Nelly was, years older than when she'd been Ari's nanny ... Ari watched her with a little worry, a little jealousy, still. Nelly was sweet, was what she was, just kind, and sweet, and loved babies until they got to be older, and contrary-minded, and did things Nelly couldn't understand. That was why Uncle Denys had had to send Nelly away from her—because she'd have driven Nelly into therapy.

She worried just a little that Giraud was going to be a handful for Nelly—but Nelly was experienced, no question, and she'd made the assignment herself: Yanni needed the help.

Nelly carried Giraud over to Yanni—put the blanket-wrapped bundle into Yanni's arms, and Yanni, thin from

his recent ordeal, and ordered not to lift heavy things, took
up a hell of a burden, took it up as gingerly as if it were a
ticking bomb, and then moved the blanket to look in its
face, and touched it, and was, Ari thought, pretty well
committed. Yanni had found arguments against it. But
there was nobody better, nobody in all the world, who'd
know how to keep ahead of Giraud Nye. For the next few
months, Nelly would do most of the work.

And that was that. Giraud was in the world. He had his
CIT number from birth—the law had changed: she was
why it had. He'd be Giraud Nye from this day on, and systems would recognize him—if they weren't locked against
him; and they were, thank God and Base One.

She cast a look at Florian and Catlin as they fell in with
her, on her way out of the labs. "I think we'll walk across,"
she said. She'd had enough of the tunnels. "It's a sunny
day."

"You didn't bring enough coat, sera," Florian said.

"I won't freeze," she said.

There might be a nip in the morning air, weather ad-
visories said so. But the pale sun had warmth, still, in
autumn.

They went out in the daylight, under Cyteen's morning
sky. There was color still in the east, a warm blush of dawn
on the cliffs that rimmed Reseune, and a gentle breeze was
moving. Florian was right: the coat wasn't quite enough,
and the chill got through, but that was proof the world was
random and she was alive in it.

That was all she asked of the day.